Kathy Reichs

DÈJÂ
DEAD

DEATH
DU JOUR

WILLIAM HEINEMANN : LONDON

This edition published by William Heinemann in 2004

Dèjâ Dead first published in the United Kingdom in 1998 by William Heinemann
Death Du Jour first published in the United Kingdom in 1999 by William Heinemann

William Heinemann
The Random House Group Ltd
20 Vauxhall Bridge Road, London SW1V 2SA

Random House Australia (Pty) Limited
20 Alfred Street, Milsons Point, Sydney,
New South Wales 2061, Australia

Random House New Zealand Limited
18 Poland Road, Glenfield
Auckland 10, New Zealand

Random House South Africa (Pty) Limited
Endulini, 5a Jubilee Road, Parktown 2193, South Africa

Random House UK Limited Reg. No. 954009

A CIP catalogue record for this book is available from the British Library

Papers used by Random House UK Limited are natural, recyclable products made from wood grown in sustainable forests. The manufacturing processes conform to the environmental regulations of the country of origin

ISBN 0 09 190407 2

Typeset by SX Composing DTP, Rayleigh, Essex
Printed and bound in Great Britain by
Cox & Wyman Ltd, Reading, Berks

Déjà Dead

'Alone and in the dark and quiet, I could no longer suppress the thought. The other homicide. The other young woman who'd come to the morgue in pieces. I saw her in vivid detail, remembered my feelings as I'd worked on her bones . . .'

Also by Kath Reichs

Death Du Jour
Deadly Decisions
Fatal Voyage

Kathy Reichs is forensic anthropologist for the Office of the Chief Medical Examiner, State of North Carolina, and the Laboratoire de Sciences Judiciaires et de Médecine Légale for the province of Quebec. She is one of only 50 forensic anthropologists certified by the American Board of Forensic Anthropology and is on the Board of Directors of the American Academy of Forensic Sciences. A professor of anthropology at The University of North Carolina at Charlotte, Dr Reichs is a native of Chicago, where she received her PhD at Northwestern. She now divides her time between Charlotte and Montreal and is a frequent expert witness in criminal trials. *Déjà Dead* is her first novel.

For Karl and Marta Reichs,
the two kindest and most generous people I know.

Paldies par jūsu mīlestību, Vecāmamma un Paps

Kārlis Reichs 1914–1996

Acknowledgments

In an attempt to create accurate fiction, I consulted experts in many fields. I wish to thank Bernard Chapais for his explanation of Canadian regulations pertaining to the housing and maintenance of laboratory animals; Sylvain Roy, Jean-Guy Hébert, and Michel Hamel for their help on serology; Bernard Pommeville for his detailed demonstration of X-ray microfluorescence; and Robert Dorion for his advice on forensic dentistry, bite mark analysis, and proper use of the French language. Last, but far from least, I wish to express my gratitude to Steve Symes for his boundless patience in discussing saws and their effects on bone.

I owe a debt of thanks to John Robinson and Marysue Rucci, without whom *Déjà Dead* may never have come to be. John brought the manuscript to Marysue's attention, and she saw merit in it. My editors, Susanne Kirk, Marysue Rucci, and Maria Rejt waded through the original version of *Déjà Dead*, improving it greatly with their editorial suggestions. A million thanks to my agent, Jennifer Rudolph Walsh. She is amazing.

Finally, on a more personal note, I want to thank the members of my family who read the embryonic work and made valuable comments. I appreciate their support, and their patience with my long absences.

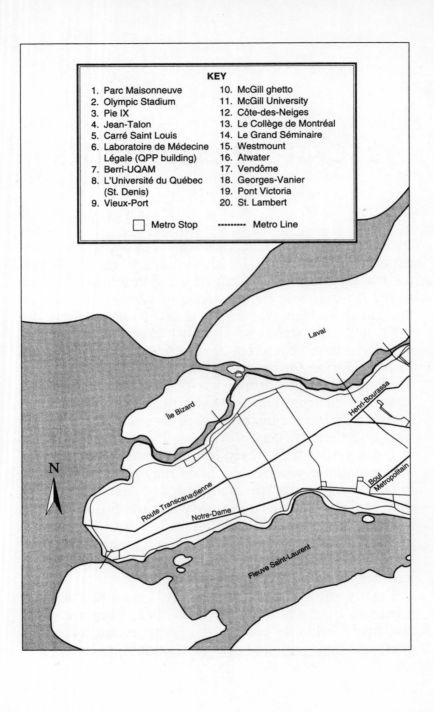

KEY

1. Parc Maisonneuve
2. Olympic Stadium
3. Pie IX
4. Jean-Talon
5. Carré Saint Louis
6. Laboratoire de Médecine Légale (QPP building)
7. Berri-UQAM
8. L'Université du Québec (St. Denis)
9. Vieux-Port
10. McGill ghetto
11. McGill University
12. Côte-des-Neiges
13. Le Collège de Montréal
14. Le Grand Séminaire
15. Westmount
16. Atwater
17. Vendôme
18. Georges-Vanier
19. Pont Victoria
20. St. Lambert

☐ Metro Stop   ---------- Metro Line

N

Laval

Île Bizard

Henri-Bourassa

Boul Metropolitain

Route Transcanadienne

Notre-Dame

Fleuve Saint-Laurent

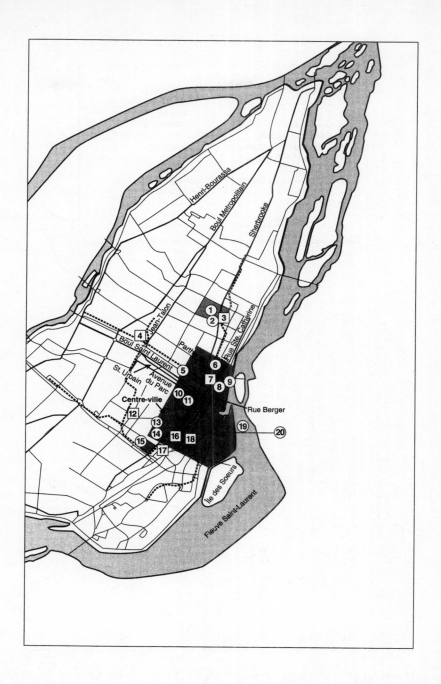

Henri-Bourassa
Boul Métropolitain
Sherbrooke
Jean-Talon
Parthe
Rue Ste. Catherine
Boul Saint-Laurent
Avenue du Parc
St. Urbain
Centre-ville
Rue Berger
Île des Soeurs
Fleuve Saint-Laurent

DÉJÀ DEAD

1

I wasn't thinking about the man who'd blown himself up. Earlier I had. Now I was putting him together. Two sections of skull lay in front of me, and a third jutted from a sand-filled stainless steel bowl, the glue still drying on its reassembled fragments. Enough bone to confirm identity. The coroner would be pleased.

It was late afternoon, Thursday, June 2, 1994. While the glue set, my mind had gone truant. The knock that would break my reverie, tip my life off course, and alter my comprehension of the bounds of human depravity wouldn't come for another ten minutes. I was enjoying my view of the St. Lawrence, the sole advantage of my cramped corner office. Somehow the sight of water has always rejuvenated me, especially when it flows rhythmically. Forget Golden Pond. I'm sure Freud could have run with that.

My thoughts meandered to the upcoming weekend. I had a trip to Quebec City in mind, but my plans were vague. I thought of visiting the Plains of Abraham, eating mussels and crepes, and buying trinkets from the street vendors. Escape in tourism. I'd been in Montreal a full year, working as a forensic anthropologist for the province, but I hadn't been up there yet, so it seemed like a good program. I needed a couple of days without skeletons, decomposed bodies, or corpses freshly dragged from the river.

Ideas come easily to me, enacting them comes harder. I usually let things go. Perhaps it's an escape hatch, my way of allowing myself to double back and ease out the side door on a lot of my schemes. Irresolute about my social life, obsessive in my work.

I knew he was standing there before the knock. Though he moved quietly for a man of his bulk, the smell of old pipe tobacco gave him away. Pierre LaManche had been director of the Laboratoire de Médecine Légale for almost two decades. His visits to my office were never social, and I suspected that his news wouldn't be good. LaManche tapped the door softly with his knuckles.

"Temperance?" It rhymed with France. He would not use the shortened version. Perhaps to his ear it just didn't translate. Perhaps he'd had a bad experience in Arizona. He, alone, did not call me Tempe.

"*Oui?*" After months, it was automatic. I had arrived in Montreal thinking myself fluent in French, but I hadn't counted on *Le Français Québecois*. I was learning, but slowly.

"I have just had a call." He glanced at a pink telephone slip he was holding. Everything about his face was vertical, the lines and folds moving from high to low, paralleling the long, straight nose and ears. The plan was pure basset hound. It was a face that had probably looked old in youth, its arrangement only deepening with time. I couldn't have guessed his age.

"Two Hydro-Quebec workers found some bones today." He studied my face, which was not happy. His eyes returned to the pink paper.

"They are close to the site where the historic burials were found last summer," he said in his proper, formal

2

French. I'd never heard him use a contraction. No slang or police jargon. "You were there. It is probably more of the same. I need someone to go out there to confirm that this is not a coroner case."

When he glanced up from the paper, the change in angle caused the furrows and creases to deepen, sucking in the afternoon light, as a black hole draws in matter. He made an attempt at a gaunt smile and four crevices veered north.

"You think it's archaeological?" I was stalling. A scene search had not been in my pre-weekend plans. To leave the next day I still had to pick up the dry cleaning, do the laundry, stop at the pharmacy, pack, put oil in the car, and explain cat care to Winston, the caretaker at my building.

He nodded.

"Okay." It was not okay.

He handed me the slip. "Do you want a squad car to take you there?"

I looked at him, trying hard for baleful. "No, I drove in today." I read the address. It was close to home. "I'll find it."

He left as silently as he'd come. Pierre LaManche favored crepe-soled shoes, kept his pockets empty so nothing jangled or swished. Like a croc in a river he arrived and departed unannounced by auditory cues. Some of the staff found it unnerving.

I packed a set of coveralls in a backpack with my rubber boots, hoping I wouldn't need either, and grabbed my laptop, briefcase, and the embroidered canteen cover that was serving as that season's purse. I was still promising myself that I wouldn't be back until Monday, but another voice in my head was intruding, insisting otherwise.

When summer arrives in Montreal it flounces in like a

3

rumba dancer: all ruffles and bright cotton, with flashing thighs and sweat-slicked skin. It is a ribald celebration that begins in June and continues until September.

The season is embraced and relished. Life moves into the open. After the long, bleak winter, outdoor cafés reappear, cyclists and Rollerbladers compete for the bike paths, festivals follow quickly one after another on the streets, and crowds turn the sidewalks into swirling patterns.

How different summer on the St. Lawrence is from summer in my home state of North Carolina, where languid lounging on beach chairs, mountain porches, or suburban decks marks the season, and the lines between spring, summer, and fall are difficult to determine without a calendar. This brash vernal rebirth, more than the bitterness of winter, had surprised me my first year in the North, banishing the homesickness I'd felt during the long, dark cold.

These thoughts were drifting through my mind as I drove under the Jacques-Cartier Bridge and turned west onto Viger. I passed the Molson brewery, which sprawled along the river to my left, then the round tower of the Radio-Canada Building, and thought of the people trapped inside: occupants of industrial apiaries who undoubtedly craved release as much as I did. I imagined them studying the sunshine from behind glass rectangles, longing for boats and bikes and sneakers, checking their watches, bitten by June.

I rolled down the window and reached for the radio.

Gerry Boulet sang "*Les Yeux du Cœur*." I translated automatically in my mind. I could picture him, an intense man with dark eyes and a tangle of curls flying around his head, passionate about his music, dead at forty-four.

Historic burials. Every forensic anthropologist handles these cases. Old bones unearthed by dogs,

4

construction workers, spring floods, grave diggers. The coroner's office is the overseer of death in Quebec Province. If you die inappropriately, not under the care of a physician, not in bed, the coroner wants to know why. If your death threatens to take others along, the coroner wants to know that. The coroner demands an explanation of violent, unexpected, or untimely death, but persons long gone are of little interest. While their passings may once have cried out for justice, or heralded warning of an impending epidemic, the voices have been still for too long. Their antiquity established, these finds are turned over to the archaeologists. This promised to be such a case. Please.

I zigzagged through the logjam of downtown traffic, arriving within fifteen minutes at the address LaManche had given me. Le Grand Séminaire. A remnant of the vast holdings of the Catholic Church, Le Grand Séminaire occupies a large tract of land in the heart of Montreal. Centre-ville. Downtown. My neighborhood. The small, urban citadel endures as an island of green in a sea of high-rise cement, and stands as mute testimony to a once-powerful institution. Stone walls, complete with watchtowers, surround somber gray castles, carefully tended lawns, and open spaces gone wild.

In the glory days of the church, families sent their sons here by the thousands to train for the priesthood. Some still come, but their numbers are few. The larger buildings are now rented out and house schools and institutions more secular in mission where the Internet and fax machine replace Scripture and theological discourse as the working paradigm. Perhaps it's a good metaphor for modern society. We're too absorbed in communicating among ourselves to worry about an almighty architect.

I stopped on a small street opposite the seminary grounds and looked east along Sherbrooke, toward the portion of the property now leased by Le Collège de Montréal. Nothing unusual. I dropped an elbow out the window and peered in the opposite direction. The hot, dusty metal seared the skin on my inner arm, and I retracted it quickly, like a crab poked with a stick.

There they were. Juxtaposed incongruously against a medieval stone tower, I could see a blue-and-white patrol unit with POLICE-COMMUNAUTÉ URBAINE DE MONTRÉAL written on its side. It blocked the western entrance to the compound. A gray Hydro-Quebec truck was parked just ahead of it, ladders and equipment protruding like appendages to a space station. Near the truck a uniformed officer stood talking with two men in work clothes.

I turned left and slid into the westbound traffic on Sherbrooke, relieved to see no reporters. In Montreal an encounter with the press can be a double ordeal, since the media turn out in both French and English. I am not particularly gracious when badgered in one language. Under dual assault I can become downright surly.

LaManche was right. I'd come to these grounds the previous summer. I recalled the case – bones unearthed during the repair of a water mains. Church property. Old cemetery. Coffin burials. Call the archaeologist. Case closed. Hopefully, this report would read the same.

As I maneuvered my Mazda ahead of the truck and parked, the three men stopped talking and looked in my direction. When I got out of the car the officer paused, as if thinking it over, then moved toward me. He was not smiling. At 4:15 P.M. it was probably past the end of his shift and he didn't want to be there. Well, neither did I.

"You'll have to move on, madame. You may not park here." As he spoke he gestured with his hand, shooing me in the direction in which I was to depart. I could picture him clearing flies from potato salad with the same

6

movement.

"I'm Dr. Brennan," I said, slamming the Mazda door. "Laboratoire de Médecine Légale."

"You're the one from the coroner?" His tone would have made a KGB interrogator sound trusting.

"Yes. I'm the *anthropologiste judiciaire*." Slowly, like a second-grade teacher. "I do the disinterments and the skeletal cases. I understand this may qualify for both?"

I handed him my ID. A small, brass rectangle above his shirt pocket identified him as Const. Groulx.

He looked at the photo, then at me. My appearance was not convincing. I'd planned to work on the skull reconstruction all day, and was dressed for glue. I was wearing faded brown jeans, a denim shirt, sleeves rolled to the elbows, Topsiders, no socks. Most of my hair was bound up in a barrette. The rest, having fought gravity and lost, spiraled limply around my face and down my neck. I was speckled with patches of dried Elmer's. I must have looked more like a middle-aged mother forced to abandon a wallpaper project than a forensic anthropologist.

He studied the ID for a long time, then returned it without comment. I was obviously not what he wanted.

"Have you seen the remains?" I asked.

"No. I am securing the site." He used a modified version of the hand flip to indicate the two men who stood watching us, conversation suspended.

"They found it. I called it in. They will lead you."

I wondered if Constable Groulx was capable of a compound sentence. With another hand gesture, he indicated the workers once again.

"I will watch your car."

I nodded but he was already turning away. The Hydro workers watched in silence as I approached. Both wore aviator shades, and the late afternoon sun shot orange beams off alternating lenses as one or the other

7

moved his head. Their mustaches looped in identical upside down U's around their mouths.

The one on the left was the older of the two, a thin, dark man with the look of a rat terrier. He was glancing around nervously, his gaze bouncing from object to object, person to person, like a bee making sorties in and out of a peony blossom. His eyes kept darting to me, then quickly away, as if he feared contact with other eyes would commit him to something he'd later come to regret. He shifted his weight from foot to foot and hunched and unhunched his shoulders.

His partner was a much larger man with a long, lank ponytail and a weathered face. He smiled as I drew near, displaying gaps that once held teeth. I suspected he'd be the more loquacious of the two.

"*Bonjour. Comment ça va?*" The French equivalent of "Hi. How are you?"

"*Bien. Bien.*" Simultaneous head nods. Fine. Fine.

I identified myself, asked if they'd reported finding the bones. More nods.

"Tell me about it." As I spoke I withdrew a small spiral notebook from my backpack, flipped back the cover, and clicked a ballpoint into readiness. I smiled encouragingly.

Ponytail spoke eagerly, his words racing out like children released for recess. He was enjoying the adventure. His French was heavily accented, the words running together and the endings swallowed in the fashion of the upriver Québecois. I had to listen carefully.

"We were clearing brush, it's part of our job." He pointed at overhead power lines, then did a sweep of the ground. "We must keep the lines clear."

I nodded.

"When I got down into that trench over there" – he turned and pointed in the direction of a wooded area running the length of the property – "I smelled some-

8

thing funny." He stopped, his eyes locked in the direction of the trees, arm extended, index finger piercing the air.

"Funny?"

He turned back. "Well, not exactly funny." He paused, sucking in his lower lip as he searched his personal lexicon for the right word. "Dead," he said. "You know, dead?"

I waited for him to go on.

"You know, like an animal that crawls in somewhere and dies?" He gave a slight shrug of the shoulders as he said it, then looked at me for confirmation. I did know. I'm on a first-name basis with the odor of death. I nodded again.

"That's what I thought. That a dog, or maybe a raccoon, died. So I started poking around in the bush with my rake, right where the smell was real strong. Sure enough, I found a bunch of bones." Another shrug.

"Uh-huh." I was beginning to get an uneasy feeling. Ancient burials don't smell.

"So I called Gil over . . ." He looked to the older man for affirmation. Gil was staring at the ground. ". . . and we both started digging around in the leaves and stuff. What we found don't look like no dog or raccoon to me." As he said it he folded his arms across his chest, lowered his chin, and rocked back on his heels.

"Why is that?"

"Too big." He rolled his tongue and used it to probe one of the gaps in his dental work. The tip appeared and disappeared between the teeth like a worm testing for daylight.

"Anything else?"

"What do you mean?" The worm withdrew.

"Did you find anything else besides bones?"

"Yeah. That's what don't seem right." He spread his arms wide, indicating a dimension with his hands.

9

"There's a big plastic sack around all this stuff, and . . ." He shrugged, turning his palms up and leaving the sentence unfinished.

"And?" My uneasiness was escalating.

"*Une ventouse.*" He said it quickly, embarrassed and excited at the same time. Gil was traveling with me, his apprehension matching mine. His eyes had left the ground and were roving in double time.

"A what?" I asked, thinking perhaps I'd misunderstood the word.

"*Une ventouse.* A plunger. For the bathroom." He imitated its use, his body thrust forward, hands wrapped around an invisible handle, arms driving upward and downward. The macabre little pantomime was so out of context it was jarring.

Gil let out a "*Sacré . . .*" and locked his eyes back on to the earth. I just stared at him. This wasn't right. I finished my notes and closed the spiral.

"Is it wet down there?" I didn't really want to wear the boots and coveralls unless it was necessary.

"Nah," he said, again looking to Gil for confirmation. Gil shook his head, eyes never leaving the dirt at his feet.

"Okay," I said. "Let's go." I hoped that I appeared calmer than I felt.

Ponytail led the way across the grass and into the woods. We descended gradually into a small ravine, the trees and brush growing thicker as we approached the bottom. I followed into the thicket, taking the larger branches in my right hand as he bent them back for me, then handing them off to Gil. Still small branches tugged at my hair. The place smelled of damp earth, grass, and rotting leaves. Sunlight penetrated the foliage unevenly, dappling the ground with puzzle piece splotches. Here and there a beam found an opening and sliced straight through to the ground. Dust particles danced in the slanted shafts. Flying insects swarmed around my face and whined in my ears, and creepers grabbed my ankles.

At the bottom of the trench the worker stopped to get his bearings, then turned to the right. I followed, slapping at mosquitoes, handing off vegetation, squinting through clouds of gnats around my eyes, and the occasional loner that went straight for the cornea. Sweat beaded my lip and dampened my hair, plastering the escapee strands to my forehead and neck. I needn't have worried about my dress or coiffure.

Fifteen yards from the corpse I no longer needed a guide. Blending with the loamy scent of woods and sunlight I detected the unmistakable smell of death. The odor of decomposing flesh is like no other, and it hung there in the warm afternoon air, faint but undeniable. Step by step, the sweet, fetid stench grew stronger, building in intensity like the whine of a locust, until it ceased blending, and overpowered all other smells. The aromas of moss and humus and pine and sky deferred to the rankness of rotting flesh.

Gil stopped and hung back at a discreet distance. The smell was enough. He didn't need another look. Ten feet farther the younger man halted, turned, and wordlessly pointed to a small heap partially covered by leaves and debris. Flies buzzed and circled around it, like academics at a free buffet.

At the sight my stomach went into a tuck, and the voice in my head started in on "I told you so." With growing dread, I placed my pack at the base of a tree, withdrew a pair of surgical gloves, and picked my way gingerly through the foliage. When I neared the mound I could see where the men had raked away the vegetation. What I saw confirmed my fears.

Protruding from the leaves and soil was an arcade of ribs, their ends curving upward like the framework of an embryonic boat. I bent down for a closer look. Flies

11

whined in protest, the sun iridescent on their blue-green bodies. When I cleared more debris I could see that the ribs were held in place by a segment of spinal column.

Taking a deep breath, I eased on the latex gloves and began to remove handfuls of dead leaves and pine needles. As I exposed the backbone to the sunlight, a knot of startled beetles flew apart. The bugs disentangled themselves and scuttled outward, disappearing one by one over the vertebral edges.

Ignoring the insects, I continued to remove sediment. Slowly, carefully, I cleared an area approximately three feet square. In less than ten minutes I could see what Gil and his partner had discovered. Brushing hair from my face with a latexed hand, I leaned back on my heels and surveyed the emerging picture.

I looked at a partially skeletonized torso, the rib cage, backbone, and pelvis still connected by dried muscle and ligament. While connective tissue is stubborn, refusing to yield its hold on the joints for months or years, the brain and internal organs are not so tenacious. With the aid of bacteria and insects, they decompose quickly, sometimes in a matter of weeks.

I could see remnants of brown and desiccated tissue clinging to the thoracic and abdominal surfaces of the bones. As I squatted there, the flies buzzing and the sunlight dappling the woods around me, I knew two things with certainty. The torso was human, and it hadn't been there long.

I knew also that its arrival in that place wasn't by chance. The victim had been killed and dumped. The remains lay on a plastic bag, the common kitchen variety used for garbage. It was ripped open now, but I guessed the bag had been used to transport the torso. The head and limbs were missing, and I could see no personal effects or objects close by. Except one.

The bones of the pelvis encircled a bathroom

12

plunger, its long wooden handle projecting upward like an inverted Popsicle stick, its red rubber cup pressed hard against the pelvic outlet. Its position suggested deliberate placement. Gruesome as the idea was, I didn't believe the association was spurious.

I stood and looked around, my knees protesting the change to upright posture. I knew from experience that scavenging animals can drag body parts impressive distances. Dogs often hide them in areas of low brush, and burrowing animals drag small bones and teeth into underground holes. I brushed dirt from my hands and scanned the immediate vicinity, looking for likely routes.

Flies buzzed and a horn blared a million miles away on Sherbrooke. Memories of other woods, other graves, other bones skittered through my mind, like disconnected images from old movies. I stood absolutely still, searching, wholly alert. Finally, I sensed, more than saw, an irregularity in my surroundings. Like a sunbeam glinting off a mirror, it was gone before my neurons could form an image. An almost imperceptible flicker caused me to turn my head. Nothing. I held myself rigid, unsure if I'd really seen anything. I brushed the insects from my eyes and noticed that it was growing cooler.

Shit. I continued looking. A slight breeze lifted the damp curls around my face and stirred the leaves. Then I sensed it again. A suggestion of sunlight skipping off something. I took a few steps, unsure of the source, and stopped, every cell of my being intent on sunlight and shadows. Nothing. Of course not, stupid. There can't be anything over there. No flies.

Then I spotted it. The wind puffed gently, flicking over a shiny surface and causing a momentary ripple in the afternoon light. Not much, but it caught my eye. Hardly breathing, I went closer and looked down. I

13

wasn't surprised at what I saw. Here we go, I thought.

Peeking from a hollow in the roots of a yellow poplar was the corner of another plastic bag. A spray of buttercups ringed both the poplar and the bag, tiptoeing off in slender tendrils to disappear into the surrounding weeds. The bright yellow flowers looked like escapees from a Beatrix Potter illustration, the freshness of the blooms in stark contrast to what I knew lay hidden in the bag.

I approached the tree, twigs and leaves snapping beneath my feet. Bracing myself with one hand, I cleared enough plastic to get a grip, took firm hold, and pulled gently. No give. Rewrapping the plastic around my hand, I pulled harder, and felt the bag move. I could tell that its contents had substance. Insects whined in my face. Sweat trickled down my back. My heart drummed like the bass in a heavy metal band.

One more tug and the bag came free. I dragged it forward far enough to allow a view inside. Or maybe I just wanted it away from Ms. Potter's flowers. Whatever it held was heavy, and I had little doubt what that would be. And I was right. As I disentangled the ends of the plastic, the smell of putrefaction was overwhelming. I unwound the edges and looked inside.

A human face stared out at me. Sealed off from the insects that hasten decomposition, the flesh had not fully rotted. But heat and moisture had altered the features, converting them into a death mask bearing scant resemblance to the person it had been. Two eyes, shriveled and constricted, peered out from under half-closed lids. The nose lay bent to one side, the nostrils compressed and flattened against a sunken cheek. The lips curled back, a grin for eternity with a set of perfect teeth. The flesh was pasty white, a blanched and soggy wrapper molding itself closely to the underlying bone. Framing the whole was a mass of dull red hair, the lusterless corkscrew curls plastered to the head by an ooze

14

of liquefied brain tissue.

Shaken, I closed the bag. Remembering the Hydro workers, I glanced over to where I'd left them. The younger was watching me closely. His companion remained some distance behind, shoulders hunched, hands thrust deep into the pockets of his work pants.

Stripping off my gloves, I walked past them, out of the woods and back toward the CUM squad car. They said nothing, but I could hear them following, scraping and rustling in my wake.

Constable Groulx was leaning against his hood. He watched me approach but didn't change position. I'd worked with more amiable individuals.

"May I use your radio?" I could be cool, too.

He pushed himself upright with both hands and circled the car to the driver's side. Leaning in through the open window, he disengaged the mike and looked at me questioningly.

"Homicide," I said.

He looked surprised, regretted it, and put through the call. *"Section des homicides,"* he said to the dispatcher. After the usual delays, transfers, and static, the voice of a detective came over the air.

"Claudel," it said, sounding irritated.

Constable Groulx handed me the mike. I identified myself and gave my location. "I've got a homicide here," I said. "Probable body dump. Probable female. Probable decapitation. You'd better get recovery out here right away."

There was a long pause. No one was finding this good news.

"Pardon?"

I repeated what I'd said, asking Claudel to pass the word along to Pierre LaManche when he called the morgue. There would be nothing for the archaeologists this time.

15

I returned the mike to Groulx, who'd been listening to every word. I reminded him to get a full report from the two workers. He looked like a man who'd just been sentenced to ten to twenty. He knew he wouldn't be going anywhere for some time. I wasn't terribly sympathetic. I wouldn't be sleeping in Quebec City this weekend. In fact, as I drove the few short blocks to my condo, I suspected that no one would be sleeping much for a long time. As things turned out, I was right. What I couldn't know then was the full extent of the horror we were about to face.

2

The next day began as warm and sunny as its predecessor, a fact that would normally draw me into high spirits. I am a woman whose moods are influenced by the weather, my outlook rising and falling with the barometer. But that day the weather would be irrelevant. By 9 A.M. I was already in autopsy room 4, the smallest of the suites at the Laboratoire de Médecine Légale, and one that is specially outfitted for extra ventilation. I often work here since most of my cases are less than perfectly preserved. But it's never fully effective. Nothing is. The fans and disinfectants never quite win over the smell of ripened death. The antiseptic gleam of the stainless steel never really eradicates the images of human carnage.

The remains recovered at Le Grand Séminaire definitely qualified for room 4. After a quick dinner the previous evening, I'd gone back to the grounds and we'd processed the site. The bones were at the morgue by 9:30 P.M. Now they lay in a body bag on a gurney to my right. Case #26704 had been discussed at the morning staff meeting. Following standard procedure, the body had been assigned to one of the five pathologists working at the lab. Since the corpse was largely skeletonized,

17

the little soft tissue that remained far too decomposed for standard autopsy, my expertise was requested.

One of the autopsy technicians had called in sick this morning, leaving us shorthanded. Bad timing. It'd been a busy night: a teenage suicide, an elderly couple found dead in their home, and a car fire victim charred beyond recognition. Four autopsies. I'd offered to work alone.

I was dressed in green surgical scrubs, plastic goggles, and latex gloves. Fetching. I'd already cleaned and photographed the head. It would be X-rayed this morning, then boiled to remove the putrefied flesh and brain tissue so that I could do a detailed examination of the cranial features.

I'd painstakingly examined the hair, searching for fibers or other trace evidence. As I separated the damp strands, I couldn't help imagining the last time the victim had combed it, wondering if she'd been pleased, frustrated, indifferent. Good hair day. Bad hair day. Dead hair day.

Suppressing these thoughts, I bagged the sample and sent it up to biology for microscopic analysis. The plunger and plastic bags had also been turned over to the Laboratoire des Sciences Judiciaires where they'd be checked for prints, traces of bodily fluids, or other minuscule indicators of killer or victim.

Three hours on our hands and knees the previous night feeling through mud, combing through grass and leaves, and turning over rocks and logs had yielded nothing else. We'd searched until darkness closed us down, but came away empty. No clothing. No shoes. No jewelry. No personal effects. The crime scene recovery team would return to dig and sift today, but I doubted they'd find anything. I would have no manufacturer's tags or labels, no zippers or buckles, no jewelry, no weapons or bindings, no slashes or entrance holes in clothing to corroborate my findings. The body

18

had been dumped, naked and mutilated, stripped of everything that linked it to a life.

I returned to the body bag for the rest of its grisly contents, ready to start my preliminary examination. Later, the limbs and torso would be cleaned, and I would do a complete analysis of all the bones. We'd recovered almost the whole skeleton. The killer had made that task easier. As with the head and torso, he, or she, had placed the arms and legs in separate plastic bags. There were four in all. Very tidy. Packaged and discarded like last week's garbage. I filed the outrage in another place and forced myself to concentrate.

I removed the dismembered segments and arranged them in anatomical order on the stainless steel autopsy table in the middle of the room. First, I transferred the torso and centered it, breast side up. It held together reasonably well. Unlike the bag holding the head, those containing the body parts had not stayed tightly sealed. The torso was in the worst shape, the bones held together only by leatherized bands of dried muscle and ligament. I noted that the uppermost vertebrae were missing, and hoped I'd find them attached to the head. Except for traces, the internal organs were long gone.

Next, I placed the arms to the sides and the legs below. The limbs hadn't been exposed to sunlight, and weren't as desiccated as the chest and abdomen. They retained large portions of putrefied soft tissue. I tried to ignore the seething blanket of pale yellow that made a languid, wavelike retreat from the surface of each limb as I withdrew it from the body bag. Maggots will abandon a corpse when exposed to light. They were dropping from the body to the table, from the table to the floor, in a slow but steady drizzle. Pale yellow grains of rice lay writhing by my feet. I avoided stepping on them. I'd never really gotten used to them.

19

I reached for my clipboard and began to fill in the form. Name: *Inconnue*. Unknown. Date of autopsy: June 3, 1994. Investigators: Luc Claudel, Michel Charbonneau, *Section des homicides*, CUM. Homicide division, Montreal Urban Community Police.

I added the police report number, the morgue number, and the Laboratoire de Médecine Légale, or LML, number and experienced my usual wave of anger at the arrogant indifference of the system. Violent death allows no privacy. It plunders one's dignity as surely as it has taken one's life. The body is handled, scrutinized, and photographed, with a new series of digits allocated at each step. The victim becomes part of the evidence, an exhibit, on display for police, pathologists, forensic specialists, lawyers, and, eventually, jurors. Number it. Photograph it. Take samples. Tag the toe. While I am an active participant, I can never accept the impersonality of the system. It is like looting on the most personal level. At least I would give this victim a name. Death in anonymity would not be added to the list of violations he or she would suffer.

I selected a form from those on the clipboard. I'd alter my normal routine and leave the full skeletal inventory for later. For now the detectives wanted only the ID profile: sex, age, and race.

Race was pretty straightforward. The hair was red, what skin remained appeared fair. Decomposition, however, could do strange things. I'd check the skeletal details after cleaning. For now Caucasoid seemed a safe bet.

I already suspected the victim was female. The facial features were delicate, the overall body build slight. The long hair meant nothing.

I looked at the pelvis. Turning it to the side I noted that the notch below the hip blade was broad and shallow. I repositioned it so that I could see the pubic bones, the region in front where the right and left halves of the pelvis meet. The curve formed by their lower borders was a wide arch. Delicate raised ridges cut across the front of each pubic bone, creating distinct triangles in the lower corners. Typical female features. Later I'd take the measurements and run discriminant function analyses on the computer, but I had no doubt these were the remains of a woman.

I was wrapping the pubic area in a wet rag when the sound of the phone startled me. I hadn't realized how quiet it was. Or how tense I was. I walked to the desk, zigzagging through maggots like a child playing jacks.

"Dr. Brennan," I answered, pushing the goggles to the top of my head and dropping into the chair. Using my pen, I flicked a maggot from the desktop.

"Claudel," a voice said. One of the two CUM detectives assigned to the case. I looked at the wall clock – ten-forty. Later than I realized. He didn't go on. Obviously he assumed his name was message enough.

"I'm working on her right now," I said. I could hear a metallic grating sound. "I shou–"

"*Elle?*" he interrupted. Female?

"Yes." I watched another maggot contract into a crescent, then double back on itself and repeat the maneuver in the opposite direction. Not bad.

"White?"

"Yes."

"Age?"

"I should be able to give you a range within an hour." I could picture him looking at his watch.

"Okay. I'll be there after lunch." Click. It was a statement, not a request. Apparently it didn't matter if it was okay with me.

I hung up and returned to the lady on the table. Picking up the clipboard, I flipped to the next page on the report form. Age. This was an adult. Earlier, I'd

21

checked her mouth. The wisdom teeth were fully erupted.

I examined the arms where they'd been detached at the shoulders. The end of each humerus was fully formed. I could see no line demarcating a separate cap on either side. The other ends were useless – they had been cleanly severed just above the wrists. I'd have to find those fragments later. I looked at the legs. The head of the femur was also completely formed on both right and left.

Something about those severed joints disturbed me. It was a feeling apart from the normal reaction to depravity, but it was vague, ill-formed. As I allowed the left leg to settle back on to the table my guts felt like ice. The cloud of dread that first touched me in the woods returned. I shook it off and forced myself to focus on the question at hand. Age. Fix the age. A correct age estimate can lead to a name. Nothing else will matter until she has a name.

I used a scalpel to peel back the flesh around the knee and elbow joints. It came away easily. Here, too, the long bones were fully mature. I'd verify this on X-ray, but knew it meant bone growth had been completed. I saw no lipping or arthritic change in the joints. Adult, but young. It was consistent with the lack of wear I'd observed on the teeth.

But I wanted more precision. Claudel would expect it. I looked at each collarbone where it met the sternum at the base of the throat. Though the one on the right was detached, the joint surface was encased in a hard knot of dried cartilage and ligament. Using a scissors, I snipped away as much of the leathery tissue as I could, then wrapped the bone in another wet rag. I returned my attention to the pelvis.

I removed that rag and, again using a scalpel, began gently sawing through the cartilage connecting the two

22

halves in front. Wetting it down had made it more pliable, easier to cut, but still the process was slow and tedious. I didn't want to risk damaging the underlying surfaces. When the pubic bones were finally separate, I cut the few strips of dried muscle uniting the pelvis to the lower end of the spine in back, freed it, carried it to the sink, and submerged the pubic portion in water.

Next I returned to the body and unwrapped the collarbone. Again, I teased off as much tissue as possible. Then I filled a plastic specimen container with water, positioned it against the rib cage, and stuck the end of the clavicle in it.

I glanced at the wall clock – 12:25 P.M. Stepping back from the table, I peeled off my gloves and straightened. Slowly. My back felt like a Pop Warner league had been practicing on it. I placed my hands on my hips and stretched, arching backward and rotating my upper body. It didn't really relieve the pain, but it didn't hurt either. My spine seemed to hurt a lot lately, and bending over an autopsy table for three hours tended to aggravate it. I refused to believe or admit it was age-related. My newly discovered need for reading glasses and the seemingly permanent upgrade from 115 to 120 in my weight were likewise not the result of aging. Nothing was.

I turned to see Daniel, one of the autopsy technicians, watching from the outer office. A tic pulled his upper lip, and his eyes pinched shut momentarily. With a jerk he shifted, placing all his weight on one leg and cocking the other. He looked like a sandpiper waiting out a wave.

"When would you like me to do the radiography?" he asked. His glasses rode low on his nose and he seemed to peer over rather than through them.

"I should finish up by three," I said, tossing my gloves into the biological waste receptacle. I suddenly realized how hungry I was. My morning coffee sat on the counter, cold and untouched. I'd completely forgotten it.

"Okay." He hopped backward, pivoted, and disappeared down the hall.

I flipped the goggles onto the counter, withdrew a white paper sheet from a drawer below the side counter, unfolded it, and covered the body. After washing my hands I returned to my office on the fifth floor, changed into street clothes, and went out for lunch. This was rare for me, but today I needed the sunshine.

Claudel was true to his word. When I returned at one-thirty he was already in my office. He sat opposite my desk, his attention focused on the reconstructed skull on my worktable. He turned his head when he heard me, but said nothing. I hung my coat on the back of the door and moved past him and into my chair.

"*Bonjour,* Monsieur Claudel. *Comment ça va?*" I smiled at him across my desk.

"*Bonjour.*" Apparently he was uninterested in how I was doing. Okay. I waited. I would not succumb to his charm.

A folder lay on the desk in front of him. He placed his hand on it and looked at me. His face brought to mind a parrot. The features angled sharply from his ears to the midline, plunging forward into a beaklike nose. Along this apex his chin, his mouth, and the tip of his nose pointed downward in a series of V's. When he smiled, which was rare, the V of his mouth sharpened and the lips drew in, rather than back.

He sighed. He was being very patient with me. I hadn't worked with Claudel before, but knew his reputation. He thought himself an exceptionally intelligent man.

"I have several names," he said. "Possibles. They all

24

disappeared within the last six months."

We'd already discussed the question of time since death. My morning's work hadn't changed my mind. I was certain she'd been dead less than three months. That would place the murder in March or later. Winters are cold in Quebec, hard on the living but kind to the dead. Frozen bodies do not decay. Nor do they attract bugs. Had she been dumped last fall, before the onset of winter, there would've been signs of insect infestation. The presence of casings or larvae would've indicated an aborted fall invasion. There were none. Given that it had been a warm spring, the abundance of maggots and the degree of deterioration were consistent with an interval of three months or less. The presence of connective tissue along with the virtual absence of viscera and brain matter also suggested a late winter, early spring death.

I leaned back and looked at him expectantly. I could be cagey too. He opened the folder and thumbed through its contents. I waited.

Selecting one of the forms, he read, "Myriam Weider." There was a pause as he sifted through the information on the form. "Disappeared April 4, 1994." Pause. "Female. White." Long pause. "Date of birth 9/6/48."

We both calculated mentally – forty-five years old.

"Possible," I said, gesturing with my hand for him to go on.

He laid the form on the desk and read from the next. "Solange Leger. Reported missing by the husband," he paused, straining to make out the date, "May 2, 1994. Female. White. Date of birth 8/17/28."

"No." I shook my head. "Too old."

He placed the form at the back of the folder and selected another. "Isabelle Gagnon. Last seen April 1, 1994. Female. White. Date of birth 1/15/71."

"Twenty-three. Yeah." I nodded slowly. "Possible." It went on the desk.

"Suzanne St. Pierre. Female. Missing since March 9, 1994." His lips moved as he read. "Failed to return from school." He paused, calculating on his own. "Age sixteen. Jesus Christ."

Again I shook my head. "She's too young. This isn't a kid."

He frowned, pulling out the last form. "Evelyn Fontaine. Female. Age thirty-six. Last seen in Sept Îles on March 28. Oh yeah. She's an Innu."

"Doubtful," I said. I didn't think the remains were those of an Indian.

"That's it," he said. There were two forms on the desk. Myriam Weider, age forty-five, and Isabelle Gagnon, age twenty-three. Maybe one of them was lying downstairs in room 4. Claudel looked at me. His eyebrows rose in the middle forming yet another V, this one inverted.

"How old *was* she?" he asked, emphasizing the verb and his long-suffering patience.

"Let's go downstairs and see." That'll bring a little sunshine into your day, I thought.

It was petty but I couldn't help it. I knew Claudel's reputation for avoiding the autopsy room, and I wanted to discomfort him. For a moment he looked trapped. I enjoyed his unease. Grabbing a lab coat from the hook on the door, I hurried down the hall and inserted my key for the elevator. He was silent as we descended. He looked like a man on the way to a prostate exam. Claudel rarely rode this elevator. It stopped only at the morgue.

The body lay undisturbed. I gloved and removed the white sheet. From the corner of my eye I could see Claudel framed in the doorway. He'd entered the room

26

just far enough to be able to say he'd been there. His eyes wandered over the steel countertops, the glass-fronted cabinets with their stock of clear plastic containers, the hanging scale, everything but the body. I'd seen it before. Photographs were no threat. The blood and gore were somewhere else. Distant. The murder scene was a clinical exercise. No problem. Dissect it, study it, solve the puzzle. But place a body on an autopsy table and it was a different matter. Claudel had put his face in neutral, hoping to look calm.

I removed the pubic bones from the water and gently pried them apart. Using a probe, I teased around the edges of the gelatinous sheath that covered the right pubic face. Gradually it loosened its hold and came away. The underlying bone was marked with deep furrows and ridges coursing horizontally across its surface. A sliver of solid bone partially framed the outer margin, forming a delicate and incomplete rim around the pubic face. I repeated the process on the left. It was identical.

Claudel hadn't moved from the doorway. I carried the pelvis to the Luxolamp, pulled the extensor arm toward me, and pressed the switch. Fluorescent light illuminated the bone. Through the round magnifying glass, details appeared that hadn't been apparent to the naked eye. I looked at the uppermost curve of each hipbone and saw what I'd been expecting.

"Monsieur Claudel," I said without looking up. "Look at this."

He came up behind me, and I moved over to allow him an unobstructed view. I pointed to an irregularity on the upper border of the hip. The iliac crest was in the process of attaching itself when death had occurred.

I set the pelvis down. He continued looking at it, but didn't touch it. I returned to the body to examine the clavicle, certain of what I'd find. I withdrew the sternal end from the water and began to tease away the tissue.

27

When I could see the joint surface I gestured for Claudel to join me. Wordlessly I pointed to the end of the bone. Its surface was billowy, like the pubic face. A small disk of bone clung to the center, its edges distinct and unfused.

"So?" Sweat beaded his forehead. He was hiding his nervousness with bravado.

"She's young. Probably early twenties."

I could have explained how bone reveals age, but I didn't think he'd be a good listener, so I just waited. Particles of cartilage clung to my gloved hands, and I held them away from my body, palms up, like a pan-handler. Claudel kept the same distance he would with an Ebola patient. His eyes stayed on me, but their focus shifted to thoughts inside his head as he ran through the data, looking for a match.

"Gagnon." It was a statement, not a question.

I nodded. Isabelle Gagnon. Age twenty-three.

"I'll have the coroner request dental records," he said.

I nodded again. He seemed to bring it out in me.

"Cause of death?" he asked.

"Nothing apparent," I said. "I may know more when I see the X rays. Or I may see something on the bones when they're cleaned."

With that he left. He didn't say good-bye. I didn't expect it. His departure was mutually appreciated.

I stripped off my gloves and tossed them. On the way out I poked my head into the large autopsy suite and told Daniel I was finished with this case for the day. I asked him to take full body and cranial X rays, A-P and lateral views. Upstairs I stopped by the histology lab and told the head technician that the body was ready for boiling, warning him to take extra care since this was a dismemberment. It was unnecessary. No one could reduce a body like Denis. In two days a skeleton would

28

appear, clean and undamaged.

I spent the rest of the afternoon with the glued-together skull. Though fragmentary, there was, indeed, enough detail to confirm the identity of its owner. He wouldn't drive any more propane tankers.

Returning home, I began to feel the sense of foreboding I'd experienced in the ravine. All day I'd used work to keep it at bay. I'd banished the apprehension by centering my mind fully on identifying the victim and on piecing together the late trucker. At lunch the park pigeons had been my distraction. Unraveling the pecking order could be all-consuming. Gray was alpha. Brown speckles seemed to be next. Blackfoot was clearly low on the list.

Now I was free to relax. To think. To worry. It started as soon as I pulled into the garage and turned off the radio. Music off, anxiety on. No, I admonished myself. Later. After dinner.

I entered the apartment and heard the reassuring beep of the security system. Leaving my briefcase in the entry hall, I closed the door and walked to the Lebanese restaurant on the corner, where I ordered a Shish Taouk and Shawarma plate to go. It's what I love most about living downtown – within a block of my condo are representative samples of all the cuisines of the world. Could the weight gain . . . ? Nah.

While I waited for the take-out I perused the buffet selections. Homos. Taboule. *Feuilles de vignes*. Bless the global village. Lebanese gone French.

A shelf to the left of the cash register held bottles of red wine. My weapon of choice. As I looked at them, for the thousandth time I felt the craving. I remembered the taste, the smell, the dry, tangy feel of the wine on my tongue. I remembered the warmth that would start in my gut and spread upward and outward, navigating a path through my body, lighting the fires of well-being along its course. The bonfires of control. Of vigor. Of invincibility. I could use that right now, I thought. Right. Who was I kidding? I wouldn't stop there. What were those stages? I'd move right on to bulletproof and then to invisible. Or was it the other way around? No matter. I'd carry it too far, and then the crash would come. The comfort would be short term, the price heavy. It'd been six years since I'd had a drink.

I took my food home and ate it with Birdie and the Montreal Expos. He slept, curled in my lap, purring softly. They lost to the Cubs by two runs. Neither mentioned the murder. I appreciated that.

I took a long, hot bath and fell into bed at ten-thirty. Alone in the dark and quiet I could no longer suppress the thought. Like cells gone mad, it grew and gathered strength, finally forcing itself into my consciousness, insisting on recognition. The other homicide. The other young woman who'd come to the morgue in pieces. I saw her in vivid detail, remembered my feelings as I'd worked on her bones. Chantale Trottier. Age sixteen. Strangled, beaten, decapitated, dismembered. Less than a year ago she'd arrived naked and packaged in plastic garbage bags.

I was ready to end the day but my mind refused to clock out. I lay there as mountains formed and the continental plates shifted. Finally, I fell asleep, the phrase ricocheting in my skull. It would haunt me all weekend. Serial murder.

3

Gabby was calling my flight. I had an enormous suitcase and couldn't maneuver it down the jetway. The other passengers were annoyed, but no one was helping me. I could see Katy leaning out to watch me from the front row of first class. She was wearing the dress we'd chosen for her high school graduation. Moss green silk. But she'd told me later she didn't like it, regretted the choice. She would've preferred the floral print. Why was she wearing it? Why was Gabby at the airport when she should have been at the university? Her voice over the loudspeaker was becoming louder, more strident.

I sat up. It was seven-twenty. Monday morning. Light illuminated the edges of the window shade, but little seeped into the room.

Gabby's voice continued. ". . . but I knew I wouldn't be able to get ya later. Guess you're an earlier riser than I thought. Anyway, about to . . ."

I picked up the phone. "Hello." I tried to sound less groggy than I was. The voice stopped in midsentence.

"Temp? Is that you?"

I nodded.

"Did I wake ya?"

"Yes." I was not yet up to a witty response.

31

"Sorry. Should I call back later?"

"No, no. I'm up." I resisted adding that I'd had to get up to answer the phone anyway.

"Butt outa bed, babe. Early worm time. Listen, about tonight. Could we make it se–" A high-pitched screech interrupted her.

"Hang on. I must've left the answering machine on automatic." I set down the receiver and walked to the living room. The red light was flashing. I picked up the portable handset, returned to the bedroom, and replaced that receiver in its cradle.

"Okay." By now I was fully awake and starting to crave coffee. I headed for the kitchen.

"I was calling about tonight." Her voice had an edge to it. I couldn't blame her. She'd been trying to finish one sentence for five minutes now.

"I'm sorry, Gabby. I spent the whole weekend reading a student thesis, and I was up pretty late last night. I was really sound asleep. I didn't even hear the phone ring." That was odd, even for me. "What's up?"

"About tonight. Uh, could we make it seven-thirty instead of seven? This project has me jumpier than a cricket in a lizard cage."

"Sure. No problem. That's probably better for me too." Cradling the phone on my shoulder, I reached into the cabinet for the jar of coffee beans, and transferred three scoops to the grinder.

"Want me to pick ya up?" she asked.

"Either way. I can drive if you want. Where should we go?" I considered grinding, decided against it. She already sounded a little touchy.

Silence. I could picture her playing with her nose ring as she thought it over. Or today it might be a stud. At first it had bothered me, and I'd had difficulty concentrating in conversations with Gabby. I'd find myself focusing on the ring, wondering how much pain was involved in piercing one's nose. I no longer noticed.

"It should be nice tonight," she said. "How 'bout someplace we can eat outside? Prince Arthur or St. Denis?"

"Great," I said. "No reason for you to come down here, then. I'll be by about seven-thirty. Think of someplace new. I feel like something exotic."

Though it could be risky with Gabby, that was our usual routine. She knew the city much better than I, so the choice of restaurant usually fell to her.

"Okay. *À plus tard*."

"*À plus tard*," I responded. I was surprised and a bit relieved. Normally she'd stay on the phone forever. I often had to manufacture excuses to escape.

The telephone has always been a lifeline for Gabby and me. I associate her with the phone as I do no one else. This pattern was set early in our friendship. Our graduate student conversations were a strange relief from the melancholy that enveloped me in those years. My daughter Katy finally fed, bathed, and in her crib, Gabby and I would log hours on the line, sharing the excitement of a newly discovered book, discussing our classes, professors, fellow students, and nothing in particular. It was the only frivolity we allowed ourselves in a nonfrivolous time in our lives.

Though we talk less frequently now, the pattern has altered little in the decades since. Together or apart, we are there for each other's highs and lows. It was Gabby who talked me through the AA days, when the need for a drink colored my waking hours and brought me to at night, trembling and sweating. It is me whom Gabby dials, exhilarated and hopeful when love enters her life, lonely and despairing when, once again, it leaves.

When the coffee was ready I took it to the glass table in the dining room. Memories of Gabby were replaying in my mind. I always smiled when I thought of her.

Gabby in grad seminar. Gabby at the Pit. Gabby at the dig, red kerchief askew, hennaed dreadlocks swinging as she scraped the dirt with her trowel. At six foot one she understood early that she'd never be a conventional beauty. She didn't try to become thin or tan. She didn't shave her legs or armpits. Gabby was Gabby. Gabrielle Macaulay from Trois-Rivières, Quebec. French mother, English father.

We'd been close in grad school. She'd hated physical anthropology, suffered through the courses I loved. I felt the same about her ethnology seminars. When we left Northwestern I'd gone to North Carolina and she'd returned to Quebec. We'd seen little of each other over the years, but the phone had kept us close. It was largely because of Gabby that I'd been offered a visiting professorship at McGill in 1990. During that year I'd begun working at the lab part time, and had continued the arrangement after returning from North Carolina, commuting north every six weeks as the caseload dictated. This year I had taken a leave of absence from UNC-Charlotte, and was in Montreal full time. I'd missed being with Gabby, and was enjoying the renewal of our friendship.

The flashing light on the answering machine caught my eye. There must've been a call before Gabby. I had it set to answer after four rings unless the tape had already been triggered. Then it would pick up after one. Wondering how I could've slept through four rings and an entire message, I went over and pressed the button. The tape rewound, engaged, and played. Silence, then a click. A short beep followed, then Gabby's voice. It was only a hang-up. Good. I hit rewind and went to dress for work.

The medico-legal lab is located in what is known as the QPP or SQ building, depending on your linguistic preference. To anglophones, it is the Quebec Provincial Police – to francophones, La Sûreté du Québec. The Laboratoire de Médecine Légale, similar to a medical examiner's office in the States, shares the fifth floor with the Laboratoire des Sciences Judiciaires, the central crime lab for the province. Together the LML and the LSJ make up a unit known as La Direction de l'Expertise Judiciaire – DEJ. There is a jail on the fourth and top three floors of the building. The morgue and autopsy suites are in the basement. The provincial police occupy the remaining eight floors.

This arrangement has its advantages. We're all together. If I need an opinion on fibers, or a report on a soil sample, a walk down the corridor takes me directly to the source. It also has its drawbacks in that we are easily accessible. For an SQ investigator, or a city detective dropping off evidence or paperwork, it is a short elevator ride to our offices.

Witness that morning. Claudel was waiting at my office door when I arrived. He was carrying a small brown envelope and repeatedly tapped its edge against the palm of his hand. To say he looked agitated would be like saying Gandhi looked hungry.

"I have the dental records," he said in way of greeting. He flourished the envelope like a presenter at the Academy Awards.

"I picked them up myself."

He read a name scrawled on the outside. "Dr. Nguyen. He's got an office over in Rosemont. I would have been here earlier but the guy's got a real cretin of a secretary."

"Coffee?" I asked. Though I'd never met Dr. Nguyen's secretary I felt empathy for her. I knew she hadn't had a good morning.

He opened his mouth to accept or decline. I don't know which. At that moment Marc Bergeron rounded

35

the corner. Seemingly unaware of our presence, he strode past the row of shiny black office doors, stopping one short of mine. Crooking a knee, he placed his brief-case on the upraised thigh. I thought of the crane maneuver in the *Karate Kid*. Thus poised, he clicked the case open, rummaged among its contents, and withdrew a set of keys.

"Marc?"

It startled him. He slammed the case shut and swung it down, all in one movement.

"*Bien fait*," I said, suppressing a smile.

"*Merci*." He looked at Claudel and me, the briefcase in his left hand, the keys in his right.

Marc Bergeron was, by any standard, peculiar-looking. In his late fifties or early sixties, his long, bony frame was slightly stooped, bent forward at midchest as if perpetually ready to absorb a blow to the stomach. His hair started midway back on his scalp and exploded in a corona of white frizz. It brought him to well over six foot three. His wire-rimmed glasses were always greasy and speckled with dust, and he often squinted, as though reading the fine print on a rebate coupon. He looked more like a Tim Burton creation than a forensic dentist.

"Monsieur Claudel has the dental records for Gagnon," I said, indicating the detective. Claudel raised the envelope, as if in proof.

Nothing clicked behind the smudged lenses. Bergeron regarded me blankly. He looked like a tall, confused dandelion, with his long, thin stem and puff of white hair. I realized he knew nothing about the case.

Bergeron was among the professionals employed part time by the LML, each a forensic specialist consulted for specific expertise. Neuropathology. Radiology. Microbiology. Odontology. He normally came to the lab once a week. The rest of the time he saw patients in

36

private practice. He hadn't been here last week.

I summarized. "Last Thursday workers found some bones on the grounds of Le Grand Séminaire. Pierre LaManche thought it was another historic cemetery situation and sent me over. It wasn't."

He set down the briefcase and listened intently.

"I found parts of a dismembered body that had been bagged and dumped, probably within the last couple of months. It's a female, white, probably in her early twenties."

Claudel's envelope tapping had become more rapid. It stopped momentarily as he looked pointedly at his watch. He cleared his throat.

Bergeron looked at him, then back at me. I continued.

"Monsieur Claudel and I narrowed the possibles to one we think is pretty good. The profile fits and the timing is reasonable. He drove the records in himself. A Dr. Nguyen over in Rosemont. Know him?"

Bergeron shook his head and extended a long, skinny hand. "*Bon*," he said. "Give them to me. I'll have a look at them. Has Denis done X rays yet?"

"Daniel did them," I said. "They should be on your desk."

He unlocked the door to his office. Claudel followed. Through the open door I could see a small brown envelope lying on his desk. Bergeron picked it up and checked the case number. From where I stood I could see Claudel charting the room, like a monarch, deciding on a place to light.

"You may call me in an hour, Monsieur Claudel," Bergeron said.

The detective stopped in mid-chart. He started to speak, then pressed his lips into a thin, tight line, readjusted his cuffs, and left. For the second time in minutes I suppressed a smile. Bergeron would never

37

tolerate an investigator peering over his shoulder as he worked. Claudel had just learned that.

Bergeron's gaunt face reappeared. "Coming in?" he asked.

"Sure," I said. "Coffee?" I still hadn't had any since getting to work. We often got it for each other, taking turns making the trek to the kitchenette in the other wing.

"Great." He dug out his mug and handed it to me. "I'll get set up here."

I got my own mug and started down the corridor. I was pleased at his invitation. We often worked the same cases, the decomposed, burned, mummified, or skeletonized, the dead who could not be identified by normal means. I thought we worked well together. It seemed he agreed.

When I returned, two sets of small black squares lay on the light box. Each X ray showed a segment of jaw, the dentition bright against a stark black background. I remembered the teeth as I'd first seen them in the woods, their flawlessness in sharp contrast to the grisly context. They looked different now. Sanitized. Neatly lined up in rows, ready for inspection. The familiar shapes of crowns, roots, and pulp chambers were illuminated by differing intensities of gray and white.

Bergeron began by arranging the antemortem radiographs to the right and the postmortem to the left. His long, bony fingers located a small bump on each X ray, and, one by one, he oriented them, placing the dot face up. When he'd finished, each antemortem radiograph lay in identical alignment to its postmortem counterpart.

He compared the two sets for discrepancies. Everything matched. Neither series showed missing teeth. All roots were complete to their tips. The outlines and curvatures on the left mirrored perfectly those on

38

the right. But most noticeable were the stark white globs representing dental restorations. The constellation of shapes on the antemortem films was mimicked in detail on the films Daniel had taken.

After studying the X rays for what seemed an interminable time, Bergeron selected a square from the right, placed it over the corresponding postmortem X ray, and positioned it for my inspection. The irregular patterns on the molars superimposed exactly. He swiveled to face me.

"*C'est positif,*" he said, leaning back and placing an elbow on the table. "Unofficially, of course, until I finish with the written records." He reached for his coffee. He would do an exhaustive comparison of the written records in addition to a more detailed X-ray comparison, but he had no doubt. This was Isabelle Gagnon.

I was glad I wouldn't be the one to face the parents. The husband. The lover. The son. I'd been present at such meetings. I knew the look. The eyes, pleading. Tell me this is a mistake. A bad dream. Make it end. Say it isn't so. Then, comprehension. In a millisecond, the world changed forever.

"Thanks for looking at this right away, Marc," I said. "And thanks for the preliminary."

"I wish they could all be this easy." He took a sip of coffee, grimaced and shook his head.

"Do you want me to deal with Claudel?" I tried to keep the distaste out of my voice. Apparently I didn't succeed. He smiled knowingly.

"I have no doubt you can handle Monsieur Claudel."

"Right," I said. "That's what he needs. A handler."

I could hear him laughing as I returned to my office.

My grandmother always told me there is good in everyone. "Just look fer it . . ." she'd say, the brogue smooth

as satin, ". . . and ye'll find it. Everyone has a virtue."
Gran, you never met Claudel.

Claudel's virtue was promptness. He was back in fifty minutes.

He stopped in Bergeron's office, and I could hear the voices through the wall. My name was repeated several times as Bergeron forwarded him to me. Claudel's cadence signaled irritation. He wanted a real opinion, but now he'd have to settle for me again. He appeared seconds later, his face hard.

Neither of us offered greeting. He waited at the door.

"It's positive," I said. "Gagnon."

He frowned, but I could see excitement collecting in his eyes. He had a victim. Now he could begin the investigation. I wondered if he felt anything for the dead woman or if it was all an exercise for him. Find the bad guy. Outwit the perp. I'd heard the banter, the comments, the jokes made over a victim's battered body. For some it was a way to deal with the obscenity of violence, a protective barrier against the daily reality of human slaughter. Morgue humor. Mask the horror in male bravado. For others it went deeper. I suspected Claudel was among the others.

I watched him for several seconds. Down the hall a phone rang. Though I truly disliked the man, I forced myself to admit that his opinion of me mattered. I wanted his approval. I wanted him to like me. I wanted all of them to accept me, to admit me to the club.

An image of Dr. Lentz flashed into my mind, a hologram psychologist, lecturing from the past.

"Tempe," she would say, "you are the child of an alcoholic father. You are searching for the attention he denied you. You want Daddy's approval, so you try to please everybody."

She made me see it, but she couldn't correct it. I had to do that on my own. Occasionally I overcompensated,

40

and many found me a genuine pain in the ass. This had not been the case with Claudel. I realized I'd been avoiding a confrontation.

I took a deep breath and began, choosing my words carefully.

"Monsieur Claudel, have you considered the possibility that this murder is connected to others that have taken place during the past two years?"

His features froze, the lips drawn in so tightly against his teeth as to be almost invisible. A cloud of red began at his collar and spread slowly up his neck and face. His voice was icy.

"Such as?" He held himself absolutely still.

"Such as Chantale Trottier," I continued. "She was killed in October of '93. Dismembered, decapitated, disemboweled." I looked directly at him. "What was left of her was found wrapped in plastic trash bags."

He raised both hands to the level of his mouth, clasped them together, fingers intertwined, and tapped them against his lips. His perfectly chosen gold cuff links, in his perfectly fitted designer shirt, clinked faintly. He looked straight at me.

"Ms. Brennan," he said, emphasizing the English label. "Perhaps you should stick to your area of expertise. I think we would recognize any links which might exist between crimes under our jurisdiction. These murders share nothing in common."

Ignoring the demotion, I forged on. "They were both women. They were both murdered within the past year. Both bodies showed signs of mutilation or attempt–"

His carefully constructed dam of control ruptured, and his anger rushed at me in a torrent.

"*Tabernac!*" he exploded. "Do you wo–"

His lips pursed to form the despised word, but he stopped himself just in time. With a visible effort, he regained his composure.

41

"Do you always have to overreact?"

"Think about it," I spat at him. I was trembling in rage as I got up to close the door.

4

It should have felt good just to sit in the steam room and sweat. Like broccoli. That had been my intention. Three miles on the StairMaster, a round on the Nautilus, then vegetate. Like the rest of the day, the gym was not living up to my expectations. The workout had dissipated some of my anger, but I was still agitated. I knew Claudel was an asshole. It was one of the names I'd stomped on his chest with each pump of the StairMaster. Asshole. Dickhead. Moron. Two syllables worked best. I'd figured that out, but little else. It distracted me for a while, but now that my mind was idle I couldn't drive the murders out. Isabelle Gagnon. Chantale Trottier. I kept rolling them around, like peas on a dinner plate.

I shifted my towel, and allowed my brain to reprocess the events of the day. When Claudel left, I'd checked with Denis to see when Gagnon's skeleton would be ready. I wanted to go over every inch of it for signs of trauma. Fractures. Gashes. Anything. Something about the way the body had been carved up bothered me. I wanted a close look at those cut marks. There was a problem with the boiling unit. The bones wouldn't be ready until tomorrow.

43

Next I'd gone to the central files and pulled the jacket for Trottier. I spent the rest of the afternoon poring over police accounts, autopsy findings, toxicology reports, photos. Something lingered in my memory cells, nagging at me, insisting the cases were linked. Some forgotten detail hovered just beyond recall, coupling the victims in a way I didn't understand. Some stored memory that I couldn't access told me it wasn't just the mutilation and bagging. I wanted to find the connection.

I readjusted my towel and wiped sweat from my face. The skin on my fingertips had gathered into little puckers. Everywhere else I was slick as a perch. I was definitely a short-timer. I couldn't take the heat for more than twenty minutes, no matter what the alleged benefits. Five more.

Chantale Trottier had been killed less than a year ago, in the fall of my first year full time at the lab. She was sixteen. I'd spread the autopsy photos on my desk this afternoon, but I didn't need them. I remembered her vividly, remembered in crisp detail the day she'd arrived at the morgue.

October 22, the afternoon of the oyster party. It was a Friday and most of the staff had quit early to drink beer and shuck their way through the crates of Malpeques that are an autumn tradition.

Through the crowd in the conference room I noticed LaManche talking on the phone. He held a hand over his free ear as a barricade against the party noise. I watched him. When he hung up he did a visual sweep of the room. Spotting me, he signaled with one hand, indicating that I should meet him in the hall. When he located Bergeron and got his attention, he repeated the message. In the elevator, five minutes later, he explained. A young girl had just come in. The body was badly beaten and dismembered. A visual ID would be impossible. He wanted Bergeron to look at the teeth. He wanted me to look at the cuts on the bones.

The mood in the autopsy room was in sharp contrast to the gaiety upstairs. Two SQ detectives stood at a distance while a uniformed officer from the identity section took photos. The technician positioned the remains in silence. The detectives said nothing. There were no jokes or wisecracks. The usual banter was completely stilled. The only sound was the click of the shutter as it recorded the atrocity that lay on the autopsy table.

What was left of her had been arranged to form a body. The six bloody pieces had been placed in correct anatomical order, but the angles were slightly off, turning her into a life-sized version of those plastic dolls designed to be twisted into distorted positions. The overall effect was macabre.

Her head had been cut off high on the neck, and the truncated muscles looked bright poppy red. The pallid skin rolled back gently at the severed edges, as if recoiling from contact with the fresh, raw meat. Her eyes were half open, and a delicate trail of dried blood meandered from her right nostril. Her hair was wet and lay plastered against her head. It had been long and blond.

Her trunk was bisected at the waist. The upper torso lay with her arms bent at the elbows, the hands drawn in and resting on her stomach. Coffin position, except her fingers were not intertwined.

Her right hand was partially detached, and the ends of the creamy white tendons jutted out like snapped electrical cords. Her attacker had been more successful with the left. The technician had placed it beside her head, where it lay alone, the fingers drawn in like the legs of a shriveled spider.

Her chest had been opened lengthwise, from throat to belly, and the pendulous breasts drooped downward toward each side of the rib cage, their weight drawing apart the two halves of divided flesh. The lower section of torso extended from her waist to her knees. Her lower legs rested side by side, positioned below their normal points of attachment. Unfettered by union at the knee joint, they lay with the feet rotated far to the sides, the toes pointed outward.

With a stab of pain, I'd noticed that her toenails were painted a soft pink. The intimacy of that simple act had caused me such an ache that I wanted to cover her, to scream at all of them to leave her alone. Instead, I'd stood and watched, waiting for my turn to trespass.

I could still close my eyes and see the jagged edges of the lacerations on her scalp, evidence of repeated blows with a blunt object. I could recall in minute detail the bruises on her neck. I could visualize the petechial hemorrhages in her eyes, tiny spots left by the bursting of small blood vessels. Caused by tremendous pressure on the jugular vessels, they are the classic sign of strangulation.

My gut had recoiled as I'd wondered what else had happened to her, this woman-child so carefully composed and nurtured by peanut butter, Scout leaders, summer camps, and Sunday schools. I'd grieved for the years she wouldn't be allowed to live, for the proms she'd never attend, and the beers she'd never sneak. We think we are a civilized tribe, we North Americans in the last decade of the second millennium. We'd promised her three score years and ten. We'd allowed her but sixteen.

Shutting out the memories of that painful autopsy, I wiped perspiration from my face and shook my head, whipping my soggy hair back and forth. The mental images were liquefying so that I could no longer separate what I was recalling from the past from what I'd seen in the detail photos that afternoon. Like life. I've long suspected that many of my memories of childhood are

46

actually drawn from old pictures, that they are a composite of snapshots, a mosaic of celluloid images reworked into a remembered reality. Kodak cast backward. Maybe it's better to recall the past that way. We rarely take pictures of sad occasions.

The door opened and a woman entered the steam room. She smiled and nodded, then carefully spread her towel on the bench to my left. Her thighs were the consistency of a sea sponge. I gathered my towel and headed for the shower.

Birdie was waiting when I got home. He watched me from across the entrance hall, his white form reflected softly in the black marble floor. He seemed annoyed. Do cats feel such emotions? Perhaps I was projecting. I checked his bowl and found it low, but not empty. Feeling guilty, I filled it anyway. Birdie had adjusted well to the move. His needs were simple. Me, Friskies Ocean Fish, and sleep. Such wants find no impediment in borders and relocate easily.

I had an hour before I was to meet Gabby so I stretched out on the sofa. The workout and steam had taken their toll, and I felt as if major muscle groups had gone off duty. But exhaustion has its rewards. I was physically, if not mentally, relaxed. As usual at such times I really wanted a drink.

Late afternoon sunlight flooded the room, its effect muted by the bleached muslin sheared across each window. It is what I love most about the apartment. The sunlight melds with the pale pastels to create a bright airiness I find soothing. It is my island of tranquillity in a world of tension.

The apartment is on the ground floor of a U-shaped building, which wraps around an inner courtyard. The unit takes up most of one wing and is free of immediate neighbors. On one side of the living room, French doors

47

open to the courtyard garden. A set opposite gives way to my own small yard. It is an urban rarity – grass and flowers in the heart of Centre-ville. I've even planted a small herb garden.

At first I'd wondered if I'd like living by myself. I'd never done it. I'd gone from home to college to marriage with Pete, raising Katy, never the mistress of my own estate. I need not have worried. I love it.

I was drifting on the boundary between sleep and wakefulness when the phone yanked me back. Headachy from a nap interrupted, I spoke into the receiver. I was rewarded by a robotic voice trying to sell me a cemetery plot.

"*Merde*," I said, swinging my legs outward and rising from the couch. It is the one drawback to living alone. I talk to myself.

The other drawback is being apart from my daughter. I dialed, and she picked up on the first ring.

"Oh, Mom, I'm so glad you called! How are you? I can't talk now, I've got someone on the other line, but can I catch you a little later?"

I smiled. Katy. Always breathless and spinning in a thousand directions.

"Sure, hon. It's nothing important, just wanted to say hi. I'm going to dinner with Gabby tonight. How about tomorrow?"

"Great. Give her a big kiss for me. Oh, I think I got an A in French if that's what's on your mind."

"Never doubted it," I said, laughing. "Talk to you tomorrow."

Twenty minutes later I parked in front of Gabby's building. By some miracle there was a spot just opposite her door. I killed the engine and got out.

Gabby lives on Carré St. Louis, a charming little square tucked between Rue St. Laurent and Rue St.

Denis. The park is surrounded by row houses with unpredictable shapes and elaborate wood trim, relics of an age of architectural whimsy. Their owners have painted them with rainbow eccentricity and filled their yards with riotous bouquets of summer flowers, making them look like a scene in a Disney animation.

There is an air of capriciousness to the park, from its central fountain, rising from the pool like a giant tulip, to the small wrought-iron fence decorating its perimeter. Little more than knee-high, its frivolous spikes and curlicues separate the public green of the plaza from the gingerbread houses encircling its perimeter. It seemed the Victorians, so prim in their sexual prudery, could be playful in their building design. Somehow, I find this reassuring, a quiet confirmation that there is balance in life.

I glanced at Gabby's building. It stands on the north side of the park, the third one in from Rue Henri-Julien. Katy would have called it "wretched excess," like the prom dresses we'd scorned in our annual spring quest. It seemed the architect couldn't stop until he'd incorporated every fanciful detail he knew.

The building is a three-story brownstone, its lower floors bulging into large bay windows, its roof rising to a truncated hexagonal turret. The roof tower is covered with small oval tiles arranged like the scales on a mermaid's tail. It's topped by a widow's walk bordered in wrought iron. The windows are Moorish, their lower edges square, their upper borders ballooning into domed arches. Every door and window is framed by intricately carved woodwork painted a light shade of lavender. Downstairs, to the left of the bay, an iron staircase sweeps from ground level to a second-story porch, the sworls and loops of its banisters echoing those of the park fence. Early June flowers bloomed in window boxes and in oversized pots lining the porch.

She must have been waiting. Before I could cross the street, the lace curtain flicked momentarily, and the front door opened. She waved, then locked the door and double-checked, shaking the handle vigorously. She swooped down the steep iron staircase, her long skirt billowing behind her like a spinnaker on a downwind run. I could hear her as she drew near. Gabby likes things that sparkle or jangle. That night a ring of small silver bells circled her ankle. It jingled with each step. She dressed in what I'd dubbed Nouveau Ashram in grad school. She always would.

"How ya doing?"

"Good," I hedged.

Even as I was saying it, I knew it wasn't true. But I didn't want to discuss the murders, or Claudel, or my lost trip to Quebec City, or my broken marriage, or anything else that had been plaguing my peace of mind lately.

"You?"

"*Bien.*"

She wagged her head from side to side and the dreadlocks flopped. *Bien. Pas Bien.* Just like old times. But not quite. I recognized my own behavior. She was hedging also, wanted to keep the conversation light. Feeling a little blue, but suspecting I'd set the mood, I let it go and joined in the conspiracy of mutual avoidance.

"So, where should we eat?"

I wasn't really changing the subject since there hadn't actually been one.

"What do ya feel like?"

I thought about it. I usually make such choices by imagining food on a plate in front of me. My mind definitely prefers a visual mode. I guess you could say, when it comes to food, it's graphics, not menu, driven. Tonight it wanted something red and heavy.

"Italian?"

50

"Okay." She considered. "Vivaldi's on Prince Arthur? We can sit outside."

"Perfect. And I won't have to waste this parking place."

We angled across the square, passing beneath the large broadleafs that arch above its lawn. Old men sat on benches, talking in groups, surveying their fellow citizens. A woman in a shower cap fed pigeons from a bag of bread, admonishing them like rowdy children. A pair of foot patrolmen strolled one of the paths that crisscross the park, their hands clasped behind them in identical V's. They stopped periodically to exchange pleasantries, ask questions, respond to quips.

We passed the cement gazebo at the west end of the square. I noted the word "Vespasian," and wondered, once again, why the name of a Roman emperor was carved above its door.

We left the square, crossed Rue Laval, and passed through a set of cement pillars marking the entrance to Rue Prince Arthur. All this time no words were spoken. This was odd. Gabby wasn't this quiet, or this passive. She was usually bursting with plans and ideas. Tonight she'd simply yielded to my suggestion.

I watched her, discreetly, from the corner of my eye. She was scanning the faces we passed while simultaneously chewing on a thumbnail. The scrutiny didn't appear to be absentminded. She seemed edgy, searching the crowded sidewalks.

The evening was warm and humid, and Prince Arthur was jammed. People swirled and eddied in all directions. The restaurants had thrown open their doors and windows, and the tables spilled out helter skelter, as though someone planned to arrange them later. Men in cotton shirts and women with bare shoulders talked and laughed under brightly colored umbrellas. Others stood in lines, waiting to be seated. I joined the line outside

51

Vivaldi's while Gabby walked to the corner dépanneur to buy a bottle of wine.

When we were finally settled Gabby ordered the fettuccine Alfredo. I asked for veal piccata, spaghetti on the side. Though seduced by the lemon, I remained partially loyal to the vision of red. While we waited for our salads, I sipped a Perrier. We spoke some, moving our mouths, forming words, saying nothing. Mostly we sat. It wasn't the comfortable silence of old friends accustomed to each other, but a dialogue of uneasiness.

I'm as familiar with the ebb and flow of Gabby's moods as I was with my own menstrual cycles. I sensed something tense in her demeanor. Her eyes didn't meet mine, but roved restlessly, continuously exploring as they had in the park. She was obviously distracted. She reached for her wine often. Each time she lifted her glass the early evening light kindled the Chianti, making it blaze like a Carolina sunset.

I knew the signs. She was drinking too much, trying to blunt the anxiety. Alcohol, the opiate of the troubled. I knew because I'd tried it. The ice in my Perrier was slowly melting, and I watched the lemon resuscitate itself. It dropped from one cube to another with a delicate fizzing sound.

"Gabby, what's up?"

The question startled her.

"Up?"

She gave a short, jittery laugh and brushed a dreadlock from her face. Her eyes were unreadable.

Taking her cue, I moved once again to a neutral topic. She would tell me when she was ready. Or perhaps I was being a coward. The price of intimacy would be its loss.

"Do you hear from anyone from Northwestern?"

We'd met as graduate students in the seventies. I'd been married. Katy was a preschooler. I envied Gabby

52

and the others their freedom back then. I'd missed the bonding experience of all-night parties and early morning philosophy sessions. I was their age but lived in a different world. Gabby was the only one with whom I'd grown close. I've never really known why. We look as different as two women can. We did back then. Perhaps it was because Gabby liked Pete, or, at least, pretended to. Flashback: Pete, military-crisp, surrounded by flower children high on grass and cheap beer. He hated my grad school parties, masked his discomfort behind cocky disdain. Only Gabby had made the effort to break through.

I'd lost contact with all but a few of our classmates. They were scattered across the States now, most at universities and museums. Over the years Gabby had been better at maintaining ties. Or perhaps they sought her out more.

"I hear from Joe now and then. He's teaching at some podunk place in Iowa, I think. Or Idaho." American geography had never been Gabby's strong suit.

"Oh yeah?" I encouraged.

"And Vern's selling real estate in Las Vegas. He came through here for some sort of conference a few months ago. He's out of anthropology and happy as a clam."

She sipped.

"Same hair, though."

This time the laugh sounded genuine. Either the wine or my personal charm was relaxing her.

"Oh, and I got an e-mail message from Jenny. She's thinking of getting back into research. You know she married some yo-yo and gave up a tenured position at Rutgers to follow him to the Keys?"

Gabby didn't usually mince words.

"Well, she's gotten some sort of adjunct affiliation and is busting her butt on a grant proposal."

Another sip.

"When he lets her. What gives with Pete?"

The question hit me broadside. Up to this point I'd been very cautious in talking about my failed marriage. It was as if the gears of my speech were jammed on the subject, and releasing them would somehow verify the truth. As if the act of arranging words in rows, of forming sentences, would validate a reality I wasn't quite ready to face. I avoided the topic. Gabby was one of the few I'd told.

"He's fine. We talk."

"People change."

"Yes."

The salads arrived and for a few minutes we concentrated on dressings and pepper grinding. When I looked up she was sitting very still, a forkful of lettuce suspended over her plate. She'd withdrawn from me once again, though this time she seemed to be examining an inner world, rather than the one around her.

I tried another tack.

"Tell me how your project is going." I speared a black olive.

"Huh? Oh, the project. Good. It's going good. I've finally gotten their confidence and some of them are really starting to open up to me."

She took a bite of salad.

"Gabby, I know you've explained this, but tell me again. I'm just a physical sciences type. What exactly is the goal of the research?"

She laughed at the familiar demarcation between the physical and cultural anthropology students. Our class had been small but diverse: some studying ethnology, others taking linguistics, archaeology, and biological anthropology. I knew as little about deconstructionism as she did about mitochondrial DNA.

"Remember the ethnographies Ray made us read? The Yanomamo, and the Semai, and the Nuer? Well,

54

it's the same idea. We're trying to describe the world of the prostitute through close observation and interviews with informants. Field work. Up close and personal." She took another bite of salad. "Who are they? Where do they come from? How do they get into hooking? What do they do on a daily basis? What support networks do they have? How do they fit into the legitimate economy? How do they view themselves? Where–"

"I get it."

Perhaps the wine was having its effect, or perhaps I'd tapped into the one passion in her life. She was becoming more animated. Though it had grown dark I could see that her face was flushed. Her eyes glistened with the light of the streetlamp. Or maybe the alcohol.

"Society has just written these women off. No one's really interested in them, except those who are somehow threatened by them and want them gone."

I nodded as we each took a bite of salad.

"Most people think girls hook because they've been abused, or because they're forced into it, or whatever. Actually, a lot of them do it simply for the money. With limited skills for the legitimate job market, they're never going to make a decent living and they know that. They make a decision to hook for a few years because it's the most profitable thing they can do. Peddling ass pays better than slinging burgers."

More salad.

"And, like any other group, they've got their own subculture. I'm interested in the networks they construct, the mental mapping they do, the support systems they rely on, that sort of thing."

The waiter returned with our entrées.

"What about the men who hire them?"

"What?" The question seemed to unnerve her.

"What about the guys who go down there? They must be an important element in the whole thing. Are you also talking to them?" I rolled a forkful of spaghetti.

"I – Yeah, some," she stammered, clearly flustered. After a pause: "Enough about me, Tempe. Tell me what you're working on. Any interesting cases?" Her eyes were focused on her plate.

The shift was so abrupt it caught me off-guard. I answered without thinking.

"These murders have me pretty uptight." I regretted saying it immediately.

"What murders?" Her voice was becoming thick, the words rounded and soft on the edges.

"A pretty nasty one came in last Thursday." I didn't go on. Gabby has never wanted to hear about my work.

"Oh?" She helped herself to more bread. She was being polite. She'd told me about her work, now she'd listen to me talk about mine.

"Yeah. Surprisingly there hasn't been much press. Her body was found off Sherbrooke last week. Came in as an unknown. Turns out she was killed last April."

"That sounds like a lot of your cases. So what's rattling ya?"

I sat back and looked at her, wondering if I really wanted to go into this. Maybe it would be better to talk about it. Better for whom? For me? There was no one else with whom I could do that. Did she really want to hear it?

"The victim was mutilated. Then the body was butchered and thrown into a ravine."

She looked at me without commenting.

"I think the MO is similar to another one I worked on."

"Meaning?"

"I see the same" – I groped for the right word – "elements in both."

"Such as?" She reached for her glass.

"Savage battering, disfiguring the body."

56

"But that's pretty common, isn't it? When women are the victims? Bash our heads in, choke us, then slash us up? Male Violence 101."

"Yes," I admitted. "And I don't really know the cause of death in this last one since she was so badly decomposed."

Gabby looked ill at ease. Maybe this was a mistake.

"What else?" She held her wine but didn't drink.

"The mutilation. Cutting up the body. Or removing parts of it. Or . . ." I trailed off, thinking of the plunger. I still wasn't sure what it meant.

"So ya think the same bastard did them both?"

"Yes. I do. But I can't convince the idiot who's working the case. He won't even look into the other one."

"The murders could be the work of one of these dirtbags who gets his rocks off butchering women?"

I answered without looking up. "Yes."

"And ya think he'll do it again?"

Her voice was sharp once more, the velvety edges gone. I put my fork down and looked at her. She was peering at me intently, her head thrust slightly forward, her fingers wrapped tightly around the stem of her wineglass. The glass was trembling, its contents rippling gently.

"Gabby, I'm sorry. I shouldn't have talked about this. Gabby, are you all right?"

She straightened in her seat and set the glass down deliberately, holding on to it a moment before letting go. She continued to stare at me. I signaled the waiter.

"Do you want coffee?"

She nodded her head.

We finished dinner, indulging ourselves in cannoli and cappuccino. She seemed to recover her humor as we laughed and mocked the memory of our student selves in the Age of Aquarius, our hair worn long and straight, our shirts tie-dyed, our jeans slung low on our

57

hips and belled at the ankles, a generation following identical escape routes from conformity. It was past midnight when we left the restaurant.

Walking along Prince Arthur, she brought up the murders again.

"What would this guy be like?"

The question took me by surprise.

"I mean, would he be wacko? Would he be normal? Would ya be able to spot him?"

My confusion was annoying her.

"Could ya pick the fucker out at a church picnic?"

"The killer?"

"Yes."

"I don't know."

She pursued it. "Would he be functional?"

"I think so. If one person did kill both these women, and I don't know that for sure, Gab, he's organized. He plans. Many serial killers fool the world for a long time before they're caught. But I'm not a psychologist. That's pure speculation."

We arrived at the car and I unlocked it. Suddenly she reached over and grabbed my arm. "Let me show ya the strip."

I didn't follow. Again the mental leap had left me out. My mind went into bridge building.

"Uh . . ."

"The red-light district. My project. Let's just drive by and I'll show ya the girls."

I glanced over just as the headlights of an oncoming car caught her. Her face looked strange in the shifting illumination. The light moved across her like the beam of a flashlight, accentuating some features, throwing others into shadow. Her eagerness was persuasive. I looked at my watch – twelve-eighteen.

"Okay." It really wasn't. Tomorrow would be tough. But she seemed so anxious I didn't have the heart to disappoint her.

She folded herself into the car and slid the seat back to its farthest position. It gave her some leg room, but not enough.

We rode in silence for a couple of minutes. Following her instructions I went west several blocks, then turned south onto St. Urbain. We skirted the easternmost edge of the McGill ghetto, a schizoid amalgam of low-rent student housing, high-rise condos, and gentrified brown-stones. Within six blocks I turned left onto Rue Ste. Catherine. Behind me lay the heart of Montreal. In the rearview mirror I could see the looming shapes of Complexe Desjardins and Place des Arts challenging each other from their opposite corners. Below them lay Complexe Guy-Favreau and the Palais des Congrès.

In Montreal, the grandeur of downtown gives way quickly to the squalor of the east end. Rue Ste. Catherine sees it all. Born in the affluence of West-mount, it strides through Centre-ville, eastward to Boulevard St. Laurent, the Main, the dividing line between east and west. Ste. Catherine is home to the Forum, Eaton's, and the Spectrum. Downtown it is lined with high-rises and hotels, with theaters and shop-ping centers. But at St. Laurent it leaves behind the office complexes and condominiums, the convention centers and boutiques, the restaurants and singles' bars. The hookers and the punks take over from there. Their turf stretches eastward, from the Main to the gay village. They share it with the drug dealers and the skinheads. Tourists and suburbanites venture in as visitors, to gawk and avoid eye contact. They see the other side and re-affirm their separateness. But they don't stay long.

We were almost at St. Laurent when Gabby indicated that I should pull to the right. I found a spot in front of La Boutique du Sex, and turned off the engine. Across the street a group of women clustered outside the Hotel

59

Granada. Its sign offered CHAMBRES TOURISTIQUES, but I doubted any tourists frequented its rooms.

"There," she said. "That's Monique."

Monique was wearing red vinyl boots that reached to midthigh. Black spandex, pulled to its tensile limits, struggled to cover her rump. Through it I could see the line of her panties, and a lumpy ridge formed by the hem of her white polyester blouse. Plastic earrings dangled to her shoulders, splashes of dazzling pink against her impossibly black hair. She seemed a caricature of a hooker.

"That's Candy."

She indicated a young woman in yellow shorts and cowboy boots. Her makeup made Bozo look drab. She was painfully young. Except for the cigarette and clown face, she could have been my daughter.

"Do they use their real names?" It was like witnessing a cliché.

"I don't know. Would you?"

She pointed to a girl in black sneakers and short shorts.

"Poirette."

"How old is she?" I was appalled.

"Says she's eighteen. She's probably fifteen."

I leaned back and rested my hands on the steering wheel. As she pointed them out, one by one, I couldn't help thinking of gibbons. Just like the small apes, the women spaced themselves at equal intervals, dividing the field into a mosaic of precise territories. Each worked her patch, excluding others of her gender, and trying to beguile a mate. The seductive poses, the taunts and jeers, were a courtship ritual, *sapiens* style. With these dancers, however, reproduction was not the goal.

I realized Gabby had stopped talking. She'd finished her roll call. I turned to look at her. She was facing in my direction, but her eyes went past me, locked on something outside my window. Perhaps outside my world.

"Let's go."

She said it so quietly I could hardly hear her. "What – ?"

"Go!"

Her ferocity stunned me. A volley flew to my lips, but the look in her eyes convinced me to say nothing.

Again we rode in silence. Gabby seemed to be deep in thought, as though mentally she'd relocated to a different planet. But as I pulled up to her apartment she blindsided me with another question.

"Are they raped?"

My mind rewound and played the tape of our conversation. No good. I'd missed another bridge.

"Who?" I asked.

"These women."

The hookers? The murder victims?

"Which women?"

For several seconds she didn't answer.

"I'm so sick of this shit!"

She was out of the car and up the stairs before I could react. Then her vehemence slapped me in the face.

5

For the next couple of weeks I heard nothing from Gabby. I was also not on Claudel's dialing list. He'd cut me out of the loop. I learned about Isabelle Gagnon's life through Pierre LaManche.

She'd lived with her brother and his lover in St. Édouard, a working-class neighborhood northeast of Centre-ville. She worked in a lover's boutique, a small shop off St. Denis specializing in unisex clothes and paraphernalia. Une Tranche de Vie. A Slice of Life. The brother, who was a baker, had thought of the name. The irony of it was depressing.

Isabelle disappeared on Friday, April 1. According to the brother, she was a regular at some of the bars on St. Denis, and had been out late the night before. He thought he'd heard her come in around 2 A.M., but didn't check. The two men left for work early the next morning. A neighbor saw her at 1 P.M. Isabelle was expected at the boutique at 4 P.M. She never showed up. Her remains were discovered nine weeks later at Le Grand Séminaire. She was twenty-three.

LaManche came into my office late one afternoon to see if I'd finished my analysis.

"There are multiple fractures of the skull," I said. "It

took quite a bit of reconstructing."

"*Oui*."

I took the skull from its cork ring.

"She was hit at least three times. This is the first."

I pointed to a small, saucerlike crater. A series of concentric circles expanded outward from its epicenter, like rings on a shooting target.

"The first blow wasn't hard enough to shatter her skull. It just caused a depression fracture of the outer table. Then he hit her here."

I indicated the center of a starburst pattern of fracture lines. Looping through the stellate system was a series of curvilinear fractures. The rays and the circles interlaced to form a spiderweb of damage.

"This blow was much harder, and caused a massive comminuted fracture. Her skull shattered."

It had taken long hours to reassemble the pieces. Traces of glue were visible along the fragment edges.

He listened, absorbed, his eyes driving back and forth from the skull to my face so intently they seemed to burrow a channel through the air.

"Then he hit her here."

I traced a runner from another starburst system toward an arm of the one I'd just shown him. The second linear break came up to the first and stopped, like a country road at a T-intersection.

"This blow came later. New fractures will be arrested by preexisting ones. New lines won't cross old ones, so this one had to have come last."

"*Oui*."

"The blows were probably delivered from the back and slightly to the right."

"*Oui*."

He did this to me often. The absence of feedback was no indication of a lack of interest. Or understanding. Pierre LaManche missed nothing. I doubt he ever

63

needed second explanations. The monosyllabic response was his way of forcing you to organize your thoughts. A sort of dry-run jury presentation. I forged on.

"When a skull is hit it acts like a balloon. For a fraction of a second the bone pushes in at the point of impact, and bulges out on the opposite side. So the damage isn't restricted to the place the head was struck."

I looked to see if he was with me. He was.

"Because of the architecture of the skull, the forces caused by a sudden impact travel along certain pathways. The bone fails, or breaks, somewhat predictably."

I pointed to the forehead.

"For example, an impact here can result in damage to the orbits or face."

I indicated the back of the skull.

"A blow here often causes side-to-side fractures of the base of the skull."

He nodded.

"In this case, there are two comminuted fractures and one depressed fracture of the posterior right parietal. There are several linear fractures that start on the opposite side of the skull and travel toward the damage in the right parietal. This suggests she was struck from the back and to her right."

"Three times," he said.

"Three times," I confirmed.

"Did it kill her?" He knew what my answer would be.

"Could have. I can't say."

"Any other signs of cause?"

"No bullets, no stab marks, no other fractures. I've got some odd gashes on the vertebrae, but I'm not really sure what they mean."

"Due to the dismemberment?"

I shook my head. "I don't think so. They're not in the right place."

I replaced the skull in its ring.

"The dismemberment was very clean. He didn't just chop the limbs off. He severed them neatly at the joints. Remember the Gagne case? Or Valencia?"

He thought a minute. In a rare display of movement he tipped his head to the right, then to the left, like a dog cuing in on the crinkle of cellophane.

"Gagne came in, oh, maybe two years ago," I prompted. "He was wrapped in layers of blankets, trussed up with packaging tape. His legs had been sawed off and packaged neatly."

At the time it had reminded me of the ancient Egyptians. Before mummification they removed the internal organs and preserved them. The viscera were then bundled separately and placed with the body. Gagne's killers had done the same with his legs.

"Ah, *oui*. I remember the case."

"Gagne's legs were sawed off below the knees. Same with Valencia. His arms and legs were cut several inches above or below the joints."

Valencia had gotten greedy on a drug deal. He came to us in a hockey bag.

"In both those cases the limbs were hacked off at the most convenient place. In this case the guy neatly disconnected the joints. Look."

I showed him a diagram. I'd used a standard autopsy drawing to indicate the points at which the body had been cut. One line ran through the throat. Others bisected the shoulder, hip, and knee joints.

"He cut the head off at the level of the sixth cervical vertebrae. He removed the arms at the shoulder joints, and the legs at the hip sockets. The lower legs were separated at the knee joints."

I picked up the left scapula.

"See how the cuts surround the glenoid fossa?"

He studied the marks, sets of parallel grooves circling the joint surface.

65

"Same thing with the leg." I switched the scapula for the pelvis. "Look at the acetabulum. He went right into the socket."

LaManche inspected the deep cup that accommodates the head of the femur. Numerous gashes scarred its walls. Silently, I took the pelvis and handed him the femur. Its neck was ringed by pairs of parallel cuts.

He looked at the bone a long time, then returned it to the table.

"The only place he deviated was with the hands. There he just sliced right through the bone."

I showed him a radius.

"Odd."

"Yes."

"Which is more typical? This or the others?"

"The others. Usually you want to cut a body up so it's easier to dispose of, so you do it the fastest way possible. Grab a saw and hack away. This guy took more time."

"Hmm. What does it mean?"

I'd given the question quite a bit of thought.

"I don't know."

Neither of us spoke for a few minutes.

"The family wants the body for burial. I'm going to hold off as long as I can, but be sure you've got good pictures and everything you will need if we go to trial on this one."

"I plan to take sections from two or three of the cut marks. I'll look at them under the microscope to see if I can pinpoint the tool type."

I chose my next words carefully, and watched him closely for a reaction.

"If I get any good features I'd like to try comparing these cuts to some I have on another case."

The corners of his mouth twitched almost imperceptibly. I couldn't tell if it was amusement or annoyance. Or perhaps I'd imagined it.

66

After a pause he said, "Yes. Monsieur Claudel has mentioned this." He looked directly at me. "Tell me why you think these cases are connected."

I outlined the similarities I saw between the Trottier and Gagnon cases. Bludgeoning. Cutting of the body after death. The use of the plastic bags. Dumping in a secluded area.

"Are these both CUM cases?"

"Gagnon is. Trottier is SQ. She was found in the St. Jerome."

As in many cities, questions of jurisdiction can be tricky in Montreal. The city lies on an island in the middle of the St. Lawrence. The Communauté Urbaine de Montréal police handle murders occurring on the island itself. Off the island, they fall to local police departments, or to La Sûreté du Québec. Coordination is not always good.

After a pause he said, "Monsieur Claudel can be" – he hesitated – "difficult. Follow through on your comparison. Let me know if you need anything."

Later that week I'd photographed the cut marks with a photomicroscope, using varying angles, magnifications, and intensities of light. I hoped to bring out details of their internal structure. I'd also removed small segments of bone from several joint surfaces. I planned to view them with the scanning electron microscope. Instead I was up to my neck in bones for the next two weeks.

A partially clothed skeleton was discovered by kids hiking in a provincial park. A badly decomposed body washed up on the shore of Lac St. Louis. While cleaning the basement of their newly purchased home, a couple found a trunk full of human skulls covered with wax, blood and feathers. Each find came to me.

The remains from Lac St. Louis were presumed to be those of a gentleman who died in a boating mishap the

67

previous fall when a competitor took exception to his freelancing as a cigarette smuggler. I was putting his skull back together when the call came.

I'd been expecting it, though not this soon. As I listened my heart raced and the blood below my breast-bone felt fizzy, like carbonated soda shaken in a bottle. I felt hot all over.

"She's been dead less than six hours," LaManche was saying. "I think you'd better take a look."

6

Margaret Adkins was twenty-four. She had lived with her common-law husband and their six-year-old son in a neighborhood nestled in the shadow of the Olympic Stadium. She was to have met her sister at ten-thirty that morning for shopping and lunch. She didn't make it. Nor did she take later phone calls after speaking with her husband at ten. She couldn't. She'd been murdered sometime between his call and noon, when her sister discovered her body. That was four hours ago. That's all we knew.

Claudel was still at the scene. His partner, Michel Charbonneau, sat on one of the plastic chairs lining the far wall of the large autopsy suite. LaManche had returned from the murder scene less than an hour ago, the body preceding him by minutes. The autopsy was underway when I arrived. I knew immediately that we'd all work overtime that night.

She lay facedown, her arms straight against her sides, hands palm up with the fingers curving inward. The paper bags placed on them at the scene had already been removed. Her fingernails had been inspected and scrapings taken. She was nude, and her skin looked waxy against the polished stainless steel. Small circles dotted

69

her back, pressure points left by drainage holes in the table's surface. Here and there a solitary hair clung to her skin, estranged forever from the curly tangle on her head.

The back of her head was distorted, the shape slightly off, like a lopsided figure in a child's drawing. Blood oozed from her hair and mingled with the water used to clean her, gathering below the body in a translucent, red pool. Her sweat suit, bra, panties, shoes, and socks had been spread across the adjacent autopsy table. They were saturated with blood, and the sticky, metallic smell hung heavy on the air. A Ziploc bag next to the sweats held an elasticized belt and sanitary pad.

Daniel was taking Polaroids. The white-bordered squares lay on the desk next to Charbonneau, their emerging images in varying degrees of clarity. Charbonneau was inspecting them, one by one, then carefully returning each to its original place. He chewed on his lower lip as he studied them.

A uniformed officer from identity was shooting with a Nikon and flash. As he circled the table, Lisa, newest of the autopsy technicians, positioned an old-fashioned screen behind the body. The painted metal frame, with its shirred white fabric, belonged to an era when such paraphernalia were used in hospital rooms to barricade patients during intimate procedures. The irony was jarring. I wondered whose privacy they were trying to protect here. Margaret Adkins was past caring.

After several shots the photographer stood down from his stool and looked questioningly at LaManche. The pathologist stepped closer to the body and pointed to a scrape on the back of the left shoulder.

"Did you get this?"

Lisa held a rectangular card to the left of the abrasion. On it were written the LML number, the morgue number, and the date: June 23, 1994. Both Daniel and the photographer took close-ups.

At LaManche's direction, Lisa shaved the hair from around the head wounds, spraying the scalp repeatedly with a nozzle. There were five in all. Each showed the jagged edges typical of blunt instrument trauma. LaManche measured and diagrammed them. The cameras captured them in close-up.

At length LaManche said, "That should do it from this angle. Please turn her back over."

Lisa stepped forward, momentarily blocking my view. She slid the body to the far left side of the table, rolled it back slightly, and snugged the left arm tightly against the stomach. Then she and Daniel turned the body onto its back. I heard a soft thunk as the head dropped onto the stainless steel. Lisa lifted the head, placed a rubber block behind the neck, and stepped back.

What I saw made my blood race even faster, as if the thumb had been slipped from the shaken soda bottle in my chest and a geyser of fear allowed to erupt.

Margaret Adkins had been ripped open from her breastbone to her pubis. A jagged fissure ran downward from her sternum, exposing along its course the colors and textures of her mutilated entrails. At its deepest points, where the organs had been displaced, I could see the glistening sheath surrounding her vertebral column.

I dragged my eyes upward, away from the terrible cruelty in her belly. But there was to be no relief there. Her head was turned slightly, revealing a pixie-like face, with upturned nose and delicately pointed chin. Her cheeks were high and sprinkled with freckles. In death, the tiny brown splotches stood out in sharp contrast to the surrounding white in which they floated. She looked like Pippi Longstocking in short brown hair. But the little elf mouth was not laughing. It was stretched wide, and a severed left breast bulged from it, the nipple resting on the delicate lower lip.

71

I looked up and met LaManche's eyes. The lines paralleling them seemed deeper than usual. There was a tension to the lower lids that caused the sagging parenthesis under each to twitch slightly. I saw sadness, but perhaps something more.

LaManche said nothing and continued the autopsy, his attention shifting back and forth between the body and his clipboard. He recorded each atrocity, noting its position and dimensions. He detailed every scar and lesion. As he worked, the body was photographed from the front as it had been from the back. We waited. Charbonneau smoked.

After what seemed like hours, LaManche finished the external exam.

"*Bon*. Take her for radiography."

He stripped off his gloves and sat down at the desk, hunching over his clipboard like an old man with a stamp collection.

Lisa and Daniel rolled a steel gurney to the right of the autopsy table. With professional agility and detachment they transferred the body and wheeled it off to be X-rayed.

Silently, I moved over and took the chair next to Charbonneau. He half rose, nodding and smiling in my direction, took a long pull on his cigarette, and stubbed it out.

"Dr. Brennan, how goes it?"

Charbonneau always spoke to me in English, proud of his fluency. His speech was an odd mixture of Québecois and Southern slang, born of a childhood in Chicoutimi, embellished by two years in the oil fields of east Texas.

"Good. And you?"

"Can't complain." He shrugged in a way only francophiles have mastered, shoulders hunched, palms raised.

72

Charbonneau had a wide, friendly face and prickly gray hair that always reminded me of a sea anemone. He was a large man, his neck disproportionately so, and his collars always looked tight. His ties, perhaps in an attempt to compensate, either rolled over and slipped sideways, or disengaged themselves and hung below the level of his first shirt button. He'd loosen them early in the morning, probably hoping to make the inevitable look intentional. Or maybe he just wanted to be comfortable. Unlike most of the CUM detectives, Charbonneau did not try to make a daily fashion statement. Or maybe he did. Today he wore a pale yellow shirt, polyester pants, and a green plaid sports jacket. The tie was brown.

"Seen the prom pics?" he asked, reaching to retrieve a brown envelope from the desk.

"Not yet."

He withdrew a stack of Polaroids and handed them to me. "These are just the backup shots that came in with the body."

I nodded and began going through them. Charbonneau watched me closely. Perhaps he hoped I would recoil from the carnage so he could tell Claudel I'd blinked. Perhaps he was genuinely interested in my reaction.

The photos were in chronological order, re-creating the scene as the recovery team had found it. The first showed a narrow street lined on both sides by old but well-kept buildings, each three stories high. Parallel rows of trees bordered the curbs on each side, their trunks disappearing into small squares of dirt surrounded by cement. The buildings were fronted by a series of postage-stamp yards, each bisected by a walkway leading to a steep metal staircase. Here and there a tricycle blocked the sidewalk.

The next several shots focused on the exterior of one

73

of the red-brick buildings. Small details caught my attention. Plaques over a pair of second-story doors bore the numbers 1407 and 1409. Someone had planted flowers below one of the ground-floor windows in front. I could make out three forlorn marigolds huddled together, their huge yellow heads shriveled and drooping in identical arcs, solitary blooms coaxed into life and abandoned. A bicycle leaned against the rusted iron fence that surrounded the tiny front yard. A rusty sign angled from the grass, leaning low to the ground, as if to hide the message: *À VENDRE*. FOR SALE.

Despite the attempts at individualization, the building looked like all the others lining the street. Same stairs, same balcony, same double doors, same lace curtains. I wondered: Why this one? Why did tragedy visit this place? Why not 1405? Or across the street? Or down the block?

One by one the photos took me closer, like a microscope shifting to higher and higher magnification. The next series showed the condo's interior, and, again, it was the minutiae that I found arresting. Small rooms. Cheap furniture. The inevitable TV. A living room. A dining room. A boy's bedroom, walls hung with hockey posters. A book lying on the single bed: *How the World Works*. Another stab of pain. I doubted the book would explain this.

Margaret Adkins had liked blue. Every door and inch of woodwork had been painted a bright, Santorini blue.

Finally, the victim. The body lay in a tiny room to the left of the front entrance. From it, doors gave on to a second bedroom and the kitchen. Through the entrance to the kitchen I could see a Formica table set with plastic place mats. The cramped space where Adkins had died held only a TV, a sofa, and a sideboard. Her body lay centered between them.

She lay on her back, her legs spread wide. She was

74

fully dressed, but the top of her sweat suit had been yanked up, covering her face. The sweatshirt pinned her wrists together above her head, elbows out, hands hanging limp. Third position, like a novice ballerina at her first recital.

The gash in her chest gaped raw and bloody, only partially camouflaged by the darkening film that surrounded the body and seemed to cover everything. A crimson square marked the place where her left breast had been, its borders formed by overlapping incisions, the long, perpendicular slashes crossing each other at ninety-degree angles at the corners. The wound reminded me of trephinations I'd seen on the skulls of ancient Mayans. But this mutilation had not been done to relieve the victim's pain, or to release imagined phantoms from her body. If any imprisoned spirit had been set free, it had not been hers. Margaret Adkins was made the trapdoor through which some stranger's twisted, tormented soul sought relief.

The bottom of her sweats had been pulled down around her spread knees, the elastic waist stretched taut. Blood trickled from between her legs and pooled below her. She'd died still wearing her sneakers and socks.

Wordless, I replaced the photos and handed the envelope to Charbonneau.

"It's a nasty one, eh?" he asked. He removed a speck from his lower lip, inspected and flicked it.

"Yes."

"Asshole thinks he's a goddamn surgeon. Real blade cowboy." He shook his head.

I was about to answer when Daniel returned with the X rays and began to clamp them to the light box on the wall. Each made a sound like distant thunder as it bowed in his hand.

We inspected them in sequence, our collective gaze moving from left to right, from her head to her feet. The

75

frontal and lateral X rays of the skull showed multiple fractures. The shoulders, arms, and rib cage were normal. There was nothing extraordinary until we arrived at the radiograph of her abdomen and pelvis. Everyone saw it at once.

"Holy shit," said Charbonneau.

"Christ."

"*Tabernouche.*"

A small human form glowed from the depths of Margaret Adkins's abdomen. We all stared at it, mute. There was but one explanation. The figure had been thrust through the vagina and high into the viscera with enough force to conceal it completely from external view. On seeing it, I felt as if a hot poker had pierced my gut. Involuntarily, I clutched my belly, as my heart hammered against my ribs. I stared at the film. I saw a statue.

Framed by the broad pelvic bones, the silhouette stood out in sharp contrast to the organs in which it was embedded. Surrounded by the grays of her intestines, the stark white figure stood with one foot forward, hands outstretched. It appeared to be a religious statue. The figure's head was bowed, like a paleolithic Venus figurine.

For a few moments no one spoke. The room was absolutely silent.

"I've seen those," Daniel said at last. With a stabbing motion he pushed his glasses back onto the bridge of his nose. A tic squeezed his features like a rubber toy.

"It's our lady of something. You know. The Virgin. Mary."

We all examined the opaque shape on the X ray. Somehow it seemed to compound the offense, making it all the more obscene.

"This sonofabitch's a real sick bastard," said Charbonneau, the practiced nonchalance of the homicide detective overridden by the emotion of the moment.

His vehemence surprised me. I was unsure if the atrocity alone had stirred something in him, or if the religious nature of the offending object was contributing to his reaction. Like most Québecois, Charbonneau had no doubt had a childhood permeated with traditional Catholicism, the rhythm of his daily life inextricably ruled by church dogma. Though many of us throw off the outward trappings, reverence for the symbols often lingers. A man might refuse to wear a scapular, but neither will he burn it. I understood. Different city, different language, but I, too, was a member of the tribe. Atavistic emotions die hard.

There was another long silence. Finally, LaManche spoke, choosing his words carefully. I couldn't tell if he realized the full implications of what we were seeing. I wasn't sure I did. Though he used milder tones than I'd have chosen, he voiced my thoughts perfectly.

"Monsieur Charbonneau, I believe you and your partner need to meet with Dr. Brennan and me. As I am sure you know, there are some unsettling aspects to this case and several others."

He paused to allow that to sink in, and to consult a mental calendar.

"I will have the results of this autopsy by later tonight. Tomorrow is a holiday. Would Monday morning be convenient?"

The detective looked at him, then at me. His face was neutral. I couldn't tell if he understood LaManche's meaning, or if he was truly unaware of the other cases. It was not beyond Claudel to have dismissed my comments without sharing them with his partner. If so, Charbonneau could not admit his ignorance.

"Yeah. Okay. I'll see what I can do."

LaManche held his melancholy eyes on Charbonneau and waited.

77

"Okay. Okay. We'll be here. Now I better get my ass back on the street and start looking for this shithook. If Claudel turns up, tell him I'll meet him back at head-quarters around eight."

He was rattled. He'd failed to switch over to French when addressing LaManche. It was clear he would have a long talk with his partner.

LaManche resumed the autopsy before the door closed behind Charbonneau. The rest was routine. The chest was opened with a Y-shaped incision. The organs were removed, weighed, sliced, and inspected. The statue's position was determined, the internal damage assessed and described. Using a scalpel, Daniel cut the skin across the crown of the head, peeled the face forward and the scalp backward, and removed a section of skullcap with a Stryker saw. I took a step backward and held my breath as the air filled with the whine of the saw and the smell of burnt bone. The brain was structurally normal. Here and there gelatinous globs clung to its surface, like black jellyfish on a slick, gray globe. Subdural hematoma from the blows to her head.

I knew what the essence of LaManche's report would be. The victim was a healthy young woman with no abnormalities or signs of disease. Then, that day, some-one had bludgeoned her head with enough force to frac-ture her skull and cause her cerebral vessels to bleed into her brain. At least five times. He had then rammed a statue into her vagina, partially disemboweled her, and slashed off her breast.

A shudder ran through me as I considered her ordeal. The wounds to her vagina were vital. Her torn flesh had bled extensively. The statue had been inserted while her heart still beat. While she was alive.

". . . tell Daniel what you want, Temperance."

I hadn't been listening. LaManche's voice brought

me back to the present. He'd finished, and was suggesting I take my bone samples. The sternum and front portions of the ribs had been removed early in the autopsy, so I told Daniel they were to be sent upstairs for soaking and cleaning.

I stepped close to the body and peered into the thoracic cavity. A number of small gashes meandered up the belly side of the vertebral bodies. They appeared as a trail of faint slits in the tough sheath covering the spine.

"I want the vertebrae from about here to here. Ribs, too." I indicated the segment containing the gashes. "Send it up to Denis. Tell him to soak, no boiling. And be very careful in removing it. Don't touch it with any kind of blade."

He listened, holding his gloved hands out. His nose and upper lip jumped as he tried to adjust his glasses. He nodded continuously.

When I stopped speaking he looked at LaManche.

"Then close?" he asked.

"Close her after that," LaManche responded.

Daniel set to the task. He would remove the bone segments, then replace the organs and close the midsection. Finally, he would restore the skullcap, reposition the face, and sew the severed borders of the scalp. Save for the Y-shaped seam down her front, Margaret Adkins would appear untouched. She would be ready for her funeral.

I returned to my office, determined to regroup mentally before driving home. The fifth floor was totally deserted. I swiveled my chair, put my feet on the window ledge, and looked out at my river world. On my shore, the Miron complex resembled a Lego creation, its eccentric gray buildings connected by a horizontal latticework of steel. Beyond the cement factory, a boat moved slowly

79

upriver, its running lights barely visible behind the gray veil of dusk.

The building was absolutely still, but the spooky quiet failed to relax me. My thoughts were black as the river. I wondered briefly if there was someone looking back at me from the factory, someone who was equally alone, equally unnerved by the after-hours solitude that rings so loudly in an empty office building.

I was having trouble sleeping and had been up since 6:30 A.M. I should have been tired. Instead I was agitated. I found myself absently playing with my right eyebrow, a nervous gesture that had profoundly irritated my husband. Years of his criticism had never broken me of the habit. Separation has its advantages. I can now fidget to my heart's content.

Pete. Our last year together. Katy's face when we'd told her about the split. Shouldn't be too traumatic, we thought, she's away at college. How wrong we'd been. The tears had almost made me reverse the decision. Margaret Adkins, her hands curled in death. She'd painted her doors blue with those hands. She'd hung her son's posters. The killer. Was he out there right now? Was he relishing what he'd done today? Was his blood lust satiated, or was his need to kill heightened by the act itself?

The phone rang, splitting the silence like a sonic boom and yanking me back from whatever private grotto I'd entered. I was so startled I jumped, upending the pencil holder with my elbow. Bics and Scripto markers went flying.

"Dr. Bren—"

"Tempe. Oh, thank God! I tried your apartment but ya weren't there. Obviously." Her laugh was high and strained. "I thought I'd try this number just for the hell of it. Didn't really think I'd find ya."

I recognized her voice, but it had a quality I'd never

heard before. It was stretched taut with fear. The tone was elevated, the cadence spiky. Her words rushed at me, breathy and urgent, like a whisper carried on sharply expelled breath. My stomach muscles contracted once again.

"Gabby, I haven't heard from you in three weeks. Why haven't y –"

"I couldn't. I've been – involved – in something. Tempe, I need help."

A soft scraping and clattering came over the line as she repositioned the receiver. In the background I could hear the hollow sound of a public place. It was punctuated by a staccato of muffled voices and metallic clangs. In my mind's eye I could see her standing at a pay phone, scanning her surroundings, her eyes never resting, broadcasting fear like Radio Free Europe.

"Where are you?" I selected a pen from the Pick-Up Sticks tumble on my desk and began to twirl it.

"I'm at a restaurant. La Belle Province. It's at the corner of Ste. Catherine and St. Laurent. Come get me, Temp. I can't go out there."

The rattling increased. She was becoming more agitated.

"Gabby, it's been a very long day here. You're only a few blocks from your apartment. Couldn't you–"

"He's going to kill me! I can't control it anymore. I thought I could, but I can't. I can't shield him anymore. I have to protect myself. He's not right. He's dangerous. He's – *complètement fou!*"

Her voice had been rising steadily, treading upward on a staircase of hysteria. It stopped suddenly, the break accentuated by the abrupt shift to French. I stopped twirling the pen and looked at my watch – 9:15 P.M. Shit.

"Okay. I'll be there in about fifteen minutes. Watch for me. I'll come across Ste. Catherine."

81

My heart was racing and my hands were trembling. I locked the office and practically ran to the car on wobbly legs. I felt as if I were on an eight-cup coffee high.

7

During the drive my emotions did acrobatics. It had turned dark, but the city was fully lit. Apartment windows glowed softly in the east end neighborhood surrounding the SQ building, and here and there a television flickered blue light into the summer night. People sat on balconies and stoops, clustered in chairs dragged outside for summer curtain calls. They talked and sipped cold drinks, having piloted the thick heat of afternoon into the renewing cool of evening.

I coveted their quiet domesticity, just wanted to go home, share a tuna sandwich with Birdie, and sleep. I wanted Gabby to be all right, but I wanted her to take a taxi home. I dreaded dealing with her hysteria. I felt relief at hearing from her. Fear for her safety. Annoyance at having to go into the Main. It was not a good mix.

I took René Lévesque to St. Laurent and hung a right, turning my back on Chinatown. That neighborhood was closing for the night, the last of the shop owners packing up their crates and display bins and dragging them inside.

The Main sprawled ahead of me, stretching north from Chinatown along Boulevard St. Laurent. The

Main is a close-packed quarter of small shops, bistros, and cheap cafés, with St. Laurent as its main commercial artery. From there it radiates out into a network of narrow, back streets packed with cramped, low-rent housing. Though French in temperament, the Main has always been a polycultural mosaic, a zone in which the languages and ethnic identities coexist but fail to blend, like the distinct smells that waft from its dozens of shops and bakeries. The Italians, the Portuguese, the Greeks, the Poles, and the Chinese cluster in enclaves along St. Laurent as it climbs its way from the port to the mountain.

The Main was once Montreal's principal switching station for immigrants, the newcomers attracted by the cheap housing and the comforting proximity of fellow countrymen. They settled there to learn the ways of Canada, each group of rookies banding together to ease its disorientation, and to buoy its confidence in the face of an alien culture. Some learned French and English, prospered, and moved on. Others stayed, either because they preferred the security of the familiar, or because they lacked the ability to get out. Today this nucleus of conservatives and losers is joined by an assortment of dropouts and predators, by a legion of the powerless, discarded by society, and by those who prey on them. Outsiders come to the Main in search of many things: wholesale bargains, cheap dinners, drugs, booze, and sex. They come to buy, to gawk, to laugh, but they don't stay.

Ste. Catherine forms the southern boundary of the Main. Here I turned right, and pulled to the curb where Gabby and I had sat almost three weeks before. It was earlier now, and the hookers were just beginning to divvy up their patches. The bikers hadn't arrived.

Gabby must have been watching. When I glanced in the rearview mirror, she was already halfway across the street, running, her briefcase clutched to her chest. Though her terror wasn't enough to launch her into full flight, her fear was evident. She ran in the manner of adults long estranged from the unfettered gallop of childhood, her long legs slightly bent, her head lowered, her shoulder bag swinging in rhythm to her stilted stride.

She circled the car, got in, and sat with eyes closed, chest heaving. She was obviously struggling for composure, clenching her hands tightly in an attempt to stop the trembling. I'd never seen her like this and it frightened me. Gabby had always had a flare for the dramatic as she threaded her way through perpetual crises, both real and imagined, but nothing had ever undone her to this extent before.

For a few moments I said nothing. Though the night was warm, I felt a chill, and my breathing became thin and shallow. Outside on the street, horns blared and a hooker cajoled a passing car. Her voice rode the summer evening like a toy plane, rising and falling in loops and spirals.

"Let's go."

It was so quiet I almost missed it. Déjà vu.

"Do you want to tell me what's going on?" I asked.

She raised a hand as if to ward off a scolding. It trembled, and she placed it flat against her chest. From across the car I could sense the fear. Her body was warm with the smell of sandalwood and perspiration.

"I will. I will. Just give me a minute."

"Don't jerk me around, Gabby," I said, more harshly than I'd intended.

"I'm sorry. Let's just get the hell out of here," she said, dropping her head into her hands.

All right, we'd follow her script. She'd have to calm down and tell me in her own way. But tell me she would.

"Home?" I asked.

85

She nodded, never taking her face from her hands. I started the car and headed for Carré St. Louis. When I arrived at her building she still hadn't spoken. Though her breathing had steadied, her hands still shook. They had resumed their clasping and unclasping, clutching each other, separating, then linking once again in an odd dance of panic. The choreography of terror.

I put the car in park and killed the engine, dreading the encounter that was to come. I'd counseled Gabby through calamities of health, parental conflict, academics, faith, self-esteem, and love. I'd always found it draining. Invariably, the next time I'd see her, she'd be cheerful and unruffled, the catastrophe forgotten. It wasn't that I was unsympathetic, but I'd been down this route with Gabby many times before. I remembered the pregnancy that wasn't. The stolen wallet that turned up beneath the couch cushions. Nevertheless, the intensity of her reaction disturbed me. Much as I longed for solitude, she didn't look as if she should be alone.

"Would you like to stay with me tonight?"

She didn't answer. Across the square an old man arranged a bundle under his head and settled onto a bench for the night.

The silence stretched for so long I thought she hadn't heard. I turned, about to repeat the invitation, and found she was staring intently in my direction. The jittery movements of a moment ago had been replaced by absolute stillness. Her spine was rigid, and her upper body angled forward, barely touching the seat back. One hand lay in her lap, the other was curled into a fist pressed tightly to her lips. Her eyes squinted, the lower lids quivering almost imperceptibly. She seemed to be weighing something in her mind, considering variables and calculating outcomes. The sudden mood swing was unnerving.

"You must think I'm crazy." She was totally calm,

her voice low and modulated.

"I'm confused." I didn't say what I really thought.

"Yeah. That's a kind way to put it."

She said it with a self-deprecating laugh, slowly shaking her head. The dreadlocks flopped.

"I guess I really freaked back there."

I waited for her to go on. A car door slammed. The low, melancholy voice of a sax floated from the park. An ambulance whined in the distance. Summer in the city.

In the dark, I felt, more than saw, Gabby's focus alter. It was as if she'd taken a road up to me, then veered off at the last minute. Like a lens on automatic, her eyes readjusted to something beyond me, and she seemed to seal herself off again. She was having another session with herself, running through her options, deciding what face to wear.

"I'll be okay," she said, gathering her briefcase and bag, and reaching for the handle. "I really appreciate your coming for me."

She'd decided on evasive.

Maybe it was fatigue, maybe it was the stress of the last few days. Whatever. I lost it.

"Wait just a minute!" I exploded. "I want to know what's going on! An hour ago you were talking about someone wanting to kill you! You come sprinting out of that restaurant and across the street, shaking and gasping like the goddamn Night Stalker's on your tail! You can't breathe, your hands are jerking like they're wired for high voltage, and now you're just going to sail out of here with a 'Thank you very much for the ride,' without any explanation?"

I'd never been so furious with her. My voice had risen, and my breath was coming in short gulps. I could feel a tiny throbbing in my left temple.

The force of my anger froze her in place. Her eyes went round and cavernous, like those of a doe caught in high beams. A car passed and her face flickered white then red, amplifying the image.

She held a moment, a catatonic cutout rigid against the summer sky. Then, as if a valve had been released, the tension seemed to drain from her body. She let go of the handle, lowered her briefcase, and settled back into the seat. Again, she turned inward, reconsidering. Perhaps she was deciding where to begin; perhaps she was scouting alternative escape routes. I waited.

At length, she took a deep breath and her shoulders straightened slightly. She'd settled on a course. As soon as she spoke I knew what she'd determined to do. She would let me in, but only so far. She chose her words carefully, threading a guarded path through the emotional quagmire in her mind. I leaned against the door and braced myself.

"I've been working with some – unusual – people lately."

I thought that an understatement, but didn't say so.

"No, no. I know that sounds banal. I don't mean the usual street people. I can handle that."

Her choice of words was tortuous.

"If you know the players, learn the rules and the lingo, you're fine down there. It's like anywhere else. You've got to observe the local etiquette and not piss people off. It's pretty simple: Don't trespass on someone else's patch, don't screw up a trick, don't talk to the cops. Except for the hours, it's not hard to work down there. Besides, the girls know me now. They know I'm no threat."

She went mute. I couldn't tell if she was closing me out again, or if she'd gone back to the shelves to continue her sorting. I decided to nudge.

"Is one of them threatening you?"

Ethics had always been important to Gabby, and I suspected she was trying to shield an informant.

88

"The girls? No. No. They're fine. They're never a problem. I think they kind of like my company. I can be as raunchy as any of them."

Great. We know what the problem isn't. I prodded some more.

"How do you avoid being mistaken for one of them?"

"Oh, I don't try. I just sort of blend in. Otherwise I'd be defeating my own purpose. The girls know I don't turn tricks, so they just, I don't know, go along with it."

I didn't ask the obvious.

"If a guy hassles me, I just say I'm not working right then. Most of them move on."

There was another pause as she continued her mental triage, considering what to tell me, what to keep to herself, and what to scoop into a heap, not tendered, but accessible if probed. She fumbled with a tassle on her briefcase. A dog barked in the square. I was sure she was protecting someone, or something, but this time I didn't goad her.

"Most of them," she continued, "except this one guy lately."

Pause.

"Who is he?"

Pause.

"I don't know, but he has me really creeped out. He's not a john, exactly, but he likes to hang out with prostitutes. I don't think the girls pay much attention to him. But he knows a lot about the street, and he's been willing to talk to me, so I've been interviewing him."

Pause.

"Lately, he's begun following me. I didn't realize it at first, but I've started noticing him in odd places. He'll be at the Métro when I come home at night, or here, in the square. Once I saw him at Concordia, outside the library building where I have my office. Or I'll see him behind me, on a sidewalk, walking in the same direction

89

I am. Last week I was on St. Laurent when I spotted him. I wanted to convince myself it was my imagination, so I tested him. If I slowed down, so did he. If I speeded up, he did the same thing. I tried to shake him by going into a patisserie. When I came out, he was across the street, pretending to window shop."

"You're sure it's always the same guy?"

"Absolutely."

There was a long, laden silence. I waited it out.

"That's not all."

She stared at her hands, which, once again, had found each other. They were tightly clenched.

"Recently he's started talking some really weird shit. I've tried to avoid him, but tonight he showed up at the restaurant. Lately it's like he's equipped with radar. Anyway, he got off on the same stuff, asking me all kinds of sick questions."

She went back inside her head. After a moment she turned to me, as if she'd found an answer there she hadn't seen before. Her voice was tinged with mild surprise.

"It's his eyes, Tempe. His eyes are so weird! They're black and hard, like a viper, and the whites are all pink and flecked with blood. I don't know if he's sick, or if he's hung over all the time, or what. I've never seen eyes like that. They make you want to crawl under something and hide. Tempe, I just freaked! I guess I've been thinking about our last conversation, and this shitfreak you're cleaning up after, and my mind took the first bus outa there."

I didn't know what to say. I couldn't read her face in the darkness, but her body spoke the language of fear. Her torso was rigid and her arms were drawn in, pressing the briefcase to her chest, as if for protection.

"What else do you know about this guy?"

"Not much."

90

"What do the girls think about him?"

"They ignore him."

"Has he ever been threatening?"

"No. Not directly."

"Has he ever been violent or out of control?"

"No."

"Is he into drugs?"

"I don't know."

"Do you know who he is or where he lives?"

"No. There are some things we don't ask. It's an unspoken rule, sort of a tacit agreement down here."

Again there was a long silence while we both weighed what she'd said. I watched a cyclist pass along the sidewalk, pedaling with unhurried strokes. His helmet seemed to pulsate, blinking on as he passed beneath a streetlamp, then off as he moved back into darkness. He crossed my field of vision then disappeared slowly into the night, a firefly signaling his passage. On. Off. On. Off.

I thought about what she'd said, wondering if I was to blame. Had I set her fears in motion by talking about my own, or had she actually encountered a psychopath? Was she amplifying a set of harmless coincidences, or was she truly in jeopardy? Should I let things ride for a while? Should I do something? Was this a police matter? I was running through my old, practiced loop.

We sat for some time, listening to the sounds of the park and smelling the soft summer night, each of us drifting alone in separate reflections. The quiet interlude had a calming effect. Eventually Gabby shook her head, dropped the briefcase to her lap, and leaned back in the seat. Though her features were obscured, the change in her was visible. When she spoke, her voice was stronger, less shaky.

"I know I'm overreacting. He's just some harmless weirdo who wants to rattle my cage. And I'm playing into his game. I'm letting this fuckhead grab my mind and shake me."

"Don't you run across a lot of 'weirdos,' as you call him?"

"Yeah. Most of my informants aren't exactly the Brooks Brothers crowd." She gave a short, mirthless laugh.

"What makes you think this guy may be different?"

She thought about it, worrying a thumbnail with her teeth.

"Ah, it's hard to put into words. There's just a – a line that divides the crackpots from the real predators. It's hard to define, but ya know when it's been crossed. Maybe it's an instinct I've picked up down there. In the business, if a woman feels threatened by someone, she won't go with him. Each one has her own little triggering devices, but they all draw that line on something. Could be eyes, could be some odd request. Hélène won't go with anyone who wears cowboy boots."

She took another time-out to debate with herself.

"I think I just got carried away by all the talk about serial killers and sexual devos."

More introspection. I tried to steal a look at my watch.

"All this guy is trying to do is shock me."

Another pause. She was talking herself down.

"What an asshole."

Or up. Her voice was growing angrier by the minute.

"Goddammit, Tempe, I'm not going to let this turd get his rocks off sniveling trash and showing me his sick pictures. I'm going to tell him to blow it out his ass."

She turned and put her hand on mine.

"I'm so sorry I dragged you down here tonight. I am such a jerk! Will ya forgive me?"

I stared mutely at her. Again, her emotional U-turn had taken me by surprise. How could she be terrified,

92

analytical, angry, then apologetic all within the space of thirty minutes? I was too tired, and it was too late at night to sort it out.

"Gabby, it's late. Let's talk about this tomorrow. Of course I'm not mad. I'm just glad you're all right. I meant it about staying at my place. You're always welcome."

She leaned over and hugged me. "Thanks, but I'll be fine. I'll call ya. I promise."

I watched her climb the stairs, her skirt floating like mist around her. In an instant she disappeared through the purple doorway, leaving the space between us empty and undisturbed. I sat alone, surrounded by the dark and the faint scent of sandalwood. Though nothing stirred, a momentary chill gripped my heart. Like a shadow, it flickered and was gone.

All the way home my mind was at warp speed. Was Gabby constructing another melodrama? Was she genuinely in danger? Were there things she wasn't telling me? Could this man be truly dangerous? Was she nurturing the seeds of paranoia planted by my talk of murder? Should I tell the police?

I refused to allow my concern for Gabby's safety to overpower me. When I got home, I resorted to a childhood ritual that works when I'm tense or overwrought: I ran a hot bath and filled it with herbal salts. I put a Chris Rea CD on full volume, and, as I soaked, he sang to me of the road to hell. The neighbors would have to survive. After my bath, I tried Katy's number, but, once again, got her machine. Then I shared milk and cookies with Birdie, who preferred the milk, left the dishes on the counter, and crawled into bed.

My anxiety was not completely dissipated. Sleep didn't come easily, and I lay in bed for some time, watching the shadows on the ceiling, and fighting the impulse to call Pete. I hated myself for needing him at such times, for craving his strength whenever I felt upset. It was one ritual I'd vowed to break.

Eventually sleep took me down like a whirlpool, swirling all thoughts of Pete, and Katy, and Gabby, and the murders from my consciousness. It was a good thing. It's what got me through the following day.

8

I slept soundly until nine-fifteen the next morning. I'm not usually a napper, but it was Friday, June 24, St. Jean Baptiste Day, *La Fête Nationale du Québec,* and I was encouraging the holiday languor allowed on such days. Since the feast of St. John the Baptist is the principal holiday for the province, almost everything is closed. There would be no *Gazette* at my door that morning, so I made coffee, then walked to the corner in search of an alternative paper.

The day was bright and vivid, the world displayed on active matrix. Objects and their shadows stood out in sharp detail, the colors of brick and wood, metal and paint, grass and flowers screaming out their separate places on the spectrum. The sky was dazzling and absolutely intolerant of clouds, reminding me of the robin's egg blue on the holy cards of my childhood, the same outrageous blue. I was certain St. Jean would have approved.

The morning air felt warm and soft, perfect with the smell of window box petunias. The temperature had climbed gradually but persistently over the past week, with each day's high surpassing its predecessor. Today's forecast: thirty-two degrees Celsius. I did a quick conversion: about eighty-nine degrees Fahrenheit. Since Montreal is built on an island, the surrounding moat of the St. Lawrence ensures constant humidity. Yahoo! It would be a Carolina day: hot and humid. Bred in the South, I love it.

I purchased *Le Journal de Montréal*. The "number one daily French paper in America" was not as fastidious about taking the day off as the English language *Gazette*. As I walked the half block back to my condo, I glanced at the front page. The headline was written in three-inch letters the color of the sky: BONNE FÊTE QUÉBEC!

I thought about the parade and the concerts to follow at Parc Maisonneuve, about the sweat and the beer that would flow, and about the political rift that divided the people of Quebec. With a fall election due, passions were high, and those pushing for separation were hoping fervently that this would be the year. T-shirts and placards already clamored: *L'an prochain mon pays!* Next year my own country! I hoped the day would not be marred by violence.

Arriving home, I poured myself a coffee, mixed a bowl of Müeslix, and spread the paper on the dining room table. I am a news junkie. While I can go several days without a newspaper, contenting myself with a regular series of eleven o'clock TV fixes, before long I have to have the written word. When traveling, I locate CNN first, then unpack. I make it through the hectic days of the work week, distracted by the demands of teaching or casework, soothed by the familiar voices of "Morning Edition" and "All Things Considered," knowing that on the weekend I will catch up.

I cannot drink, loathe cigarette smoke, and was logging a lean year for sex, so Saturday mornings I reveled in journalistic orgies, allowing myself hours to devour the tiniest minutiae. It isn't that there's anything new in the news. There isn't. I know that. It's like balls in a

Bingo hopper. The same events keep coming up over and over. Earthquake. Coup d'état. Trade war. Hostage taking. My compulsion is to know which balls are up on any given day.

Le Journal is committed to the format of short stories and abundant pictures. Though not *The Christian Science Monitor*, it would do. Birdie knew the routine, and hoisted himself onto the adjacent chair. I'm never sure if he's attracted by my company, or by hopes of Müeslix leavings. He arched his back, settled with all four feet drawn primly in, and fixed his round yellow eyes on me, as if seeking the answer to some profound feline mystery. As I read, I could feel his gaze on the side of my face.

I found it on page two, between a story about a strangled priest and coverage of World Cup soccer.

VICTIM FOUND MURDERED AND MUTILATED

A twenty-four-year-old woman was found murdered and savagely disfigured in her east end home yesterday afternoon. The victim, identified as Margaret Adkins, was a homemaker and the mother of a six-year-old son. Mme. Adkins was last known to be alive at 10 A.M., when she spoke by phone to her husband. Her brutally beaten and mutilated body was discovered by her sister around noon.

According to CUM police, there were no signs of forced entry, and it is unclear how her attacker gained access to the home. An autopsy was performed at the Laboratoire de Médecine Légale by Dr. Pierre LaManche. Dr. Temperance Brennan, an American forensic anthropologist and expert in skeletal trauma, is examining the bones of the victim for indications of knife marks. . . .

The story continued with a patchwork of speculations on the victim's final comings and goings, a synopsis of

97

her life, a heartrending account of the reaction of her family, and promises that the police were doing everything possible to apprehend the killer.

Several photos accompanied the article, depicting the grizzly drama and its cast of characters. There, in shades of gray, were the apartment and its staircase, the police, the morgue attendants pushing the gurney with its sealed body bag. A scattering of neighbors lined the sidewalk, held back by crime scene tape, their curiosity frozen in grainy black and white. Among the figures inside the tape I recognized Claudel, his right arm raised like the conductor of a high school band. A circular inset presented a close-up of Margaret Adkins, a blurred but happier version of the face I'd seen on the autopsy table.

A second photograph showed an older woman with bleached hair curled tightly around her head, and a young boy in shorts and an Expos T-shirt. A bearded man in wire-rimmed glasses had one arm placed protectively around the shoulders of each. All three stared from the page with grief and puzzlement, the expression common to those left in the wake of violent crime, a look with which I've become all too familiar. The caption identified them as the mother, son, and common-law husband of the victim.

I was dismayed to see the third photo: a shot of me at a disinterment. I was familiar with it. Taken in 1992 and kept on file, it was frequently exhumed and reprinted. I was, as usual, identified as ". . . *une anthropologiste américaine.*"

"Damn!"

Birdie flicked his tail and looked disapproving. I didn't care. My vow to banish the murders from my mind for the entire holiday weekend had been short-lived. I should have known the story was going to be in today's paper. I finished the last, cold dregs of my coffee and tried Gabby's number. No answer. Though there could be a million explanations, that, too, made me cranky.

I went to the bedroom to dress for Tai Chi. The class normally met on Tuesday nights, but since no one was working, they'd voted to hold a special session today. I hadn't been sure I wanted to go, but the article and the unanswered phone settled it. At least for an hour or two my mind would be clear.

Again, I was wrong. Ninety minutes of "stroking the bird," "waving hands like clouds," and "needle at the bottom of the sea" did nothing to put me in a holiday mood. I was so distracted that I was out of sync the entire workout, and came away more aggravated than before.

Driving home, I turned on the radio, bent on herding my thoughts like a shepherd tends his flock, nurturing the frivolous and driving off the macabre. I was determined that the weekend could still be salvaged.

". . . was killed sometime around noon yesterday. Mme. Adkins was expected by her sister, but did not keep the appointment. The body was discovered at 1327 Desjardins. Police could find no evidence of a break-in, and suspect Mme. Adkins may have known her assailant."

I knew I should change the station. Instead, I let the voice suck me in. It stirred what was simmering on my mental back burner, bringing my frustrations to the surface and demolishing with finality any possibility of a weekend furlough.

". . . the results of an autopsy have not been released. Police are scouring east end Montreal, questioning everyone who knew the victim. The incident is the twenty-sixth homicide this year in the CUM. Police are asking anyone with information to call the homicide squad at 555-2052."

99

Without making a conscious decision, I did an about-face and headed toward the lab. My hands steered and my feet worked the pedals. Within twenty minutes I was there, determined to accomplish something, but unsure what.

The SQ building was quiet, the usual tumult hushed by the desertion of all but an unlucky few. The lobby guards eyed me suspiciously, but said nothing. It may have been the ponytail and spandex, or it may have been a general surliness at having drawn holiday duty. I didn't care.

The LML and LSJ wings were completely abandoned. The empty offices and labs seemed to lie in repose, regrouping for the aftermath of a long, hot weekend. My office was as I'd left it, the pens and markers still scattered across the desktop. As I picked them up I looked around, my eyes roving over unfinished reports, uncataloged slides, and an ongoing project on maxillary sutures. The empty orbits of my reference skulls regarded me blankly.

I still wasn't sure why I was there or what I planned to do. I felt tense and out of sorts. Again I thought of Dr. Lentz. She'd led me to recognize my alcohol addiction, to face my growing alienation from Pete. Gently but relentlessly her words had picked at the scabs that covered my emotions. "Tempe," she'd say, "must you always be in control? Can no one else be trusted?"

Maybe she was right. Perhaps I was just trying to escape the guilt that always plagued me when I couldn't resolve a problem. Maybe I was simply evading inactivity and the feeling of inadequacy that accompanied it. I told myself the murder investigation really wasn't my responsibility, that the homicide detectives had that duty, and my job was to assist them with complete and accurate technical support. I chided myself for being there simply for lack of alternative invitations. It didn't work.

100

Although I recognized the logic of my own arguments by the time the pencil clean-up was complete, I still couldn't escape the feeling that there was something I needed to do. It gnawed at me, like a hamster with a carrot. I couldn't shake the nagging sensation that I was missing some tiny element that was important to these cases in a way I didn't yet understand. I needed to do something.

I pulled a file jacket from the cabinet where I keep old case reports, and another from my current case pile, and laid them beside the Adkins dossier. Three yellow folders. Three women yanked from their surroundings and slaughtered with psychopathic malevolence. Trottier. Gagnon. Adkins. The victims lived miles apart and were dissimilar in background, age, and physical characteristics, yet I couldn't shake the conviction that the same hand had butchered all three. Claudel could see only the differences. I needed to find the link that would convince him otherwise.

Tearing off a sheet of lined paper, I constructed a crude chart, heading the columns with categories I thought might be relevant. Age. Race. Hair color/length. Eye color. Height. Weight. Clothing when last seen. Marital status. Language. Ethnic group/religion. Place/type of residence. Place/type of employment. Cause of death. Date and time of death. Post-mortem body treatment. Location of body.

I started with Chantale Trottier, but realized quickly that my files wouldn't contain all the information I needed. I wanted to see the full police reports and scene photos. I looked at my watch – 1:45 P.M. Trottier had been an SQ case, so I decided to drop down to the first floor. I doubted there would be much activity in the homicide squad room, so it might be a good time to request what I wanted.

I was right. The huge room was almost empty, its

101

colony of regulation gray metal desks largely uninhabited. Three men clustered together in the far
corner of the room. Two occupied adjoining desks,
facing each other across stacks of file folders and overflowing in-baskets.

A tall, lanky man with hollow cheeks and hair the
color of hand-rubbed pewter sat with his chair tipped
back, feet propped high and ankles crossed. His name
was Andrew Ryan. He spoke in the hard, flat French of
an anglophone, stabbing the air with a ballpoint pen.
His jacket hung from the chair back, its empty arms
swinging in rhythm to the pen thrusts. The tableau
reminded me of firemen at a firehouse, relaxed but
ready at a moment's notice.

Ryan's partner watched him from across the desk,
head tilted to one side, like a canary inspecting a face
outside its cage. He was short and muscular, though his
body was beginning to take on the bulges of middle age.
He had the unlined tan of a bronzing salon, and his thick
black hair was styled and perfectly combed. He looked
like a would-be actor in a promo shot. I suspected even
his mustache was professionally coifed. A wooden
plaque on his desk said Jean Bertrand.

The third man perched on the edge of Bertrand's
desk, listening to the banter and inspecting the tassles
on his Italian loafers. When I saw him my spirits
dropped like an elevator.

". . . like a goat shitting cinders."

They laughed simultaneously, with the throaty sound
men seem to share when enjoying a joke at the expense
of women. Claudel looked at his watch.

You're being paranoid, Brennan, I told myself. Get a
grip. I cleared my throat and began weaving my way
through the labyrinth of desks. The trio fell silent and
turned in my direction. Recognizing me, the SQ detectives smiled and rose. Claudel did not. Making no

attempt to mask his disapproval, he flexed and lowered his feet, and resumed his tassle inspection, abandoning it only to consult his watch.

"Dr. Brennan. How are you?" Ryan asked, switching to English and extending his hand in my direction. "You been home lately?"

"Not for several months." His grip was firm.

"I've been meaning to ask you, do you pack an AK-47 when you go out down there?"

"No, we keep those mostly for home use. Mounted."

I was used to their quips about American violence.

"They got indoor toilets down there yet?" asked Bertrand. His topic of choice was the South.

"In some of the bigger hotels," I responded.

Of the three men, only Ryan looked embarrassed.

Andrew Ryan was an unlikely candidate for an SQ homicide detective. Born in Nova Scotia, he was the only son of Irish parents. Both were physicians who trained in London, arriving in Canada with English as their sole language. They expected their son to follow into the professional ranks, and, having chafed under the confines of their own unilingualism, vowed to ensure his fluency in French.

It was during his junior year at St. Francis Xavier that things began to go bad. Enticed by the thrill of life on the edge, Ryan got into trouble with booze and pills. Eventually, he was spending little time on campus, preferring the dark, stale beer-smelling haunts of dopers and drunks. He became known to the local police, his benders frequently concluding on the floor of a cell, his finales played facedown in vomit. He ended up one night in St. Martha's Hospital, a cokehead's blade having pierced his neck, nearly severing his carotid artery.

As with a born-again Christian, his conversion was swift and total. Still drawn to life in the underbelly, Ryan

103

merely changed sides. He finished his undergraduate studies in criminology, applied for and got a job with the SQ, eventually rising to the rank of detective lieutenant.

His time on the streets served him well. Though usually polite and soft-spoken, Ryan had the reputation of a brawler who could take the lowlifes on their own terms and match them trick for trick. I'd never worked with him. All this had come to me through the squad room grapevine. I'd never heard a negative comment about Andrew Ryan.

"What are you doing here today?" he asked. He swept his long arm toward the window. "You should be out enjoying the party."

I could see a thin scar winding out of his collar and up the side of his neck. It looked smooth and shiny, like a latex snake.

"Lousy social life, I guess. And I don't know what else to do when the stores are closed."

I said it brushing bangs back from my forehead. I remembered my gym gear, and felt a bit intimidated by their impeccable tailoring. The three of them looked like an ad for *GQ*.

Bertrand came from behind his desk, and extended his hand, nodding and smiling. I shook it. Claudel continued not to look at me. I needed him here like I needed a yeast infection.

"I wondered if I could take a look at a file from last year. Chantale Trottier. She was killed in October of '93. The body was found in St. Jerome."

Bertrand snapped his fingers into a pointing gesture, which he aimed at me.

"Yes. I remember that one. The kid in the dump. We still haven't nailed the bastard that did that one."

From the corner of my eye I saw Claudel's eyes go to Ryan. Though the movement was almost imperceptible, it triggered my curiosity. I doubted Claudel was there on a social call, was certain they'd talked about yesterday's murder. I wondered if they'd discussed Trottier or Gagnon.

"Sure," said Ryan, his face smiling but impassive. "Whatever you need. You think there's something in there we missed?"

He reached for a pack of cigarettes and shook one loose. Placing it in his mouth, he extended the pack toward me. I shook my head.

"No, no. Nothing like that," I said. "I've got a couple of cases upstairs I'm working on, and they keep making me think of Trottier. I'm not really sure what I'm looking for. I'd just like to go over the scene photos and maybe the incident report."

"Yeah, I know the feeling," he said, blowing a stream of smoke out the side of his mouth. If he knew any of my cases were also Claudel's, he didn't let on. "Sometimes you just have to follow a hunch. What do you think you've got?"

"She thinks there's a psychopath out there responsible for every murder since Cock Robin."

Claudel's voice was flat, and I saw that his eyes were back on the tassles. His mouth barely moved when he spoke. It seemed to me that he did not try to disguise his contempt. I turned away and ignored him.

Ryan smiled at Claudel. "Come on, Luc, ease back, it never hurts to take another look. We sure aren't setting any speed records clipping this worm."

Claudel snorted and shook his head. Again he consulted his watch.

Then, to me, "What've you got?"

Before I could answer the door flew open and Michel Charbonneau burst into the far end of the room. He jogged toward us, weaving through the desks and waving a paper in his left hand.

"We've got him," he said. "We've got the sonofabitch."

105

His face was red and he was breathing hard.

"About time," said Claudel. "Let's see." He addressed Charbonneau as one would a delivery boy, his impatience obliterating any pretense of courtesy.

Charbonneau's brow furrowed, but he handed the paper to Claudel. The three men huddled, their heads bent close, like a team consulting the playbook. Charbonneau spoke to their backs.

"The dumb fucker used her bank card an hour after he iced her. Apparently he hadn't had enough fun for the day, so he went to the corner dépanneur to score some change. Only this place don't cater to the quiche and Brie crowd, so they've got a video camera pointed at the money machine. Ident hammered the transaction and, *voilà*, we've got us a Kodak moment."

He nodded at the photocopy.

"He's a real beauty, eh? I took it by there this morning, but the night clerk didn't know the guy's name. Thought he recognized the face. Suggested we talk to the guy comes in after nine. Apparently our boy's a regular."

"Holy shit," said Bertrand.

Ryan just stared at the picture, his tall, lean frame hunched over that of his shorter partner.

"So this is the cocksucker," said Claudel, scrutinizing the image in his hand. "Let's get this asshole."

"I'd like to ride along."

They'd forgotten I was there. All four turned toward me, the SQ detectives half amused and curious as to what would happen next.

"*C'est impossible*," said Claudel, the only one now using French. His jaw muscles bunched and his face went taut. There was no smile in his eyes.

Showdown.

"Sergeant Detective Claudel," I began, returning his French and choosing my words carefully. "I believe I see

106

significant similarities in several homicide victims whom I have been asked to examine. If this is so, there may be one individual, a psychopath as you call him, behind all of their deaths. Maybe I'm right, maybe I'm wrong. Do you really want to assume responsibility for ignoring the possibility and risking the lives of more innocent victims?"

I was polite but unyielding. I, too, was unamused.

"Oh hell, Luc, let her ride along," said Charbonneau. "We're just going to do some interviews."

"Go on, this guy's going down whether you cut her in or not," said Ryan.

Claudel said nothing. He took out his keys, stuffed the photo into his pocket, and brushed past me on his way to the door.

"Let's boogie," said Charbonneau.

I had a hunch yet another day might go into overtime.

9

Getting there was no small task. As Charbonneau fought his way west along De Maisonneuve, I sat in the back, gazing out the window and ignoring the bursts of static that erupted from the radio. The afternoon was sweltering. As we inched along, I watched heat rise from the pavement in undulating waves.

Montreal was preening itself with patriotic fervor. The fleur-de-lis was everywhere, hung from windows and balconies, worn on T-shirts, hats, and boxer shorts, painted on faces, and waved on flags and placards. From Centre-ville eastward to the Main, sweaty revelers clogged the streets, choking off traffic like plaque in an artery. Thousands of people filled the streets, ebbing and flowing in streams of blue and white. Though seemingly without orientation, the throng oozed generally northward, toward Sherbrooke and the parade, punks moving next to mothers with strollers. The marchers and floats had left St. Urbain at 2 P.M., twirling and high-stepping eastward along Sherbrooke. At that moment they were just above us.

Over the hum of the air conditioner I could hear a lot of laughter and sporadic bursts of song. Already there was some fighting. As we waited out the light at

Amherst, I watched a lummox push his girlfriend against a wall. He had hair the color of unbrushed teeth, burred on top and long in the back. His chicken-white skin was moving toward grenadine. We pulled away before the scene could play itself out, leaving me with an image of the girl's startled face superimposed on the breasts of a naked woman. Eyes squinting and mouth in an O, she was framed by a poster for a Tamara de Lempicka exposition at the Musée des Beaux Arts. "*Une femme libre*," it whooped. "A free woman." Another of life's ironies. I took some satisfaction in knowing the oaf wouldn't have a good night. He might even blister.

Charbonneau turned to Claudel. "Lemme see that picture a minute."

Claudel pulled it from his pocket. Charbonneau studied it, shifting his eyes from the traffic to the photo in his hand.

"He sure don't look like much, does he?" he said to no one in particular. Wordlessly he extended the picture to me over the seat back.

What I held was a black-and-white print, a blowup of a single frame taken from high up and to the subject's right. It showed a blurred male figure with face averted, concentrating on the task of inserting or retracting a card at an automatic teller machine.

His hair was short and wispy in front, splayed downward into a fringe on his forehead. The top of his head was almost bare, and he had combed as many long strands as possible from left to right in an attempt to hide his baldness. My favorite male "do." About as attractive as a Speedo bathing suit.

His eyes were shielded by bushy brows, and his ears flared out like petals on a pansy. His skin looked deathly pale. He wore a plaid shirt and what looked like work pants. The graininess and poor angle obscured any other details. I had to agree with Charbonneau. He

109

didn't look like much. It could have been anyone. Silently, I handed the photo back.

Dépanneurs are the convenience stores of Quebec. They are found anywhere shelves and a refrigerator can be packed into a covered space. Scattered throughout the city, dépanneurs survive by providing grocery, dairy, and alcohol essentials. They dot every neighborhood, forming a capillary bed that feeds the needs of locals and foot travelers. They can be counted on for milk, cigarettes, beer, and cheap wine, the remainder of their inventory determined by neighborhood preferences. They provide no glitz and no parking. The upscale version may have a bank machine. It was to one such that we were heading.

"Rue Berger?" Charbonneau asked Claudel.

"*Oui*. It runs south from Ste. Catherine. Take René Lévesque to St. Dominique then go back north. That's a snakepit of one-ways in there."

Charbonneau turned left and began creeping south. In his impatience he kept goosing the gas then tapping the brake, causing the Chevy to lurch like a Ferris wheel seat. Feeling a bit seasick, I focused on the action at the boutiques, bistros, and modern brick buildings of L'Université du Québec, which lined St. Denis.

"*Sacré bleu!*"

"*Ca-lice!*" said Charbonneau as a dark green Toyota station wagon cut him off.

"Bastard," he added as he hit the brake then shot up to its bumper. "Look at that oily little freak."

Claudel ignored him, apparently used to his partner's erratic driving. I thought of Dramamine, but held my tongue.

Eventually we reached René Lévesque and turned west, then cut north onto St. Dominique. We doubled back at Ste. Catherine and, once again, I found myself in the Main, less than one block from Gabby's girls.

110

Berger is one of a small checkerboard of side streets sandwiched between St. Laurent and St. Denis. It lay directly ahead.

Charbonneau turned the corner and slid to the curb in front of the Dépanneur Berger. A dingy sign above its door promised "*bière et vin*." Sun-bleached ads for Molson and Labatt covered the windows, the tape yellowed and peeling with age. Rows of dead flies lined the sill below, their bodies stratified according to season of death. Iron bars safeguarded the glass. Two geezers sat on kitchen chairs outside the door.

"Guy's name is Halevi," said Charbonneau, consulting his notebook. "He probably won't have much to say."

"They never do. His memory may improve if we sweat him a little," said Claudel, slamming the car door.

The geezers watched us silently.

A string of brass bells jangled as we entered. The interior was hot and smelled of dust and spices and old cardboard. Two rows of back-to-back shelves ran the length of the store, forming one center and two side aisles. The dusty shelves held an assortment of aging canned and packaged goods.

On the far right a horizontal refrigerator case held vats of nuts, dal, dried peas, and flour. An assembly of limp vegetables lay in its far end. Something from another era, the case no longer refrigerated.

Upright coolers with wine and beer lined the left wall. In the rear, a small, open case, draped with plastic to conserve the cold, held milk, olives, and feta cheese. To its right, in the far corner, was the bank machine. Except for this, the place looked as if it hadn't been renovated since Alaska applied for U.S. statehood.

The counter was directly to the left of the front door. Mr. Halevi sat behind it, speaking heatedly into a cellular phone. He kept running his hand over his naked head, the maneuver a holdover from a hairier youth. A

111

sign on the cash register read SMILE. GOD LOVES YOU. Halevi was not taking his own advice. His face was red, and he was clearly piqued. I stood back and watched.

Claudel positioned himself directly in front of the counter and cleared his throat. Halevi showed him a palm and nodded his head in a "hold on" gesture. Claudel flashed his badge and shook his head. Halevi looked momentarily confused, said something in rapid Hindi, and clicked off. His eyes, huge behind thick lenses, moved from Claudel to Charbonneau and back.

"Yes," he said.

"You Bipin Halevi?" asked Charbonneau in English.

"Yes."

Charbonneau placed the photo face up on the counter. "Take a look. You know this guy?"

Halevi rotated the picture and leaned over it, his jittery fingers holding down the edges. He was nervous and trying hard to please, or at least to give the impression of cooperation. Many dépanneur operators sell smuggled cigarettes or other black market goodies, and police visits are as popular as tax audits.

"No one could recognize a man from this. Is this from the video? Men were here earlier. What did this man do?"

He spoke English with the singsong cadence of northern India.

"Any idea who he is?" said Charbonneau, ignoring the questions.

Halevi shrugged. "With my customers, you don't ask. Besides, this is too fuzzy. And his face is turned away."

He shifted on his stool. He was relaxing somewhat, realizing that he wasn't the object of the inquiry, that it had to do with the security video the police had confiscated.

"He a local?" asked Claudel.

"I tell you, I don't know."

112

"Does this even remotely remind you of anyone comes in here?"

Halevi stared at the picture.

"Maybe. Maybe, yes. But it's just not clear. I wish I could help. I . . . Maybe this could be a man I've seen."

Charbonneau looked at him hard, probably thinking what I was. Was Halevi trying to please, or did he really see something familiar in the photo?

"Who?"

"I – I don't know him. Just a customer."

"Any pattern to what he does?"

Halevi looked blank.

"Does the guy come at the same time of day? Does he come from the same direction? Does he buy the same stuff? Does he wear a goddamn tutu?" Claudel was becoming annoyed.

"I told you. I don't ask. I don't notice. I sell my stuff. At night I go home. This face is like many others. They come and they go."

"How late is this place open?"

"Till two."

"He come in at night?"

"Maybe."

Charbonneau was taking notes in a leather-bound pad. So far he'd written little.

"You work yesterday afternoon?"

Halevi nodded. "It was busy, the day before the holiday, eh? Maybe people think I won't be open today."

"You see this guy come in?"

Halevi studied the picture again, ran both hands to the back of his head, then scratched his halo of hair vigorously. He blew out a puff of air and raised his hands in a gesture of helplessness.

Charbonneau slipped the photo into his notebook and snapped it shut. He placed his card on the counter.

"If you think of anything else, Mr. Halevi, give us a call. We thank you for your time."

"Sure, sure," he said, his face brightening for the first time since seeing the badge. "I will call."

"Sure, sure," said Claudel when we were outside. "That toad'll call when Mother Teresa screws Saddam Hussein."

"He works a dépanneur. He's got chili for brains," Charbonneau responded.

As we crossed to the car I looked back over my shoulder. The two geezers were still flanking the door. They seemed a permanent fixture, like stone dogs at the entrance to a Buddhist temple.

"Let me have the picture a minute," I told Charbonneau.

He looked surprised but dug it out. Claudel opened the car door, and baked air rolled out like heat from a smelter. He draped one arm over the door, propped a foot on the frame, and watched me. As I recrossed the street, he said something to Charbonneau. Fortunately, I didn't hear.

I walked over to the old man on the right. He wore faded red running shorts, a tank top, dress socks, and leather oxfords. His bony legs were cobwebbed by varicose veins, and looked as if the pasty, white skin had been stretched over knots of spaghetti. His mouth had the collapsed look of toothlessness. A cigarette jutted from one corner at a downward angle. He watched me approach with unmasked curiosity.

"*Bonjour*," I said.

"Hey," he said, leaning forward to peel his sweat-slicked back from the cracked vinyl of the chair. He'd either heard us talking or picked up on my accent.

"Hot day."

"I seen hotter." The cigarette jumped as he spoke.

"You live near here?"

114

He flapped a scrawny arm in the direction of St. Laurent.

"Could I ask you something?"

He recrossed his legs and nodded.

I handed him the photo.

"Have you ever seen this man?"

He held the picture at arm's length in his left hand, and shaded it from the sun with his right. Smoke floated across his face. He studied the image for so long, I thought perhaps he'd drifted off. I watched a gray-and-white cat covered with raw, red patches slither behind his chair, skirt the building, and disappear around the corner.

The second old man placed both hands on his knees and raised himself with a low grunt. His skin had once been fair, but now looked as if he'd been sitting in that chair a hundred and twenty years. Adjusting first the suspenders and then the belt that held his gray work pants, he shuffled over to us. He brought the rim of his Mets cap to the level of his companion's shoulder, and squinted at the photo. Finally, spaghetti legs handed it back.

"A man's own mother wouldn't know him from this. Picture's shit."

The second geezer was more positive.

"He lives over there somewhere," he said, aiming a yellowed finger down the block at a seedy brick three-flat, and speaking in a joual so thick I could barely understand him. He, too, was without teeth or dentures, and, as he spoke, his chin seemed to reach for his nose. When he paused, I pointed to the photo and then to the building. He nodded his head.

"*Souvent?*" Often? I asked.

"Mmm, *oui*," he responded, raising his eyebrows and shoulders, thrusting forward his lower lip, and giving the palm up, palm down gesture with his hands. Often. Sort of.

115

The other geezer shook his head and snorted in disgust.

I signaled to Charbonneau and Claudel to join me, and explained what the old man had said. Claudel looked at me as he might a buzzing wasp, an annoyance that must be dealt with. I met his eyes, daring him to say something. He knew they should have questioned the men.

Without comment, Charbonneau turned his back and focused on the pair. Claudel and I stood and listened. The joual was rapid as gunfire, the vowels so stretched and the endings so truncated, I caught little of the exchange. But the gestures and signals were clear as a headline. Suspenders said he lived down the block. Spaghetti legs disagreed.

At length Charbonneau turned back to us. He tipped his head in the direction of the car, gesturing Claudel and me to follow. As we crossed the street, I could feel two sets of rheumy eyes burning the back of my neck.

10

Leaning on the Chevy, Charbonneau shook free a cigarette and lit it. His body looked as tense as an unsprung
trap. For a moment he was quiet, seeming to sort
through what the old men had said. Finally he spoke, his
mouth a straight line, his lips hardly moving.

"What do you think?" he asked.

"Click and clack look like they spend a lot of time
here," I offered. Inside my T-shirt, a rivulet of sweat ran
down my back.

"Could be a pair of real head cases," said Claudel.

"Or it could be they've actually seen the prick-ass,"
said Charbonneau. He inhaled deeply then flicked at the
cigarette with his middle finger.

"They weren't exactly star witnesses on details," said
Claudel.

"Yeah," said Charbonneau, "but we all agreed. The
guy ain't much to remember. And mutants like him
usually keep a pretty low profile."

"And grandpa number two seemed pretty sure," I
added.

Claudel snorted. "Those two may not be sure of anything but the wine shop and the blood bank. Probably
the only two landmarks they can map."

Charbonneau took one last drag, dropped the butt, and ground it with his toe. "It could be nothing, or it could be he's in there. Me, I don't want to guess wrong. I say we take a look, bust his ass if we find him."

I observed yet another of Claudel's shrugs. "Okay. But I'm not about to get my bacon fried. I'll call for backup."

He flicked his eyes to me and back to Charbonneau, brows raised.

"She don't bother me," Charbonneau said.

Shaking his head, Claudel rounded the car and slid in on the passenger side. Through the windshield I could see him reach for his handset.

Charbonneau turned to me. "Stay alert," he said. "If anything breaks, get down."

I appreciated his refraining from telling me not to touch anything.

In less than a minute Claudel's head reappeared above the door frame.

"*Allons-y*," he said. Let's roll.

I climbed into the backseat, and the two detectives got in front. Charbonneau put the car in gear and we crept slowly up the block. Claudel turned to me.

"Don't touch anything in there. If this is the guy, we don't want anything screwed up."

"I'll try," I said, fighting to suppress the sarcasm in my voice. "I'm one of the nontestosterone gender, and we sometimes have trouble remembering things like that."

He blew out a puff of air and pivoted back in his seat. I was sure if he'd had an appreciative audience he'd have rolled his eyes and smirked.

Charbonneau pulled to the curb in midblock, and we all considered the building. It sat surrounded by empty lots. The cracked cement and gravel were overgrown with weeds and strewn with the broken bottles, old tires, and the usual debris that accumulates on abandoned urban spaces. Someone had painted a mural on the wall facing the lot. It depicted a goat with an automatic weapon slung from each ear. In its mouth it held a human skeleton. I wondered if the meaning was clear to anyone but the artist.

"The old boy hadn't seen him today," said Charbonneau, drumming his fingers on the steering wheel.

"When did they go on neighborhood watch?" asked Claudel.

"Ten," said Charbonneau. He looked at his watch, and Claudel and I followed suit. Pavlov would have been proud – 3:10 P.M.

"Maybe the guy's a late sleeper," said Charbonneau. "Or maybe he's worn out from his little field trip yesterday."

"Or maybe he's not there at all and these geeks are getting ready to bust their balls laughing."

"Maybe."

I watched a group of girls cross the vacant lot behind the building, their arms intertwined in teenage comraderie. Their shorts formed a row of Quebec flags, a chorus line of fleur-de-lis swaying in unison as they picked their way through the weeds. Each had braided her hair in tiny cornrows and sprayed it bright blue. As I watched them laugh and jostle in the summer heat, I thought how easily such youthful high spirits could be extinguished forever by the act of a madman. I fought back a wave of anger. Was it possible we were sitting not ten yards from such a monster?

At that moment a blue-and-white patrol unit slipped quietly in behind us. Charbonneau got out and spoke to the officers. In a minute he was back.

"They'll cover the back," he said, nodding toward the squad car. His voice had an edge to it, all sarcasm gone.

"*Allons-y.*"

When I opened the door Claudel started to speak, changed his mind, and walked toward the apartment. I followed with Charbonneau. I noticed that he had unbuttoned his jacket and his right arm was tense and slightly bent. Reflex readiness. For what? I wondered.

The red-brick building stood alone, its neighbors long since gone. Trash littered the adjacent lots, and large blocks of cement dotted them helter-skelter, like boulders left in a glacial retreat. A rusted and sagging chain-link fence ran along the building's south side. The goat faced north.

Three ancient white doors, side by side, opened onto Berger at street level. In front of them, the ground was covered by a patch of asphalt running to the curb. Once painted red, the pavement was now the color of dried blood.

In the window of the third door, a handwritten sign rested at an angle against a limp and grayed lace curtain. I could barely read through the dirty glass, "*Chambres à louer, #1.*" Rooms to rent. Claudel put one foot on the step and pressed on the higher of two buttons next to the door frame. No answer. He rang again, then, after a brief pause, pounded on the door.

"*Tabernac!*" shrieked a voice directly in my ear. The piercing Québecois expletive sent my heart leaping into my throat.

I turned and saw that the voice came from a first-floor window eight inches to my left. A face scowled through the screen in undisguised annoyance.

"What do you think you're doing? You break that door, *trou de cul*, and you're going to pay for it."

"Police," said Claudel, ignoring the asshole reference.

"Yeah? You show me something."

Claudel held his shield close to the screen. The face

leaned forward and I could see it was that of a woman. It was flushed and porcine, its perimeter bordered by a diaphanous lime scarf, knotted with exuberance on the top of her head. The ends sprouted upward, bobbing on the air like chiffon ears. Save for the absence of armaments and ninety extra pounds, she bore a noticeable resemblance to the goat.

"So?" The scarf tips floated as she looked from Claudel to Charbonneau to me. Deciding I was the least threatening, she pointed them in my direction.

"We'd like to ask you a few questions," I said, feeling instantly as if I'd done a Jack Webb imitation. It sounded as clichéd in French as it would have in English. At least I hadn't added "ma'am" at the end.

"Is this about Jean-Marc?"

"We really shouldn't do this in the street," I said, wondering who Jean-Marc was.

The face hesitated then disappeared. In a moment we heard the rattle of locks being turned, and the door was opened by an enormous woman in a yellow polyester housedress. Her underarms and midsection were dark with perspiration, and I could see sweat mixed with grime in the folds that circled her neck. She held the door for us, then turned and waddled down a narrow hall, disappearing through a door on the left. We followed in single file, Claudel leading, me bringing up the rear. The corridor smelled of cabbage and old grease. The temperature inside was at least ninety-five degrees.

Her tiny apartment was rank with the stench of overused cat litter, and was crammed with the dark, heavy furniture mass-produced in the twenties and thirties. I doubted the fabric had been changed from the original. A clear vinyl runner cut diagonally across the living room carpet, which was a threadbare imitation of a Persian original. There wasn't an uncluttered surface in sight.

121

The woman lumbered to an overstuffed chair by the window and dropped heavily into it. A metal TV table to her right teetered, and a can of diet Pepsi wobbled with the tremor. She settled in and glanced nervously out the window. I wondered if she was expecting someone, or if she simply hated to have her surveillance interrupted.

I handed her the photo. She looked at it, and her eyes took on the shape of larvae, burrowing between their well-padded lids. She raised them to the three of us and realized, too late, that she had placed herself at a disadvantage. Standing, we had the benefit of height. She craned up at us, shifting the larvae from one of us to the other. Her mood seemed to change from belligerent to cautious.

"You are . . .?" began Claudel.

"Marie-Eve Rochon. What is this all about? Is Jean-Marc in trouble?"

"You are the concierge?"

"I collect the rent for the owner," she answered. Though there wasn't much room, she shifted in the chair. Its protest was audible.

"Know him?" asked Claudel, gesturing at the photo.

"Yes and no. He's staying here but I don't know him."

"Where?"

"Number 6. First entrance, room on the ground level," she said, making a wide gesture with her arm. The loose, lumpy flesh jiggled like tapioca.

"What's his name?"

She thought for a moment, fidgeting absently with a scarf tip. I watched a bead of sweat reach its hydrostatic maximum, burst, and trickle down her face. "St. Jacques. Course, they don't usually use their real names."

Charbonneau was taking notes.

122

"How long has he been here?"

"Maybe a year. That's a long time for here. Most are vagrants. Course, I don't see him much. Maybe he comes and goes. I don't pay attention." She flicked her eyes down and crimped her lips at the obviousness of her lie. "I don't ask."

"You get any references?"

Her lips fluttered with a loud puff of air, and she shook her head slowly.

"He have any visitors?"

"I told you, I don't see him much." For a time she was silent. Her fidgeting had pulled the scarf to the right, and the ears were now off center on her head. "Seems like he's always alone."

Charbonneau looked around. "The other apartments like this?"

"Mine's the biggest." The corners of her mouth tightened and there was an almost imperceptible lift to her chin. Even in shabbiness there was room for pride. "The others are broken up. Some are just rooms with hot plates and toilets."

"He here now?"

The woman shrugged.

Charbonneau closed his notebook. "We need to talk to him. Let's go."

She looked surprised. "*Moi?*"

"We may need to get into the flat."

She leaned forward in the chair and rubbed both hands on her thighs. Her eyes widened and her nostrils seemed to dilate. "I can't do that. That would be a violation of privacy. You need a warrant or something."

Charbonneau fixed her with a level stare and did not answer. Claudel sighed loudly, as though bored and disappointed. I watched a rivulet of condensed water run down the Pepsi can and join a ring at its base. No one spoke or moved.

123

"Okay, okay, but this is your idea."

Shifting her weight from ham to ham, she scooted forward in diagonal thrusts, like a sailboat on a series of short tacks. The housedress crept higher and higher, exposing enormous stretches of marbleized flesh. When she had maneuvered her center of gravity to the chair's edge, she placed both hands on the arms and levered herself up.

She crossed to a desk on the far side of the room and gophered around in a drawer. Shortly, she withdrew a key and checked its tag. Satisfied, she held it out to Charbonneau.

"Thank you, madame. We will be happy to check your property for irregularities."

As we turned to leave, her curiosity overcame her. "Hey, what's this guy done?"

"We'll return the key on our way out," said Claudel. Once again, we left with eyes fixed on our backs.

The corridor inside the first entrance was identical to the one we'd just left. Doors opened to the left and right, and, at the rear, a steep staircase led to an upper floor. Number 6 was the first on the left. The building was stifling and eerily quiet.

Charbonneau stood to the left, Claudel and I to the right. Both their jackets hung loose, and Claudel rested his palm on the butt of his .357. He knocked on the door. No answer. He knocked a second time. Same response.

The two detectives exchanged glances, and Claudel nodded. The corners of his mouth were tucked in tightly, beaking his face even more than usual. Charbonneau fitted the key into the lock and swung the door in. We waited, rigid, listening to dust motes settle back into place. Nothing.

"St. Jacques?"

Silence.

"Monsieur St. Jacques?"

Same answer.

Charbonneau raised a palm in my direction. I waited while the detectives entered, then followed, my heart pounding in my chest.

The room held little furniture. In the left-rear corner a pink plastic curtain hung by rusted rings from a semicircular rod, separating the area into a makeshift bathroom. Below the curtain I could see the base of a commode and a set of pipes that probably led to a sink. The pipes were badly rusted and supported a thriving colony of a soft, green life-form. To the right of the curtain, the back wall had been fitted with a Formica-topped counter. It held a hot plate, several plastic tumblers, and an unmatched collection of dishes and pans.

In front of the curtain, an unmade bed ran the length of the left wall. A table fashioned from a large plywood plank was placed along the right. Its base was formed by two sawhorses, each clearly stamped as property of the city of Montreal. The surface was heaped with books and papers. The wall above was covered with maps, photos, and newspaper articles, forming a cut-and-paste mosaic that extended the length of the table. A metal folding chair was tucked below. The room's only window was to the right of the front door, identical to that used by Madame Rochon. Two bare bulbs jutted from a hole in the ceiling.

"Nice place," said Charbonneau.

"Yeah. A thing of beauty. I'd rank it up there with herpes and Burt Reynolds's hairpiece."

Claudel moved to the toilet area, withdrew a pen from his pocket, and gingerly drew back the curtain.

"Defense Ministry might want to take scrapings. This stuff may have potential for biological warfare." He

125

dropped the curtain and moved toward the table.

"Dickhead isn't even here," said Charbonneau, flipping a blanket edge onto the bed with the tip of his shoe.

I was surveying the kitchenware on the Formica counter. Two Expos beer tumblers. A dented saucepan encrusted with something resembling SpaghettiOs. A half-eaten chunk of cheese congealed in the same substance in a blue china bowl. A cup from Burger King. Several cellophane packages of saltine crackers.

It hit me when I leaned over the hot plate. The lingering warmth made my blood turn to ice, and I spun toward Charbonneau.

"He's here!"

My words hit the air at the exact moment a door exploded open in the right-hand corner of the room. It slammed into Claudel, knocking him off balance and pinning his right arm and shoulder against the wall. A figure lunged across the room, body doubled over, legs thrusting toward the open front door. I could hear breath rasping in his throat.

For just an instant in his headlong plunge across the room, the fugitive raised his head, and two flat, dark eyes met mine, peering out from under the orange brim of a cap. In that brief flash I recognized the look of a terrified animal. Nothing more. Then he was gone.

Claudel regained his balance, unsnapped his gun, and bolted out the door. Charbonneau was right behind him. Without thinking, I plunged into the chase.

11

When I shot onto the street the sunlight blinded me. I squinted up Berger trying to locate Charbonneau and Claudel. The parade was over, and large numbers of people were drifting down from Sherbrooke. I spotted Claudel shouldering his way through the crowd, his face red and contorted as he demanded passage through the sticky bodies. Charbonneau was close behind. He was holding his badge straight arm in front of him, using it like a chisel to gouge his way forward.

The throng partied on, unaware that anything unusual was taking place. A heavy blonde swayed on her boyfriend's shoulders, her head thrown back, her arms held high, wagging a bottle of Molson's at the sky. A drunken man wearing a Quebec flag like a Superman cape hung from a lamppost. He prompted the crowd in chanting, "*Québec pour les Québecois!*" I noticed the chorus had a stridence that hadn't been there earlier.

I veered into the vacant lot, climbed onto a cement block, and stood on tiptoe to scan the crowd. St. Jacques, if that's who it had been, was nowhere to be seen. He had the home-court advantage, and had used it to put as much geography as possible between himself and us.

I could see one of the backup team replacing his handset and joining the chase. He'd radioed for reinforcements, but I doubted a cruiser could penetrate the mob. He and his partner were elbowing their way toward Berger and Ste. Catherine, well behind Claudel and Charbonneau.

Then I spotted the orange baseball cap. It was ahead of Charbonneau, who had turned east on Ste. Catherine, unable to see it through the mass of bodies. St. Jacques was heading west. As quickly as I saw him, he disappeared. I waved my arms for attention, but it was useless. I'd lost sight of Claudel, and neither of the patrolmen could see me.

Without thinking, I jumped from the block and plunged into the crowd. The smell of sweat, suntan lotion, and stale beer seemed to seep from the bodies around me, forming a bubble of human smog. I lowered my head and plowed through the swarm with less than my usual courtesy, bulldozing a path toward St. Jacques. I had no badge to excuse my roughness, so I pushed and shoved and avoided eye contact. Most people took the jostling with good humor, others paused to fling insults at my back. The majority were gender specific.

I tried to see St. Jacques's baseball cap through the hundreds of heads surrounding me, but it was impossible. I set a course toward the point where I'd spotted him, driving through the bodies like an ice-breaker on the St. Lawrence.

It almost worked. I was close to Ste. Catherine when I was grabbed roughly from behind. A hand the size of a Prince tennis racket wrapped itself around my throat and my ponytail was yanked sharply downward. My chin shot up, and I felt, or heard, something snap in my neck. The hand jerked me backward, and pressed me flat against the chest of a Yeti construction worker. I

128

could feel his heat and smell his perspiration as it soaked my hair and back. A face came close to my ear, and I was enveloped in the odor of sour wine, cigarette smoke, and stale nacho chips.

"Hey, *plotte*, who the fuck you shoving?"

I could not have answered were I inclined. This seemed to anger him further and he released my hair and neck, placed both hands on my back, and shoved violently. My head snapped forward like a catapult launcher, and the force of the movement propelled me into a woman in short shorts and stiletto heels. She screamed, and the people around us separated slightly. I threw my hands out in an attempt to regain my balance, but it was too late. I went down, bouncing hard off someone's knee.

As I hit the pavement I slid and scraped my cheek and forehead, and threw my arms over my head in a reflex of self-preservation. The blood was pounding in my ears. I could feel surface gravel grinding into my right cheek, and knew I had lost some of the skin. As I attempted to push off the pavement with my hands, a boot came down hard on my fingers, mashing them. I could see nothing but knees, legs, and feet as the crowd rolled over me, seeming not to see me until the instant of tripping over me.

I rolled on to my side and tried again to come to my hands and knees. Unintended blows from feet and legs kept me from righting myself. No one stopped to shield me or help me up.

Then I heard an angry voice, and felt the crowd recede slightly. A small pocket of space formed around me, and a hand appeared at my face, its fingers gesturing impatiently. I grasped it and pulled myself up, rising, unbelievably, to sunlight and oxygen.

The hand was attached to Claudel. He held back the crowd with his other arm as I got painfully to my feet. I

129

saw his lips move but couldn't understand what he was saying. As usual, he seemed to be annoyed. Nonetheless, he'd never looked so good. He finished speaking, paused, and looked me over. He took in the jagged tear in my right knee and the abrasions on my elbows. His eyes came to rest on my right cheek. It was scraped and bleeding, and the eye on that side was beginning to swell shut.

Dropping my hand, he withdrew a handkerchief from his pocket and gestured at my face. When I reached for it my hand was trembling. I blotted away blood and gravel, refolded to a clean surface, and held the linen to my cheek.

Claudel leaned close and shouted in my ear, "Stay with me!"

I nodded.

He worked his way toward the west side of Berger, where the crowd was a little thinner. I followed on rubbery legs. Then he turned and began to worm his way in the direction of the car. I lunged and grabbed his arm. He stopped and looked a question at me. I shook my head vehemently, and his eyebrows went from a deep V to a Stan Laurel imitation.

"He's over there!" I screamed, pointing in the opposite direction. "I saw him."

A man in a Tweedledee costume brushed past me. He was eating a snow cone, and the drops from the melt-off were painting a red trail down his belly. It looked like a blood-splatter pattern.

Claudel's brows dived in the midline. "You are going to the car," he said.

"I saw him on Ste. Catherine!" I repeated, thinking perhaps he hadn't heard. "Outside Les Foufounes Électriques! He was going toward St. Laurent!" Even to me, my voice was sounding a bit hysterical.

It got his attention. He hesitated for a second, assess-

130

ing the damage to my cheek and limbs.

"You're okay?"

"Yeah."

"You will go to the car?"

"Yes!" He turned to go. "Wait." One by one I lifted my trembling legs over a rusted metal cable that looped knee-high around the edge of the lot, crossed to another cement block, and stepped on to it. I scanned the sea of heads, looking for the orange baseball cap. Nothing. Claudel watched impatiently as I surveyed the crowd, shifting his eyes from me to the intersection then back again. He reminded me of a sled dog waiting for the gun.

Finally, I shook my head and raised my hands.

"Go. I'll keep looking."

Skirting the open lot, he began elbowing his way in the direction I'd indicated. The mob on Ste. Catherine was bigger than ever, and, in a few minutes, I watched his head disappear into it. The swarm seemed to absorb him, like an army of antibodies seeking out and surrounding a foreign protein. One moment he was an individual, the next a dot in the pattern.

I searched until my vision blurred, but hard as I tried I couldn't locate Charbonneau or St. Jacques. Beyond St. Urbain, I could see a squad car nibbling its way into the edge of the crowd, its lights flashing red and blue. The revelers ignored its whining insistence on right of way. Once I caught a flash of orange, but it turned out to be a tiger wearing tails and high-top sneakers. Moments later she passed closer, carrying her costume head and drinking a Dr Pepper.

The sun was burning, and my head pounded. I could feel a crust hardening on my abraded cheek. I kept scanning and rescanning, sweeping the crowd. I refused to quit until Charbonneau and Claudel returned. But I knew it was a farce. St. Jean and the day had smiled on our quarry, and he had escaped.

An hour later we were gathered around the car. Both detectives had removed their jackets and ties and tossed them in the backseat. Beads of sweat glistened on their faces and flowed into their collars. Their underarms and backs were saturated, and Charbonneau's face was the color of a raspberry tart. His hair stood on end in front, reminding me of a schnauzer with a bad clip. My T-shirt hung limp, and my spandex workout pants felt as if I'd put them on straight from the washer. Our breathing had slowed to normal, and "fuck" had been said at least a dozen times, with everyone contributing.

"*Merde*," said Claudel. It was an acceptable alternative.

Charbonneau leaned into the car and extracted a pack of Players from his jacket pocket. He slumped against a fender, lit up, and blew the smoke out the corner of his mouth.

"Bastard can cut a crowd like a cockroach through shit."

"He knows his way around here," I said, resisting the urge to explore the damage to my cheek. "That helps him."

He smoked for a moment.

"Think it was our guy from the cash machine?"

"Hell, I don't know," I said. "I didn't get a look at his face."

Claudel snorted, then pulled a handkerchief from his pocket and began wiping the perspiration from the back of his neck.

I locked my one good eye on him. "Were you able to ID him?"

Another snort.

I looked at him shaking his head, and my plan of zero commentary evaporated.

132

"You're treating me like I'm not quite bright, Monsieur Claudel, and you're starting to piss me off."

He gave another in his series of smirks.

"How's your face feel?" he asked.

"Peachy!" I shot back between clenched teeth. "At my age free dermabrasion is a bonus."

"Next time you decide to go on a wild-assed crime fighting spree, don't expect me to scrape you up."

"Next time do a better job of controlling an arrest scene and I won't have to." The blood was pounding in my temples, and my hands were clenched so tightly the nails were digging small crescents into the flesh of my palms.

"Okay. Knock this shit off," said Charbonneau, flipping his cigarette in a wide arc. "Let's toss the apartment."

He turned to the patrolmen, who had been standing by quietly.

"Call in recovery."

"You got it," said the taller, moving toward the squad car.

Silently, the rest of us followed Charbonneau to the red-brick building and reentered the corridor. The other patrolman waited outside.

In our absence someone had closed the outer door, but the one leading to number 6 still stood wide. We entered the room and spread out as before, like characters in a stage play following directions for blocking.

I moved toward the back. The hot plate was cold now, and the SpaghettiOs had not improved with age. A fly danced on the edge of the pan, reminding me of other, grislier leftovers that may have been abandoned by the occupant. Nothing else had changed.

I walked over to the door in the far right corner of the room. Small chunks of plaster littered the floor, the result of a doorknob slammed against the wall with great

133

force. The door was half open, revealing a wooden staircase descending to a lower floor. It dropped one step to a small landing, made a ninety-degree turn to the right, and disappeared into darkness. The landing was lined with tin cans where it met the back wall. Rusted hooks jutted from the wood at eye level. I could see a light switch on the wall to the left. The plate was missing, and the exposed wires looped around themselves like worms in a bait carton.

Charbonneau joined me and eased the door back with his pen. I indicated the switch, and he used the pen to flip it. A bulb went on somewhere below, casting the bottom steps into shadowy relief. We listened to the gloom. Silence. Claudel came up behind us.

Charbonneau stepped on to the landing, paused, and descended slowly. I followed, feeling each riser protest softly under my feet. My battered legs trembled as though I'd just run a marathon, but I resisted the temptation to touch the walls. The passage was narrow, and all I could see were Charbonneau's shoulders ahead of me.

At the bottom, the air was dank and smelled of mildew. Already my cheek felt like molten lava, and the coolness was a welcome relief. I looked around. It was a standard basement, roughly half the size of the building. The back wall was constructed of unfinished cinder blocks, and must have been added later to subdivide a larger area. A metal washtub stood ahead and to the right, with a long wooden workbench snugged up against it. Pink paint was peeling from the bench. Below it lay a collection of cleaning brushes, their bristles yellowed and covered in cobwebs. A black garden hose was coiled neatly on the wall.

A behemoth furnace filled the space to the right, its round metal ducts branching and rising like the limbs of an oak. A midden of trash circled its base. In the dim

134

light I could identify broken picture frames, bicycle wheels, bent and twisted lawn chairs, empty paint cans, and a commode. The castoffs looked like offerings to a Druid god.

A bare bulb hung in the middle of the room, throwing about one watt of light. That was it. The rest of the cellar was empty.

"Sonofabitch must've been waiting at the top," said Charbonneau, gazing up the stairs, hands on his hips.

"Madame Fatass might have told us the guy had this little hidey-hole," said Claudel, teasing at the trash pile with the tip of his shoe. "Regular Salman Rushdie down here."

I was impressed by the literary reference, but having returned to my original plan of neutral observation, said nothing. My legs were beginning to ache, and something was very wrong in my neck.

"Fucker could've scrambled us from behind that door."

Charbonneau and I didn't reply. We'd had the same thought.

Dropping his hands, Charbonneau crossed to the stairs and started up. I followed, beginning to feel a bit like Tonto. When I emerged into the room, the heat rolled over me. I crossed to the makeshift table and started examining the collage on the wall above.

The central piece was a large map of the Montreal area. Cutouts from magazines and newspapers surrounded it. Those on the right were standard issue pornography shots, the progeny of *Playboy* and *Hustler*. Young women stared from them, their bodies in distorted positions, their clothes absent or in disarray. Some pouted, some invited, and some feigned looks of orgasmic bliss. None was very convincing. The collagist was eclectic in his taste. He exhibited no preference as to body type, race, or hair color. I noted that the edges

135

of each picture were carefully trimmed. Each was set equidistant from its neighbors and stapled in place.

A grouping of newspaper articles occupied the space to the left of the map. Although a few were in English, the majority were drawn from the French press. I noticed that those in English were always accompanied by pictures. I leaned close and read a few sentences about a groundbreaking at a church in Drummondville. I moved to a French article on a kidnapping in Senneville. My eyes shifted to an ad for Videodrome, claiming to be the largest distributor of pornographic films in Canada. There was a piece from *Allo Police* on a nude dance bar. It showed "Babette" dressed in leather cross garters and draped with chains. There was another on a break-in in St.-Paul-du-Nord in which the burglar had constructed a dummy of his victim's nightclothes, stabbed it repeatedly, then left it on her bed. Then I spotted something that again turned my blood to ice.

In his collection St. Jacques had carefully clipped and stapled three articles side by side. Each described a serial killer. Unlike the others, these appeared to be photocopies. The first describe Léopold Dion, "The Monster of Pont-Rouge." In the spring of 1963 police had discovered him at home with the bodies of four young men. They had all been strangled.

The second recounted the exploits of Wayne Clifford Boden, who strangled and raped women in Montreal and Calgary beginning in 1969. When arrested in 1971, his final count was four. In the margin someone had written "Bill *l'étrangleur*."

The third article covered the career of William Dean Christenson, alias Bill *l'éventreur*, Montreal's own Ripper. He'd killed, decapitated, and dismembered two women in the early 1980s.

"Look at this," I said to no one in particular. Though the room was stifling, I felt cold all over.

Charbonneau came up behind me. "Oh, baby, baby," he intoned flatly, as his eyes swept over the arrangement to the right of the map. "Love in wide angle."

"Here," I said, pointing at the articles. "Look at these."

Claudel joined us and the two men scanned them wordlessly. They smelled of sweat and laundered cotton and aftershave. Outside I could hear a woman calling to Sophie, and wondered briefly if she beckoned a pet or a child.

"Holy fuck," breathed Charbonneau, as he grasped the theme of the stories.

"Doesn't mean he's Charlie Manson," scoffed Claudel.

"No. He's probably working on his senior thesis."

For the first time I thought I detected a note of annoyance in Charbonneau's voice.

"The guy could have delusions of grandeur," Claudel went on. "Maybe he watched the Menendez brothers and thought they were keen. Maybe he thinks he's Dudley DoRight and wants to fight evil. Maybe he's practicing his French and finds this more interesting than Tin Tin. How the fuck do I know? But it doesn't make him Jack the Ripper." He glanced toward the door. "Where the hell is recovery?"

Sonofabitch, I thought, but held my tongue.

Charbonneau and I turned our attention to the desktop. A stack of newspapers leaned against the wall. Charbonneau used his pen to rifle through them, lifting the edges then allowing the sections to drop back into place. The stack contained only want ads, most from *La Presse* and the *Gazette*.

"Maybe the toad was looking for a job," said Claudel sardonically. "Thought he'd use Boden as a reference."

"What was that underneath?" I'd seen a flash of yellow as the bottom section was lifted briefly.

137

Charbonneau nudged the pen under the last section in the pile and levered it upward, tipping the stack toward the wall. A yellow tablet lay under it. I wondered briefly if pen manipulation was required training for detectives. He allowed the newspapers to drop back to the desktop, slid the pen to the back of the stack, and pushed at the tablet, sliding it forward and into view.

It was a lined yellow pad, the type favored by attorneys. We could see that the top page was partially filled with writing. Bracing the stack with the back of his hand, Charbonneau teased the tablet out and slid it into full view.

The impact of the serial killer stories was nothing compared to the jolt I felt on seeing what was scrawled there. The fear that I'd kept down deep in its lair lunged out and grabbed me in its teeth.

Isabelle Gagnon. Margaret Adkins. Their names leapt out at me. They were part of a list of seven that ran along the bound edge of the tablet. Beside each, running sideways across the page, was a series of columns separated by vertical lines. It looked like a crude spreadsheet containing personal data on each of the individuals listed. It did not look unlike my own spreadsheet, except I didn't recognize the other five names.

The first column listed addresses, the second phone numbers. The next held brief notations on the residence. Apt. w/ outsd. entr., condo, 1st flr.; house w/ yd. The next column contained sets of letters behind some names, for others it was blank. I looked at the Adkins entry. Hu. So. The combinations looked familiar. I closed my eyes and ran a key word search. Kinship charts.

"Those are people they live with," I said. "Look at Adkins. Husband. Son."

"Yeah. Gagnon's got Br and Bf. Brother, boyfriend," said Charbonneau.

"Big fag," added Claudel. "What's Do mean?" he asked, referring to the last column. St. Jacques had written it behind some names, left no notation for others.

No one had an answer.

Charbonneau flipped back the first sheet and everyone fell silent reading the next set of notations. The page was divided in half with one name at the top and another halfway down. Below each was another set of columns. That on the left was headed "Date," the next two were marked "In" and "Out." The empty spaces were filled with dates and times.

"Jesus H. Christ, he stalked them. He picked them out and tracked them like goddamn quail or something," exploded Charbonneau.

Claudel said nothing.

"This sick sonofabitch hunted women," repeated Charbonneau, as if rephrasing it would somehow make it more believable. Or less.

"Some research project," I said softly. "And he hasn't turned it in yet."

"What?" asked Claudel.

"Adkins and Gagnon are dead. These dates are recent. Who are the others?"

"Shit."

"Where the fuck is recovery?" Claudel strode over to the door and disappeared into the corridor. I could hear him swearing at the patrolman.

My eyes wandered back to the wall. I didn't want to think about the list anymore today. I was hot and exhausted and in pain, and there was no satisfaction in the realization that I was probably right, and that now we would work together. That even Claudel would come on board.

I looked at the map, searching for something to divert myself. It was a large one showing in rainbow detail the island, the river, and the jumble of communities comprising the CUM and surrounding areas. The pink municipalities were crisscrossed by small white streets, and linked by red arterial roads and large blue autoroutes. They were dotted by the green of parks, golf courses, and cemeteries, the orange of institutions, the lavender of shopping centers, and the gray of industrial areas.

I found Centre-ville and leaned closer to try to locate my own small street. It was only one block long and, as I searched for it, I began to understand why taxis had so much difficulty finding me. I vowed to be more patient in the future. Or at least more specific. I traced Sherbrooke west to intersect Guy, but found I'd gone too far. It was then I had my third shock of the afternoon.

My finger hovered above Atwater, just outside the orange polygon demarcating Le Grand Séminaire. My eye was drawn to a small symbol sketched in pen at its southwest corner, a circle enclosing an X. It lay close to the site where Isabelle Gagnon's body had been discovered. With my heart pounding, I shifted to the east end and tried to find the Olympic Stadium.

"Monsieur Charbonneau, look at this," I said, my voice strained and shaky.

He came closer.

"Where's the stadium?"

He touched it with his pen and looked at me.

"Where's Margaret Adkins's condo?"

He hesitated a minute, leaned in, and started to point to a street running south from Parc Maisonneuve. His pen rested in midair as we both stared at the tiny figure. It was an X drawn and circled in pen.

"Where did Chantale Trottier live?"

"Ste. Anne-de-Bellevue. Too far out."

We both stared at the map.

"Let's search it systematically, sector by sector," I

140

suggested. "I'll start in the upper left-hand corner and work down, you start with the lower right and work up."

He found it first. The third X. The mark was on the south shore, near St. Lambert. He knew of no homicides in that district. Neither did Claudel. We looked for another ten minutes, but found no other X's.

We were just starting a second search when the crime scene van pulled up in front.

"Where the fuck have you been?" asked Claudel as they came through the door with their metal cases.

"It's like driving through Woodstock out there," said Pierre Gilbert, "only less mud." His round face was completely encircled by curly beard and curlier hair, reminding me of a Roman god. I could never remember which one. "What've we got here?"

"Girl killed over on Desjardins? Pussbag that lifted her card calls this little hole home," said Claudel. "Maybe."

He indicated the room with a sweep of his arm. "Put a lot of himself into it."

"Well, we'll take it out," said Gilbert with a smile. His hair was clinging in circles to his wet forehead. "Let's dust."

"There's a basement, too."

"*Oui.*" Save for the inflection, dropping then rising, it sounded more like a question than an assent. *Whyyyy?*

"Claude, why don't you start down below? Marcie, take the counter back there."

Marcie moved to the back of the room, removed a canister from her metal suitcase, and began brushing black powder on the Formica counter. The other technician headed downstairs. Pierre put on latex gloves and began removing sections of newspaper from the desktop and placing them in a large plastic sack. It was then I had my final shock of the day.

"*Qu'est-ce que c'est?*" he said, lifting a small square

141

from what had been the middle of the stack. He studied it a long time. *"C'est toi?"*

I was surprised to see him look at me.

Wordlessly I walked over and glanced at what he had. I was unnerved to see my own familiar jeans, my "Absolutely Irish" T-shirt, my Bausch and Lomb aviator sunglasses. In his gloved hand he held the photo which had appeared in *Le Journal* that morning.

For the second time that day I saw myself locked at an exhumation two years in the past. The picture had been cut and trimmed with the same careful precision as those on the wall. It differed in only one respect. My image had been circled and recircled in pen, and the front of my chest was marked with a large X.

12

I slept a lot of the weekend. Saturday morning I had tried getting up, but that was short-lived. My legs trembled, and if I turned my head long fingers of pain shot up my neck and grabbed the base of my skull. My face had crusted over like crème brûlée, and my right eye looked like a purple plum gone bad. It was a weekend of soup, aspirin, and antiseptic. I spent the days dozing on the couch, keeping abreast of O.J. Simpson's escapades. At night I was asleep by nine.

By Monday the jackhammer had stopped pounding inside my cranium. I could walk stiffly and rotate my head somewhat. I got up early, showered, and was in my office by eight-thirty.

There were three requisitions on my desk. Ignoring them, I tried Gabby's number, but got only her machine. I made myself a cup of instant coffee and uncurled the phone messages I'd taken from my slot. One was from a detective in Verdun, another from Andrew Ryan, the third a reporter. I threw the last away and set the others by the phone. Neither Charbonneau nor Claudel had called. Nor had Gabby.

I dialed the CUM squad room and asked for Charbonneau. After a pause I was told he wasn't there.

Neither was Claudel. I left a message, wondering if they were out on the street early or starting the day late.

I dialed Andrew Ryan but his line was busy. Since I was accomplishing nothing by phone, I decided to drop by in person. Maybe Ryan would discuss Trottier.

I rode the elevator to the first floor and wound my way back to the squad room. The scene was much livelier than during my last visit. As I crossed to Ryan's desk I could feel eyes on my face. It made me vaguely uncomfortable. Obviously they knew about Friday.

"Dr. Brennan," said Ryan in English, unfolding from his chair and extending a hand. His elongated face broke into a smile when he saw the scab that was my right cheek. "Trying out a new shade of blusher?"

"Right. Crimson cement. I got a message you called?"

For a moment he looked blank.

"Oh yeah. I pulled the jacket on Trottier. You can take a look if you want."

He leaned over and fiddled with some folders on his desk, spreading them out in a fan-shaped heap. He selected one and handed it to me just as his partner entered the room. Bertrand strode toward us wearing a light gray sports jacket monochromatically blended to darker gray pants, a black shirt, and a black-and-white floral tie. Save for the tan, he looked like an image from 1950s TV.

"Dr. Brennan, how goes it?"

"Great."

"Wow, nice effect."

"Pavement is impersonal," I said, looking around for a place to spread the file. "May I . . ." I gestured to an empty desk.

"Sure, they're out already."

I sat down and began sorting the contents of the folder, leafing through incident reports, untangling

144

interviews, and turning over photos. Chantale Trottier. It was like walking barefoot across hot asphalt. The pain came back as though it had happened yesterday, and I had to keep looking away, allowing my mind breaks from the surging sorrow.

On October 16, 1993, a sixteen-year-old girl rose reluctantly, ironed her blouse, and spent an hour shampooing and preening. She refused the breakfast her mother offered, and left her suburban home to join friends for the train ride to school. She wore a plaid uniform jumper and knee socks and carried her books in a backpack. She chatted and giggled, and ate lunch after math class. At the end of the day she vanished. Thirty hours later her butchered body was found in plastic garbage bags forty miles from her home.

A shadow fell across the desk and I looked up. Bertrand held two mugs of coffee. The one he offered me said "Monday I Start My Diet." Gratefully, I reached out and took it.

"Anything interesting?"

"Not much." I took a sip. "She was sixteen. Found in St. Jerome."

"Yup."

"Gagnon was twenty-three. Found in Centre-ville. Also in plastic bags," I mused aloud.

He tipped his head.

"Adkins was twenty-four, found at home, over by the stadium."

"She wasn't dismembered."

"No, but she was cut up and mutilated. Maybe the killer got interrupted. Had less time."

He sipped his coffee, slurping loudly. When he lowered the mug, milky brown breads clung to his mustache.

"Gagnon and Adkins were both on St. Jacques's list." I assumed the story had spread by now. I was right.

145

"Yeah but the media went snake over those cases. The guy had clipped *Allo Police* and *Photo Police* articles on both of them. With pictures. He could just be a maggot that feeds on that kind of crap."

"Could be." I took another sip, not really believing it.

"Didn't he have a whole dungheap of stuff?"

"Yeah," said Ryan from behind us. "Dickhead had clippings on all kinds of weird shit. Francoeur, didn't you catch some of those dummy cases when you were with property?" This to a short, fat man with a shiny brown head who was eating a Snickers bar four desks over.

Francoeur put down the candy, licking his fingers and nodding. His rimless glasses blinked as his head moved up and down.

"Um. Hum. Two." Lick. "Damnedest thing." Lick. "This squirrel creeps the place, rifles the bedroom, then makes a big doll with a nightgown or a sweat suit, something that belongs to the lady of the house. He stuffs it, dresses it up in her underwear, then lays it out on the bed and slashes it. Probably makes him harder than a math final." Lick. Lick. "Then he gets his sorry ass out of there. Doesn't even take anything."

"Sperm?"

"Nope. Believes in safe sleaze, I guess."

"What's he use?"

"Probably a knife, but we never found it. He must bring it with him."

Francoeur peeled back the wrapper and took another bite of Snickers.

"How's he get in?"

"Bedroom window." It came out through caramel and peanuts.

"When?"

"Night, usually."

"Where's he put on these little freak shows?"

146

Francoeur chewed slowly for a moment, then, using a thumbnail, removed a speck of peanut from his molar. He inspected and flicked it.

"One was in St. Calixte, and I think the other was St. Hubert. The one this guy clipped went down a couple of weeks ago in St. Paul-du-Nord." His upper lip bulged as he ran his tongue over his incisors. "And I think one fell to the CUM. I sort of remember a call about a year ago from someone over there."

Silence.

"They'll pop him, but this squirrel isn't exactly high priority. He doesn't hurt anybody and he doesn't take anything. He's just got a twisted idea of a cheap date."

Francoeur crumbled the Snickers wrapper and arced it into the wastebasket beside his desk.

"I hear the concerned citizen in St. Paul-du-Nord refused to follow up with a complaint."

"Yeah," said Ryan, "those cases are about as rewarding as a lobotomy with a Scout knife."

"Our hero probably clipped the story because he gets a hard-on reading about busting someone's bedroom. He had a story on that girl out in Senneville and we know he wasn't the one grabbed her. Turned out the father had the kid stashed the whole time." Francoeur leaned back in his chair. "Maybe he just identifies with a kindred pervert."

I listened to this exchange without really looking at the participants. My eyes drifted over a large city map behind Francoeur's head. It was similar to the one I'd seen in the Berger apartment, but drawn to a smaller scale, extending out to include the far eastern and western suburbs off the island of Montreal.

The discussion snaked around the squad room, scooping up anecdotes of Peeping Toms and other sexual perverts. As it meandered from desk to desk, I rose quietly and crossed to the map for a closer view,

147

hoping to draw as little attention to myself as possible. I studied it, replaying the exercise Charbonneau and I had gone through on Friday, mentally plotting the location of the X's. Ryan's voice startled me.

"What are you thinking?" he asked.

I took a container of pins from a ledge below the map. Each was topped by a large, brightly colored ball. Choosing a red one, I placed it at the southwest corner of Le Grand Séminaire.

"Gagnon," I said.

Next I placed one below the Olympic Stadium.

"Adkins."

The third went in the upper-left corner, near a broad expanse of river known as Lac des Deux-Montagnes.

"Trottier."

The island of Montreal is shaped like a foot with its ankle dipping in from the northwest, its heel to the south, and its toes pointing northeast. Two pins marked the foot, just above the sole, one in the heel of Centreville, another to the east, halfway up the toes. The third lay up the ankle, on the far western end of the island. There was no apparent pattern.

"St. Jacques marked this one and this one," I said, pointing to one of the downtown pins, then to the one on the east end.

I searched the south shore, following the Victoria Bridge across to St. Lambert, then dropping south. Finding the street names I'd seen on Friday, I took a fourth pin and pushed it in on the far side of the river, just below the arch of the foot. The scatter made even less sense. Ryan looked at me quizzically.

"That was his third X."

"What's there?"

"What do you think?" I asked.

"Hell if I know. Could be his dead dog Spike." He glanced at his watch. "Look, we've got this . . ."

148

"Don't you think it would be a good idea to find out?"

He looked at me for a long time before he answered. His eyes were neon blue, and I was mildly surprised that I'd never noticed them before. He shook his head.

"It just doesn't feel right. It isn't enough. Right now your serial killer idea's got more holes than the Trans-Canada. Fill them in. Get me something else, or get Claudel to do a request for an SQ search. So far, this isn't our baby."

Bertrand was signaling to him, pointing at his watch, then hitching his thumb at the door. Ryan looked at his partner, nodded, then turned the neon back on me.

I said nothing. My eyes roved over his face, rummaging for a sign of encouragement. If it was there, I couldn't find it.

"Gotta go. Just leave the file on my desk when you're done."

"Right."

"And . . . Uh . . . Keep your head up."

"What?"

"I heard what you found in there. This prick could be more than just your average dirtbag." He reached into his pocket, withdrew a card, and wrote something on it. "You can get me at this number just about any time. Call if you need help."

Ten minutes later I was sitting at my desk, frustrated and antsy. I was trying to concentrate on other things, but having little success. Every time a phone rang in an office along the corridor, I reached for mine, willing it to be Claudel or Charbonneau. At ten-fifteen I called again.

A voice said, "Hold, please." Then.

"Claudel."

"It's Dr. Brennan," I said.

The silence was deep enough to scuba.

"*Oui.*"

"Did you get my messages?"

"*Oui.*"

I could tell he was going to be as forthcoming as a bootlegger at a tax audit.

"I wondered what you dug up on St. Jacques?"

He gave a snort. "Yeah, St. Jacques. Right."

Though I felt like reaching across the line to rip out his tongue, I decided the situation called for tact, rule number one in the care and handling of arrogant detectives.

"You don't think that's his real name?"

"If that's his real name, I'm Margaret Thatcher."

"So, where are you?"

There was another pause, and I could see him turning his face to the ceiling, deciding how best to rid himself of me.

"I'll tell you where we are, we're nowhere. We didn't get piss all. No dripping weapons. No home movies. No rambling confession notes. No souvenir body parts. Zip."

"Prints?"

"None usable."

"Personal effects?"

"The guy's taste falls somewhere between severe and stark. No decorative touches. No personal effects. No clothes. Oh yeah, one sweatshirt and an old rubber glove. A dirty blanket. That's it."

"Why the glove?"

"Maybe he worried about his nails."

"What *do* you have?"

"You saw it. His collection of Miss Show Me Your Twangie shots, the map, the newspapers, the clippings, the list. Oh, and some Franco-American spaghetti."

"Nothing else?"

150

"Nothing."

"No toiletries? Drugstore items?"

"*Nada.*"

I picked through that for a moment.

"Doesn't sound like he really lives there."

"If he does, he's the filthiest sonofabitch you'll ever meet. He doesn't brush his teeth or shave. No soap. No shampoo. No floss."

I gave that some thought.

"How do you read it?"

"Could be the little freak just uses the place as a hidey-hole for his true crime and porno hobby. Maybe his old lady doesn't like his taste in art. Maybe she doesn't let him jack off at home. How should I know?"

"What about the list?"

"We're checking out the names and addresses."

"Any in St. Lambert?"

Another pause.

"No."

"Any more information on how he might have gotten Margaret Adkins's bank card?"

This time the pause was longer, more palpably hostile.

"Dr. Brennan, why don't you stick to what you do and let us catch the killers?"

"Is he?" I couldn't resist asking.

"What?"

"A killer?"

I found myself listening to a dial tone.

I spent what was left of the morning estimating the age, sex, and height of an individual from a single ulna. The bone was found by children digging a fort near Pointe-aux-Trembles, and probably came from an old cemetery.

At twelve-fifteen I went upstairs for a Diet Coke. I

151

brought it back to my office, closed the door, and took out my sandwich and peach. Swiveling to face the river, I encouraged my thoughts to wander. They didn't. Like a Patriot missile, they homed in on Claudel.

He still rejected the idea of a serial killer. Could he be right? Could the similarities be coincidental? Could I be manufacturing associations that weren't there? Could St. Jacques merely have a grotesque interest in violence? Of course. Movie producers and publishing houses make millions off the same theme. Maybe he wasn't a killer himself, maybe he just charted the murders or played some kind of voyeuristic tracking game. Maybe he found Margaret Adkins's bank card. Maybe he stole it before her death and she hadn't yet missed it. Maybe. Maybe. Maybe.

No. It didn't tally. If not St. Jacques, there was someone out there responsible for several of these deaths. At least some of the murders were linked. I didn't want to wait for another butchered body to prove me right.

What would it take to convince Claudel I wasn't a dimwit with an overactive imagination? He resented my involvement in his territory, thought I was overstepping my bounds. He'd told me to stick to what I do. And Ryan. What had he said? Potholes. Not enough. Find stronger evidence of a link.

"All right, Claudel, you sonofabitch, that's exactly what you'll get."

I said it aloud, snapping my chair into full upright position and tossing my peach pit into the wastebasket.

So.

What do I do?

I dig up bodies. I look at bones.

13

In the histology lab I asked Denis to pull out cases 25906-93 and 26704-94. I cleared the table to the right of the operating scope and placed my clipboard and pen. I took out two tubes of vinyl polysiloxane and positioned them, along with a small spatula, a tablet of coated papers, and a digital caliper accurate to .0001 inch.

Denis placed two cardboard boxes on the end of the table, one large and one small, each sealed and carefully labeled. I eased the lid from the larger box, selected portions of Isabelle Gagnon's skeleton, and laid them out on the right half of the table.

Next I opened the smaller box. Though Chantale Trottier's body had been returned to her family for burial, segments of bone had been retained as evidence, a standard procedure in homicide cases involving skeletal injury or mutilation.

I removed sixteen Ziploc bags and put them on the left side of the table. Each was marked as to body part and side. Right wrist. Left wrist. Right knee. Left knee. Cervical vertebrae. Thoracic and lumbar vertebrae. I emptied each bag and arranged the contents in anatomical order. The two segments of femur went next to their

153

corresponding portions of tibia and fibula to form the knee joints. Each wrist was represented by six inches of radius and ulna. The ends of the bones sawed at autopsy were clearly notched. I would not confuse these cuts with those made by the killer.

I pulled the mixing pad toward me, opened one of the tubes, and squeezed a bright blue ribbon of dental impression material onto the top sheet. Next to it I squirted a white ribbon from the second tube. Selecting one of Trottier's arm bones, I placed it in front of me and picked up the spatula. Working quickly, I mixed the blue catalyst and the white base, kneading and scraping the two squiggles into a homogenous goo. I scraped the compound into a plastic syringe, then squeezed it out like cake decoration, carefully covering the joint surface.

I laid the first bone down, cleaned the spatula and syringe, tore off the used sheet, and began the process anew with another bone. As each mold hardened I removed it, marked it as to case number, anatomical site, side, and date, and placed it next to the bone on which it had been formed. I repeated the procedure until a rubbery blue mold sat next to each of the bones in front of me. It took over two hours.

Next I turned to the microscope. I set the magnification and adjusted the fiber-optic light to angle across the viewing plate. Starting with Isabelle Gagnon's right femur I began a meticulous examination of each of the small nicks and scratches I had just cast.

The cut marks seemed to be of two types. Each arm bone had a series of trench-like troughs lying parallel to its joint surfaces. The walls of the troughs were straight and dropped to meet their floors at ninety-degree angles. Most of the trench-like cuts were less than a quarter of an inch in length and averaged five hundredths of an inch across. The leg bones were circled by similar grooves.

154

Other marks were V-shaped, narrower, and lacked the squared-off walls and floors of the trench-like grooves. The V-shaped cuts lay parallel to the trenches on the ends of the long bones, but were unaccompanied in the hip sockets and on the vertebrae.

I diagrammed the position of each mark, and recorded its length, width, and, in the case of the trenches, depth. Next I observed each trench and its corresponding mold from above and in cross-section. The molds allowed me to see minute features not readily apparent when viewing the trenches directly. Tiny bumps, grooves, and scratches marking the walls and floors appeared as three-dimensional negatives. It was like viewing a relief map, the islands, terraces, and synclines of each trench replicated in bright blue plastic.

The limbs had been separated at the joints, leaving the long bones intact. With one exception. The bones of the lower arms had been severed just above the wrists. Turning to the bisected ends of the radius and ulna, I noted the presence and position of breakaway spurs, and analyzed the cross-sectional surface of each cut. When I'd finished with Gagnon, I repeated the whole process for Trottier.

At some point Denis asked if he could lock something up, and I agreed, paying no attention to his question. I didn't notice the lab grow quiet.

"What are you still doing here?"

I almost dropped the vertebra I was removing from the microscope.

"Jesus Christ, Ryan! Don't do that!"

"Don't go bughouse, I just saw the light and thought I'd drop in to see if Denis was putting in overtime slicing up something entertaining."

"What time is it?" I gathered the other cervical vertebrae and placed them in their bag.

155

Andrew Ryan looked at his watch. "Five-forty." He watched me lift the bags into the smaller cardboard box and set the cover on top.

"Find anything useful?"

"Yup."

I tapped the cover into place and picked up Isabelle Gagnon's pelvic bones.

"Claudel doesn't put much stock in this cut-mark business."

It was precisely the wrong thing to say. I put the pelvic bones in the larger box.

"He thinks a saw's a saw."

I laid the two scapulae in the box and reached for the arm bones.

"What do you think?"

"Shit, I don't know."

"You are of the carpentry and grout gender. What do you know about saws?" I continued laying bones in the box.

"They cut things."

"Good. What things?"

"Wood. Shrubbery. Metal." He paused. "Bone."

"How?"

"How?"

"How."

He thought a minute. "With teeth. The teeth go back and forth and cut through the material."

"What about radial saws?"

"Oh well, they go around."

"Do they slice through the material or chisel through it?"

"What do you mean?"

"Are the teeth sharp on the edge or flat? Do they cut the material or rip their way through it?"

"Oh."

"And do they cut when they go back or when they go

forth?"

"What do you mean?"

"You said the teeth go back and forth. Do they cut on the back or on the forth? On the push stroke or on the pull stroke?"

"Oh."

"Are they designed to cut on the grain or across the grain?"

"Does that matter?"

"How far apart are the teeth? Are they evenly spaced? How many are on the blade? What's their shape? How are they angled front to back? Is their edge pointed or squared off? How are they set relative to the plane of the blade? What kind of . . ."

"Okay, okay, I see. So, tell me about saws."

As I spoke, I placed the last of Isabelle Gagnon's bones in the box and tapped on the cover.

"There must be hundreds of different kinds of saws. Crosscut saws. Ripsaws. Pruning saws. Hacksaws. Keyhole saws. Kitchen and meat saws. Ryoba saws. Gigli and rod saws. Bone and metacarpal saws. And those are just the hand-powered ones. Some run on muscle, and some are powered by electricity or gas. Some move with a reciprocating action, some use continuous action, some move back and forth, some use a rotating blade. Saws are designed to cut different types of materials and to do different things as they cut. Even if we just stick to handsaws, which is what we've got here, they vary as to blade dimensions, and the size, spacing, and set of their teeth."

I looked to see if he was still with me. He was, eyes as blue as the flame in a gas burner.

"What all this means is that saws leave characteristic marks in materials such as bone. The troughs they leave are of different widths and contain certain patterns in their walls and floors."

"So if you've got a bone you can tell the specific saw that cut it?"

"No. But you *can* determine the most likely class of saw that made the cuts."

He digested that. "How do you know this is a handsaw?"

"Power saws don't depend on muscle, so they tend to leave more consistent cuts. The scratches in the cuts, the striae, are more evenly patterned. The direction of the cut is also more uniform; you don't see a lot of directional changes like you do with a handsaw." I thought for a minute. "Since there isn't a lot of human energy required, people using power saws often leave a lot of false starts. And deeper false starts. Also, because the saw is heavier, or sometimes because the person working it is putting pressure on the object being cut, power saws tend to leave larger breakaway spurs when the bone finally gives."

"What if a really strong person is working a handsaw?"

"Good point. Individual skill and strength can be factors. But power saws often leave scratches at the start of the cut, since the blade is already moving when it makes contact. Exit chipping is also more marked with a power saw." I paused, but this time he waited me out. "The greater transfer of energy with power saws can also leave a sort of polish on the cut surface. Handsaws don't usually do that."

I took a breath. He waited to be sure I was actually through.

"What's a false start?"

"When the blade first enters the bone it forms a trough, or kerf, with corners at the initial striking surface. As the saw moves deeper and deeper into the bone, the initial corners become walls and the kerf develops a distinct floor. Like a trench. If the blade jumps out, or is

158

pulled out, before going all the way through the bone, the kerf that's left is known as a false start. A false start contains all kinds of information. Its width is determined by the width of the saw blade and the set of its teeth. A false start will also have a characteristic shape in cross-section, and the teeth of the blade may leave marks on its walls."

"What if the saw goes straight through the bone?"

"If the cut progresses all the way through the bone, the kerf floor can still partially be seen in a breakaway spur. That's a spike that's left at the edge of the bone where it finally breaks. Also, individual tooth marks may be left on the cut surface."

I dug Gagnon's radius back out, found a partial false start on the breakaway spur, and angled the fiber-optic beam across it.

"Here, look at this."

He leaned over and squinted into the eyepiece, fiddling with the focus knob.

"Yeah. I see it."

"Look at the kerf floor. What do you see?"

"It looks lumpy."

"Right. Those lumps are bone islands. They mean that the teeth were set at alternating angles from the saw blade. That kind of set causes a phenomenon known as blade drift."

He raised his head from the microscope and looked at me blankly. The eyepiece had left double rings, grooving his face like that of a swimmer with tight goggles.

"When the first tooth cuts into the bone it tries to align itself to the plane of the blade. It seeks the midline, and the blade goes along with that. When the next tooth enters the bone it tries to do the same thing, but it's set in the opposite direction. The blade readjusts. This happens as each tooth comes along, so the forces acting on the blade change constantly. As a result, it sort of drifts back and forth in the kerf. The more set to the teeth, the

159

more the blade is forced to drift. A very wide set causes successive teeth to drift so much that material is actually left in the midline of the kerf. Bone islands. Lumps."

"So they tell you the teeth were angled."

"Actually, they tell more than that. Since each directional change of a tooth is caused by the introduction of a new tooth, the distance between these directional changes can tell the distance between teeth. Since islands represent the widest points of bone drift, the distance from island to island is equal to the distance between two teeth. Let me show you something else."

I withdrew the radius and inserted the ulna so that the cut surface at its wrist end was illuminated, then I stepped back from the microscope.

"Can you see those wavy lines on the cut surface?"

"Yeah. Looks kind of like a washboard, only curvy."

"That's called harmonics. Blade drift leaves those peaks and valleys on the wall of the cut just as it leaves bone islands on the floor. The peaks and islands correspond to the wide points in drift; the valleys and narrow aspects of the floor correspond to the points in drift when the blade is closest to the midline."

"So you can measure these peaks and valleys like you do the islands?"

"Exactly."

"How come I don't see anything farther down in the kerf?"

"Drift occurs mostly at the beginning or end of a cut, when the blade is free, not embedded in bone."

"Makes sense." He looked up. The goggles were back.

"Can you tell anything about direction?"

"Of blade stroke or blade progress?"

"What's the difference?"

"Direction of stroke has to do with whether the blade is cutting on the push or the pull. Most Western saws

160

are designed to cut on the push. Some Japanese saws cut on the pull. Some can cut on both. Progress has to do with the direction the blade moves through the bone."

"Can you determine that?"

"Yup."

"So what do you have?" he asked, rubbing his eyes and trying to look at me at the same time.

I took my time answering, kneading the small of my back, then reaching for my clipboard. I flipped through my notes, selecting relevant points.

"Isabelle Gagnon's bones have quite a few false starts. The kerfs measure about .05 inches in width and have floors that, in most cases, have some dip to them. Harmonics are present, and there are bone islands. Both are measurable." I flipped a page. "There's some exit chipping."

He waited for me to go on. When I didn't, he said, "What does all that mean?"

"I think we're dealing with a handsaw with alternating set teeth, probably a TPI of 10."

"TPI?"

"Teeth per inch. In other words, tooth distance is about a tenth of an inch. The teeth are chisel type, and the saw cuts on the push stroke."

"I see."

"The blade drift is extreme and there's a lot of exit chipping, but the blade seems to cut efficiently by chiseling the material clear. I think it's probably a saw designed like a very large hacksaw. The islands mean the set has to be pretty wide, to avoid binding."

"That narrows it to what?"

I was pretty sure I knew what had made the cuts, but wasn't ready to share my thoughts.

"There's someone else I want to talk to before I reach a conclusion."

"Anything else?"

I flipped to the first page of my notes, and summarized the observations I'd made.

"The false starts are on the anterior surfaces of the long bones. Where there are breakaway spurs, they're on the posterior aspects. That means the body was probably lying on its back when it was cut up. The arms were detached at the shoulders, and the hands were cut off. The legs were removed at the hips and the knee joints were severed. The head was removed at the level of the fifth cervical vertebrae. The thorax was opened with a vertical slash that penetrated all the way to the vertebral column."

He shook his head. "Guy was a real whiz with a saw."

"It's more complicated than that."

"*More* complicated?"

"He also used a knife."

I adjusted the ulna and refocused. "Take another look."

He bent over the scope, and I couldn't help noticing his nice, tight butt. Jesus, Brennan . . .

"You don't have to press quite so hard against the eyepieces."

His shoulders relaxed somewhat, and he shifted his weight.

"See the kerfs we've been talking about?"

"Uh-huh."

"Now, look to the left. See the narrow slash?"

He was silent for a moment as he adjusted the focus. "Looks more like a wedge. Not square. It's not as wide."

"Right. That's made by a knife."

He stood up. Goggles.

"The knife marks have a definite pattern. A lot of them parallel the saw false starts, some even cross them. Also, they're the only kind I see in the hip joint and on the vertebrae."

"Meaning?"

162

"Some of the knife marks overlie saw marks and some are underneath, so the cutting probably came before and after the sawing. I think he cut the flesh with the knife, separated the joints with the saw, then finished with the knife, maybe disconnecting any muscles or tendons that still held the bones together. Except for the wrists, he went right into the joints. For some reason he just sawed the hands off above the wrists, going right through the lower arm bones."

He nodded.

"He decapitated Isabelle Gagnon and opened her chest using just the knife. There are no saw marks on any of the vertebrae."

We were both silent for a few moments thinking about that. I wanted all this to sink in before I dropped the bombshell.

"I also examined Trottier."

The brilliant blue eyes met mine. His gaunt face looked tense, stretched, as he prepared it to receive what I was about to say.

"It's identical."

He swallowed and took a deep breath. Then he spoke very quietly. "This guy must run Freon through his veins."

Ryan pushed off from the counter just as a janitor poked his head through the door. We both turned to look at him, and, seeing our somber expressions, the man left quickly. Ryan's eyes reengaged mine. His jaw muscles flexed.

"Run this by Claudel. You're getting there."

"I've got a couple of others things I want to check out first. Then I'll approach Capitaine Congenial."

He departed without saying good-bye, and I finished repacking the bones. I left the boxes on the table and locked the lab behind me. As I passed through the main reception area, I noted the clock above the elevators:

163

6:30 P.M. Once again it was me and the cleaning crew. I knew it was too late to accomplish either of the last two things I'd planned to do, but decided to try anyway.

I walked past my own office and down the corridor to the last door on the right. A small plaque said, INFORMATIQUE, with the name LUCIE DUMONT printed neatly below.

It had been long in arriving, but the LML and LSJ were finally coming on-line. Complete computerization had been achieved in the fall of '93, and data were continually being fed into the system. Current cases could now be tracked, with reports from all divisions coordinated into master files. Cases from years past were gradually being entered into the database. L'Expertise Judiciaire had roared into the computer age, and Lucie Dumont was leading the charge.

Her door was closed. I knocked, knowing there would be no answer. At 6:30 P.M. even Lucie Dumont was gone.

I trudged back to my office, pulled out my membership directory for the American Academy of Forensic Sciences, and found the name I was looking for. I glanced at my watch, quickly calculating. It would be only four-forty there. Or would it be five-forty? Was Oklahoma on Mountain or Central time?

"Oh hell," I said, punching in the area code and number. A voice answered and I asked for Aaron Calvert. I was told, in a friendly, twangy way, that I was speaking with the night service, but that they'd be glad to take a message. I left my name and number and hung up, still not knowing into what time zone I'd been speaking.

This was not going well. I sat a moment, regretful that my burst of resolve hadn't come earlier in the day. Then, undaunted, I reached for the receiver again. I dialed Gabby's number and got no response.

Apparently, even the answering machine had dropped out. I tried her office at the university, and listened to the line roll over after four rings. As I was about to hang up, the phone was answered. It was the departmental office. No, they hadn't seen her. No, she hadn't picked up her mail for a few days. No, that wasn't unusual, it was summer. I thanked them and hung up.

"Strike three," I said to the empty air. No Lucy. No Aaron. No Gabby. God, Gabby, where are you? I wouldn't let myself think about it.

I tapped the blotter with a pen.

"High and outside."

I tapped some more.

"Fourth and long," I added, ignoring the mixed metaphor. Tap. Tap.

"D.Q."

I leaned back and flipped the pen end on end into the air.

"Double fault."

I caught the pen and sent it airborne again.

"Personal foul."

Another launch.

"Time to switch to a new game plan."

Catch. Launch.

"Time to dig in and hold the line."

I caught the pen and held it. Dig in. I looked at the pen. Dig in. That's it.

"Okay," I said, pushing back my chair and reaching for my purse.

"Try batting from the other side of the plate."

I slung the purse over my shoulder and turned out the light.

"In your face, Claudel!"

14

When I got to the Mazda I tried resuming my sports cliché soliloquy. It was no good. The genius was gone. Anticipation of what I had planned for the evening had me too wired for creative thought. I drove to the apartment, stopping only at Kojax to pick up a souvlaki plate.

Arriving home, I ignored Birdie's accusatory greeting, and went directly to the refrigerator for a Diet Coke. I set it on the table next to the grease-stained bag containing my dinner, and glanced at the answering machine. It stared back, silent and unblinking. Gabby hadn't called. A growing sense of anxiety was wrapping itself around me and, like a conductor high on his music, my heart was beating prestissimo.

I went to the bedroom and rifled through the bedside stand. What I wanted was buried in the third drawer. I took it to the dining room, spread it on the table, and opened my drink and carry-out. No go. The sight of greasy rice and overcooked beef made my stomach withdraw like a sand crab. I reached for a slice of pita.

I located my street on the now familiar foot, and traced a route out of Centre-ville and across the river

166

onto the south shore. Finding the neighborhood I wanted, I folded the map with the cities of St. Lambert and Longueuil showing. I tried another bite of souvlaki as I studied the landmarks, but my stomach hadn't altered its negativism. It would accept no input.

Birdie had oozed to within three inches of me. "Knock yourself out," I said, sliding the aluminium container in his direction. He looked astounded, hesitated, then moved toward it. The purring had already begun.

In the hall closet I found a flashlight, a pair of garden gloves, and a can of insect repellent. I threw them into a backpack along with the map, a tablet and a clipboard. I changed into a T-shirt, jeans, and sneakers, and braided my hair back tightly. As an afterthought, I grabbed a long-sleeved denim shirt and stuffed it into the pack. I got the pad from beside the phone and scribbled: "Gone to check out the third X – St. Lambert." I looked at my watch: 7:45 P.M. I added the date and time, and laid the tablet on the dining room table. Probably unnecessary, but in case I got into trouble I had at least left a trail.

Slinging the pack over my shoulder, I punched in the code for the security system, but in my building excitement I got the numbers wrong and had to start over. After messing up a second time, I stopped, closed my eyes, and recited every word of "I Wonder What the King Is Doing Tonight." Clear the mind with an exercise in trivia. It was a trick I'd learned in grad school, and, as usual, it worked. The time-out in Camelot helped me reestablish control. I entered the code without a slip, and left the apartment.

Emerging from the garage, I circled the block, took Ste. Catherine east to De la Montagne, and wound my way south to the Victoria Bridge, one of three linking the island of Montreal with the south shore of the St.

167

Lawrence River. The clouds that had tiptoed across the afternoon sky were now gathering for serious action. They filled the horizon, dark and ominous, turning the river a hostile, inky gray.

I could see Île Notre-Dame and Île Ste. Hélène upriver, with the Jacques-Cartier Bridge arching above them. The little islands lay somber in the deepening gloom. They must have throbbed with activity during Expo '67, but were idle now, hushed, dormant, like the site of an ancient civilization.

Downriver lay Ile des Soeurs. Nuns' Island. Once the property of the church, it was now a Yuppie ghetto, a small acropolis of condos, golf courses, tennis courts, and swimming pools, the Champlain Bridge its lifeline to the city. The lights of its high-rise towers flickered, as if in competition with the distant lightning.

Reaching the south shore, I exited on to Sir Wilfred Laurier Boulevard. In the time it took to cross the river, the evening sky had turned an eerie green. I pulled over to study the map. Using the small emerald shapes that represented a park and the St. Lambert golf course, I fixed my location, then replaced the map on the seat beside me. As I shifted into gear, a snap of lightning electrified the night. The wind had picked up, and the first fat drops began to splatter on the windshield.

I crept along through the spooky, prestorm darkness, slowing at each intersection to crane forward and squint at the street signs. I followed the route I'd plotted in my head, turning left here, right there, then two more lefts . . .

After ten minutes I pulled over and put the car in park. My heart sounded like a Ping-Pong ball in play. I rubbed my damp palms on my jeans and looked around.

The sky had deepened and the darkness was almost

168

total. I'd come through residential neighborhoods of small bungalows and tree-lined streets, but now found myself on the edge of an abandoned industrial park, marked as a small gray crescent on the map. I was definitely alone.

A row of deserted warehouses lined the right side of the street, their lifeless shapes illuminated by a single functioning streetlamp. The building closest to the lamppost stood out in eerie clarity, like a stage prop under studio lights, while its neighbors receded into ever-deepening murkiness, the farthest disappearing into pitch blackness. Some of the buildings bore realtors' signs offering them for sale or rent. Others had none, as if their owners had given up. Windows were broken, and the parking lots were cracked and strewn with debris. The scene was an old black-and-white of London during the Blitz.

The view to the left was no less desolate. Nothing. Total darkness. This emptiness corresponded to the unmarked green space on the map where St. Jacques had placed his third X. I'd hoped to find a cemetery or a small park.

Damn.

I put my hands on the wheel and stared into the blackness.

Now what?

I really hadn't thought this through.

Lightning flashed, and for a moment the street was aglow. Something flew out of the night and slapped against the windshield. I jumped and gave a yelp. The creature hung there a moment, beating a spastic tattoo against the glass, then flew off into the dark, an erratic rider on the mounting wind.

Cool it, Brennan. Deep breath. My anxiety level was in the ionosphere.

I reached for the backpack, put on the denim shirt,

shoved the gloves into my back pocket and the flashlight into my waistband, leaving the notepad and pen.

You won't be taking any notes, I told myself.

The night smelled of rain on warm cement. The wind was chasing debris along the street, swirling leaves and paper upward into small cyclones, dropping them into piles, then stirring them up anew. It caught my hair and grabbed at my clothes, snapping my shirttails like laundry on a line. I tucked in the shirt and took the flashlight in my hand. The hand trembled.

Sweeping the beam in front of me, I crossed the street, then stepped up the curb onto a narrow patch of grass. I'd been right. A rusted iron fence, about six feet high, ran along the edge of the property. On the far side of the fence, trees and bushes formed a thick tangle, a wildwood forest that stopped abruptly, held in check by the iron barrier. I aimed the light straight ahead, trying to peer through the trees, but I couldn't tell how far they extended or what lay beyond them.

As I followed the fence line, overhanging branches dipped and rose in the wind, shadows dancing across the small, yellow circle of my flashlight. Raindrops slapped the leaves above my head, and a few penetrated to strike my face. The downpour was not far off. Either the dropping temperature or the hostile setting was making me shiver. More like both. I cursed myself for bringing the bug spray instead of a jacket.

Three quarters of the way up the block I stepped down hard at a drop in elevation. I swept the light along what seemed to be a driveway or service road leading forward to a break in the trees. At the fence, a set of gates was held shut by a length of chain and a combination padlock.

The entrance didn't look recently used. Weeds grew in the gravel roadbed, and the border of litter that ran the length of the fence was uninterrupted at the gate. I

170

aimed the light through the opening, but it penetrated the darkness only a little. It was like using a Bic to light the Astrodome.

I inched along for another fifty yards or so until I reached the end of the block. It took a decade. At the corner I looked around. The street I'd been following ended at a T-intersection. I peered into the gloom on the far side of the intersecting, equally dark and deserted street.

I could make out a sea of asphalt running the length of the block and surrounded by a chain-link fence. I guessed it had been a parking area for a factory or warehouse. The crumbling compound was lit by a single bulb suspended from a makeshift arch on a telephone pole. The bulb was hooded by a metal shade, and threw light for approximately twenty feet. Debris skittered across the empty pavement, and here and there I could see the silhouette of a small shack or storage shed.

I listened for a moment. A cacophony. Wind. Raindrops. Distant thunder. My pounding heart. The light from across the way compromised the blackness just enough to reveal my unsteady hands.

Okay, Brennan, I chided myself, cut the crap. No pain, no gain.

"Hmm. Good one," I said aloud. My voice sounded strange, muffled, as if the night were swallowing my words before they could reach my ears.

I turned back to the fence. At the end of the block it rounded the corner and took a hard left, paralleling the street I'd just reached. I turned with it. Within ten feet the iron uprights ended at a stone wall. I stepped back and played the light over it. The wall was grayish, about eight feet high, topped by a border of stones jutting six inches laterally from the face. As best I could see in the darkness, it ran the length of the street, with

171

an opening near midblock. It looked to be the front of the property.

I followed the wall, noting the soggy paper, broken glass, and aluminium containers that had collected at its base. I stepped on a variety of objects I didn't care to identify.

Within fifty yards the wall gave way, once again, to rusted iron grillwork. More gates, secured like the set at the side entrance. When I held the flashlight close to inspect the chain and padlock, the metal links gleamed. This chain looked new.

I tucked the flashlight into my waistband, and yanked the chain sharply. It held. I tried again, with the same result. I stepped back, retrieved the light, and began passing the beam slowly up and down the bars.

Just then something grabbed my leg. As I clawed at my ankle, I dropped the flashlight. In my mind I could see red eyes and yellow teeth. In my hand I felt a plastic sack.

"Shit," I said, my mouth dry, my hands shakier than before as I disentangled myself from the bag. "Assaulted and battered by a Pharmaprix sack."

I released the bag and it went whipping off in the wind. I could hear it rustling as I groped for my flashlight. It had gone out when it hit the ground. I found it but it was reluctant to serve. At first nothing. I pounded it against the palm of my hand, and the bulb flicked on, then died. Another tap and the beam stayed on, but the light looked shaky and uncertain. I had little confidence in its long-term commitment.

I hovered a moment in the dark, considering my next move. Did I really want to go further with this? What in God's name did I hope to accomplish? Home to a hot bath and bed seemed the better plan.

I closed my eyes and concentrated on sound, straining to filter any signs of human presence from the bustle of the elements. Later, in the many times I would replay that scene in my mind, I would ask myself if there wasn't something I missed. The crunch of tires on gravel. The creak of a hinge. The hum of a car engine. Perhaps I was sloppy, perhaps the building storm was a co-conspirator, but I noticed nothing.

I took a deep breath, squared my shoulders, and peered into the darkness beyond the wall. Once in Egypt I had been in a tomb in the Valley of the Kings when the lights failed. I remember standing in that small space, engulfed not just in darkness, but in a total absence of light. I had felt as if the world had been snuffed out. As I tried to tease something from the void beyond the fence, that feeling returned. What held darker secrets? The pharaoh's tomb or the blackness inside that wall?

The X marks something. It's in there. Go.

I retraced my steps to the corner and down the fence to the side gate. How could I disengage the lock? I was playing the light over the metal bars, searching for an answer, when lightning lit the scene like a camera flash. I smelled ozone in the air and felt a tingling in my scalp and hands. In the brief burst of light I spied a sign to the right of the gates.

By the flashlight beam it looked to be a small metal plaque bolted to the bars. Though rusted and obscured, the message was clear. *Entrée interdite.* Entrance forbidden. Keep out. I held the light close and tried to make out the smaller print below. Something de Montreal? It looked like Archduke. Archduke de Montreal? I didn't think there was one.

I peered at a tiny circle below the writing. Gently, I dislodged some rust with my thumbnail. An emblem began to appear, resembling a crest or coat of arms that looked vaguely familiar. Then it hit me. Archdiocese. Archdiocese of Montreal. Of course. This was church

173

property, probably an abandoned convent or monastery. Quebec was peppered with them.

Okay, Brennan, you're Catholic. Protected on church property. Full-court press. Where were these clichés coming from? Pumping out with the rushes of adrenaline that alternated with the trembling apprehension.

I stuck the flashlight into my jeans, took the chain in my right hand, and grasped a rusty metal upright with my left. I was about to yank, but there was no resistance. Link by link the chain slithered through the bars, looping over my wrist like a snake coiling onto a branch. I let go of the gate and reeled in the chain with both hands. It didn't come loose completely, but stopped when the padlock wedged between the bars. I looked at it in disbelief. It was hooked through the last link, but the prongs had been left unclasped.

I unhooked the lock, pulled the rest of the chain through the bars, and stared at them both. The wind had stopped during my labors, leaving an unsettling hush. The quiet pounded on my ears.

I looped the chain over the right gate, and pulled the left one toward me. The hinges seemed to scream in the void left by the wind. No other sound breached the silence. No frogs. No crickets. No distant train whistles. It was as if the universe were holding its breath, awaiting the storm's next move.

The gate moved grudgingly and I passed through, easing it closed behind me. I followed a roadbed, my shoes making soft crunching sounds on the gravel. I kept the light roving from the road to the thicket of trees on each side. After ten yards I stopped and directed the beam upward. The branches, ominously still, were interlaced in an arch above my head.

Here's the church. Here's the steeple. Great. My mind had switched to children's rhymes. I was shivering from tension and wound up with enough energy to repaint the Pentagon. You're losing it, Brennan, I warned myself. Think about Claudel. No. Think about Gagnon and Trottier and Adkins.

I turned to my right and swept the beam as far as it would reach, allowing it to linger briefly on each of the trees bordering the road. They marched along in endless rank. When I did the same on my left, I thought I saw a narrow break about ten yards up.

I kept the beam focused on that spot and crept forward. What looked like a gap wasn't. The trees didn't break rank, yet the place looked different somehow, disturbed. Then it struck me. It wasn't the trees, it was the underbrush. The ground cover was sparse and patchy, and the vines and creepers looked stunted compared with those nearby. Like a clearing partly overgrown again.

They're younger, I thought. More recent. I shone the light in all directions. The undersized vegetation seemed to flow in a narrow strip, like a stream meandering through the trees. Or a path. I gripped the flashlight tighter and followed the diversion. As I took my first step, the storm broke.

The steady drizzle gave way to a sudden torrent, and the trees burst into motion, leaping and diving like a thousand kites. Lightning flashed and thunder responded, over and over, like demon creatures seeking each other. Snap. Where are you? Boom. Over here. The wind returned with full fury, driving the water sideways.

Water soaked my clothes and plastered my hair to my head. It streamed down my face, blurred my vision, and stung the abrasion on my cheek. Blinking, I tucked some loose hair behind my ears and ran a hand over my eyes. I pulled out a shirttail and held it over the flashlight to try to keep the water from getting inside the casing.

175

Hunching my shoulders, I edged up the path, oblivious of everything beyond the ten-foot diameter of my pale yellow beacon. I swung the beam back and forth across the path, allowing it to probe the woods on either side, like a dog on a leash, sniffing and poking its way along.

In about fifty feet I spotted it. Looking back, I realized that an instant synapse occurred, that in a nanosecond my brain linked the visual input of the moment to a past experience recently stored. At some level of awareness I knew what I was seeing before my conscious mind developed the picture.

As I closed in and the beam teased its find from the covering darkness, recognition broke the surface. I could taste my stomach contents in my throat.

In the wobbling shaft of light I saw a brown plastic garbage bag poking through the dirt and leaves, its open end twisted and tied back unto itself. The knot rose from the earth like a sea lion surfacing for air.

I watched rain pound down on the bag and the surrounding soil. The water nibbled at the edges of the shallow burial, turning the dirt to mud and slowly but persistently uncovering the hole. I could feel a weakness at the back of my knees as more of the bag was exposed.

A flash of lightning snapped me out of my reverie. I jumped more then stepped toward the bag, and bent down to examine it. Tucking the flashlight back into my jeans, I grabbed the knotted end of the bag and pulled. It was still buried too deep to budge. I tried to undo the knot, but my wet fingers got a poor grip on wet plastic. It wouldn't give. I placed my nose close to the sealed opening and inhaled. Mud and plastic. No other smell.

I made a small perforation in the bag with my thumbnail and sniffed again. Though faint, the odor

176

was identifiable. The sweet, fetid smell of rotted flesh and damp bone. Before I could decide on flight or fury, a twig snapped and I sensed movement behind me. As I tried to leap sideways, lightning flashed inside my head, sending me plunging back into that pharaoh's tomb.

15

I hadn't been this hungover in a very long time. As usual I was too sick to remember much. When I moved, harpoons of pain shot into my brain and forced me to be still. I knew if I opened my eyes I'd vomit. My stomach also recoiled at the thought of motion, yet I had to get up. Above all, I was cold. My body was gripped by a chill that had taken over its core. I began to shake uncontrollably, and thought I needed another blanket.

I sat up with my eyes still tightly shut. The pain in my head was so fierce I retched up a small quantity of bile. I lowered my head to my knees and waited for the nausea to pass. Still unable to open my eyes, I spit the bile into my left hand, and felt for my comforter with my right.

Through the throbbing and shivering, I began to realize I wasn't in bed. My groping hand encountered twigs and leaves. That got my eyes open, pain or no pain.

I was sitting in a wood, in wet clothes and covered with mud. The ground around me was littered with leaves and small branches, and the air was heavy with the smell of earth and things that would become earth.

Above me I could see a latticework of branches, their dark, spidery fingers intertwining against a black velvet sky. Behind them, a million stars flickered through the leafy cover.

Then memory logged in. The storm. The gates. The path. But how had I come to be lying here? This was not a hangover night, only a parody of one.

I ran an exploratory hand over the back of my head. A knob the size of a lime was palpable beneath my hair. Great. Bashed twice in one week. Most boxers are punched less often.

But *how* had I been bashed? Had I tripped and fallen? Had a tree limb struck me? The storm had been churning things up pretty well, but no large branches lay next to me. I couldn't remember, and I didn't care. I just wanted to be gone.

Fighting back nausea, on my hands and knees I fumbled for the flashlight. I found it half buried in mud, wiped it clean, and flicked the switch. Amazingly, it worked. Controlling my trembling legs, I stood and more fireworks exploded in my head. I braced myself against a tree and retched again.

The taste of bile filled my mouth and triggered more questions by my consciousness. When did I eat? Last night? Tonight? What time is it? How long have I been here? The storm had ended and stars emerged. And it was still night. And I was freezing. That's all I knew.

When the abdominal contractions stopped, I straightened slowly and played the flashlight around me, looking for the path. The beam dancing across the ground cover tripped another cognitive wire. The buried bag. The burst of memory brought with it a wave of fear. I gripped the flashlight tighter, and turned a complete rotation, assuring myself that no one was behind me. Back to the bag. Where had it been? Recall was creeping back, but in still frames. I

179

could see the bag in my mind, but couldn't fix a location on the ground.

I probed in the adjacent vegetation searching for the burial. My head pounded and nausea kept rising in my throat, but there was nothing left, and the dry heaving made my sides ache and my eyes tear. I kept stopping and bracing against a tree, waiting for the spasms to subside. I noted crickets warming up for a post-storm gig, and their music had the feel of gravel sucked into my ears and dragged across my brain.

The bag was not ten feet away when I finally found it. Shaking so I could hardly hold the flashlight steady, I saw it as I remembered, though with more plastic exposed. A moat of rainwater circled its perimeter, and small pools had collected in the folds and creases of the bag itself.

In no condition to recover it, I just stood staring. I knew the scene had to be processed correctly, but was afraid someone might disturb it, or remove the remains before a unit could get there. I wanted to cry in frustration.

Oh, there's a good idea, Brennan. Weep. Maybe someone will come and rescue you.

I stood, trembling from cold and whatever, trying to think but my brain cells not cooperating, slamming their doors and refusing all callers. Phone it in. That thought got through.

I identified the borders of the brushy path and picked my way out of the woods. Or hoped I was. Couldn't remember coming in and had only a vague notion of the way out. My sense of direction had left with my short-term memory. Without warning, the flashlight died, and I was plunged into the near darkness of filtered starlight. Shaking the flashlight did not help, nor swearing at it.

"Shit!" At least I tried.

180

I listened for some audible direction finder. All I heard were crickets from every direction. Chirping in the round. That wouldn't work.

I tried to distinguish shadowy small growth from shadowy larger growth, and crept forward in the direction my face was pointing. As good a plan as any. Unseen branches grabbed my hair and clothing, and vines and creepers tugged at my feet.

You're off the path, Brennan. This stuff's getting thicker.

I was deciding which way to veer when one foot met air and dropped off the earth. I followed it forward, landing hard on my hands and one knee. My feet were trapped, and my forward knee pressed against what felt like loose earth. The flashlight had flown from my hand and jarred to life when it hit the ground. It had tumbled and was now casting an eerie yellow glow back toward me. I looked down and saw my feet disappearing into a tight, dark space.

My heart in my throat, I clawed my way out and scrambled toward the light, sideways like a crab on a beach. Pointing the beam to where I'd fallen, I saw a small crater. It gaped fresh and raw, like an unhealed wound in the earth. Loose dirt rimmed its perimeter and gathered in a small mound behind it.

I shone the light into the opening. It was not large, perhaps two feet across and three feet deep. In my stumbling, I planted a foot too close to the rim, sending a stream of soil dribbling into the pit. Like Grape-Nuts pouring from a box, I thought. They joined those I'd dislodged by my fall.

I stared at the soil as it collected in a small heap at the bottom of the hole. Something about it. Then realization. The dirt was practically dry. Even to my scrambled brain the inference was clear. This hole had either been covered, or dug since the rain.

181

An involuntary tremor seized me, and I wrapped my arms across my chest for warmth. I was still soaking and the storm had left cold air in its wake. The arm movement didn't really warm me, and drew the light away from the pit. I unfolded my arms and readjusted the beam. Why would someone . . .

The real question slammed home, making my stomach recoil like a .45 caliber pistol. *Who?* Who had come here to dig, or empty, this hole? Is he, or she, here now? That thought jolted me into action. I spun and swept the flash around in a 360. A geyser of pain vented in my head and my heartbeat tripled.

I don't know what I expected to see. A slathering Doberman? Norman Bates with his mother? Hannibal Lecter? A George Burns god in a baseball cap? None of them showed. I was alone with the trees and the creepers and the star-pierced darkness.

What I did see in the rotating light was the path. I left the fresh hole and staggered back to the half-buried bag. I kicked a blanket of leaves over it. The crude camouflage wouldn't fool the person who brought it there, but it might conceal the bag from casual eyes.

When satisfied with my ground cover, I took the can of insect repellent from my pocket and jammed it into the fork of an adjacent tree as a marker. Moving down the path, I tripped on weeds and roots and barely kept my feet. My legs felt as if they'd been deadened with drugs, and I moved in slow motion.

At the junction of the path with the roadbed, I stuck each of my gloves into a tree fork, and plunged on toward the gate. I was sick and exhausted, and feared I might pass out. The adrenaline would soon give out, and collapse would come. When it did, I wanted to be elsewhere.

My old Mazda was parked where I'd left it. Looking neither left nor right, I stumbled headlong across the

182

street, mindless of who might be waiting for me. Almost past feeling, I plunged my hands into pocket after pocket, groping for keys. On finding them I cursed myself for carrying so many on the same ring. Shaking, cursing, and dropping the keys twice, I disentangled the car key, opened the door, and threw myself behind the wheel.

Locking the door, I draped my arms across the steering wheel and rested my head. I felt a need to sleep, to escape my circumstances by drifting out of them. I knew I had to fight the urge. Someone could be out there, watching me, deciding on a course of action.

Another mistake, I reminded myself, as my eyelids drifted toward each other, would be to just rest here a second.

My mind went into random scan. George Burns appeared again and said, "I'm always interested in the future. I plan to spend the rest of my life there."

I sat up smartly and dropped my hands to my lap. The stab of pain helped clear my mind. I didn't throw up. Progress.

"If you're going to *have* a future, you'd better get your ass out of here, Brennan."

My voice sounded heavy in the closed space, but it, too, helped orient me to the present reality. I started the engine, and the digits on the console clock glowed green: 2:15 A.M. When had I set out?

Still shivering, I flicked the heat to high, though I wasn't sure it would help. The chill I was feeling was only partly due to the wind and the night air. There was a deeper cold in my soul that would not be warmed by a mechanical heater. I pulled away without a backward glance.

I slid the soap over my breasts, circling each again and again, willing the sweet-smelling lather to cleanse me

183

of the night's events. I raised my face to the spray that was pounding my head and coursing over my body. The water would grow cold soon. I'd been showering for twenty minutes, trying to drive out the cold and silence the voices in my head.

The heat and the steam and the scent of jasmine should have relaxed me, loosened the tension in my muscles and carried away the soreness. They hadn't. The whole time I was listening for a sound outside my rectangle of steam. I was waiting for the phone to ring. Fearful I'd miss Ryan's call, I had brought the handset into the bathroom.

I'd called the station immediately on reaching home, even before stripping off my wet clothes. The dispatcher had been skeptical, reluctant to disturb a detective in the middle of the night. She'd been adamant in her refusal to give me Ryan's home number, and I'd left his card at work. Standing in my living room, shivering, my head still pounding and my stomach regrouping for another attack, I'd been in no mood for discussion. My words, as well as my tone, persuaded her. I would apologize tomorrow.

That had been half an hour ago. I felt the back of my head. The lump was still there. Under my wet hair it felt like a hard-boiled egg, and was tender to the touch. Before getting into the shower I'd gone through the instructions I'd been given following previous thumps on the head. I checked my pupils, rotated my head hard right and hard left, and pricked my hands and feet to test for feeling. All parts seemed to be in their proper places and in working order. If I'd suffered a concussion, it was a mild one.

I turned off the water and stepped from the shower. The phone lay where I'd left it, mute and disinterested.

Damn. Where is he?

I dried myself, slipped into my ratty old terry cloth

robe, and wrapped a towel around my hair. I checked the answering machine to be sure I hadn't missed a call. No red light. Damn. Retrieving the handset, I clicked it on to see if it was working. Dial tone. Of course it was working. I was just agitated.

I lay down on the couch and placed the phone on the coffee table. Surely he'd call soon. No point going to bed. I closed my eyes, planning to rest a few minutes before making something to eat. But the cold and the stress and the fatigue and the jolt to my brain melded into a tidal wave of exhaustion that rose up and crashed over me, plunging me into a deep but troubled sleep. I didn't drift off, I passed out.

I was outside a fence, watching someone dig with an enormous shovel. Each time the blade came out of the ground it seethed with rats. When I looked down, there were rats everywhere. I had to keep kicking at them to keep them off my feet. The figure wielding the shovel was shadowy, but when it turned I could see it was Pete. He pointed at me and said something, but I couldn't make out the words. He started to shout and beckon to me, his mouth a round, black circle that grew larger and larger, engulfing his face and turning it into a hideous clown mask.

Rats ran across my feet. One was dragging Isabelle Gagnon's head. Its teeth were clamped onto her hair as it yanked the head across the lawn.

I tried to run, but my legs didn't move. I'd sunk into the earth, and was standing in a grave. Dirt was trickling in around me. Charbonneau and Claudel were peering down at me. I tried to speak, but words wouldn't come. I wanted them to pull me out. I held my hands out to them, but they ignored me.

Then they were joined by another figure, a man in long robes and an odd hat. He looked down and asked me if I'd been confirmed. I couldn't answer. He told

185

me I was on church property, and had to leave. He said only those who worked for the church could enter its gates. His cassock flapped in the wind, and I worried that his hat would fall into the grave. He tried to restrain his vestments with one hand, and dial a flip phone with the other. It started to ring, but he ignored it. It rang and rang.

So did the phone on my coffee table, which I eventually distinguished from the phone in my dream. Awakening through layers of resistance, I reached for the handset.

"Um. Hm," I said, groggily.

"Brennan?"

Anglophone. Gruff. Familiar. I fought to clear my head.

"Yes?" I looked at my wrist. No watch.

"Ryan. This better be good."

"What time is it?" I had no idea if I'd been asleep five minutes or five hours. This was getting old.

"Four-fifteen."

"Just a sec."

I set the phone down and stumbled to the bathroom. I threw cold water on my face, sang one chorus of "The Drunken Sailor" as I jogged in place. Rewrapping my turban, I returned to Ryan. I didn't want to increase his annoyance by making him wait, but, even more, I didn't want to sound groggy, or to ramble. Better to take a minute to slap myself into shape.

"Okay, I'm back. Sorry."

"Was someone singing?"

"Hm. I went out to St. Lambert tonight," I began. I wanted to tell him enough, but didn't want to go into the details at 4:15 A.M. "I found the spot where St. Jacques put the X. It's some sort of abandoned church property."

"You called to tell me this at four in the morning?"

186

"I found a body. It's badly decomposed, probably already skeletal from the smell. We need to get out there right away before someone stumbles on it, or the neighborhood dogs organize a church supper."

I took a breath and waited.

"Are you fucking crazy?"

I wasn't sure if he was referring to what I'd found, or to my going out alone. Since he was probably right about the latter, I went for the former.

"I know a body when I find one."

There was a long silence, then, "Buried or surface?"

"Buried, but very shallow. The portion I saw was exposed, and the rain was making it worse."

"You sure this isn't another pissant cemetery eroding out?"

"The body's in a plastic bag." Like Gagnon. And Trottier. It didn't need saying.

"Shit." I could hear a match being struck, then the long expulsion of breath that meant a cigarette had been lit.

"Think we should go now?"

"No fucking way." I could hear him pull on the cigarette. "And what is this 'we'? You have something of a reputation as a freelancer, Brennan, which doesn't particularly impress me. Your go-to-hell attitude may work with Claudel, but it's not going to slice with me. The next time you feel an urge to go waltzing around a crime scene, you might just politely inquire as to whether someone in the homicide squad has an opening on his dance card. We do still fit that sort of thing into our busy schedules."

I hadn't expected gratitude, but I was unprepared for the vehemence of his response. I was starting to get angry, and it was causing the hammering in my head to escalate. I waited, but he didn't go on.

"I appreciate your calling back so soon."

187

"Hm."

"Where are you?" With my brain fully functional, I would never have asked. I regretted it immediately.

After a pause, "With a friend."

Good move, Brennan. No wonder he was annoyed.

"I think someone was out there tonight."

"What?"

"While I was looking at the burial, I thought I heard something then I took a shot to the head that knocked me out. All hell was breaking loose with the storm, so I can't be sure."

"Are you hurt?"

"No."

Another pause. I could almost hear him turning things over in his head.

"I'll send a squad to secure the site until morning. Then I'll get recovery out there. Think we'll need the dogs?"

"I only saw the one bag, but there must be more. Also, it looked like there'd been other digging going on in the area. It's probably a good idea."

I waited for a response. There was none.

"What time will you pick me up?" I asked.

"I won't be picking you up, *Doctor* Brennan. This is real life homicide, as in the jurisdiction of the homicide squad, not *Murder She Wrote*."

Now I was furious. My temples were pounding and I could feel a small cloud of heat directly between them, deep in my brain.

"'More holes than the TransCanada,'" I spat at him. "'Get me something else.' Those are your words, Ryan. Well, I got it. And I can take you right to it. Besides, this involves skeletal remains. Bones. That's *my* jurisdiction, unless I'm mistaken."

The line was silent for so long I thought he might have hung up. I waited.

188

"I'll come by at eight."

"I'll be ready."

"Brennan?"

"Yeah?"

"Maybe you should invest in a helmet."

The line went dead.

16

Ryan was true to his word, and by eight forty-five we were sliding in behind the recovery van. It sat not ten feet from where I'd parked the night before. But it was a different world from the one I'd visited hours earlier. The sun was shining and the street throbbed with activity. Cars and police cruisers lined both curbs, and at least twenty people, in plainclothes and uniform, stood talking in clumps.

I could see DEJ, SQ, and cops from St. Lambert scattered here and there, each wearing a different uniform and distinctive insignia. The assemblage reminded me of the mixed flocks birds will sometimes form, spontaneous jamborees of twittering and chirping, each bird declaring its species by the color of its plumage and the stripes on its wings.

A woman with a large shoulder bag and a young man draped with cameras smoked and leaned against the hood of a white Chevy. Yet another species: the press. Further up the block, on the grassy strip adjacent to the fence, a German shepherd panted and sniffed around a man in a dark blue jumpsuit. The dog kept bolting off on short forays, nose to the ground, then darting back to its handler, tail wagging and face upturned. It seemed

190

anxious to go, confused by the delay.

"The gang's all here," said Ryan, putting the car in park and releasing his seat belt.

He hadn't apologized for his rudeness on the phone, and I hadn't expected it. No one is at his best at 4 A.M. He'd been cordial throughout the ride, almost jocular, pointing out places where incidents had occurred, recounting anecdotes of blunder and humiliation. War stories. Here, in this three-flat, a woman assaulted her husband with a frying pan, then turned it on us. There, in that Poulet Kentucky Frites, we found a nude man stuck in the ventilator shaft. Cop talk. I wondered if their cognitive maps were based on sites of police happenings chronicled in incident reports, rather than on the names of rivers and streets and the numbers on buildings that the rest of us use.

Ryan spied Bertrand and headed toward him. He was part of a clump composed of an SQ officer, Pierre LaManche, and a thin, blond man in dark aviator glasses. I followed him across the street, scanning the crowd for Claudel or Charbonneau. Though this was officially an SQ party, I thought they might be here. Everyone else seemed to be. I saw neither.

As we drew closer I could tell the man in the sunglasses was agitated. His hands never rested, but continuously worried a wispy fringe of mustache that crawled across his upper lip. His fingers kept teasing out a few sparse hairs, then stroking them back into place. I noticed that his skin was peculiarly gray and unblemished, having neither color nor texture. He wore a leather bomber jacket and black boots. He could have been twenty-five or sixty-five.

I could feel LaManche's eyes on me as we joined the group. He nodded, but said nothing. I began to have doubts. I'd choreographed this circus, brought all these people here. What if they found nothing? What if some-

191

one had removed the bag? What if it did turn out to be just another "pissant cemetery" burial? Last night was dark, I was hyped. How much had I imagined? I could feel a growing tightness in my stomach.

Bertrand greeted us. As usual, he looked like a short, stocky version of a men's fashion model. He'd chosen earth colors for the exhumation, ecologically correct tans and browns, no doubt made without chemical dyes.

Ryan and I acknowledged those we knew, then turned to the man in the shades. Bertrand introduced us.

"Andy. Doc. This is Father Poirier. He's here representing the diocese."

"*Arch*diocese."

"Pardon me. Archdiocese. Since this is church property." Bertrand jerked his thumb toward the fence behind him.

"Tempe Brennan," I volunteered, offering my hand.

Father Poirier fixed his aviators on me and accepted it, wrapping my palm in a weak, spiritless grip. If people were graded on handshakes, he'd get a D-minus. His fingers felt cold and limp, like carrots kept too long in a cooler bin. When he released my hand, I resisted the urge to wipe it on my jeans.

He repeated the ritual with Ryan, whose face revealed nothing. Ryan's early morning joviality had flown, replaced by stark seriousness. He'd gone into cop mode. Poirier looked as if he wanted to speak, but, seeing Ryan's face, reconsidered and crimped his lips into a tight line. Somehow, with nothing said, he recognized that authority had shifted, that Ryan was now in charge.

"Has anyone been in there yet?" asked Ryan.

"No one. Cambronne got here about 5 A.M.," said Bertrand, indicating the uniformed officer to his right. "No one's gone in or out. Father tells us that only two people have access to the grounds, himself and a care-

192

taker. The guy's in his eighties, been working here since Mamie Eisenhower made bangs popular." In French it came out Eesenhure, and sounded comical.

"The gate could not have been open," said Poirier, turning his aviators back on me. "I check it every time I am here."

"And when is that?" asked Ryan.

The shades released me and fastened on Ryan. They rested there a full three seconds before he responded.

"At least once a week. The Church feels a responsibility for all its properties. We do not simp–"

"What is this place?"

Again, the pause. "Le Monastère St. Bernard. Closed since 1983. The Church felt the numbers did not warrant its continued operation."

I found it strange that he spoke of the Church as an animate being, an entity with feelings and will. His French was also odd, subtly different from the flat, twangy form I'd grown used to. He wasn't Québecois, but I couldn't place the accent. It wasn't the precise but throaty sound of France, what North Americans call Parisian. I suspected he was Belgian or Swiss.

"What goes on here?" Ryan pursued.

Another pause, as if the sound waves had to travel a long distance to strike a receptor.

"Today, nothing."

The priest stopped speaking and sighed. Perhaps he recalled happier times when the Church thrived and the monasteries bustled. Perhaps he was collecting his thoughts, wanting to be precise in his statements to the police. The aviator lenses hid his eyes. An odd candidate for a priest, with his pristine skin, leather jacket, and biker footwear.

"Now, I come to check the property," he continued. "A caretaker keeps things in order."

"Things?" Ryan was taking notes in a small spiral.

"The furnace, the pipes. Shoveling the snow. We live in a very cold place." Poirier made a sweeping gesture with one thin arm, as if to take in the whole province. "The windows. Sometimes boys like to throw rocks." He looked at me. "The doors and the gates. To make certain they remain locked."

"When did you last check the padlocks?"

"Sunday at 6 P.M. They were all secure."

His prompt answer struck me. He hadn't stopped to think on this one. Maybe Bertrand had already posed the question, or maybe Poirier just anticipated it, but the speed of his response made it sound pre-cooked.

"You noticed nothing out of the ordinary?"

"*Rien.*" Nothing.

"When does this caretaker – what's his name?"

"Monsieur Roy."

"When does he come?"

"He comes on Fridays, unless there is some special task for him."

Ryan didn't speak, but continued looking at him.

"Like clearing snow, or repairing a window."

"Father Poirier, I believe Detective Bertrand has already questioned you about the possibility of burials on the grounds?"

Pause. "No. No. There are none." He wagged his head from side to side and the sunglasses shifted on his nose. A bow popped off one ear and the frames came to rest at a twenty-degree angle. He looked like a tanker listing to port.

"This was a monastery, always a monastery. No one is buried here. But I have called our archivist and asked her to check the records to be absolutely certain." As he spoke, he moved both hands to his temples and adjusted the glasses, realigning them carefully.

"You're aware of why we're here?"

Poirier nodded and the glasses tilted again. He

194

started to speak, then said nothing.

"Okay," said Ryan, closing the spiral and sliding it into his pocket. "How do you suggest we do this?" He directed that question to me.

"Let me take you in, show you what I found. After we remove it, bring in the dog to see if there's anything else." I was hoping my voice conveyed more confidence than I felt. Shit. What if there was nothing there?

"Right."

Ryan strode over to the man in the jumpsuit. The shepherd bounded up to him and nuzzled his hand for attention. He stroked its head as he spoke to the handler. Then he rejoined us and led the whole group to the gate. As we walked I scanned my surroundings discreetly, looking for signs showing I'd been there the night before. Nothing.

We waited at the gate as Poirier withdrew an enormous ring of keys from his pocket and selected one. He grasped the padlock and yanked, making a show of testing it against the bars. It clanged softly in the morning air, and a shower of rust drifted to the ground. Had I locked it hours earlier? I couldn't remember.

Poirier released the mechanism, unhooked the padlock, and swung the gate open. It creaked softly. Not the piercing screech of metal I recalled. He stepped back to clear the way for me, and everyone waited. LaManche still hadn't spoken.

I hitched the backpack higher on to my shoulder, brushed past the priest, and started up the roadbed. In the clear, crisp light of morning the woods seemed friendly, not malevolent. The sun shone through broad leaves and conifer needles, and the air was thick with the smell of pine. A collegial smell that evoked visions of lake houses and summer camps, not corpses and night shadows. I moved slowly, examining every tree, every inch of ground for broken branches, displaced vege-

195

tation, disturbed soil, anything to attest to human presence. Especially mine.

My anxiety level rose with every step, and my heart slipped in extra beats. What if I hadn't locked the gate? What if someone had been here after me? What had been done after I'd left?

The atmosphere was that of a place I'd never visited, but which seemed familiar because I'd read about it, or seen it in photographs. I tried to sense by time and distance where the path should be. But I had heavy misgivings. My recollection was jumbled and fuzzy, like a dream partly remembered. Major events were vivid, but details as to sequencing and duration were muddy. Let me see something to serve as a prompt, I prayed.

The prayer was answered in the form of gloves. I'd forgotten them. There, on the left side of the roadbed, just at eye level, three white fingertips poked from the fork of a tree. Yes! I scanned the adjacent trees. The second glove showed in a notch in a small maple about four feet off the ground. An image flashed of me, trembling, probing in the darkness to jam the gloves into place. I gave myself high marks for forethought, and low for recall. I thought I'd put them higher. Perhaps, like Alice, I'd had a size-altering experience in these woods.

I veered off between the gloved trees, on what I could barely make out as a path. Its impact on the thicket was so subtle that, without the markers, I might not have spotted it. In the daylight, the trail was little more than a change in texture, the vegetation along its length stunted and more sparse than that to either side. In a narrow line the ground cover did not intertwine. Weeds and small bushes stood alone, isolated from neighbors, exposing the coarse, burnt sienna of dead leaves and soil on which they stood. That was all.

I thought of the jigsaw puzzles I'd worked as a child. Gran and I pored over the pieces, searching for the right one, our eyes and brains calibrating minute variations in grain and shade. Success depended on the ability to perceive subtle differences in tone and texture. How the hell had I spotted this path in the dark?

I could hear the rustling of leaves and the snapping of twigs behind me. I didn't point out the gloves, but let them be impressed with my land navigational skills. Brennan the Pathfinder. Within a few yards I spotted the can of insect repellent. No subtlety there. The bright orange cap shone like a beacon in the foliage.

And there was my camouflaged mound. Below a white oak the ground swelled into a small protuberance covered by leaves and bordered by bare earth. In the exposed soil I could see the marks left by my fingers as I'd scratched up leaves and dirt to conceal the plastic. The results of my hurried camouflage job may have revealed more than concealed, but it seemed the thing to do at the time.

I've done many body recoveries. Most hidden corpses are found because of a lucky tip or a lucky break. Informants rat out their accomplices. Excited kids point out their finds. *It smelled awful so we started poking around, and there it was!* It felt odd to be one of the kids.

"There." I indicated the leafy hump.

"You sure?" Ryan asked.

I just looked at him. The others said nothing. I set down my backpack and withdrew another pair of garden gloves. Crossing to the mound, I placed my feet carefully to minimize the disturbance. Absurd, in light of my thrashing about the night before, but at an official scene proper technique is expected.

I squatted down and brushed back enough leaves to expose a small portion of the plastic bag. The bulk of it was still embedded in the earth, and the irregular contour suggested that the contents were secure within. It looked undisturbed. When I turned, Poirier was crossing himself.

Ryan spoke to Cambronne. "Let's get some shots for the travel brochure."

I rejoined the others and waited silently as Cambronne followed his ritual. He unpacked his equipment, filled out a marker board, and photographed the mound and the bag from several distances and directions. Finally, he lowered his camera and stepped back.

Ryan turned to LaManche. "Doc?"

LaManche said his first word since I'd arrived. "Temperance?"

Taking a trowel from the backpack, I crossed back to the mound. I swept away the remaining leaves, carefully uncovering as much of the bag as possible. It looked as I remembered it. I could even see the small perforation I'd made with my thumbnail.

Using the trowel, I scraped soil upward and outward around the periphery, slowly exposing more and more of the bag. The dirt smelled ancient and musty, as if bound in its molecules it held a minute part of everything it had nurtured since the glaciers released it from their icy grip.

I heard voices drifting from the law enforcement carnival on the street, but where I worked, the only sounds came from the birds, insects, and the steady scraping of my trowel. Branches lifted and fell in the breeze, a gentler version of the dance they'd done the night before. The night theater had been Masai warriors leaping and lunging in mock battle. The morning show was the "Anniversary Waltz." Shadows moved across the bag, and across the faces of the solemn group witnessing its emergence. I watched the shapes move on the plastic, like puppets in a shadow play.

Within fifteen minutes the mound had become a pit, with more than half the bag visible. I suspected the contents had rearranged themselves as decomposition progressed and bones were freed of their anatomical responsibilities. If there were bones.

Thinking I'd removed enough soil to free the bundle, I put down my trowel, took hold of the twisted plastic, and slowly pulled. It wouldn't budge. Last night all over again. Was someone underground, holding the other end of the bag, challenging me to a macabre game of tug-of-war?

Cambronne had photographed as I dug, and was now behind me, positioned to fix on Kodachrome the moment of the bag's release. The phrase popped into my mind: Capture the moments of our lives. And deaths, I thought.

I brushed my gloves along the sides of my jeans, grabbed the sack as far down as I could, and gave a short, sharp yank. Movement. The pit wouldn't yield its cache with ease, but I'd weakened its grip. I felt the bag shift and the contents relocate slightly. I took a breath and pulled again, harder. I wanted to dislodge the bag, but not rip it. It gave way and then resettled.

Bracing my feet, I gave one more tug, and my underground opponent gave up the contest. The sack started to slide free. I rewrapped my fingers around the twisted plastic, and inching backward, step by step, teased the bag out of the pit.

When I'd pulled it free of the rim, I released my grip and stepped back. A common garbage bag, the kind found in kitchens and garages across North America. Intact. The contents made it lumpy. It wasn't heavy. That was not a good sign, or was it? Would I rather find the remains of someone's dog and be humiliated, or the remains of a human body and be vindicated?

Cambronne snapped into action. He placed his placard and took a series of shots. I removed one glove, and dug my Swiss army knife from my pocket.

When Cambronne finished, I knelt beside the bag.

199

My hands shook slightly, but I finally got my thumbnail into the small crescent of the blade and opened it. The stainless steel glinted as sunlight struck it. I selected a spot at the bound end for my incision. I felt five sets of eyes on me.

I glanced at LaManche. His features changed shape as the shadows shifted. I wondered, briefly, how my own sullied face looked in the light. LaManche nodded, and I placed pressure on the blade.

Before the steel could pierce the plastic, my hands stopped, checked by a sound like an invisible tether. We all heard it at once, but Bertrand voiced our collective thought.

"What the fuck?" he said.

17

The sudden din was a cacophony of sounds. The frantic barking of a dog mingled with human voices raised in excitement. Shouts rang back and forth, tense and clipped, but too indistinct to make out the words. The bedlam was within the monastery grounds, somewhere off to our left. My first thought was that the night prowler had returned, and that every cop in the province, and at least one German shepherd, were in pursuit.

I looked at Ryan and the others. Like me, they were frozen in place. Even Poirier had stopped fidgeting with his mustache and stood with hands fixed to upper lip.

Then the approaching sound of a body tunneling swiftly and indiscriminantly through foliage broke the spell. Heads turned simultaneously, as if operated by one switch. From somewhere in the trees, a voice called out.

"Ryan? You over there?"

"Here."

We oriented in the direction of the voice.

"*Sacré bleu.*" More thrashing and crunching. "Aiee."

An SQ officer came into view, wrestling back branches and muttering audibly. His beefy face was red, and his breathing was noisy. Sweat beaded his brow and flattened the fringe of hair circling his mostly bald head. Spotting us, he planted a hand on each knee, and bent to catch his breath. I could see scratches where twigs had dragged across the top of his exposed scalp.

After a moment he raised up and jerked a thumb in the direction from which he'd come. In a wheezy voice, like air through a clogged filter, he panted, "You better get over there, Ryan. The goddamn dog's acting like a crackhead with a bad load."

Out of the corner of my eye I saw Poirier's hand jerk to his forehead and slide to his chest. The sign of the cross called upon once more.

"What?" Ryan's eyebrows rose in puzzlement.

"DeSalvo took him around the grounds, like you said, and the sonofabitch started circling this one spot and barking like he thinks Adolf Hitler and the whole goddamn German army's buried there." He paused. "Listen to him!"

"And?"

"And??? The little bastard's about to blow a vocal chord. You don't get over there pretty quick he's going to circle right up his own asshole."

I suppressed a smile. The image was pretty comical.

"Just hold him back a few more minutes. Give him a Milk-Bone or pop him a Valium if you have to. We've got something here we need to finish." He looked at his watch. "Get back here in ten minutes."

The officer shrugged, released the branch he was holding, and turned to go.

"Eh, Piquot."

The corpulent face swiveled back.

"There's a path here."

"Sacrifice," Piquot hissed, picking his way through the tangle toward the trail Ryan had indicated. I was sure he'd lose it within fifteen yards.

"And Piquot . . ." Ryan continued.

202

The face looked back again.

"Don't let Rin Tin Tin disturb anything."

He turned back to me. "You waiting to have a birthday, Brennan?"

We heard Piquot thrashing his way out of earshot as I slit the bag from end to end.

The odor didn't leap out and grab me as it had with Isabelle Gagnon. Freed of its confines, it spread outward slowly, asserting itself. My nose identified soil and plant decay, and an overlay of something else. It wasn't the fetid smell of putrefaction, but a more primeval scent. It was a smell that spoke of passing, of origins and extinctions, of life recycled. I had smelled it before. It told me the sack held something dead, and not newly dead.

Don't let it be a dog or a deer, I thought, as my gloved hands separated the opening. My hands shook again and the plastic quivered in them. Yes, I changed my mind, let it be a dog or a deer.

Ryan, Bertrand, and LaManche pressed in as I laid back the severed plastic. Poirier stood like a headstone, rooted to the spot.

First I saw a scapula. Not much, but enough to confirm this was no hunter's cache or family pet. I looked at Ryan. I could see pinching at the corners of his eyes and tension in his jaw muscles.

"It's human."

Poirier's hand flew to his forehead for another go-around.

Ryan reached for his spiral and turned a page. "What have we got?" he asked. His voice was as sharp as the blade I'd just used.

I gently moved the bones. "Ribs . . . shoulder blades . . . collarbones . . . vertebrae," I ticked off. "Looks like they're all thoracic."

"Sternum," I added, on finding the breastbone.

I probed among the bones, looking for more body

203

parts. The others watched in silence. When I reached into the back of the bag, a large brown spider skittered across my hand and up my arm. I could see its eyes rising on stalks, tiny periscopes seeking the cause of this intrusion. Its fuzzy legs felt light and delicate, like a lace hanky brushing across my skin. I jerked back, flinging the spider into space.

"That's it," I said, straightening and stepping back. My knees popped in protest. "Upper torso. No arms." My skin was crawling, but not from the spider.

My gloved hands hung at my sides. I felt no joy in the vindication of my judgment, just a dulling numbness, like someone in shock. My emotional being had shut down, hung up a sign and gone to lunch. It's happened again, I thought. Another human being dead. A monster is out there.

Ryan scribbled in his spiral. His neck tendons bulged.

"Now what?" Poirier's voice was little more than a squeak.

"Now we find the rest," I said.

Cambronne was positioning for photos when we heard the return of Piquot. Again, he came cross country. He joined us, looked at the bones, and released a whispered expletive.

Ryan turned to Bertrand. "Can you take over here while we check out the dog?"

Bertrand nodded. His body was as rigid as the pines around us.

"Let's bag what we've got, then recovery can go over this whole area. I'll send them."

We left Bertrand and Cambronne and followed Piquot toward the barking. The animal sounded almost distraught.

Three hours later I sat on a grassy strip examining the contents of four body bags. The sun was high and hot on my shoulders, but did little to warm the chill inside me. Fifteen feet away the dog lay near its handler, its head angled across enormous brown paws. It had finished a big morning.

Conditioned to respond to the smell of decomposed or decomposing body tissue, body dogs ferret out hidden corpses like infrared systems pinpoint heat. Even after its removal they detect the former resting places of decaying flesh. They are the bloodhounds of the dead. This dog had performed well, zeroing in on three more burial sites. At each strike it announced its find with zeal, barking and snapping and circling the spot in a frenzied display. I wondered if all cadaver dogs were as passionate about their work.

Two hours were needed to excavate, process, and bag the remains. A preliminary inventory before removal, and now a more detailed list, logging every fragment of bone.

I glanced at the dog. It looked as tired as I felt. Only its eyes moved, the chocolate orbs revolving like radar dishes. It shifted its gaze without moving its head.

The dog had a right to be exhausted, but so did I. When it finally raised its head, a long, thin tongue dropped into view and hung quivering. I kept my tongue in my mouth and turned back to the inventory.

"How many?"

I hadn't heard him approach, but I knew the voice. I braced myself.

"*Bonjour*, Monsieur Claudel. *Comment ça va?*"

"How many?" he repeated.

"One," I answered, never raising my eyes.

"Anything missing?"

I finished writing and turned to look at him. He was standing with his feet spread, jacket hung from one arm, peeling the cellophane from a vending machine sandwich.

Like Bertrand, Claudel had chosen natural textiles,

205

cotton for the shirt and pants, linen for the jacket. He'd stayed with the greens, however, preferring a more verdant look. The only color contrast was in the pattern of his tie. Here and there it introduced a tasteful splash of tangerine.

"Can you tell what we've got?" He gestured with bread and lunch meat.

"Yes."

"Yes?"

Less than thirty seconds since his arrival and I wanted to rip the sandwich from his hand and insert it forcefully up his nose, or any other orifice. Claudel did not bring out the best in me when I was relaxed and rested. This morning I was neither. Like the dog, I'd had it. I lacked the energy or the inclination to play games.

"What *we* have is a partial human skeleton. There's almost no soft tissue. The body was dismembered, placed in garbage bags, and buried in four separate locations in there." I pointed to the monastery grounds. "I found one bag last night. The dog smelled out the other three this morning."

He took a bite, and gazed in the direction of the trees.

"What's missing?" The words garbled in ham and Muenster.

I stared at him without speaking, wondering why I found a routine question so annoying. It was his manner. I played myself a variation on my Claudel lecture. Ignore it. This is Claudel. The man is a reptile. Expect condescension and arrogance. He knows you were right. He's heard the story by now. He's not going to say 'bully for you.' It must be killing him. That's good enough. Let it go.

When I didn't answer he returned his attention to me.

"Anything missing?"

"Yes."

I put down the skeletal inventory sheet and looked him full in the eye. He squinted back, chewing. I wondered briefly why he had no sunglasses.

"The head."

He stopped chewing.

"What?"

"The head is missing."

"Where is it?"

"Monsieur Claudel, if I knew that, it wouldn't be missing."

I saw the jaw muscles bunch, then release, not from mastication.

"Anything else?"

"Anything else what?"

"Missing?"

"Nothing significant."

His mind gnawed on those facts while his teeth gnawed on the sandwich. As he chewed, his fingers crumpled the cellophane, compressing it into a tight ball. Placing the ball in his pocket, he wiped each corner of his mouth with an index finger.

"I don't suppose you will tell me anything else?" More a statement than a question.

"When I have had time to examine the . . ."

"Yes." He turned and walked away.

Cursing under my breath, I zipped each of the body bags. The dog's head snapped up at the sound. Its eyes followed me as I stuffed the clipboard into my pack and crossed the street toward a morgue attendant with a waist the size of an inner tube. I told him I'd finished, that the remains could be loaded, and that then they should wait.

Up the street, I could see Ryan and Bertrand talking with Claudel and Charbonneau. The SQ meets the CUM. My paranoia made me suspicious of their talking. What was Claudel saying to them? Was it

207

disparaging of me? Most cops are as territorial as howler monkeys, jealous of *their* turf, guarding *their* cases, wanting *their own* collars. Claudel was worse than the others, but why so specifically disdainful of me?

Forget it, Brennan. He's a bastard, and you've embarrassed him in his own backyard. You're not at the top of his hit parade. Stop worrying about feeling and think about the job. You haven't been innocent of possessive casework either.

The talk stopped as I neared. Their manner removed some of the punch from the peppy approach I'd planned, but I hid my discomfort.

"Hey, Doc," said Charbonneau.

I nodded and smiled in his direction.

"So, where are we?" I asked.

"Your boss took off about an hour ago. So did the good father. Recovery is finishing up," said Ryan.

"Anything?"

He shook his head.

"Metal detector hits?"

"Every bloody pop top tab in the province." Ryan sounded exasperated. "Oh, and we're good for one parking meter. How 'bout you?"

"I'm done. I told the morgue boys they could load up."

"Claudel says you've got no head."

"That's right. The skull, jaw, and first four neck vertebrae are missing."

"Meaning?"

"Meaning the victim was decapitated and the killer put the head somewhere. He might've buried it here, but separately, like he did with the other body parts. They were pretty scattered."

"So we've got another bag out there?"

"Maybe. Or he could've disposed of it somewhere else."

208

"Like where?"

"In the river, down a latrine, in his furnace. How the hell would I know?"

"Why would he do that?" asked Bertrand.

"Maybe so the body couldn't be identified."

"Could it?"

"Probably. But it's a hell of a lot easier with teeth and dental records. Besides, he left the hands."

"So?"

"If a corpse is mutilated to prevent identification, usually the hands are removed too."

He looked at me blankly.

"Prints can be taken from badly decomposed bodies, as long as there's still some preserved skin. I've gotten prints from a five-thousand-year-old mummy."

"Did you get a match?" Claudel's voice was flat.

"The guy wasn't entered," I responded with equal lack of mirth.

"But this is just bones," said Bertrand.

"The killer wouldn't know that. He couldn't be sure when the body would be found." Like Gagnon, I thought. Only this one he buried.

I stopped for a minute, and pictured the killer prowling the dark woods, distributing the bags and their grisly contents. Had he carved the victim elsewhere, bagged the bloody pieces, and brought them here by car? Did he park where I had parked, or was he able, somehow, to drive onto the grounds? Had he dug the holes first, planning the location of each? Or had he just carried in bags of body parts, digging one pit here and another there on four trips from his car? Was the dismemberment a panicky attempt to conceal a passion crime, or had both the murder and the mutilation been coldly premeditated?

An appalling possibility struck me. Had he been here with me last night? Back to the present.

"Or . . ."

They all looked at me.

"Or, he could still have it."

"Still have it?" scoffed Claudel.

"Shit," said Ryan.

"Like Dahmer?" asked Charbonneau.

I shrugged.

"We better take Fang back for another sweep," said Ryan. "They never brought him near the torso site."

"Right," I said. "He'll be pleased."

"Mind if we watch?" Charbonneau asked. Claudel shot him a look.

"Not as long as you think happy thoughts," I said. "I'll get the dog. Meet me at the gate."

Striding off, I heard the word "bitch" in Claudel's nasal tone. No doubt a reference to the animal, I told myself.

The dog leapt to its feet when I approached, its tail wagging slowly. It looked from me to the man in the blue jumpsuit, seeking permission to approach the newcomer. I could see "DeSalvo" stamped on the jumpsuit.

"Fido ready for another go?" I asked, extending a hand, palm down, toward the dog. DeSalvo gave an almost imperceptible nod, and the animal leapt forward and wetly nuzzled my fingers.

"Her name's Margot," he said, speaking in English, but giving the name the French pronunciation.

His voice was low and even, and he moved with the fluid, unhurried ease of those who spend their days with animals. His face was dark and deeply lined, a fan of small creases radiating from the corner of each eye. He looked like a man who'd lived outdoors.

"French or English?"

"She's bilingual."

"Hey, Margot," I said, crouching on one knee to

210

scratch behind her ears. "Sorry about the gender thing. Big day, eh?"

Margot's tail picked up velocity. When I rose, she leapt back, pivoted full circle, then froze, studying my face intently. She tilted her head from side to side, and the crease between her eyes furrowed and unfurrowed.

"Tempe Brennan," I said, offering my hand to DeSalvo.

He clipped one end of Margot's lead to a belt at his waist and grasped the other end with one hand. He reached out his other hand to me. It felt hard and rough, like distressed metal. His grip was an uncontested A.

"David DeSalvo."

"We think there may be more in there, Dave. Margot good for another go-round?"

"Look at her."

On hearing her name Margot pricked her ears, crouched with head down, hips in the air, then sprang forward in a series of short hops. Her eyes were glued to DeSalvo's face.

"Right. What've you covered so far?"

"We zigzagged the whole grounds, 'cept where you were working."

"Any chance she missed something?"

"Nah, not today." He shook his head. "Conditions are perfect. Temperature's just right, it's nice and moist from the rain. Plenty of breeze. And Margot's in top form."

She nuzzled his knee and was rewarded by strokes.

"Margot don't miss much. She wasn't trained to nothing but corpse scent, so she won't get sidetracked by nothing else."

Like trackers, cadaver dogs are taught to follow specific scents. In their case, it's the smell of death. I remembered an Academy meeting at which an exhibitor had given away samples of bottled corpse scent. Eau de

211

putrefaction. A trainer I knew used extracted teeth, bummed from his dentist and aged in plastic vials.

"Margot's 'bout the best I've worked with. Something else's out there, she'll scent it."

I looked at her. I could believe it.

"Okay. Let's take her over to that first site."

DeSalvo clipped the lead's free end to Margot's harness and she led us to the gate where the four detectives waited. We moved along the now familiar route, Margot in the lead, straining at her leash. She sniffed her way along, exploring nooks and crannies with her nose the way my flashlight had with its beam. Occasionally she stopped, inhaled rapidly, then expelled the air in a burst that sent dead leaves eddying around her snout. Satisfied, she'd move on.

We stopped where the path branched off into the woods.

"The part we haven't done is just off here."

DeSalvo gestured in the general direction of our first find.

"I'm gonna swing her around, bring her in downwind. She scents better that way. She thinks she's got something, I'll let her have her head."

"Will we bother her if we go into the area?" I asked.

"Nah. Your smell don't do nothing for her."

Dog and trainer continued up the roadbed for about ten yards, then disappeared into the woods. The detectives and I took the path. The crush of feet had made it more obvious. In fact, the burial site itself could now qualify as a tiny clearing. The vegetation was trampled and some of the overhead branches had been clipped.

At the center, the abandoned hole gaped dark and empty, like a plundered grave. It was much larger than when we'd left it, and the surrounding earth was bare and scuffed. A mound of dirt lay off to the side, an earthen cone with sloping sides and truncated top, its particles unnaturally uniform. Backdirt from the screening.

In less than five minutes we heard barking.

"He behind us?" asked Claudel.

"She," I corrected.

He opened his mouth, then crimped it shut. I could see a small vein pulsing in his temple. Ryan shot me a look. All right, maybe I was goading him.

Wordlessly, we moved back down the path. Margot and DeSalvo were off to the left, rustling through the leaves. In less than a minute they came into view. Margot's body was as tense as a violin string, her shoulder muscles bulging, her chest straining against the leather harness. She held her head high, jerking it from side to side, testing the air in all directions. Her nostrils twitched feverishly.

Suddenly, she stopped and grew rigid, ears extended, tips trembling. A noise started somewhere deep inside her, faint at first, then building, half growl, half whine, like the keening of a mourner in some primordial ritual. As it grew in intensity, I felt the hairs rise on the back of my neck and a chill travel down my body.

DeSalvo reached down and released the lead. For a moment Margot held her stance, as though confirming her position, recalibrating her heading. Then she bolted.

"What the fuck . . ." said Claudel.

"Where the . . ." said Ryan.

"Hot damn!" said Charbonneau.

We'd expected her to scent on the burial site behind us. Instead, she cut straight across the path and tore into the trees below. We watched in silence.

Six feet in, she stopped, lowered her snout, and inhaled several times. Exhaling sharply, she moved to her left and repeated the maneuver. Her body was tense, every muscle taut. As I watched her, images formed in my mind. Flight through darkness. A hard fall. A flash

213

of lightning. An empty hole.

Margot recaptured my attention. She'd stopped at the base of a pine, her whole being focused on the ground in front of her. She lowered her snout and inhaled. Then, as if triggered by some feral instinct, the fur rose along her spine, and her muscles twitched. Margot raised her nose high in the air, blew out one last puff of air, and flew into a frenzy. She lunged forward and jerked back, tail between her legs, snarling, and snapping at the ground in front of her.

"Margot! *Ici!*" ordered DeSalvo. He plunged through the branches and grabbed her harness, dragging her back from the source of her agitation.

I didn't have to look. I knew what she'd found. And what she hadn't. I remembered staring at the dry earth and the empty hole. Dug with intent to bury or intent to uncover? Now I knew.

Margot was yapping and growling at the pit I'd fallen into last night. It was still empty, but her nose told me what it had held.

18

The beach. Rolling surf. Sandpipers skittering on spindly legs. Pelicans gliding like paper airplanes, then folding their wings to plummet into the sea. Gone to Carolina in my mind. I could smell the brackish inland marshes, the ocean's salt spray, wet sand, beached fish, and drying seaweed. Hatteras, Ocracoke, and Bald Head to the north. Pawley's, Sullivan's, and Kiawah to the south. I wanted to be home, and which island didn't matter. I wanted palmetto palms and shrimp boats, not butchered women and body parts.

I opened my eyes to pigeons on a statue of Norman Bethune. The sky was graying, yielding pink and yellow remains of a departing sunset to the advance guard of approaching darkness. Streetlights and store signs announced evening's arrival with neon winks. Cars streamed by on three sides, a four-wheeled motorized herd grudgingly parting for the small triangle of green at Guy and De Maisonneuve.

I sat sharing a bench with a man in a Canadiens jersey. His hair flowed to his shoulders, neither blond nor white. Backlit by passing cars, it haloed his head like spun glass. His eyes were the color of denim that's been washed a thousand times, red-rimmed, a yellow crust

215

trickling from each corner. He picked at the crust with pasty, white fingers. From a chain around his neck hung a metal cross the size of my hand.

I'd gotten home by late afternoon, switched the phone to the answering machine, and slept. Ghosts of people I knew alternated with unrecognized figures in a parade without a theme. Ryan chased Gabby into a boarded building. Pete and Claudel dug a hole in my courtyard. Katy lay on a brown plastic bag on the deck of the beach house, burning her skin and refusing lotion. A menacing figure stalked me on St. Laurent.

I woke several times, finally rising at 8 P.M., headachy and famished. A reflection on the wall near the phone pulsed red, red, red, dim; red, red, red, dim. Three messages. I stumbled to the machine and hit play.

Pete was considering an offer with a law firm in San Diego. Terrific. Katy was thinking of dropping out of school. Wonderful. One hang up. At least that wasn't bad news. Still no word from Gabby. Great.

Twenty minutes of talking with Katy did little to ease my mind. She was polite, but noncommital. Finally, a long silence, then, "Talk to you later." Dial tone. I'd closed my eyes and stood very still. An image of Katy at thirteen filled my mind. Ear to ear with her Appaloosa, her blond hair mingled with his dark mane. Pete and I had gone to visit her at camp. On seeing us her face lit up and she'd left the horse to throw her arms around me. We'd been so close then. Where had the intimacy gone? Why was she unhappy? Why did she want to leave school? Was it the separation? Were Pete and I to blame?

Burning with parental inadequacy, I tried Gabby's apartment. No answer. I remembered a time Gabby had disappeared for ten days. I was crazy worrying about her. Turned out she'd gone on retreat to discover her inner self. Maybe I couldn't get in touch with her

216

because she was getting in touch with herself again.

Two Tylenol relieved my head, and a # 4 special at the Singapore sated my hunger. Nothing calmed my discontent. Neither pigeons nor park bench strangers distracted me from the constant themes. Questions crashed and rebounded like bumper cars inside my head. Who was this killer? How did he choose his victims? Did they know him? Did he gain their confidence, worm his way into their homes? Adkins was killed at home. Trottier and Gagnon? Where? At a predesignated place? A place chosen for death and dismemberment? How did the killer get around? Was it St. Jacques?

I stared at the pigeons without seeing them. I imagined the victims, imagined their fear. Chantale Trottier was only sixteen. Had he forced her at knife point? When had she known she was going to die? Had she begged him not to hurt her? Begged for her life? Another image of Katy. Other people's Katys. Empathy to the point of pain.

I focused on the present moment. In the morning, lab work on the recovered bones. Dealing with Claudel. Tending the scabs on my face. So Katy aspired to a career as an NBA groupie, and nothing I said would dissuade her. Pete might split for the Coast. I was horny as Madonna, with no relief in sight. And where the *hell* was Gabby?

"That's it," I said, startling the pigeons and the man beside me. I knew one thing I could do.

I walked home, went directly to the garage, and drove to Carré St. Louis. I parked on Henri-Julien and rounded the corner to Gabby's apartment. Sometimes her building made me think of Barbie's Dreamhouse. Tonight it was Lewis Carroll. I almost smiled.

A single bulb lit the lavender porch, casting shadow petunias across the boards. The looking-glass windows stared at me darkly. "Alice isn't home," they said.

217

I rang the bell to number 3. Nothing. I rang again. Silence. I tried number 1, then 2 and 4. No response. Wonderland had closed for the night.

Circling the park, I looked for Gabby's car. Not there. Without plan, I drove south, then east toward the Main.

After twenty frustrating minutes looking for a parking place, I left the car on one of the unpaved alleys that feed St. Laurent. The alley was remarkable for flattened beer cans and the stink of stale urine. Piles of trash abounded, and I could hear jukebox noise through the brick on the left. It was a setting which called for that popularly advertised auto security device known as the Club. Lacking one, I entrusted the Mazda to the god of parking, and joined the flow on the strip.

Like a rain forest, the Main is inhabited by sympatric breeds, populations living side by side but occupying different niches. One group is active by day, the other exclusively nocturnal.

In the hours from dawn to dusk the Main is the realm of deliverymen and shopkeepers, of schoolchildren and housewives. The sounds are those of commerce and play. The smells are clean, and speak of food: fresh fish at Waldman's, smoked meat at Schwartz's, apples and strawberries at Warshaw's, baked goods at La Boulangerie Polonaise.

As shadows lengthen and streetlamps and bar lights come on, as shops close and taverns and porn mills open, the day crowd surrenders the sidewalks to different creatures. Some are harmless. Tourists and college kids who come for bargain booze and cheap thrills. Others are more toxic. Pimps, dealers, hookers, and crackheads. The users and the used, the predators and prey in a food chain of human misery.

At eleven-fifteen, the night shift was in full control. The streets were thronged and the low-rent bars and

218

bistros were packed. I walked to Ste. Catherine and stood on the corner, La Belle Province at my back. It seemed a good place to start. Entering, I walked past the pay phone where Gabby had made her panicky call.

The restaurant smelled of Pine-Sol, grease, and over-fried onions. It was too late for dinner and too early for the après booze set. Only four booths were occupied.

A couple with identical Mohawks stared glumly at each other over half-eaten bowls of chili. Their spiny hackles were an identical inky black, as if they'd split the cost of the Clairol. They wore enough studded leather to open a combination kennel and motorcycle outfitter.

A woman with arms the size of Number 2 pencils and platinum bouffant hair smoked and drank coffee in a booth at the back. She wore a red tube top and what my mother would've called capri pants. She'd probably had that look since she dropped out of school to join the war effort.

As I watched, she drained the last of her coffee, took a long pull on her cigarette, and stubbed the butt into the small metal disk that served as an ashtray. Her painted eyes surveyed the room listlessly, not really expecting to find a mark, but prepared to dance the dance. Her face displayed the joyless look of someone who'd been on the street a long time. No longer able to compete with the young, she probably specialized in alley quickies and backseat blow jobs. Late night bliss at bargain prices. She hiked the tube higher on her bony chest, picked up her bill, and walked to the counter. Rosie the Riveter hitting the streets again.

Three young men occupied a booth near the door. One lay sprawled across the table, an arm cradling his head, another disappearing limply into his lap. All three wore T-shirts, cutoffs, and baseball caps. Two had their bills turned backward. The third, in a defiant disregard for fashion, wore his brim planted firmly across his fore-

219

head. The upright pair downed cheeseburgers, seemingly unconcerned about their companion. They looked about sixteen.

The only other patron was a nun. No Gabby.

I left the restaurant and looked up and down Ste. Catherine. The bikers had been drifting in, and Harleys and Yamahas lined both sides of the street to the east. Their owners straddled them, or drank and talked in packs, leathered and booted despite the warm evening.

Their women sat behind them, or formed conversational clusters of their own. It reminded me of junior high. But these women chose a world of violence and male dominance. Like hamadryas baboons, the females in the troop were herded and controlled. Worse. They were pimped and swapped, tattooed and burned, beaten and killed. And yet they stayed. If this was improvement, it was hard to imagine what they'd left behind.

I scanned to the west of St. Laurent. Right away I saw what I was looking for. Two hookers lounged outside the Granada, smoking cigarettes and playing the crowd. I recognized Poirette, but wasn't sure about the other.

I fought an impulse to give this up and head for home. What if I'd guessed wrong on the dress? I'd chosen a sweatshirt, jeans, and sandals, hoping they'd be nonthreatening, but I didn't know. I'd never done this kind of fieldwork.

Cut the crap, Brennan, you're stalling. Get your sorry butt up there. The worst that can happen is they blow you off. Won't be the first time.

I moved up the block and planted myself in front of the two women.

"*Bonjour.*" My voice sounded quavery, like a cassette tape stretched and rewound. I was annoyed with myself, and coughed to create a cover.

The women stopped talking and inspected me much as they would an unusual insect, or something odd found in a nostril. Neither spoke. Their faces were flat and devoid of emotion.

Poirette shifted her weight, thrusting one hip forward. She was wearing the same black high-tops she'd had on when I first saw her. Wrapping an arm across her waist and resting the opposite elbow on it, she regarded me with veiled eyes. Pulling hard on her cigarette, she breathed the smoke deep into her lungs, then pooched out her lower lip and blew it upward in a stream. The smoke looked like haze in the pulsating neon glow of the hotel sign. The sign's blinking cast nets of red and blue across her cocoa skin. Wordlessly, her dark eyes left my face and returned to the sidewalk parade.

"What you wantin', chère?"

The street woman's voice was deep and raspy, as if the words were formed by particles of sound with empty gaps floating among them. She addressed me in English, with a cadence that spoke of hyacinths and cypress swamps, of gumbo and zydeco bands, of cicadas droning on soft summer nights. She was older than Poirette.

"I'm a friend of Gabrielle Macaulay. I'm trying to find her."

She shook her head. I wasn't sure if she meant she didn't know Gabby, or was unwilling to answer.

"She's an anthropologist? She works down here?"

"Sugar, we all work down here."

Poirette snorted and shifted her feet. I looked at her. She was wearing shorts and a bustier made of shiny black vinyl. I was certain she knew Gabby. She'd been one of the women we'd seen that night. Gabby had pointed her out. Up close she looked even younger. I concentrated on her companion.

"Gabby's a large woman," I went on. "About my age. She has" – I groped for a color term – "reddish dreadlocks?"

Blank indifference.

221

"And a nose ring."

I was hitting a brick wall.

"I haven't been able to reach her for a while. I think her phone's out of order, and I'm a little worried about her. Surely y'all must know her?"

I drew out my vowels and emphasized the Southern version of *vous*. Appeal to regional loyalties. Daughters of Dixie unite.

Louisiana shrugged, a fluid, Cajun version of the universal French response. More shoulder, less palm.

So much for the Daughters of Dixie approach. This was going nowhere. I was beginning to understand what Gabby had meant. You don't ask questions on the Main.

"If you run into her, will you tell her Tempe's looking for her?"

"That a Southern name, chère?"

She slipped a long, red nail into her hair, and scratched her scalp with the tip. The updo was so lacquered, it would've held in a hurricane. It moved as one mass, creating the illusion that her head was changing shape.

"Not exactly. Can you think of anywhere else I might look?"

Another shrug. She withdrew her nail and inspected it.

I pulled a card from my back pocket.

"If you think of anything, this is where you can get in touch with me." As I walked away I could see Poirette reaching for the card.

Approaches to several streetwalkers along Ste. Catherine yielded much the same result. Their reactions ranged from indifference to contempt, uniformly leavened by suspicion and distrust. No information. If Gabby had ever existed down here, no one would admit it.

222

I went from bar to bar, moving through the seedy haunts of the night people. One was as the next, brain-children of a single warped decorator. Ceilings were low, and walls cinder block. All painted with Day-Glo murals, or covered with fake bamboo or cheap wood. Dark and dank, they smelled of stale beer, smoke, and human sweat. In the better ones, the floors were dry and the toilets flushed.

Some bars had raised platforms on which strippers writhed and slithered, their teeth and G-strings glowing purple in the black lights, their faces fixed in boredom. Men in tank tops and five o'clock shadows drank beer from bottles and watched the dancers. Imitation elegant women sipped cheap wine, or nursed soft drinks disguised to look like highballs, rousing themselves to smile at passing men, hoping to lure a trick. Aiming for seductive, they looked mostly tired.

The saddest were the women at the borders of this flesh trade life, those just crossing the start and finish lines. There were the painfully young, some still flying the colors of puberty. Some were out for fun and a quick buck, others were escaping some private hell at home. Their stories had a central theme. Hustle long enough to make a stake, then on to a respectable life. Adventurers and runaways, they'd arrive by bus from Ste. Thérèse and Val d'Or, from Valleyfield and Pointe-du-Lac. They came with gleaming hair and fresh faces, confident of their immortality, certain of their ability to control the future. The pot and the coke were just a lark. They never recognized them as the first rungs on a ladder of desperation until they were too high up to get off except by falling.

Then there were those who'd managed to grow old. Only the truly canny and exceptionally strong had prospered and gotten out. The ill and weak were dead. The strong-bodied but weak-willed endured. They saw the future, and accepted it. They would die in the streets because they knew nothing else. Or because they loved or feared some man enough to peddle ass to buy his dope. Or because they needed food to eat and a place to sleep.

I appealed to those entering or those leaving the sisterhood. I avoided the senior generation, the hardened and street smart, still able to rule their patches just as they in turn were ruled by their pimps. Perhaps the young, naive and defiant, or the old, jaded and spent, might be more open. Wrong. In bar after bar they turned away from me, allowing my questions to dissolve into the smoky air. The code of silence held. No access to strangers.

By three-fifteen I'd had it. My hair and clothes smelled of tobacco and reefer, and my shoes of beer. I'd downed enough Sprite to reclaim the Kalahari, and my eyes were seeded with gravel. Leaving yet another loony on yet another bar, I gave up.

19

The air had the texture of dew. A mist had risen from the river, and tiny droplets sparkled like glitter in the streetlights. The chill and damp felt good against my skin. A knot of pain between my neck and shoulder blades made me suspect I'd been tensed for hours, coiled and ready to bolt. Maybe I had been. If so, the tension came only in part from my search for Gabby. Approaching the hookers had grown routine. So had their rejection. Fending off the cruisers and the gropers had become a reflex response.

It was the battle inside that was wearing me down. I'd spent four hours fighting off an old lover, a lover from whom I'd never be free. All night I'd gazed temptation in the face – the chestnut glow of scotch on ice, the amber beer poured from bottles into throats. I'd smelled my moonshine sweetheart and seen his light in the eyes around me. I'd loved it once. Hell, I loved it still. But the enchantment would destruct. For me, any trifling dalliance and the affair would consume and overpower. So I'd walked away from it, with twelve slow steps. And I had stayed away. Having been lovers, we could never be friends. Tonight we'd almost been thrown into each other's arms.

I breathed deeply. The air was a cocktail of motor oil, wet cement, and fermenting yeast from the Molson brewery. Ste. Catherine was almost deserted. An old man in a tuque and parka slumbered against a storefront, a scruffy mongrel at his side. Another sorted through trash on the far side of the street. Perhaps there was a third shift on the Main.

Discouraged and exhausted, I headed toward St. Laurent. I'd tried. If Gabby was in trouble, these folks would not help me reach her. This club was as closed as the Junior League.

I passed the My Kinh. A sign above the window advertised CUISINE VIETNAMIENNE, and promised it all night. I glanced through the grimy glass with little interest, then stopped. Seated at a rear booth was Poirette's companion, her hair still frozen in an apricot pagoda. I watched her for a moment.

She dipped an egg roll into a cherry red sauce, then raised it to her mouth and licked the tip. After a moment she inspected the roll, then nibbled at the wrapping with her front teeth. She dipped again, and repeated the maneuver without hurry. I wondered how long she'd been working that egg roll.

No. Yes. It's too late. Hell. One last shot. I pushed open the door, and entered.

"Hi."

Her hand jumped at the sound of my voice. She looked puzzled at first, then relieved, as recognition surfaced.

"Hey, chère. You still out?" She returned to her roll.

"May I join you?"

"Suit yourself. You're not working my ground, sugar, I got no grievance with you."

I slid into the booth. She was older than I'd thought, late thirties, maybe early forties. Though the skin on her throat and forehead was taut and there were no bags under her eyes, in the harsh fluorescent light I could see small creases radiating from her lips. Her jawline was beginning to sag.

The waiter brought a menu and I ordered Soupe Tonqinoise. I wasn't hungry, but I wanted an excuse to stay.

"You find your friend, chère?" She reached for her coffee, and the plastic bracelets on her wrist clacked. I could see gray scar lines across her inner elbow.

"No."

We waited while an Asian boy of about fifteen brought water and a paper place mat.

"I'm Tempe Brennan."

"I remember. Jewel Tambeaux may hawk pussy, darlin', but she's not stupid." She licked at the egg roll.

"Ms. Tambeaux, I–"

"You call me Jewel, baby."

"Jewel. I just spent four hours trying to find out if a friend is all right, and no one will even admit they've heard of her. Gabby's been coming down here for *years* so I'm sure they know who I'm talking about."

"Might be they do, chère. But they got no idea why you askin'." She put down the roll, and drank the coffee with a soft slurping sound.

"I gave you my card. I'm not hiding who I am."

She looked at me hard for a moment. The smell of drugstore cologne, smoke, and unwashed hair floated from her and filled the small booth. The neck of her halter was rimmed with makeup.

"Who *are* you, Miss 'Person with a Card Says Tempe Brennan'? You heat? You inta some kind of weird hustle?" It came out sounding like "wired." "You someone got a grudge?" As she spoke she raised one long, red talon from her cup and pointed it at me, emphasizing each possibility.

"Do I look like a threat to Gabby?"

227

"All folks know, chère, is you're down here in your Charlotte Hornets sweatshirt and Yuppie sandals, and you're asking a lot of questions, trying real hard to shake someone loose. You ain't pussy on the hoof and you ain't trying to score rocks. Folks don't know where to put you."

The waiter brought my soup and we sat in silence while I squeezed small cubes of lime and added red pepper paste with a tiny china spoon. As I ate, I watched Jewel nibble her egg roll. I decided to try humble.

"I guess I went about it all wrong."

She raised hazel eyes to me. One false lash had loosened, and it curved upward on her lid, like a millipede rising to test the air. Dropping her eyes, she laid down the remains of the egg roll, and slid her coffee directly in front of her.

"You're right. I shouldn't have just charged up to people and started asking questions. It's just that I'm worried about Gabby. I've called her apartment. I've stopped by. I've called her at school. No one seems to know where she is. It's not like her."

I took a spoonful of soup. It tasted better than I'd anticipated.

"What's your friend Gabby do?"

"She's an anthropologist. She studies people. She's interested in life down here."

"Coming of Age on the Main."

She laughed to herself, watching carefully for my response to the Margaret Mead reference. I gave none, but began to agree that Jewel Tambeaux was no dummy. I sensed I was being tested.

"Maybe she doesn't want to be found right now."

You may open your exam booklets.

"Maybe."

"So what's the problem?"

You may pick up your pencils.

228

"She seemed very troubled the last time I was with her. Scared, almost."

"Troubled 'bout what, sugar?"

Ready.

"Some guy she thought was following her. Said he was strange."

"Lot of strange ones down here, chère."

Okay, class, begin.

I told her the whole story. As she listened, she swirled the dregs in her cup, watching the black-brown liquid intently. When I'd finished, she continued with the cup, as if scoring my answer. Then she signaled for a refill. I waited to find out my grade.

"I don't know his name, but I most likely know who you talkin' about. Skinny dude, personality of a meal-worm. He's strange, all right, and whatever's ailing him ain't no small thing. But I don't think he's dangerous. I doubt he's got the brains to read a ketchup label."

I'd passed.

"Most of us avoid him."

"Why?"

"I'm only passing on the word from the street, 'cause I don't do business with him myself. The guy makes my skin crawl like a gator in mud." She grimaced and gave a small shudder. "Word is he's got peculiar wants."

"Peculiar?"

She put her cup on the table and looked at me, evaluating.

"He pays for it, but he doesn't want to fuck."

I scooped noodles from my soup and waited.

"Girl named Julie goes with him. No one else will. She's about as smart as a runner bean, but that's another story. She told me it's the same show every time. They go to the room, our hero brings a paper bag with a nightie inside. Nothing kinky, lacy kinds of stuff. He watches her put it on, then tells her to lie on the bed.

229

Okay, no big deal. Then he strokes the nightie with one hand and his dick with the other. Pretty soon he gets hard as an oil derrick and blows a gusher, grunting and groaning like he's off in some other creation. Then he makes her take off the gown, thanks her, pays her, and leaves. Julie figures it's easy money."

"What makes you think this is the guy worrying my friend?"

"One time, he's stuffing Granny's nightie back in the ditty bag, Julie sees a big ol' knife handle. She tells him, you want more pussy, cowboy, lose the knife. He tells her it's his sword of righteousness or some damned thing, goes on about the knife, and his soul, and ecological balance, and crap like that. Scares the shit out of her."

"And?"

Another shrug.

"He still around?"

"Haven't seen him for a while, but that don't mean much. I never did see him regular. He'd kind of drift in and drift out."

"Did you ever talk to him?"

"Cutie, we've all talked to him. When he's around he's like a case of the drips, irritating as hell but you can't shake it. That's how I know he's got the personality of road larvae."

"Ever see him with Gabby?" I slurped some more noodles.

She sat back and laughed. "Nice try, sugar."

"Where could I find him?"

"Hell if I know. Wait long enough, he'll show up."

"How about Julie?"

"It's a free trade zone here, chère, folks come and go. I don't keep track."

"Have you seen her lately?"

She gave it some thought. "Can't say as I have."

230

I studied the noodles at the bottom of the bowl and I studied Jewel. She had lifted the lid a tiny crack, allowed a peek inside. Could I raise it farther? I took the chance.

"There may be a serial killer out there, Jewel. Someone murdering women and slicing them up."

Her expression never changed. She just looked at me, a stony gargoyle. Either she hadn't understood, or she was dulled to thoughts of violence and pain, even death. Or perhaps she'd thrown on a mask, a facade to conceal a fear too real to validate by speech. I suspected the latter.

"Jewel, is my friend in danger?"

Our eyes locked.

"She female, chère?"

I motored my way home, letting my thoughts drift, paying little attention to my driving. De Maisonneuve was deserted, the traffic lights playing to an empty house. Suddenly, a pair of headlights appeared in my rearview mirror and bore down on me.

I crossed Peel and slid to my right to allow the vehicle to pass. The lights moved with me. I shifted back to the inner lane. The driver followed, shifting to high beam.

"Asshole."

I sped up. The car stayed on my bumper.

A prickle of fear. Maybe it wasn't just a drunk. I squinted into the rearview mirror, trying to make out the driver. All I could see was a silhouette. It looked large. A man? I couldn't tell. The lights were blinding. The car unidentifiable.

Hands slick on the wheel, I crossed Guy, turned left around the block, ignoring red lights, shot up my street, and dived underground into the garage of my building.

I waited until the electric door had settled, then bolted, key ready, ears alert for the sound of footsteps. No one followed. As I passed through the first-floor

231

lobby, I peeked through the curtains. A car idled at the curb on the far side of the street, lights burning, its driver a black profile in the predawn dimness. Same car? I couldn't be certain. Was I losing it?

Thirty minutes later I lay watching the curtain of darkness outside my window fade from charcoal to mourning dove gray. Birdie purred in the crook of my knee. I was so exhausted I'd pulled off my clothes and fallen into bed, skipping the preliminaries. Not like me. Usually I'm compulsive about teeth and makeup. Tonight, I didn't care.

20

Wednesday is garbage day on my block. I slept through the sound of the sanitation truck. I slept through Birdie's nudging. I slept through three phone calls.

I woke at ten-fifteen feeling sluggish and headachy. I was definitely not twenty-four anymore. All-nighters took their toll, and it made me cranky to admit it.

My hair, my skin, even the pillow and sheets smelled of stale smoke. I bundled the linens and last night's clothes into the washer, then took a long, sudsy shower. I was spreading peanut butter on a stale croissant when the phone rang.

"Temperance?" LaManche.

"Yes."

"I have been trying to reach you."

I glanced at the phone machine. Three messages.

"Sorry."

"*Oui*. We will be seeing you today? Already Monsieur Ryan is calling."

"I'll be there within the hour."

"*Bon*."

I played the messages. A distraught graduate student. LaManche. A hang-up. I wasn't up to student problems, so I tried Gabby. No answer. I dialed Katy and got

233

her machine.

"Leave a short message, like this one," it chirped cheerily. I did, not cheerily.

In twenty minutes I was at the lab. Stuffing my purse in a desk drawer, and ignoring the pink slips scattered across the blotter, I went directly downstairs to the morgue.

The dead come first to the morgue. There, they are logged in and stored in refrigerated compartments until assigned to an LML pathologist. Jurisdiction is coded by floor color. The morgue opens directly onto the autopsy rooms, the red floor of each morgue bay stopping abruptly at the autopsy room threshold. The morgue is run by the coroner, the LML controls the operatories. Red floor: coroner. Gray floor: LML. I do my initial examinations in one of the four autopsy rooms. Afterward, the bones are sent up to the histology lab for final cleaning.

LaManche was making a Y incision in the chest of an infant, her tiny shoulders propped on a rubber headrest, her hands spread at her sides as if poised to make a snow angel. I looked at LaManche.

"*Secouée*," was all he said. Shaken.

Across the room Nathalie Ayers bent over another autopsy as Lisa lifted the breastplate from a young man. Below a shock of red hair his eyes bulged purple and swollen, and I could see a small, dark hole on his right temple. Suicide. Nathalie was a new pathologist at the LML, and didn't yet do homicides.

Daniel put down the scalpel he was sharpening. "Do you need the bones from St. Lambert?"

"*S'il vous plaît*. In number 4?"

He nodded and disappeared into the morgue.

The skeletal autopsy took several hours, and I confirmed my initial impression that the remains were of

234

one individual, a white female around thirty years of age. Though little soft tissue remained, the bones were in good condition and retained some fat. She'd been dead two to five years. The only oddity was an unfused arch on her fifth lumbar vertebra. Without the head, a positive ID would be tough.

I asked Daniel to transfer the bones to the histo lab, washed, and went upstairs. The pile of pink slips had grown. I phoned Ryan and gave him my summary. He was already working missing persons reports with the St. Lambert police.

One of the calls was from Aaron Calvert in Norman, Oklahoma. Yesterday. When I tried his number, a syrupy voice told me he was away from his desk. She assured me she was devastatingly sorry, and guaranteed that he'd get the message. Professionally affable. I set the other messages aside and went to see Lucie Dumont.

Lucie's office was crammed with terminals, monitors, printers, and computer paraphernalia of all kinds. Cables climbed walls to disappear into the ceiling, or were taped in bundles along the floor. Stacks of printouts drooped on shelves and file cabinets, fanning out like alluvium seeking the lowest point.

Lucie's desk faced the door, the control panel of cabinets and hardware forming a horseshoe behind her. She worked by rolling from station to station, sneakered feet propelling her chair across the gray tile. To me, Lucie was the back of a head silhouetted against a glowing green screen. I rarely saw her face.

Today the horseshoe held five Japanese in business suits. They circled Lucie, arms held close to their bodies, nodding gravely as she pointed to something on a terminal and explained its significance. Cursing my timing, I went on to the histo lab.

The St. Lambert skeleton had arrived from the

morgue, and I set about analyzing the cuts the same way I had with Trottier and Gagnon. I described, measured, and plotted the location of each mark, and made impressions of the false starts. As with the others, the tiny gashes and trenches suggested a knife and a saw. Microscopic details were similar, and placements of cuts almost identical to those in the earlier cases.

The woman's hands had been sawed at the wrists, the rest of her limbs detached at the joints. Her belly had been slashed along the midline deep enough to leave cuts on the spine. Although the skull and upper neck bones were missing, marks on the sixth cervical vertebra told me that she had been decapitated at the midthroat. The guy was consistent.

I repacked the bones, gathered my notes, and returned to my office, diverting up the corridor to see if Lucie was free. She and her Japanese suits were nowhere to be seen. I left a Post-it note on her terminal. Maybe she'd thank me for an excuse to bolt.

In my absence Calvert had called. Naturally. As I dialed his number, Lucie appeared in my doorway, her hands clasped tightly in front of her.

"You left me a message, Dr. Brennan?" she asked, flashing a quick smile. She spoke not a word of English.

She was thin as soup in a homeless shelter, with a burr haircut that accentuated the length of her skull. The absence of hair and pale skin magnified the effect of her eyeglasses, making her seem little more than a mannequin for the oversized frames.

"Yes, Lucie, thank you for stopping by," I said, rising to clear a chair.

She tucked her feet behind the chair leg, one behind the other, as she slid into her seat. Like a cat oozing onto a cushion.

"Did you get stuck with tour duty?"

She twitched a smile, then looked blank.

236

"The Japanese gentlemen."

"Yes. They are from a crime lab in Kobe, chemists mostly. I do not mind."

"I'm not sure you can help me, but I wanted to ask," I began.

Her lenses focused on a row of skulls I keep on the shelf behind my desk.

"For comparison," I explained.

"Are they real?"

"Yes, they're real."

She shifted her gaze and I could see a distorted version of myself in each pink lens. The corners of her lips jumped and resettled. Her smiles came and went like light from a bulb with a bad connection. Reminded me of my flashlight in the woods.

I explained what I wanted. When I'd finished, she tipped her head and stared upward, as if the answer might be on the ceiling. Taking her time. I listened to the whir of a printer somewhere down the hall.

"There won't be anything before 1985, I know that." Facial flicker. On. Off.

"I realize it's a bit unusual, but see what you can do."

"Quebec City, also?"

"No, just the LML cases for now."

She nodded, smiled, and left. As if on cue, the phone rang. Ryan.

"How about someone younger?"

"How much younger?"

"Seventeen."

"No."

"Maybe someone with some sort of–"

"No."

Silence.

"I've got one sixty-seven."

"Ryan, this woman belongs neither to the Clearasil nor the Geritol set."

He continued with the relentlessness of a busy signal. "What if she had some kind of bone condition or something? I read abou–"

"Ryan, she was between twenty-five and thirty-five."

"Right."

"She probably went missing somewhere between '89 and '92."

"So you've said."

"Oh. One other thing. She probably had kids."

"What?"

"I found pitting on the inside of the pubic bones. You're looking for someone's mother."

"Thanks."

In less time than he could have punched the numbers, the phone rang again.

"Ryan, I–"

"It's me, Mom."

"Hi, darlin', how are you?"

"Good, Mom." Pause. "Are you mad about our conversation last night?"

"Of course not, Katy. I'm just worried about you."

Long pause.

"So. What else is new? We didn't really talk about what you've been up to this summer." There was so much I wanted to say, but I'd let her take the lead.

"Not much. Charlotte's boring as ever. Nothing to do."

Good. Another dose of adolescent negativity. Just what I needed. I tried to hold my annoyance in check.

"How's the job?"

"Okay. Tips are good. I made ninety-four dollars last night."

"That's great."

"I'm getting a lot of hours."

"Terrific."

"I want to quit."

238

I waited.

She waited.

"Katy, you're going to need that money for school."
Katy, don't mess up your life.

"I told you. I don't want to go back right away. I'm thinking of taking a year off to work."

Here we go again. I had an idea what was coming, and launched my offensive.

"Honey, we've gone over this. If you don't like the University of Virginia, you could try McGill. Why don't you take a couple of weeks, come up here, check it out?" Talk fast, Mom. "We could make a vacation of it. I'll take some time off. Maybe we could drive out to the Maritimes, bum around Nova Scotia for a few days." God. What was I saying? How could I work that? No matter. My daughter comes first.

She didn't answer.

"It's not grades, is it?"

"No, no. They were fine."

"Then your credits should transfer. We coul–"

"I want to go to Europe."

"Europe?"

"Italy."

"Italy?"

I didn't have to think that one through.

"Is that where Max is playing?"

"Yes." Defensive. "So?"

"So?"

"They're giving him a lot more money than the Hornets."

I said nothing.

"And a house."

Nothing.

"And a car. A Ferrari."

Nothing.

"Tax free." Her tone was becoming more defiant.

239

"That's great for Max, Katy. He gets to play a sport he loves and gets paid for it. But what about you?"

"Max wants me to come."

"Max is twenty-four and has a degree. You're nineteen and have one year of college."

She heard the irritation in my voice.

"You got married when you were nineteen."

"Married?" My stomach did a triple gainer.

"Well, you did."

She had a point. I held my tongue, anxious with concern for her but knowing I was helpless to do anything.

"I just said that. We're not getting married."

We sat and listened to the air between Montreal and Charlotte for what seemed like forever.

"Katy, will you think about coming up here?"

"Okay."

"Promise you won't do anything without talking to me?"

More silence.

"Katy?"

"Yes, Mom."

"I love you, sweetheart."

"I love you, too."

"Say hi to your dad for me."

"Okay."

"I'll leave something on your e-mail tomorrow, okay?"

"Okay."

I hung up with an unsteady hand. What next? Bones were easier to read than kids. I got a cup of coffee, then dialed.

"Dr. Calvert, please."

"May I ask who's calling?" I told her. "Just a minute, please." Put on hold.

"Tempe, how are you? You spend more time on the phone than an MCI salesman. You surely are hard to

240

reach." He out-twanged both the day and night shifts.

"I'm sorry, Aaron. My daughter wants to drop out of school and run off with a basketball player," I blurted.

"Can he go to his left or shoot the three?"

"I guess."

"Let her go."

"Very funny."

"Nothing funny about someone who can go left or shoot from outside the arc. Money in the bank."

"Aaron. I've got another dismemberment." I'd called Aaron about cases past. We often bounced ideas off each other.

I heard him chuckle. "You may not have guns up there, but you sure do like to cut."

"Yes. I think this sicko has cut several. They're all women, otherwise there doesn't seem to be much linking them. Except the cut marks. They're going to be critical."

"Serial or mass?"

"Serial."

He digested that for a second. "So. Tell me."

I described the kerfs and the cut ends of the arm bones. He interrupted occasionally to ask a question, or to slow me down. I could picture him taking notes, his tall, gaunt frame bent over some scrap of discarded paper, finding every usable millimeter of blank space. Though Aaron was forty-two, his somber face and dark, Cherokee eyes made him look about ninety. Always had. His wit was as dry as the Gobi, and his heart about that size.

"Any really deep false starts?" he asked, all business.

"No. They're pretty superficial."

"Harmonics are clear?"

"Very."

"You said blade drift in the kerf?"

"Uh. Huh. Yes."

241

"Are you confident in the tooth distance measures?"

"Yeah. The scratches were distinct in several places. So were some of the islands."

"Otherwise you got pretty flat floors?"

"Yeah. It's really obvious on the impressions."

"And exit chipping," he mumbled, more to himself than me.

"Lots."

A long pause while his mind picked its way through the information I'd given him, sorting the possibilities. I watched people drift past my door. Phones rang. Printers clicked to life, whirred, then rested. I swiveled and gazed out. Traffic rolled across the Jacques-Cartier Bridge, Lilliputian Toyotas and Fords. Minutes ticked by. Finally.

"I'm kinda workin' blind here, Tempe. I'm not sure how you get me to do this. But here goes."

I swiveled back and leaned my elbows on the desk.

"I'd bet the farm this isn't a power saw. Sounds like some kinda specialty handsaw. Probably a kitchen saw of some type."

Yes! I slapped my hand on the desktop, raised a clenched fist, and lowered it sharply, like an engineer pulling the whistle cord. Pink slips sailed up, then fluttered down.

Aaron went on, oblivious to my theatrics. "Kerfs're too big to be any kinda fine-toothed bow saw, or a serrated knife. Besides, sounds like there's too much set to the teeth. With those floor shapes I doubt you're talking about any kinda cross cut. Got to be chisel. All that, 'thout seein' 'em, of course, tells me chef's saw or meat saw."

"What's it look like?"

"Kinda like a big hacksaw. Teeth set pretty wide, so as not to bind. That's why you sometimes get the islands you're describing in the false starts. Usually there's a

242

lotta drift, but the blade chisels through bone just fine and cuts real clean. They're mighty efficient little saws. Cut right through bone, gristle, ligaments, whatever."

"Anything else that might be consistent?"

"Well, there's always the chance you can get something doesn't fit the regular pattern. These saws don't read the books, you know. But right offhand, I can't think of anything else fits all you've told me."

"You are fantastic. That's exactly what I was thinking, but I wanted to hear it from you. Aaron, I can't tell you how much I appreciate your doing this."

"Ah."

"You want to see the photos and impressions?"

"Sure."

"I'll send them out tomorrow."

Aaron's second passion in life was saws. He cataloged written and photographic descriptions of features produced in bone by known saws, and spent hours poring over cases sent to his lab from all over the world.

A hitch in his breathing told me he had something more to say. As I waited, I gathered pink slips.

"Did you say the only completely sectioned bones are in the lower arms?"

"Yep."

"Went into the joints for the others?"

"Yep."

"Neat?"

"Very."

"Hm."

I stopped gathering. "What?"

"What?" Innocent.

"When you say 'Hm' like that, it means something."

"Just a mighty interesting association."

"Which is?"

"Guy uses a chef's saw. And he goes about cuttin' up a body like he knows what he's doing. Knows what's

243

where, how to get at it. And does it the same way every time."

"Yeah. I thought of that."

A few seconds ticked off.

"But he just whacks off the hands. What about that?"

"That, Dr. Brennan, is a question for a psychologist, not a saw man."

I agreed and changed the subject. "How're the girls?"

Aaron had never married, and, though I'd known him for twenty years, I'm not sure I'd ever seen him with a date. His horses were his first passion. From Tulsa to Chicago to Louisville, and back to Oklahoma City, he traveled where the quarter horse circuit took him.

"Pretty excited. I bid a stallion this past fall and got 'im. The ladies been actin' like yearlings ever since."

We exchanged news of our lives and small talk about mutual friends, and we agreed to get together at the Academy meeting in February.

"Well, good luck nailin' this guy, Tempe."

"Thanks."

My watch read four-forty. Once again the offices and corridors had grown quiet around me. I jumped at the sound of the phone.

Too much coffee, I thought.

As I answered, the receiver was still warm against my ear.

"I saw you last night."

"Gabby?"

"Don't do that again, Tempe."

"Gabby, where are you?"

"You're just going to make things worse."

"Goddammit, Gabby, don't play with me! Where are you? What's going on?"

"Never mind that. I can't be seeing you right now."

I couldn't believe she was doing this again. I could feel the anger rising in my chest.

244

"Stay away, Tempe. Stay away from me. Stay away from my—"

Gabby's self-centered rudeness ignited my pent-up anger. Fueled by Claudel's arrogance, the inhumanity of a psychopathic killer, and by Katy's youthful folly, I exploded with the fury of a flash fire, rolling over Gabby and charring her.

"Who the hell do you think you are?" I seethed into the phone, my voice cracking. Squeezing the receiver with enough force to break the plastic, I raved on.

"I'll leave you alone! I'll leave you alone, all right! I don't know what bugass little game you're playing, Gabby, but I'm out! Gone! Game, set, match, finished! I'm not buying into your schizophrenia! I'm not buying into your paranoia! And I'm not, repeat *not*, playing Masked Avenger to your damsel in and out of distress!"

Every neuron in my body was overcharged, like a 110 appliance in a 220 socket. My chest was heaving, and I could feel tears behind my eyes. Tempe's temper.

From Gabby, a dial tone.

I sat for a moment, doing nothing, thinking nothing. I felt giddy.

Slowly, I replaced the receiver. I closed my eyes, ran through the sheet music, and made a selection. This one's going out to me. In a low, throaty voice I hummed the tune:

Busted flat in Baton Rouge . . .

21

At 6 A.M. a steady rain drummed against my windows. An occasional car made soft shishing sounds as it passed on some predawn journey. For the third time in as many days I saw daybreak, an event I embrace as eagerly as Joe Montana welcomes an all-out blitz. While not a day napper, neither am I an early riser. Yet three mornings this week I'd seen the sun come up, twice as I fell asleep, today as I tossed and turned after eleven hours in bed, feeling neither sleepy nor rested.

Home after Gabby's call, I'd gone on an eating binge. Greasy fried chicken, rehydrated mashed potatoes with synthetic gravy, mushy corn on the cob, and soggy apple pie. *Merci*, Colonel. Then a hot bath and a long pick at the scab on my right cheek. The microsurgery didn't help. I still looked like I'd been dragged. Around seven I turned on the Expos game, and fell asleep to the play-by-play.

I switched on my computer – 6 A.M. or 6 P.M., it was alert and ready to perform. I had sent a message to Katy, relaying through the e-mail system at McGill to my mail server at UNC-Charlotte. She could access the message with her laptop and modem, and reply right from her bedroom. Yahoo! Hop aboard the

Internet.

The screen's cursor blinked at me, insisting there was nothing in the document I'd created. It was right. The spreadsheet I had started on paper had only column headings but no content. When had I begun this? The day of the parade. Just one week, but it seemed like years. Today was the thirtieth. Four weeks to the day since Isabelle Gagnon's body was found, one week since Margaret Adkins had been murdered.

What had we accomplished since then except discover another body? A stakeout on the Rue Berger apartment confirmed that its occupant had not returned. Big surprise. The bust had turned up nothing useful. We had no leads on the identity of "St. Jacques," and we hadn't identified the latest body. Claudel still wouldn't acknowledge the cases were linked, and Ryan thought of me as a "freelancer." Happy day.

Back to the spreadsheet. I expanded the column headings. Physical characteristics. Geography. Living arrangements. Jobs. Friends. Family members. Dates of birth. Dates of death. Dates of discovery. Times. Places. I entered everything I could think of that might reveal a link. At the far left I entered four row headings: Adkins, Gagnon, Trottier, *Inconnue.* I'd replace the unknown designation when we tied a name to the St. Lambert bones. At seven-thirty I closed the file, packed the laptop, and got ready for work.

Traffic was clogged, so I cut down to the Ville-Marie tunnel. Full morning, but dark, heavy clouds trapped the city in murky gloom. The streets were covered with a wet sheen that reflected the brake lights of the morning rush hour.

My wipers beat a monotonous refrain, slapping water from two fan-shaped patches on the windshield. I leaned forward, bobbing my head like a palsied tortoise, searching for clear glass between the streaks. Time for new wipers, I told myself, knowing I wouldn't get them. It took a good half hour to reach the lab.

I wanted to get right to the files, to dig out minutiae and enter them into the spreadsheet, but there were two requisitions on my desk. A baby boy had been found in a municipal park, his tiny body wedged in the rocks of a creek bed. According to LaManche's note, the tissue was desiccated and the internal organs unrecognizable, but otherwise the corpse was well preserved. He wanted an opinion on the infant's age. That wouldn't take long.

I looked at the police report attached to the other form. "*Ossements trouvés dans un bois.*" Bones found in the woods. My most common case. Could mean anything from a multiple ax murder to a dead cat.

I called Denis and requested radiographs of the infant, then went downstairs to look at the bones. Lisa brought a cardboard box from the morgue and placed it on the table.

"*C'est tout?*"

"*C'est tout.*" That's all.

She handed me gloves, and I withdrew three clods of hard clay from the box. Bones protruded from each clump. I chipped at the soil, but it was hard as cement.

"Let's get photos and radiographs, then put these in a screen and get them soaking. Use dividers to keep the chunks separate. I'll be back down after the meeting."

The four other pathologists at the LML meet with LaManche each morning to review cases and receive autopsy assignments. On the days I'm present, I attend. When I got upstairs LaManche, Natalie Ayers, Jean Pelletier, and Marc Bergeron were already seated around the small conference table in LaManche's office. From the activity board in the corridor, I knew that Marcel Morin was in court, and Emily Santangelo

248

had taken a personal day.

Everyone shifted to make room, and a chair was shuffled into the circle. *Bonjour*'s and *Comment ça va*'s were exchanged.

"Marc, what brings you in on a Thursday?" I asked.

"Holiday tomorrow."

I'd completely forgotten. Canada Day.

"Going to the parade?" asked Pelletier, poker-faced. His French wore the trappings of the Quebec back country, making it difficult for me to unravel his words. For months I hadn't understood him at all, and had missed his wry comments. Now, after four years, I caught most of what he said. I had no trouble following his drift this morning.

"I think I'll skip this one."

"You could just get your face painted at one of those booths. It might be easier."

Chuckles all around.

"Or maybe a tattoo. Less painful."

"Very funny."

Feigned innocence, eyebrows raised, shoulders hoisted, palms up. What? Settling back, he clamped the last two inches of an unfiltered cigarette between yellowed fingers, and inhaled deeply. Someone once told me that Pelletier had never traveled outside Quebec Province. He was sixty-four years old.

"There are only three autopsies," LaManche began, distributing the list of that day's cases.

"Pre-holiday lull," said Pelletier, reaching for his printout. His dentures clicked softly when he spoke. "Things'll get busier."

"Yes." LaManche picked up his red marker. "At least the weather is cooler. Perhaps that will help."

He went over the day's melancholy roster, supplying additional information on each case. A suicide by carbon monoxide. An old man found dead in his bed. A

249

baby tossed into a park.

"The suicide looks pretty straightforward." LaManche scanned the police report. "White male . . . Age twenty-seven . . . Found behind the wheel in his own garage . . . fuel tank empty, key in the ignition, turned to the 'on' position."

He laid several Polaroids on the table. They showed a dark blue Ford centered in a one-car garage. A length of flexible tubing, the type used to vent clothes dryers, ran from the exhaust pipe into the car's right rear window. LaManche read on.

"History of depression . . . *Note d'adieu.*" He looked at Nathalie. "Dr. Ayers?"

She nodded and reached for the paperwork. He marked "Ay" in red on the master list, and picked up the next set of forms.

"Number 26742 is a white male . . . Age seventy-eight . . . Controlled diabetic." His eyes skipped through the summary report, pulling out the pertinent information. "Hadn't been seen for several days . . . Sister found him . . . No signs of trauma." He read to himself for a few seconds. "Curious thing is there was a delay between the time she found him and the time she called for help. Apparently the lady did some housecleaning in between." He looked up. "Dr. Pelletier?"

Pelletier shrugged and extended his hand. LaManche placed a red "Pe" on his list, then passed him the forms. They were accompanied by a plastic bag full of prescription and over-the-counter drugs. Pelletier took the materials, making a wisecrack which I missed.

My attention was turned to the stack of Polaroids accompanying the baby case. Taken from several angles, they showed a shallow creek with a small foot-bridge arching across it. A little body lay among the rocks, its tiny muscles shriveled, its skin yellowed like old parchment. A fringe of fine hair floated round its head, another rimmed its pale blue eyelids. The child's fingers were splayed wide, as if grasping for help, for something to cling to. He was nude, and lay half in and half out of a dark green plastic bag. He looked like a miniature pharaoh, exposed and discarded. I was beginning to dislike plastic bags intensely.

I returned the photos to the table and listened to LaManche. He'd finished his summary, and was marking "La" on the master sheet. He would do the autopsy, I would narrow the age range by assessing skeletal development. Bergeron would have a go at the teeth. Nods all around. There being no further discussion, the meeting broke up.

I got coffee and returned to my office. A large brown envelope lay on the desk. I opened it and slipped the first of the baby's X rays onto the light box. Withdrawing a form from the drawer in my worktable, I started my survey. Only two carpals were present in each hand. No caps at the ends of the finger bones. I looked at the lower arms. No cap on either radius. I finished with the upper body, listing on my inventory sheet those bony elements that were present, and noting which had not yet formed. Then I did the same for the lower body, shifting from film to film to be sure of my observations. The coffee grew cold.

An infant is born with its skeleton incomplete. Some bones, such as the carpals in the hand, are absent at birth, appearing months, or even years later. Other bones lack knobs and ridges that will eventually give them their adult form. The missing parts emerge in predictable succession, allowing for fairly accurate age estimates for very young children. This baby had lived only seven months.

251

I summarized my conclusions on yet another form, placed all the paperwork in a yellow file folder, and dropped it on the stack for the secretarial pool. It would come back with the report typed in my preferred format, with all supporting materials and diagrams duplicated and assembled. They would also polish my French. I made a verbal report to LaManche. Then I moved on to my clumps.

The clay hadn't dissolved, but had softened enough to allow me to pry out the contents. After fifteen minutes of scraping and teasing, the matrix yielded eight vertebrae, seven long bone fragments, and three chunks of pelvis. All showed evidence of butchering. I spent thirty minutes washing and sorting the mess, then cleaned up and jotted a few notes. On my way upstairs, I asked Lisa to photograph the partial skeletons of the three victims: two white-tailed deer and one medium-sized dog. I filled out another report form and dropped this folder on top of the earlier one. Odd, but not a forensic problem.

Lucie had left a note on my desk. I found her in her office, back to the door, eyes shifting between a terminal screen and an open dossier. She typed with one hand and held her place in the dossier with the other, her index finger moving slowly from entry to entry.

"Got your note," I said.

She raised the finger, typed a few more strokes, then laid a ruler across the file. Pivoting and thrusting in one motion, she rolled to her desk.

"I pulled up what you asked for. Sort of."

She dug through one stack of paper, shifted to another, then returned to the first, searching more slowly. Finally she withdrew a small stack of papers stapled at the corner, scanned a few pages, then extended the collection to me.

"Nothing before '88."

I leafed through the pages, dismayed. How could there be so many?

"First I tried calling up cases with 'dismemberment' as my key word. That's the first list. The long one. I got all the people who threw themselves in front of trains, or fell into machinery and had limbs ripped off. I didn't think you wanted that."

Indeed. It seemed to be a list of every case in which an arm, leg, or finger had been traumatically severed at or even near the time of death.

"Then I tried adding 'intentional,' to limit the selections to cases in which the dismemberment was done on purpose."

I looked at her.

"I got nothing."

"None?"

"That doesn't mean there weren't any."

"How come?"

"I didn't enter this data. Over the past two years we've had special funding to hire part-time workers to get historical data on-line as quickly as possible." She gave an exasperated sigh and shook her head. "The ministry dragged its heels for years getting computerized, now they want everything up to date overnight. Anyway, the data entry people have standard codes for the basics: date of birth, date of death, cause of death, and so on. But for something that's odd, something that occurs only rarely, they're pretty much on their own. They make up a code."

"Like a dismemberment."

"Right. Someone might call it an amputation, someone else might use the term disjointing, usually they just use the same word the pathologist put in the report. Or they might just enter it as cutting or sawing."

I looked back at the lists, thoroughly discouraged.

253

"I tried all of those, and a few others. No go."

So much for this idea.

"'Mutilation' brought up the other really long list." She waited while I turned to the second page. "That was even worse than 'dismemberment.'

"Then I tried 'dismemberment' in combination with 'postmortem' as a limiter, to select out the cases in which the" – she turned her palms upward and made a scratching motion with her fingers, as if trying to tease the word from the air – "the event took place after death."

I looked up, hopeful.

"All I got was the guy with his dick chopped off."

"Computer took you literally."

"Huh?"

"Never mind." Another joke that didn't travel.

"Then I tried 'mutilation' in combination with the 'postmortem' limiter, and . . ." She reached across the desk and displayed the last printout. "Bango! Is that what you say?"

"Bingo."

"Bingo! I think this may be what you want. You can ignore some of it, like those drug things where they used acid." She pointed to several lines she'd penciled out. "Those are probably not what you want."

I nodded absently, totally absorbed by page three. It listed twelve cases. She'd drawn lines through three of them.

"But I think maybe some of the others might be of interest to you."

I was hardly hearing her. My eyes had been drifting through the list, but were now riveted on the sixth name down. A tingle of uneasiness passed through me. I wanted to get back to my office.

"Lucie, this is great," I said. "This is better than I'd hoped for."

"Anything you can use?"

"Yes. Yes, I think so," I said, trying to sound casual.

"Do you want me to call these cases up?"

"No. Thanks. Let me look this over, then I think I'd rather pull the complete files." Let me be wrong on this one, I prayed to myself.

"*Bien sûr.*"

She took off her glasses and began polishing a lens on the hem of her sweater. Without them she looked incomplete, wrong somehow, like John Denver after he switched to contacts.

"I'd like to know what happens," she said, the pink rectangles back flanking the bridge of her nose.

"Of course. I'll tell you if anything breaks."

As I walked away I heard the wheels of her chair gliding across the tile.

In my office, I laid the printout on my desk and looked at the list. One name stared at me. Francine Morisette-Champoux. Francine Morisette-Champoux. I'd forgotten all about her. Stay cool, I told myself. Don't jump to conclusions.

I forced myself to go over the other entries. Gagne and Valencia were in there, a pair of drug dealers with a lousy business sense. So was Chantale Trottier. I recognized the name of a Honduran exchange student whose husband had put a shotgun to her face and pulled the trigger. He had driven her from Ohio to Quebec, cut off her hands, and dumped her nearly headless body in a provincial park. As a parting gesture, he'd carved his initials on her breasts. I didn't recognize the other four cases. They were before 1990, before my time. I went to the central files and pulled them, along with the jacket on Morisette-Champoux.

I stacked the files according to their LML numbers, thus achieving chronological order. I'd go about this

255

systematically. Violating that resolution as soon as I made it, I went right to the Morisette-Champoux folder. Its contents made my anxiety rocket.

22

Francine Morisette-Champoux was beaten and shot to death in January 1993. A neighbor had seen her walking her small spaniel around ten one morning. Less than two hours later her husband discovered her body in the kitchen of their home. The dog was in the living room. Its head was never found.

I remembered the case, though I wasn't involved in the investigation. I'd commuted to the lab that winter, flying north for one week of every six. Pete and I were at each other constantly, so I'd agreed to spend the whole summer of '93 in Quebec, optimistic the three-month separation might rejuvenate the marriage. Right. The brutality of the attack on Morisette-Champoux had shocked me then and did still. The crime scene photos brought it all back.

She was lying half under a small wooden table, her arms and legs spread wide, white cotton panties stretched taut between her knees. A sea of blood surrounded her, giving way at its perimeter to the geometric pattern of the linoleum. Dark smears covered the walls and counter fronts. From off camera, the legs of an upturned chair seemed to point at her. You are here.

257

Her body looked ghostly white against the crimson background. A pencil-thin line looped across her abdomen, a happy-face smile just above her pubis. She was slit from this scar upward to her breastbone, and her innards protruded from the opening. The handle of a kitchen knife was barely visible at the apex of the triangle formed by her legs. Five feet from her, between a work island and the sink, lay her right hand. She'd been forty-seven years old.

"Jesus," I whispered softly.

I was picking my way through the autopsy report when Charbonneau appeared in my doorway. I guessed his mood was not congenial. His eyes looked bloodshot and he didn't bother with greetings. He entered without asking and took the chair opposite my desk.

Watching him, I felt a momentary sense of loss. The lumbering walk, the looseness in his movement, just the *largeness* of him touched something I thought I'd abandoned. Or been abandoned by.

For a moment I saw Pete sitting across from me, and my mind flew backward in time. What an intoxicant his body had been. I never knew if it was his size, or the relaxed way he had of moving it. Maybe it was *his* fascination with *me*. That had seemed genuine. I could never get enough of him. I'd had sexual fantasies, damn good ones, but from the moment I saw him standing in the rain outside the law library they'd always involved Pete. I could use one right now, I thought. Jesus, Brennan. Get a grip. I snapped back to the present.

I waited for Charbonneau to begin. He was staring down at his hands.

"My partner can be a sonofabitch." He spoke in English. "But he's not a bad guy."

I didn't respond. I noticed that his pants had four-inch hems, hand sewn, and wondered if he'd done the job himself.

"He's just – set in his ways. Doesn't like change."

"Yes."

He wouldn't meet my eyes. I felt unease.

"And?" I encouraged.

He leaned back and picked at a thumbnail, still avoiding eye contact. From a radio down the hall Roch Voisine sang softly of Hélène.

"He says he's going to file a complaint." He dropped both hands and shifted his gaze to the window.

"A complaint?" I tried to keep my voice flat.

"With the minister. And the director. And LaManche. He's even looking up your professional board."

"And what is Monsieur Claudel unhappy about?" Stay calm.

"He says you're overstepping your bounds. Interfering in stuff you got no business in. Messing up his investigation." He squinted into the bright sunlight.

I felt my stomach muscles tighten, and a hotness spread upward.

"Go on." Flat.

"He thinks you're . . ." He fumbled for a word, no doubt seeking a substitute for the one Claudel had actually used. ". . . overreaching."

"And what exactly does that mean?"

He still avoided eye contact.

"He says you're trying to make the Gagnon case into a bigger deal than it really is, seeing all kinds of shit that isn't there. He says you're trying to turn a simple murder into an American-style psycho extravaganza."

"And why am I trying to do that?" My voice wavered slightly.

"Shit, Brennan, this isn't my idea. I don't know." For the first time his eyes met mine. He looked miserable. It was obvious he didn't want to be there.

I stared back, not really seeing him, just using the

259

time to quell the alarm call going out to my adrenals. I had some idea of the type of inquiry a letter of complaint could set in motion, and I knew it wouldn't be good. I'd investigated such charges when I sat on the board's ethics committee. Regardless of outcome, it was never pretty. Neither of us spoke.

"Hélène the things you do. Make me crazy 'bout you," crooned the radio.

Don't kill the messenger, I told myself. My eyes dropped to the dossier on my desk. A body with skin the color of milk reproduced in a dozen glossy rectangles. I considered the photos, then looked at Charbonneau. I hadn't wanted to broach this yet, didn't feel ready, but Claudel was forcing my hand. What the hell. Things couldn't get worse.

"Monsieur Charbonneau, do you remember a woman named Francine Morisette-Champoux?"

"Morisette-Champoux." He repeated the name several times, twirling through his mental Rolodex. "That was several years ago, eh?"

"Almost two. January of 1993." I handed him the photos.

He thumbed through them, nodding his head in recognition. "Yeah, I remember. So?"

"Think, Charbonneau. What do you recall about the case?"

"We never got the turd that did it."

"What else?"

"Brennan, tell me you're not trying to hook this one in, too?"

He went through the photos again, the nodding transformed to negative shaking.

"No way. She was shot. Doesn't fit the pattern."

"The bastard slit her open and cut her hand off."

"She was old. Forty-seven, I think."

I gave him an icy stare.

260

"I mean, older than the others," he mumbled, reddening.

"Morisette-Champoux's killer drove a knife up her vagina. According to the police report there was extensive bleeding."

I let that sink in.

"She was still alive."

He nodded. I didn't need to explain that a wound inflicted after death will bleed very little since the heart is no longer pumping and blood pressure is gone. Francine Morisette-Champoux had bled profusely.

"With Margaret Adkins it was a metal statue. She was also alive."

Silently, I reached behind me and pulled the Gagnon file. I withdrew the scene photos and spread them in front of him. There was the torso lying on its plastic bag, dappled by the four o'clock sunlight. Nothing had been moved but the covering of leaves. The plunger lay in place, its red rubber cup snug against the pelvic bones, its handle projecting toward the body's severed neck.

"I believe Gagnon's killer shoved that plunger into her with enough force to drive the handle through her belly and clear up to her diaphragm."

He studied the photos for a long time.

"Same pattern with all three victims," I hammered on. "Forceful penetration with a foreign object while the victim is alive. Body mutilation after death. Coincidence, Monsieur Charbonneau? How many sadists do we want out there, Monsieur Charbonneau?"

He ran his fingers through the bristle on his head, then drummed them on the arm of the chair.

"Why didn't you tell us this sooner?"

"I just realized the Morisette-Champoux connection today. With only Adkins and Gagnon, it seemed a bit thin."

"What does Ryan say?"

261

"Haven't told him."

Unconsciously I fingered the scab on my cheek. I still looked like I'd gone to a TKO with George Foreman.

"Shit." He said it with little force.

"What?"

"I think I'm beginning to agree with you. Claudel's going to bust my balls about this." More drumming. "What else?"

"The saw marks and pattern of dismemberment are almost identical for Gagnon and Trottier."

"Yeah. Ryan told us that."

"And the unknown from St. Lambert."

"A fifth?" It came out "fit."

"You're very quick."

"Thanks." Back to drumming. "Know who she is yet?"

I shook my head. "Ryan's working on it."

He ran a meaty hand over his face. His knuckles were covered with patches of coarse gray hair, miniature versions of the crop on his head.

"So what do you think about victim selection?"

I gave a palm up gesture. "They're all female."

"Great. Ages?"

"Sixteen to forty-seven."

"Physicals?"

"A mix."

"Locations?"

"All over the map."

"So what's the sicko bastard go for? The way they look? The boots they wear? The place they shop?"

I replied with silence.

"You find *anything* common to all five?"

"Some sonofabitch beat the crap out of them, then killed them."

"Right." Tilting forward, he placed his hands on his knees, hunched and lowered his shoulders, and gave a deep sigh. "Claudel's going to shit flaming bullets."

When he'd gone I called Ryan. Neither he nor Bertrand was in, so I left a message. I went through the other dossiers, but found little of interest. Two drug dealers blasted and sawed up by former friends in crime. A man killed by his nephew, dismembered with a power saw, then stored in the basement freezer. A power failure had brought him to the attention of the rest of the family. A female torso washed up in a hockey bag, with head and arms found downriver. The husband was convicted.

I closed the last file and realized I was starving – 1:50 P.M. No wonder. I bought a ham and cheese croissant and a Diet Coke in the cafeteria on the eighth floor, and returned to my office, ordering myself to take a break. Ignoring the order, I tried Ryan again. Still out. A break it would be. I bit the sandwich and allowed my thoughts to meander. Gabby. Nope. Out of bounds. Claudel. Veto. St. Jacques. Off limits.

Katy. How could I get through to her? Right now, no way. By default, back to Pete, and I felt a familiar flutter in my stomach. Remember the tingling skin, the pounding blood, the warm wetness between my legs. Yes, there had been passion. You're just horny, Brennan. I took another bite of my sandwich.

The other Pete. The nights of anger. The arguments. The dinners alone. The cold shroud of resentment that had smothered the lust. I took a swig of Coke. Why was I thinking about Pete so often? If we had a chance to do it all again . . . Thanks, Ms. Streisand.

Relaxation therapy wasn't working. I reread Lucie's printout, careful not to drip mustard on it. I reviewed the list on page three, trying to read the items Lucie had crossed out, but her pencil marks obscured the letters. Out of curiosity, I erased each of her lines and read the entries. Two cases involved bodies stuffed into barrels

263

then doused with acid. A new twist on the ever-popular drug burn.

The third item puzzled me. Its LML number indicated a 1990 case, and that Pelletier had been the pathologist. No coroner was listed. In the name field it read: Singe. The data fields for date of birth, date of autopsy, and cause of death were empty. The entry "*démembrement/postmortem*" had prompted the computer to include the case in Lucie's list.

Finishing the croissant, I went to the central files and pulled the jacket. It contained only three items: a police incident report, a one-page opinion by the pathologist, and an envelope of photographs. I thumbed through the pictures, read the reports, then went in search of Pelletier.

"Got a minute?" I said to his hunched back.

He turned from the microscope, glasses in one hand, pen in the other. "Come in, come in," he urged, sliding his bifocals on to his face.

My office had a window; his had space. He strode across it and gestured to one of two chairs flanking a low table in front of his desk. Reaching into his lab coat, he withdrew a pack of du Maurier's and extended it to me. I shook my head. We'd been through the ritual a thousand times. He knew I didn't smoke, but would always offer. Like Claudel, Pelletier was set in his ways.

"What can I help you with?" he said, lighting up.

"I'm curious about an old case of yours. Goes back to 1990."

"Ah, *Mon Dieu*, can I remember that far back? I can barely remember my own address sometimes." He leaned forward, cupped his mouth, and looked conspiratorial. "I write it on matchbooks, just in case."

We both laughed. "Dr. Pelletier, I think you remember just about everything you want to remember."

He shrugged and wagged his head, all innocence.

264

"Anyway, I brought the file." I held it up, then opened it. "Police report says the remains were found in a gym bag behind the Voyageur bus station. Wino opened it, thinking maybe he could find the owner."

"Right," said Pelletier. "Honest rubbies are so common they should form their own fraternal organization."

"Anyway, he didn't like the aroma. Said" – I skimmed the incident report to find the exact phrase – "'the smell of Satan rose up out of the bag and surrounded my soul.' Unquote."

"A poet. I like that," said Pelletier. "Wonder what he'd say about my shorts."

I ignored that and read on. "He took the bag to a janitor, who called the police. They found a collection of body parts wrapped up in some sort of tablecloth."

"Ah, *oui*. I remember that one," he said, pointing a yellowed finger at me. "Grisly. Horrible." He had that look.

"Dr. Pelletier?"

"The case of the terminal monkey."

"Then I read your report correctly?"

He raised his eyebrows questioningly.

"It really was a monkey?"

He nodded gravely. "Capucin."

"Why did it come here?"

"Dead."

"Yes." Everyone's a comedian. "But why a coroner case?"

The look on my face must have prompted a straight answer. "Whatever was in there was small, and someone had skinned it and cut it up. Hell, it could have been anything. Cops thought it might be a fetus or a neonate, so they sent it to us."

"Was there anything odd about the case?" I wasn't sure what I was looking for.

"Nah. Just another sliced-up monkey." The corners

265

of his mouth twitched slightly.

"Right." Dumb question. "Anything strike you about the way the monkey was cut up?"

"Not really. These monkey dismemberments are all the same."

This was going nowhere.

"Did you ever find out whose monkey it was?"

"Actually we did. A blurb appeared in the paper, and some guy called from the university."

"UQAM?"

"Yeah, I think so. A biologist or zoologist or something. Anglophone. Ah. Wait."

He went to a desk drawer, pushed the contents around, then withdrew a stack of business cards bound with a rubber band. Rolling the band off, he flicked through the cards and handed one to me.

"That's him. I saw him when he came to ID the deceased."

The card read: Parker T. Bailey, Ph.D., Professeur de Biologie, Université du Québec à Montrèal, and gave e-mail, telephone, and fax numbers, along with an address.

"What was the story?" I asked.

"The gentleman keeps monkeys at the university for his research. One day he came in and found one less subject."

"Stolen?"

"Stolen? Liberated? Escaped? Who knows? The primate was AWOL." The expression sounded odd in French.

"So he read about the dead monkey in the paper and called here?"

"*C'est ça.*"

"What happened to it?"

"The monkey?"

I nodded.

266

"We released it to . . ." He gestured at the card.

"Dr. Bailey," I supplied.

"*Oui*. There were no next of kin. At least, not in Quebec." Not a twitch.

"I see."

I looked at the card again. This is nothing, my left brain said, while at the same time I heard myself asking, "May I keep this?"

"Of course."

"One other thing." I laid the trap for myself. "Why do you call it the case of the terminal monkey?"

"Well, it was," he answered, surprised.

"Was what?"

"The monkey. It was terminal."

"Yes. I see."

"Also, that's *where* it was."

"Where?"

"The terminal. The bus terminal."

Some things do translate. Unfortunately.

For the rest of the afternoon I pulled details from the four principal files and entered them into the spreadsheet I'd created. Color of hair. Eyes. Skin. Height. Religion. Names. Dates. Places. Signs of the Zodiac. Anything and everything. Doggedly, I plugged it in, planning to search for links later. Or perhaps I thought the patterns would form by themselves, the interconnecting bits of information drawn to each other like neuropeptides to receptor sites. Or maybe I just needed a rote task to occupy my mind, a mental jigsaw puzzle to give the illusion of progress.

At four-fifteen I tried Ryan again. Though he wasn't at his desk, the operator thought she'd seen him, and reluctantly began a search. While I waited, my eye fell on the monkey file. Bored, I dumped out the photos. There were two sets, one of Polaroids, the other of five-by-seven color prints. The operator came back on to tell

267

me Ryan was not in any of the offices she'd rung. Yes, sigh, she'd try the coffee room.

I thumbed through the Polaroids. Obviously taken when the remains arrived in the morgue. Shots of a purple and black nylon gym bag, zipped and unzipped, the latter showing a bundle in its interior. The next few showed the bundle on an autopsy table, before and after it was unrolled.

The remaining half dozen featured the body parts. The scale on the ID card confirmed that the subject was, indeed, tiny, smaller than a full-term fetus or newborn. Putrefaction was advancing nicely. The flesh had begun to blacken and was smeared with something that looked like rancid tapioca. I thought I could identify the head, the torso, and the limbs. Other than that, I couldn't tell squat. The pictures had been taken from too far away, and the detail was lousy. I rotated a few, looking for a better angle, but it was impossible to make out much.

The operator came back with resolve in her voice. Ryan was not there. I'd have to try tomorrow. Denying her the opportunity to launch the argument she'd prepared, I left another message, and hung up.

The five-by-seven close-ups had been taken following cleaning. The detail that had escaped the Polaroids was fully captured in the prints. The tiny corpse had been skinned and disjointed. The photographer, probably Denis, had arranged the pieces in anatomical order, then carefully photographed each in turn.

As I worked my way through the stack, I couldn't help noting that the butchered parts looked vaguely like rabbit about to become stew. Except for one thing. The fifth print showed a small arm ending in four perfect fingers and a thumb curled onto a delicate palm.

The last two prints focused on the head. Without the outer covering of skin and hair it looked primordial, like an embryo detached from the umbilicus, naked and vulnerable. The skull was the size of a tangerine. Though the face was flat and the features anthropoid, it didn't take Jane Goodall to know that this was no human primate. The mouth contained full dentition, molars and all. I counted. Three premolars in each quadrant. The terminal monkey had come from South America.

It's just another animal case, I told myself, returning the pictures to their envelope. We'd get them occasionally, because someone thought the remains to be human. Bear paws skinned and left behind by hunters, pigs and goats slaughtered for meat, the unwanted portions discarded by a roadside, dogs and cats abused and thrown in the river. The callousness of the human animal always astounded me. I never got used to it.

So why did this case hold my attention? Another look at the five-by-sevens. Okay. The monkey had been cut up. Big deal. So are a lot of animal carcasses that we see. Some asshole probably got his jollies tormenting and killing it. Maybe it was a student, pissed off at his grade.

With the fifth photo I stopped, my eyes cemented to the image. Once again, my stomach muscles knotted. I stared at the photo, then reached for the phone.

23

There's nothing emptier than a classroom building after hours. It's how I imagine the aftermath of a neutron bomb. Lights burn. Water fountains spew forth on command. Bells ring on schedule. Computer terminals glow eerily. The people are absent. No one quenching a thirst, scurrying to class, or clicking on keyboards. The silence of the catacombs.

I sat on a folding chair outside Parker Bailey's office at the Université du Québec à Montréal – UQAM. Since leaving the lab, I'd worked out at the gym, bought groceries at the Provigo, and fed myself a meal of vermicelli and clam sauce. Not bad for a quick and dirty. Even Birdie was impressed. Now I was impatient.

To say the biology department was quiet would be like saying a quark is small. Up and down the corridor every door was closed. I'd perused the bulletin boards, read the graduate school brochures, the field school announcements, the offers to do word processing or tutoring, the notices announcing guest speakers. Twice.

I looked at my watch for the millionth time – 9:12 P.M. Damn. He should be here by now. His class ended at nine. At least, that's what the secretary had told me.

270

I got up and paced. Those who wait must pace – 9:14. Damn.

At 9:30 I gave up. As I slung my purse over my shoulder, I heard a door open somewhere out of sight. In a moment a man with an enormous stack of lab books hurried around the corner. He kept adjusting his arms to keep the books from falling. His cardigan looked as if it had left Ireland before the potato famine. I guessed his age at around forty.

He stopped when he saw me, but his face registered nothing. I started to introduce myself when a notebook slipped from the stack. We both lunged for it. Not a good move by him. The better part of the pile followed, scattering across the floor like confetti on New Year's Eve. We gathered and restacked for several minutes, then he unlocked his office and dumped the books on his desk.

"Sorry," he said in heavily accented French. "I–"

"No problem," I responded in English. "I must have startled you."

"Yes. No. I should have made two trips. This happens a lot." His English was not American.

"Lab books?"

"Yeah. I just taught a class in ethological methodology."

He was brushed with all the shades of an Outer Banks sunset. Pale pink skin, raspberry cheeks, and hair the color of a vanilla wafer. His mustache and eyelashes were amber. He looked like a man who'd burn, not tan.

"Sounds intriguing."

"Wish more of them thought so. Can I–"

"I'm Tempe Brennan," I said, reaching into my bag and offering him a card. "Your secretary said I could catch you now."

As he read the card, I explained my visit.

"Yeah, I remember. I hated losing that monkey. It

271

really cheesed me off at the time." Suddenly, "Would you like to sit?"

Without waiting for a reply, he began shoveling objects from a green vinyl chair and heaping them onto the office floor. I stole a peek around. His tiny quarters made mine look like Yankee Stadium.

Every inch of wall space that wasn't covered with shelves was blanketed with pictures of animals. Sticklebacks. Guinea fowl. Marmosets. Warthogs. Even an aardvark. No level of the Linnaean hierarchy had been neglected. It reminded me of the office of an impressario, with celebrity associations displayed like trophies. Only these photos weren't signed.

We both sat, he behind his desk, feet propped on an open drawer, I in the recently cleared visitor's chair.

"Yeah. It really cheesed me off," he repeated, then switched the topic suddenly. "You're an anthropologist?"

"Um. Hm."

"Do much with primates?"

"No. Used to, but not anymore. I'm on the anthropology faculty at the University of North Carolina at Charlotte. Occasionally I teach a course on primate biology or behavior, but I'm really not involved in that work anymore. I'm too busy with forensic research and consulting."

"Right." He waved the card. "What did you do with primates?"

I wondered who was interviewing who. Whom. "I was interested in osteoporosis, especially the interplay between social behavior and the disease process. We worked with animal models, rhesus mostly, manipulating the social groups, creating stress situations, then monitoring the bone loss."

"Do any work in the wild?"

"Just island colonies."

"Oh?" The amber eyebrows arched with interest.

"Cayo Santiago in Puerto Rico. For several years I taught a field school on Morgan Island, off the coast of South Carolina."

"Rhesus monkeys?"

"Yes. Dr. Bailey, I wonder if you can tell me anything about the monkey that disappeared from your facility?"

He ignored my not so smooth segue. "How'd you get from monkey bones to corpses?"

"Skeletal biology. It's the crux of both."

"Yeah. True."

"The monkey?"

"The monkey. Can't tell you much." He rubbed one Nike against the other, then leaned over and flicked at something. "I came in one morning and the cage was empty. We thought maybe someone had left the latch unhooked and that Alsa, that was her name, maybe she let herself out. They'll do that, you know. She was smart as a pistol and had phenomenal manual dexterity. She had the most amazing little hands. Anyway, we searched the building, alerted campus security, jumped through all the hoops. But we never found her. Then I saw the article in the paper. The rest is history."

"What were you doing with her?"

"Actually, Alsa wasn't my project. A graduate student was working with her. I'm interesting in animal communication systems, particularly, but not exclusively, those relying on pheromones and other olfactory signals."

The change in cadence, along with the shift to jargon, clued me that he'd given this synopsis before. He'd launched into his "my research is" spiel, the scientist's oral abstract for public consumption. "The spiel" is based on the KISS principle: Keep It Simple Stupid. It is trotted out for cocktail parties, fund-raisers, first meetings, and other social occasions. We all have one. I was hearing his.

273

"What was the project?" Enough about you.

He gave a wry smile and shook his head. "Language. Language acquisition in a New World primate. That's where she got her name. L'Apprentissage de la Langue du Singe Americain. ALSA. Marie-Lise was going to be Quebec's answer to Penny Patterson, and Also would be the KoKo of South American monkeys." He flourished a pen above his head, gave a derisive snort, then let his arm drop heavily. It made a soft thud against the desk. I studied his face. He looked either tired or discouraged, I couldn't tell which.

"Marie-Lise?"

"My student."

"Was it working?"

"Who knows? She didn't really have enough time. The monkey disappeared five months into the project." More wry. "Followed shortly thereafter by Marie-Lise."

"She left school?"

He nodded.

"Do you know why?"

He paused a long time before answering. "Marie-Lise was a good student. Sure, she had to start over on her thesis, but I have no doubt she could have completed her master's. She loved what she was doing. Yeah, she was devastated when Alsa was killed, but I don't think that was it."

"What do you think it was?"

He drew small triangles on one of the lab books. I let him take his time.

"She had this boyfriend. He'd hassle her all the time about being in school. Badgered her to quit. She only talked to me about it once or twice, but I think it really got to her. I met him at a couple of department parties. I thought the guy was spooky."

"How so?"

"Just . . . I don't know, antisocial. Cynical. Antago-

274

nistic. Rude. Like he had never absorbed the basic . . . skills. He always reminded me of a Harlow monkey. You know? Like he was raised in isolation and never learned to deal with other beings. No matter what you said to him, he'd roll his eyes and smirk. God, I hated that."

"Did you ever suspect him? That maybe he killed Alsa to sabotage Marie-Lise's work, to get her to quit school?"

His silence told me that he had. Then, "He was supposedly in Toronto at the time."

"Could he verify that?"

"Marie-Lise believed him. We didn't pursue it. She was too upset. What was the point? Alsa was dead."

I wasn't sure how to ask the next question. "Did you ever read Marie-Lise's project notes?"

He stopped doodling and looked at me sharply. "What do you mean?"

"Is there any chance of something she wanted to cover up? Some reason to want to dump the project?"

"No. Absolutely not." His voice held conviction. His eyes did not.

"Did she keep in touch?"

"No."

"Is that common?"

"Some do, some don't." The triangles were spreading.

I changed tack. "Who else had access to the . . . is it a lab?"

"Just a small one. We keep very few animal subjects here on campus. We just don't have the space. Every species has to be kept in a separate room, you know."

"Oh?"

"Yes. The CCAC has specific guidelines for temperature control, space, diet, social and behavioral parameters, you name it."

"The CCAC?"

275

"The Canadian Council on Animal Care. They publish a guide for the care and use of experimental animals. It's our bible. Everyone using research animals has to conform to it. Scientists. Breeders. Industry. It also covers the health and safety of personnel working with animals."

"What about security?"

"Oh yeah. The guidelines are very specific."

"What security measures did you follow?"

"I'm working with sticklebacks right now. Fish."

He swiveled and waved his pen at the fish on the wall.

"They don't require a whole lot. Some of my colleagues keep lab rats. They don't either. The animal activists don't usually get wrought up over fish and rodents."

His face did the World Cup of wry.

"Alsa was the only other mammal, so security wasn't all that stringent. She had her own little room, which we kept locked. And, of course, we locked her cage. And the outer lab door."

He stopped.

"I've gone over it in my mind. I can't remember who was the last to leave that night. I know I didn't have a night class, so I don't think I was here late. Probably one of the grad students did the last check. The secretary won't check those doors unless I specifically ask her to."

He paused again.

"I suppose an outsider could have gotten in. It's not impossible someone left the doors unlocked. Some of the students are less dependable than others."

"What about the cage?"

"The cage was certainly no big deal. Just a padlock. We never found it. I suppose it could have been cut."

I tried to broach the next topic delicately. "Were the missing parts ever found?"

"Missing parts?"

"Alsa had been" – now I groped for a word. KISS –

276

"cut up. Parts of her weren't in the bundle that was recovered. I wondered if anything showed up here."

"Like what? What was missing?" His pastel face looked puzzled.

"Her right hand, Dr. Bailey. Her right hand had been severed at the wrist. It wasn't there."

There was no reason to tell him about the women who'd suffered the same violation, about the real reason I was there.

He was silent. Linking his fingers behind his head, he leaned back and focused on something above me. The raspberry in his cheeks moved toward rhubarb. A small clock radio hummed quietly on his file cabinet.

After a decade, I broke the silence.

"In retrospect, what do you think happened?"

He didn't answer right away. Then, when I was convinced he never would, "I think it was probably one of the mutant life-forms that are spawned in the cesspool around this campus."

I thought he'd finished. The source of his breathing seemed to have moved deeper into his chest. Then he added something, almost in a whisper. I didn't catch it.

"Sorry?" I asked.

"Marie-Lise deserved better."

I found it an odd thing to say. So did Alsa, I thought, but held my tongue. Without warning, a bell split the silence, firing a current through every nerve in my body. I looked at my watch – 10:00 P.M.

Sidestepping his question about my interest in a monkey dead four years, I thanked him for his time and asked him to call me should he think of anything else. I left him sitting there, refocusing on whatever had floated above his head. I suspected he was gazing into time, not space.

Not too familiar with the territory, I'd parked in the

277

same alley as the night I'd cruised the Main. Stick with what works. I'd come to think of that outing as the Great Gabby Grope. It seemed like eons ago. It had been two days.

Tonight was cooler, and a soft rain still fell. I zipped my jacket and started back to my car.

Leaving the university, I walked north on St. Denis, past a cavalcade of upscale boutiques and bistros. Though just a few blocks east, St. Denis is a galaxy away from St. Laurent. Frequented by the young and affluent, St. Denis is the place to go seeking – a dress, silver earrings, a mate, a one-night stand. The street of dreams. Most cities have one. Montreal has two: Crescent for the English, St. Denis for the French.

I thought about Alsa as I waited for the light at De Maisonneuve. Bailey was probably right. Ahead and to my right sat the bus station. Whoever had killed her hadn't gone far to ditch the body. That suggested a local.

I watched a young couple emerge from the Berri-UQAM Métro station. They ran through the rain, clinging together like socks just out of the dryer.

Or it could have been a commuter. Right, Brennan, grab a monkey, take the Métro home, whack it, cut it up, then haul it back on the Métro and leave it at the bus station. Great thinking.

The light turned green. I crossed St. Denis and walked west on De Maisonneuve, still thinking about my conversation with Bailey. What was it about him that bothered me? Did he show too much emotion for his student? Too little for the monkey? Why had he seemed so – what? – negative about the Alsa project? Why didn't he know about the hand? Hadn't Pelletier told me Bailey inspected the cadaver? Wouldn't he have noticed the missing hand? The remains had been released to him, and he'd taken them from the lab.

278

"Shit," I said aloud, mentally smacking my forehead.

A man in coveralls turned to look at me, registering apprehension. He wore no shirt or shoes and carried a shopping bag in both arms, its torn paper handles pointing at odd angles. I smiled to reassure him, and he shuffled on, shaking his head at the state of humanity and the universe.

You're a regular Columbo, I berated myself. You didn't even ask Bailey what he did with the body! Good job.

Having chastised myself, I made amends by proposing consumption of a hot dog.

Knowing I wouldn't sleep anyway, I accepted. That way I could blame it on the food. I went into the Chien Chaud on St. Dominique, ordered a dog all dressed, fries, and a Diet Coke. "No Coke, Pepsi," I was told by a John Belushi look-alike with thick black hair and a heavy accent. Life really does imitate art.

I ate my food in a red-and-white plastic booth, contemplating travel posters peeling from the walls. That would do, I thought, gazing at the too blue skies and blindingly white buildings of Paros, Santorini, Mykonos. Yes. That would do nicely. Cars began to crowd the wet pavement outside. The Main was revving up.

A man arrived and engaged Belushi in loud conversation, presumably Greek. His clothes were damp and smelled of smoke and fat and a spice I didn't recognize. Droplets sparkled in his thick hair. When I glanced over he smiled at me, cocked one bushy eyebrow and ran his tongue slowly along his upper lip. He might as well have shown me his hemorrhoid. Matching his maturity level, I showed him middle man, and turned my attention to the scene outside the window.

Through rain-streaked glass I could make out a row of shops across the street, dark and silent on the eve of

279

a holiday. La Cordonnerie la Fleur. Why would a shoe-maker call his shop "The Flower"?

La Boulangerie Nan. I wondered if that was the name of the bakery, the name of the owner, or just an ad for Indian bread. Through the windows I could see empty shelves, ready for the morning's harvest. Do bakers bake on national holidays?

La Boucherie St. Dominique. Its windows were covered with news of weekly specials. *Lapin frais. Boeuf. Agneau. Poulet. Saucisse.* Fresh rabbit. Beef. Lamb. Chicken. Sausage. Monkey.

That's it. You're out of here. I wadded the wrapper into the paper tray that had held my hot dog. The things for which we kill trees. I added my Pepsi can, threw the whole mess into the trash, and left.

The car was where I'd left it and as I'd left it. Driving, my brain looped back to the murders.

Each slap of the wipers brought up a new image. Alsa's truncated arm. Slap. Morisette-Champoux's hand lying on her kitchen floor. Slap. Chantale Trottier's tendons. Slap. Arm bones with clean cut lower ends. Slap.

Was it always the same hand? Couldn't remember. Have to check. No human hand had been missing. Just coincidence? Was Claudel right? Was I getting para-noid? Maybe Alsa's abductor collected animal paws. Was he just an over-zealous Poe fan? Slap. Or she?

At eleven-fifteen I pulled into my garage. Even my bone marrow was exhausted. I'd been up over eighteen hours. No hot dog would keep me awake tonight.

Birdie hadn't waited up. As was his habit when alone, he'd curled up in the small wooden rocker by the fire-place. He looked up when I came in, blinking round yel-low eyes at me.

"Hey, Bird, how was it being a cat today?" I purred, scratching under his chin. "Does anything ever keep you up?"

280

He closed his eyes and stretched his neck, either ignoring or enhancing the feel of my stroking. When I withdrew my hand he yawned widely, nestled his chin back on to his paws, and regarded me from under heavy lids. I went to the bedroom, knowing he'd follow eventually. Unclasping the barrettes in my hair and dumping my clothes in a heap on the floor, I threw back the covers and dropped into bed.

In no time I fell into a dense and dreamless sleep. I hosted no phantom apparitions, no menacing stage plays. At one point I sensed a warm heaviness against my leg, and knew that Birdie had joined me, but I slept on, enveloped in a black void.

Then, my heart was pounding and my eyes were open. I was wide awake, felt alarm, and didn't know why. The transition was so abrupt I had to orient myself.

The room was pitch black. The clock read one twenty-seven. Birdie was gone. I lay in the dark holding my breath, listening, straining for a clue. Why had my body gone to red alert? Had I heard something? What blip had my personal radar detected? Some sensory receptor had sent a signal. Had Birdie heard something? Where was he? It was unlike him to prowl at night.

I relaxed my body and listened harder. The only sound was my heart hammering against my chest. The house was eerily silent.

Then I heard it. A soft clunk followed by a faint metallic rattle. I waited, rigid, not breathing. Ten. Fifteen. Twenty seconds. A glowing digit changed shape on the clock. Then, when I thought I might have imagined it, I heard it again. Clunk. Rattle. My molars compressed like a Black & Decker vise, and my fingers curled into fists.

Was someone in the apartment? I'd grown accustomed to the ordinary sounds of the place. This sound was different, an acoustic intruder. It didn't belong.

281

Silently, I eased back the quilt and swung my legs out of bed. Blessing last night's sloppiness, I reached for my T-shirt and jeans and slipped them on. I stole across the carpet.

I stopped at the bedroom door to look back in search of a possible weapon. Nothing. There was no moon, but light from a streetlamp oozed through the window in the other bedroom and partly lit the hall with a faint glow. I stole forward, past the bathroom, toward the hall with the courtyard doors. Every few steps I stopped to listen, breath frozen, eyes wide. At the entrance to the kitchen, I heard it again. Clunk. Rattle. It was coming from somewhere near the French doors.

I turned right into the kitchen and peered toward the French doors on the patio side of the apartment. Nothing moved. Silently cursing my aversion to guns, I scanned the kitchen for a weapon. It wasn't exactly an arsenal. Noiselessly, I slid my trembling hand along the wall, feeling for the knife holder. Choosing a bread knife, I wrapped my fingers around the handle, pointed the blade backward, and dropped my arm into full extension.

Slowly, testing with one bare foot at a time, I tiptoed forward far enough to see into the living room. It was as dark as the bedroom and kitchen.

I made out Birdie in the gloom. He was sitting a few feet from the doors, his eyes fixed on something beyond the glass. The tip of his tail twitched back and forth in jittery little arcs. He looked tense as an unshot arrow.

Another clunk-rattle stopped my heart and froze my breath. It came from outside. Birdie's ears went horizontal.

Five tremorous steps brought me alongside Birdie. Unconsciously, I reached out to pat his head. He recoiled at the unexpected touch and went tearing across the room with such force that his claws left divots in the carpet. They looked like small, black commas in the murky darkness. If a cat could be said to scream, Birdie did it.

His flight totally unnerved me. For a moment I was paralyzed, frozen in place like an Easter Island statue.

Do like the cat and get yourself out of here! the voice of panic told me.

I took a step backward. Clunk. Rattle. I stopped, clutching the knife as if it were a lifeline. Silence. Blackness. Da-dum. Da-dum. I listened to my heartbeat, searching my mind for a sector still able to think critically.

If someone is in the apartment, it told me, he is behind you. Your escape route is forward, not backward. But if someone is just outside, don't provide him with a way in.

Da-dum. Da-dum.

The noise is outside, I argued. What Birdie heard is outside.

Da-dum. Da-dum.

Take a look. Flatten yourself against the wall next to the courtyard doors and move the curtains just enough to peer outside. Maybe you can see a shape in the darkness.

Reasonable logic.

Armed with my Chicago Cutlery, I unglued one foot from the carpet, inched forward, and reached the wall. Breathing deeply, I moved the curtain a few inches. The shapes and shadows in the yard were poorly defined but recognizable. The tree, the bench, some bushes. Nothing identifiable as movement, except for branches pushed by wind. I held my position for a long moment. Nothing changed. I moved toward the center of the curtains and tested the door handle. Still locked.

Knife at the ready, I sidled along the wall toward the main entrance door. Toward the security system. The warning light glowed evenly, indicating no breach. On impulse I pressed the test button.

A noise split the silence, and despite my anticipating it, I jumped. My hand jerked upward, bringing the knife into readiness.

Stupid! the functioning brain fragment told me. The security system is operating and it hasn't been breached! Nothing has been opened! No one has entered.

Then he's out there! I responded, still quite shaken.

Maybe, said my brain, but that's not so bad. Turn on some lights, show some activity, and any prowler with sense will beat it out of here.

I tried to swallow, but my mouth was too dry. In a gesture of bravado, I switched on the hall light rapidly followed by every light between there and my bedroom. No intruders anywhere. As I sat on the edge of my bed holding the knife I heard it again. A muffled clunk, rattle. I jumped and almost cut myself.

Emboldened by my conviction that no intruder was inside, I thought, All right you bastard, let me catch just one glimpse, and I'm gonna call the cops.

I moved back to the French doors adjacent to the side yard, quickly this time. That room was still unlit, and I moved the curtain edge once more and peered out, bolder than before.

The scene was the same. Vaguely familiar shapes, some moved by the wind. Clunk, rattle! I started involuntarily, then thought, That noise is back from the doors, not at the doors.

I remembered the side yard floodlight, and moved to find the switch. This was no time to worry about annoying the neighbors. With the light on I returned to my curtain edge. The floodlight was not powerful, but it displayed the yard's features well enough.

The rain had stopped but a breeze had picked up. A fine mist danced in the beam of the light. I listened for a while. Nothing. I scanned my available field of vision several times. Nothing. Recklessly, I deactivated the security system, opened the French door, and stuck my head outside.

To the left, against the wall, the black spruce lived up to its name, but no foreign shape mingled with its branches. The wind gusted slightly, and the branches moved. Clunk. Rattle. A new surge of fright.

The gate. The noise was coming from the gate. My gaze whipped to it in time to catch a slight movement as it settled into place. As I watched, the wind surged again and the gate moved slightly within the boundaries of its latch. Clunk. Rattle.

Chagrined, I marched into the yard and up to the gate. Why had I never noticed that sound? Then I flinched once more. The lock was gone. The padlock that prevented any movement of the latch was missing. Had Winston neglected to replace it after cutting the grass? He must have.

I gave the gate a sharp shove to secure the latch as tightly as I could and turned back toward the door. Then I heard the other sound, more delicate and muffled.

Looking toward it, I saw a foreign object in my herb garden. Like a pumpkin impaled on a stick coming out of the ground. The wispy rustle was that of a plastic covering, moved by the wind.

A horrifying realization overtook me. Without knowing why I knew, I sensed what was beneath that plastic cover. My legs trembled as I crossed the grass and yanked the plastic upward.

At the sight, nausea overcame me and I turned to retch. Wiping my hand across my mouth, I charged back inside, slammed and locked the door, and reset my security alarm.

I fumbled for a number, lurched to the phone, and

willed myself to punch the correct buttons. The call was answered on the fourth ring.

"Get over here, please. Right now!"

"Brennan?" Groggy. "What the f–"

"This goddamn minute, Ryan! *Now!*"

24

A gallon of tea later I was curled in Birdie's rocker, dully observing Ryan. He was on his third call, this one personal, assuring someone he'd be a while. Judging by his end, the call's recipient wasn't happy. Tough.

Hysteria has its rewards. Ryan had arrived within twenty minutes. He searched the apartment and yard, then contacted the CUM to arrange for a patrol unit to stake out the building. Ryan had placed the bag and its grisly contents into another, larger bag, sealed it, and put it in a corner of the dining room floor. He would take it to the morgue tonight. The recovery team would come in the morning. We were in the living room, me sitting and sipping tea, Ryan pacing and talking.

I wasn't sure which had the more calming effect, the tea or Ryan. Probably not the tea. What I really wanted was a serious drink. Want didn't really describe it. Crave came closer. Actually, I wanted many drinks. A bottle I could pour from until there was no more. Forget it, Brennan. The cap's on and it's going to stay on.

I sipped my tea and watched Ryan. He wore jeans and a faded denim shirt. Good choice. The blues lit his eyes like colorizing on old film. He finished his calls and sat down.

287

"That should do it," he said, tossing the phone onto the couch and running a hand over his face. His hair was disheveled and he looked tired. But, then, I probably didn't look like Claudia Schiffer.

Do what? I wondered.

"I appreciate your coming," I said. "I'm sorry I over-reacted." I'd already said this, but repeated myself.

"No. You didn't."

"I don't usually—"

"It's okay. We're going to get this psycho."

"I could've just—"

He leaned forward and rested his elbows on his knees. The blue lasers grabbed my eyes and held them. A fleck of lint rode one of his lashes, like a pollen grain clinging to a pistil.

"Brennan, this is serious. There's a guy out there that's some sort of mental mutant. He's psychologically malformed. He's like the rats that tunnel under garbage heaps and slink through sewer pipes in this city. He's a predator. His wiring's twisted, and now he's fed you into whatever degenerate nightmare he's spinning for himself. But he's made a mistake, and we're going to flush him out and squash him. That's what you do with vermin."

The intensity of his response startled me. I could think of nothing to say. Pointing out his mixed metaphors seemed unwise.

He took my silence for skepticism.

"I mean it, Brennan. This asshole has dog food for brains. Which means you can't pull any more of your stunts."

His comment turned me churlish, a swing that didn't need much of a push. I was feeling vulnerable and dependent and hating myself for it, so I turned my frustration on him.

"Stunts?" I spat at him.

288

"Shit, Brennan, I don't mean tonight."

We both knew what he did mean. He was right, which increased my annoyance and made me even more contentious. I swirled my tea, now cold, and held my silence.

"This animal's obviously been stalking you," he drummed on, persistent as a jackhammer. "He knows where you live. He knows how to get in."

"He didn't really get in."

"He planted a goddamn human head in your back-yard!"

"I know!" I screamed, my composure developing a major fault line.

My eyes slid to the dining room corner. The thing from the garden lay there, silent and inert, an artifact waiting to be processed. It could have been anything. A volleyball. A globe. A melon. The round object in its shiny black bag looked harmless inside the clear plastic into which Ryan had sealed it.

I stared at it, and images of the grisly contents washed over my mind. I saw the skull rising on its scrawny, picket neck. I saw empty orbits staring straight ahead and pink neon glinting off the white enamel in the gaping mouth. I imagined the intruder cutting the lock and boldly crossing the yard to plant his gruesome memento.

"I know," I repeated, "you're right. I'll have to be more careful."

I swirled my cup again, looking for answers in the leaves.

"Want some tea?"

"No. I'm fine." He got up. "I'll check to see if the unit's here."

He disappeared into the back of the apartment, and I made myself another cup. I was still in the kitchen when he returned.

289

"There's one unit parked in the alley across the street. There'll be another one around back. I'll check with them when I leave. No one should be able to get near this building without being seen."

"Thanks." I took a sip and leaned against the counter.

He took out a pack of du Maurier's and raised his eyebrows at me.

"Sure."

I hated smoke in the apartment. But, then, he probably hated being there. Life is compromise. I thought about searching out my one ashtray, but didn't bother. He smoked and I sipped without speaking, leaning against the counter, each lost in thought. The refrigerator hummed.

"You know, it wasn't really the skull that freaked me. I'm used to skulls. It was just so . . . so out of context."

"Yeah."

"It's a cliché, I know, but I feel so violated. Like some alien creature breached my personal space, rooted about, and left when he lost interest in anything more."

I gripped the mug tightly, feeling vulnerable and hating it. Also feeling stupid. He'd no doubt heard some version of that speech many times. If so, he didn't mention it.

"Do you think it's St. Jacques?"

He looked at me, then flicked his ash into the sink. Leaning back against the counter, he took a deep pull. His legs stretched almost to the refrigerator.

"I don't know. Hell, we can't even pin down who it is we rousted. St. Jacques is probably an alias. Whoever was using that shithole probably didn't really live there. Turns out the landlady only saw him twice. We've staked the place for a week, and no one's gone in or out."

Hummm. Pull, exhale. Swirl.

290

"He had my picture in his collection. He'd cut it out and marked it."

"Yep."

"Be straight with me."

He paused a minute, then, "He'd be my pick. Coincidence is just too improbable."

I knew it, but didn't want to hear it. Even more, I didn't want to think about what it meant. I gestured toward the skull.

"From the body we found in St. Lambert?"

"Whoa, that's your country."

He took a last drag, ran tap water over the butt, and looked around for someplace to put it. I pushed off the counter and opened a cabinet containing a trash bag. As he raised up, I laid a hand on his forearm.

"Ryan, do you think I'm crazy? Do you think this serial killer idea is just in my head?"

He straightened and fixed his eyes on me.

"I don't know. I just don't know. You could be right. Four dead women over a two-year period who've all been sliced up or dismembered or both. Maybe a fifth. Maybe some similarities with the mutilation. The object insertion. But that's all. So far, no other tie. Maybe they're linked. Maybe they're not. Maybe there's a truckload of sadists out there operating independently. Maybe St. Jacques did all of them. Maybe he just likes to collect stories about the exploits of others. Maybe it's only one person, but that person is someone else. Maybe he's fantasizing his next outing right now. Maybe the bastard just planted a skull in your yard, maybe he didn't. I don't know. But I do know some sicko asshole parked a skull in your petunias tonight. Look, I don't want you taking chances. I want your word you'll be careful. No more expeditions."

Again the paternalism. "It was parsley."

"What?" The edge on his voice was sharp enough to

291

cut off any more flippant remarks.

"Just what *do* you want me to do?"

"For now, no more secret sorties." He hooked a thumb at the evidence bag. "And tell me who that is over there."

He looked at his watch.

"Christ. It's three-fifteen. You going to be all right?"

"Yes. Thanks for coming."

"Right."

He checked the phone and the security system again, collected the plastic bag, and I let him out the front. As I watched his retreat I couldn't help noticing that his eyes weren't the only feature the jeans showed off well. Brennan! Too much tea. Or too little of something else.

At exactly four twenty-seven the nightmare started again. At first I thought I was dreaming, replaying earlier events. But I'd never really fallen asleep. I'd been lying there, urging myself to relax, allowing my thoughts to fragment and reassemble like shapes in a kaleidoscope. But the sound I now heard was present and real. I recognized what it was and what it meant. The beep of the security alarm told me a door or window had been opened. The intruder was back and had gotten inside.

My heart rate launched into orbit and I felt the fear return, first suffocating and paralyzing, then triggering a rush of adrenaline that left me alert but uncertain. What to do? Fight? Flight? My fingers gripped the edge of the blanket, and my mind flew in a thousand directions. How had he gotten past the police units? Which room was he in? The knife! It was on the kitchen counter! I lay there, rigid, gauging options. Ryan had checked the phones, but I wanted to sleep undisturbed and had unplugged the one in the bedroom. Could I find the cord, locate the little triangular plug, and make a call before being overpowered? Where had Ryan said the

292

police cars were parked? If I threw open the bedroom window and screamed, could the police hear me and react in time?

I strained to hear every movement in the darkness around me. There! A soft click. In the entrance hall? I stopped breathing. My front teeth clamped my lower lip.

A scrape against the marble floor. Near the entrance hall. Could it be Birdie? No, this sound had weight behind it. Again! A gentle brushing, as though against a wall, not the floor. Too high for a cat.

An image from Africa jumped into my head. A night drive in the Amboseli. A leopard, frozen in the jeep headlights, crouched, muscles taut, nostrils sucking the night air, soundlessly closing in on the unsuspecting gazelle. Was my stalker similarly in command of the darkness, picking a deliberate path to my bedroom? Cutting off escape routes? What was he doing? Why had he come back? What should I do? Something! Don't lie there and wait. Do something!

The phone! I'd try for the phone. There were police units right outside. The dispatcher would reach them. Could I reach it without giving myself away? Did it really matter?

Slowly, I raised the blankets and rolled flat on my back. The rustling of the sheets sounded like thunder in my ears.

Something brushed the wall again. Louder. Closer. As if the intruder was more sure of himself, less inclined to be cautious.

Every muscle and tendon tense, I inched toward the left side of the bed. The pitch black of the room made it hard to get my bearings. Why had I drawn the shade? Why had I unplugged that phone for a little extra sleep? Stupid. Stupid. Stupid. Find the cord, find the plug, punch 911 in the dark. I made a mental inventory of the objects on the nightstand, mapping the route my hand would take. I would have to slide down to the floor to reach the telephone jack.

At the left side of the bed, I raised onto my elbows. My eyes probed the darkness, but it was too deep to distinguish features except for the bedroom door. It was faintly backlit by some appliance with a glowing dial. There was no silhouette in the doorway.

Encouraged, I eased my left leg clear of the bed and slowly, blindly, groped for the floor. Then a shadow crossed the doorway, freezing my leg in midair and locking my muscles in catatonic fear.

This is the end, I thought. In my own bed. Alone. Four cops outside, oblivious. I pictured the other women, their bones, their faces, their gutted bodies. The plunger. The statue. No! screamed a voice in my head. Not me. Please. Not me. How many screams could I manage before he was on me? Before he silenced them with one sweep of his blade across my throat? Enough to alert the police outside?

My eyes darted back and forth, frantic, like those of an animal in a trap. A dark mass filled the doorway. A human figure. I lay speechless, motionless, unable even to launch my final screams.

The figure hesitated, as though uncertain of its next move. No features. Only a silhouette framed in the entrance. The only entrance. The only exit. God! Why didn't I keep a gun?

Seconds dragged by. Maybe the figure could not make out my outline on the very edge of the bed. Maybe the room looked empty from the doorway. Did he have a flashlight? Would he turn on the wall switch?

My mind snapped out of its paralysis. What had they taught in self-defense class? Run if you can. I can't. If cornered, fight to win. Bite. Gouge. Kick. Hurt him! First rule: Don't let him get on top! Second rule: Never

294

let him pin you down! Yes. Surprise him. If I could get to any exit door, the cops outside could save me.

My left foot was already on the floor. Still on my back, I eased my right leg toward the edge of the bed, millimeter by millimeter, pivoting on my buttocks. I had both feet on the floor when the figure made a jerky motion and I was blinded by the glare of light.

My hand flew to my eyes and I lurched forward in a desperate effort to knock the figure aside and escape the bedroom. My right foot caught the sheet, sending me headlong onto the carpet. I rolled quickly to my left and scrambled on to my knees, turning to face my attacker. Third rule: Never turn your back.

The figure remained on the far side of the room, hand on the light switch. Only now it had a face. A face distorted by some inner turmoil at which I could only guess. A face I knew. My own face was fast forwarding through a series of expressions. Terror. Recognition. Confusion. Our eyes locked and held. Neither moved. Neither spoke. We stared at each other across the air in my bedroom.

I screamed.

"Goddamn you, Gabby! You stupid bitch! What are you doing? What have I done to you? You bitch! You goddamn bitch!"

I sat back on my heels, hands on my thighs, making no attempt to control the tears bathing my face or the sobs racking my body.

25

I rocked back and forth from my knees to heels, sobbing and shouting. My words made little sense and when mingled with the sobbing became incoherent. I knew the voice was mine, but I had no power to stop it. Gibberish I didn't recognize flew from my mouth as I rocked and sobbed and shrieked.

Soon the sobbing won out over the shrieking and receded to a muffled sucking sound. With one last shudder, I stopped my rocking and focused on Gabby. She, too, was crying.

She stood across the room, one hand clutching the light switch, the other pressed to her chest. Her fingers twitched open then closed. Her chest heaved with each intake of breath, and tears ran down her face. She wept silently, and seemed frozen in place except for that one clutching hand.

"Gabby?" My voice broke, and it came out "–by?"

She gave a tight nod, her dreadlocks bobbing about her ashen face. She started making little sucking sounds, as if trying to pull back her tears. Speech seemed beyond her capabilities.

"Jesus Christ, Gabby! Are you crazy?" I whispered, reasonably controlled. "What are you doing here? Why didn't you call?"

She seemed to consider the second question, but attempted to answer the first.

"I needed to . . . talk to you."

I just stared at her. I'd been trying to find this woman for three weeks. She'd avoided me. It was four-thirty in the morning, she'd just broken into my home, and aged me at least a decade.

"How did you get in here?"

"I still have a key." More gulping sounds, but quieter, slower. "From last summer."

She moved a trembling hand from the light switch and displayed a key dangling from a small chain.

I felt anger rising in me, but my exhaustion held it in check.

"Not tonight, Gabby."

"Tempe, I . . ."

I gave her a look intended to freeze her in place once more. She stared back, not comprehending, plaintive.

"Tempe, I can't go home."

Her eyes were dark and round, her body rigid. She looked like an antelope cut from the herd and cornered. A very large antelope, but terrified nonetheless.

Wordlessly, I pushed to my feet, got towels and linens from the hall closet and dropped them on the guest room bed.

"We'll talk in the morning, Gabby."

"Tempe, I . . ."

"In the morning."

As I fell asleep I thought I heard her dial the phone. It didn't matter. Tomorrow.

And talk we did. For hours and hours. Over bowls of cornflakes and plates of spaghetti. Sipping endless cappuccinos. We talked curled on the couch and on long walks up and down Ste. Catherine. It was a weekend of

297

words, most of them pouring from Gabby. At first I was convinced she had come unglued. By Sunday night I wasn't so sure.

The recovery team came by late Friday morning. In deference to me, they called ahead, arrived without fanfare, and worked quickly and efficiently. They accepted Gabby's presence as a natural development. The comfort of a friend after a night of fright. I told Gabby there had been an intruder in the garden, leaving out mention of the head. She had enough on her mind. The team left with encouraging words. "Don't worry, Dr. Brennan. We'll get the bastard. You hang in there."

Gabby's situation was as harrowing as mine. Her former informant had become her stalker. He was everywhere. Sometimes she'd see him on a bench in the park. Other times he'd follow her on the street. At night he'd hang around St. Laurent. Though she now refused to talk to him, he was always there. He kept his distance, but his eyes never left her. Twice she thought he'd been in her apartment.

I said, "Gabby, are you sure?" I meant, Gabby are you losing it?

"Did he take anything?"

"No. At least, I don't think so. Nothing I've noticed. But I know he went through my things. You know how you can tell. Nothing was gone, but things were a bit off. Just sort of rotated in place."

"Why didn't you return my calls?"

"I stopped answering the phone. It rang a dozen times a day and no one would be on the other end. Same with the answering machine. Lots of hang-ups. I just stopped using it."

"Why didn't you call me?"

"And say what? I'm being stalked? I've made myself a victim? I can't handle my own life? I thought if I treated him like the maggot he is he'd lose interest.

298

Slither away and pupate somewhere else."

Her eyes looked tortured.

"And I knew what you'd say. You're losing it, Gabby. You're letting your paranoia control you, Gabby. You need help, Gabby."

I felt a stab of guilt, remembering the way I'd hung up with her last. She was right.

"You could have called the police. They'd give you protection." Even as I said it I didn't believe it.

"Right." And then she told me about Thursday night.

"I got home about 3:30 A.M. and I could tell someone had entered the apartment. I'd used the old trick of stretching a thread across the lock. Well, seeing it gone totally unnerved me. I had been in a pretty good mood since I hadn't seen the creep all night. Also, I'd just had the locks changed, so I was feeling secure about the apartment for the first time in months. Seeing that thread on the floor just destroyed me. I couldn't believe he'd gotten in again. I didn't know if he was still inside and I didn't want to find out. I bolted and came here."

Bit by bit she talked of the past three weeks, recounting incidents as they came into her head. As her narrative unfolded over the weekend, my mind rearranged the disjointed episodes into a chronology. Though the man harassing her had done nothing overtly aggressive, I saw a pattern of increasing boldness. By Sunday I began to share her fear.

We decided she would stay with me for the time being, though I wasn't so sure what score my place would earn in a safety check. Late Friday Ryan had called to tell me the patrol unit would be there through Monday. I'd nod to them as we set out on our walks. Gabby thought they were a response to the garden intruder. I didn't suggest otherwise. I needed to bolster her newborn sense of safety, not wreck it.

I suggested we contact the police about her stalker,

but she adamantly refused, fearing their involvement would compromise her girls. I also suspected she was afraid of losing their trust and her access to them. Reluctantly, I agreed.

On Monday I left her and went to work. She planned to gather some things from her apartment. She'd agreed to stay off the Main for a while, and meant to spend time writing. For that she needed her laptop and files.

When I got to my office it was past nine. Ryan had already phoned. The scrawled message read: "Got a name. AR." He was out when I returned his call, so I went to the histo lab to check on my garden memento.

It was drying on the counter, cleaned and marked, the absence of soft tissue having made boiling unnecessary. It looked like a thousand other skulls, with its empty orbits and neatly penned LML number. I stared at it, recalling the terror it had triggered three nights earlier.

"Location. Location. Location," I said to the empty lab.

"Pardon?"

I hadn't heard Denis come in.

"Something a realtor once told me."

"*Oui?*"

"It isn't *what* something is, so much as *where* it is that often shapes our reaction."

He looked blank.

"Never mind. You took soil samples before you washed this?"

"*Oui.*" He held up two small plastic vials.

"Let's get them over to trace."

He nodded.

"Have X rays been done?"

"*Oui.* I just gave the bitewings and apicals to Dr. Bergeron."

"He's here on a Monday?"

300

"He's going on holiday for two weeks so he came to finish some reports."

"Happy day." I put the skull in a plastic tub. "Ryan thinks he's got a name."

"Ah, *oui?*" His eyebrows shot up.

"He must have been up with the birds today. The message was taken by the night service."

"For the St. Lambert skeleton or for your chum there?"

He indicated the skull. Apparently the story had already made the rounds.

"Maybe both. I'll let you know."

I headed for my office, stopping by Bergeron's on the way. He'd spoken with Ryan. The detective had found a missing person match promising enough to request a *mandat du coroner* for the antemortem records, and was on his way.

"Know anything about her?"

"*Rien.*" Nothing.

"I'll finish with the skull before lunch. If you need it, just come by."

I spent the next two hours assessing the sex, race, and age of the skull. I observed features of the face and braincase, took measurements, and ran discriminant functions on my computer. We agreed. The skull was that of a white female. Like the St. Lambert skeleton.

Age was frustrating. All I had to go on was closure of the cranial sutures, a notoriously untrustworthy system for evaluating age. The computer couldn't help. I estimated she'd been in her late twenties to mid-thirties when she died. Maybe forty. Again, consistent with the bones from St. Lambert.

I looked for other indicators of congruity. Overall size. Robusticity of muscle attachments. Degree of arthritic change. Condition of the bone. State of preser-

301

vation. Everything matched. I was convinced this was the head missing from the Monastère St. Bernard skeleton, but I needed more. Then I turned the skull over and examined the base.

Coursing across the occipital bone, close to the point where the skull sits on the vertebral column, I could see a series of slashes. They were V-shaped in cross-section and ran from high to low, following the contour of the bone. Under the Luxolamp they looked similar to the marks I'd observed on the long bones. I wanted to be sure.

I took the skull back to the histo lab, set it next to the operating scope, and got out the headless skeleton. I withdrew the sixth cervical vertebra, placed it under the scope, and reexamined the cuts I'd described the week before. Then I switched to the skull, focusing on the gashes scoring its back and base. The marks were identical, the contours and cross-sectional dimensions matching perfectly.

"Grace Damas."

I switched off the fiber-optic light and turned toward the voice.

"*Qui?*"

"Grace Damas," repeated Bergeron. "Age thirty-two. According to Ryan, she went missing in February of '92."

I calculated. Two years and four months. "That fits. Anything else?"

"I really didn't ask. Ryan said he'd stop in after lunch. He's tracking something else down."

"Does he know the ID's positive?"

"Not yet. I just finished." He looked at the bones. "Anything?"

"They're a match. I wanted to see what the trace evidence folks have to say about the soil samples. Maybe we can get a pollen profile. But I'm convinced. Even the cut marks are the same. I wish I had the upper neck vertebrae, but it's not critical."

Grace Damas. All through lunch the name echoed in my head. Grace Damas. Number five. Or was it? How many more would we find? Each of the names was burned into my mind, like a brand on a heifer's rump. Morisette-Champoux. Trottier. Gagnon. Adkins. Now another. Damas.

At one-thirty Ryan came to my office. Bergeron had already given him the positive on the skull. I told him it was good for the skeleton as well.

"What do you know about her?" I asked.

"She was thirty-two. Three kids."

"Christ."

"Good mother. Faithful wife. Active in the church." He glanced at his notes. "St. Demetrius, over on Hutchinson. Near Avenue du Parc and Fairmont. Sent the kids off to school one day. Never seen again."

"Husband?"

"Looks clean."

"Boyfriend?"

He shrugged. "It's a very traditional Greek family. If you don't talk about it, those things can't be true. She was a good girl. Lived for her husband. They've got a friggin' shrine set up for her in the living room." Another shrug. "Maybe she was a saint. Maybe she wasn't. We're not going to find out from Mama or Hubby. It's like talking to barnacles. You mention hanky-panky, they pull in and slam shut."

I told him about the cut marks.

"Same as Trottier. And Gagnon."

"Hm."

"Hands were cut off. Like Gagnon, and one each for Morisette-Champoux and Trottier."

"Hm."

When he'd gone I turned on the computer and pulled

303

up my spreadsheet. I erased *"Inconnue"* from the name column and typed in Grace Damas, then entered the scanty information Ryan had given me. In a separate file I summarized what I knew about each of the women, arranging them by date of death.

Grace Damas had disappeared in February of 1992. She was thirty-two, married, the mother of three. She lived in the near northeast part of the city, in an area known as Parc Extension. Her body had been dismembered and buried in a shallow grave at the St. Bernard Monastery in St. Lambert, where it was found in June of 1994. Her head showed up in my garden several days later. Cause of death was unknown.

Francine Morisette-Champoux was beaten and shot in January of 1993. She was forty-seven. Her body was found less than two hours later, just south of Centreville, in the condo she shared with her husband. Her killer had slit her belly, cut off her right hand, and forced a knife into her vagina.

Chantale Trottier disappeared in October of 1993. She was sixteen. She lived with her mother off the island, in the lake community of Ste. Anne-de-Bellevue. She'd been beaten, strangled, and dismembered, her right hand partially severed, her left one completely detached. Her body was found two days later in St. Jerome.

Isabelle Gagnon disappeared in April of 1994. She'd lived with her brother in St. Édouard. In June of this year her dismembered body was found on the grounds of Le Grand Séminaire in Centre-ville. Though cause of death could not be determined, marks on her bones indicated she'd been dismembered, her belly slit. Her hands had been removed, and her killer had inserted a plunger in her vagina. She was twenty-three.

Margaret Adkins was killed on June 23, just over a week ago. She was twenty-four, had one son, and lived

304

with her common-law husband. She'd been beaten to death. Her belly was slit and one breast had been sliced off and forced into her mouth. A metal statue had been rammed up her vagina.

Claudel was right. There was no pattern in MO. They were all beaten, but Morisette-Champoux was also shot. Trottier was strangled. Adkins was bludgeoned. Hell, we didn't even have a cause for Damas and Gagnon.

I went over and over what had been done to each of them. There was variation, but there was also a theme. Sadistic cruelty and mutilation. It had to be one person. One monster. Damas, Gagnon, and Trottier were dismembered and dumped in plastic bags. Their bellies had been slit. Gagnon and Trottier had had their hands severed. Morisette-Champoux was slashed and had a hand cut off, but she wasn't dismembered. Adkins, Gagnon, and Morisette-Champoux had suffered genital penetration with a foreign object. The others hadn't. Adkins's breast was mutilated. No one else was disfigured in that way. Or were they? There hadn't been enough of Damas and Gagnon to say.

I stared at the screen. It has to be here, I told myself. Why can't I see it? What's the link? Why these women? Their ages are up and down the charts. It's not that. They're all white. Big deal, this is Canada. Francophone. Anglophone. Allophone. Married. Single. Common law. Choose another category. Let's try geography.

I got out a map and plotted where each of the bodies had been found. It made even less sense than when I'd done it with Ryan. Now there were five points in the scatter. I tried plotting their homes. The pins looked like paint flung at a canvas by an abstract artist. There was no pattern.

What did you expect, Brennan, an arrow pointing to a flat on Sherbrooke? Forget place. Try time.

305

I looked at the dates. Damas was the first. In early 1992. I calculated in my head. Eleven months between Damas and Morisette-Champoux. Nine months later, Trottier. Six months to Gagnon. Two months between Gagnon and Adkins.

The intervals were decreasing. Either the killer was growing bolder, or his blood lust was growing stronger. My heart pounded hard against my ribs as I considered the implication. Over a week had passed since Margaret Adkins died.

26

I felt trapped inside my skin. Anxious and frustrated. The visions in my head annoyed me, but I couldn't turn them off. I watched a candy wrapper dance on the wind outside my window, tossed by puffs of shifting air.

That piece of paper is you, Brennan, I chided myself. Can't control your own fate, much less anyone else's. There's nothing on St. Jacques. No word on who put the skull in your yard. Gabby's nut case is still out there. Claudel is probably lodging a complaint against you. Your daughter is about to drop out of school. And five dead women are living in your head, and likely to be joined by a sixth or seventh at the rate your investigation is going.

I looked at my watch – 2:15 P.M. I couldn't stand my office another minute. I had to do something.

But what?

I glanced at Ryan's incident report. An idea began to form.

They'll be furious, I told myself.

Yes.

I checked the report. The address was there. I pulled up my spreadsheet on the computer screen. They were all there, along with the phone numbers.

You would do better to go to the gym and work off your frustration there.

Yes.

Solo sleuthing won't help the situation with Claudel.

No.

You may lose Ryan's support.

True.

Tough.

I printed the data from the screen, made a choice, and dialed. A man answered on the third ring. He was surprised but agreed to see me. Grabbing my purse, I fled into the summer sunshine.

It was hot again, the air so thick with humidity you could take your finger and write your initials in it. The haze refracted the sun's glare and spread it all around like a cloak. I drove toward the home Francine Morisette-Champoux had shared with her husband. I'd chosen her case for no other reason than proximity. She had lived just below Centre-ville, not ten minutes from my condo. If I bombed, well, I was on my way home.

I found the address and pulled to a stop. The street was lined with brick town houses, each with its iron balcony, below-ground garage, and brightly colored door.

Unlike most communities in Montreal, this one had no name. Urban renewal had transformed what had been part of the Canadian National yards, replacing tracks and toolsheds with residences, barbecue grills, and tomato plants. The neighborhood was neat and middle class, but suffered from an identity crisis. It was too close to the city core to be truly suburban, but just a hair outside the arc defining trendy downtown. It wasn't old and it wasn't new. Functional and convenient, it lacked bouquet.

I rang the bell and waited. Fresh-cut grass and ripe garbage tinged the hot air. Two doors down a sprinkler arced water across a Chiclet-sized lawn. A central air

308

compressor hummed to life, its sound challenging the sprinkler's steady click.

When he opened the door I thought of the Gerber baby grown up. His hair was blond and receding, the center patch swirling into a curl on his forehead. His cheeks and chin were round and padded, his nose short and angled upward. He was a large man, not yet gone to fat, but moving down that road. Though it was ninety degrees, he wore jeans and a sweatshirt. Calgary Stampede – 1985.

"Monsieur Champoux, I'm . . ."

He pulled the door wide and stepped back, ignoring the ID I held for his inspection. I followed him down a narrow hall to a narrow living room. Fish tanks lined one wall, tinting the room an eerie aquamarine. At the far end I could see a counter stacked with small nets, boxes of food, and other fish paraphernalia. Louvered doors opened onto the kitchen. I recognized the kitchen work island and looked away.

Monsieur Champoux cleared a spot on the sofa and indicated I should sit. He dropped into a recliner.

"Monsieur Champoux," I began again, "I'm Dr. Brennan from the Laboratoire de Médecine Légale."

I left it at that, hoping to avoid further explanations about my precise role in the investigation. I didn't really have any.

"Have you found something? I . . . It's been so long I don't let myself think about it anymore." He spoke to the parquet floor. "It's been a year and a half since Francine died, and I haven't heard from you people in over a year."

I wondered where he thought I fit in with "you people."

"I answered so many questions, talked to so many people. The coroner. The cops. The press. I even hired my own investigator. I really wanted to nail this guy.

Didn't do any good. They never found a clue. We can pinpoint the time he killed her to within an hour, you know. The coroner said she was still warm. This maniac kills my wife, walks out, and disappears without a trace." He shook his head in disbelief. "Have you finally got something?"

His eyes held a mixture of anguish and hope. Guilt sliced to my core.

"No, Monsieur Champoux, not really." Except four other women may have been killed by the same animal. "I just want to go over a few details, see if there's anything we overlooked."

The hope vanished and resignation surfaced. He leaned back in his chair and waited.

"Your wife was a nutritionist?"

He nodded.

"Where did she work?"

"All over, really. She was paid by the MAS, but on any given day she could have been anywhere."

"The MAS?"

"Ministère des Affaires Sociales."

"She moved around?"

"Her job was to advise food cooperatives, immigrant groups mostly, about how to buy stuff. She'd help them form these collective kitchens, then teach them how to make whatever it is they like to eat so it would be cheap, but still healthy. She'd help them get produce and meat and things. Usually in bulk. She was always visiting the kitchens to be sure they were running okay."

"Where were these collectives?"

"All over the place. Parc Extension. Côtes des Neiges. St. Henri. Little Burgundy."

"How long had she been working for the MAS?"

"Maybe six, seven years. Before that she worked at the Montreal General. Had much better hours."

"Did she enjoy her work?"

310

"Oh yeah. She loved it." The words caught briefly in his throat.

"Were her hours irregular?"

"No, they were regular. She worked all the time. Mornings. Evenings. Weekends. There was always a problem and Francine was the one to fix it." His jaw muscles clenched and unclenched.

"Had you and your wife disagreed about her work?"

He fell silent for a moment. Then, "I wanted to see more of her. I wished she was still at the hospital."

"What do you do, Monsieur Champoux?"

"I'm an engineer. I build things. Only no one wants much built these days." He gave a mirthless smile and tipped his head to one side. "I was downsized." He used the English phrase.

"I'm sorry."

"Do you know where your wife was going the day she was killed?"

He shook his head. "We'd hardly seen each other that week. There was a fire in one of her kitchens and she'd been there day and night. She may have been going back there, or she may have been heading for another one. She didn't keep any kind of journal or log that I know of. They never found one in her office and I never saw one here. She'd been talking about getting her hair cut. Hell, she may have been going to do that."

He looked at me, his eyes tortured.

"Do you know what that feels like? I don't even know what my wife was planning to do on the day she died."

The circulating water of the tanks murmured softly in the background.

"Had she spoken about anything unusual? Odd phone calls? A stranger at the door?" I thought of Gabby. "Someone on the street?"

Another head shake.

"Would she have?"

"Probably, if we'd spoken. We really hadn't had time those last few days."

I tried a new tack.

"It was January. Cold. The doors and windows would have been closed. Was your wife in the habit of keeping them locked?"

"Yes. She never liked living here, didn't like being right on the street. I talked her into buying this place, but she preferred high-rise buildings with security systems or guards. We get some pretty seedy characters down here, and she was always on edge. That's why we were leaving. She liked the extra space, and the little yard out back, but she never really got used to being here. Her work took her to some rough areas, and when she came home she wanted to feel safe. Untouchable. That's what she said. Untouchable. You know?"

Yes. Oh yes.

"When was the last time you saw your wife, Monsieur Champoux?"

He breathed deeply, exhaled. "She got killed on a Thursday. She'd worked late the night before, because of the fire, so I'd already gone to bed when she got home."

He dropped his head and talked again to the parquet. A patch of tiny vessels colored each of his cheeks.

"She came to bed full of her day, trying to tell me where she'd been and what she'd been doing. I didn't want to hear it."

I saw his chest rise and fall under the sweatshirt.

"The next day I got up early and left. Didn't even say good-bye."

We were quiet a moment.

"That's what I did and there's no way out. I don't get another shot." He raised his eyes and stared into the turquoise of the tanks. "I resented her working when I couldn't, so I froze her out. Now I live with it."

Before I could think of a response he turned to me, his face taut, his voice harder than it had been.

"I went to see my brother-in-law. He had some job leads for me. I was there all morning, then I fou– Then I came back here around noon. She was already dead. They checked all that out."

"Monsieur Champoux, I'm not suggesting y–"

"I don't see that this is going anywhere. We're just rehashing old words."

He rose. I was being dismissed.

"I'm sorry to bring up painful memories."

He regarded me without comment, then moved toward the hall. I followed.

"Thanks for your time, Monsieur Champoux." I handed him my card. "If there's anything you think of later, please give me a call."

He nodded. His face had the numbed look of a person swept into a calamity who can't forget that his last words and last acts toward the wife he loved were petty and far from a proper good-bye. Is there ever a proper good-bye?

As I left I could feel his eyes on my back. Through the heat I felt cold inside. I hurried to my car.

The interview with Champoux left me shaken. As I drove toward home, I asked myself a thousand questions.

What right had I to dredge up this man's pain?

I pictured Champoux's eyes.

Such sorrow. Brought on by my forced reminders?

No. I wasn't the architect of his house of regret. Champoux was a man living with remorse of his own construction.

Remorse for what? For harming his wife?

No. That was not his character.

Remorse for ignoring her. For leaving her thinking she was not important. Simple as that. On the eve of her

313

death, he rejected conversation, turned his back and went to sleep. He didn't say good-bye in the morning. Now he never would.

I turned north onto St. Marc, passing into the shadow of the overpass. Would my inquiries do anything but drag memories to the surface where they would again cause pain?

Could I really help where an army of professionals had failed, or was I just on a personal quest to show up Claudel?

"No!"

I banged the steering wheel with the heel of my hand.

No, dammit, I thought to myself. That is not my goal. No one but me is convinced that there is a single killer and that he will kill again. If I am to prevent more deaths, I have to dig up more facts.

I emerged from shadow into sunlight. Instead of turning east, toward home, I crossed Ste. Catherine, doubled back on Rue du Fort, and merged onto the 20 West. Locals called it the 2 and 20, but I'd yet to find anyone who could explain or locate the 2.

I edged out of the city, drumming my impatience on the steering wheel. It was three-thirty and traffic was already backed up at the Turcot Interchange. Bad timing.

Forty-five minutes later I found Geneviève Trottier weeding tomatoes behind the faded green house she had shared with her daughter. She looked up when I pulled onto the drive, and watched me cross the lawn.

"*Oui?*" Friendly, sitting back on her heels, squinting up at me.

She wore bright yellow shorts and a halter too big for her small breasts. Sweat glistened on her body and curled her hair tightly around her face. She was younger than I'd expected.

314

When I explained who I was and why I was there, the friendliness turned somber. She hesitated, put down her trowel, then rose, brushing dirt from her hands. The smell of tomatoes hung heavy around us.

"We'd better go inside," she said, dropping her eyes. Like Champoux she didn't question my right to ask.

She started across the yard and I followed, hating the conversation about to ensue. The knotted halter hung loose across the knobs of her spine. Blades of grass stuck to the backs of her legs and rode the tops of her feet.

Her kitchen gleamed in the afternoon sunlight, its porcelain and wood surfaces testimony to years of care. Potted kalanchoe lined the windows, framed by yellow gingham. Yellow knobs dotted the cabinets and drawers.

"I've made some lemonade," she said, her hands already moving to the task. Comfort in the familiar.

"Yes, thank you. That would be nice."

I sat at a scrubbed wooden table and watched her twist ice cubes from a plastic tray, drop them into glasses, and add the lemonade. She brought the drinks and slid in across from me, her eyes avoiding mine.

"It's hard for me to talk about Chantale," she said, studying her lemonade.

"I understand, and I am so sorry for your loss. How are you doing?"

"Some days it's easier than others."

She folded her hands and tensed, her thin shoulders rising under the halter.

"Have you come to tell me something?"

"I'm afraid not, Madame Trottier. And I don't really have any specific questions for you. I thought there might be something you've remembered, perhaps something you didn't think important earlier?"

Her eyes stayed on the lemonade. A dog barked outside.

"Has anything occurred to you since you last spoke

315

with the detectives? Any detail about the day Chantale disappeared?"

No response. The air in the kitchen was hot and dense with humidity. It smelled faintly of lemon disinfectant.

"I know this is awful for you, but if we're to have any hope of finding your daughter's killer, we still need your help. Is there anything that's been bothering you? Anything you've been thinking about?"

"We fought."

Again. The guilt of nonclosure. The wish to take back words and substitute others.

"She wouldn't eat. She thought she was getting fat."

I knew all this from the report.

"She wasn't fat. You should have seen her. She was beautiful. She was only sixteen." Her eyes finally met mine. A single tear spilled over each lower lid, and trickled down each cheek. "Like the English song."

"I'm so sorry," I said, gently as I could. Through the screened window I could smell sun on geraniums. "Was Chantale unhappy about anything?"

Her fingers tightened around her glass.

"That's what's so hard. She was such an easy child. Always happy. Always full of life, bubbling with plans. Even my divorce didn't seem to upset her. She took it in stride and never missed a step."

Truth or retrospective fantasy? I remembered the Trottiers had divorced when Chantale was nine. Her father was living somewhere in the city.

"Can you tell me anything about those last few weeks? Had Chantale altered her routine in any way? Had any odd calls? Made any new friends?"

Her head moved slowly in continuous negation. No.

"Did she have trouble making friends?"

No.

"Were you uneasy about any of her friends?"

316

No.

"Did she have a boyfriend?"

No.

"Did she date?"

No.

"Did she have problems at school?"

No.

Poor interrogation technique. Need to get the witness to do the talking instead of me.

"What about that day? The day Chantale disappeared?"

She looked at me, her eyes unreadable.

"Can you tell me what took place that day?"

She took a sip of lemonade, swallowed deliberately, set the glass back on the table. Deliberately.

"We got up around six. I made breakfast." She clutched the glass so tightly I feared it would shatter. "Chantale left for school. She and her friends rode the train since the school is in Centre-ville. They say she went to all her classes. And then she . . ."

A breeze teased the gingham off the window frame.

"She never came home."

"Did she have any special plans that day?"

"No."

"Did she normally come right home after classes?"

"Usually."

"Did you expect her home that day?"

"No. She was going to see her father."

"Did she do that often?"

"Yes. Why do I have to keep answering these questions? It's useless. I've told all this to the detectives. Why do I have to keep repeating the same things over and over? It doesn't do any good. It didn't then, it won't now."

Her eyes fixed on mine, the pain almost palpable.

"You know what? All the time I was filling out

317

missing persons forms and answering questions, Chantale was already dead. She was lying in pieces in a dump. Already dead."

She dropped her head and the thin shoulders shuddered. She was right. We had nothing. I was fishing. She was learning to bury the pain, to plant tomatoes and live, and I'd ambushed her and forced an exhumation.

Be kind. Get out.

"It's all right, Madame Trottier. If you can't remember further details, they are probably not important."

I left my card and standard request. Call if you think of anything. I doubted she would.

Gabby's door was closed when I got home, her room quiet. I thought of looking in, resisted. She could be so touchy about her privacy. I got into bed and tried to read, but Geneviève Trottier's words kept jamming my mind. *Déjà mort.* Already dead. Champoux had used the same phrase. Yes. Déjà dead. Five. That was the chilling truth. Like Champoux and Trottier, I too had thoughts that would not lie quiet in my mind.

27

I woke to the sound of the morning news. July 5. I'd slipped through Independence Day and not even noticed. No apple pie. No "Stars and Stripes Forever." Not a single sparkler. Somehow the thought depressed me. Every American anywhere on the globe should stand up and strut on the Fourth. I had allowed myself to become a Canadian spectator of American culture. I made plans to go to the ball park at the next opportunity and cheer for whichever American team was in town.

I showered, made coffee and toast, and scanned the *Gazette*. Endless talk of separation. What would happen to the economy? To aboriginals? To English speakers? The want ads embodied the fear. Everyone selling, no one buying. Maybe I should go home. What was I accomplishing here?

Brennan. Stow it. You're surly because you have to take the car in.

It was true. I hate errands. I hate the minutiae of making do in a techno-nation-state in the closing years of the second millennium. Passport. Driver's license. Work permit. Income tax. Rabies shot. Dry cleaning. Dental appointment. Pap smear. My pattern: put it off

319

until unavoidable. Today the car had to be serviced.

I am a daughter of America in my attitude toward the automobile. I feel incomplete without one, cut off and vulnerable. How will I escape an invasion? What if I want to leave the party early, or stay after the Métro stops? Go to the country? Haul a dresser? Gotta have wheels. But I am not a worshipper. I want a car that will start when I turn the key, get me where I want to go, keep doing it for at least a decade, and not require a lot of pampering.

Still no sounds from Gabby's room. Must be nice. I packed my gear and left.

The car was in the shop and I was on the Métro by nine. The morning rush was over, the railcar relatively empty. Bored, I grazed through the ads. See a play at Le Théâtre St. Denis. Improve your job skills at Le Collège O'Sullivan. Buy jeans at Guess, Chanel perfume at La Baie, color at Benetton.

My eyes drifted to the Métro map. Colored lines crossed like the wiring on a motherboard, white dots marked the stops.

I traced my route eastward along the green line from Guy-Concordia to Papineau. The orange line looped around the mountain, north-south on its eastern slope, east-west below the green line, then north-south again on the west side of the city. Yellow dived below the river, emerging on Île Ste. Hélène and at Longueuil on the south shore. At Berri-UQAM the orange and yellow lines crossed the green. Big dot. Major switching point.

The train hummed as it slithered through its underground tunnel. I counted my stops. Seven dots.

Compulsive, Brennan. Want to wash your hands?

My eyes moved north along the orange line, visualizing the changing landscape of the city. Berri-UQAM. Sherbrooke. Mount Royal. Eventually, Jean-Talon

320

near St. Édouard. Isabelle Gagnon had lived in that neighborhood.

Oh?

I looked for Margaret Adkins's neighborhood. Green line. Which station? Pie IX. I counted from Berri-UQAM. Six stops east.

How many was Gagnon? Back to orange. Six.

Tiny hairs tingled at the back of my neck.

Morisette-Champoux. Georges-Vanier Métro. Orange. Six stops west from Berri-UQAM.

Jesus.

Trottier? No. The Métro doesn't go to Ste. Anne-de-Bellevue.

Damas? Parc Extension. Close to the Laurier and Rosemont stations. Third and fourth stops from Berri-UQAM.

I stared at the map. Three victims lived exactly six stops from the Berri-UQAM station. Coincidence?

"Papineau," said a mechanical voice.

I grabbed my things and bolted onto the platform.

Ten minutes later I heard the phone as I unlocked my office door.

"Dr. Brennan."

"What the hell are you doing, Brennan?"

"Good morning, Ryan. What can I help you with?"

"Claudel's trying to nail my butt to the wall because of you. Says you've been running around bothering victims' families."

He waited for me to say something but I didn't.

"Brennan, I've been defending you because I respect you. But I can see what's shaping up here. Your prying could really hang me up on this case."

"I asked a few questions. That's not illegal." I did nothing to defuse his anger.

"You didn't tell anyone. You didn't coordinate. You

321

just went off knocking on doors." I could hear breath being drawn through nostrils. They sounded clenched.

"I called first." Not quite true for Geneviève Trottier.

"You're not an investigator."

"They agreed to see me."

"You're confusing yourself with Mickey Spillane. It's not your job."

"A well-read detective."

"Christ, Brennan, you are pissing me off!"

Squad room noise.

"Look." Controlled. "Don't get me wrong. I think you're solid. But this isn't a game. These people deserve better." His words were hard as granite.

"Yes."

"Trottier is my case."

"What exactly is being done on *your* case?"

"Bren–"

"And what about the others? Where are they going?"

I was on a roll.

"These investigations aren't exactly heading everyone's agenda right now, Ryan. Francine Morisette-Champoux was killed over eighteen months ago. It's been eight months since Trottier. I have this bizarre notion that whoever killed these women ought to be reeled in and locked up. So I take an interest. I ask a few questions. What happens? I'm told to butt out. And because Mr. Claudel thinks I'm about as helpful as a boil, these cases will drop lower and lower until they're off the charts and out of everyone's minds. Again."

"I didn't tell you to butt out."

"What are you saying, Ryan?"

"I understand Claudel wants your ass in a sling. You want to fry his balls. I might too if he'd stonewalled me. I just don't want you two screwing up my case."

"What's that supposed to mean?"

322

He took a long time to answer.

"I'm not saying I don't want your input. I just want the priorities in this investigation perfectly clear."

For a long time no one spoke. Anger rushed the line in both directions.

"I think I've found something."

"What?" He hadn't expected that.

"I may have a connection."

"What do you mean?" A little of the edge was gone from his voice.

I wasn't sure what I meant. Maybe I just wanted to derail him.

"Meet me for lunch."

"This better be good, Brennan." Pause. "I'll see you at Antoine's at noon."

Fortunately I had no new cases, so I was able to get right to work. So far nothing had fit together. Maybe the Métro was the tie.

I opened the computer and pulled up the file to check addresses. Yes. I had the right stops. I dug out a map and plotted the stations, just as Ryan and I had done with the victims' homes. The three pins formed a triangle, with Berri-UQAM in the center. Morisette-Champoux, Gagnon, and Adkins had each lived within six stops of the station. St. Jacques's apartment was a short walk away.

Could that be it? Catch a train at Berri-UQAM. Pick a victim who gets off six stops away. Hadn't I read about that type of behavior? Fixate on a color. A number. A series of actions. Follow a pattern. Never deviate. Be in control. Wasn't careful planning characteristic of serial killers? Could our boy take it one step further? Could he be a serial killer with some sort of compulsive behavior pattern into which the killings fit?

But what about Trottier and Damas? They didn't fit. It couldn't be that simple. I stared at the map, willing an answer to materialize. The feeling that something lurked just over the wall of my conscious nagged stronger than ever. What? I hardly heard the tap.

"Dr. Brennan?"

Lucie Dumont stood in my doorway. That's all it took. The wall was breached.

"Alsa!"

I'd forgotten all about the little monkey.

My outburst startled Lucie. She jerked, almost dropping her printout.

"Shall I come back?"

I was already digging for Lucie's earlier printout. Yes. Of course. The bus terminal. It's practically next to the Berri-UQAM station. I plotted Alsa. Her pin went right in the center of the triangle.

Was that it? The monkey? Did she tie in? If so, how? Another victim? An experiment? Alsa died two years before Grace Damas. Hadn't I read about that pattern also? Teenage peeping and fantasy escalating to animal torture and, finally, human rape and murder? Wasn't that Dahmer's chilling progression?

I sighed and sat back. If that was the bulletin my subconscious was trying to post, Ryan wouldn't be impressed.

Out the door and down to the central files. Lucie had vanished. I'd apologize later. I was doing that a lot lately. Back to my desk.

The Damas folder held little save my report. I opened the jacket marked Adkins and leafed through. The contents were beginning to look archival, I'd handled them so often. Nothing clicked. On to Gagnon. Morisette-Champoux. Trottier.

I spent an hour poring over the files. Gran's puzzle pieces again. Jumbled bits of information. Feed them in, let your mind rotate and arrange. It was the arranging that wasn't going well. Coffee time.

324

I brought it back, along with the morning's *Journal*. Sip and read. Regroup. The news varied little from the English language *Gazette*, the editorials enormously. What did Hugh MacLennan call it? The Two Solitudes.

I sat back. There it was again. The subliminal itch. I had the pieces, but wasn't making the fit.

Okay, Brennan. Be systematic. The feeling started today. What have you been doing? Not much. Read the paper. Took the car in. Rode the Métro. Reviewed files.

Alsa? My mind wasn't satisfied. There's more.

Car?

Nothing.

Paper?

Maybe.

I leafed back through it. Same stories. Same editorials. Same want ads.

I stopped.

Want ads. Where had I seen want ads? Stacks of them.

St. Jacques's room.

I went through them slowly. Jobs. Lost and found. Garage sales. Pets. Real estate.

Real estate? Real estate!

I pulled the Adkins folder and withdrew the pictures. Yes. There it was. The tilting, rusty sign, barely visible in the untended yard. *À Vendre*. Someone was selling a condo in Margaret Adkins's building.

So?

Think.

Champoux. What had he said? She didn't like it there. That's why we were leaving. Something like that.

I reached for the phone. No answer.

What about Gagnon? Didn't the brother rent?

325

Perhaps the landlord was selling the building.

I checked the photos. No sign. Damn.

I tried Champoux again. Still no answer.

I dialed Geneviève Trottier. It was answered on the second ring.

"*Bonjour.*" Cheerful.

"Madame Trottier?"

"*Oui.*" Curious.

"This is Dr. Brennan. We spoke yesterday."

"*Oui.*" Fearful.

"I have one question, if I may?"

"*Oui.*" Resigned.

"Did you have your home on the market when Chantale disappeared?"

"*Pardonnez-moi?*"

"Were you trying to sell your home in October of last year?"

"Who told you that?"

"No one. I was just curious."

"No. No. I have lived here since my husband and I separated. I have no intention of leaving. Chantale . . . I . . . it was our home."

"Thank you, Madame Trottier. I'm sorry to have disturbed you." Again I'd violated the accord she'd reached with her memories.

This is going nowhere. Maybe it's a stupid idea.

I tried Champoux. A male voice answered as I was about to hang up.

"*Oui.*"

"Monsieur Champoux?"

"*Un instant.*"

"*Oui.*" A second male voice.

"Monsieur Champoux?"

"*Oui.*"

I explained who I was and posed my question. Yes, they had been trying to sell the property. It was listed

326

with ReMax. When his wife was killed he took it off the market. Yes, he thought ads had run, but he couldn't be sure. I thanked him and hung up.

Two out of five. Could be. Maybe St. Jacques used want ads.

I called recovery. The materials from the Berger Street apartment were in property.

I glanced at my watch – eleven forty-five. Time to meet Ryan. He wouldn't bite. I needed more.

Once again I spread the Gagnon photos and studied them, one by one. This time I saw it. Grabbing a magnifying glass, I moved the lens until the object came into focus. I leaned closer, adjusting and readjusting to be sure.

"Hot damn."

I scooped the pictures into their envelope, stuffed them into my briefcase, and almost ran to the restaurant.

Le Paradis Tropique is directly across from the SQ building. The food is lousy, the service slow, but the tiny restaurant is always crowded at noon, due largely to the effervescence of its owner, Antoine Janvier. Today's greeting was typical.

"Ah, madame, you are hoppy today? Yes! I am so glad to see you. It has been a very long time." His ebony face showed mock disapproval.

"Yes, Antoine, I've been very busy." True, but Caribbean food would never be my daily fare.

"Ah, so hard, you work too hard. But today I have some nice fish. Fresh. Barely dead. The ocean is still dripping from his back. You will eat him and feel better. I have a beautiful table for you. The best in the house. Your friends, they are here."

Friends? Who else?

"Come. Come. Come."

There must have been a hundred people inside,

sweating and eating under brightly colored umbrellas. I followed Antoine through the maze of tables to a raised platform in the far corner. Ryan sat silhouetted against a fake window hung with yellow and lavender curtains tied back to show a painted sunset. A ceiling fan revolved slowly above his head as he talked to a man in a linen sports jacket. Though his back was to me, I recognized the razor cut and perfect creases.

"Brennan." Ryan half rose from his chair. Catching my expression, his eyes narrowed in warning. Bear with me.

"Detective Lieutenant Ryan." Okay. But this better be good.

Claudel remained seated and nodded.

I took the seat next to Ryan. Antoine's wife appeared and, after the pleasantries, the detectives ordered beer. I asked for Diet Coke.

"So. What's this breakthrough?" No one could do condescending like Claudel.

"Why don't we order first?" Ryan the peacemaker.

Ryan and I exchanged thoughts on the weather. We agreed it was warm. When Janine returned I asked for the fish special. Jamaican plates for the detectives. I was beginning to feel the outsider.

"So. What have you come up with?" Ryan the moderator.

"The Métro."

"The Métro?"

"That narrows it to four million people. Two if we stick to males."

"Let her talk, Luc."

"What about the Métro?"

"Francine Morisette-Champoux lived six stops from the Berri-UQAM station."

"Now we're getting somewhere."

Ryan shot him a look that could have cut glass.

328

"So did Isabelle Gagnon. And Margaret Adkins."

"Hm."

Claudel said nothing.

"Trottier is too far out."

"Yes. And Damas is too close."

"The St. Jacques apartment is a few blocks away."

We ate in silence for a while. The fish was dry, the fries and dirty rice were greasy. Hard combination to get just right.

"It may be more complicated than simply the Métro stops."

"Oh?"

"Francine Morisette-Champoux and her husband had their home on the market. Listed with ReMax."

No one said anything.

"There was a sign outside Margaret Adkins's building. ReMax."

They waited for me to go on. I didn't. I reached into my purse, extracted the Gagnon photos, and placed one on the table. Claudel forked a fried plantain.

Ryan picked up the photo, studied it, then looked at me quizzically. I handed him the magnifying glass and pointed to an object barely visible at the far left edge of the photo. He examined it for a long time, then, saying nothing, he extended the picture and lens across the table.

Claudel wiped his hands, wadded the paper napkin, and tossed it on to his plate. Taking the photo, he repeated Ryan's actions. When he recognized the object his jaw muscles bunched. For a long time he stared at it, saying nothing.

"Neighbor?" Ryan asked.

"Looks like it."

"ReMax?"

"I think so. You can just see the R and part of the E. We can get the print blown up."

"Should be easy to track. The listing would only be four months old. Hell, in this economy it's probably still active." Ryan was already making notes.

"What about Damas?"

"I don't know." Wouldn't want to bother a victim's family. I didn't say it.

"Trottier?"

"No. I talked to Chantale's mother. She wasn't selling. Never listed the property."

"Could be the father."

We both turned to Claudel. He was looking at me, and this time his voice held no condescension.

"What?" Ryan.

"She spent a lot of time at the father's place. Could be he was selling." Endorsement?

"I'll check." More notes.

"She was going there the day she was killed," I said.

"She stayed there a couple of days every week." Patronizing, but not contemptuous. Progress.

"Where does he live?"

"Westmount. Billion-dollar condo on Barat, off Sherbrooke."

I tried to place that. Just over the border from Centre-ville. Not far from my condo.

"Just above the Forum?"

"Right."

"What Métro station?"

"Must be Atwater. It's just a couple of blocks up from there."

Ryan looked at his watch, waved to catch Janine's attention, then pantomimed a signature in the air. We paid, receiving handfuls of candy from Antoine.

The minute I reached my office I pulled out the map, located the Atwater station, and counted the stops to Berri-UQAM. One. Two. Three. Four. Five. Six. The phone rang as I was reaching out for it.

28

Robert Trottier's condo had been listed for a year and a half.

"Guess things are slow in that price range."

"I wouldn't know, Ryan. I've never been there."

"I've seen it on television."

"ReMax?"

"Royal Lepage."

"Ads?"

"He thinks so. We're checking."

"Sign outside?"

"Yes."

"Damas?" I asked.

She, her husband, and three kids lived with his parents. The senior Damases had owned their home since dirt was invented. Would die in it.

I thought about that for a while.

"What did Grace Damas do?"

"Raised kids. Crocheted doilies for the church. Hopped around in part-time jobs. You ready for this? Once worked in a boucherie."

"Perfect." Who butchered the butcher?

"The husband?"

"Clean. Drives a truck." Pause. "Like his father

331

before him."

Silence.

"Think it means anything?"

"The Métro or the listings?"

"Either."

"Hell, Brennan, I don't know." More silence. "Give me a scenario."

I'd been trying to concoct one.

"Okay. St. Jacques reads the real estate ads, picks an address. Then he stakes it out until he spots his victim. He stalks her, waits for his opportunity. Then the ambush."

"How does the Métro figure in?"

Think. "It's a sport to him. He's the hunter, she's the prey. The hidey-hole on Berger is his blind. He flushes her with the want ads, tracks her, then moves in for the kill. He only uses certain hunting areas."

"The sixth stop out."

"Got a better idea?"

"Why real estate notices?"

"Why? Vulnerable target, a woman home alone. Figures if she's selling she'll be there to show the property. Maybe he calls. The ad would give him an entrée."

"Why six?"

"I don't know. The guy's nuts."

Brilliant, Brennan.

"Must know the city pretty damn well."

We chewed on that.

"Métro worker?"

"Cabby?"

"Utilities?"

"Cop?"

There was an interval of tense silence.

"Brennan, I wouldn–"

"No."

"What about Trottier and Damas? They don't fit."

"No."

Silence.

"Gagnon was found in Centre-ville, Damas in St. Lambert, Trottier in St. Jerome. If our boy's a commuter, how does he handle that?"

"I don't know, Ryan. But it's four for five on both the ads and the Métro stops. Look at St. Jacques, or whoever this rodent is. His hole is right at Berri-UQAM, and he collected want ads. It's worth some follow-up."

"Yep."

"Might start with the St. Jacques collection, see what the guy saved."

"Yep."

Another thought occurred to me.

"What about profiling? We've got enough to give it a try now."

"Very trendy."

"Could help."

I could read his thoughts across the line.

"Claudel doesn't have to know. I could poke around unofficially, find out if it's worth pursuing. We've got crime scenes for Morisette-Champoux and Adkins, manner of death and body disposal for the others. I think they can work with that."

"Quantico?"

"Yeah."

He snorted. "Right. They're so backed up they won't return your call until the turn of the century."

"I know someone there."

"I'm sure you do." Sigh. "Why not. But just an inquiry at this point. Don't go committing us to anything. The request will have to come from Claudel or me."

A minute later I was dialing a Virginia area code. I asked for John Samuel Dobzhansky and waited. Mr. Dobzhansky was unavailable. I left a message.

333

I tried Parker Bailey. Another secretary, another message.

I called Gabby to find out her dinner plans. My own voice asked for a message.

Called Katy. Message.

Doesn't anybody stay in one place anymore?

I spent the rest of the afternoon on correspondence and student recommendations, listening for the phone. I wanted to talk to Dobzhansky. I wanted to talk to Bailey. A clock ticked inside my head, making it hard to concentrate. Countdown. How long until the next victim? At five I gave up and went home.

The condo was silent. No Birdie. No Gabby.

"Gab?" Maybe she was napping.

The guest room door was still closed. Birdie was asleep on my bed.

"You two really have it rough." I stroked his head. "Whoo. Time to clean your pan." The odor was noticeable.

"Too much on my mind, Bird. Sorry."

No acknowledgment.

"Where's Gabby?"

Blank stare. Stretch.

I replaced the litter. Birdie acknowledged by using it, pawing a large portion onto the floor.

"Come on, Bird, try to keep it in the pan. Gabby's not the neatest bathroom mate, but do your part." I looked at her jumble of cleansers and cosmetics. "I think she cleaned up a little."

I got a Diet Coke and changed into cutoffs. Plan dinner? Who was I kidding? We'd go out.

The answering machine blinked. One message. Me. I'd called around one. Hadn't Gabby heard it? Had she ignored it? Maybe she'd turned the phone off. Maybe she was sick. Maybe she wasn't here. I went to her door.

"Gab?"

I knocked softly.

"Gabby?"

Harder.

I opened the door and looked in. The usual Gabby mess. Jewelry. Papers. Books. Clothes everywhere. A bra hung from the back of a chair. I checked the closet. Shoes and sandals tossed in heaps. Amid it all, the neatly made bed. The incongruity of it struck me.

"Sonofabitch."

Birdie slithered past my legs.

"Was she here at all last night?"

He looked at me, jumped to the bed, circled twice, and settled. I dropped next to him, the familiar knot tightening in my stomach.

"She's done it again, Bird."

He spread his toes and began to lick.

"Not so much as a stinking note."

Birdie focused on inter-toe spaces.

"I will not think about this." I went to unload the dishwasher.

Ten minutes later I had calmed enough to dial her number. No answer. Of course. I tried the university. No answer.

I wandered into the kitchen. Opened the refrigerator. Closed it. Dinner? Reopened it. Diet Coke. Wandered to the living room, set the new Coke next to the earlier can, clicked on the TV, surfed the channels, chose a sitcom I wouldn't watch. My mind raced from the murders to Gabby to my garden skull and back, unable to fix on anything. The cadence of dialogue and canned laughter provided background noise as my thoughts bounced around like atomic particles.

Anger at Gabby. Resentment at letting myself be used. Hurt that she would do it. Apprehension about her safety. Fear for a new victim. Frustration over my

335

helplessness. I felt emotionally bruised, but couldn't stop beating myself.

I'm not sure how long I'd been there when the phone rang, the sound sending adrenaline pouring from wherever it rooms when not on duty.

Gabby!

"Hello."

"Tempe Brennan, please." A male voice. Familiar as my Midwest childhood.

"J.S.! God, am I glad to hear from you!"

John Samuel Dobzhansky. My first love. Counselors. Camp Northwoods. The romance outlasted that summer and the next, thrived until our freshman year of college. I went South, J.S. went North. I chose anthropology, met Pete. He trained in psychology, married, divorced. Twice. Years later we'd reconnected at the Academy. J.S. specialized in sexual homicide.

"You got that Camp Northwoods feeling?" he asked.

"Up in my head," I finished the line from the camp song. We both laughed.

"I wasn't sure if you'd want me to call at home, but you left the number so I figured I'd try."

"Glad you did. Thank you." Thank you. Thank you. "I want to pick your brain about a situation we've got up here. If that's okay?"

"Tempe, when will you stop disappointing me?" Feigned hurt.

We'd had dinner at Academy meetings, the possibility of a fling hanging heavy between us at first. Should we tamper with teenaged memories? Was the passion still there? Nothing verbalized, the idea waned bilaterally. Better to leave the past intact.

"What about the new love interest you were telling me about last year?"

"Gone."

"Sorry. J.S., we've had some murders here that I

336

think are tied together. If I give you an overview, can you opine on whether we have a serial?"

"I can opine on anything." One of our old pet phrases.

I described the Adkins and Morisette-Champoux scenes, and outlined what had been done to the victims. I described how and where the other bodies were found, and how they'd been mutilated. Then I added my theories about the Métro and want ads.

"I'm having trouble convincing the cops these cases are connected. They keep saying there's no pattern. They're right to some extent. The victims are all different, one is shot, the others aren't. They lived all over the place. Nothing hooks together."

"Whoa. Whoa. Slow down. You're going about this all wrong. First of all, most of what you've described has to do with modus operandi."

"Yes."

"Similarities in MO can be useful, don't get me wrong, but disparities are extremely common. A perpetrator may gag or tie his victim with the phone cord at one scene, then bring his own rope to the next. He may stab or slash one victim, shoot or strangle the next, steal from one, not from another. I profiled one guy who used a different kind of weapon at every scene. You still there?"

"Yes."

"A criminal's MO is never static. It's like anything else, there's a learning curve. These guys get better with practice. They learn what works and what doesn't. They're continually improving their technique. Some more than others, of course."

"Comforting."

"Also, there are all kinds of random events that can affect what a perpetrator does, regardless of his best-laid plans. A phone rings. A neighbor shows up. A cord breaks. He has to improvise."

"I see."

"Don't misunderstand. Patterns in MO are useful, and we use that. But variations don't mean much."

"What *do* you use?"

"Ritual."

"Ritual?"

"Some of my colleagues call it a signature, or a calling card, and it's only seen at some crime scenes. Most perpetrators develop an MO because once a plan works a couple of times they gain confidence in it and believe it lowers their risk of getting caught. But with violent, repetitive offenders there's something else operating. These people are driven by anger. Their anger leads them to fantasize about violence, and eventually they act out the fantasies. But the violence isn't enough. They evolve rituals for expressing the anger. It's these rituals that give them away."

"What sort of rituals?"

"Usually they involve controlling, maybe humiliating the victim. You see, it isn't really the victim that's important. Her age, her appearance may be irrelevant. It's the need to express the anger. I did one guy whose victims ranged from seven to eighty-one years in age."

"So, what would you look for?"

"How does he encounter his victim? Does he jump her? Does he use a verbal approach? How does he control her once he's made contact? Does he assault her sexually? Does he do it before or after he kills her? Does he torture his victim? Does he mutilate the body? Does he leave anything at the scene? Take anything away?"

"But can't those things be affected by unexpected contingencies also?"

"Of course. But the critical thing is he does these things as part of his fantasy enactment, his anger dissipation ritual, not just to cover his ass."

338

"So, what do you think? Does what I described have a signature?"

"Off the record?"

"Of course."

"Absolutely?"

"Really?" I began taking notes.

"I'd bet my ass on it."

"Your buns are safe, J.S. Do you think it's a sexual sadist?"

I heard a rattling as he switched the phone. "Sexual sadists are turned on by their victim's pain. They don't just want to kill, they want their victims to suffer. And – and this is critical – they're sexually aroused by it."

"And?"

"Part of your pattern says yes. Insertion of objects into the vagina or rectum is very common with these guys. Were your victims alive when this was done?"

"At least one. Hard to tell with the other two since the bodies were so decomposed."

"Sounds like sexual sadism is a possibility. The real question remains, was the killer sexually aroused by his actions?"

I couldn't answer that. No semen was found on any of the victims. I said this.

"Useful, but doesn't rule out SS. I had one guy who'd masturbate in his victim's hand, cut it off, then grind it up in a blender. Never found semen at the scenes."

"How'd you get him?"

"One time his aim wasn't so good."

"Three of these women were dismembered. We know that for certain."

"That may show a pattern, but it's not proof of sexual sadism. Unless it was done before the victim's death. Serial killers, whether sexual sadists or not, are very cunning. They put a lot of planning into their crimes. Postmortem mutilation doesn't necessarily mean there's

339

a sexual or sadistic component. Some cut the body up just to make it easier to hide."

"What about the mutilation? The hands?"

"Same answer. It's a pattern, it's overkill, but it may or may not be sexual. Sometimes it's just a way of rendering the victim powerless. I do see some indicators, however. You say the victims were unknown to their killer. They were savagely beaten. Three suffered object insertion, probably antemortem. That combination is characteristic."

I was writing furiously.

"Check whether the objects were brought to the scene or were already there. That could be part of this guy's signature, planned as opposed to opportunistic cruelty."

I noted it, starred it.

"What are some other characteristics of sexual sadism?"

"Patterned MO. Use of a pretext to make contact. A need to control and humiliate the victim. Excessive cruelty. Sexual arousal from the victim's fear and pain. Keeping victim memorabilia. The—"

"What was the last one?" I was writing so fast my hand was cramping.

"Memorabilia. Souvenirs."

"What kinds of souvenirs?"

"Items from the murder scene, pieces of the victim's clothing, jewelry, that sort of thing."

"Newspaper clippings?"

"Sexual sadists love their own press."

"Would they keep records?"

"Maps, diaries, calendars, drawings, you name it. Some of them make tapes. The fantasy isn't just the kill. The stalk before and the reenactment afterward can be a big part of the turn-on."

"If they're so good at avoiding detection, why would

they keep that stuff? Isn't it risky?"

"Most of them think they're superior to the cops. Too smart to get caught."

"What about body parts?"

"What *about* body parts?"

"Do they keep them?"

Pause. "Not common, but sometimes."

"So what do you think about the Métro and want ad idea?"

"The fantasies these guys act out can be incredibly elaborate and very specific. Some need special locations, exact sequences of events. Some sexual sadists need specific victim responses, so they script the whole thing, force the victim to say certain things, perform certain acts, wear certain clothes. But, Tempe, these behaviors aren't just typical of sexual sadists. They characterize a lot of personality disorders. Don't get hung up on the sexual sadist angle. What you want to look for is that signature, that calling card that only your killer leaves. That's how you'll nail him, regardless of how psychiatrists classify him. Using the Métro and newspaper could figure into your boy's fantasy."

"J.S., based on what I've told you, what do you think?"

There was a long pause, a slow expulsion of breath.

"I think you've got a real nasty one up there, Tempe. Tremendous anger. Extreme violence. If it is this St. Jacques character, his using the victim's bank card bothers me. Either he's incredibly stupid, and it doesn't look that way, or he's getting sloppy for some reason. Maybe sudden financial pressure. Or he's getting bolder. The skull in your garden is a flag. He was sending a message. Maybe a taunt. Or, it's possible that at some level he wants to be caught. I don't like what you're telling me about how you figure in. And it looks like you *do* figure in. The picture. The skull. Based on what you've told

341

me, looks more like he's taunting you."

I told him about the night at the monastery and the car that had tailed me.

"Christ, Tempe, if this guy's refocusing on you, don't play games. He's dangerous."

"J.S., if it was him on the monastery grounds, why didn't he just kill me then?"

"It goes back to what I was saying before. You probably surprised him out there, so he wasn't prepared to kill in the way he likes. He wasn't in control. Maybe he didn't have his kit. Maybe the fact that you were unconscious robbed him of the rush he gets at seeing his victim's fear."

"No death ritual."

"Exactly."

We chatted for a while, other places, old friends, the time before murder became part of our lives. When we hung up it was after eight.

I leaned back, stretched my arms and legs, and went limp. For some time I lay there, a rag doll recalling its past. Eventually hunger roused me, and I went to the kitchen, warmed a tray of frozen lasagna and forced myself to eat it. Then I spent an hour reconstructing from my notes what J.S. had said. His parting words kept coming back to me.

"The intervals are getting shorter."

Yes, I knew that.

"He's upping the stakes."

I knew that too.

"He may now have his sights trained on you."

At ten I went to bed. I lay in the dark, staring at the ceiling, feeling alone and sorry for myself. Why did I carry the burden of these women's deaths? Did someone have me in the crosshairs of his psychopathic fantasy? Why wouldn't anyone take me seriously? Why was I getting old, eating frozen dinners in front of a television I didn't watch? When Birdie nestled at my knee, that tiny bit of contact triggered the tears I'd been holding back since talking to J.S. I cried into the pillowcase Pete and I had bought in Charlotte. Or, rather, I had bought while he stood around looking impatient.

Why had my marriage failed? Why was I sleeping alone? Why was Katy so discontented? Why had my best friend been inconsiderate of me again? Where was she? No. I wouldn't think about that. I don't know how long I lay there, feeling the emptiness of my life, listening for Gabby's key.

29

The next morning I gave Ryan a summary of my discussion with J.S. A week crept by. Nothing.

The weather stayed hot. Days, I worked through
bones. Remains found in a septic tank in Cancún had
been a tourist missing for nine years. Bones scavenged
by dogs had been a teenage girl before homicide by a
blunt instrument. A cadaver in a box, hands severed,
face mutilated beyond recognition, revealed only that it
had been a white male, skeletal age thirty-five to forty.

Nights, I visited the jazz festival, milling with the
sticky crowds that clogged Ste. Catherine and Jeanne-
Mance. I heard Peruvians, their music a blend of wood-
wind and rain forest. I wandered from Place des Arts to
Complexe Desjardins, enjoying the saxophones and gui-
tars and summer nights. Dixieland. Fusion. R&B.
Calypso. I willed myself not to look for Gabby. I refused
to fear for the women about me. I listened to the music
of Senegal, Cape Verde, Rio, and New York, and, for a
while, I forgot. The five.

Then, on Thursday, a call came. LaManche.
Meeting on Tuesday. Important. Please be there.

I arrived not knowing what to expect, most certainly
not what greeted me. Seated with LaManche were

344

Ryan, Bertrand, Claudel, Charbonneau, and two detectives from St. Lambert. The director of the lab, Stefan Patineau, sat at the far end of the table, a crown prosecutor on his right.

They rose as one when I arrived, sending my anxiety level into the cheap seats. I shook hands with Patineau and the attorney. The others nodded, their faces neutral. I tried to read Ryan's eyes, but they would not meet mine. As I took the one remaining chair, my palms felt sweaty and the familiar knot had hold of my gut. Had this meeting been called to discuss me? To review allegations made against me by Claudel?

Patineau wasted no time. A task force was being formed. The possibility of a serial killer would be examined from every angle, all suspect cases investigated, every lead aggressively pursued. Known sex offenders would be pulled in and questioned. The six detectives would be assigned full time, Ryan would coordinate. I would continue my normal casework, but serve as an ex-officio member of the team. Space had been set aside downstairs, all dossiers and relevant materials were being moved to that location. Seven cases were under consideration. The task force would hold its first meeting that afternoon. We would keep Monsieur Gauvreau and the prosecutor's office informed of all progress.

Just like that. Done. I returned to my office, more stunned than relieved. Why? Who? I'd been arguing the serial killer theory for almost a month. What had happened to suddenly give it credence? Seven cases? Who were the other two?

Why ask, Brennan? You'll find out.

And I did. At one-thirty I entered a large room on the second floor. Four tables formed an island in the middle, portable chalk and bulletin boards lined the walls. The detectives were clumped at the back of the room, like buyers at a trade show booth. The board

345

they were viewing held the familiar Montreal and Métro maps, colored pins jutting from each. Seven more boards stood side by side, each topped by a woman's name and picture. Five were as familiar as my own family, the others I didn't know.

Claudel favored me with a half second of eye contact, the others greeted me cordially. We exchanged comments about the weather, then moved to the table. Ryan distributed legal pads from a stack in the center, then launched right in.

"You all know why you're here, and you all know how to do your jobs. I just want to make sure of a few things at this point."

He looked from face to face, then gestured at a stack of folders.

"I want everyone to study these files. Go through them carefully. Digest everything in them. We're getting the information on computer, but it's slow. For now we'll use the old-fashioned way. If there's anything you think is relevant, anything at all, get it up on that victim's board."

Nods.

"We'll have an updated printout of the pervert parade today. Divide it up, roust these guys, see where they've been partying."

"Usually in their own shorts." Charbonneau.

"Could be one of them crossed the line, now finds his shorts lacking."

Ryan looked at each of us in turn.

"It's absolutely critical we work as a team. No individuals. No heroes. Talk. Exchange information. Bounce ideas off each other. That's how we're going to nail this bastard."

"If there is one." Claudel.

"If not, Luc, we'll clean house, nail a whole lot of bastards. Nothing lost."

346

Claudel tucked down the corners of his mouth and drew a series of short, quick lines on his tablet.

"It's equally important we be concerned about security," Ryan continued. "No leaks."

"Patineau going to announce our little civic group?" Charbonneau.

"No. In a sense, we're working undercover."

"Public hears the words serial killer, they'll go ape shit. Surprised they haven't already." Charbonneau.

"Apparently the press hasn't picked up on the connection. Don't ask me why. Patineau wants to keep it that way for now. That may change."

"Press has the memory of a gnat." Bertrand.

"Nah, that's the IQ score."

"They'd never make that cutoff."

"Okay. Okay. Let's go. Here's what we've got."

Ryan summarized each case. I listened mutely as my ideas, even my words, filled the air and were scribbled onto legal pads. Okay, some of Dobzhansky's ideas as well, but passed on by me.

Mutilation. Genital penetration. Real estate ads. Métro stops. Someone had been listening. What's more, someone had been checking. The boucherie where Grace Damas had once worked was a block off St. Laurent. Close to the St. Jacques apartment. Close to the Berri-UQAM Métro. It plotted. That made four for five. That's what had tipped the balance. That and J.S.

Following our talk, Ryan had convinced Patineau to forward a formal request to Quantico. J.S. had agreed to give the Montreal cases top priority. A flurry of faxes provided him with what he needed, and Patineau had a profile three days later. That had done it. Patineau had decided to move. *Voilà.* Task force.

I felt relieved, but also slighted. They'd taken my labor and left me to sweat. On walking into that meeting, I had feared personal censure, had not expected

347

tacit acknowledgment of work well done. Nevertheless. I steadied my voice to hide my anger.

"So what does Quantico tell us to look for?"

Ryan pulled a thin folder from the stack, opened it, and read.

"Male. White. Francophone. Probably not educated beyond secondary level. Probably a history of NSO's . . ."

"*C'est quoi, ça?*" Bertrand.

"Nuisance sexual offenses. Peeping. Obscene phone calls. Indecent exposure."

"The cute stuff." Claudel.

"Dummy man." Bertrand.

Claudel and Charbonneau snorted.

"Shit." Claudel.

"My hero." Charbonneau.

"Who the hell's dummy man?" Ketterling, St. Lambert.

"Little maggot busts apartments so he can stuff the lady's nightie, then slash it. Been working his act about five years."

Ryan continued, selecting phrases from the report.

"Careful planner. Probably uses ruse to approach victim. Possibly the real estate angle. Probably married . . ."

"*Pourquoi?*" Rousseau, St. Lambert.

"The hidey-hole. Can't bring the victims home to wifey."

"Or Mommy." Claudel.

Back to the report.

"Probably selects, prepares isolated location in advance."

"The basement?" Ketterling, St. Lambert.

"Hell, Gilbert sprayed the shit out of that place with Luminol. If there was any blood there, it would have lit up like Tomorrowland." Charbonneau.

Report. "Excessive violence and cruelty suggest

348

extreme anger. Possible revenge orientation. Possible sadistic fantasies involving domination, humilation, pain. Possible religious overlay."

"*Pourquoi, ça?*" Rousseau.

"The statue, the body dumps. Trottier was at a seminary, so was Damas."

For the next few moments no one said a word. The wall clock buzzed softly. In the corridor, a pair of high heels clicked closer, receded. Claudel's pen made short, tense strokes.

"*Beaucoup de* 'possibles' *et* 'probables.'" Claudel.

Claudel's continued resistance to the one-killer theory annoyed me.

"It's also *possible* and *probable* we're going to have another murder soon," I snapped.

Claudel's face hardened into its usual mask, which he pointed at his tablet. The lines in his cheeks tensed, but he said nothing.

Buzz.

"Does Dr. Dobzhansky have a long-term forecast?" I asked, calmer.

"Short term," Ryan said somberly and returned to the profile. "Indications of loss of control. Increasing boldness. Intervals shortening." He closed the folder and shoved it toward the center of the table. "Will kill again."

Silence again.

Eventually, Ryan looked at his watch. We all followed suit, like assembly line robots.

"So. Let's get into these files. Add anything you have that's not here. Luc, Michel, Gautier was CUM, so you guys might have more on that one."

Nods from Charbonneau and Claudel.

"Pitre fell to the SQ. I'll double-check her. The others are more recent, should be pretty complete."

Since I was all too familiar with the five recents, I

349

started with Pitre and Gautier. The files had been open since '88 and '89 respectively.

Constance Pitre's semi-nude, badly decomposed body was found in an abandoned house at Khanawake, an Indian reserve upriver from Montreal. Marie-Claude Gautier was discovered behind the Vendôme Métro, a switching point for trains to the western suburbs. Both women had been savagely beaten, their throats slashed. Gautier had been twenty-eight, Pitre thirty-two. Neither had been married. Each lived alone. The usual suspects had been questioned, the usual leads pursued. Dead end in each case.

I spent three hours going over the files, which, compared to those I'd studied for the past six weeks, were relatively sparse. Both women had been prostitutes. Was that the reason for the limited investigations? Exploited in life, ignored in death? Good riddance? I refused to allow myself to pursue it.

I looked at family snapshots of each victim. Their faces were different, yet similar in some disturbing way. The yeasty white pallor, the lavish makeup, the cold, flat stare. Their expressions brought to recall my night on the Main, when I'd viewed the street production from a front-row seat. Resignation. Desperation. There I'd seen it live. Here it was in stills.

I spread the crime scene photos, knowing beforehand the story they'd tell. Pitre: the yard, the bedroom, the body. Gautier: the station, the bushes, the body. Pitre's head was almost severed. Gautier's throat had also been slashed, her right eye stabbed into a pulpy mush. The extreme savagery of the attacks had prompted their inclusion in our investigation.

I read the autopsy, toxicology, and police reports. I dissected each interview and investigator's summary. I pulled out every detail of the victims' comings and goings, every particular of their lives and deaths. All the

350

minutiae I could suck from each folder went on to a crude spreadsheet. It wasn't much.

I heard the others moving around, scraping chairs, exchanging banter, but I paid no attention. When I finally closed the files, it was past five. Only Ryan remained. I looked up to see him watching me.

"Wanna see the Gypsies?"

"What?"

"Heard you like jazz."

"Yeah, but the festival is over, Ryan." Heard from whom? How? Was this a social invitation?

"True. But the city isn't. Les Gitanes are playing in the Old Port. Great group."

"Ryan, I don't think so." But I *did* think. Had thought. That's why I'd refuse. Not now. Not until the investigation was over. Not until the animal was netted.

"Good enough." The electric eyes. "But you gotta eat."

That was true. Another frozen dinner, solo, was decidedly unappealing. No. Don't even give Claudel the appearance of impropriety.

"It's probably not a g—"

"We could chew over some of your thoughts on this stuff while we put away a pizza."

"Business meeting."

"*Certainement.*"

Buzz.

Did I want to discuss the cases? Of course. Something about the added two didn't ring true. Even more, I was curious about the task force. Ryan had given us the official version; what were the real dynamics? Were there threads in the web I should know about? Avoid?

Buzz.

Would the others think twice? Of course not.

"Sure, Ryan. Where do you want to go?"

351

Shrug. "Angela's?"

Close to my condo. I thought of the 4 A.M. call last month, the "friend" he'd been with. You're paranoid, Brennan. The man wants a pizza. He knows you can park at home.

"Is that convenient for you?"

"Right on the way."

To what? I didn't ask.

"Fine. See you there in" – I looked at my watch – "thirty minutes?"

I stopped home, fed Birdie, barred myself from mirrors. No hair combing. No blusher. Business.

At six-fifteen Ryan sipped a cold beer, I a Diet Coke as we waited for a veggie supreme. No goat cheese on his half.

"You're making a mistake."

"I don't like it."

"Rigid."

"In touch with myself."

We exchanged small talk for a while, then I switched lanes. "Tell me about these other cases. Why Pitre and Gautier?"

"Patineau had me pull all unsolved SQ homicides that fit a certain profile. Back to '85. Basically the pattern you've been hammering on. Females, overkill, mutilation. Claudel searched the CUM cases. Local PD's were asked to do the same. So far, these two have come up."

"Just the province?"

"Not exactly."

We fell silent as the waitress arrived, sliced, and served the pizza. Ryan ordered another Belle Gueule. I passed, mildly resentful. Your own fault, Brennan.

"Don't even think about touching my half."

"Don't like it." He drained his glass. "Do you know

352

what goes through goats?"

I did, but blocked it.

"What do you mean, not exactly?"

"Initially, Patineau asked for a search of cases in and around Montreal. When the profile arrived from Quantico, he sent a composite description, our stuff and theirs, to the RCMP to see if the Mounties had similar cases in their files."

"And?"

"Negative. Looks like we've got a homeboy."

We ate in silence for a while.

Finally, "What's your take?"

I took my time answering.

"I only spent three hours with the new files, but somehow they don't seem to fit."

"The hooker angle?"

"That. But something else. The killings are violent, no question about that, but they're just too . . ."

I'd been trying to put a word to the feeling all afternoon, but hadn't found one. I dropped a piece of pizza to my plate, watched tomato and artichoke ooze off the soggy dough.

". . . messy."

"Messy?"

"Messy."

"Jesus, Brennan, what do you want? Did you see the Adkins apartment? Or Morisette-Champoux? Looked like Wounded Tree."

"Knee."

"What?"

"Knee. It was Wounded Knee."

"The Indians?"

I nodded.

"I don't mean blood. The Pitre and Gautier scenes looked, what . . . ?" Again, I groped for a word. "Disorganized. Unplanned. With the others, you get the

353

sense this guy knew exactly what he was doing. Got into their homes. Brought his own weapon. Took it away with him. Never found one at the other scenes, right?"

He nodded.

"They recovered the knife with Gautier."

"No prints. That could suggest planning."

"It was winter. The guy probably wore gloves."

I swirled my Coke.

"The bodies look like they were just left. Quickly. Gautier was facedown. Pitre was lying on her side, her clothes were torn, her pants were at her ankles. Take another look at the Morisette-Champoux and Adkins photos. The bodies almost look posed. They were both lying on their backs, their legs were spread, their arms were positioned. Like dolls. Or ballerinas. Christ, Adkins looked like she'd been laid down while doing a pirouette. Their clothing wasn't torn, it was opened, neatly. It's as if he wanted to display what he'd done to them."

Ryan said nothing. The waitress appeared, wanting assurance we'd enjoyed our meal. Anything else? Just a check.

"I just get a different feeling with these other two cases. I could be dead wrong."

"That's what we're supposed to figure out."

Ryan took the check, raising a hand in a "don't argue" gesture. "This one's on me. Next one's yours."

He cut my protest short by reaching out to touch my upper lip. Slowly, he ran his index finger around the corner of my mouth, then held it up for my inspection.

"Goat," he said.

Fire ants would have had less effect on my face.

I arrived home to an empty apartment. No surprise. But I was becoming anxious about Gabby, and hoped she would reappear. Mainly so I could send her packing.

354

I lay on the couch and turned on the Expos game. Martinez had just beaned one off the batter. The announcer was going crazy. Tough moving back up to starter.

I watched until the announcer's voice faded to a hum and the noise in my head took over. How did Pitre and Gautier fit in? What did Khanawake mean? Pitre was Mohawk. The others had all been white. Four years ago the Indians had barricaded the Mercier Bridge, making life hell for commuters. Feelings between the reserve and its neighbors remained less than cordial. Was that significant?

Gautier and Pitre were hookers. Pitre had been busted several times. None of the other victims had police records. Did that mean anything? If victims had been selected at random, what would be the odds that two out of seven would be hookers?

Had the Morisette-Champoux and Adkins scenes really shown premeditation? Was I imagining the staging? Was it accidental?

Was there a religious angle? That was one I hadn't really explored. If so, what did it mean?

Eventually, I drifted into uneasy sleep. I was on the Main. Gabby was beckoning to me from the upstairs window of a run-down hotel. The room behind her was dimly lit, and I could see figures moving about. I tried to cross the street to her, but women outside the hotel threw rocks when I moved. They were angry. A face appeared beside Gabby's, backlit against the room. It was Constance Pitre. She tried to put something over Gabby's head, a dress or gown of some sort. Gabby resisted, her gestures to me becoming more frantic.

A rock hit me in the gut, wrenching me hard into the present. Birdie stood on my stomach, tail in landing position, eyes fixed on my face.

"Thanks."

355

I dislodged him and swung to a sitting position.

"What the hell did that mean, Birdie?"

My dreams are not particularly disingenuous. My subconscious takes recent experience and throws it back at me, often in riddle form. Sometimes I feel like Arthur, frustrated with Merlin's cryptic answers. Just tell me! Think, Arthur. Think!

The rock-throwing. Obvious: Martinez's bean ball. Gabby. Obvious: She's on my mind. The Main. The hookers. Pitre. Pitre trying to dress Gabby. Gabby beckoning for help. A tingle of fear began to form.

Hookers. Pitre and Gautier were hookers. Pitre and Gautier are dead. Gabby works with hookers. Gabby was being harassed. Gabby is gone. Could there be a connection? Could she be in trouble?

No. She used you, Brennan. She does it often. You always fall for it.

The fear would not recede.

What about the guy shadowing her? She seemed genuinely frightened.

She split. Not even a note. Thanks. Gotta go. Nothing.

Isn't that a bit much, even for Gabby? The fear became stronger.

"Okay, Dr. Macaulay, let's find out."

I went to the guest room and looked around. Where to begin? I had already gathered her belongings and heaped them on the closet floor. I hated to go through them.

Trash. It seemed less invasive. I dumped the wastebasket onto the desk. Tissues. Candy wrappers. Tinfoil. A sales slip from Limité. An ATM receipt. Three balls of crumpled paper.

I opened a yellow ball. Gabby's scrawl on lined paper:

"I'm sorry. I can't deal with this. I would never forgive myself if . . ."

356

It broke off there. A note to me?

I opened the other yellow ball:

"I will not succumb to this harassment. You are an irritant that must . . ."

Again, she'd given up. Or been interrupted. What had she been trying to say? To whom?

The other ball was white and larger. When I unwadded it, runaway fear shot through me, vaporizing all the unkind thoughts I'd been nurturing. I flattened the paper with trembling hands and stared.

What I saw was a pencil drawing, the central figure clearly female, her breasts and genitalia depicted in minute detail. The torso, arms, and legs were crudely sketched, the face an oval with features vaguely shadowed in. The woman's abdomen was open, the organs rising from it to circle the central figure. In the lower left-hand corner in a stranger's hand was written:

"Every move you make. Every step you take. Don't cut me."

30

I felt cold all over. Oh, God, Gabby. What have you gotten into? Where are you? I looked at the mess around me. Was it normal Gabby chaos, or the aftermath of panicky flight?

I reread the unfinished notes. For whom were they intended? Me? Her stalker? I would never forgive myself if *what*? An irritant that must be *what*? I looked at the drawing and sensed what I'd felt when viewing Margaret Adkins's X rays. Foreboding. No. Not Gabby.

Calm down, Brennan. Think!

The phone. I tried Gabby's apartment and office. Answering machine. Voice mail. Bless the electronic age.

Think.

Where did her parents live? Troi-Rivières? 411. Only one Macaulay. Neal. An old woman's voice. French. So glad to hear from you. Been such a long time. How are you? No, they hadn't talked to Gabrielle in several weeks. No, that wasn't unusual. Young people, so busy. Is anything wrong? Assurances. Promises to visit soon.

Now what? I didn't know any of Gabby's current friends.

Ryan?

No. He's not your guardian. Anyway, what would you tell him?

Slow down. Think. I got a Diet Coke. Was I overreacting? I returned to the guest room and reexamined the sketch. Overreacting? Hell, I was underreacting. I checked a number, reached for the phone, and dialed.

"Y'allo."

"Hey, J.S. Tempe." I struggled to keep my voice steady.

"My God. Two calls in one week. Admit it. You can't stay away from me."

"It's been over a week."

"Anything under a month I interpret as irresistible attraction. What's up?"

"J.S., I . . ."

He caught the tremor in my voice and his demeanor changed, the flipness replaced by genuine concern.

"Are you okay, Tempe? What is it?"

"It's these cases I talked to you about last week."

"What's happened? I profiled the guy right away. Hope they realize that was your influence. Did they get my report?"

"Yes. You made the difference, actually. They've decided to form a task force. That part's moving right along."

I wasn't sure how to broach my anxiety about Gabby, didn't want to abuse our friendship.

"Could I ask you a few more questions? There's something else I'm concerned about, and I really don't know wh–"

"Why do you even ask, Brennan? Fire away."

Where to begin? I should have made a list. My head was like Gabby's room, thoughts and images scattered haphazardly.

"This is something else."

"Yes. You said that."

359

"I guess I'm interested in what you call nuisance sexual offenders?"

"Okay."

"Would that include things like following someone, calling her, but not doing anything overtly threatening?"

"It could."

Start with the sketch.

"You told me last time that violent offenders often make records? Like tapes and drawings?"

"Right."

"Do nuisance offenders?"

"Do they what?"

"Make sketches and things."

"They might."

"Can the content of a drawing indicate the level of violence someone is capable of?"

"Not necessarily. For one person drawing could be a release valve, a way of acting out without actually engaging in violence. For another, it could be the trigger that sets him off. Or a reenactment of what he's already done."

Great.

"I found a drawing of a woman with her stomach slit and her guts spread out around her. What does that suggest?"

"The Venus de Milo has no arms. G.I. Joe has no dick. What does that mean? Art? Censorship? Sexual deviance? Tough call when seen in a vacuum."

Silence. What should I tell him?

"Did this drawing come from the St. Jacques gallery?" he asked.

"No." I found it in my guest room trash. "You said offenders often escalate to higher and higher levels of violence, right?"

"Yeah. At first they might just engage in peeping, or obscene phone calls. Some stay with that, others move

360

on to bigger challenges: self-exposure, stalking, even breaking and entering. For still others that's not enough; they progress to rape and even murder."

"So some sexual sadists might not actually be violent?"

"There you go with the sexual sadist business again. But in answer to your question, yes. Some of these guys play out their fantasies in other ways. Some use inanimate objects, or animals, some find consenting partners."

"Consenting partners?"

"A compliant partner, someone who'll permit whatever it is the fantasy requires. Subordination, humiliation, even pain. Could be a wife, a girlfriend, someone he pays."

"A prostitute?"

"Sure. Most prostitutes will do some role playing, within limits."

"That can defuse violent tendencies?"

"It can as long as she goes along. Same with a wife or girlfriend. It's often when the compliant partner gets fed up that things go bad. She's been his punching bag, then she pulls the plug, maybe even threatens to tell. He gets enraged, kills her, finds he enjoys it. On to the next."

Something he'd said was bothering me.

"Let's back up. What kind of inanimate objects?"

"Pictures, dolls, clothing. Anything, really. I had one guy used to beat the crap out of a life-size blowup of Flip Wilson in drag."

"I hate to ask."

"Deep-seated rage against blacks, gays, and women. Hat trick every time he jerked off."

"Of course."

I could hear the *Phantom of the Opera* in the background.

"J.S., if a guy does that, makes pictures or uses a doll,

361

for instance, does that mean he probably won't kill?"

"Maybe, but again, who knows what's going to alter his curve and nudge him over that line? One day a naughty picture is enough, the next it's not."

"Could a guy do both?"

"Both what?"

"Flip-flop back and forth. Kill some victims, just stalk and harass others?"

"Sure. For one thing, a victim's behavior can alter the equation. He feels insulted or rejected by her. She says the wrong thing, turns left instead of right. She wouldn't even have to know. Don't forget, most serial killers have never met their victims. But these women star in the fantasy. Or he might see one woman in one role, cast another differently. Love your wife, then go out and kill. Cast one stranger as prey, another as friend."

"So, once someone starts killing, he could still revert to his earlier, less violent tactics on occasion?"

"He might."

"So someone who is seemingly just a nuisance could be a lot more?"

"Definitely."

"Someone who phones a victim, follows her, sends her gory sketches isn't necessarily harmless, even though he keeps his distance?"

"You are talking about St. Jacques, aren't you?"

Was I?

"Does it sound like him?"

"I just assumed we were discussing him. Or whoever it was kept the bridal suite you guys tossed."

Open up your mind, let the fantasy unwind . . .

"J.S. I – It's gotten personal."

"What do you mean?"

I told him everything. Gabby. Her fear. Her exit. My anger, now my fear.

"Shit, Brennan, how do you get yourself into these

362

things? Look, this guy sounds like bad news. Gabby's creep may or may not be St. Jacques, but it's possible. He stalks women. St. Jacques stalks women. He draws pictures of eviscerated females, doesn't exactly have a normal sex life, and carries a knife. St. Jacques, or whoever this devo is, is killing women, then cutting them up or disfiguring them. What do you think?"

Turn your face away from the garish light of day . . .

"When did she first notice this guy?" J.S. asked.

"I don't know."

"Before or after this whole thing broke?"

"I don't know."

"What *do* you know about him?"

"Not much. He hangs out with hookers, pays for sex, then plays a scene with lingerie. Carries a knife. Most of the women won't have anything to do with him."

"That sound good to you?"

"No."

"Tempe, I want you to report this to the guys you work with. Let them check it out. You say Gabby is unpredictable, so it's probably nothing. She may have just taken off. But she's your friend. You've been threatened. The skull. The guy who followed you in the car."

"Maybe."

"Gabby was staying with you. She's disappeared. It warrants a look."

"Right. Claudel will rush right out and collar nightie man."

"Nightie man? You've been hanging with cops too long."

I stopped. Where had I gotten that? Of course. Dummy man.

"We have a fruitcake that breaks in, stuffs lingerie, stabs it, then leaves. Been at it for years. They call him dummy man."

"If he's been at it for years he can't be that dumb."

363

"No, no. It's what he makes with the lingerie. It's like a dummy."

Synapse. Or a doll.

Feel me, touch me . . .

J.S. said something, but my mind was veering off at warp speed. Dummy. Lingerie. Knife. A hooker named Julie who plays games with a nightie. A sketch of carnage with the words "don't cut me." News articles found in a Berger Street room, one about a break-in with a nightgown dummy, one with my picture, clipped and marked with an X. A skewered skull, grinning from my shrubbery. Gabby's face in 4 A.M. terror. A bedroom in chaos.

Help me make the music of the night . . .

"I've got to go, J.S."

"Tempe, promise me you'll do what I say. It's a long shot, but it could be that Gabby's creep is the sicko that kept the Berger Street nest. He could be your killer. If so, you're in danger. You're blocking him, so you're a threat to him. He had your picture. He may have put Grace Damas's skull in your yard. He knows who you are. He knows where you are."

I wasn't hearing J.S. In my mind I was already moving.

It took thirty minutes to cross Centre-ville, go up the Main, and find my alley spot. As I stepped over the splayed legs of a wino who sat slumped against the wall, his head bobbing to the muted thud of C&W coming through the brick, he smiled and raised a hand in a one-finger wave, then opened his palm and extended it toward me.

I dug in my pocket and gave him a loony. Maybe he'd watch my car.

The Main was a smorgasbord of night dwellers through which I nibbled a path. Panhandlers, hookers,

364

druggies, and tourists. Accountants and salesmen jostled in clumps, reckless with binge merriment. For some it was a boisterous romp, for others a joyless reality. Welcome to the Hotel St. Laurent.

Unlike my last visit, this time I had a plan. I worked my way toward Ste. Catherine, hoping to find Jewel Tambeaux. Not so easy. Though the usual pack was gathered outside the Hotel Granada, Jewel wasn't part of it.

I crossed the street and considered the women. No one reached for a rock. I took this as a good sign. Now what? From my last social call on these ladies, I had a pretty good idea as to what I shouldn't do. That, however, gave me no clues as to what I should do.

I have a rule that has served me well in life. When in doubt, do nothing. If you're not sure, don't buy it, don't comment, don't commit. Sit tight. Deviation from this maxim has usually caused me regret. The red dress with the ruffled neck. The promise to debate Creationism. The angry letter fired off to the Vice Chancellor. This time I stuck to my policy.

I found a cement block, brushed off the broken glass, and sat. Knees drawn, eyes on the Granada, I waited. And waited. And waited.

For a while I was intrigued by the soap opera playing around me. As the Main Turns. Midnight came and went – 1 A.M. Then 2. The script unwound its tale of seduction and exploitation. Maul My Children. The Young and the Hopeless. I played mental games, creating all sorts of clever titles.

By 3 A.M. screenwriting no longer held my interest. I was tired, discouraged, and bored. I knew surveillance was not glamorous, but I hadn't been prepared for just how numbing it was. I'd had enough coffee to fill an aquarium, prepared endless lists in my head, composed several letters I would never write, and played "guess the life story" of a great many citizens of Quebec. Hookers and johns had come and gone, but Jewel Tambeaux was not to be seen.

I stood and flexed backward, considered rubbing my anesthetized ass, decided against it. Next time, no cement. Next time no sitting up all night, watching for a hooker who could be in Saskatoon.

As I started to step off toward my car, a white Pontiac station wagon swung to the curb across the street. Orange Chihuly hair emerged, followed by a familiar face and halter.

Jewel Tambeaux slammed the Pontiac door, then leaned inside the passenger window to say something to the driver. A moment later the car sped off, and Jewel joined two women sitting on the hotel steps. In the pulsating neon they looked like a trio of housewives gossiping on a suburban stoop, their laughter sailing into the predawn air. After a moment, Jewel stood, hiked her spandex mini-skirt, and moved off up the block.

The Main was winding down, the action seekers gone, the scavengers just emerging. Jewel walked slowly, swinging her hips to some private rhythm. I angled across and fell in behind her.

"Jewel?"

She turned, her face a smiling question mark. I was not what she expected. Her eyes moved over my face, puzzled, disappointed. I waited for her to recognize me.

"Margaret Mead."

I smiled. "Tempe Brennan."

"Researching a book?" She moved her hand in a horizontal swath, indicating a title. "Ass on the Hoof, or My Life Among Hookers." Soft, Southern English, with a bayou cadence.

I laughed. "Might sell. May I walk with you?"

She shrugged and blew a puff of air, then turned and resumed her slow pelvic swing. I fell in beside her.

366

"You still looking for your friend, chère?"

"Actually, I was hoping to find you. I didn't expect you this late."

"Kindergarten's still open, sugar. Gotta *do* business to stay in business."

"True."

We walked a few steps in silence, my sneakers echoing her metallic clip.

"I've given up on finding Gabby. I don't think she wants to be found. She came to see me about a week ago, then took off again. I guess she'll turn up when she turns up."

I looked for a reaction. Jewel shrugged, said nothing. Her lacquered hair moved in and out of shadow as we walked. Here and there a neon sign blinked off as the last of the taverns closed their doors, sealing in the smells of stale beer and cigarette smoke for another night.

"Actually, I'd like to talk to Julie."

Jewel stopped walking and turned to me. Her face looked tired, as though emptied by the night. The life. She pulled a pack of Players from the V in her halter, lit one, blew the smoke upward.

"Maybe you should go on home, cutie."

"Why do you say that?"

"You're still chasing killers, aren't you, chère?"

Jewel Tambeaux was no fool.

"I believe there's one out there, Jewel."

"And you think it's this cowboy Julie plays with?"

"I'd sure like to talk to him."

She took a pull on her cigarette, tapped it with a long red nail, then watched the sparks float to the pavement.

"I told you last time, he's got the brains of a liverwurst sandwich and the personality of roadkill, but I doubt he's killed anybody."

"Do you know who he is?" I asked.

"No. These morons are about as scarce as pigeon shit. I pay them about as much mind."

"You said this guy could be bad news."

"There really hasn't been much good news down here, sugar."

"Has he been around lately?"

She considered me, then something else, turning inward to an image or remembered thought at which I could only guess. Some other bad news.

"Yeah. I've seen him."

I waited. She drew on her cigarette, watched a car move slowly up the street.

"Haven't seen Julie."

She took another pull, closed her eyes and held the smoke, then sent it upward into the night.

"Or your friend Gabby."

An offering. Should I push?

"Do you think I could find him?"

"Frankly, sugar, I don't think you could find your own butt without a map."

Nice to be respected.

Jewel took one last drag, flipped the butt, and ground it with her shoe.

"Come on, Margaret Mead. Let's bag us some road-kill."

31

Jewel walked with purpose now, her heels clicking a rapid tattoo on the pavement. I wasn't sure where she was taking me, but it had to beat my cement perch.

We went east two blocks, then left Ste. Catherine and cut across an open lot. Jewel's apricot sculpture moved smoothly through the dark while I stumbled behind, threading my way through chunks of asphalt, aluminum cans, broken glass, and dead vegetation. How could she do that in stilettos?

We emerged on the far side, turned down an alley, and entered a low wooden building with no sign to indicate its calling. The windows were painted black and strings of Christmas lights provided the only illumination, giving the interior the reddish glow of a nocturnal animal exhibit. I wondered if that was the intent. Rouse the occupants to late night action?

Discreetly, I glanced about. My eyes needed little adjustment, since the amount of light inside differed only slightly from that outdoors. Staying with the Christmas theme, the decorator had gone with cardboard pine for the walls and cracked red vinyl for the stools, accessorizing with beer adds. Dark wooden booths lined one wall, cases of beer were stacked

369

against another. Though the bar was almost empty, the air was heavy with the smell of cigarette smoke, cheap booze, vomit, sweat, and reefer. My cement block began to hold more appeal.

Jewel and the bartender exchanged nods. He had skin the color of day-old coffee and heavy brows. From under them, he tracked our movement.

Jewel walked slowly through the bar, checking each face with seeming disinterest. An old man called to her from a corner stool, waving a beer and gesturing to her to join him. She blew a kiss. He gave her the finger.

As we passed the first booth a hand reached out and grasped Jewel's wrist. With the other hand, she uncurled the fingers and laid the hand back in front of its owner.

"Playpen's closed, sugar."

I shoved my hands into my pockets and kept my eyes on Jewel's back.

At the third booth Jewel stopped, folded her arms, and shook her head slowly.

"*Mon Dieu*," she said, clicking her tongue against her upper teeth.

The booth's single occupant sat staring into a glass of watery brown liquid, elbows on the table, cheeks propped on curled fists. All I could see was the top of a head. Greasy brown hair divided unevenly along the crown and hung limply to either side of the face. White flecks littered the area of the part.

"Julie," said Jewel.

The face did not look up.

Jewel clicked again, then slid into the booth. I followed, grateful for the meager cover. The tabletop was slick with something I didn't want to identify. Jewel leaned an elbow on its edge, jerked back with a wiping gesture. She dug out a cigarette, lit it, blew the smoke in an upward jet.

"Julie." Sharper.

Julie caught her breath and raised her chin.

"Julie?" The girl repeated her own name, sounding as if she'd been roused from sleep.

My heart slipped in an extra beat and my teeth grabbed for my lower lip.

Oh, God.

I was looking at a face that had lived no more than fifteen years. Its color could be described only in shades of gray. The pallid skin, the cracked lips, the vacant, recessed eyes with their somber underlining looked like those of someone long deprived of sunlight.

Julie stared at us without expression, as if our images were slow in forming in her brain, or recognition a complex exercise. Then.

"Can I have one, Jewel?" English. She reached a trembling hand across the table. The inside of her elbow looked purple in the room's muted glow. Slender gray worms crawled across the veins on her inner wrist.

Jewel lit a Player and handed it to her. Julie pulled the smoke deep into her lungs, held it, then blew it upward in a Jewel pantomime.

"Yeah. Oh yeah," she said. A tiny scrap of cigarette paper stuck to her lower lip.

She drew again, eyes closed, completely absorbed by the smoking ritual. We waited. Double tasking was not within Julie's capacity.

Jewel looked at me, eyes unreadable. I let her lead.

"Julie, darlin', you been workin'?"

"Some." The girl sucked another long drag, blew two streams of smoke from her nose. We watched them dissolve, silvery clouds in the reddish light.

Jewel and I were silent while Julie smoked. She didn't seem to question our being there. I doubted she questioned much of anything.

371

After a while she finished, stubbed out the butt, and looked at us. She seemed to consider what benefit our presence might hold.

"I haven't eaten today," she said. Like her eyes, her voice was flat and empty.

I glanced at Jewel. She shrugged and reached for another cigarette. I looked around. No menus. No blackboards.

"They got burgers."

"Would you like one?" How much cash did I bring?

"Banco does them."

"Okay."

She leaned from the booth and called to the bartender.

"Banco. Can I get a burger? With cheese?" She sounded six years old.

"You've got a tab, Jules."

"I'll get it," I said, sticking my head out of the booth.

Banco was leaning against the bar sink, arms folded across his chest. They looked like baobab branches.

"One?" He pushed off.

I looked at Jewel. She shook her head.

"One."

I turned back to the booth. Julie had slumped into the corner, her drink held loosely in two hands. Her jaw hung slack, leaving her mouth partially open. The paper still rode her lower lip. I wanted to pick it off, but she seemed unaware. A microwave beeped, then hummed. Jewel smoked.

Shortly, the microwave gave four beeps, and Banco appeared with the burger, steaming in its plastic wrapper. He placed it in front of Julie and looked from Jewel to me. I ordered club soda. Jewel shook her head.

Julie tore the cellophane, then lifted the top to inspect the contents of the bun. Satisfied, she took a

372

bite. When Banco brought my drink, I stole a peek at my watch. Three-twenty. I began to think Jewel would never speak again.

"Where you been workin', sugar?"

"Nowheres special." Through a mouthful of bun and burger.

"Haven't seen you lately."

"I was sick."

"You feelin' better now?"

"Mm."

"Working the Main?"

"Some."

"You still doing that little creep with the nightie?" Casual.

"Who?" She ran her tongue around the edge of the burger, like a child with an ice cream cone.

"Guy with the knife."

"Knife?" Absently.

"You know, chère, little man likes to stroke his tallywacker while you model his mama's sleepwear?"

Julie's chewing slowed then stopped, but she didn't answer. Her face looked like putty, smooth, gray, and without expression.

Jewel's nails clicked against the tabletop. "Come on, sugar, let's turn it up a notch. You know who I'm talking about?"

Julie swallowed, glanced up, then returned her attention to the burger.

"What about him?" She took a bite.

"Just wonderin' if he's still around."

"Who's she?" Garbled.

"Tempe Brennan. She's a friend of Dr. Macaulay. You know her, don't you, chère?"

"Something wrong with this guy, Jewel? He got the gon or AIDS or something? Why you asking about him?"

373

It was like interrogating a magic eight ball. If answers floated up at all they were random, not tied to specific questions.

"No, honey, I just wondered if he's still comin' around."

Julie's eyes met mine. They looked uninhabited.

"You work with her?" she asked me, her chin glistening with grease.

"Something like that," Jewel answered for me. "She'd like to talk to this nightie guy."

"'Bout what?"

"Usual stuff," said Jewel.

"She a deaf-mute or something? Why can't she talk for herself?"

I started to speak, but Jewel wagged me silent.

Julie didn't seem to expect an answer. She finished the last of the burger and licked her fingers, one by one. Finally.

"What's with this guy? Jesus, he was talking about her, too."

Fear surged through every nerve in my body.

"Talking about who?" I blurted.

Julie regarded me, jaw slack, mouth half open as before. When not speaking or eating she seemed unable, or unwilling, to maintain its closure. I could see specks of food in her lower teeth.

"Why do you want to turn this guy?" she asked.

"Turn him?"

"He's the only steady bang I've got."

"She's not interested in turning anybody, she'd just like to talk to him." Jewel.

Julie sipped her drink. I tried again.

"What did you mean, 'he was talking about her, too'? Who was he talking about, Julie?" A look of bewilderment crossed her face, as if she'd already forgotten her words.

374

"Who was your regular talking about, Julie?" Jewel's voice was growing weary.

"You know, the old lady that hangs around, kinda butchy, with the nose ring and the weird hair?" She tucked one of her own lank strands behind an ear. "She's nice, though. She bought me doughnuts a couple of times. Isn't that who you're talking about?"

I ignored Jewel's warning squint.

"What was he saying about her?"

"He was pissed off at her or something. I don't know. I don't listen to what a trick says. I just fuck 'em and keep my ears and my mouth shut. It's healthier."

"But this guy's a regular."

"Kinda."

"Any particular times?" I couldn't help myself. Jewel gave me an "Okay, you're on your own" gesture.

"What is this, Jewel? Why's she asking me all this?" Again, she sounded like a child.

"Tempe wants to talk to him. That's all."

"I can really do without this guy getting busted. He's a creep, but it's regular money, and I need it real bad."

"I know, sugar."

Julie swirled the last of her drink then tossed it back. Her eyes avoided mine.

"And I'm not going to quit doing him. I don't care what anybody says. So he's weird, so what, it's not like he's going to kill me or nothing. Hell, I don't even have to fuck him. And what else would I do with my Thursdays? Take a class? Go to the opera? If I don't do him some other whore will."

It was the first emotion she'd shown, the adolescent bravado a contrast to her previous listlessness. I ached for her. But I feared for Gabby, and wouldn't let up.

"Have you seen Gabby lately?" I tried to sound softer.

"What?"

"Dr. Macaulay. Have you seen her recently?"

The lines between her eyes deepened, reminding me of Margot, though the shepherd probably had better short-term memory.

"The old lady with the nose ring," said Jewel, emphasizing the age indicator.

"Oh." Julie closed her mouth, then let it drop back open. "No. I've been sick."

Stay cool, Brennan. You almost have enough.

"Are you better now?" I asked.

She shrugged.

"Will you be okay?"

She nodded.

"Do you want anything else?"

She shook her head.

"Do you live close?" I hated using her like this, but I wanted a bit more.

"At Marcella's. You know, Jewel, over on St. Dominique? A lot of us crash there." She refused to look at me.

Yes. I had what I needed. Or would, very soon.

The burger and the booze and whatever else she'd taken were having their effect on Julie. The bravado ebbed, the apathy returned. She slumped in the corner of the booth, eyes staring out like the darkened circles on a gray-faced mime. She closed them and took a deep breath, swelling her bony chest inside its cotton tank. She looked exhausted.

Suddenly the Christmas glow was gone. Fluorescent brightness filled the bar and Banco was bellowing its imminent closing. The few remaining patrons moved toward the door, grumbling their dissatisfaction. Jewel tucked her Players into her halter and indicated we should follow. I checked my watch – 4 A.M. I looked across at Julie and the guilt I'd been beating back all

376

night surged up with full force.

In the unforgiving light Julie looked like a near cadaver, like someone slowly shuffling toward death. I wanted to wrap my arms around her and hold her for a moment. I wanted to take her home to Beaconsfield, or Dorval, or North Hatley, where she would eat fast food and go to the prom and order jeans from the Lands' End catalog. But I knew it would not happen. I knew Julie would be a statistic, and, sooner or later, she would be in the basement at Parthenais.

I paid the bill and we left the bar. The early morning air was moist and cool and carried the scents of river and brewery.

"Good night, ladies," said Jewel. "Don't y'all go out dancing now."

She wiggled her fingers, turned, and clicked rapidly up the alley. Without a word, Julie departed in the opposite direction. The vision of home and bed pulled like a magnet, but there was one more bit of information I had to have.

I hung back and watched Julie scurry up the alley, assuming she'd be easy to follow. Wrong. When I looked up the alley, she was already disappearing around the next corner, and I had to race to catch up.

She took a zigzag path, cutting through lots and alleys to reach a run-down three-flat on St. Dominique, where she mounted the stairs, fumbled for a key, and disappeared through a peeling green door. I watched the tattered door curtain sway, then settle, barely disturbed by her indifferent slam. I noted the number.

Okay, Brennan. Bedtime. I was home in twenty minutes.

Under the covers, with Birdie at my knee, I formed a plan. It was easy to decide what *not* to do. Don't call Ryan. Don't spook Julie. Don't tip the little cretin with the knife and nightie act. Find out if it's St. Jacques. Find out where he lives. Or where his current hidey-hole is. Get something concrete. Then bring in the clod squad. You are here, boys. Bust this place.

It sounded so simple.

32

I dragged through Wednesday in a fog of exhaustion. I hadn't intended to go to the lab but LaManche called, needing a report. Once there, I decided to stay. I sorted through old cases, sluggish and irritable, clearing those that Denis could discard. It's a task I hate, and one I'd been putting off for months. I lasted until 4 P.M. Once home I ate an early supper, took a long bath, and was under the covers by 8 o'clock.

When I woke on Thursday, sunlight was streaming into the bedroom, and I knew it was late. I stretched, rolled, and looked at the clock. Ten twenty-five. Good. I'd recouped some lost sleep. Phase One of the Plan. I had no intention of going to work.

I took my time getting up, running through a checklist of what I intended to do. From the moment I'd opened my eyes I felt charged, like a runner on marathon day. I wanted to set a pace. Control, Brennan. Run a smart race.

I went to the kitchen, made coffee, and read the *Gazette*. Thousands fleeing the war in Rwanda. Parizeau's Parti Québecois ten points ahead of Premier Johnson's Liberals. The Expos out of first place in the NL East. Laborers working during the annual construction holiday. No kidding. I could never understand the genius who thought that one up. In a country with four or five months of good weather for building, construction stops for two weeks in July while the workers go on holiday. Brilliant.

I had a second cup and finished the paper. So far so good. On to Phase Two. Mindless Activity.

I threw on shorts and a T and went to the gym. Thirty minutes on the StairMaster and a round on the Nautilus. Next, the Provigo, where I bought enough groceries to feed Cleveland. Back home I spent the afternoon mopping, scouring, dusting, and vacuuming. At one point I considered cleaning the refrigerator, but decided against it. Too extreme.

By 7 P.M. my nesting frenzy was sated. The place reeked of spray cleaners and lemon polish, the dining room table was covered with drying sweaters, and I had clean panties to last a month. I, on the other hand, looked and smelled as if I had been camping for weeks. I was ready to go.

The day had been sweltering and the evening promised no relief. I chose another shorts and T combo, accessorized with worn Nikes. Perfect. Not your street professional, but someone prowling the Main in search of recreational chemicals or a companion for the evening, or both. As I drove toward St. Laurent I ran through the Plan. Find Julie. Follow Julie. Find nightie man. Follow nightie man. Don't be seen. Simplicity itself.

I drove across Ste. Catherine, scanning the sidewalks on both sides. A few women had opened shop at the Granada, but there was no sign of Julie. I wouldn't expect her this early. I was allowing myself extra time to get into place.

The first glitch came when I turned into my alley. Like a genie from a bottle, a large woman materialized and bore down on me. She had Tammy Bakker makeup and the neck of a bull terrier. Though I couldn't catch all her words, there was no mistaking her message. I backed out and drove off in search of other parking arrangements.

I found a spot six blocks north, on a narrow side street lined with three-flats. Hot town. Summer in the city. Neighborhood watch was underway. Men's eyes tracked me from a balcony, others from a stoop, conversation suspended, beer cans resting on sweaty knees. Were they hostile? Curious? Disinterested? Very interested? I didn't stay in place long enough for anyone to approach. I locked the car and covered the distance to the end of the block at a brisk pace. Perhaps I was overly nervous, but I didn't want complications to sabotage my mission.

I breathed easier when I rounded the corner and entered the flow on St. Laurent. A clock in Le Bon Deli said eight-fifteen. Damn. I'd wanted to be in position by now. Should I modify the Plan? What if I missed her?

At Ste. Catherine I crossed St. Laurent and rechecked the crowd in front of the Granada. No Julie. Would she even come here? What route would she take? Damn. Why hadn't I started earlier? No time for indecision.

I hurried east, scanning the faces on both sides of the street, but the pedestrian flow had grown, making it harder to be sure she didn't slip past. I cut north at the vacant lot, retracing the path Jewel and I had taken two nights earlier. I hesitated at the alley bar, moved on, gambling again that Julie was not an early starter.

A few minutes later I stood hunched behind a utility pole on the far side of St. Dominique. The street was deserted and still. Julie's building showed no signs of life, windows dark, porch light dead, paint peeling

381

grimly in the muggy dusk. The scene brought to mind photos I had seen of the Towers of Silence, platforms maintained by the Parsi sect in India on which they placed their dead to have the bones picked clean by vultures. I shivered in the heat.

Time crept by. I watched. An old woman trudged up the block, dragging a cart loaded with rags. She muscled her evening's take along the uneven pavement, then disappeared around a corner. The cart's tinny squeak-bump sound ebbed, then stilled. Nothing else disturbed the street's ragged ecosystem.

I looked at my watch – eight-forty. It had grown very dark. How long should I wait? What if she'd already left? Should I ring the bell? Damn. Why hadn't I gotten the time out of her? Why hadn't I gotten here earlier? Already the Plan was showing deficiencies.

Another expanse of time went by. A minute, maybe. I was debating leaving when a light went on in an upstairs room. Not long after, Julie emerged in bustier, mini-skirt, and over-the-knee boots. Her face, midriff, and thighs were splotches of white in the porch shadow. I drew back behind my pole.

She hesitated a moment, chin raised, arms wrapped around her midriff. She seemed to be testing the night. Then she plunged down the steps and walked quickly toward Ste. Catherine. I followed, trying to keep her in view, yet remain unnoticed.

At the corner she surprised me, turning left, away from the Main. Good call on the Granada, Brennan, but where is she going? Julie wended her way quickly through the crowd, boot fringe swinging, oblivious to cat calls and wolf whistles. She was a good wender and I had to work to keep up.

The crowd grew smaller as we moved east, and eventually ceased being one. I'd been lengthening the distance between us in direct response to the thinning

382

out of sidewalk people, but it was probably unnecessary. Julie seemed focused on a destination and disinterested in other foot traffic.

The streets not only grew emptier, the neighborhood changed flavor. We now shared Ste. Catherine with dandies in *GQ* haircuts, hardbodies in tanks and spray paint jeans, unisex couples, and the occasional transvestite. We had crossed into the gay village.

I followed Julie past coffeehouses, bookstores, and ethnic restaurants. Eventually she turned north, then east, then south on to a dead-end street of warehouses and seedy wooden buildings, many with corrugated metal covering the windows. Some had the appearance of having been upfitted for business space at street level, though they probably hadn't seen customers in years. Papers, cans, and bottles littered both curbs. The place looked like a set for the Jets and the Sharks.

Julie went straight to an entrance halfway up the block. She opened a dirty glass door covered with metal latticework, spoke briefly, then disappeared inside. I could see the glow of a beer sign through a window to the right. It was also armored with metal grillwork. A sign above the door said simply: BIÈRE ET VIN.

Now what? Was this the place of assignation, with a private room upstairs or in the back? Or was this a rendezvous bar they would leave together? I needed it to be the latter. If they left separately, their business concluded, the Plan was foiled. I wouldn't know what man to follow.

I couldn't just stand in front and wait. I spotted an even darker gap in the darkness across the street. An alleyway? I walked past the beer joint Julie had entered, and diagnaled toward the strip of blackness. It was a passageway between an abandoned barbershop and a

383

storage company, about two feet wide and dark as a crypt.

Heart pounding, I slipped in and pressed against a wall, taking cover behind a cracked and yellowed barber pole that projected over the sidewalk. Several minutes passed. The air hung dead and heavy, the only movement my breathing. Suddenly, a rustling made me jump. I wasn't alone. As I was about to bolt, a dark blob shot from the trash at my feet and scurried toward the back of the passageway. My chest constricted, and once again a chill passed through me, despite the heat.

Ease back, Brennan. Just a rodent. Come on, Julie!

As if in response, Julie reappeared, followed by a man in dark sweats, L'UNIVERSITÉ DE MONTRÉAL arced across his chest. He cradled a paper bag in his left arm.

My pulse hammered even faster. Is it him? Is it the face in the ATM photo? Is it the Berger Street runner? I strained to see the man's features, but it was too dark and he was too far away. Would I recognize St. Jacques even if I got a good look? Doubtful. The photo had been too blurry, the man in the apartment too quick.

The pair looked straight ahead and didn't touch or speak. Like homing pigeons they retraced the path Julie and I had just taken, only digressing at Ste. Catherine, where they continued south instead of turning west. They made several more turns, snaking through streets of run-down apartments and abandoned businesses, streets that were dark and sincerely unfriendly.

I trailed half a block behind, conscious of every scrape and crunch, wary of discovery. There was no cover. If they turned and saw me, I would have no excuse, no windows to shop, no doorways to enter, nothing to hide behind, physical or fictional. My only option would be to keep walking and hope to find a turnoff before Julie recognized me. They didn't look back.

We worked our way through a tangle of alleys and lanes, each emptier than the one before. At one point two men passed from the opposite direction, arguing in tense, hard voices. I prayed Julie and her john wouldn't follow the men with their eyes. They didn't. They kept on and disappeared around another corner. I sped up, fearful of losing them in the seconds they were out of sight.

My fears were well grounded. When I made the turn, they had vanished. The block was still and empty.

Shit!

I checked the buildings on both sides, running my eyes up and down each iron staircase, probing each entranceway. Nothing. Not a sign.

Damn!

I dashed up the sidewalk, furious with myself for losing them. I was halfway to the next corner when a door opened and Julie's regular stepped onto a rusted iron balcony just twenty feet ahead and to my right. He was at shoulder level, his back to me, but the sweatshirt looked the same. I froze, incapable of thought or action.

The man hawked a glob of phlegm and sent it rocketing onto the sidewalk. Drawing the back of his hand across his mouth, he went back inside and closed the door, oblivious to my presence.

I stood as I was, legs rubbery, unable to move.

Great move, Brennan. Panic and rush the play! Why not light a flare and sound a siren?

The building into which he'd disappeared was one in a row that seemed to cling together for support. Take one out and the block would crumble. A sign identified it as LE ST. VITUS, and offered CHAMBRES TOURISTIQUES. Tourist rooms. Right.

385

Was this home or merely his trysting place? I resigned myself to more waiting.

Again I looked for a place to hide. Again I spotted what I thought was a gap on the far side of the street. Again I crossed and found that it was. Maybe I was showing a learning curve. Maybe I was lucky.

I took a breath and slipped into the darkness of my new passageway. It was like crawling into a Dumpster. The air was warm and heavy and smelled of urine and things gone bad.

I stood in the narrow space, shifting my weight from foot to foot. The belly-up spiders and roaches I'd seen entombed in the barber pole kept me from leaning against the wall. There was no question of sitting.

Time dragged by. My eyes never left the St. Vitus, but my thoughts traveled the galaxy. I thought of Katy. I thought of Gabby. I thought of Saint Vitus. Who was he anyway? How would he feel about having the rathole across the street named in his honor? Wasn't Saint Vitus a disease? Or was that Saint Elmo?

I thought of St. Jacques. The ATM photo was so poor you really couldn't see the face. The geezer was right. The guy's own mother wouldn't know him from that shot. Besides, he could have changed his hair, grown a beard, gotten glasses.

The Incas built a road system. Hannibal crossed the Alps. Seti occupied the throne. No one entered or left the St. Vitus. I tried not to think about what was unfolding in one of its rooms. I hoped the guy was a short timer. There's a first, Brennan.

There was no breeze in my tiny crevice, and the brick walls on either side still held the heat that had built up all day. My shirt grew clammy and clung to my skin. My scalp was sweaty damp, and an occasional bead broke free and trickled down my face or neck.

I shifted and watched and thought. The air was

386

breathless. The sky flickered and rumbled softly. Celestial grumbling, nothing more. Now and then a car lighted the street, then passed on, casting it back into obscurity.

The heat and smell and confinement began to crowd in on me. I felt a dull pain in the space between my eyes, and the back of my throat was doing pre-nausea things. I thought about hanging it up. I tried squatting on my haunches.

Suddenly a form loomed over me! My mind exploded in a million directions. Was the passage open behind me? Stupid! I hadn't checked for an escape route!

The man stepped into the alley, fumbling for something at his waist. I looked down the corridor in back but it was pitch black. I was trapped!

Then it was like a physics experiment, with equal and opposite forces responding. I shot up and stumbled back on deadened legs. The man also staggered backward, a look of shock on his face. I could see he was Asian, though only his teeth and astonished eyes were clear in the murky shadows.

I pressed against the wall, as much for support as for cover. He leered at me in a bewildered way, shook his head as though perplexed, then lurched off down the block, tucking his shirt and zipping his fly.

For a moment I just stood there, talking my heart rate down from the stratosphere.

A wino who only wanted to pee. He's gone.

What if it had been St. Jacques?

It wasn't.

You left yourself no out. You're being stupid. You're going to get yourself killed.

It was just a wino.

Go home. J.S. is right. Leave this to the cops.

They won't do it.

It's not your problem.

Gabby is.

She's probably in Ste. Adele.

Had me there.

Calmer, I resumed my surveillance. I thought some more about Saint Vitus. Saint Vitus's dance. That's it. It was widespread in the 1500s. People grew nervous and irritable, then their limbs started twitching. They thought it was a form of hysteria and hiked off to the saint. Then what about Saint Anthony? The fire. Saint Anthony's fire. Something to do with ergot in grain. Didn't it also make people act crazy?

I thought about cities I'd like to visit. Abilene. Bangkok. Chittagong. I'd always liked that name, Chittagong. Maybe I'd go to Bangladesh. I was in the D's when Julie came out of the St. Vitus and walked calmly up the block. I held my ground. She was no longer my mark.

I didn't have to hold for long. My prey was also leaving.

I gave him half a block, then dropped in behind. His movements reminded me of the trash rat. He scurried, shoulders hunched, head tucked, bag clutched to his chest. As I followed, I compared the figure ahead to the one I'd seen bolt from the Berger Street room. Not a good match as memory went, but St. Jacques had been too quick and his appearance too unexpected. This *could* be the same man, but I just hadn't gotten a good enough look the other time. This guy was definitely not moving as fast.

For the third time in as many hours I wove my way through a labyrinth of unlit side streets, tailing a quarry as close as I dared. I prayed he wouldn't stop off at another beer joint. I wasn't up to any more surveillance.

I needn't have worried. After snaking through a

maze of tributary streets and side alleys, the man made one final turn and went directly to a bow-fronted graystone. It was like a hundred others I'd passed tonight, though a bit less seedy, the stone a little less dirty, the rusted stairs curving to doors slightly less in need of paint.

He took the stairs quickly, the metallic slap of his footfalls sharp against the air, then disappeared through an ornately carved door. A light went on almost immediately on the second floor of the bow, showing windows half open, curtains hanging limp and lifeless. A shadowy figure moved about the room, veiled by the graying lace.

I crossed the street and waited. No alley this time.

For a while the figure shifted back and forth, then it disappeared.

I waited.

It's him, Brennan. Outa here.

He could be visiting someone. Dropping something off.

You've got him. Let's go.

I checked my watch – eleven-twenty. Still early. Ten more minutes.

It took less. The figure reappeared, raised the windows to full open, and vanished again. Then the room went black. Bedtime!

I waited five minutes to be sure no one left the building, then needed no more convincing. Ryan and the boys could take it from here.

I noted the address and began winding my way back to the car, hoping I could find it. The air was still leaden, the heat as intense as midafternoon. Leaves and curtains hung motionless, as if laundered and left to dry. The neon of St. Laurent glowed over the tops of the darkened buildings, backlighting the maze of streets through which I hurried.

The clock on the dash said midnight when I pulled into the garage. I *was* improving. Home before dawn.

The noise didn't register at first. I was across the garage and singling out my key when it finally intruded on my conscious mind. I stood still to listen. A high-pitched beeping was coming from behind me, near the main auto entrance.

As I walked in that direction, trying to pinpoint its source, the tone clarified into a sharp, pulsating beat. When I drew near I could see that the noise came from a door to the right of the car ramp. Though the door appeared closed, the lock was only partly engaged, thus triggering the alarm.

I pushed, then pulled on the safety bar, slamming the door fully shut. The beeping stopped abruptly, leaving the garage deathly quiet. I reminded myself to mention the apparent malfunction to Winston.

The condo felt cool and fresh after my hours in hot, dirty crevices. For a moment I just stood in the hall, allowing the refrigerated air to roll over my hot skin. Birdie brushed back and forth against my leg, arching his back and purring in greeting. I looked down at him. Soft, white hairs clung to my sweaty legs. I stroked his head, fed him, and checked my messages. One hang-up. I headed for the shower.

As I lathered and relathered I ran over the events of the evening in my mind. What had I accomplished? Now I knew where Julie's lingerie loony lived. At least I assumed that's who he was since today was Thursday. So what? He might have nothing to do with the murders.

But I couldn't quite convince myself. Why? Why did I think this guy was hooked in? Why did I think it was my job to nail him? Why was I afraid for Gabby? Julie had been fine.

After my shower I was still keyed up and knew I

wouldn't sleep, so I dug a chunk of Brie and a wedge of *tomme de chèvre de savoie* from the refrigerator and poured myself a ginger ale. Wrapping myself in a quilt, I stretched out on the couch, peeled an orange, and ate it with the cheese. Letterman couldn't hold my attention. Back to the debate.

Why did I just spend four hours packed in with spiders and rats to spy on some guy who likes to see whores in lingerie? Why not let the cops handle it?

It kept coming back to that. Why didn't I just tell Ryan what I knew and ask him to roust this guy?

Because it was personal. But not in the way I'd been telling myself. It wasn't just a threat in my garden, an attack on my safety or Gabby's. Something else was causing me to obsess over these cases, something deeper and more troubling. For the next hour, little by little, I admitted it to myself.

The truth was that, lately, I was scaring myself. I saw violent death every day. Some woman killed by some man and thrown into a river, a wood, a dump. Some child's fractured bones uncovered in a box, a culvert, a plastic bag. Day after day I cleaned them up, examined them, sorted them out. I wrote reports. Testified. And sometimes I felt nothing. Professional detachment. Clinical disinterest. I saw death too often, too close, and I feared I was losing a sense of its meaning. I knew I couldn't grieve for the human being that each of my cadavers had been. That would empty my emotional reservoir for sure. Some amount of professional detachment was mandatory in order to do the work, but not to the extent of abandoning all feeling.

The deaths of these women had stirred something in me. I ached for their fear, their pain, their helplessness in the face of madness. I felt anger and outrage, and a need to root out the animal responsible for the slaughter. I felt for these victims, and my response to their

391

deaths was like a lifeline to my feelings. To my own humanity and my celebration of life. I felt, and I was grateful for the feeling.

That's how it was personal. That's why I wouldn't stop. That's why I'd prowl the monastery grounds, and the woods, and the bars and back streets of the Main. I'd persuade Ryan to follow this up. I'd figure out Julie's client. I'd find Gabby. Maybe this was connected. Maybe not. No matter. One way or another, I'd flush out the sonofabitch responsible for this shedding of female blood, and I'd help shut him down. For good.

33

Spurring the investigation turned out to be harder than I thought. Partly because of me.

By five-thirty on Friday afternoon my head and my stomach ached from the endless cups of machine coffee. We'd been discussing the files for hours. No one had turned up much, so we kept rehashing the same things over and over, sifting through the mountains of information, desperately searching for something new. There was little.

Bertrand was working the realtor angle. Morisette-Champoux and Adkins had listed their condos with ReMax. So had Gagnon's neighbor. Huge firm, three different offices, three separate agents. None of them remembered the victims, or even the properties. Trottier's father had used Royal Lepage.

Pitre's former boyfriend was a doper who'd killed a prostitute in Winnipeg. Could be a break. Could be nothing. Claudel was on that.

The questioning of known sex offenders was continuing, coming up empty. Big surprise.

Teams of uniformed officers were canvassing the neighborhoods around the Adkins and Morisette-Champoux condos. Zero.

We had nowhere to turn so we were turning on one another. The mood was gloomy and patience was in short supply, so I bided my time, waiting for the right opening. They listened politely as I told them about the situation with Gabby, about the night in the car. I described the drawing, my conversation with J.S., and my surveillance of Julie.

When I finished, no one spoke. Seven women watched mutely from portable bulletin boards. Claudel's pen wove complex webs and grids. He'd been silent and withdrawn all afternoon, as if disconnected from the rest of us. My account made him even more sullen. The sound of the large electric clock began to dominate the room.

Buzzzz.

"And you have no idea if this is the same sack of shit we chased from Berger?" Bertrand.

I shook my head.

Buzzzz.

"I say we bust the cocksucker." Ketterling.

"For what?" Ryan.

Buzzzz.

"We could just be there for him, see how he deals with pressure." Charbonneau.

"If he is our boy that might spook him. The last thing we want is for him to panic and blow town." Rousseau.

"No. The last thing we want is for him to shove a plastic Jesus up someone else's sweet spot." Bertrand.

"The guy's probably just a wienie wagger."

"Or he could be Bundy with an underwear twist."

Buzzzz.

Round and round it went like that, zigging and zagging from French to English. Eventually, everyone was drawing Claudel lines.

Buzzzz.

Then.

394

"How unreliable *is* this Gabby?" Charbonneau.

I hesitated. Somehow daylight colored things differently. I'd sent these men on a chase before, and we still didn't know if it had been for wild geese.

Claudel looked up at me, eyes reptilian cold, and I felt the tightening in my stomach. This man despised me, wanted to destroy me. What was he doing behind my back? How far had his complaint gone? What if I was wrong?

And then I did something I would forever be unable to change. Deep down maybe I didn't think anything bad would really happen to Gabby. She'd always landed on her feet before. Maybe I just took the safe path. Who knows? I did not elevate concern for my friend's safety to the level of urgency. I backed off.

"She has taken off before."

Buzzzz.

Buzzzz.

Buzzzz.

Ryan was the first to respond.

"Like this? Without a word?"

I nodded.

Buzzzz.

Buzzzz.

Buzzzz.

Ryan's expression was grim. "All right. Let's get a name, run a check. But we'll keep it low profile for now. Without something else, we couldn't get a warrant anyway." He turned to Charbonneau. "Michel?"

Charbonneau nodded. We discussed a few other points, gathered our things, and broke.

In the many times I'd look back on that meeting, I'd always wonder if I could have altered later events. Why had I not sounded the cry over Gabby? Had the sight of Claudel dampened my resolve? Had I sacrificed the

395

previous evening's zeal on the altar of professional caution? Had I compromised Gabby's survival rather than risk my professional standing? Would an all-out search begun that day have made any difference?

That night I went home and warmed a TV dinner. Swiss steak, I think. When the microwave beeped I removed the tray and peeled back the foil.

I stood there a moment, watching the synthetic gravy congeal on synthetic mashed potatoes, feeling loneliness and frustration tune up for the overture. I could eat this and spend another night fighting back demons, with the cat and the sitcoms, or I could be the conductor of the evening's performance.

"Fuck this. Maestro . . . ?"

I threw the dinner into the trash and walked to Chez Katsura on Rue de la Montagne, where I treated myself to sushi and exchanged small talk with a card salesman from Sudbury. Then, declining his invitations, I moved on and caught the late showing of *The Lion King* at Le Faubourg.

It was ten-forty when I left the theater and took the escalator to the main level. The tiny mall was largely deserted, the vendors gone, their wares stowed and sealed in carts. I passed the bagel bakery, the frozen yogurt stand, the Japanese carry-out, their shelves and counters stripped and barricaded behind collapsible security gates. Knives and saws hung in neat rows behind the butcher's empty cases.

The movie had been just what I needed. Singing hyenas, pounding African rhythms, and lion cub romance kept me from thinking of the murders for hours.

Well orchestrated, Brennan. Hakuna Matata.

I crossed Ste. Catherine and walked toward home. It was still hot and very humid. Mist haloed the streetlamps and hovered over the pavement, like steam from a hot tub on a cold winter night.

I saw the envelope as soon as I left the lobby and turned down my hall. It was wedged between the brass knob and the doorjamb. My first thought was Winston. Perhaps he needed to fix something and would be turning off the power or the water. No. He'd post a notice. A complaint about Birdie? A note from Gabby?

It wasn't. In fact, it wasn't a note at all. The envelope held two items, which lay on the table now, silent and terrible. I stared at them, heart pounding, hands trembling, knowing, yet refusing to admit their meaning.

The envelope contained a plastic ID. Gabby's name, date of birth, and *numéro d'assurance maladie* appeared in raised white letters below a red sunset on the left-hand side of the card. Her image was at the upper right, dreadlocks swinging, something silver dangling from each ear.

The other item was a two-inch square cut from a large-scale city map. The map was in French, and showed streets and green spaces in an agonizingly familiar color code. I looked for landmarks or names that would help me pinpoint the neighborhood. Rue Ste. Hélène. Rue Beauchamp. Rue Champlain. I didn't know those streets. Could be Montreal, could be a score of other cities. I hadn't lived in Quebec long enough to know. The map contained no highways or features I could identify. Except one. A large black X covered the center of the map.

I stared numbly at the X. Terrible images formed in my mind but I fought them off, denying the one acceptable conclusion. It was a bluff. It was like the skull in the garden. This maniac was toying with me. Seeing how frightened he could make me.

I don't know how long I looked at Gabby's face, remembering it in other places, other times. A happy face in a clown hat at Katy's third birthday party. A face bathed in tears as she told me of her brother's suicide.

397

The house was silent around me, the universe at a standstill. Then horrible certainty overtook me.

It wasn't a bluff. Dear God, dear God, dear Gabby. I'm so very, terribly sorry.

Ryan picked up on the third ring.

"He's got Gabby," I whispered, knuckles white on the receiver, voice steady by sheer strength of will.

He wasn't fooled.

"Who?" he asked, sensing the underlying terror and going straight to the crux.

"I don't know."

"Where are they?"

"I – I don't know."

I heard the sound of a hand passing over a face.

"What do you have?"

He heard me out without interrupting.

"Shit."

Pause.

"Okay. I'll take the map in so ident can pinpoint the location, then we'll get a team out there."

"I can take the map in," I said.

"I think you should stay there. And I want a surveillance unit back on your building."

"I'm not the one in danger," I snapped. "This bastard's got Gabby! He's probably killed her already!"

My mask was crumbling. I fought to control the trembling in my hands.

"Brennan, I feel sick about your friend. I would help her in any way I could. Believe that. But you have to use your head. If this psychopath only got her purse but not her, she's probably okay, wherever she is. If he has her and has shown us where to find her, he will have left her in whatever state he wants her found. We can't change that. Meanwhile, someone put a note on your door, Brennan. This sonofabitch was in your building. He knows your car. If this guy is the killer, he won't hesitate

398

to add you to his list. Respect for life is not among his personality traits, and he seems to have focused on yours right now."

He had a point.

"And I'll get somebody on the guy you followed."

I spoke slowly and softly. "I want ident to call me as soon as they pull up the location."

"Bren–"

"Is that a problem?" Not so softly.

It was irrational and I knew it, but Ryan was sensitive to my growing hysteria, or was it rage? Maybe he just didn't want to deal with me.

"No."

Ryan got the envelope around midnight, and the ident unit called an hour later. They lifted one print from the card. Mine. The X marked an abandoned lot in St. Lambert. An hour later I got a second call from Ryan. A patrol unit had checked the lot and all surrounding buildings. Nothing. Ryan had arranged for recovery in the morning. Including dogs. We were going back to the south shore.

"What time tomorrow?" I said, my voice shaking, my grief for Gabby already too dreadful to bear.

"I'll set it up for seven."

"Six."

"Six. Want a ride?"

"Thanks."

He hesitated. "She may be fine."

"Yeah."

I went through the normal bedtime motions, though I knew I wouldn't sleep. Teeth. Face. Hand lotion. Nightshirt. Then I wandered from room to room, trying not to think about the women on the bulletin boards. Murder scene photos. Autopsy descriptions. Gabby.

I adjusted a picture, repositioned a vase, picked fluff from the carpet. I felt cold, made myself a cup of tea, and turned down the air-conditioning. Minutes later, I shot it back up. Birdie withdrew to the bedroom, fed up with the pointless movement, but I couldn't stop myself. The feeling of helplessness in the face of impending horror was unbearable.

Around two, I stretched out on the couch, closed my eyes, and tried to will myself to relax. Concentrate on night sounds. AC compressor. Ambulance. Trickle of taps on the floor above. Water flowing through a pipe. Wood creaking. Walls settling.

My mind drifted to a visual mode. Images floated past, spinning and tumbling like parts of a Hollywood dream sequence. I saw Chantale Trottier's plaid jumper. Morisette-Champoux's gutted belly. The putrefied head that was Isabelle Gagnon. A severed hand. A mangled breast cupped in bone-white lips. A lifeless monkey. A statue. A plunger. A knife.

I couldn't help myself. I produced a cinema of death, tortured by the thought that Gabby had joined the cast. Darkness was fading into light when I got up to dress.

34

The sun had barely climbed above the horizon when we uncovered Gabby's body. Margot had gone directly to it, scarcely hesitating when released inside the plywood fence surrounding the property. She'd scented for a moment, then raced across the wooded lot, the saffron dawn tinging her fur and illuminating the dust around her feet.

The grave was hidden inside a crumbling house foundation. It was shallow, dug quickly, filled with haste. Standard. But then the killer had added a personal touch, outlining the burial with a carefully placed oval of bricks.

Her corpse lay on the ground now, zippered in its body bag. We'd sealed the scene with sawhorses and yellow tape, but it hadn't been necessary. The early hour and the plywood barrier had been protection enough. No one had come to gawk as we unearthed the body and went through our macabre routines.

I sat in a patrol unit, sipping cold coffee from a Styrofoam cup. The radio cackled and the usual motion swirled around me. I'd come to do my job, to be a professional, but found I couldn't do it. The others would have to manage. Perhaps later my brain would accept the messages it was currently rejecting. For now, I was numb and my brain was numb. I didn't want to see her in the trench, to replay the scene of the marbled and bloated body emerging as the layers of dirt were lifted off. I'd recognized the silver earrings instantly. Ganesh. I recalled an image of Gabby explaining about the little elephant. A friendly god. A happy god. Not a god of pain and death. Where were you, Ganesh? Why didn't you protect your friend? Why didn't *any* of her friends protect her? Agony. Push it away.

I'd done a visual ID on the body, then Ryan had taken charge of the scene. I watched as he conferred with Pierre Gilbert. They spoke a moment, then Ryan turned and walked in my direction.

He hitched his pant legs and squatted next to the open car door, one hand on the armrest. Though it was only midmorning, the temperature was already twenty-seven Celsius, and perspiration soaked his hair and armpits.

"I'm so sorry," he said.

I nodded.

"I know how hard this is."

No. You don't. "The body isn't too bad. I'm surprised, considering this heat."

"We don't know how long she's been here."

"Yes."

He reached over and took my hand. His palm left a small saddle of perspiration on the vinyl armrest. "There was noth–"

"Have you found anything?"

"Not much."

"No footprints, no tire tracks, nothing in this whole bloody field?"

He shook his head.

"Latents on the bricks?" I knew that was stupid even as I said it.

402

His eyes held mine.

"Nothing down in the pit?"

"There was one thing, Tempe. Lying on her chest." He hesitated a moment. "A surgical glove."

"A little sloppy for this guy. He never left anything before. Might be prints inside." I was fighting for control. "Anything else?"

"I don't think she was killed here, Tempe. She was probably transported from somewhere else."

"What is this place?"

"A tavern that closed down years ago. The property was sold, the building was knocked down, then the buyer went belly-up. The lot's been boarded up for six years."

"Who owns it?"

"You want a name?"

"Yes, a name," I snarled.

He checked his notebook. "Guy named Bailey."

Behind him I could see two attendants lift Gabby's remains onto a stretcher, then wheel it toward the coroner's van.

Oh, Gabby! I'm so sorry!

"Can I get you anything?" The ice blue eyes were studying my face.

"What?"

"Do you want a drink? Something to eat? Would you like to go home?"

Yes. And never come back.

"No. I'm fine."

For the first time I noticed the hand he'd placed over mine. The fingers were slender, but the hand itself was broad and angular. A dashed semicircle arced across his thumb knuckle.

"She wasn't mutilated."

"No."

"Why the bricks?"

403

"I've never been able to understand how these mutants think."

"It's a taunt, isn't it? He wanted us to find her, and he wanted to make a statement. There won't be any prints inside the glove."

He didn't say anything.

"This is different, isn't it, Ryan?"

"Yes."

The heat in the car was like molasses against my skin. I got out and lifted my hair to feel the breeze on my neck. There was none. I watched them secure the body bag with black canvas straps and slide it into the van. I felt a sob build in my chest and fought it back.

"Could I have saved her, Ryan?"

"Could any of us have saved her? I don't know." He let out a deep breath and squinted up into the sun. "Weeks ago, maybe. Probably not yesterday or the day before." He turned back and locked his gaze on me. "What I do know is we'll get this cocksucker. He's a dead man."

I spotted Claudel walking toward us, carrying a plastic evidence bag. He says one thing to me and I'll rip his goddamn lips off, I promised myself. I meant it.

"Very sorry," Claudel mumbled, avoiding my eyes. To Ryan. "We're about done here."

Ryan raised his eyebrows. Claudel gave him an "over there" head signal.

My pulse quickened. "What? What did you find?" Ryan placed a hand on each of my shoulders.

I looked at the bag in Claudel's hand. I could see a pale yellow surgical glove, dark brown stains mottling its surface. Protruding from the glove's rim was a flat object. Rectangle. White border. Dark background. A snapshot. Ryan's hands squeezed hard on my shoulders. I stared a question at him, already fearing the answer.

"Let's do this later."

404

"Let me see it." I reached out a trembling hand.

Claudel hesitated, extended the bag. I took it, grasped one glove finger through the plastic, and tapped gently until the photo slid free. I reoriented the bag and stared through the plastic.

Two figures, arms entwined, hair whipping, ocean breakers rolling behind. Fear gripped me. My breathing quickened. Calm. Stay calm.

Myrtle Beach – 1992. Me. Katy. The bastard had buried a picture of my daughter with my murdered friend.

No one spoke. I watched Charbonneau approach from the grave site. He joined us, looked at Ryan, who nodded. The three men stood in silence. No one knew how to act, what to say. I didn't feel like helping them out. Charbonneau broke the silence.

"Let's go nail this sonofabitch."

"Got the warrant?" Ryan.

"Bertrand will meet us. They issued as soon as we found the . . . body." He looked at me, quickly away.

"Is our boy there now?"

"No one's gone in or out since they staked the place. I don't think we should wait."

"Yeah."

Ryan turned to me. "Judge Tessier bought probable cause and cut a warrant this morning, so we're going to bust the guy you tailed Thursday night. I'll drop y–"

"No way, Ryan. I'm in."

"Br–"

"In case you forgot, I just identified my best friend. She was holding a picture of me and my daughter. It may be this slimy piece of shit, or it may be some other psychopath that killed her, but I'm going to find out, and I'm going to do everything I can to fry his sorry ass. I will hunt him down and flush him out with or without you and your Merry Men." My finger was stabbing the

405

air like a hydraulic piston. "I will be there! Starting now!"

My eyes burned and my chest began to heave. Don't cry. Don't you dare cry. I forced calmness over my hysteria. For a long time no one spoke.

"*Allons-y*," said Claudel. Let's go.

35

By noon the temperature and humidity were so high the city was rendered lifeless. Nothing moved. Trees, birds, insects, and humans held themselves as still as possible, immobilized by the stifling heat. Most stayed out of sight.

The drive was St. Jean Baptiste Day all over again. The tense silence. The smell of air-conditioned sweat. The fear in my gut. Only Claudel's surliness was absent. He and Charbonneau were meeting us there.

And the traffic was different. On our trip to Rue Berger we had fought holiday crowds. Today we breezed through empty streets, arriving at the suspect's place in less than twenty minutes. When we turned the corner I could see Bertrand, Charbonneau, and Claudel in an unmarked car, Bertrand's unit parked behind. The crime scene van was at the end of the block, Gilbert behind the wheel, a tech slumped against the passenger side window.

The three detectives got out as we walked toward them. The street was as I remembered it, though daylight showed it to be even plainer and more worn than it had appeared in the dark. My shirt was pasted to my clammy skin.

"Where's the stakeout team?" Ryan asked by way of greeting.

"They circled round back." Charbonneau.

"He in there?"

"No activity since they got here around midnight. He could be asleep inside."

"There's a back entrance?"

Charbonneau nodded. "Been covered all night. We've got units at each end of the block, and there's one on Martineau." He jerked a thumb toward the opposite side of the street. "If lover boy's in there, he's not going anywhere."

Ryan turned to Bertrand. "Got the paper?"

Bertrand nodded. "It's 1436 Séguin. Number 201. Come on down." He mimicked the game show invitation.

We stood a moment, sizing up the building as one would an adversary, preparing ourselves for assault and capture. Two black kids rounded the corner and started up the block, rap music blaring from an enormous boom box. They wore Air Jordans and pants big enough to house a nuclear family. Their T-shirts bore totems of violence, one a skull with melting eyeballs, the other the grim reaper with beach umbrella. Death on Vacation. The taller boy had shaved his scalp, leaving only an oval cap on top. The other had dreadlocks.

A mental flash of Gabby's dreadlocks. A stab of pain.

Later. Not now. I yanked my attention back to the moment.

We watched the boys enter a nearby building, heard the rap truncated as a door closed behind them. Ryan looked in both directions, then back at us.

"We set?"

"Let's get the sonofabitch." Claudel.

"Luc, you and Michel cover the back. If he bolts,

408

squash him."

Claudel squinted, tipped his head as though to speak, then shook it, exhaling sharply through his nose. He and Charbonneau moved off, turned back at Ryan's voice.

"We do this by the books." His eyes were hard. "No mistakes."

The CUM detectives crossed the street and disappeared around the graystone.

Ryan turned to me.

"Ready?"

I nodded.

"This could be the guy."

"Yes, Ryan, I know that."

"You all right?"

"Jesus, Ryan . . ."

"Let's go."

I felt a bubble of fear swell in my chest as we mounted the iron stairs. The outer door was unlocked. We entered a small lobby with a grimy tile floor. Mailboxes lined the right wall, circulars lay on the floor beneath them. Bertrand tried the inner door. It was also open.

"Great security," said Bertrand.

We crossed into a poorly lit corridor shrouded in heat and the smell of cooking grease. A threadbare carpet ran toward the back of the building and up a staircase to the right, secured at three-foot intervals by thin metal strips. Over it someone had laid a vinyl runner, at one time clear, now opaque with age and grime.

We climbed to the second floor, our feet making faint tapping sounds on the vinyl – 201 was first on the right. Ryan and Bertrand placed themselves on either side of the dark wooden door, backs to the wall, jackets unbuttoned, hands resting loosely on their weapons.

Ryan motioned me beside him. I flattened myself

409

against the wall, felt the rough plaster pluck at my hair. I took a deep breath, drawing in the mildew and dust. I could smell Ryan's sweat.

Ryan nodded to Bertrand. The anxiety bubble swelled up into my throat.

Bertrand knocked.

Nothing.

He knocked again.

No response.

Ryan and Bertrand tensed. My breath was coming fast.

"Police. Open up."

Down the hall a door opened quietly. Eyes peered through a crack the width of a security chain.

Bertrand knocked harder, five sharp raps in the sweltering silence. Silence.

Then. *"Monsieur Tanguay n'est pas ici."*

Our heads whipped toward the sound of the voice. It was soft and high-pitched, and came from across the corridor.

Ryan gave Bertrand a stay-here gesture and we crossed. The eyes watched, their irises magnified behind thick lenses. They were barely four feet off the floor, and angled higher and higher as we approached.

The eyes shifted from Ryan to me and back, seeking the least threatening place to land. Ryan squatted to meet them at their level.

"Bonjour," he said.

"Hi."

"Comment ça va?"

"Ça va."

The child waited. I couldn't tell if it was a boy or girl.

"Is your mother home?"

Head shake.

"Father?"

"No."

"Anyone?"

"Who are you?"

Good, kid. Don't tell a stranger anything.

"Police." Ryan showed him his badge. The eyes grew even larger.

"Can I hold it?"

Ryan passed the badge through the crack. The child studied it solemnly, handed it back.

"Are you looking for Monsieur Tanguay?"

"Yes, we are."

"Why?"

"We want to ask him some questions. Do you know Monsieur Tanguay?"

The child nodded, offered nothing.

"What's your name?"

"Mathieu." Boy.

"When will your mother be home, Mathieu?"

"I live with my grammama."

Ryan shifted his weight and a joint cracked loudly. He dropped one knee to the floor, propped an elbow on the other, rested chin on knuckles, and looked at Mathieu.

"How old are you, Mathieu?"

"Six."

"How long have you lived here?"

The child looked puzzled, as though other possibilities had never occurred to him.

"Always."

"Do you know Monsieur Tanguay?"

Mathieu nodded.

"How long has he lived here?"

Shrug.

"When will your grammama be home?"

"She cleans for people." Pause. "Saturday." Mathieu rolled his eyes and nibbled his lower lip. "Just a minute." He disappeared into the apartment, reappeared in less than a minute. "Three-thirty."

"Sh . . . Shoot," said Ryan, uncoiling from his hunched position. He spoke to me, his voice tense, just above a whisper. "That asshole may be in there and we've got an unattended kid here."

Mathieu watched like a barn cat with a cornered rat, his eyes never leaving Ryan's face.

"Monsieur Tanguay's not here."

"Are you sure?" Ryan crouched again.

"He's gone away."

"Where?"

Another shrug. A chubby finger pushed his glasses up the bridge of his nose.

"How do you know he's away?"

"I'm taking care of his fish." A smile the size of the Mississippi lit his face. "He's got tetras, and angelfish, and white clouds." He used the English names. "They're fantastic!" *Fantastique!* Such a perfect word. Its English counterpart never quite matches it.

"When will Monsieur Tanguay be back?"

Shrug.

"Did Grammama write it on the calendar?" I asked.

The child regarded me, surprised, then disappeared as he had before.

"What calendar?" Ryan asked, looking up.

"They must keep one. He went to check something when he wasn't sure when Grammama would be home today."

Mathieu returned. "Nope."

Ryan stood. "Now what?"

"If he's right, we go in and toss the place. We've got a name, we'll run Monsieur Tanguay down. Maybe Grammama knows where he's gone. If not, we'll pop him as soon as he comes anywhere near here."

Ryan looked to Bertrand, pointed at the door.

412

Five more raps.

Nothing.

"Break it?" asked Bertrand.

"Monsieur Tanguay won't like it."

We all looked at the boy.

Ryan lowered himself a third time.

"He gets really mad if you do something bad," said Mathieu.

"It's important that we look for something in Monsieur Tanguay's apartment," explained Ryan.

"He won't like it if you break his door."

I squatted next to Ryan.

"Mathieu, do you have Monsieur Tanguay's fish in your apartment?"

Head shake.

"Do you have a key to Monsieur Tanguay's apartment?"

Mathieu nodded.

"Could you let us in?"

"No."

"Why not?"

"I can't come out when Grammama's gone."

"That's good, Mathieu. Grammama wants you to stay inside because she thinks it's safer for you. She's right, and you're a good boy to listen to her."

The Mississippi smile spread north again.

"Do you think we could use the key, Mathieu, just for a few minutes? It's very important police business and you are correct that we shouldn't break the door."

"I guess that would be okay," he said. "Because you're police."

Mathieu darted out of sight, returned with a key. He pressed his lips together and looked straight at me as he held it through the crack.

"Don't break Monsieur Tanguay's door."

"We'll be very careful."

413

"And don't go in the kitchen. That's bad. You can't ever go in the kitchen."

"You close the door and stay inside, Mathieu. I'll knock when we've finished. Don't open the door until you hear my knock."

The small face nodded solemnly, then disappeared behind the door.

We rejoined Bertrand, who knocked again, called out. There was an awkward pause, then Ryan nodded, and I slipped the key into the lock.

The door opened directly into a small living room, its color scheme shades of maroon. Shelves stretched from floor to ceiling on two sides, the other walls were wood, every surface darkened by years of varnishing. Crushed red velvet looped across the windows, backed by graying lace, which blocked most of the sunlight. We stood absolutely still, listening and peering into the unlit room.

The only sound I heard was a faint buzzing, erratic, like electricity jumping a broken circuit. Bzzt. Bzzzzzt. Bzt. Bzt. It came from behind double doors ahead and to the left. Otherwise, the place was deathly quiet.

Poor choice of adverb, Brennan.

I looked around and furniture shapes emerged from the deep shadow, looking old and worn. The center of the room was occupied by a carved wooden table with matching chairs. A well-used couch sagged in the front bay, a Mexican blanket stretched across it. Opposite, a wooden trunk served as a stand for a Sony Trinitron.

Scattered about the room were small wooden tables and cabinets. Some were quite nice, not unlike pieces I'd unearthed at flea markets. I doubted any of these had been afternoon finds, purchased as bargains to strip and refinish. They looked as though they'd been in the place for years, ignored and unappreciated as successive tenants came and went.

414

The floor was covered by an aging dhurrie. And plants. Everywhere. They were tucked in corners and strung along baseboards and hung from hooks. What the occupant lacked in furnishings, he'd made up for in greenery. Plants dangled from wall brackets and rested on windowsills, tabletops, sideboards, and shelves.

"Looks like a fucking botanical garden," said Bertrand.

And smells, I thought. A musty odor permeated the air, a blend of fungus, and leaves, and damp earth.

Across from the main entrance a short hall led to a single closed door. Ryan gestured me back with the same move he'd used in the hall, then slid along the wall, shoulders hunched, knees bent, back pressed to the plaster. He inched up to the door, paused, then shot a foot hard against the wood.

The door flew in, hit the wall, and recoiled toward the frame, then came to rest half open. I strained for sounds of movement, my heart beating with the erratic buzzing. Bzzzzzzt. Bzt. Bzt. Bzzzzt. Da dum dum dum. Da dum. Da dum dum.

An eerie glow seeped from behind the half-open door, accompanied by a soft gurgling.

"Found the fish," said Ryan, moving through the door.

He flicked a switch with his pen and the room was thrown into brightness. Standard bedroom. Single bed, Indian print spread. Nightstand, lamp, alarm, nasal spray. Dresser, no mirror. Tiny bath to the rear. One window. Heavy drapes blocked a view of a brick wall.

The only uncommon items were the tanks that lined the brick wall. Mathieu was right, they were *fantastique*. Electric blues, canary yellows, and black-and-white stripes darted in and out of rose and white coral and foliage of every shade of green imaginable. Each tiny

415

ecosystem was illuminated in aquamarine and lulled by a rolling oxygen sonata.

I watched, mesmerized, feeling an idea about to form. Coaxing it. What? Fish? What? Nothing.

Ryan moved around me, using his pen to sweep back the shower curtain, open the medicine cabinet, poke among the food and nets surrounding the tanks. He used a hanky to open dresser drawers, then the pen to leaf through underwear, socks, shirts, and sweaters.

Forget the fish, Brennan. Whatever idea was in my mind, it was as elusive as the bubbles in the tanks, rising toward the surface only to disappear.

"Anything?"

He shook his head. "Nothing obvious. Don't want to piss off recovery, so I'm just doing a quick check. Let's case the other rooms, then I'll turn it over to Gilbert. Pretty clear Tanguay's elsewhere. We'll nail his ass, but in the meantime we might as well find out what he has here."

Back in the living room Bertrand was inspecting the TV.

"State of the art," he said. "Boy likes his tube."

"Probably needs a regular Cousteau fix," said Ryan absently, body tense, eyes scanning the gloom around us. No one would surprise us today.

I wandered to the shelves containing the books. The range of topics was impressive, and, like the TV, the books looked new. I scanned the titles. Ecology. Ichthyology. Ornithology. Psychology. Sex. Lots of science, but the guy's taste was eclectic. Buddhism. Scientology. Archaeology. Maori art. Kwakiutl wood carving. Samurai warriors. World War II artifacts. Cannibalism.

The shelves held hundreds of paperbacks, including modern fiction, both French and English. Many of my favorites were present. Vonnegut. Irving. McMurtry.

416

But the majority were crime fiction novels. Brutal murderers. Deranged stalkers. Violent psychopaths. Heartless cities. I could quote their cover blurbs without even reading them. There was also an entire shelf of nonfiction devoted to the lives of serial and spree killers. Manson. Bundy. Ramirez. Boden.

"I think Tanguay and St. Jacques belong to the same book club," I said.

"This butt wipe probably *is* St. Jacques," said Bertrand.

"No, this guy brushes his teeth," said Ryan.

"Yeah. When he's Tanguay."

"If he reads this stuff, his interests are incredibly broad," I said. "And he's bilingual." I glanced over the collection again. "And he's compulsive as hell."

"What are you now, Dr. Ruth?" asked Bertrand.

"Look at this."

They joined me.

"Everything's arranged by topic, alphabetically." I pointed to several shelves. "Then by author within each category, again alphabetically. Then by year of publication for each author."

"Doesn't everyone do that?"

Ryan and I looked at him. Bertrand was not a reader.

"Look how every book is aligned with the edge of the shelf."

"He does the same with his shorts and socks. Must use a square edge to stack them," said Ryan.

Ryan voiced my thoughts.

"Fits the profile."

"Maybe he just keeps the books for show. Wants his friends to think he's an intellectual," said Bertrand.

"I don't think so," I said. "They're not dusty. Also, look at the little yellow slips. He not only reads this stuff, he marks certain things to go back to. Let's point

417

that out to Gilbert and his commandos so they don't lose the markers. Could be useful."

"I'll have them seal the books before they dust."

"Something else about Monsieur Tanguay."

They stared at the shelves.

"He reads some weird shit," said Bertrand.

"Besides the crime stories, what interests him most?" I asked. "Look at the very top shelf."

They looked again.

"Shit," said Ryan. "*Gray's Anatomy. Cunningham's Manual of Practical Anatomy. Color Atlas of Human Anatomy. Handbook of Anatomical Dissection. Medical Illustration of the Human Body.* Christ, look at this. *Sabiston's Principles of Surgery.* He's got more of this shit than a med school library. Looks like he's heavy into knowing what a body's got inside."

"Yeah, and not just the software. This squirrel's into the hardware."

Ryan reached for his radio. "Let's get Gilbert and his raiders up here. I'll tell the teams out back to go to ground and watch for Dr. Prick. We don't want to spook him when he shows up. Christ, Claudel's probably got his nuts in a half hitch by now."

Ryan spoke into his handset. Bertrand continued to skim the titles behind me.

"Bzt. Bzzzzzzt. Bzzt. Bzt.

"Hey, this is your kind of stuff." He used a hanky to withdraw something. "Looks like there's just this one."

He laid a single volume of the *American Anthropologist* on the table. July 1993. I didn't have to open it. I knew one entry on its table of contents. "A major hit," she'd called it. "Fodder for promotion to full professor."

Gabby's article. The sight of the *AA* hit me like a snapped cable. I wanted out of there. I wanted to be gone to a sunny Saturday where I was safe, and no one

418

was dead, and my best friend would be calling with plans for dinner.

Water. Cold water on your face, Brennan.

I lurched toward the double doors and flipped one open with my foot, looking for the kitchen.

BZZZZZT. BZZZZZT. BZT. BZZZZZZT. BZT.

The room had no window. A digital clock to my right gave off a luminous orange glow. I could make out two white shapes and another pale stretch at waist level. Refrigerator, stove, sink, I assumed. I felt for a switch. The hell with procedure. They could sort out my prints.

The back of my hand pressed to my mouth, I stumbled to the sink and splashed cold water on my face. When I straightened and turned, Ryan was standing in the doorway.

"I'm fine."

Flies shot around the room, startled at the sudden intrusion.

BZZT. BZT. BZZZZT.

"Mint?" He offered a roll of Life Savers.

"Thanks." I took one. "The heat."

"It's a cooker."

A fly careened off his cheek. "What the fu–" He swatted at the air. "What's this guy do in here?"

Ryan and I saw them at the same time. Two brown objects lay on the counter, halos of grease staining the paper towels on which they dried. Flies danced around them, landing and taking off in nervous agitation. A surgical glove lay to their left, a twin to the one we'd just unearthed. We went closer, fomenting the flies to excited flight.

I looked at each shriveled mass and thought of the roaches and spiders in the barber pole, their legs dried and constricted in rigor. These objects had nothing to do with arachnids, however. I knew instantly what they

419

were, though I'd only seen the others in photos.

"They're paws."

"What?"

"Paws from some kind of animal."

"Are you sure?"

"Flip one over."

He did. With his pen.

"You can see the ends of the lower limb bones."

"What's he doing with them?"

"How the hell should I know, Ryan?" I thought of Alsa.

"Christ."

"Check the refrigerator."

"Oh, Christ."

The tiny corpse was there, skinned and wrapped in clear plastic. Along with several others.

"What are they?"

"Small mammals of some sort. Without the skin I can't tell. They're not horses."

"Thanks, Brennan."

Bertrand joined us. "What've you got?"

"Dead animals." Ryan's voice betrayed his aggravation. "And another glove."

"Maybe the guy eats roadkill," said Bertrand.

"Maybe. And maybe he makes lampshades out of people. That's it. I want this place sealed. I want every friggin' thing confiscated. Bag his cutlery, bag that blender, bag everything in the goddamn refrigerator. I want that disposal scraped and every inch of this place hosed with Luminol. Where the hell's Gilbert?"

Ryan moved toward a wall phone to the left of the door.

"Hold it. That phone got a redial button?"

Ryan nodded.

"Hit it."

"Probably his priest. Or Grammama."

Ryan pushed the button. We listened to a seven-note melody followed by four rings. Then a voice answered, and the bubble of fear I'd been carrying all day rose to my head and I felt faint.

"*Veuillez laisser votre nom et numéro de téléphone. Je vais vous rappeler le plutôt possible. Merci.* Please leave your name and number and I'll return your call as soon as possible. Thanks. This is Tempe."

36

The sound of my own voice hit me like a blow to the head. My legs buckled and my breath came in rapid gasps.

Ryan helped me to a chair, brought water, asked no questions. I have no idea how long I sat there, feeling nothing but emptiness. Eventually, my composure crept back, and I began to assess the reality.

He'd phoned me. Why? When?

I watched Gilbert don rubber gloves and slide his hand around the inside of the disposal. He drew something out and dropped it in the sink.

Was he trying to reach me? Or Gabby? What had he intended to say? Had he intended to speak at all, or just check whether I was there?

A photographer moved from room to room, his flash like a firefly in the gloomy flat.

The hang-ups. Was it he?

A tech in rubber gloves and coveralls taped books and sealed them into evidence bags, marking each, then signing across the seal. Another brushed white powder across the red-black varnish of the shelves. A third emptied the refrigerator, removing packages in plain brown wrappers, and placing them in a cooler.

Had she died here, her last visual images the ones I now saw?

Ryan spoke to Charbonneau. Snatches of the conversation floated to me through the suffocating heat. Where's Claudel? Took off. Roust the superintendent. Find out about basements, storage areas. Get keys. Charbonneau left, returned with a middle-aged woman in housecoat and slippers. They disappeared again, accompanied by the book packer.

Again and again Ryan offered to take me home. There was nothing I could do, he told me gently. I knew that, but I couldn't leave.

Grammama arrived around four. She was neither hostile nor cooperative. Reluctantly, she provided a description of Tanguay. Male. Quiet. Brown hair, thinning. Medium everything. Could have fit half the men in North America. She had no idea where he was or how long he'd be gone. He'd left before, but never for long. She only noticed because Tanguay asked Mathieu to feed the fish. He was nice to Mathieu and gave him money when he cared for the fish. She knew little else about him, rarely saw him. She thought he worked, thought he had a car. Wasn't sure. Didn't care. Didn't want to get involved.

The recovery team spent all afternoon and late into the night dissecting the apartment. I didn't. By five I needed out. I accepted Ryan's offer of a ride and left.

We spoke little in the car. Ryan repeated what he'd said on the phone. I was to stay home. A team would watch my building around the clock. No late night sorties. No solo expeditions.

"Don't ride me, Ryan," I said, my voice betraying my emotional brittleness.

The rest of the drive was spent in strained silence. When we reached my building Ryan put the car in park and turned to me. I could feel his eyes on the side of my face.

"Listen, Brennan. I'm not trying to give you a hard time. This scum is going down. You can take that to the bank. I'd just like you to live to see it."

His concern touched me more than I was willing to admit.

They pulled out all stops. APB's went out to every cop in Quebec, to the Ontario Provincial Police, the RCMP, and the state forces in New York and Vermont. But Quebec is big, its borders easy to cross. Lots of places to hide or slip out.

In the days that followed I grappled with the possibilities. Tanguay could be lying low, biding his time. He could be dead. He could have taken off. Serial killers do that. Sensing danger, they pack up and relocate. Some are never caught. No. I refused to accept that.

Sunday I never left home. Birdie and I did what the French call *coconer*. We cocooned. I didn't get dressed, avoided the radio and television. I couldn't bear to see Gabby's photo, or hear the overdone descriptions of the victim and suspect. I made only three calls, first to Katy, then to my aunt in Chicago. Happy Birthday, Auntie! Eighty-four. Well done.

I knew Katy was in Charlotte, just wanted to reassure myself. No answer. Of course. Curse the distance. No. Bless the distance. I didn't want my daughter anywhere near the place a monster had held her picture. She would never know what I'd found.

The last call was to Gabby's mother. She was sedated, couldn't come to the phone. I spoke to Mr. Macaulay. Assuming they released the body, the funeral would be on Thursday.

For a time, I sat sobbing, my body rocking as though to a metronome. The demons that live in my bloodstream screamed for alcohol. Pleasure-pain, such a

424

simple principle. Feed us. Numb us. Make it go away.

But I didn't. That would have been easy. You're down love-forty, so lob one in, shake hands at the net, and it's Miller time. Except this wasn't tennis. If I gave up in this game, I would lose my career, my friends, my self-respect. Hell, I might as well let St. Jacques/ Tanguay do me in.

I would not give in. Not to the bottle, and not to the maniac. I owed it to Gabby. I owed it to myself and to my daughter. So I stayed sober and waited, desperately wishing I had Gabby to talk me through. I checked frequently to be sure the surveillance team was in place.

On Monday Ryan called around eleven-thirty. LaManche had completed the autopsy. Cause of death: ligature strangulation. Though the body was decomposed he'd found a groove buried deep in the flesh of Gabby's neck. Above and below it the skin was torn in a series of gouges and scratches. The vessels in the throat tissue showed hundreds of tiny hemorrhages.

Ryan's voice receded. I pictured Gabby desperately clawing to breathe, to live. Stop. Thank God we found her so quickly. I couldn't have faced the horror of Gabby on my autopsy table. The pain of losing her was unbearable enough.

". . . hyoid was broken. Also, whatever he used had links or loops or something, left a spiral pattern in the skin."

"Was she raped?"

"He couldn't tell because of the decomposition. Negative for sperm."

"Time of death?"

"LaManche is giving it a minimum of five days. We know the upper limit is ten."

"Pretty wide window."

"Given this heat and the shallow burial, he thinks the

body should be in worse shape."

Oh, God. She may not have died the day she disappeared.

"Have you checked her apartment?"

"No one saw her, but she'd been there."

"What about Tanguay?"

"Ready for this? The guy's a teacher. Small school out on the west island." I heard the rustle of paper. "St. Isidor's. Been there since 1991. He's twenty-eight. Single. For next of kin on his application he put 'none.' We're checking it. He's been living on Séguin since '91. Landlady thinks he was somewhere in the States before that."

"Prints?"

"Lots. We ran them, came up empty. Sent them south this morning."

"Inside the glove?"

"At least two readable and a smudged palm."

An image of Gabby. The plastic bag. Another glove. I jotted down a single word. Glove.

"He has a degree?"

"Bishops. Bertrand's out in Lennoxville now. Claudel's trying to roust someone at St. Isidor's, not having much luck. The caretaker is about a hundred and no one else is around. They're closed for the summer."

"Any names turn up in the apartment?"

"None. No pictures. No address books. No letters. Guy must live in a social vacuum."

A long silence as we mulled that over, then Ryan said,

"Might explain his unusual hobbies."

"The animals?"

"That. And the cutlery collection."

"Cutlery?"

"This squirrel had more blades than an orthopedic surgeon. Surgical tools mostly. Knives. Razors. Scalpels. Kept them stashed under the bed. Along with a box of surgical gloves. Original."

"A loner with a blade fetish. Great."

"And the standard porn gallery. Well thumbed."

"What else?"

"Guy's got a car." More rustling. "A 1987 Ford Probe. It's not in the neighborhood. They're looking for it. We got the driver's license photo this morning and sent that out too."

"And?"

"I'll let you judge for yourself, but I think Grammama was right. He's not memorable. Or maybe the Xerox/fax reproduction doesn't do him justice."

"Could it be St. Jacques?"

"Could be. Or Jean Chrétien. Or the guy that sells hot dogs on Rue St. Paul. Richard Petty's out. He's got a mustache."

"You're a laugh riot, Ryan."

"This guy doesn't even have a parking ticket. He's been a real good boy."

"Right. A real good boy who collects knives and porn and carves up small mammals."

Pause.

"What were they?"

"We're not sure yet. They're asking some guy over at U of M."

I looked at the word I'd written, swallowed hard.

"Any prints inside the glove we found with Gabby?" It was difficult to say her name.

"No."

"We knew there wouldn't be."

"Yeah."

I heard squad room noises in the background.

"I want to drop off a copy of this license photo so you'll have some idea what he looks like in case you meet him up close and personal. I still think it's better if you stick near home until we pop this asshole."

427

"I'm coming in. If ident is done with the gloves I want to take them over to biology. Then Lacroix."

"I think you sh–"

"Cut the macho crap, Ryan."

A breath drawn deeply, expelled.

"Are you holding out on me?"

"Brennan, what we know, you know."

"I'll be there in thirty minutes."

In less than half an hour I arrived at the lab. Ident had finished and sent the gloves to the biology section.

I looked at my watch – twelve-forty. I called the ident section at CUM headquarters to ask if I could see the photos taken at the St. Jacques apartment on Rue Berger. Lunchtime. The desk clerk would leave a message.

At one o'clock I walked over to the biology section. A woman with flyaway hair and a plump, Christmas angel face was shaking a glass vial. Two latex gloves lay on the counter behind her.

"*Bonjour*, Françoise."

"Ah. I thought I might see you today." The cherub eyes took on a worried expression. "I'm sorry. I don't quite know what to say to you."

"*Merci*. It's okay." I nodded at the gloves. "What have you got?"

"This one is clean. No blood." She gestured at Gabby's glove. "I'm just starting on the one from the kitchen. Would you like to watch?"

"Thank you."

"I've taken scrapings from these brown spots and rehydrated the sample in saline."

She examined the liquid and placed the vial in a test tube tray. Then she withdrew a glass pipette with a long, hollow projection, held it over a flame to seal it, and twisted off the tip.

"I'll test for human blood first."

Removing a tiny bottle from the refrigerator, she broke the seal and inserted the thin, tubular point of a fresh pipette. Like a mosquito sucking blood, the antiserum moved up the tiny pipeline. She sealed the other end with her thumb.

She then inserted the long beak of the pipette into the fire-sealed pipette, released her thumb, and allowed the antiserum to dribble out. She spoke as she worked.

"The blood knows its own proteins, or antigens. If it recognizes foreigners, antigens that don't belong, it tries to destroy them with antibodies. Some antibodies blow up foreign antigens, others clump them together. That clumping is called an agglutination reaction.

"Antiserum is created in an animal, usually a rabbit or a chicken, by injecting it with the blood of another species. The animal's blood recognizes the invaders and produces antibodies to protect itself. Injecting an animal with human blood produces human antiserum. Injecting it with goat blood produces goat antiserum. Horse blood produces horse antiserum.

"Human antiserum creates an agglutination reaction when mixed with human blood. Watch. If this is human blood a visible precipitate will form in the test tube, right where the sample solution and the antiserum meet. We'll compare to the saline as a control."

She tossed the pipette into a biological waste container and picked up the vial with the Tanguay sample solution. Using another pipette, she sucked the sample up the tube, released it into the antiserum, and set the pipette into a holder.

"How long will it take?" I asked.

"That depends on the strength of the antiserum. Anywhere from three to fifteen minutes. This is pretty good. Shouldn't be more than five or six minutes."

We checked it after five, Françoise holding the pipettes under the Luxolamp, a black card behind for

429

background. We checked again after ten. Fifteen. Nothing. No white band appeared between the antiserum and the sample solution. The mixture stayed as clear as the control saline.

"So. It's not human. Let's see if it's animal."

She went back to the refrigerator and withdrew a tray of small bottles.

"Can you tell the exact species?" I asked.

"No. Usually just family. Bovid. Cervid. Canid."

I looked at the tray. Written next to each bottle was an animal name. Goat. Rat. Horse. I pictured the paws in Tanguay's kitchen.

"Let's try dogs."

Nothing.

"What about something like a squirrel or a gopher?"

She thought a minute then reached for a bottle. "Maybe rat."

In less than four minutes a tiny parfait had formed in the tube, yellow above, clear below, a layer of foggy white between.

"*Voilà*," said Françoise. "It's animal blood. Something small, a mammal, like a rodent or a ground hog or something. That's about all I'll be able to determine. I don't know if that helps you."

"Yes," I said. "That helps. May I use your phone?"

"*Bien sûr*."

I dialed an extension down the hall.

"Lacroix."

I identified myself and explained what I wanted.

"Sure. Give me twenty minutes, I'm just finishing up a run."

I signed for the gloves, returned to my office, and spent the next half hour proofing and signing reports. Then I walked back to the corridor occupied by biology, and entered a door marked *Incendie et Explosifs*. Fire and Explosives.

430

A man in a lab coat stood in front of an enormous piece of machinery. A label identified it as an X-ray diffractometer. He didn't speak and I didn't say anything until he had removed a slide with a small white smear and dropped it on a tray. Then he gave me eyes as soft as a Disney fawn, lids drooping, lashes curling back like petals on a daisy.

"*Bonjour*, Monsieur Lacroix. *Comment ça va?*"

"*Bien. Bien.* You have them?"

I held up two plastic bags.

"Let's get started."

He led me into a small room with an apparatus the size of a photocopier, two monitors, and a printer. A periodic chart of the elements hung on the wall above.

Lacroix laid the evidence bags on a counter and pulled on surgical gloves. Gingerly, he withdrew each suspect glove, inspected it, then laid it on its plastic bag. The gloves stretched across his hands looked identical to those on the counter.

"First we look for gross characteristics, details of manufacturing. Weight. Density. Color. How the rims are finished." He turned each glove over and over, examining as he spoke. "These two look quite similar. Same rim technique. See?"

I looked. The wrist of each glove ended in a border that rolled outward onto itself.

"They're not all like that?"

"No. Some roll in, some roll out. These are both outies. So. Now we see what's in them."

He carried Gabby's glove to the machine, raised the cover, and placed it on a tray inside.

"With very small samples I use those little holders." He pointed to a tray of small plastic tubes. "I stretch a square of polypropylene window film across the holder, then use press-on tabs to make a sticky spot to hold the fragment. That's not necessary with this. We'll just put

431

the whole glove in."

Lacroix flipped a switch and the apparatus whirred to life. A box positioned on a pole in one corner lit up, the word X RAY white against a red background. A panel of buttons glowed, indicating the machine's condition. Red: X rays. White: Power. Orange: Shutter open.

For a few moments Lacroix adjusted dials, then he closed the cover and moved to a chair in front of the monitors.

"*S'il vous plaît.*" He indicated the other chair.

A desert landscape appeared on the first monitor, a granular backdrop of synclines and anticlines, with shadows and boulders scattered here and there. Superimposed on that scene was a series of concentric circles, the two smallest and most central shaped like footballs. Two hashed lines intersected at right angles, forming a cross directly over the bull's-eye circles.

Lacroix adjusted the image by manipulating a joy stick. Boulders shifted in and out of the circles.

"That's the glove we're looking at, magnified eighty times. I'm just picking a target location. Each run samples an area of about three hundred microns, approximately the area inside the dotted circle. So you want to direct your X rays onto the best part of your sample."

He shifted the crosshairs a few more moments, then settled on a boulderless patch.

"There. That should be good."

He flipped a switch and the machine hummed.

"Now we're creating a vacuum. That'll take a couple of minutes. Then the scan. That's very quick."

"And this will determine what's in the glove."

"*Oui.* It's a form of X-ray analysis. X-ray micro-fluorescence can determine what elements are present in a sample."

The humming stopped and a pattern began to form on the right-hand monitor. A series of tiny red mounds

432

sprouted across the bottom of the screen, then grew against a bright blue background, a thin yellow stripe up the middle of each. In the lower left-hand corner was an image of a keyboard, each key marked with the abbreviation for an element.

Lacroix typed in commands, and letters appeared on the screen. Some mounds remained small, others grew into tall peaks, like the giant termite castles I'd seen in Australia.

"*C'est ça.*" That's it. Lacroix pointed at a column on the far right. It rose from the bottom to the top of the screen, where its top was truncated. A smaller peak to its right climbed to a quarter of its height. Both were marked Zn.

"Zinc. That's standard. It's found in all these gloves."

He indicated a pair of peaks to the far left, one low, the other rising three quarters of the distance up the screen. "That low one is magnesium. Mg. The tall one marked Si is silicon." Farther to the right a double peak bore the letter S.

"Sulfur."

A Ca peak spired halfway up the screen.

"Quite a bit of calcium."

Beyond the calcium a gap, then a series of low mounds, foothills to the zinc pinnacle. Fe.

"A little iron."

He leaned back and summarized. "Pretty common cocktail. Lots of zinc, with silicon and calcium, the other major components. I'll print these, then let's test another spot."

We ran ten tests. All showed the same combination of elements.

"Right, then. The other glove."

We repeated the procedure with the glove from Tanguay's kitchen.

The peaks for zinc and sulfur were similar, but this

433

glove contained more calcium, and had no iron, silicon, or magnesium. A small spike indicated the presence of potassium. It was the same on every run.

"What does this mean?" I asked, already certain of the answer.

"Each manufacturer uses a slightly different recipe for the latex. There will even be variations among gloves from the same company, but it will be within limits."

"So these gloves are not a pair?"

"They weren't even made by the same company."

He got up to remove the glove. My mind was stumbling over our finding.

"Would X-ray diffraction give more information?"

"What we've done, X-ray microfluorescence, tells what elements are present in an object. X-ray diffraction can describe the actual mixture of the elements. The chemical structure. For example, with microfluorescence we can know that something contains sodium and chloride. With diffraction we can tell that it is made up of sodium-chloride crystals.

"To oversimplify, in the X-ray diffractometer a sample is rotated and hit with X rays. The X rays bounce off the crystals, and their pattern of diffraction indicates the structure of those crystals.

"So one limitation with diffraction is that it can only be done on materials with a crystalline structure. That's about eighty percent of everything that comes in. Unfortunately, latex is not crystalline in structure. Diffraction probably wouldn't add much anyway. These gloves are definitely made by different manufacturers."

"What if they're just from different boxes? Surely individual batches of latex must vary."

He was silent for a moment. Then:

"Wait. Let me show you something."

He disappeared into the main lab and I could hear him talking to the technician. He reappeared with a

434

stack of printouts, each composed of seven or eight sheets showing the familiar spire and steeple patterning. He unfolded each series and we looked at the variations in pattern.

"Each of these shows a sequence of tests done on gloves from a single manufacturer, but sampled from different boxes. There is variation, but the differences are never as great as those in the gloves we just analyzed."

I examined several series. The size of the peaks varied, but the components showed consistency.

"Now. Look at this."

He unfurled another series of printouts. Again, there were some differences, but overall the mix was the same.

Then I caught my breath. The configuration looked familiar. I looked at the symbols. Zn. Fe. Ca. S. Si. Mg. High zinc, silicon, and calcium content. Traces of the other elements. I laid the printout from Gabby's glove above the series. The pattern was almost identical.

"Monsieur Lacroix, are these gloves from the same manufacturer?"

"Yes, yes. That's my point. From the same box, probably. I just remembered this."

"What case is this?" My heart rate had picked up tempo.

"It came in just a few weeks ago." He flipped to the first sheet in the series. *Numéro d'événement:* 327468. "I can pull it up on the computer."

"Please."

Data filled the screen in seconds. I scanned it.

Numéro d'événement: 327468. Numéro de LML: 29427. Requesting Agency: CUM. Investigators: L. Claudel and M. Charbonneau. Recovery location: 1422 Rue Berger. Recovery date: 24/06/94.

An old rubber glove. Maybe the guy worried about his nails. Claudel! I thought he'd meant a glove for household cleaning! St. Jacques had a surgical glove! It matched the one in Gabby's grave!

I thanked Monsieur Lacroix, gathered the printouts, and left. I returned the gloves to property, my mind tearing through what I'd just learned. The glove from Tanguay's kitchen did not match the one buried with Gabby's body. Tanguay's prints were on it. The outside stains were animal blood. The glove found with Gabby was clean. No blood. No prints. St. Jacques had a surgical glove. It matched the one in Gabby's grave. Was Bertrand right? Were Tanguay and St. Jacques the same person?

A pink slip waited on my desk. CUM Ident had called. The photos of the Rue Berger flat had been archived on a CD-ROM disk. I could view it there or check it out. I called to request the latter, told them I'd be there shortly.

I fought my way to CUM headquarters, cursing the rush-hour traffic and the tourists that clogged the Old Port area. Leaving the car double-parked, I bolted the steps and went directly to the desk sergeant on the third floor. Amazingly, he had the disk. I signed it out, dashed back to the car, and stuffed it in my briefcase.

All the way home I kept looking over my shoulder, watching for Tanguay. Watching for St. Jacques. I couldn't stop myself.

37

I got home about five-thirty and sat in the silence of the apartment, assessing what else I could do. Nothing. Ryan was right. Tanguay could be out there, waiting for his chance at me. I wouldn't make it easier for him.

But I had to eat. And keep busy.

As I let myself out the front door, I scanned the street. There. In the alley to the left of the pizza parlor. I nodded to the two uniforms and pointed in the direction of Ste. Catherine. I could see them confer, then one got out.

My street crosses Ste. Catherine, not far from Le Faubourg. As I walked toward the market I could sense the annoyance of the cop on my tail. No matter. The day was glorious. I hadn't noticed at the lab. The heat had broken and huge white clouds floated in a dazzling blue sky, casting islands of shadow over the day and its players. It felt good to be outside.

Veggies. At La Plantation I squeezed avocados, evaluated the color of bananas, chose broccoli, brussels sprouts, and baking potatoes with the concentration of a neurosurgeon. A baguette at the *boulangerie*. A chocolate mousse at the pâtisserie. I picked up pork chops, ground beef, and a *tourtière* at the boucherie.

"C'est tout?"

"No, what the hell. Give me a T-bone. Really thick." I held my thumb and index finger an inch apart.

As I watched him remove the saw from its hook, the cognitive itch began again. I tried to scratch it into a full-blown idea, but with no more success than I'd had before. The saw? Too obvious. Anyone can buy a chef's saw. The SQ had run that lead to a dead end, contacting every outlet in the province. Thousands had been sold.

What, then? I'd learned that trying to pry an idea out of the subconscious only drives it deeper. If I let it drift, eventually it will float to the surface. I paid for my meat and went home, with a brief detour at the Rue Ste. Catherine Burger King.

What greeted me was the last thing I wanted to see. Someone had called. For several minutes I sat on the edge of the couch, clutching my packages and staring at the tiny indicator light. One message. Was it Tanguay? Would he speak to me, or would I hear the sound of his listening, followed by a dial tone?

"You're being hysterical, Brennan. It's probably Ryan."

I dried my palm, reached out, and pushed the button. It wasn't Tanguay. It was worse.

"Hey, Mom. Y'all out having a good time? Hello? Are you there? Pick u-up." I could hear what sounded like traffic, as if she were calling from an outside phone. "Guess not. Well, I can't talk anyway. I'm on the road. On the road again . . ." She did a Willie Nelson imitation. "Pretty good, eh? Anyway, I'm coming to visit, Mom. You're right. Max is a pecker head. I don't need that." I heard a voice in the background. "Okay, just give me a minute," she said to whoever it was. "Listen, I got a chance to visit New York. The Big Apple. I hooked a free trip, so here I am. Anyway, I can

438

get a ride to Montreal, so I'm coming up. See you soon!"

Click.

"No! Don't come here, Katy. No!" I spoke to the empty air.

I listened to the tape rewind. Jesus, what a nightmare! Gabby is dead. A psychopath placed a picture of Katy and me in her grave. Now Katy is on her way here. Blood pounded in my temples. My mind raced. I have to stop her. How? I don't know where she is.

Pete.

As his phone rang I had a flashback. Katy at three. At the park. I was talking to another mother, my eyes on Katy as she poured sand into plastic containers. Suddenly, she dropped her shovel and ran to the swings. She hesitated a moment, watching the iron pony swing back, then ran to it, her face exuberant with the feel of spring and the sight of the colorful mane and bridle moving through the air. I knew it would hit her and I could not stop it. It was happening again.

No answer on Pete's direct line.

I tried his switchboard number. A secretary told me he was away, taking a deposition. Of course. I left a message.

I stared at the answering machine. I shut my eyes and took several long, deep breaths, willing my heart to a slower pace. The back of my head felt as though it were clamped in a vise, and I was hot all over.

"This will not happen."

I opened my eyes to see Birdie gazing at me from across the room.

"This will not happen," I repeated to him.

He stared, his yellow eyes unblinking.

"I can do something."

He arched, placed all four paws in a tight little

439

square, curled his tail, and sat, his eyes never leaving my face.

"I will do something. I will not just sit around and wait for this fiend to pounce. Not on my daughter."

I took the groceries to the kitchen and placed them in the refrigerator. Then I got out my laptop, logged in, and pulled up the spreadsheet. How long had it been since I'd started it? I checked the dates I'd entered. Isabelle Gagnon's body was found on June 2. Seven weeks. It seemed like seven years.

I went to the study and brought out my case files. Maybe the effort I'd spent photocopying wouldn't be wasted after all.

For the next two hours I scrutinized every photograph, every name, every date, literally every word in every interview and police report I had. Then I did it again. I went over and over the words, hoping to find some little thing I'd missed. The third time through I did.

I was reading Ryan's interview with Grace Damas's father when I noticed it. Like a sneeze that's been building, taunting but refusing to break, the message finally burst into my conscious thought.

A boucherie. Grace Damas had worked at a boucherie. The killer used a chef's saw, knew something about anatomy. Tanguay dissected animals. Maybe there was a link. I looked for the name of the boucherie but couldn't find it.

I dialed the number in the file. A man answered.

"Mr. Damas?"

"Yes." Accented English.

"I'm Dr. Brennan. I'm working on the investigation of your wife's death. I wonder if I could ask you a couple of questions."

"Yes."

"At the time she disappeared, was your wife working

440

outside the home?"

Pause. Then, "Yes."

I could hear a television in the background.

"May I ask where, please?"

"A bakery on Fairmont. Le Bon Croissant. It was just part time. She never worked full time, with the kids and all."

I thought that over. So much for my link.

"How long had she worked there, Mr. Damas?" I hid my disappointment.

"Just a few months, I think. Grace never lasted any-wheres very long."

"Where did she work before that?" I dogged on.

"A boucherie."

"Which one?" I held my breath.

"La Boucherie St. Dominique. Belongs to a man in our parish. It's over on St. Dominique, just off St. Laurent, ya know?"

Yes. I pictured the rain against its windows.

"When did she work there?" I kept my voice calm.

"Almost a year, I guess. Most of '91, seems like. I can check. Think it's important? They never asked nothing about the dates before."

"I'm not sure. Mr. Damas, did your wife ever speak of someone named Tanguay?"

"Who?" Harsh.

"Tanguay."

An announcer's voice promised he'd be right back after the commercial break. My head throbbed and a dry scratching was beginning in my throat.

"No."

The vehemence startled me.

"Thank you. You've been very helpful. I'll let you know if there are any new developments."

I hung up and phoned Ryan. He'd left for the day. I tried his home number. No answer. I knew what I had

441

to do. I made one call, picked up a key, and headed out.

La Boucherie St. Dominique was busier than the day I'd first noticed it. The same signs occupied its windows, but tonight the store was lit and open for business. There wasn't much. An old woman moved slowly down the glass case, her face flaccid in the fluorescent glare. I watched her double back and point to a rabbit. The stiff little carcass reminded me of Tanguay's sad collection. And Alsa.

I waited until the woman left, then approached the man behind the counter. His face was rectangular, the bones large, the features coarse. The arms that hung from his T-shirt looked surprisingly thin and sinewy in contrast. Dark splotches marred the white of his apron, like dried petals on a linen tablecloth.

"*Bonjour.*"

"*Bonjour.*"

"Slow tonight?"

"It's slow every night." English, accented like Damas's.

I could hear someone rattling utensils in a back room.

"I'm working on the Grace Damas murder investigation." I pulled out my ID and flashed it. "I need to ask you a few questions."

The man stared at me. In the back, a faucet went on, off.

"Are you the owner?"

Nod.

"Mr.?"

"Plevritis."

"Mr. Plevritis, Grace Damas worked here for a short time, did she not?"

"Who?"

442

"Grace Damas. Fellow parishioner at St. Demetrius?"

The scrawny arms folded across his chest. Nod.

"When was that?"

"About three, four years ago. I don't know exactly. They come and go."

"Did she quit?"

"Without notice."

"Why was that?"

"Hell if I know. Everyone was doing it about then."

"Did she seem unhappy, upset, nervous?"

"What do I look like, Sigmund Freud?"

"Did she have any friends here, anyone she was particularly close to?"

His eyes lighted on mine and a smile teased the corners of his mouth. "Close?" he asked, his voice oily as Valvoline. I returned his gaze, unsmiling.

The smile disappeared and his eyes left mine to wander the room.

"It's just me and my brother here. There's no one to get *close* with." He drew the word out, like an adolescent with a dirty joke.

"Did she have any peculiar visitors, anyone who might have been hassling her?"

"Look, I gave her a job. I told her what to do and she did it. I didn't keep track of her social life."

"I thought perhaps you might have noticed—"

"Grace was a good worker. I was mad as hell when she quit. Everyone splitting at the same time really left me with my nuts in a vise, so I was pissed. I admit it. But I don't hold a grudge. Later, when I heard she was missing, at church, ya know, I thought she'd taken off. Didn't really seem like her, but her old man can be pretty heavy sometimes. I'm sorry she got killed. But I really hardly remember her."

"What do you mean 'heavy'?"

443

A blank expression crossed his face, like a sluice gate dropping. He lowered his eyes and scratched with his thumbnail at something on the counter. "You'll have to talk to Nikos about that. That's family."

I could see what Ryan meant. Now what? Visual aids. I reached in my purse and pulled out the picture of St. Jacques.

"Ever see this guy?"

Plevritis leaned forward to take it. "Who is he?"

"Neighbor of yours."

He studied the face. "Not exactly a prizewinning photo."

"It was taken by a video camera."

"So was the Zapruder film, but at least you could see something."

I wondered at his reference but said nothing. Spare me another conspiracy buff. Then I saw something cross his face, a subtle squint that puckered then flattened his lower lids.

"What?"

"Well . . ." He stared at the photo.

"Yes?"

"This guy looks a little like the other shitrag that bailed on me. But maybe that's because you put me in mind of him with all your questions. Hell, I don't know." He thrust the picture across the counter at me. "I gotta close up."

"Who? Who was that?"

"Look, it's a lousy picture. Looks like a lot of guys with bad hair. Don't mean nothing."

"What did you mean, someone else bailed on you? When?"

"That's why I was so cheesed off about Grace. The guy I had before her quit without so much as a goodbye, then Grace takes a walk, then not long after that this other guy. He and Grace were part-timers, but they were the only help I had. My brother was down in the States and I was running this place all by myself that year."

"Who was he?"

"Fortier. Lemme think. Leo. Leo Fortier. I remember 'cause I got a cousin named Leo."

"He worked here at the same time Grace Damas did?"

"Yeah. I hired him to replace the guy quit just before Grace started. I figured with two part-timers to split the hours, in case one didn't come in, I'd only be short-handed half the day. Then they both left. *Tabernac*, that was a mess. Fortier worked here maybe a year, year and a half, then just stopped coming. Never even turned in his keys. I had to start back at zero. I don't want to go through that again."

"What can you tell me about him?"

"That's an easy one. Nothing. He saw my sign, walked in off the street wanting to work part time. He fit in where I needed him, early morning to open, late night for closing and clean up, and he had experience cutting up meat. Turned out to be real good, actually. Anyway, I hired him. He had some other kind of job during the day. He seemed okay. Real quiet. Did his work, never opened his mouth. Hell, I never even knew where he lived."

"How did he and Grace get along?"

"Hell if I know. He'd be gone when she came in, then he'd come back after she'd left for the day. I'm not sure they even knew each other."

"And you think the man in this picture looks like Fortier?"

"Him and every other guy with bad hair and an attitude about it."

"Do you know where Fortier is now?"

He shook his head.

445

"You know anyone named St. Jacques?"

"Nope."

"Tanguay?"

"Sounds like a bronzer for queers."

My head was pounding and my throat was starting to scratch. I left my card.

38

I arrived home to find Ryan fuming on my doorstep. He wasted no time.

"I just can't get through to you, can I? No one can. You're like one of those Ghost Dance Indians. Dress the dress and dance the dance and you're bulletproof."

His face was flushed, and I could see a tiny vessel throbbing in his temple. I thought it unwise to comment just yet.

"Whose car was it?"

"Neighbor."

"Do you find all this amusing, Brennan?"

I said nothing. The headache had spread from the back to encompass my entire cranium, and a dry cough told me my immune system was about to have callers.

"Is there anyone on this planet who can get through to you?"

"Would you like to come in for coffee?"

"What makes you think you can just sail off like that and leave everyone sucking wind? These guys don't exactly live to be out here protecting your sorry ass, Brennan. Why the hell didn't you call or page me?"

"I did."

"You couldn't wait ten minutes?"

"I didn't know where you were or how long it would be. I didn't think I'd be gone long. Hell, I wasn't."

"You could have left a message."

"I'd have left *War and Peace* if I'd known you were going to overreact like this." Not quite true. I knew.

"Overreact?" His voice went icy calm. "Let me review for you. Five, maybe seven women have been brutally murdered and mutilated in this town. The most recent was four weeks ago." He ticked points off on his fingers. "One of these women made a partial appearance in your garden. A nutcase had your picture in his spice collection. He's gone missing. A loner who collects knives and pornography, frequents hookers, and likes to slice and dice little animals dialed up your apartment. He'd been stalking your best friend. She is now dead. She was buried clutching a picture of you and your daughter. This loner has also gone missing."

A couple passed on the sidewalk, dropping their eyes and quickening their pace, embarrassed to witness a lovers' quarrel.

"Ryan, come inside. I'll make coffee." My voice sounded raspy and speech was starting to hurt.

He raised a hand in exasperation, fingers splayed, then dropped it to his side. I returned the keys to my neighbor, thanked her for the use of her car, and let Ryan and myself into the apartment.

"Decaf or high test?"

Before he could answer his beeper sounded, causing us both to jump.

"Better go with decaf. You know where the phone is."

I listened, rattling cups and pretending not to.

"Ryan." Pause. "Yeah." Pause. "No shit." Long pause. "When?" Pause. "Okay. Thanks. I'll be right there."

He came to the kitchen door and stood there, his face

448

tense. My temperature, blood pressure, and pulse all began to rise. Stay calm. I poured two cups of coffee, forcing my hand not to tremble. I waited for him to speak.

"They got him."

My hand froze, the pot suspended in midair.

"Tanguay?"

He nodded. I returned the pot to its warmer. Carefully. I took out milk, poured a dollop in my cup, offered some to Ryan. Carefully. He shook his head. I put the carton back in the refrigerator. Carefully. I took a sip. Okay. Speak.

"Tell me."

"Let's sit."

We moved to the living room.

"They arrested him about two hours ago driving east on the 417. An SQ unit spotted the tag and pulled him."

"It's Tanguay?"

"It's Tanguay. Prints match."

"He was heading toward Montreal?"

"Apparently."

"What are they charging him with?"

"For now, possession of open alcohol in a moving vehicle. Jerk was thoughtful enough to crack a bottle of Jim Beam and leave it in the backseat. They also confiscated some skin magazines. He thinks that's the beef. They're letting him sweat for a while."

"Where was he?"

"Claims he has a cabin in the Gatineau. Inherited it from Daddy. Get this. He'd been fishing. Crime scene's sending out a team to take the place apart."

"Where is he now?"

"Parthenais."

"You're heading over there?"

"Yeah." He took a deep breath, expecting a fight. I had no desire to see Tanguay.

449

"Okay." My mouth was dry, and a languor was spreading through my body. Tranquillity? I hadn't felt that in a long time.

"Katy is coming," I said with a nervous laugh. "That's why I . . . why I went out tonight."

"Your daughter?"

I nodded.

"Bad timing."

"I thought I might find something. I . . . never mind."

For a few seconds neither of us spoke.

"I'm glad it's over." Ryan's anger was gone. He rose to his feet. "Would you like me to stop by after I've talked to him? Could be late."

Bad as I felt, there was no chance I'd sleep until I knew the outcome. Who was Tanguay? What would they find in his cabin? Had Gabby died there? Had Isabelle Gagnon? Grace Damas? Or had they been taken there, postmortem, merely to be butchered and packaged?

"Please."

When he'd gone I realized I'd forgotten to tell him about the gloves. I tried Pete again. Though Tanguay was in custody, I was still uneasy. I didn't want Katy anywhere near Montreal yet. Perhaps I'd go South.

This time I reached him. Katy had left several days earlier. She'd told her father I proposed the trip. True. And approved the plans. Not quite. He wasn't sure of the itinerary. Typical. She was traveling with friends from the university, driving to D.C. to stay with one set of parents, then to New York to visit the other friend's home. Then she planned to continue on to Montreal. Sounded okay to him. He was sure she'd call.

I started to tell him about Gabby and what had been going on in my life, but couldn't. Not yet. No matter. It was over. As usual he had to rush off to prepare for an early morning deposition, regretted he couldn't talk longer. What's new?

I felt too ill and weary even to take a bath. For the next few hours I sat wrapped in a quilt, shivering and staring at the empty fireplace, wishing I had someone to feed me soup, stroke my forehead, and say I would be better soon. I dozed and woke, drifting in and out of dream fragments, while microscopic beings multiplied in my bloodstream.

Ryan buzzed at one-fifteen.

"Jesus, you look awful, Brennan."

"Thanks." I rewrapped my quilt. "I think I'm getting a cold."

"Why don't we do this tomorrow?"

"No way."

He looked at me strangely then followed me in, threw his jacket on the couch, and sat.

"Name's Jean Pierre Tanguay. Twenty-eight. Homeboy. Grew up in Shawinigan. Never married. No kids. He has one sister living in Arkansas. His mother died when he was nine. Lot of hostility there. Father was a plasterer, pretty much raised the two kids. The old man died in a car wreck when Tanguay was in college. Apparently it hit him pretty hard. He dropped out of school, stayed with the sister for a while, then wandered around down in the States. You ready for this? While he was in Dixie he got a call from God. Wanted to be a Jesuit or something, but flunked the interview. Apparently they didn't think his personality was priestly enough. Anyway, he resurfaced in Quebec in '88 and managed to get back into Bishops. Finished his degree about a year and a half later."

"So he's been in the area since '88?"

"Yep."

"That would put him back here about the time Pitre and Gautier were murdered."

Ryan nodded. "And he's been here ever since."

451

I had to swallow before I spoke.

"What's he say about the animals?"

"Claims he teaches biology. We've checked that out. Says he's building a reference collection for his classes. Boils down the carcasses and mounts the skeletons."

"That would explain the anatomy books."

"Might."

"Where does he get them?"

"Roadkills."

"Oh, Christ, Bertrand was right." I could picture him skulking around at night, scraping up corpses and dragging them home in plastic bags.

"He ever work in a butcher shop?"

"He didn't say. Why?"

"What did Claudel find out from the people he works with?"

"Nothing we didn't know. Keeps to himself, teaches his classes. Nobody really knows him all that well. And they're not thrilled at a call late in the evening."

"Sounds like Grammama's profile."

"The sister says he's always been antisocial. Can't remember him having friends. But she's nine years older, doesn't remember much about him as a kid. She did throw us one interesting tidbit."

"Yes"

Ryan smiled. "Tanguay's impotent."

"The sister volunteered that?"

"She thought it might explain his antisocial tendencies. Sis thinks he's harmless, just suffers from low self-esteem. She's big into the self-help literature. Knows all the jargon."

I didn't reply. In my mind I was seeing lines from two autopsy reports.

"That makes sense. Adkins and Morisette-Champoux tested negative for sperm."

"Bingo."

452

"How did he become impotent?"

"Combination congenital and trauma. He was born a one-baller, then wrecked it in a soccer accident. Some freak thing where another player was carrying a pen. Tanguay caught it with his one good nut. Bye-bye spermatogenesis."

"And that's why he's a hermit?"

"Hey. Maybe Sis is right."

"Could explain his lack of sparkle with the girls." I thought of Jewel's comments. And Julie.

"And everyone else."

"Isn't it odd he'd choose teaching?" Ryan mused. "Why work in a setting where you have to interact with so many people? If you really feel inadequate, why not choose something less threatening, more private? Computers? Or lab work?"

"I'm not a psychologist, but teaching might be perfect. You don't interact with equals – you know, with adults; you interact with kids. You're the one in charge. You have the power. Your classroom is your little kingdom and the kids have to do what you say. No way they're going to ridicule or second-guess you."

"At least not to your face."

"Could be the perfect balance for him. Satisfy his need for power and control by day, feed his sexual fantasies at night."

"And that's the best-case scenario," I said. "Think of the opportunities for voyeurism, or even for physical contact that he has with those kids."

"Yeah."

We sat in silence for a while, Ryan's eyes sweeping the room much as they had in Tanguay's apartment. He looked exhausted.

"Guess the surveillance unit isn't necessary anymore," I said.

"Yeah." He stood.

453

I walked him to the door.

"What's your take on him, Ryan?"

He didn't answer right away. Then he spoke very carefully.

"He claims he's innocent as little Orphan Annie, but he's nervous as hell. He's hiding something. By tomorrow we'll know what's in the little country getaway. We'll use that and hit him with the whole thing. He'll roll over."

When he left I took a heavy dose of cold medicine and slept soundly for the first time in weeks. If I dreamed, I couldn't remember.

The next day I felt better, but not well enough to go to the lab. Maybe it was avoidance, but I stayed home. Birdie was the only one I wanted to see.

I kept busy reading a student thesis and responding to correspondence I'd been ignoring for weeks. Ryan called around one as I was unloading the dryer. I knew from his voice things weren't going well.

"Crime scene turned the cabin inside out and came up empty. Nothing there to suggest the guy even cheats at solitaire. No knives. No guns. No snuff films. None of Dobzhansky's victim souvenirs. No jewelry, clothing, skulls, body parts. One dead squirrel in the refrigerator. That's it. Otherwise zipp-o."

"Signs of digging?"

"Nothing."

"Is there a toolshed or a basement where he might have saws or old blades?"

"Rakes, hoes, wooden crates, an old chain saw, a broken wheelbarrow. Standard garden stuff. And enough spiders to populate a small planet. Apparently Gilbert's going to need therapy."

"Is there a crawl space?"

"Brennan, you're not listening."

454

"Luminol?" I asked, depressed.

"Clean."

"Newspaper clippings?"

"No."

"Is there anything to tie this place to the room we busted on Berger?"

"No."

"To St. Jacques?"

"No."

"To Gabby?"

"No."

"To *any* of the victims?"

He didn't answer.

"What do you think he does out there?"

"Fishes and thinks about his missing nut."

"What now?"

"Bertrand and I are going up to have a long talk with Monsieur Tanguay. Time to drop some names and start turning up the heat. I still think he'll give it up."

"Does it add up to you?"

"Maybe. Maybe Bertrand's idea isn't so bad. Maybe Tanguay's one of these split personalities. One side is the biology teacher who lives clean, fishes, and collects specimens for his students. The other side has uncontrollable rage against women and feels sexually inadequate, so he gets his rocks off stalking them and beating them to death. Maybe he keeps the two personalities apart, even to the extent of having a separate place for the stalker to enjoy his fantasies and admire his souvenirs. Hell, maybe Tanguay doesn't even know he's nuts."

"Not bad. Mr. Peepers and Mr. Creeper."

"Who?"

"Never mind. Old sitcom." I told him what I'd found out with Lacroix.

"Why didn't you tell me about this sooner?"

"You're a little hard to pin down, Ryan."

"So Rue Berger is definitely tied in."

"Why do you think there were no prints there?"

"Shit, Brennan, I don't know. Maybe Tanguay's just slick as black ice. If it's any comfort to you Claudel's already got this guy convicted."

"Why?"

"I'll let him tell you. Look, I've got to get up there."

"Keep in touch."

I finished my letters and decided to take them to the post office. I checked the refrigerator. My pork chops and ground beef wouldn't do for Katy. I smiled, remembering the day she announced she'd no longer eat meat. My fourteen-year-old zealot vegetarian. I thought she'd last three months. It had been over five years.

I made a mental list. Humus. Tabouli. Cheese. Fruit juices. No sodas for my Katy. How had I produced this child?

The scratch in my throat was back and I felt hot again, so I decided to stop by the gym. I'll blast these buggers with exercise and steam, I thought. One of us will come out the victor.

The exercise turned out to be a bad idea. After ten minutes on the StairMaster my legs trembled and perspiration poured down my face. I had to quit.

The steam had mixed results. It soothed my throat and released the bands that squeezed my forehead and facial bones. But as I sat there with the vapor swirling around me, my mind reached for something to play with. Tanguay. I ran through what Ryan had said, Bertrand's theory, J.S.'s prediction, and what I knew. Something about Tanguay bothered me. As my thoughts gathered speed I could feel myself tensing. The gloves. Why had I blocked their relevance before?

Did Tanguay's physical handicap really lead him to sexual fantasies that ended in violence? Was he really a

456

man with a desperate need to control? Was killing the ultimate act of control for him? *I can just watch you, or I can hurt you or even kill you?* Did he also play out the fantasy with animals? With Julie? Then why murder? Did he keep the violence in check, then suddenly succumb to a need to act out? Was Tanguay the product of abandonment by his mother? His deformity? A bad chromosome? Something else?

And why Gabby? She didn't fit the picture. He knew her. She was one of the few who would talk to him. I felt a wave of anguish.

Yes. Of course she fit the picture. A picture that included me. I found Grace Damas. I identified Isabelle Gagnon. I was interfering, challenging his authority. His manhood. Killing Gabby vented his rage against me and reestablished his sense of control. What next? Did the picture mean he would have gone for my daughter?

A teacher. A killer. A man who likes to fish. A man who likes to mutilate. My mind continued to drift. I closed my eyes and felt heat trapped below the lids. Bright colors swam back and forth, like goldfish in a pond.

A teacher. Biology. Fishing.

Again the nagging. It was there. Come on. Come on. What? A teacher. A teacher. That's it. A teacher. Since 1991. St. Isidor's. Yes. Yes. We know that. So what? My head was too heavy to think. Then:

The CD-ROM. I'd forgotten all about it. I grabbed for my towel. Maybe there was something there.

39

I was perspiring heavily and felt weak all over, but I managed to drive. Bonehead move, Brennan. Microbes win this one. Reduce your speed. You don't want to be stopped. Get home. Find it. There's got to be something.

I flew along Sherbrooke, circled the block, and shot down the drive. The garage door was beeping again. Damn. Why can't Winston fix that? I parked the car and hurried to my apartment. Check the dates.

A satchel rested on the floor outside my door.

"Shit. Now what?"

I looked down at the backpack. Black leather. Made by Coach. Expensive. A gift from Max Ferranti. A gift to Katy. It was lying outside my door.

My heart froze in my chest.

Katy!

I opened the door and called her name. No answer. I punched in the security code and tried again. Silence.

I raced from room to room, searching for signs of my daughter, knowing I would find none. Did she remember to bring her key? If she had, she wouldn't have left her pack in the hall. She had been here, found me not home, left her pack, and gone somewhere.

458

I stood in the bedroom, trembling, a victim of virus and fear. Think, Brennan. Think! I tried. It wasn't easy.

She arrived and couldn't get in. She's gone for coffee, or window shopping, or to look for a phone. She'll call in a few minutes.

But if she didn't have the key, how did she get through the outer door into the corridor to my unit door? The garage. She must have come through the pedestrian door into the garage, the one that's not latching as it closes.

The phone!

I ran to the living room. No message. Could it be Tanguay? Did he have her?

That's impossible. He's in jail.

The teacher is in jail. But he's not the one. The teacher isn't the one. Or is he? Did he keep the Rue Berger room? Did he bury the glove with Katy's picture in Gabby's grave?

The fear sent a wave of nausea rising up my esophagus. I swallowed and my swollen throat screamed in protest.

Check the facts, Brennan. They may have been holidays.

I booted the computer with shaking hands, my fingers barely able to work the keys. The spreadsheet filled the screen. Dates. Times.

Francine Morisette-Champoux was killed in January. She died between 10 A.M. and noon. It was a Thursday.

Isabelle Gagnon disappeared in April, between 1 and 4 P.M. It was a Friday.

Chantale Trottier disappeared on an afternoon in October. She was last seen at her school in Centre-ville, miles from the west island.

They died or disappeared during the week. During the day. The school day. Trottier may have been abducted after school hours. The other two were not.

459

I grabbed the phone.

Ryan was out.

I slammed the receiver. My head felt like lead and my thoughts were coming in slow motion.

I tried another number.

"Claudel."

"Monsieur Claudel, this is Dr. Brennan."

He didn't answer.

"Where is St. Isidor's?"

He hesitated, and I didn't think he was going to answer.

"Beaconsfield."

"That's what, about thirty minutes from downtown?"

"Without traffic."

"Do you know what the school hours are?"

"What's this about?"

"Can I just have an answer?" I was pushing the envelope and about to crack. My voice must have told him.

"I can ask."

"Also, find out if Tanguay ever missed any days, if he called in sick or took personal leave, particularly on the days Morisette-Champoux and Gagnon were killed. They'll have a record. They'd have needed a substitute unless school was not in session for some reason."

"I'm going out there tom—"

"Now. I need it now!" I was poised on the edge of hysteria, toes clutching the end of the board. Don't make me jump.

I could hear his face muscles harden. Go ahead, Claudel. Hang up. I'll have your ass.

"I'll get back to you."

I sat on the edge of the bed, staring numbly at dust playing tag in a shaft of sunlight.

Move.

I went to the bathroom and splashed cold water on my face. Then I fished a plastic square from my brief-

460

case and returned to the computer. The case was labeled with the Rue Berger address and the date 94/06/24. I raised the lid, removed a CD-ROM disk, and set it in the drive.

I opened a program for image viewing, bringing up a row of icons. I chose *Album* then *Open*, and a single album name appeared in the window. *Berger.abm*. I double-clicked and three rows of pictures filled the screen, each displaying six still photos of St. Jacques's apartment. A line at the bottom told me the album contained a hundred and twenty shots.

I clicked to maximize the first image. Rue Berger. The second and third showed the street from different angles. Next, the apartment building, front and back. Then the corridor leading to the St. Jacques apartment. Views of the apartment's interior started with image twelve.

I moved through the pictures, scrutinizing every detail. My head pounded. My shoulder and back muscles were like high-tension wires. I was back there again. The suffocating heat. The fear. The odors of filth and corruption.

Image by image I searched. For what? I wasn't sure. It was all there. The *Hustler* centerfolds. The newspapers. The city map. The staircase landing. The filthy toilet. The greasy countertop. The Burger King cup. The bowl of SpaghettiOs.

I stopped, stared at the still life. File 102. A grimy plastic bowl. Fatty white rings congealing in red sludge. A fly, front legs clasped as if in prayer. An orange boulder rising from the sauce and pasta.

I squinted, leaned in. Could I be seeing what I thought I was seeing? There. Coursing across the orange chunk. My heart pounded. It couldn't be. We couldn't be that lucky.

I double-clicked, and a dotted line appeared. I

dragged the cursor, and the line became a rectangle, its borders a string of rotating dots. I positioned the rectangle directly over the orange blob and zoomed in, magnifying the image again and again. Double. Triple. Up to eight times its actual size. I watched as the faint parabola I had spotted became an arched trail of dots and dashes.

I zoomed out and examined the entire arc.

"Oh, Jesus."

Using the image editor, I manipulated the brightness and contrast, modified the hue and saturation. I tried reversing the color, changing each pixel to its complement. I used a command to emphasize edges, sharpening the tiny trail against the orange background.

I leaned back and stared. It is. I inhaled deeply. Sweet Jesus, it really is.

With a trembling hand I reached for the phone.

A recorded message told me Bergeron was still on vacation. I was on my own.

I sifted the possibilities. I'd seen him do it several times. I could try. I had to know.

I looked up another number.

"*Centre de Détention Parthenais.*"

"This is Tempe Brennan. Is Andrew Brennan there? He'd be with a prisoner named Tanguay."

"*Un instant. Gardez la ligne.*"

Voices in the background. Come on. Come on.

"*Il n'est pas ici.*"

Damn. I looked at my watch. "Is Jean Bertrand there?"

"*Oui.* Un instant."

More voices. Clatter.

"Bertrand."

I identified myself, explained what I'd found.

"No shit. What did Bergeron say?"

"He's on vacation until next Monday."

462

"Cheese, that's beautiful. Kind of like your false starts, eh? What do you want me to do?"

"Find a piece of plain Styrofoam and get Tanguay to bite down on it. Don't stick it too far into his mouth. I just need the front six teeth. Have him bite edge to edge so you get nice clean tooth marks, one arch on each side of the plate. Then I want you to take the Styrofoam downstairs to Marc Dallair in photography. He's way in back, behind ballistics. You got that?"

"Yeah. Yeah. How do I get Tanguay to agree to this?"

"That's your problem. Figure something out. If he's screaming innocent he should be delighted."

"Where am I supposed to come up with Styrofoam at four-forty in the afternoon?"

"Go buy yourself a bloody Big Mac, Bertrand. I don't know. Just get it. I've got to catch Dallair before he leaves. Get moving!"

Dallair was waiting for an elevator when my call came. He took it at the reception desk.

"I need a favor."

"*Oui.*"

"Within the hour Jean Bertrand will bring bite mark specimens to your office. I need to have the image scanned into a Tif file and sent to me electronically as soon as possible. Can you do that?"

There was a long pause. In my mind I could see him glance at the elevator clock.

"Does this have to do with Tanguay?"

"Yes."

"Sure. I'll wait."

"Angle the light across the Styrofoam as close to parallel as possible to really bring the marks out. And be sure to include a scale, a ruler or something. And please make sure the image is exactly one to one."

"No problem. I think I have an ABFO ruler here

463

somewhere."

"Perfect." I gave him my e-mail address and asked him to call when he'd sent the file.

Then I waited. Seconds crept by with glacial slowness. No phone. No Katy. The digits on the clock glowed green. I heard them change. Click, click, click as the rotors turned.

When the phone rang I grabbed it.

"Dallair."

"Yes." I swallowed and the pain was excruciating.

"I sent the file about five minutes ago. It's called *Tang.tif*. It's compressed, so you'll have to unencode. I'll stick here until you've downloaded, to be sure there's no problem. Just send a reply. And good luck."

I thanked him and hung up. Moving to the computer I logged into my mailbox at McGill. The *Mail Waiting!!!* message glowed brightly. Ignoring other unread mail, I downloaded the file Dallair had sent, and returned it to its graphic format. A dental imprint arched across the screen, each tooth clearly visible against a white background. To the left and below the impression was a right-angle ABFO ruler. I sent Dallair a reply and logged off.

Back in the imaging program, I called up *Tang.tif* and double-clicked it open. Tanguay's impression filled the screen. I retrieved the bite mark in the Rue Berger cheese, and tiled the two images side by side.

Next I converted both images to an RGB scale, to maximize the amount of information in the pictures. I adjusted tone, brightness, contrast, and saturation. Finally, using the image editor I sharpened the edges on the Styrofoam impression as I had with the indentations in the cheese.

For the type of comparison I planned to try, both images had to be to the same scale. I got out a needle point caliper and checked the ruler in the Tanguay

464

photo. The distance between hash marks was exactly one millimeter. Good. The image was one to one.

There was no ruler in the Berger photo. Now what?

Use something else. Go back to the full image. There has to be a known.

There was. The Burger King cup touched the bowl adjacent to the cheese, its red and yellow logo clear and recognizable. Perfect.

I ran to the kitchen. Let it still be here! Throwing open the cabinet doors, I rummaged through the trash under the sink.

Yes! I washed off the coffee grounds and carried the cup to the computer. My hands trembled as I spread the calipers. The upright arm of the logo B measured exactly 4 millimeters across.

Selecting the resize function in the image editor I clicked on one edge of the B on the Rue Berger cup, dragged the cursor to the far border, and clicked again. Having chosen my calibration points I told the program to resize the entire image so that the B measured exactly 4 millimeters across at that position. Instantly the picture changed dimension.

Both images were now one to one. I looked at them side by side on the computer screen. The impression Tanguay had given showed a complete dental arch, with eight teeth on each side of the midline.

Only five teeth had registered in the cheese. Bertrand was right. It was like a false start. The teeth had gripped, slid, or been retracted, then bitten a chunk from behind the mark I was now seeing.

I stared at the trail of indentations. I was sure it was an upper arch. I could see two long depressions to either side of the midline, probably the central incisors. Lateral to them were two similarly oriented but slightly shorter grooves. Farther out, on the left of the arcade, was a small, circular dent, probably made by the canine. No other teeth had registered.

I ran my sweaty palms down the sides of my shirt, arched my back, and took a deep breath.

Okay. Position.

Choosing the *Effect* function, I clicked on *Rotate*, and slowly maneuvered Tanguay's dental impression, hoping to achieve the same orientation as the mark in the cheese. Click by click I rotated the central incisors clockwise. Forward, then backward, then forward again, a few degrees at a time, my anxiousness and clumsiness prolonging the process. It took an entire growing season, but at last I was satisfied. Tanguay's front teeth lay at the same angle and position as their counterparts in the cheese.

Back to the *Edit* menu. *Stitch* function. I selected the cheese as the active image and the Tanguay impression as the floating image. I set the transparency level at 30 percent, and Tanguay's bite mark grew cloudy.

I clicked on a spot directly between Tanguay's front teeth, and again on the corresponding gap in the cheese arcade, defining a stitch point on each image. Satisfied, I activated the *Place* function, and the image editor superimposed Tanguay's bite mark directly over that in the cheese. Too opaque. The cheese trail was completely obliterated.

I raised the transparency level to 75 percent, and watched the Styrofoam dots and dashes fade to ghostly transparency. I now had a clear view of the dents and hollows in the cheese through the impression made by Tanguay.

Dear God.

I knew instantly the bites were not by the same person. No amount of manual manipulation or fine tuning of the images could alter that impression. The mouth that had bitten into the Styrofoam had not left the marks in the cheese.

466

Tanguay's dental arch was too narrow, the curve at the front much tighter than that preserved in the cheese. The composite image showed a horseshoe overlying a partial semicircle.

More striking, the person eating cheese at the Rue Berger flat had an irregular break to the right of the normal midline gap, and the adjacent tooth shot off at a thirty-degree angle, making the tooth row look like a picket fence. The cheese eater had a badly chipped central incisor, and a sharply rotated lateral.

Tanguay's teeth were even and uninterrupted. His bite showed neither of these traits. He had not bitten that cheese. Either Tanguay had entertained a guest at Rue Berger, or the Rue Berger apartment had nothing to do with Tanguay at all.

40

Whoever used Rue Berger had killed Gabby. The gloves matched. The strong probability was that Tanguay was not that person. His teeth had not bitten the cheese. St. Jacques was not Tanguay.

"Who the hell are you?" I asked, my voice raspy in the silence of my empty home. Fears for Katy erupted full force. Why hadn't she called?

I tried Ryan at home. No answer. I tried Bertrand. He'd gone. I tried the task force room. No one.

I went to the yard and peeked through the fence at the pizza parlor across the street. The alley was empty. The surveillance team had been pulled. I was on my own.

I ran through my options. What could I do? Not much. I couldn't leave. I had to be here if Katy came back. *When* Katy came back.

I looked at the clock – 7:10 P.M. The files. Back to the files. What else could I do from inside these walls? My refuge had become my prison.

I changed clothes and went to the kitchen. Though my head was swimming, I took no medication. My mind was dull enough without sedation. I'd blast the germs with vitamin C. I got a can of frozen orange juice from the freezer and dug for the opener. Damn. Where is it?

Too impatient to look for long, I grabbed a steak knife and sawed the top of the cardboard can to remove the metal lid. Pitcher. Water. Stir. You can do it. Clean up the mess later.

Moments later I was settled on the couch, tightly quilted, tissues and juice within arm's reach. I played with my eyebrow to hold my nerves together.

Damas. I descended into the file, revisiting names, places, and dates I'd visited before. The Monastère St. Bernard. Nikos Damas. Father Poirier.

Bertrand had done a follow-up on Poirier. I reread it, my mind resisting concentration. The good father checked out. I reviewed the original interview, looking for other names to chase after, like clues in a road rally scavenger hunt. Next I'd rehash dates.

Who was the caretaker? Roy. Emile Roy. I dug for his statement.

It wasn't there. I went through everything in the jacket. Nothing. Surely someone had talked to him. I couldn't recall seeing the report. Why wasn't it here?

I sat for a moment, the friction of my breath the only sound in my universe. The pre-idea sensation was back, like an aura presaging a migraine. The sense that I was missing something was stronger than ever, but the elusive fact would not come into focus.

I went back to Poirier's statement. Roy tends the building and grounds. Fixes the furnace, shovels the snow.

Shovels snow? At age eighty? Why not? George Burns could do it. Past images drifted into my mind. I thought of the apparition I'd had, alone in the car, Grace Damas's bones lying behind me in the rain-soaked woods.

I thought of my other dream that night. The rats. Pete. Isabelle Gagnon's head. Her grave. The priest. What had he said? Only those who worked for the church could enter its gates.

Could that be it? Is that how he got onto the grounds of the monastery and Le Grand Séminaire? Is our killer someone who works for the church?

Roy!

Right, Brennan, an eighty-year-old serial killer.

Should I wait to hear from Ryan? Where the hell is he? I pulled out the phone book with trembling hands. If I can find the caretaker's number, I'll call.

There was one E. Roy listed in St. Lambert.

"*Oui.*" A gravelly voice.

Be careful. Take your time.

"Monsieur Emile Roy?"

"*Oui.*"

I explained who I was and why I was calling. Yes, I had the right Emile Roy. I asked about his duties at the monastery. For a long time he said nothing. I could hear him wheezing, the breath drawing in and out like air through a blowhole. Finally:

"I don't want to lose my job. I take good care of the place."

"Yes. Do you do it by yourself?"

I heard his breath catch, as though a pebble had clogged the blowhole.

"I just need a little help from time to time. It don't cost them nothing more. I pay for it myself, out of my wages." He was almost whining.

"Who helps you, Monsieur Roy?"

"My nephew. He's a good boy. Mostly he does the snow. I was going to tell Father, but . . ."

"What's your nephew's name?"

"Leo. He's not going to get in no trouble, is he? He's a good boy."

The receiver felt slick in my palm.

"Leo what?"

"Fortier. Leo Fortier. He's my sister's grandson."

470

His voice receded. I was pouring sweat. I said the necessary things and hung up, my mind flailing, my heart racing.

Calm down. It could be a coincidence. Being a caretaker and a part-time butcher's helper doesn't make one a killer. Think.

I looked at the clock and reached for the phone. Come on. Be there.

She picked up on the fourth ring.

"Lucie Dumont."

Yes!

"Lucie, I can't believe you're still there."

"I had some trouble with a program file. I was just leaving."

"There's something I need, Lucie. It's extremely important. You may be the only one who can get it for me."

"Yes?"

"I want you to run a check on someone. Do whatever it is you do to pull up everything there is on this guy. Can you do that?"

"It's late and I wa–"

"This is critical, Lucie. My daughter may be in danger. I really need this!"

I made no attempt to hide the desperation in my voice.

"I can link through to the SQ files and see if he's there. I have clearance. What do you want to know?"

"Everything."

"What can you give me?"

"Just a name."

"Anything else?"

"No."

"Who is it?"

"Fortier. Leo Fortier."

"I'll call you back. Where are you?"

I gave her the number and hung up.

I paced the apartment, crazy with fear for Katy. Was it Fortier? Had his psychotic rage fixed on me because I had thwarted him? Had he killed my friend to vent this rage? Did he plan the same for me? For my daughter? How did he know about my daughter? Had he stolen the photo of Katy and me from Gabby?

The cold, numbing fear went deep into my soul. I had the worst thoughts I've ever known. I pictured Gabby's last moments, imagined what she must have felt. The phone exploded into my train of thought.

"Yes!"

"It's Lucie Dumont."

"Yes." My heart was pounding so hard I thought she might hear it.

"Do you know how old your Leo Fortier is?"

"Uh . . . thirty, forty."

"I came up with two; one has a date of birth 2/9/62, so he'd be about thirty-two. The other was born 4/21/16, so he'd be, what . . . seventy-eight."

"Thirty-two," I said.

"That's what I thought, so I ran him. He's got a big jacket. Goes back to juvenile court. No felonies, but a string of misdemeanor problems and psychiatric referrals."

"What kind of problems?"

"Caught for voyeurism at age thirteen." I could hear her fingers clicking on the keyboard. "Vandalism. Truancy. There was an incident when he was fifteen. Kidnapped a girl and kept her for eighteen hours. No charges. You want it all?"

"What about recent things?"

Click. Clickety. Click. I could picture her leaning into the monitor, her pink lenses bouncing back the green glow.

"The most recent entry is 1988. Arrested for assault.

472

Looks like a relative, victim has the same name. No jail time. Did six months in Pinel."

"When did he get out?"

"The exact date?"

"Do you have it?"

"Looks like November 12, 1988."

Constance Pitre died in December of 1988. The room was hot. My body was slick with sweat.

"Does the file list the name of his attending psychiatrist at Pinel?"

"There's reference to a Dr. M. C. LaPerrière. Doesn't say who he is."

"Is his number there?"

She gave it to me.

"Where is Fortier now?"

"The file ends in 1988. You want that address?"

"Yes."

I was on the verge of tears as I punched in a number and listened to a phone ring on the far northern end of the island of Montreal. *Composer*, they say in French. *Composer le numéro.* Compose yourself, Brennan. I tried to think what to say.

"*L'hôpital Pinel. Puis-je vous aider?*" A female voice.

"Dr. LaPerrière, *s'il vous plaît.*" Please let him still work there.

"*Un instant, s'il vous plaît.*"

Yes! He was still on staff. I was put on hold, then led through the same ritual by a second female voice.

"*Qui est sur la ligne, s'il vous plaît?*"

"Dr. Brennan."

The sound of more empty air. Then.

"Dr. LaPerrière." A female voice, this one sounding tired and impatient.

"I'm Dr. Temperance Brennan," I said, fighting to keep the tremor from my voice, "forensic anthropologist at the Laboratoire de Médecine Légale, and I'm

473

involved in the investigation of a series of murders which have taken place over the past several years in the Montreal area. We have reason to believe one of your former patients may be involved."

"Yes." Wary.

I explained about the task force, and asked what she could tell me about Leo Fortier.

"Dr. . . . Brennan, is it? Dr. Brennan, you know I can't discuss a patient file on the basis of a phone call. Without court authorization, that would be a breach of confidentiality."

Stay cool. You knew that would be the response.

"Of course. And that authorization will be forthcoming, but we are in an urgent situation, Doctor, and we cannot delay in speaking with you. And at this point that authorization really isn't necessary. Women are dying, Dr. LaPerrière. They're being brutally murdered and disfigured. The individual doing this is capable of extreme violence. He mutilates his victims. We think he's someone with tremendous rage against women, and someone with enough intelligence to plan and carry out these killings. And we think he'll strike again soon." I swallowed, my mouth dry from fear. "Leo Fortier is a suspect, and we need to know whether, in your opinion, there is anything in Fortier's history to suggest he could fit this profile? The paperwork for production of his records will catch up, but if you have a recollection of this patient, information you provide now may help us stop the killer before he strikes again."

I had wrapped another quilt around myself, this one a blanket of icy calm. I could not let her hear the fear in my voice.

"I simply cannot . . ."

My blanket was slipping.

"I have a child, Dr. LaPerrière? Do you?"

"What?" Affront vied with the weariness.

474

"Chantale Trottier was sixteen years old. He beat her to death, then cut her up and left her in a dump."

"Jesus Christ."

Though I'd never met Marie Claude LaPerrière, her voice painted a vivid scene, a triptych done in metal gray, institutional green, and dirty brick.

I could picture her: middle-aged, disillusionment etched deeply in her face. She worked for a system in which she'd long ago lost faith, a system unable to understand, much less curb, the cruelty of a society gone mad on its fringes. The gang bang victims. The teenagers with vacant eyes and bleeding wrists. The babies, scalded and scarred by cigarette burns. The fetuses floating in bloody toilet bowls. The old, starved and tethered in their own excrement. The women with their battered faces and pleading eyes. Once, she'd believed she could make a difference. Experience had convinced her otherwise.

But she'd taken an oath. To what? For whom? The dilemma was now as familiar to her as her idealism had once been. I heard her take a deep breath.

"Leo Fortier was committed for a six-month period in 1988. During that time I was his attending psychiatrist."

"Do you remember him?"

"Yes."

I waited, heart pounding. I heard her click a lighter open and shut, then breathe deeply.

"Leo Fortier came to Pinel because he beat his grandmother with a lamp." She spoke in short sentences, treading carefully. "The old woman needed over a hundred stitches. She refused to press charges against her grandson. When Fortier's period of involuntary commitment ended, I recommended continued treatment. He refused."

She paused to select just the right words.

475

"Leo Fortier watched his mother die while his grandmother stood by. Grandma then raised him, engendering in him an extremely negative self-image that resulted in an inability to form appropriate social relationships.

"Leo's grandmother punished him excessively, but protected him from the consequences of his acts outside the home. By the time Leo was a teen, his activities suggest he was suffering severe cognitive distortion along with an overwhelming need to control. He'd developed an excessive sense of entitlement, and exhibited intense narcissistic rage when thwarted.

"Leo's need to control, his repressed love and hatred toward his grandmother, and his increasing social isolation led him to spend more and more time in his own fantasy world. He had also developed all the classic defense mechanisms. Denial, repression, projection. Emotionally and socially, he was extremely immature."

"Do you think he is capable of the behavior I have described?" I was surprised at how steady my voice sounded. Inside I was churning, terrified for my daughter.

"At the time I worked with Leo his fantasies were fixed and definitely negative. Many involved violent sexual behaviors."

She paused and I heard another deep breath.

"In my opinion, Leo Fortier is a very dangerous man."

"Do you know where he lives now?" This time my voice trembled.

"I have had no contact with him since his release."

I was about to say good-bye when I thought of another question. "How did Leo's mother die?"

"At the hands of an abortionist," she answered.

When I hung up, my mind was racing. I had a name. Leo Fortier worked with Grace Damas, had access to church properties, and was extremely dangerous. Now what?

I heard a soft rumble and noticed that the room had turned purple. I opened the French doors and looked out. Heavy clouds had gathered over the city, casting the evening into premature darkness. The wind had shifted and the air was dense with the smell of rain. Already the cypress was whipping to and fro, and leaves were dancing along the ground.

One of my earliest cases unexpectedly came to mind. Nellie Adams, five years old, missing. I'd heard it on the news. There had been a violent thunderstorm the day she was reported missing. I'd thought of her that night from the safety of my bed. Was she out there, alone and terrified in that storm? Six weeks later I'd identified her from a skull and rib fragments.

Please, Katy! Please come back now!

Stop it! Call Ryan.

Lightning flickered on the wall. I latched the doors shut and walked over to a lamp. Nothing. The timer, Brennan. It's set for eight. It's still too early.

I slid my hand behind the couch and flicked the timer button. Nothing. I tried the wall switch. Nothing. I felt my way along the wall and rounded the corner into the kitchen. The lights would not respond. With growing alarm, I stumbled down the hall and into the bedroom. The clock was dark. No power. I stood for a moment, my mind grasping at explanations. Had there been a lightning strike? Had the wind felled branches onto a feeder line?

I realized the apartment was unnaturally quiet, and closed my eyes to listen. A mélange of sounds filled the vacuum left by stilled appliances. The storm outside. My own heartbeat. And then, something else. A faint click. A door closing? Birdie? Where was it? The other bedroom?

477

I crossed to the bedroom window. Lights glowed along the street and from the apartments on De Maisonneuve. I ran back down the hall to the courtyard doors. I could see the lights in my neighbors' windows gleaming through the rain. It was just me! Only my power was off! Then I remembered: the safety alarm had not beeped when I opened the French doors. I had no security system!

I jumped for the telephone.

The line was dead.

41

I hung up and my eyes swept through the dimness around me. No threatening form met them, but I could sense another presence. I trembled and then tensed, my thoughts running through my options like a deck of cards.

Stay calm, I told myself. Make a break for it through the French doors into the garden.

But the garden gate was locked and the key was in the kitchen. I pictured the fence. Could I scale it? If not, at least in the garden I'd be outside and someone might hear me scream. *Would* anyone hear? The storm was raging out there.

I strained to hear the slightest sound, my heart banging against my ribs like a moth against a screen. My mind flew in a thousand directions. I thought of Margaret Adkins, of Pitre and the others, of their slashed throats, their sightless, staring eyes.

Take action, Brennan. Make a move! Don't wait to be his victim! My fear for Katy was making rational thought difficult. What if I get away and he waits for her? No, I told myself, he won't wait for anything. He needs to be in control. He'll disappear and plan for next time.

I swallowed and nearly screamed in pain, my throat parched from illness and fear. I decided to run, to throw open the French doors, and fling myself into the rain and freedom. My body rigid, every muscle and tendon taut, I sprang for the door. In five steps I rounded the couch and was there, one hand on the handle, the other turning the latch. The brass felt cold in my feverish fingers.

From nowhere a hand like a ham whipped across my face and jerked me back, pressing my skull against a body solid as concrete, crushing my lips and twisting my jaw out of alignment. The hard palm covered my mouth, and a familiar scent filled my nostrils. The hand felt unnaturally smooth and slippery. From the corner of my eye I saw a glint of metal, and felt something cold against my right temple. My fear was like white noise, overpowering my mind and obliterating everything beyond my body and his.

"Well, Dr. Brennan. I believe we have a date this evening." Spoken in English, but with a French pronunciation. Soft and low, like a love song with the lyrics recited.

I struggled, my body twisting, my hands flailing. His grip was like a vise. Desperate, I lashed out and clawed the air.

"No, no. Don't fight. You're with me tonight. There's no one else in the world but us." I could feel his heat against my neck as he pressed me back against him. Like his hand, his body felt oddly smooth and compact. Panic overwhelmed me. I felt helpless.

I couldn't think. I couldn't speak. I didn't know whether to beg, to fight, to reason with him. He held my head immobile, his hand mashing my lips against my teeth. I could taste blood in my mouth.

"Nothing to say? Well, we'll talk later." As he spoke he did something odd with his lips, wetting them then

480

sucking them back against his teeth.

"I brought you something." I felt his body twist, and the hand came off my mouth. "A present."

A slithery metallic sound, then he pulled my head forward and slid something cold past my face and on to my neck. Before I could react, his arm jerked and I was yanked into a place far beyond thinking, a place of bursting light and choking and gagging. At this point I could do nothing but categorize my pain according to the moves he made.

He released, then pulled up hard on the chain once more, crushing my larynx and twisting my jaw and vertebrae. The pain was unendurable.

I clawed and gasped for air and he spun me, grabbed my hands, and circled my wrists with another chain. He pulled it tight with one sharp tug, clipped it to the neck chain, then yanked and held both high above his head. Fire roared through my lungs and my brain begged for air. I fought to remain conscious, tears running down my face.

"Oh, did that hurt? I'm sorry."

He lowered the chain and my tortured throat gasped for breath.

"You look like a big fish dangling there, sucking for air."

I was facing him now, his eyes but inches from mine. Through my pain I registered little. His could have been anyone's face, an animal's face. The corners of his mouth quivered, as though teased by an inner joke. He circled my lips with the tip of a knife.

My mouth was so dry my tongue stuck to it when I tried to talk. I swallowed.

"I'd li–"

"Shut up! You shut your fucking mouth! I know what you'd like. I know what you think about me. I know what you all think about me. You think I'm some kind

481

of genetic freak that ought to be exterminated. Well, I'm as good as anybody. And I'm in charge here."

He gripped the knife so hard his hand trembled. It looked ghostly pale in the gloom of the hallway, the knuckles bulging white and round. Surgical gloves! That's what I'd smelled. The blade bit into my cheek, and I could feel warmth trickle down my chin. I felt utterly without hope.

"Before I'm through you'll be tearing your panties off, you'll want me so bad. But that's later, *Doctor* Brennan. For now, you speak when I tell you to."

He was breathing hard, his nostrils white. His left hand toyed with the choke chain, wrapping and rewrapping the links around his palm.

"Now. Tell me." Calm again. "What are you thinking?" His eyes looked cold and hard, like some Mesozoic mammal.

"You think I'm crazy?"

I held my tongue. Rain pounded the window behind him.

He pulled in the chain, drawing my face close to his. His breath brushed the sweat on my skin.

"Worried about your daughter?"

"What do you know about my daughter?" I choked.

"I know everything about you, Dr. Brennan." His voice was low and syrupy again. It felt like something obscene crawling in my ear. I swallowed through my pain, needing to speak, not wanting to provoke him. His moods were swinging like a hammock in a hurricane.

"Do you know where she is?"

"I might." He raised the chain again, this time slowly, forcing my chin into full extension, then he drew the knife across my throat in a slow backhand motion.

Lightning flashed and his hand jumped. "Tight enough?" he asked.

"Please–" I gagged.

482

He eased off on the chain, allowing me to drop my chin. I swallowed and took a deep breath. My throat was on fire and my neck was bruised and swollen. I raised my hands to rub it, and he jerked them down with the wrist chain. His mouth did another rodent twitch.

"Nothing to say?" He stared at me, his eyes black and all pupil. The lower lids quivered, like his lips.

Terrified, I wondered what the others had done. What Gabby had done.

He lifted the chain above my head and began to increase the tension, a child torturing a puppy. A homicidal child. I remembered Alsa. I remembered the marks in Gabby's flesh. What had J.S. said? How could I use it?

"Please. I'd like to talk to you. Why don't we go somewhere where we can have a drink and– ?"

"Bitch!"

His arm snapped and the chain tightened savagely. Flames shot through my head and neck. I raised my hands in reflex, but they were cold and useless.

"The great *Doctor* Brennan doesn't drink, does she? Everyone knows that."

Through my tears I could see his lids jump wildly. He was reaching the edge. Oh, God! Help me!

"You're like all the others. You think I'm a fool, don't you?"

My brain was sending two messages: Get away! Find Katy!

He held me while the wind moaned and rain lashed the windows. Far away I heard a horn honk. The smell of his sweat mingled with my own. His eyes, glassy with madness, bore into my face. My heart was beating wildly.

Then something plupped in the silence of the bedroom, and his lids tightened momentarily as he paused. Birdie appeared in the doorway and emitted a noise

483

between a squeak and a growl. Fortier's eyes shifted to the white shadow and I took my chance.

I shot my leg out and brought it up between his legs, concentrating all my fear and hatred in the force of that blow. My shin slammed hard into his crotch. He screamed and doubled over. I jerked the chain ends from his hand, spun, and flung myself down the hall, terror and desperation propelling me forward. I felt as if I were moving in slow motion.

He recovered quickly, his scream of pain converted into a howl of anger.

"*Bitch!*"

I pitched down the narrow hall, nearly tripping over the dragging chain.

"*You're dead, bitch!*"

I could hear him behind me, lurching through the dark, breathing like a desperate animal. "*You're mine! You won't get away!*"

I staggered around the corner, twisting my hands, fighting to loosen the wrist chain. Blood pounded in my ears. I was a robot, my sympathetic nervous system working the controls.

"*Cunt!*"

He was between me and the front door, forcing me to cut through the kitchen! One thought drove me: Get to the French doors!

My right hand slipped free of the chain.

"*Whore! You're mine!*"

Two steps into the kitchen the pain slammed into me again and I thought my neck had snapped. My left arm flew up and my head whipped back. He had gotten a hand on the trailing neck chain. I felt my insides heave as my air supply was again choked off.

With my unbound hand I tried to free my throat, but the harder I clawed the tighter he pulled. I twisted and pulled, but the chain only cut deeper.

Slowly, he reeled in the chain, drawing me back toward him. I could smell his frenzy, feel his body tremble in the shake of the chain. Loop by loop he shortened my leash. I began to feel dizzy, and thought I was fainting.

"You'll pay for that, bitch." His voice was a hiss.

My face and fingertips tingled from lack of oxygen, and my ears filled with a hollow ringing. The room began to heave about me. A spatter of dots formed in the middle of my field of vision, coalesced, then spread outward as a black cumulus. Through the growing cloud I saw ceramic tile rise toward me, as if in slow motion. I watched my hands reach out as I floated forward, an insensible host tumbling with its parasite rider.

As we pitched forward, my stomach struck a section of counter, and my head slammed into an overhead cabinet. He lost his grip on the chain, but pushed up hard behind me.

He spread his legs and molded his body against mine, pressing me against the counter. The edge of the dishwasher cut painfully across my left pelvic bone, but I could breathe.

His chest heaved, and every fiber of his tissue felt taut, like a slingshot stretched to deliver. With a looping wrist motion he retrieved his grip on the chain and forced my head into a backward arch. Then he reached across my throat and placed the tip of the knife under the angle of my jaw. My carotid throbbed against cold steel. I felt his breath on my left cheek.

He held me for an eternity, head back, hands straight out and useless, like a carcass dangling on a hook. I seemed to be watching myself from across a wide gulf, a spectator, horrified but powerless to help.

I got my right hand on to the counter, trying to push against it to elevate myself and slacken the chain. Then I touched something on the countertop. The orange

485

juice container. The knife.

Silently, my fingers wrapped around the handle. I moaned and tried to sob. Divert his attention.

"Quiet, bitch! We're going to play a game now. You like games, don't you?"

Carefully I rotated the knife, gagging loudly to cover the tiniest scrape.

My hand trembled, hesitated.

Then I saw the women again, saw what he'd done to them. I felt their terror and knew their final desperation.

Do it!

Adrenaline spread through my chest and limbs like lava rolling down a mountainside. If I was going to die, it would not be like a rat in a hole. I would die charging the enemy, guns blazing. My mind refocused and I became an active participant in my own fate. I gripped the knife blade upward, and estimated the angle. Then I thrust across my body and over my left shoulder with all the strength that fear, desperation, and vengeance could muster.

The point struck bone, slipped a little, then plunged into mushy softness. His earlier scream was nothing compared with what now ripped from his throat. As he lurched backward his left hand dropped and his right hand passed across my throat. The chain end slithered to the floor, releasing its death hold.

I felt a dull ache across my throat, then something wet. It didn't matter. All I wanted was air. I gulped hungrily, reaching up to loosen the links and feeling what I knew must be my own blood.

From behind me, another scream, high-pitched, primal, like the death cry of a feral animal. Panting and holding the counter for support, I turned to look.

He stumbled backward across the kitchen, one hand to his face, the other thrown out in an attempt at balance. Horrible sounds gurgled from his open mouth

486

as he slammed against the far wall and slid slowly to the floor. The outthrust hand left a black streak snaking down the plaster. For a moment his head rolled back and forth, then a thin moan rose from his throat. His hands dropped and his head settled, chin down, eyes fixed on the floor.

I stood frozen in the sudden stillness, the only sounds my rasping breath and his fading whimpers. Through my pain, my surroundings began to register. Sink. Stove. Refrigerator, deathly still. Something slippery underfoot.

I stared at the form slumped inert on my kitchen floor, legs splayed forward, chin on chest, back propped against the wall. In the dimness I could see a dark smear trailing down his chest toward his left hand.

Lightning sparked like a welder's torch, and illuminated my handiwork.

His body looked sleek, smoothed by the peacock blue membrane that encased it. A blue and red cap stretched across his scalp, flattening his hair and turning his head into a featureless oval.

The handle of the steak knife rose from his left eye like a flagpin on a putting green. Blood streamed down his face and throat, darkening the spandex on his chest. He had stopped moaning.

I gagged and the flotilla of spots sailed back into my field of vision. My knees buckled and I tried to lean against the counter.

I tried to breathe more deeply and raised my hands to my throat to remove the chain. I felt a warm slipperiness. I lowered one hand and stared. Oh yes. I'm bleeding.

I was moving toward the door, thinking of Katy, of getting help, when a sound froze me in place. The slither of steel links! The room flickered white, black.

Too beaten to run, I turned. A dark silhouette moved

487

silently toward me.

I heard my own voice, then saw a thousand spots, and the black cloud rolled over everything.

Sirens wailing in the distance. Voices. Pressure on my throat.

I opened my eyes to light and movement. A form loomed over me. A hand pressed something against my neck.

Who? Where? My own living room. Memory. Panic. I struggled to sit up.

"*Attention. Attention. Elle se lève.*"

Hands pressed me gently down.

Then, a familiar voice. Unexpected. Out of context.

"Don't move. You've lost a lot of blood. There is an ambulance on the way."

Claudel.

"Where. I . . . ?"

"You're safe. We've got him."

"What's left of him." Charbonneau.

"Katy?"

"Lie back. You've got a gash on your throat and right neck and if you move your head, it bleeds. You've lost a good amount of blood and we don't want you to lose any more."

"My daughter?"

Their faces floated above me. A bolt of lightning flared, turning them white.

"Katy?" My heart pounded. I couldn't breathe.

"She's fine. Anxious to see you. Friends are with her."

"*Tabernac.*" Claudel moved away from the couch. "*Où est cette ambulance?*"

He strode into the hall, glanced at something on the kitchen floor, then back at me, an odd expression on his face.

A siren's wail grew louder, filled my tiny street. Then a second. I saw red and blue pulse outside the French doors.

"Relax now," said Charbonneau. "They're here. We'll see your daughter is looked after. It's over."

42

There's still a gap in my official memory files. The next two days are there, but they're fuzzy and out of synch, a disjointed collage of images and feelings that come and go, but have no rational pattern.

A clock with numbers that were never the same. Pain. Hands tugging, probing, lifting my eyelids. Voices. A light window. A dark window.

Faces. Claudel in harsh fluorescence. Jewel Tambeaux silhouetted against a white hot sun. Ryan in yellow lamplight, slowly turning pages. Charbonneau dozing, TV blue flickering across his features.

I had enough pharmaceuticals in me to numb the Iraqi army, so it's hard to sort drugged sleep from waking reality. The dreams and memories spin and swirl like a cyclone circling its eye. No matter how often I retrace my steps through that time, I cannot sort out the images.

Coherence returned on Friday.

I opened my eyes to bright sunlight, saw a nurse adjusting an IV drip, and knew where I was. Someone to my right was making soft clicking noises. I turned my head and pain shot through it. A dull throbbing in my neck told me further movement was ill advised.

Ryan sat in a vinyl chair, entering something into a pocket organizer.

"Am I going to live?" My words sounded slurred.

"*Mon Dieu.*" Smiling.

I swallowed and repeated the question. My lips felt stiff and swollen.

The nurse reached for my wrist, placed her fingertips on it, focused on her watch.

"That's what they say." Ryan slid the organizer into his shirt pocket, rose, and crossed to the bed. "Concussion, laceration of the right neck and throat region with significant loss of blood. Thirty-seven stitches, each carefully placed by a fine plastic surgeon. Prognosis: she'll live."

The nurse gave him a disapproving glance. "Ten minutes," she said, and left.

A flash of memory shot fear through the layer of drugs.

"Katy?"

"Relax. She'll be here in a while. She was in earlier, but you were out cold."

I looked a question mark at him.

"She showed up with a friend just before you left in the ambulance. Some kid she knows at McGill. She'd been dropped at your place sans key that afternoon, but talked her way through the outer door. Seems some of your neighbors aren't exactly security conscious." He hooked a thumb inside his belt. "But she couldn't get into your unit. She called you at the office, but no score. So she left her pack to flag you that she was in town, and reconnected with her friend. Sayonara, Mom.

"She meant to get back by dinnertime, but the storm hit, so the two of them hung tight at Hurley's and sipped a few. She tried to call, but couldn't get through. She nearly blew a valve when she arrived, but I was able to calm her down. One of the victim assistance officers is staying in close touch with her, making sure she knows what's up. Several people here offered to take her in, but she preferred to crash with her friend. She's been here every day and is going snake wanting to see you."

Despite my best efforts, tears of relief. A tissue and a kind look from Ryan. My hand looked strange against the green hospital blanket, as though it belonged to someone else. A plastic bracelet circled my wrist. I could see tiny flecks of blood under my nails.

More memory bytes. Lightning. A knife handle.

"Fortier?"

"Later."

"Now." The ache in my neck was intensifying. I knew I wouldn't feel like conversation for long. Also, Florence Nightingale would be back soon.

"He lost a lot of blood, but modern medicine saved the bastard. As I understand it, the blade slashed the orbit but then slid into the ethmoid without penetrating the cranium. He will lose his eye, but his sinuses should be great."

"You're a riot, Ryan."

"He got into your building through the faulty garage door, then picked your lock. No one was home, so he disabled the security system and the power. You didn't notice since your computer goes to battery when the power fails, and the regular phone isn't tied in to the electricity, just the portable. He must have cut the phone line right after you made your last call. He was probably in there when Katy tried the door and left her pack."

Another icicle of fear. A crushing hand. A choke collar.

"Where is he now?"

"He's here."

I struggled to sit up and my stomach felt as if it were doing the same. Ryan gently pushed me back against the pillow.

"He's under heavy guard, Tempe. He's not going anywhere."

"St. Jacques?" I heard a tremor in my voice.

"Later."

I had a thousand questions, but it was too late. I was slipping back into the hollow where I'd been curled the past two days.

The nurse returned and shot Ryan a withering look. I didn't see him leave.

The next time I woke Ryan and Claudel were talking quietly by the window. It was dark outside. I'd been dreaming of Jewel and Julie.

"Was Jewel Tambeaux here earlier?"

They turned in my direction.

"She came on Thursday." Ryan.

"Fortier?"

"They've taken him off critical."

"Talking?"

"Yes."

"Is he St. Jacques?"

"Yes."

"And?"

"Maybe this should wait until you're stronger."

"Tell me."

The two exchanged glances, then approached. Claudel cleared his throat.

"Name's Leo Fortier. Thirty-two years old. Lives off the island with his wife and two kids. Drifts from job to job. Nothing steady. He and Grace Damas had an affair back in 1991. Met at a butcher shop where they both worked."

"La Boucherie St. Dominique."

"*Oui.*" Claudel gave me an odd look. "Things start going bad. She threatens to blow the whistle to wifey,

493

starts dunning lover boy for money. He's had it, so he asks her to meet him at the shop after hours, kills her, and cuts her body up."

"Risky."

"The owner's out of town, place is closed up for a couple of weeks. All the equipment is there. Anyway, he cuts her up, hauls her out to St. Lambert, and buries her on the monastery grounds. Seems his uncle is custodian. Either the old man gave him a key or Fortier helped himself."

"Emile Roy."

"*Oui.*"

Again the look.

"That isn't all," said Ryan. "He used the monastery to do Trottier and Gagnon. Took them there, killed them, dismembered their bodies in the basement. He cleaned up after himself, so Roy wouldn't suspect, but when Gilbert and the boys gave the cellar a Luminol spray this morning it lit up like halftime at the Orange Bowl."

"That's how he also had access to Le Grand Séminaire," I said.

"Yeah. Says he got that idea when he was following Chantale Trottier. Her father's condo is right around the corner. Roy keeps a board at the monastery with all kinds of church keys hanging on hooks, neatly marked. Fortier just lifted the one he wanted."

"Oh. And Gilbert has a chef's saw for you. Says it glows." Ryan.

He must have seen something in my face.

"When you're feeling better."

"I can hardly wait." I was trying, but my bruised brain was withdrawing again.

The nurse came in.

"This is police business," Claudel said.

She folded her arms and shook her head.

494

"Merde."

She ushered them out quickly, but returned in a moment. With Katy. My daughter crossed the room without a word and clasped both my hands in hers. Tears filled her eyes.

Softly, "I love you, Mom."

For a moment I just looked at her, a thousand emotions boiling inside me. Love. Gratitude. Helplessness. I cherished this child as no other being on earth. I desperately wished for her happiness. Her safety. I felt completely unable to assure her of either. I could feel tears of my own.

"And I love you, darling."

She dragged a chair close and sat alongside my bed, not releasing my hands. The fluorescent light gleamed a halo of blond around her head.

She cleared her throat. "I'm staying at Monica's. She's commuting to McGill for summer school and living at home. Her family is taking good care of me." She paused, unsure what to say, what to hold back. "Birdie is with us."

She looked toward the window, back at me.

"There's a policewoman who talks to me twice a day and will bring me here whenever I want." She leaned forward, resting her forearms on the bed. "You haven't been awake very much."

"I plan to do better."

A nervous smile. "Dad calls every day to make sure I don't need anything and to ask about you."

Guilt and loss joined the emotions that were churning in me. "Tell him I'm fine."

The nurse returned quietly and stood next to Katy, who took her cue. "I'll be back tomorrow."

It was morning when I got the next installment on Fortier.

495

"He's been a nuisance sex offender for years. Got a sheet going back to 1979. Kept a girl locked up for a day and a half when he was fifteen, but nothing ever came of it. The grandmother kept it out of court, no arrest record. Mostly, he'd pick out a woman, follow her, keep records of her activities. He finally got busted for assault in 1988–"

"The grandmother."

Another Claudel look. I noticed his silk tie was the exact mauve of his shirt.

"*Oui*. An evaluation by a court-appointed psychiatrist at that time described him as paranoid and compulsive." He turned to Ryan. "What else did that shrink write? Tremendous anger, potential for violence, especially against women."

"So he got six months and walked. Typical."

This time Claudel just stared at me. He pinched his eyes at the bridge of his nose and continued.

"Except for the kid and Granny, Fortier up to that point hasn't really done much beyond nuisance stuff. But he gets a real rush killing Grace Damas, decides to move on to bigger things. It's right after that he rents his first hidey-hole. The one on Berger was only his latest."

"Didn't want to share his hobby with the little woman at home." Ryan.

"Where did he get the rent money with only a part-time job?"

"Wife works. He probably squeezed it from her, told her some lie. Or maybe he had another hobby we don't know about. We're sure going to find out."

Claudel continued in his detached, case-discussing voice.

"The next year he begins stalking in earnest, going about it systematically. You were right about the Métro. He's got a thing about the number six. He starts out riding six stops, then follows a woman that fits his profile.

496

His first random hit is Francine Morisette-Champoux. Our boy gets on at Berri-UQAM, gets off at Georges-Vanier and follows her home. He tracks her for several weeks, then makes his move."

I thought of her words and felt a rush of anger. She wanted to feel safe. Untouchable in her home. The ultimate female fantasy. Claudel's voice reconnected.

"But the free stalk is too risky, not controlled enough for him. He gets the idea of using real estate signs from the one on the Morisette-Champoux condo. It's the perfect in."

"Trottier?" I felt sick.

"Trottier. This time he takes the green line, rides his six stops, and gets off at Atwater. He walks around until he spots a sign. Daddy's condo. He watches, takes his time, sees Chantale come and go. Says he spotted the Sacré Cœur logo on her uniform, even went to the school some days. Then the ambush."

"By this time he'd also found a safer killing spot," added Ryan.

"The monastery. Perfect. How did he get Chantale to go with him?"

"One day he waits until he knows she's alone, rings the bell, asks to see the condo. He's a potential buyer, right? But she won't let him in. A few days later he pulls up next to her as she's leaving school. What a coincidence. Claims he had an appointment with her father, but no one showed up. Chantale knows how badly the old man wants to sell the place, so she agrees to walk him through. The rest we know."

The fluorescent tube above my bed buzzed softly. Claudel went on.

"Fortier doesn't want to risk another body on the monastery grounds, so he drives her all the way up to St. Jerome. But he doesn't like that either. It's too long in the car. What if he got stopped? He's seen the seminary,

497

remembers the key. Next time he'll do even better."

"Gagnon."

"Learning curve."

"*Voilà.*"

At that moment the nurse appeared, a younger, gentler version of my weekday keeper. She read my chart, felt my head, took my pulse. For the first time I noticed that the IV was gone from my arm.

"Are you getting tired?"

"I'm fine."

"You can have another painkiller if you need it."

"Let's see how it goes," I said.

She smiled and left.

"What about Adkins?"

"He gets agitated when he talks about Adkins," said Ryan. "Closes up. It's almost as if he's proud of the others, but feels different about her."

A medicine cart passed in the corridor, rubber wheels gliding silently over tile.

Why didn't Adkins fit the pattern?

A robotic voice urged someone to dial 237.

Why so messy?

Elevator doors opened, whooshed shut.

"Think about this," I said. "He's got the place on Berger. His system is working. He finds his victims with the Métro and the 'for sale' signs, then he tracks them until the right moment. He has a safe place to kill and a safe place to dump the bodies. Maybe it's working too well. Maybe the rush isn't there anymore, so he has to up the stakes. He decides to go back into the victim's home, like he did with Morisette-Champoux."

I remembered the photos. The disheveled warm-up suit. The dark red pool around the body.

"But he gets sloppy. We found out he called ahead to make an appointment with Margaret Adkins. What he didn't count on was the husband phoning during his

498

visit. He has to kill her quickly. He has to cut her fast, mutilate her with something close at hand. He pulls it off, gets away, but it's rushed. He's not in control."

The statue. The severed breast.

Ryan nodded.

"Makes sense. The kill is just the final act in his fantasy of control. I can kill you or let you live. I can hide your body or display it. I can deprive you of your gender by mutilating your breasts or vagina. I can render you powerless by cutting off your hands. But then the husband calls and threatens his whole fantasy satisfaction."

"Spoiled the rush." Ryan.

"He never used stolen items before Adkins. Maybe he used her bank card afterward to reassert control."

"Or maybe he had a cash flow problem, needed to blow something up his nose and had no purchasing power." Claudel.

"It's weird. Can't shut him up on the others, but he turns into a potted palm on Adkins." Ryan.

For a while no one said anything.

"Pitre and Gautier?" I asked, avoiding what I really had to know.

"Claims they're not his."

Ryan and Claudel exchanged words. I didn't hear them. A chill spread and filled my rib cage, a question taking form. It coalesced, hung there, then slithered up and forced itself into language.

"Gabby?"

Claudel dropped his eyes.

Ryan cleared his throat.

"You've had a–"

"Gabby?" I repeated. Tears burned the insides of my eyelids.

Ryan nodded.

"Why?"

No one spoke.

499

"It's because of me, isn't it?" I fought to keep my voice even.

"This fuckhead's a nutcase," said Ryan. "He's crazy for control. He won't open up much about his childhood, but he's got so much rage against the grandmother you have to scrape it off your teeth when you leave the room. Blames all of his problems on her. Keeps saying she ruined him. From what we've learned, she was a very domineering woman, and fanatically religious. His feelings of powerlessness probably stem from whatever went on between them."

"Meaning the guy's a real loser with women and blames it on the old lady," added Claudel.

"What does this have to do with Gabby?"

Ryan seemed reluctant to continue.

"At first Fortier gets a sense of control through peeping. He can watch his victims, track them, learn all about them, and they aren't even aware of him. He keeps his notebooks and clippings and runs a fantasy show in his head. An added bonus is that there's no risk of rejection. But eventually, that's not enough. He kills Damas, finds he likes it, and decides on a career move. He starts kidnapping and killing his victims. The ultimate control. Life and death. He's in charge and unstoppable."

I stared into the flame blue irises.

"Then you come along and dig up Isabelle Gagnon."

"I'm a threat," I said, anticipating where he was going.

"His perfect MO is jeopardized, he feels a threat. And Dr. Brennan is the cause. You may topple the whole fantasy in which he's the supreme player."

I ran over the events of the past six weeks.

"I dig up and identify Isabelle Gagnon in early June. Three weeks later Fortier kills Margaret Adkins, and the next day we show up on Rue Berger. Three days after

500

that I find Grace Damas's skeleton."

"You've got it."

"He's furious."

"Exactly. The hunt is his way of acting out his contempt for women—"

"Or his anger at Granny." Claudel.

"Maybe. Anyway, he sees you as blocking him."

"And I'm a woman."

Ryan reached for a cigarette, remembered where he was.

"Also, he made a mistake. Adkins was sloppy. Using the bank card almost cost him."

"So he needs someone to blame."

"This guy can't admit he's screwed up. And he definitely can't deal with a woman catching him out."

"But why Gabby? Why not me?"

"Who knows? Chance? Timing? Maybe she walked out before you did."

"I don't think so," I said. "It's obvious he'd been stalking me for some time. He put the skull in my yard?"

Nods.

"He could have waited, then grabbed me like he did the others."

"This is one sick fucker." Claudel.

"Gabby wasn't like the others, she wasn't a random-stranger killing. Fortier knew where I lived. He knew she was staying with me."

I was talking more to myself than to Ryan and Claudel. An emotional aneurysm, formed over the past six weeks and held in check by force of will, was threatening to burst.

"He did it on purpose. The psycho prick wanted me to know. It was a message, like the skull."

My voice was rising but I couldn't hold it back. I pictured an envelope on my door. An oval of bricks. Gabby's bloated face with its tiny silver gods. A picture

501

of my daughter.

The thin wall of my emotional balloon ruptured, and weeks of pent-up grief and tension rushed through the puncture.

Razors of pain shot through my throat but I screamed, "No! No! No! You goddamn sonofabitch!"

I heard Ryan speak sharply to Claudel, felt his hands on my arms, saw the nurse, felt the needle. Then nothing.

43

Ryan came to see me at home on Wednesday. The earth had turned seven times since my night in hell, and I'd had time to construct an official version for myself. But there were holes I wanted to fill.

"Has Fortier been charged?"

"Monday. Five counts of first degree."

"Five?"

"Pitre and Gautier are probably unrelated."

"Tell me something. How did Claudel know Fortier would show up here?"

"He didn't, really. From your questions about the school, he realized Tanguay couldn't be the perp. He checked, found out the kids are in at eight, out at three-fifteen. Tanguay earned a perfect attendance ribbon. Hadn't missed a day since he started, and there were no school holidays on the days you asked about. Also he'd learned about the glove business.

"He knew you were exposed, so he hauled ass back to your place to keep watch until he could get a unit back on site. Got here, tried the phone and found it dead. He vaulted the garden gate and found the French doors unlocked. You two were too busy dancing to hear him. He would have broken the glass, but you must have

503

gotten the latch open when you tried to split."

Claudel. My rescuer again.

"Anything new turn up?"

"They found an athletic bag in Fortier's car with three choke collars, a couple of hunting knives, a box of surgical gloves, and a set of street clothes."

I packed as he talked, perched on the end of the bed.

"His kit."

"Yes. I'm sure we'll tie the Rue Berger glove and the one with Gabby to the box in his car."

I pictured him that night, Spiderman smooth, gloved hands bone white in the darkness.

"He'd wear the cycling suit and gloves whenever he went out to play. Even at Berger. That's why we always came up empty. No hairs, no fibers, no latents."

"No sperm."

"Oh yeah. He also had a box of condoms."

"Perfect."

I went to the closet for my old sneakers, tucked them into the duffel.

"Why did he do it?"

"I doubt we'll ever know. Apparently the grand-mother could have run the showers and sifted the gold crowns out of the ovens."

"Meaning?"

"She was tough. And fanatic."

"About?"

"Sex and God. Not necessarily in that order."

"For example?"

"Gave little Leo an enema and dragged him to church every morning. To cleanse body and soul."

"The daily Mass and swish protocol."

"We talked to a neighbor who remembers one time the kid was wrestling on the floor with the family dog. The old biddy nearly stroked out because the schnauzer had a hard-on. Two days later the pup turned up with a

504

belly full of rat poison."

"Did Fortier know?"

"He doesn't talk about it. He does talk about a time he was seven and she caught him jacking off. Granny tied little Leo's wrists to her own and dragged him around for three days. He's got spiders in his head when it comes to hands."

I paused in the middle of folding a sweater.

"Hands."

"Yeah."

"That's not all. There was also an uncle, a priest who'd been forced to take early retirement. Hung around the house in his bathrobe, probably abused the kid. It's another topic he goes mute on. We're checking it out."

"Where is the grandmother now?"

"Dead. Right before he killed Damas."

"The trigger?"

"Who knows."

I started going through bathing suits, gave up, stuffed them all in the duffel.

"What about Tanguay?"

Ryan shook his head and expelled a long breath. "Looks like he's just another citizen with a seriously impaired approach to sex."

I stopped sorting socks and looked at him.

"He's mainline fruitcake, but probably harmless."

"Meaning?"

"He was a biology teacher. Collected roadkill, boiled the carcasses down and mounted the skeletons. He was building a display for his classroom."

"The paws?"

"Dried them for a vertebrae paw collection."

"Did he kill Alsa?"

"He claims he found her dead on the street near UQAM and brought her home for the collection. He'd

505

just cut her up when he read the article in the *Gazette*. Scared him, so he stuffed her in a bag and left her at the bus station. We'll probably never know how she got out of the lab."

"Tanguay *is* Julie's client, isn't he?"

"None other. Gets his jolts by hiring a hooker to dress in Mama's nightie. And . . ."

He hesitated.

"And?"

"You ready for this? Tanguay was dummy man."

"No. The bedroom burglar?"

"You got it. That's why his butt was sucked right up his throat when we were questioning him. He thought we'd hauled him on that. The dumb little bastard came out with it all by himself. Apparently, when he couldn't score on the street, he'd use plan B."

"Break in and crank up on someone else's jammies."

"You've got it. Better than bowling."

There was something else that had been bothering me.

"The phone calls?"

"Plan C. Phone a woman, hang up, feel your genitals twinkle. Typical peeper stuff. He had a list of numbers."

"Any theories on how he got mine?"

"Probably lifted it from Gabby. He was peeping her."

"The picture I found in my wastebasket?"

"Tanguay. He's into aboriginal art. It was a copy of something he saw in a book. Did it to give to Gabby. Wanted to ask her not to cut him out of the project."

I looked at Ryan. "Pretty ironic. She thought she had a stalker when she actually had two."

I felt my eyes well with tears. The emotional scar tissue was forming, but was still embryonic. It would take time until I could think of her.

Ryan rose and stretched. "Where's Katy?" he asked, changing the subject.

506

"Gone for suntan lotion." I pulled the drawstring on the duffel and dropped it to the floor.

"How's she doing?"

"She seems fine. Looks after me like a private duty nurse."

Unconsciously, I scratched at the stitches in my neck.

"But it may trouble her more than she lets on. She knows about violence, but it's evening news violence, in South L.A. and Tel Aviv and Sarajevo. It's always been something that happens to other people. Pete and I purposely sheltered her from what I do, kept Katy apart from my work. Now it's real and close and personal. She's had her world tipped, but she'll come around."

"And you?"

"I'm fine. Really."

We stood in silence and studied each other. Then he reached for his jacket and folded it over his arm.

"Going to a beach?" His affected indifference was not quite convincing.

"Every one we can find. We've dubbed it 'The Great Sand and Surf Quest.' First Ogonquit, then a swing down the coast. Cape Cod. Rehobeth. Cape May. Virginia Beach. Our only plan is to be at Nags Head on the fifteenth."

Pete had arranged that. He planned to be there.

Ryan placed a hand on my shoulder. His eyes spoke of more than professional interest.

"Are you coming back?"

I'd been asking myself all week. Am I? To what? The work? Could I go through this again with yet another twisted psychopath? To Quebec? Could I bear to let Claudel carve me up and serve me to some hearing commission? What about my marriage? That wasn't in Quebec. What would I do about Pete? What would I feel when I saw him?

I'd made only one decision: I wouldn't think about it

for now. I'd vowed to put tomorrow's uncertainties aside and leave my time with Katy unblemished.

"Of course," I said. "I'll have to finish my reports, then testify."

"Yeah."

A tense silence. We both knew it was a non-answer.

He cleared his throat and reached into his jacket pocket.

"Claudel asked me to give this to you."

He held out a brown envelope with the CUM logo on the upper left-hand corner.

"Great."

I stuck it in my pocket and followed him to the door. Not now.

"Ryan."

He turned.

"Can you do this day after day, year after year, and not lose faith in the human species?"

He didn't answer right away, seemed to focus on a point in space between us. Then his eyes met mine.

"From time to time the human species spawns predators that feed on those around them. They're not the species. They're mutations of the species. In my opinion these freaks have no right to suck oxygen from the atmosphere. But they're here, so I help cage them up and put them where they can't hurt others. I make life safer for the folks who get up, go to work each day, raise their kids or their tomatoes, or their tropical fish, and watch the ball game in the evening. *They* are the human species."

I watched him walk away, admiring once again the way he filled his 501's. And brains, too, I thought as I closed the door. Maybe, I said to myself, smiling. May, by God, be.

Later that evening Katy and I went for ice cream, then

508

drove up the mountain. Sitting on my favorite overlook we could see the whole valley, the St. Lawrence a black cutout in the distance, Montreal a twinkling panorama spreading from its edges.

I looked down from my bench, like a passenger on Mr. Toad's Wild Ride. But the ride was finally over. Perhaps I'd come to say good-bye.

I finished my cone and jammed the napkin in my pocket. My hand touched Claudel's envelope.

Hell, why not.

I opened it and withdrew a handwritten note. Odd. It was not the formal complaint I'd expected. The message was written in English.

Dr. Brennan,

You are right. No one should die in anonymity. Thanks to you, these women did not. Thanks to you, Leo Fortier's killing days are over.

We are the last line of defense against them: the pimps, the rapists, the cold-blooded killers. I would be honored to work with you again.

Luc Claudel

Higher up the mountain, the cross glowed softly, sending its message out over the valley. What was it Kojak said? Somebody loves ya, baby.

Ryan and Claudel had it figured. And we were the last line.

I looked at the city below. Hang in there. Somebody loves ya.

"*A la prochaine,*" I said to the summer night.

"What's that?" asked Katy.

"Until the next time."

My daughter looked puzzled.

"Let's go to the beach."

DEATH DU JOUR

To all who survived
the Great Quebec Ice Storm of 1998.

Nous nous souvenons.

Acknowledgements

Grateful thanks are extended to Dr. Ronald Coulombe, specialiste en incendies; to Ms. Carole Péclet, specialiste en chimie; and to Dr. Robert Dorion, Responsable d'Odontologie, Laboratoire de Sciences Judiciaires et de Médecine Légale; and to Mr. Louis Metivier, Bureau du Coroner de la Province de Québec, for sharing their knowledge with me.

Dr. Walter Birkby, forensic anthropologist for the Office of the Medical Examiner of Pima County, Arizona, provided information on the recovery of burned remains. Dr. Robert Brouillette, Head of the Divisions of Newborn Medicine and of Respiratory Medicine at the Montreal Children's Hospital helped with data on infant growth.

Mr. Curt Copeland, the Beaufort County coroner; Mr. Carl McCleod, the Beaufort County sheriff; and Detective Neal Player of the Beaufort County sheriff's department were most helpful. Detective Mike Mannix of the Illinois State Police also answered many questions pertaining to the investigation of a homicide. Dr. James Tabor, Professor of Religious Studies at the University of North Carolina at Charlotte, supplied information on cults and religious movements.

Mr. Leon Simon and Mr. Paul Reichs provided information on Charlotte and its history. I am also indebted to the latter for his comments on the manuscript. Dr. James Woodward, chancellor at the University of North Carolina at Charlotte, supported me unquestioningly throughout the writing of this book.

Special thanks must go to three individuals. Dr. David Taub, mayor of Beaufort and primatologist extraordinaire, was steadfastly helpful despite the barrage of questions I sent his way. Dr. Lee Goff, Professor of Entomology at the University of Hawaii at Manoa, did not abandon me as I pestered him endlessly for advice on bugs. Dr. Michael Bisson, Professor of Anthropology at McGill University, was a resource on McGill University, on Montreal, and on basically anything I needed to know.

Two books were particularly useful in the writing of this story. *Plague: A Story of Smallpox in Montreal* (1991), by Michael Bliss, Harper Collins, Toronto; and *Cults in Our Midst: The Hidden Menace in Our Everyday Lives* (1995), by Margaret Thaler Singer with Janja Lalich, Jossey-Bass Publishers, San Francisco.

I am grateful for the loving care of my agent, Jennifer Rudolph Walsh, and my editors Susanne Kirk and Maria Rejt. Without them Tempe could not tell the stories that she does.

1

If the bodies were there, I couldn't find them.

Outside, the wind howled. Inside the old church, just the scrape of my trowel and the hum of a portable generator and heater echoed eerily in the huge space. High above, branches scratched against boarded windows, gnarled fingers on plywood blackboards.

The group stood behind me, huddled but not touching, fingers curled tightly in pockets. I could hear the shifting from side to side, the lifting of one foot, then the other. Boots made a crunching sound on the frozen ground. No one spoke. The cold had numbed us into silence.

I watched a cone of earth disappear through quarter-inch mesh as I spread it gently with my trowel. The granular subsoil had been a pleasant surprise. Given the surface, I had expected permafrost the entire depth of the excavation. The last two weeks had been unseasonably warm in Quebec, however, allowing snow to melt and ground to thaw. Typical Tempe luck. Though the tickle of spring had been blown away by another arctic blast, the mild spell had left the dirt soft and easy to dig. Good. Last night the temperature had dropped to seven degrees Fahrenheit. Not good. While the ground had not refrozen, the air was frigid. My fingers were so cold I could hardly bend them.

We were digging our second trench. Still nothing but pebbles and rock fragments in the screen. I didn't anticipate much at this depth, but you could never tell. I'd yet to do an exhumation that had gone as planned.

I turned to a man in a black parka and a tuque on his head. He wore leather boots laced to the knee, two pairs of socks rolled over the tops. His face was the color of tomato soup.

"Just a few more inches." I gave a palm-down gesture, like stroking a cat. Slowly. Go slowly.

The man nodded, then thrust his long-handled spade into the shallow trench, grunting like Monica Seles on a first serve.

"*Par pouces!*" I yelped, grabbing the shovel. By inches! I repeated the slicing motion I'd been showing him all morning. "We want to take it down in thin layers." I said it again, in slow, careful French.

The man clearly did not share my sentiment. Maybe it was the tediousness of the task, maybe the thought of unearthing the dead. Tomato soup just wanted to be done and gone.

"Please, Guy, try again?" said a male voice behind me.

"Yes, Father." Mumbled.

Guy resumed, shaking his head, but skimming the soil as I'd shown him, then tossing it into the screen. I shifted my gaze from the black dirt to the pit itself, watching for signs that we were nearing a burial.

We'd been at it for hours, and I could sense tension behind me. The nuns' rocking had increased in tempo. I turned to give the group what I hoped was a reassuring look. My lips were so stiff it was hard to tell.

Six faces looked back at me, pinched from cold and anxiousness. A small cloud of vapor appeared and

2

dissolved in front of each. Six smiles in my direction. I could sense a lot of praying going on.

Ninety minutes later we were five feet down. Like the first, this pit had produced only soil. I was certain I had frostbite in every toe, and Guy was ready to bring in a backhoe. Time to regroup.

"Father, I think we need to check the burial records again."

He hesitated a moment. Then, "Yes. Of course. Of course. And we could all use coffee and a sandwich."

The priest started toward a set of wooden doors at the far end of the abandoned church and the nuns followed, heads down, gingerly navigating the lumpy ground. Their white veils spread in identical arcs across the backs of their black wool coats. Penguins. Who'd said that? The Blues Brothers.

I turned off the mobile spotlights and fell in step, eyes to the ground, amazed at the fragments of bone embedded in the dirt floor. Great. We'd dug in the one spot in the entire church that didn't contain burials.

Father Ménard pushed open one of the doors and, single file, we exited to daylight. Our eyes needed little adjustment. The sky was leaden and seemed to hug the spires and towers of all the buildings in the convent's compound. A raw wind blew off the Laurentians, flapping collars and veils.

Our little group bent against the wind and crossed to an adjacent building, gray stone like the church, but smaller. We climbed steps to an ornately carved wooden porch and entered through a side door.

Inside, the air was warm and dry, pleasant after the bitter cold. I smelled tea and mothballs and years of fried food.

Wordlessly, the women removed their boots, smiled at me one by one, and disappeared through a doorway to the right just as a tiny nun in an enormous ski

3

sweater shuffled into the foyer. Fuzzy brown reindeer leaped across her chest and disappeared beneath her veil. She blinked at me through thick lenses and reached for my parka. I hesitated, afraid its weight would tip her off balance and send her crashing to the tile. She nodded sharply and urged me with upturned fingertips, so I slipped the jacket off, laid it across her arms, and added cap and gloves. She was the oldest woman that I had ever seen still breathing.

I followed Father Ménard down a long, poorly lit hallway into a small study. Here the air smelled of old paper and schoolhouse paste. A crucifix loomed over a desk so large I wondered how they'd gotten it through the door. Dark oak paneling rose almost to the ceiling. Statues stared down from the room's upper edge, faces somber as the figure on the crucifix.

Father Ménard took one of two wooden chairs facing the desk, gestured me to the other. The swish of his cassock. The click of his beads. For a moment I was back at St. Barnabas. In Father's office. In trouble again. Stop it, Brennan. You're over forty, a professional. A forensic anthropologist. These people called you because they need your expertise.

The priest retrieved a leather-bound volume from the desktop, opened it to a page with a green ribbon marker, and positioned the book between us. He took a deep breath, pursed his lips, and exhaled through his nose.

I was familiar with the diagram. A grid with rows divided into rectangular plots, some with numbers, some with names. We'd spent hours poring over it the day before, comparing the descriptions and records for the graves with their positions on the grid. Then we'd paced it all off, marking exact locations.

Sister Élisabeth Nicolet was supposed to be in the second row from the church's north wall, third plot

4

from the west end. Right next to Mother Aurélie. But she wasn't. Nor was Aurélie where she should have been.

I pointed to a grave in the same quadrant, but several rows down and to the right. "O.K. Raphael seems to be there." Then down the row. "And Agathe, Véronique, Clément, Marthe, and Eléonore. Those are the burials from the 1840s, right?"

"*C'est ça.*"

I moved my finger to the portion of the diagram corresponding to the southwest corner of the church. "And these are the most recent graves. The markers we found are consistent with your records."

"Yes. Those were the last, just before the church was abandoned."

"It was closed in 1914."

"Nineteen fourteen. Yes, 1914." He had an odd way of repeating words and phrases.

"Élisabeth died in 1888?"

"*C'est ça*, 1888. Mère Aurélie in 1894."

It didn't make sense. Evidence of the graves should be there. It was clear that artifacts from the 1840 burials remained. A test in that area had produced wood fragments and bits of coffin hardware. In the protected environment inside the church, with that type of soil, I thought the skeletons should be in pretty good shape. So where were Élisabeth and Aurélie?

The old nun shuffled in with a tray of coffee and sandwiches. Steam from the mugs had fogged her glasses, so she moved with short, jerky steps, never lifting her feet from the floor. Father Ménard rose to take the tray.

"*Merci*, Sister Bernard. This is very kind. Very kind."

The nun nodded and shuffled out, not bothering to clear her lenses. I watched her as I helped myself to coffee. Her shoulders were about as broad as my wrist.

5

"How old is Sister Bernard?" I asked, reaching for a croissant. Salmon salad and wilted lettuce.

"We're not exactly sure. She was at the convent when I first started coming here as a child, before the war. World War II, that is. Then she went to teach in the foreign missions. She was in Japan for a long time, then Cameroon. We think she's in her nineties." He sipped his coffee. A slurper.

"She was born in a small village in the Saguenay, says she joined the order when she was twelve." Slurp. "Twelve. Records weren't so good in those days in rural Quebec. Not so good."

I took a bite of sandwich then rewrapped my fingers around the coffee mug. Delicious warmth.

"Father, are there any other records? Old letters, documents, anything we haven't looked at?" I wriggled my toes. No sensation.

He gestured to the papers littering the desk, shrugged. "This is everything Sister Julienne gave me. She is the convent archivist, you know."

"Yes."

Sister Julienne and I had spoken and corresponded at length. It was she who had initially contacted me about the project. I was intrigued from the outset. This case was very different from my usual forensic work involving the recently dead who end up with the coroner. The archdiocese wanted me to exhume and analyze the remains of a saint. Well, she wasn't really a saint. But that was the point. Élisabeth Nicolet had been proposed for beatification. I was to find her grave and verify that the bones were hers. The saint part was up to the Vatican.

Sister Julienne had assured me that there were good records. All graves in the old church were cataloged and mapped. The last burial had taken place in 1911. The church was abandoned and sealed in 1914 following a

6

fire. A larger one was built to replace it, and the old building was never used again. Closed site. Good documentation. Piece of cake.

So where was Élisabeth Nicolet?

"It might not hurt to ask. Perhaps there's something Sister Julienne didn't give you because she thought it unimportant."

He started to say something, changed his mind. "I'm quite sure she's given me everything, but I'll ask. Sister Julienne has spent a great deal of time researching this. A great deal."

I watched him out the door, finished my croissant, then another. I crossed my legs, tucked my feet under me, and rubbed my toes. Good. Feeling was returning. Sipping my coffee, I lifted a letter from the desk.

I'd read it before. August 4, 1885. Smallpox was out of control in Montreal. Élisabeth Nicolet had written to Bishop Édouard Fabre, pleading that he order vaccinations for parishioners who were well, and use of the civic hospital by those who were infected. The handwriting was precise, the French quaint and outdated.

The Convent Notre-Dame de l'Immaculée-Conception was absolutely silent. My mind drifted. I thought of other exhumations. The policeman in St-Gabriel. In that cemetery the coffins had been stacked three deep. We'd finally found Monsieur Beaupré four graves from his recorded location, bottom position, not top. And there was the man in Winston-Salem who wasn't in his own coffin. The occupant was a woman in a long floral dress. That had left the cemetery with a double problem. Where was the deceased? And who was the body in the coffin? The family never was able to rebury Grandpa in Poland, and the lawyers were girding for war when I left.

Far off, I heard a bell toll, then, in the corridor, shuffling. The old nun was heading my way.

7

"*Serviettes*," she screeched. I jumped, rocketing coffee onto my sleeve. How could so much volume come from so small a person?

"*Merci*." I reached for the napkins.

She ignored me, closed in, and began scrubbing my sleeve. A tiny hearing aid peeked from her right ear. I could feel her breath and see fine white hairs ringing her chin. She smelled of wool and rose water.

"Eh, *voilà*. Wash it when you get home. Cold water."

"Yes, Sister." Reflex.

Her eyes fell on the letter in my hand. Fortunately, it was coffee-free. She bent close.

"Élisabeth Nicolet was a great woman. A woman of God. Such purity. Such austerity." *Pureté. Austérité.* Her French sounded as I imagined Élisabeth's letters would if spoken.

"Yes, Sister." I was nine years old again.

"She will be a saint."

"Yes, Sister. That's why we're trying to find her bones. So they can receive proper treatment." I wasn't sure just what proper treatment was for a saint, but it sounded right.

I pulled out the diagram and showed it to her. "This is the old church." I traced the row along the north wall, and pointed to a rectangle. "This is her grave."

The old nun studied the grid for a very long time, lenses millimeters from the page.

"She's not there," she boomed.

"Excuse me?"

"She's not there." A knobby finger tapped the rectangle. "That's the wrong place."

Father Ménard returned at that moment. With him was a tall nun with heavy black eyebrows that angled together above her nose. The priest introduced Sister Julienne, who raised clasped hands and smiled.

It wasn't necessary to explain what Sister Bernard

8

had said. Undoubtedly they'd heard the old woman while in the corridor. They'd probably heard her in Ottawa.

"That's the wrong place. You're looking in the wrong place," she repeated.

"What do you mean?" asked Sister Julienne.

"They're looking in the wrong place," she repeated. "She's not there."

Father Ménard and I exchanged glances.

"Where is she, Sister?" I asked.

She bent to the diagram once again, then jabbed her finger at the southeast corner of the church. "She's there. With Mère Aurélie."

"But, Sis –"

"They moved them. Gave them new coffins and put them under a special altar. There."

Again she pointed at the southeast corner.

"When?" we asked simultaneously.

Sister Bernard closed her eyes. The wrinkled old lips moved in silent calculation.

"Nineteen eleven. The year I came here as a novice. I remember, because a few years later the church burned and they boarded it up. It was my job to go in and put flowers on their altar. I didn't like that. Spooky to go in there all alone. But I offered it up to God."

"What happened to the altar?"

"Taken out sometime in the thirties. It's in the Holy Infant Chapel in the new church now." She folded the napkin and began gathering coffee things. "There was a plaque marking those graves, but not anymore. No one goes in there now. Plaque's been gone for years."

Father Ménard and I looked at each other. He gave a slight shrug.

"Sister," I began, "do you think you could show us where Élisabeth's grave is?"

"*Bien sûr.*"

9

"Now?"

"Why not?" China rattled against china.

"Never mind the dishes," said Father Ménard. "Please, get your coat and boots on, Sister, and we'll walk over."

Ten minutes later we were all back in the old church. The weather had not improved and, if anything, was colder and damper than in the morning. The wind still howled. The branches still tapped.

Sister Bernard picked an unsteady path across the church, Father Ménard and I each gripping an arm. Through the layers of clothing, she felt brittle and weightless.

The nuns followed in their spectator gaggle, Sister Julienne ready with steno pad and pen. Guy hung to the rear.

Sister Bernard stopped outside a recess in the southeast corner. She'd added a hand-knitted chartreuse hat over her veil, tied under her chin. We watched her head turn this way and that, searching for markers, getting her bearings. All eyes focused on the one spot of color in the dreary church interior.

I signaled to Guy to reposition a light. Sister Bernard paid no attention. After some time she moved back from the wall. Head left, head right, head left. Up. Down. She checked her position once more, then gouged a line in the dirt with the heel of her boot. Or tried to.

"She's here." The shrill voice echoed off stone walls.

"You're sure?"

"She's here." Sister Bernard did not lack self-assurance.

We all looked at the mark she'd made.

"They're in little coffins. Not like regular ones. They were just bones, so everything fit into small coffins." She held her tiny arms out to indicate a child-size

10

dimension. An arm trembled. Guy focused the light on the spot at her feet.

Father Ménard thanked the ancient nun and asked two of the sisters to help her back to the convent. I watched their retreat. She looked like a child between them, so small that the hem of her coat barely cleared the dirt floor.

I asked Guy to bring the other spotlight to the new location. Then I retrieved my probe from the earlier site, positioned the tip where Sister Bernard had indicated, and pushed on the T-bar handle. No go. This spot was less defrosted. I was using a tile probe to avoid damaging anything underground, and the ball-shaped tip did not pass easily through the partially frozen upper layer. I tried again, harder.

Easy, Brennan. They won't be happy if you shatter a coffin window. Or poke a hole through the good sister's skull.

I removed my gloves, wrapped my fingers around the T-bar, and thrust again. This time the surface broke, and I felt the probe slide into the subsoil. Suppressing the urge to hurry, I tested the earth, eyes closed, feeling for minute differences in texture. Less resistance could mean an airspace where something had decomposed. More could mean that a bone or artifact was present underground. Nothing. I withdrew the probe and repeated the process.

On the third try I felt resistance. I withdrew, reinserted six inches to the right. Again, contact. There was something solid not far below the surface.

I gave the priest and nuns a thumbs-up, and asked Guy to bring the screen. Laying aside the probe, I took up a flat-edged shovel and began to strip thin slices of earth. I peeled soil, inch by inch, tossing it into the screen, my eyes moving from the fill to the pit. Within thirty minutes I saw what I was looking for. The last few

11

tosses were dark, black against the red-brown dirt in the screen.

I switched from shovel to trowel, bent into the pit, and carefully scraped the floor, removing loose particles and leveling the surface. Almost immediately I could see a dark oval. The stain looked about three feet long. I could only guess at its width since it lay half hidden under unexcavated soil.

"There's something here," I said, straightening. My breath hung in front of my face.

As one, the nuns and priest moved closer and peered into the pit. I outlined the oval with my trowel tip. At that moment Sister Bernard's escort nuns rejoined the flock.

"It could be a burial, though it looks rather small. I've dug a bit to the left, so I'll have to take this portion down." I indicated the spot where I was squatting. "I'll excavate outside the grave itself and work my way down and in. That way we'll have a profile view of the burial as we go. And it's easier on the back to dig that way. An outside trench will also allow us to remove the coffin from the side if we have to."

"What is the stain?" asked a young nun with a face like a Girl Scout.

"When something with a high organic content decays, it leaves the soil much darker. It could be from the wooden coffin, or flowers that were buried with it." I didn't want to explain the decomposition process. "Staining is almost always the first sign of a burial."

Two of the nuns crossed themselves.

"Is it Élisabeth or Mère Aurélie?" asked an older nun. One of her lower lids did a little dance.

I raised my hands in a "beats me" gesture. Pulling on my gloves, I started troweling the soil over the right half of the stain, expanding the pit outward to expose the oval and a two-foot strip along its right.

12

Again, the only sounds were scraping and screening. Then,

"Is that something?" The tallest of the nuns pointed to the screen.

I rose to look, grateful for an excuse to stretch.

The nun was indicating a small, reddish-brown fragment.

"You bet your a—. That sure is, Sister. Looks like coffin wood."

I got a stack of paper bags from my supplies, marked one with the date, location, and other pertinent information, set it in the screen, and laid the others on the ground. My fingers were now completely numb.

"Time to work, ladies. Sister Julienne, you record everything we find. Write it on the bag, and enter it in the log, just as we discussed. We're at" – I looked into the pit – "about the two-foot level. Sister Marguerite, you're going to shoot some pictures?"

Sister Marguerite nodded, held up her camera.

They flew into action, eager after the long hours of watching. I troweled, Sisters Eyelid and Girl Scout screened. More and more fragments appeared, and before long we could see an outline in the stained soil. Wood. Badly deteriorated. Not good.

Using my trowel and bare hands, I continued to uncover what I hoped was a coffin. Though the temperature was below freezing and all feeling had left my fingers and toes, inside my parka I sweated. Please let this be her, I thought. Now who was praying?

As I inched the pit northward, exposing more and more wood, the object expanded in breadth. Slowly, the contour emerged: hexagonal. Coffin shape. It took some effort not to shout "Hallelujah!" Churchy, but unprofessional, I told myself.

I teased away earth, handful by handful, until the top of the object was fully exposed. It was a small casket,

13

and I was moving from the foot toward the head. I put down my trowel and reached for a paintbrush. My eyes met those of one of my screeners. I smiled. She smiled. Her right lid did a jitterbug.

I brushed the wooden surface again and again, teasing away decades of encrusted soil. Everyone stopped to watch. Gradually, a raised object emerged on the coffin lid. Just above the widest point. Exactly where a plaque would be. My heart did its own fast dance.

I brushed dirt from the object until it came into focus. It was oval, metallic, with a filigreed edge. Using a toothbrush, I gently cleaned its surface. Letters emerged.

"Sister, could you hand me my flashlight? From the pack?"

Again, they leaned in as one. Penguins at a watering spot. I shone the beam onto the plaque. "Élisabeth Nicolet – 1846–1888. *Femme contemplative.*"

"We've got her," I said to no one in particular.

"Hallelujah!" shouted Sister Girl Scout. So much for church etiquette.

For the next two hours we exhumed Élisabeth's remains. The nuns, and even Father Ménard, threw themselves into the task like undergraduates on their first dig. Habits and cassock swirled around me as dirt was screened, bags were filled, labeled, and stacked, and the whole process was captured on film. Guy helped, though still reluctant. It was as odd a crew as I've ever directed.

Removing the casket was not easy. Though it was small, the wood was badly damaged and the coffin interior had filled with dirt, increasing the weight to about ten tons. The side trench had been a good call, though I'd underestimated the space we'd need. We had to expand outward by two feet to allow plywood to slide under the coffin. Eventually, we were able to raise the whole assemblage using woven polypropylene rope.

By five-thirty we were drinking coffee in the convent kitchen, exhausted, fingers, toes, and faces thawing. Élisabeth Nicolet and her casket were locked in the back of the archdiocese van, along with my equipment. Tomorrow, Guy would drive her to the Laboratoire de Médecine Légale in Montreal, where I work as Forensic Anthropologist for the Province of Quebec. Since the historic dead do not qualify as forensic cases, special permission had been obtained from the Bureau du Coroner to perform the analysis there. I would have two weeks with the bones.

I set down my cup and said my good-byes. Again. The sisters thanked me, again, smiling through tense faces, nervous already about my findings. They were great smilers.

Father Ménard walked me to my car. It had grown dark and a light snow was falling. The flakes felt strangely hot against my cheeks.

The priest asked once more if I wouldn't prefer to overnight at the convent. The snow sparkled behind him as it drifted in the porch light. Again, I declined. A few last road directions, and I was on my way.

Twenty minutes on the two-lane and I began to regret my decision. The flakes that had floated lazily in my headlights were now slicing across in a steady diagonal curtain. The road and the trees to either side were covered by a membrane of white that was growing more opaque by the second.

I clutched the wheel with both hands, palms clammy inside my gloves. I slowed to forty. Thirty-five. Every few minutes I tested the brakes. While I have been living in Quebec off and on for years, I have never grown accustomed to winter driving. I think of myself

15

as tough, but put me on wheels in snow and I am Princess Chickenheart. I still have the typical Southern reaction to winter storms. Oh. Snow. Then we won't be going out, of course. Les québécois look at me and laugh.

Fear has a redeeming quality. It drives away fatigue. Tired as I was, I stayed alert, teeth clenched, neck craned, muscles rigid. The Eastern Townships Autoroute was a bit better than the back roads, but not much. Lac Memphrémagog to Montreal is normally a two-hour drive. It took me almost four.

Shortly after ten, I stood in the dark of my apartment, exhausted, glad to be home. Quebec home. I'd been away in North Carolina almost two months. *Bienvenue.* My thought process had already shifted to French.

I turned up the heat and checked the refrigerator. Bleak. I micro-zapped a frozen burrito and washed it down with room temperature root beer. Not haute cuisine, but filling.

The luggage I'd dropped off Tuesday night sat unopened in the bedroom. I didn't consider unpacking. Tomorrow. I fell into bed, planning to sleep at least nine hours. The phone woke me in less than four.

"*Oui*, yes," I mumbled, the linguistic transition now in limbo.

"Temperance. It is Pierre LaManche. I am very sorry to disturb you at this hour."

I waited. In the seven years I'd worked for him, the lab director had never called me at three in the morning.

"I hope things went well at Lac Memphrémagog." He cleared his throat. "I have just had a call from the coroner's office. There is a house fire in St-Jovite. The firefighters are still trying to get it under control. The arson investigators will go in first thing in the morning, and the coroner wants us there." Again the throat. "A neighbor says the residents are at home. Their cars are in the driveway."

"Why do you need me?" I asked in English.

"Apparently the fire is extremely intense. If there are bodies, they will be badly burned. Perhaps reduced to calcined bone and teeth. It could be a difficult recovery."

Damn. Not tomorrow.

"What time?"

"I will come for you at six A.M.?"

"O.K."

"Temperance. It could be a bad one. There were children living there."

I set the alarm for five-thirty.

Bienvenue.

2

I have lived in the South all of my adult life. It can never be too hot for me. I love the beach in August, sundresses, ceiling fans, the smell of children's sweaty hair, the sound of bugs at window screens. Yet I spend my summers and school breaks in Quebec. Most months during the academic year, I fly from Charlotte, North Carolina, where I am on the anthropology faculty at the university, to work at the medicolegal lab in Montreal. This is a distance of approximately twelve hundred miles. Due north.

When it is deep winter, I often have a talk with myself before deplaning. It will be cold, I remind myself. It will be very cold. But you will dress for it and be ready. Yes. I will be ready. I never am. It's always a shock to leave the terminal and take that first, startling breath.

At 6 A.M., on the tenth day of March, the thermometer on my patio read two degrees Fahrenheit. Seventeen below, Celsius. I was wearing everything I possibly could. Long underwear, jeans, double sweaters, hiking boots, and woolen socks. Inside the socks, I had sparkly insulated liners designed to keep astronaut feet toasty on Pluto. Same provocative combo as the day before. I'd probably stay just as warm.

When LaManche honked, I zipped my parka, pulled on gloves and ski hat, and bolted from the lobby. Unenthused as I was for the day's outing, I didn't want to keep him waiting. And I was extremely over-heated.

I had expected a dark sedan, but he waved at me from what would probably be called a sport utility vehicle. Four-wheel drive, bright red, with racing stripes.

"Nice car," I said as I climbed in.

"*Merci.*" He gestured to a center rack. It held two Styrofoam cups and a Dunkin' Donuts bag. Bless you. I chose an apple crunch.

On the drive to St-Jovite, LaManche related what he knew. It went little beyond what I'd heard at 3 A.M. From across the road a neighbor couple saw occupants enter the residence at nine in the evening. The neighbors left after that and visited friends some distance away, where they stayed late. When they were returning around two they noted a glow from down the road, and then flames shooting from the house. Another neighbor thought she'd heard booming sounds some-time after midnight, wasn't sure, and went back to sleep. The area is remote and sparsely populated. The volunteer fire brigade arrived at two-thirty, and called in help when they saw what they had to deal with. It took two squads over three hours to put out the flames. LaManche had talked to the coroner again at five forty-five. Two deaths were confirmed, others anticipated. Some areas were still too hot, or too dangerous, to search. Arson was suspected.

We drove north in the predawn darkness, into the foothills of the Laurentian Mountains. LaManche talked little, which was fine with me. I am not a morning person. He is an audio junkie, however, and kept an unbroken succession of cassettes playing.

19

Classics, pop, even C&W, all converted to easy listenin'. Perhaps it was meant to calm, like the numbing music piped to elevators and waiting rooms. It made me jittery.

"How far is St-Jovite?" I picked a double-chocolate honey-glazed.

"It will take us about two hours. St-Jovite is about twenty-five kilometers this side of Mont Tremblant. Have you skied there?" He wore a knee-length parka, army green with a fur-lined hood. From the side, all I could see was the tip of his nose.

"Um. Beautiful."

I nearly got frostbite on Mont Tremblant. It was the first time I'd skied in Quebec, and I was dressed for the Blue Ridge Mountains. The wind at the summit was cold enough to freeze liquid hydrogen.

"How did things go at Lac Memphrémagog?"

"The grave wasn't where we expected, but, what's new? Apparently she was exhumed and reburied in 1911. Odd that there was no record of it." Very odd, I thought, taking a sip of tepid coffee. Instrumental Springsteen. "Born in the U.S.A." I tried to block it. "Anyway, we found her. The remains will be delivered to the lab today."

"It is too bad about this fire. I know you were counting on a free week to concentrate on that analysis."

In Quebec, winters can be slow for the forensic anthropologist. The temperature rarely rises above freezing. The rivers and lakes ice over, the ground turns rock hard, and snow buries everything. Bugs disappear, and many scavengers go underground. The result: Corpses do not putrefy in the great outdoors. Floaters are not pulled from the St. Lawrence. People, too, burrow in. Hunters, hikers, and picnickers quit roaming the woods and fields, and some of last season's dead are not found until the spring melt. The cases that are assigned to me, the faceless in need of a name, decline in number between November and April.

The exception is house fires. During the cold months, these increase. Most burned bodies go to the odontologist and are identified by dental records. The address and its occupant are generally known, so antemortem files can be pulled for comparison. It is when charred strangers turn up that my help may be requested.

Or in difficult recovery situations. LaManche was right. I'd been counting on an open agenda, and did not appreciate having to go to St-Jovite.

"Maybe I won't be involved in the analysis." A million and one strings began "I'm Sitting on Top of the World." "They'll probably have records on the family."

"Probably."

We arrived in St-Jovite in less than two hours. The sun had risen and was painting the town and countryside in icy, dawn tones. We turned west onto a winding two-lane. Almost immediately two flatbeds passed us, heading in the opposite direction. One carried a battered gray Honda, the other a red Plymouth Voyager.

"I see they have impounded the cars," said LaManche.

I watched the vehicles disappear in the side mirror. The van had infant carriers in the backseat and a yellow smiley face on the rear bumper. I pictured a child in the window, tongue out, fingers in ears, mugging at the world. Googly eyes, my sister and I had called it. Perhaps that child lay charred beyond recognition in an upstairs room ahead.

Within minutes we saw what we were looking for. Police cruisers, fire engines, utility trucks, mobile press units, ambulances, and unmarked cars lined the road and flowed up either side of a long, gravel driveway.

Reporters stood in clusters, some talking, some adjusting equipment. Others sat in cars, keeping warm while waiting out the story. Thanks to the cold and the early hour, there were surprisingly few sightseers. Now and then a car passed, then returned slowly for a second sweep. Round-trip gawkers. Later, there would be many more.

LaManche signaled a turn and angled onto the drive, where a uniformed officer waved us to a stop. He wore an olive green jacket with black fur collar, dark olive muffler, and olive hat, earflaps tied in the up position. His ears and nose were raspberry red, and when he spoke, a cloud of vapor billowed from his mouth. I wanted to tell him to cover his ears, immediately felt like my mother, and didn't. He's a big boy. If his lobes crack off, he'll deal with it.

LaManche showed ID, and the guard waved us in, indicating we should park behind the blue crime scene recovery truck. SECTION D´IDENTITÉ JUDICIAIRE it said in bold black letters. The Crime Scene Recovery unit was already here. The arson boys, too, I suspected.

LaManche and I tugged on hats and gloves and got out. The sky was azure now, the sunlight dazzling off last night's snow. The air was so frigid it felt crystalline and made everything look sharp and clear. Cars, buildings, trees, and utility poles cast dark shadows on the snowy ground, clean-edged, like images on high-contrast film.

I looked around. The blackened remains of a house, as well as an intact garage and a smaller outbuilding of some sort clustered at the head of the drive, all done in cheap Alpine style. Footpaths formed a triangle in the snow, linking the three buildings. Pines circled what was left of the house, their branches so laden with snow

22

that the tips bowed downward. I watched a squirrel scamper along a limb, then retreat to the safety of the trunk. In its wake, clumps of snow cascaded down, pockmarking the white below.

The house had a high-pitched roof of red-orange tile, partially standing but darkened now and coated in ice. That portion of the exterior surface which had not burned was covered in cream-colored siding. The windows gaped black and empty, the glass shattered, the turquoise trim burned or darkened with soot.

The left half of the house was charred, its rear largely destroyed. On the far side I could see blackened timbers where roof and walls had once met. Wisps of smoke still rose from somewhere in the back.

The front was less badly damaged. A wooden porch ran its length, and small balconies jutted from upstairs windows. The porch and balconies were constructed of pink pickets, round at the top, with heart-shaped cutouts at regular intervals.

I looked behind me, down the drive. Across the road sat a similar chalet, this one trimmed in red and blue. A man and woman stood in front, arms folded, mittened hands tucked under armpits. They watched silently, squinting into the morning glare, their faces grim below identical orange hunting caps. The neighbors who had reported the fire. I scanned the road. There were no other homes within visual distance. Whoever thought she had heard muffled booms must have good ears.

LaManche and I started toward the house. We passed dozens of firefighters, colorful in their yellow suits, red hard hats, blue utility belts, and black rubber boots. Some wore oxygen tanks strapped to their backs. Most seemed to be gathering equipment.

We approached a uniformed officer standing by the porch. Like the driveway guard, he was Sûreté du Québec, probably from a post in St-Jovite or a nearby

23

town. The SQ, or Quebec Provincial Police, have jurisdiction everywhere off the island of Montreal, except in towns that maintain their own police. St-Jovite would be too small for that, so the SQ had been called, maybe by the fire chief, maybe by the neighbor. They, in turn, had called the arson investigators from our lab. Section d'Incendie et Explosif. I wondered who had made the decision to call the coroner. How many victims would we find? In what condition would they be? Not good, I was sure. My heart stepped up its tempo.

Again LaManche held up his badge, and the man inspected it.

"Un instant, Docteur, s'il vous plaît," he said, holding up a gloved palm. He called to one of the firefighters, said something, and pointed at his head. In seconds we had hard hats and masks. We put on the former, hung the latter over our arms.

"Attention!" said the officer, inclining his head toward the house. Then he stepped aside to let us pass. Oh yes. I'd be careful.

The front door was wide open. When we crossed the threshold out of the sunshine the temperature dropped twenty degrees. The air inside felt damp and smelled of charred wood and soggy plaster and fabric. A dark goo covered every surface.

Straight ahead a staircase rose to a second story, to the left and right gaped what must have been the living and dining rooms. What remained of the kitchen was in back.

I'd been to other fire scenes, but few as devastated as this. Charred boards lay everywhere, like debris hurled against a seawall. They crisscrossed on top of tangled chair and sofa frames, angled against stairs, and trellised against walls and doors. Remnants of household furnishings lay in blackened heaps. Wires dangled from

24

walls and ceilings, and pipes twisted inward from their points of attachment. Window frames, stair rails, boards, everything was edged in black icicle lace.

The house was crawling with people in hard hats, talking, taking measurements, photos, and videos, collecting evidence, and scribbling on clipboards. I recognized two arson investigators from our lab. They held a measuring tape between them and one squatted at a fixed point while the other circled, recording data every few feet.

LaManche spotted a member of the coroner's staff, and began picking his way forward. I followed, snaking between twisted metal shelving, broken glass, and what looked like a tangled red sleeping bag, its stuffing spewed like charcoal innards.

The coroner was very fat and very flushed. He straightened slightly when he saw us, blew a puff of air, pooched out his lower lip, and gestured an upturned mitten at the devastation around us.

"So, Monsieur Hubert, there are two dead?"

LaManche and Hubert were design opposites, like contrasting shades on a color wheel. The pathologist was tall and rangy, with a long, bloodhound face. The coroner was round in every way. I thought of Hubert in horizontals, LaManche in verticals.

Hubert nodded, and three chins rippled above his muffler. "Upstairs."

"Others?"

"Not yet, but they haven't finished in the lower level. The fire was much more intense in the back. They think it probably started in a room off the kitchen. That area burned completely, and the floor collapsed into the basement."

"Have you seen the bodies?"

"Not yet. I'm waiting for clearance to go upstairs. The fire chief wants to be sure it's safe."

I shared the chief's sentiment.

We stood in silence, surveying the mess. Time passed. I curled and uncurled my fingers and toes, trying to keep them flexible. Eventually three firemen descended. They wore hard hats and goggle masks, and looked as if they'd been rummaging for chemical weapons.

"It's O.K.," said the last fireman, unsnapping and removing his mask. "You can go up now. Just watch your step and keep the hard hats on. That whole damn ceiling could come down. But the floors look O.K." He continued toward the door, then turned back. "They're in the room on the left."

Hubert, LaManche, and I worked our way up the stairs, shards of glass and charred rubble crunching under our feet. Already my stomach was tightening and a hollow feeling was building in my chest. Though it is my business, I have never grown immune to the sight of violent death.

At the top a door opened to the left, another to the right, there was a bath straight ahead. Though badly smoke damaged, compared with the downstairs, things seemed to be reasonably intact at this level.

Through the left doorway I could see a chair, a bookcase, and the end of a twin bed. On it was a pair of legs. LaManche and I entered the left-hand room, Hubert went to check the one on the right.

The back wall was partially burned, and at places two-by-fours were exposed behind the flowered wallpaper. The beams were charcoal black, their surfaces rough and checked, like the skin on a croc. "Alligatored," the arson boys would write. Charred and frozen debris lay underfoot, and soot covered everything.

LaManche took a long look around, then pulled a tiny Dictaphone from his pocket. He recorded the date, time, and location, and began describing the victims.

The bodies lay on twin beds that formed an L in the far corner of the room, a small table between them. Strangely, both individuals appeared to be fully clothed, though smoke and charring had obscured all indicators of style or gender. The victim along the back wall wore sneakers, the one on the side had died in stocking feet. I noticed that one athletic sock was partly off, exposing a smoke-stained ankle. The tip of the sock hung limply over the toes. Both victims were adult. One appeared more robust than the other.

"Victim number one . . ." continued LaManche.

I forced myself to take a closer look. Victim number one held its forearms high, flexed as if ready to fight. Pugilistic pose. While not long enough or hot enough to consume all the flesh, the fire that raced up the back wall had produced sufficient heat to cook the upper limbs and cause the muscles to contract. Below the elbows the arms were stick-thin. Clumps of scorched tissue clustered along the bones. The hands were blackened stumps.

The face reminded me of Rameses' mummy. The lips had burned away, exposing teeth with dark and cracked enamel. One incisor was delicately outlined in gold. The nose was burned and squashed, the nostrils pointing upward like the snout of a fruit bat. I could see individual muscle fibers circling the orbits and streaming across the cheekbones and mandible, like a line drawing in an anatomy text. Each socket held a dried and shriveled eyeball. The hair was gone. So was the top of the head.

Victim number two, though equally dead, was more intact. Some of the skin was blackened and split, but in most places it was merely smoked. Tiny white lines radiated from the corners of the eyes, and the ears were pale on the insides and underneath the lobes. The hair had been reduced to a frizzled cap. One arm lay flat, the

27

other was flung wide, as if reaching for its partner in death. The outstretched hand had been reduced to a bony, blackened claw.

LaManche's somber monotone droned on, describing the room and its lifeless occupants. I half listened, relieved that I wouldn't be needed. Or would I? There were supposed to be kids. Where were they? Through the open window I could see sunshine, pine trees, and glistening white snow. Outside, life went on.

Silence interrupted my thoughts. LaManche had stopped dictating and replaced wool gloves with latex. He began to examine victim number two, lifting the eyelids and observing the inside of the nose and mouth. Then he rolled the body toward the wall and raised the shirttail.

The outer layer of skin had split and the edges were curling back. The peeling epidermis looked translucent, like the delicate film inside an egg. Underneath, the tissue was bright red, mottled white where it had lain in contact with the crumpled sheets. LaManche pressed a gloved finger into the back muscle and a white spot appeared in the scarlet flesh.

Hubert rejoined us as LaManche was returning the body to its supine position. We both looked a question at him.

"Empty."

LaManche and I did not change expression.

"There are a couple of cribs in there. Must be the kids' room. Neighbors say there were two babies." He was breathing hard. "Twin boys. They're not in there."

Hubert took out a hankie and wiped his chapped face. Sweat and arctic air are not a good combination. "Anything here?"

"Of course this will require a full autopsy," answered LaManche in his melancholy bass. "But based on my preliminary, I would say that these people were alive when the fire broke out. At least this one was."

He indicated body number two.

"I'll be here another thirty minutes or so, then you may remove them."

Hubert nodded and left to tell his transport team.

LaManche crossed to the first body, then returned to the second. I watched in silence, breathing warmth onto my mittened fingers. Finally, he finished. I didn't have to ask.

"Smoke," he said. "Around the nostrils, in the nose and air passages." He looked at me.

"They were still breathing during the fire."

"Yes. Anything else?"

"The lividity. The cherry red color. That suggests carbon monoxide in the blood."

"And . . .?"

"The blanching when you applied pressure. Livor isn't fixed yet. Blanching only occurs for a matter of hours after lividity first develops."

"Yes." He looked at his watch. "It's just past eight now. This one could have been alive as late as three or four A.M." He pulled off the latex gloves. "*Could* have been, but the fire brigade got here at two-thirty, so death was before that. Livor is extremely variable. What else?"

The question went unanswered. We heard commotion below, then feet pounded up the stairs. A fireman appeared in the doorway, flushed and breathing hard.

"*Estidecolistabernac!*"

I ran through my québécois lexicon. Not there. I looked at LaManche. Before he could translate the man went on.

"Someone here named Brennan?" he asked LaManche.

The hollow feeling spread to my innards.

29

"We've got a body in the basement. They say we're going to need this Brennan guy."

"I'm Tempe Brennan."

He looked at me for a long time, helmet under one arm, head tipped. Then he wiped his nose with the back of his hand, and looked back at LaManche.

"You can go down there as soon as the chief clears you through. And better bring a spoon. There's not much left of this one."

3

The volunteer fireman led us down the stairs and into the back of the house. Here, most of the roof was gone and sunlight poured into the gloomy interior. Particles of soot and dust danced on the wintry air.

We stopped at the entrance to the kitchen. On the left I could make out the remains of a counter, sink, and several large appliances. The dishwasher was open, its contents black and melted. Charred boards lay everywhere, the same giant pickup sticks I'd seen in the front rooms.

"Keep back by the walls," said the fireman, gesturing with his arm as he disappeared around the doorjamb.

He reappeared seconds later, working his way along the west side of the room. Behind him, the countertop curled upward like a giant licorice twist. Embedded in it were fragments of shattered wine bottles and unidentifiable globs of various sizes.

LaManche and I followed, sliding along the front wall, then rounding the corner and moving down the counter. We stayed as far from the center of the room as possible, picking our way through burned rubble, imploded metal containers, and scorched propane tanks.

I stopped next to the fireman, back to the counter, and surveyed the damage. The kitchen and an adjacent room were incinerated. The ceilings were gone, the separating wall reduced to a few charred timbers. What had been the floor was now a yawning black hole. An extension ladder angled from it in our direction. Through the opening I could see men in hard hats lifting debris and either flinging or carrying it out of sight.

"There is a body down there," said my guide, tipping his head at the opening. "Found it when we began to clear rubble from the floor collapse."

"Just one, or more?" I asked.

"Hell if I know. It doesn't hardly look human."

"Adult or child?"

He gave me a "lady, are you stupid?" look.

"When can I get down there?"

His eyes slid to LaManche, back to me. "That's up to the chief. They're still clearing the area. We wouldn't want anything to split your pretty skull."

He gave me what he no doubt felt was an engaging smile. He probably practiced it in the mirror.

We watched as firemen below pitched boards and tramped back and forth with loads of debris. From out of sight I could hear banter and the sound of things being dislodged and dragged.

"Have they considered that they might be destroying evidence?" I asked.

The fireman looked at me as if I'd suggested the house had been hit by a comet.

"It's just floorboards and shit that fell down from this level."

"That 'shit' may help establish sequence," I said, my voice as chilly as the icicles on the counter behind us. "Or body position."

His face went rigid.

32

"There could still be hot spots down there, lady. You don't want one flaring up in your face, do you?"

I had to admit I didn't.

"And that guy's past caring."

Inside my hard hat I could feel a throbbing along the side of my pretty skull.

"If the victim is as burned as you suggest, your colleagues could be obliterating major body parts."

His jaw muscle bunched as he looked past me for support. LaManche said nothing.

"The chief's probably not gonna let you in there, anyway," he said.

"I need to get in now to stabilize what's there. Especially the teeth." I thought of baby boys. I hoped for teeth. Lots of them. All adult. "If there are any left."

The fireman gave me a head to toe, sizing up my five-foot-five, one-hundred-twenty-pound frame. Though the thermal outfitting disguised my shape and the hard hat hid my long hair, he saw enough to convince himself I belonged elsewhere.

"She's not really going down there?" He looked to LaManche for an ally.

"Dr. Brennan will be doing the recovery."

"*Estidecolistabernac!*"

This time I didn't need translation. Fireman Macho thought the job required testicles.

"Hot spots are no problem," I said, looking him dead in the eye. "In fact, I usually prefer to work right in the flames. I find it warmer."

With that he gripped the side rails, swung onto the ladder, and slid down, never touching the rungs with his feet.

Great. He also does tricks. I could imagine what he was scripting for the chief.

"These are volunteers," said LaManche, almost

33

smiling. He looked like Mr. Ed in a hard hat. "I must finish upstairs, but I will rejoin you shortly."

I watched him weave a path to the door, his large, hooded frame hunched in concentration. Seconds later the chief emerged on the ladder. It was the same man who'd directed us to the upstairs bodies.

"You're Dr. Brennan?" he asked in English.

I nodded once, ready for a fight.

"Luc Grenier. I head up the St-Jovite volunteer squad." He unsnapped his chin strap and let it dangle. He was older than his misogynous teammate.

"We're going to need another ten, fifteen minutes to secure the lower level. This was the last section we put down, so there could still be hot spots." The strap jumped as he talked. "This was a pisser, and we don't want a flare-up." He pointed behind me. "See how that pipe's deformed?"

I turned to look.

"That's copper. To melt copper you've got to get up over eleven hundred degrees centigrade." He shook his head, and the strap swung back and forth. "This was a real pisser."

"Do you know how it started?" I asked.

He pointed to a propane tank near my feet. "So far we've counted twelve of those suckers. Either someone knew exactly what he was doing, or he really fucked up the family barbecue." His face reddened slightly. "Sorry."

"Arson?"

Chief Grenier shrugged both shoulders and raised his eyebrows. "Not my call." He snapped his chin strap and gripped the sides of the ladder. "All we're doing is moving debris to be sure the fire's completely cold. This kitchen was full of junk. That's what provided the fuel to burn right through the floor. We'll take extra care around the bones. I'll give a whistle when it's safe."

34

"Don't spray any water on the remains," I said.

He gave a hand salute and disappeared down the ladder.

It took thirty minutes before I was allowed into the basement. During that time I went to the crime scene truck to collect my equipment and arrange for a photographer. I located Pierre Gilbert and asked to have a screen and spotlight set up below.

The basement was one large open space, dark and damp and colder than Yellowknife in January. At the far end loomed a furnace, its pipes rising, black and gnarled, like the limbs of a giant dead oak. It reminded me of another cellar I'd visited not long ago. That one had hidden a serial killer.

The walls were cinder block. Most of the large debris had been cleared and heaped against them, exposing a dirt floor. In places the fire had turned it reddish brown. In others it was black and rockhard, like ceramic tile fired in an oven. Everything was covered by a thin membrane of frost.

Chief Grenier took me to a spot on the right edge of the floor collapse. He said that no victims had been found elsewhere. I hoped he was right. The thought of sifting the entire basement almost made me weep. Wishing me good luck, he left to rejoin his men.

Little of the kitchen sun made it this far back, so I took a high powered flashlight from my kit and shone it around me. One look caused adrenaline to report for duty. This was not what I'd expected.

The remains were strewn over an area at least ten feet in length. They were largely skeletonized, and showed varying degrees of heat exposure.

In one cluster I could see a head surrounded by fragments of differing shapes and sizes. Some were black and shiny, like the skull. Others were chalky white and looked ready to crumble. Which is exactly what

35

they would do if not handled properly. Calcined bone is featherlight and extremely fragile. Yes. This would be a difficult recovery.

Five feet south of the skull an assortment of vertebrae, ribs, and long bones lay in rough anatomical position. Also white and fully calcined. I noted the orientation of the vertebrae and the position of the arm bones. The remains were lying faceup, one arm crossing the chest, the other flung above the head.

Below the upper arms and chest lay a heart-shaped black mass with two fractured long bones projecting distally. The pelvis. Beyond this, I could see the charred and fragmented bones of the legs and feet.

I felt relief, but some confusion. This was a single, fully grown victim. Or was it? Infant bones are tiny and extremely fragile. They could easily be hidden below. I prayed I'd find none when I sifted through the ash and sediment.

I made notes, took Polaroids, then began to sweep away soil and ash using a soft-bristle paintbrush. Slowly, I exposed more and more bone, carefully inspecting the displaced debris, collecting it for later screening.

LaManche returned as I was clearing the last of the muck that lay in direct contact with the bones. He watched silently as I took four stakes, a ball of string, and three retractable measuring tapes from my kit.

I hammered a stake into the ground just above the cranial cluster, and hooked the ends of two tapes onto a nail I'd driven into the top. I ran one tape ten feet south and pounded in a second stake.

LaManche held that tape at the second stake while I went back to the first and ran the other tape perpendicular, ten feet toward the east. Using the third tape, I measured off a hypotenuse of fourteen feet one and three-quarter inches from LaManche's stake to the northeast corner. Where the second and third tapes met, I hammered in a third stake. Thanks to Pythagoras, I now had a perfect right triangle with two ten-foot sides.

I unhooked the second tape from the first stake, hooked it to the northeast stake, and ran it ten feet south. LaManche brought his tape ten feet east. Where these tapes met I hammered in the fourth stake.

I ran a string around the four stakes, enclosing the remains in a ten-by-ten-foot square with ninety-degree corners. I would triangulate from the stakes when taking measurements. If needed, I could divide the square into quadrants, or break it into grid units for more precise observations.

Two evidence recovery techs arrived as I was placing a north arrow near the cranial cluster. They wore dark blue arctic suits, SECTION D´IDENTITÉ JUDICIAIRE stamped on their backs. I envied them. The damp cold in the basement was like a knife, cutting right through my clothes and into my flesh.

I'd worked with Claude Martineau before. The other tech was new to me. We introduced ourselves as they set up the screen and portable light.

"It's going to take some time to process this," I said, indicating the staked-out square. "I want to locate any teeth that might have survived, and stabilize them if necessary. I may also have to treat the pubes and rib ends if I find any. Who's going to shoot pics?"

"Halloran is coming," said Sincennes, the second tech.

"O.K. Chief Grenier says there's nobody else down here, but it wouldn't hurt to walk off the basement."

"There were supposed to be kids living in this house," said Martineau, his face grim. He had two of his own.

"I'd suggest a grid search."

I looked to LaManche. He nodded agreement.

"You've got it," said Martineau. He and his partner flicked on the lights on their hard hats, then moved to the far end of the basement. They would walk back and forth in parallel lines, first proceeding north to south, then crisscrossing east to west. When they'd finished, every inch of floor would have been searched twice.

I took several more Polaroids, then began to clear the square. Using a trowel, a dental pick, and a plastic dustpan, I loosened and dislodged the filth that encased the skeleton, leaving each bone in place. Every pan of dirt went into the screen. There I separated silt, cinders, fabric, nails, wood, and plaster from bone fragments. The latter I placed on surgical cotton in sealed plastic containers, noting their provenance in my notes. At some point, Halloran arrived and began shooting.

Now and then I glanced at LaManche. He watched silently, his face its usual solemn mask. In the time I'd known the chief, I'd rarely seen him express emotion. LaManche has witnessed so much over the years, perhaps sentiment is just too costly for him. After some time, he spoke.

"If there is nothing for me to do here, Temperance, I will be upstairs."

"Sure," I responded, thinking of the warming sun. "I'll be at this awhile."

I looked at my watch. Ten past eleven. Behind LaManche I could see Sincennes and Martineau, creeping along shoulder to shoulder, heads down, like miners seeking a rich vein.

"Do you require anything?"

"I'm going to need a body bag with a clean white sheet inside. Be sure they put a flat board or a gurney tray under it. Once I get these fragments out I don't want everything slumping together in transport."

"Of course."

38

I went back to troweling and screening. I was so cold I was shaking all over, and had to stop now and then to warm my hands. At one point the morgue transport team brought the tray and body bag. The last firemen left. The basement grew quiet.

Eventually, I had exposed the entire skeleton. I made notes and sketched its disposition, while Halloran took photos.

"Mind if I grab a coffee?" he asked when we'd finished.

"No. I'll holler if I need you. I'll just be transferring bones for a while."

When he left I began to move the remains to the body bag, starting at the feet and working toward the head. The pelvis was in good condition. I picked it up and placed it on the sheet. The pubic symphyses were embedded in charred tissue. They would not need stabilizing.

The leg and arm bones I left encased in sediment. It would hold them together until I could clean and sort them in the autopsy room. I did the same with the thoracic region, carefully lifting out sections with a flat-blade shovel. Nothing of the anterior rib cage had survived, so I did not have to worry about damaging the ends. For now I left the skull in place.

When I had removed the skeleton, I began to screen the top six inches of sediment, starting at the southwest stake and working northeast. I was finishing the last corner of the square when I spotted it, approximately a foot and a half east of the skull, at a depth of two inches. My stomach did a little flip. Yes!

The jaw. Gingerly, I teased away soil and ash to reveal a complete right ascending ramus, a fragment of the left ramus, and a portion of the mandibular body. The latter contained seven teeth.

The outer bone was checked by a latticework of

39

cracks. It was thin and powdery white. The spongy interior looked pale and brittle, as if each filament had been spun by a Lilliputian spider then left to air dry. The enamel on the teeth was already splintering, and I knew the whole thing would crumble if disturbed.

I took a bottle of liquid from my kit, shook it, and checked to be sure no crystals remained in the solution. I dug out a handful of five-milliliter disposable pipettes.

Working on hands and knees, I opened the bottle, unwrapped a pipette, and dipped it in. I squeezed the bulb to fill the pipette with solution, then allowed the fluid to drip onto the jaw. Drop by drop I soaked each fragment, watching to be sure I was getting good penetration. I lost all track of time.

"Nice angle." English.

My hand jumped, splattering Vinac on the sleeve of my jacket. My back was stiff, my knees and ankles locked, so lowering my rear quickly was not an option. Slowly, I sat back on my haunches. I didn't have to look.

"Thank you, Detective Ryan."

He circled to the far side of the grid and looked down at me. Even in the dim light of the basement I could see that his eyes were as blue as I remembered. He wore a black cashmere coat and a red wool muffler.

"Long see, no time," he said.

"Yes. No time. When was it?"

"The courthouse."

"The Fortier trial." We'd both been waiting to testify.

"Still dating Perry Mason?"

I ignored the question. The previous fall I'd briefly dated a defense attorney I'd met through my Tai Chi course.

"Isn't that fraternizing with the enemy?"

I still didn't answer. Obviously my sex life was a topic of interest to the homicide squad.

40

"How have you been?"

"Great. You?"

"Can't complain. If I did, no one would listen."

"Get a pet."

"Could try that. What's in the eyedropper?" he asked, pointing a leather-gloved finger at my hand.

"Vinac. It's a solution of a polyvinyl acetate resin and methanol. The mandible is toast and I'm trying to keep it intact."

"And that will do it?"

"As long as the bone is dry this will penetrate and hold things together pretty well."

"And if it's not dry?"

"Vinac won't mix with water, so it'll just stay on the surface and turn white. The bones will come out looking like they've been sprayed with latex."

"How long does it take to dry?"

I felt like Mr. Wizard.

"It dries quickly through evaporation of the alcohol, usually in thirty to sixty minutes. Although being in the subarctic won't speed things up."

I checked the jaw fragments, hit one with a few more drops, then rested the pipette on the solution jar cover. Ryan came around and held out a hand. I took it and rose to my feet, wrapping my arms around my middle and tucking my hands under my pits. I could feel nothing in my fingers, and suspected my nose was the shade of Ryan's scarf. And running.

"It's colder than a witch's tit down here," he agreed, surveying the basement. He held one arm behind him at an odd angle. "How long have you been down here?"

I looked at my watch. No wonder I was hypothermic. One-fifteen.

"Over four hours."

"Che-rist. You're going to need a transfusion."

It suddenly dawned. Ryan worked homicide.

41

"So it's arson?"

"Probably."

He pulled a white bag from behind his back, withdrew a Styrofoam cup and a machine sandwich, and waggled them in front of me.

I lunged. He backed up.

"You'll owe me."

"It's in the mail."

Soggy bologna and lukewarm coffee. It was wonderful. We talked while I ate.

"Tell me why you think it's arson," I said as I chewed.

"Tell me what you've got here."

O.K. He was a sandwich up.

"One person. Could be young, but it's not a little kid."

"No babies?"

"No babies. Your turn."

"Looks like someone used the old tried and true. The fire burned in trails way down between the floorboards. Where there still *are* floorboards, that is. That means liquid accelerant, probably gasoline. We found dozens of empty gas cans."

"That's it?" I finished the sandwich.

"The fire had more than one point of origin. Once it started it burned like a son of a bitch, because it set off the world's largest indoor collection of propane tanks. Big boom every time one went. Another tank, another big boom."

"How many?"

"Fourteen."

"It started in the kitchen?"

"And the adjoining room. Whatever that was. Hard to tell now."

I thought it over.

"That explains the head and jaw."

"What about the head and jaw?"

"They were about five feet away from the rest of the body. If a propane tank fell through with the victim and exploded later, that could have caused the head to relocate after it burned away from the trunk. Same with the jaw."

I finished the coffee, wishing I had another sandwich.

"Could the tanks have ignited accidentally?"

"Anything's possible."

I flicked crumbs from my jacket and thought of LaManche's doughnuts. Ryan fished in the bag and handed me a napkin.

"O.K. The fire had multiple points of origin and there's evidence of an accelerant. It's arson. Why?"

"Got me." He gestured at the body bag. "Who's this?"

"Got me."

Ryan headed upstairs, and I went back to the recovery. The jaw was not quite dry, so I turned my attention to the skull.

The brain contains a large amount of water. When exposed to fire, it boils and expands, setting up hydrostatic pressure inside the head. Given enough heat, the cranial vault may crack or even explode. This person was in pretty good shape. Though the face was gone and the outer bone was charred and flaking, large segments of the skull were intact. I was surprised, given the intensity of this fire.

When I cleaned away the mud and ash and looked closely, I saw why. For a moment I just stared. I rolled the skull over and inspected the frontal bone.

Sweet Jesus.

I climbed the ladder and poked my head into the kitchen. Ryan stood by the counter talking with the photographer.

"You'd better come down," I said.

43

They both raised eyebrows and pointed to their chests.

"Both of you."

Ryan set down the Styrofoam cup he was holding. "What?"

"This one may not have lived to see the fire."

4

It was late afternoon before the last of the bone was packaged and ready for transport. Ryan watched as I carefully extracted and wrapped the skull fragments and placed them in plastic containers. I would analyze the remains at the lab. The rest of the investigation would be his baby.

Dusk was easing in when I emerged from the basement. To say I was cold would be like saying Lady Godiva was underdressed. For the second day in a row I finished the afternoon with no feeling in any digit. I hoped amputation would not be necessary.

LaManche was gone, so I rode to Montreal with Ryan and his partner, Jean Bertrand. I sat in back, shivering and asking for more heat. They sat up front, sweating, now and then removing an article of outerwear.

Their conversation wafted in and out of my consciousness. I was fully drained and just wanted to take a hot bath and crawl into my flannel nightgown. For a month. My mind drifted. I thought about bears. There was an idea. Curl up and sleep until spring.

Images floated in my head. The victim in the basement. A sock dangling over singed and stiffened

45

toes. A nameplate on a tiny casket. A happy-face sticker.

"Brennan."

"What?"

"Good morning, starshine. Earth says 'Hello.'"

"What?"

"You're home."

I'd been sound asleep.

"Thanks. Talk to you on Monday."

I stumbled from the car and up the stairs of my building. A light snow was topping the neighborhood like frosting on a sticky bun. Where did so much snow come from?

The grocery situation had not improved, so I ate soda crackers spread with peanut butter and washed them down with clam chowder. I found an old box of Turtles in the pantry, dark chocolate, my favorite. They were stale and hard, but I was not in a position to be choosy.

The bath was all I'd hoped it would be. Afterward, I decided to light a fire. I was finally warm, but felt very tired and very alone. The chocolate had been some comfort, but I needed more.

I missed my daughter. Katy's school year was divided into quarters, my university was on a semester system, so our spring breaks did not coincide. Even Birdie had stayed south this trip. He hated air travel and voiced that opinion loudly through each flight. Since I'd be in Quebec less than two weeks this time, I'd decided to spare both the cat and the airline.

As I held the match to the starter log I considered fire. *Homo erectus* first tamed it. For almost a million years we'd been using it to hunt, cook, keep warm, and light our way. That had been my last lecture before break. I thought of my students in North Carolina. While I'd been searching for Élisabeth Nicolet, they'd been taking their midterm exam. The little blue books

46

would arrive here tomorrow by overnight delivery, while the students split for the beaches.

I turned off the lamp and watched the flames lick and twist among the logs. Shadows danced around the room. I could smell pine and hear moisture hiss and pop as it boiled to the surface. That's why fire has such appeal. It involves so many senses.

I synapsed back to childhood Christmases and summer camps. Such a dicey blessing, fire. It could give solace, rekindle gentle memories. But it could also kill. I did not want to think about St-Jovite anymore tonight.

I watched snow gather on the windowsill. My students would be planning their first beach day by now. While I was fighting frost-bite, they were preparing for sunburn. I didn't want to think about that, either.

I considered Élisabeth Nicolet. She'd been a recluse. "*Femme contemplative*," the plaque had said. But she hadn't done any contemplating for over a century. What if we had the wrong casket? Something else I didn't want to think about. At least for tonight, Élisabeth and I had little in common.

I checked the time. Nine-forty. Her sophomore year Katy was voted one of the "Beauties of Virginia." Though she maintained a grade point average of 3.8 while working on dual degrees in English and psychology, she'd never been a slouch socially. Not a chance she'd be home on a Friday night. Ever the optimist, I brought the phone to the hearth and dialed Charlottesville.

Katy answered on the third ring.

Expecting her voice mail, I stuttered something unintelligible.

"Mom? Is that you?"

"Yes. Hello. What are you doing home?"

47

"I've got a zit on my nose the size of a hamster. I'm too ugly to go out. What are you doing home?"

"There is no way you are ugly. No comment on the zit." I settled against a cushion and put my feet up on the hearth. "I've spent two days digging up dead people and I'm too tired to go out."

"I won't even ask." I heard cellophane crinkle. "This zit is pretty gross."

"It, too, will pass. How is Cyrano?" Katy had two rats, Templeton and Cyrano de Bergerat.

"He's better. I got some medicine at the pet store and I've been giving it to him with an eyedropper. He's pretty much stopped that sneezing thing."

"Good. He's always been my favorite."

"I think Templeton knows that."

"I'll try to be more discreet. What else is new?"

"Not much. Went out with a guy named Aubrey. He was pretty cool. Sent me roses the next day. And I'm going on a picnic tomorrow with Lynwood. Lynwood Deacon. He's first-year-law."

"Is that how you pick them?"

"What?"

"The names."

She ignored that. "Aunt Harry called."

"Oh?" My sister's name always made me slightly apprehensive, like a bucket of nails balanced too close to an edge.

"She's selling the balloon business or something. She was actually calling to find you. Sounded a little weirded out."

"Weirded out?" On a normal day my sister sounded a little weirded out.

"I told her you were in Quebec. She'll probably call tomorrow."

"O.K." Just what I needed.

48

"Oh! Dad bought a Mazda RX-7. It is so sweet! He won't let me drive it, though."

"Yes, I know." My estranged husband was undergoing a mild midlife crisis.

There was a slight hesitation. "Actually, we were just going out to grab a pizza."

"What about the zit?"

"I'm going to draw ears and a tail on it and claim it's a tattoo."

"Should work. If caught, use a false name."

"Love you, Mom."

"I love you, too. Talk to you later."

I finished the rest of the Turtles and brushed my teeth. Twice. Then I fell into bed and slept eleven hours.

I spent the rest of the weekend unpacking, cleaning, shopping, and grading exams. My sister called late Sunday to say she'd sold her hot air balloon. I felt relieved. I'd spent three years inventing excuses to keep Katy on the ground, dreading the day she'd finally go up. That creative energy could now be turned elsewhere.

"Are you at home?" I asked.

"Yep."

"Is it warm?" I checked the drift on the windowsill. It was still growing.

"It's always warm in Houston."

Damn her.

"So why are you selling the business?"

Harry has always been a seeker, though her grail has never been in focus. For the past three years she'd been gung-ho buggers over ballooning. When not floating safaris over Texas, she and her crew packed an old pickup and zigzagged the country to balloon rallies.

"Striker and I are splitting."

49

"Oh."

She'd also been gung-ho buggers over Striker. They met at a rally in Albuquerque, married five days later. That had been two years ago.

For a long time no one spoke. I cracked first.

"What now?" I asked.

"I may go into counseling."

That surprised me. My sister rarely did the obvious.

"It might help you get through this."

"No. No. Striker's got Kool-Aid for brains. I'm not crying over him. That just makes me puffy." I heard her light a cigarette, draw deeply, exhale. "There's this course I've heard about. You take it, then you can advise people on holistic health and stress relief and stuff. I've been reading about herbs and meditation and metaphysics and it's pretty cool. I think I'll be good at this."

"Harry. That sounds a little flaky." How many times had I said that?

"Duh. Of course I'll check it out. I'm not flat-ass stupid."

No. She was not stupid. But when Harry wants something, she wants it intensely. And there is no dissuading her.

I hung up feeling a little shaken. The thought of Harry advising people with problems was unnerving.

Around six I made myself a dinner of sautéed chicken breast, boiled red potatoes with butter and chives, and steamed asparagus. A glass of Chardonnay would have made it perfect. But not for me. That switch had been in the off position for seven years and it was staying there. I'm not flat-ass stupid either. At least not when I'm sober. The meal still beat the hell out of last night's soda crackers.

As I ate, I thought about my baby sister. Harry and formal education have never been compatible. She

50

married her high school sweetheart the day before graduation, three others after that. She's raised Saint Bernards, managed a Pizza Hut, sold designer sunglasses, led tours in the Yucatán, done PR for the Houston Astros, started and lost a carpet-cleaning business, sold real estate, and, most recently, taken up riders in hot air balloons.

When I was three and Harry was one, I broke her leg by rolling over it with my tricycle. She never slowed down. Harry learned to walk while dragging a cast. Unbearably annoying and totally endearing, my sister offsets with pure energy what she lacks in training or focus. I find her thoroughly exhausting.

At nine-thirty I turned on the hockey game. It was the end of the second period and the Habs were losing four-zip to St. Louis. Don Cherry blustered about the ineptness of the Canadiens management, his face round and flushed above his high-collar shirt. He looked more like a tenor in a barbershop quartet than a sports commentator. I watched, bemused that millions listened to him every week. At ten-fifteen I turned off the TV and went to bed.

The next morning I got up early and drove to the lab. Monday is a busy day for most medical examiners. The random acts of cruelty, senseless bravado, lonely self-loathing, and wretched bad timing that result in violent death accelerate on weekends. The bodies arrive and are stored in the morgue for Monday autopsy.

This Monday was no exception. I got coffee and joined the morning meeting in LaManche's office. Natalie Ayers was at a murder trial in Val-d'Or, but the other pathologists were present. Jean Pelletiér had just returned from testifying in Kuujjuaq, in far northern Quebec. He was showing snapshots to Emily Santangelo and Michael Morin. I leaned in.

51

Kuujjuaq looked as if it had been flown in and assembled the night before.

"What's that?" I asked, indicating a prefab building with a plastic outer layer.

"The aqua center." Pelletier pointed to a red hexagonal sign with unfamiliar characters above, *Arrêt* below in bold white letters. "All the signs are in French and Inuktitut." His upriver accent was so heavy, to my ear he might have been speaking the latter. I'd known him for years and still had trouble understanding his French.

Pelletiér pointed at another prefab building. "That's the courthouse."

It looked like the pool, sans plastic. Behind the town, the tundra stretched gray and bleak, a Serengeti of rocks and moss. A bleached caribou skeleton lay by the roadside.

"Is that common?" asked Emily, studying the caribou.

"Only when they're dead."

"There are eight autopsies today," said LaManche, handing out the roster. He went over them all. A nineteen-year-old male had been hit by a train, his torso bisected. It happened on a barricaded trestle frequented by teens.

A snowmobile had gone through the ice on Lac Megantic. Two bodies recovered. Alcohol intoxication suspected.

An infant had been found dead and putrefied in its bed. Mama, who was downstairs watching a game show when authorities arrived, said ten days earlier God told her to stop feeding the baby.

An unidentified white male was found behind a Dumpster on the McGill campus. Three bodies were recovered from a house fire in St-Jovite.

Pelletiér was assigned the infant. He indicated that he

52

might request an anthropology consult. While the baby's identity was not in question, cause and time of death would be tough.

Santangelo got the bodies from Lac Megantic, Morin the train and Dumpster cases. The victims from the bedroom in St-Jovite were intact enough for normal autopsy. LaManche would perform them. I would do the bones from the basement.

After the meeting, I went to my office and opened a dossier by transferring the information from the morning etiquette sheet onto an anthropology case form. Name: *Inconnu*. Unknown. Date of birth: blank. Laboratoire de Médecine Légale number: 31013. Morgue number: 375. Police incident number: 89041. Pathologist: Pierre LaManche. Coroner: Jean-Claude Hubert. Investigators: Andrew Ryan and Jean Bertrand, Escouade de Crimes Contre la Personne, Sûreté du Québec.

I added the date and slipped the form into a file folder. Each of us uses a different color. Pink is Marc Bergeron, the odontologist. Green is Martin Levesque, the radiologist. LaManche uses red. A bright yellow jacket means anthropology.

I keyed in and rode the elevator to the basement. There I asked an autopsy technician to place LML 31013 in room three, then went to change into surgical scrubs.

The four autopsy rooms of the Laboratoire de Médecine Légale are adjacent to the morgue. The LML controls the former, the Bureau du Coroner the latter. Autopsy room two is large and contains three tables. The others have one each. Number four is equipped with special ventilation. I often work there since many of my cases are less than fresh. Today I left room four to Pelletiér and the baby. Charred bodies do not have a particularly offensive odor.

When I got to room three, a black body bag and four plastic containers lay on a gurney. I peeled the lid from a tub, removed the cotton padding, and checked the skull pieces. They had weathered the trip without damage.

I filled out a case identification card, unzipped the body bag, and pulled back the sheet that wrapped the bones and debris. I took several Polaroids, then sent everything for X-rays. If there were teeth or metal objects, I wanted to pinpoint them before disturbing the fill.

As I waited I thought of Élisabeth Nicolet. Her coffin was locked in a cooler ten feet from me. I was anxious to see what was in it. One of my messages this morning had been from Sister Julienne. The nuns were impatient, too.

After thirty minutes Lisa wheeled the bones back from radiography and handed me an envelope of films. I popped several onto a view box, starting with the foot end of the body bag.

"They're O.K.?" asked Lisa. "I wasn't sure what setting to use with all that rubble in there, so I did several exposures of each."

"They're good."

We were looking at an amorphous mass surrounded by two tiny white railroad tracks: the bag's contents and metal zipper. The fill was speckled with construction debris, and here and there, a particle of bone appeared pale and honeycombed against the neutral background.

"What's that?" Lisa pointed to a white object.

"Looks like a nail."

I replaced the first films with three more. Soil, pebbles, scraps of wood, nails. We could see the leg and hip bones with attached charred flesh. The pelvis looked intact.

"Looks like metallic fragments in the right femur," I

54

said, indicating several white spots in the thigh bone. "Let's be careful when we handle that. We'll get another shot later."

The next films showed the ribs to be as fragmented as I remembered. The arm bones were better preserved, though fractured and badly jumbled. Several vertebrae looked salvageable. Another metal object was visible to the left of the thorax. It didn't look like a nail.

"Let's watch for that, too."

Lisa nodded.

Next we examined the X-rays of the plastic tubs. They showed nothing unusual. The mandible had held together well, the slender tooth roots still solidly encased in bone. Even the crowns were intact. I could see bright blobs in two of the molars. Bergeron would be pleased. If there were dental records, the fillings would be useful in establishing positive ID.

Then I noticed the frontal bone. It was speckled with tiny white dots, as though someone had seasoned it with salt.

"I'm going to want another shot of that, too," I said softly, staring at the radiopaque particles near the left orbit.

Lisa gave me an odd look.

"O.K. Let's get him out," I said.

"Or her."

"Or her."

Lisa spread a sheet over the autopsy table and set a screen across the sink. I took a paper apron from one of the stainless steel counter drawers, slipped it over my head, and tied it around my waist. Then I placed a mask over my mouth, pulled on surgical gloves, and unzipped the body bag.

Starting at the feet and working north, I removed the largest and most easily identifiable objects and pieces of bone. Then I went back and sifted the fill to locate any small items or bone fragments I might have missed. Lisa screened each handful under gently running water. She washed and placed artifacts on the counter, while I arranged skeletal elements in anatomical order on the sheet.

At noon Lisa broke for lunch. I worked through, and by two-thirty the painstaking process was done. A collection of nails, metal caps, and one exploded cartridge lay on the counter, along with a small plastic vial containing what I thought could be a scrap of fabric. A charred and disconnected skeleton lay on the table, the skull bones fanning out like petals on a daisy.

It took over an hour to do an inventory, identifying each bone and determining if it came from the left or right side. Then I turned my attention to the questions Ryan would ask. Age. Sex. Race. Who is it?

I picked up the mass that contained the pelvis and thigh bones. The fire had cooked the soft tissue, turning it black and leathery hard. A mixed blessing. The bones had been protected, but it might be a bitch getting them out.

I rotated the pelvis. The flesh on the left had burned away, causing the femur to split. I could see a perfect cross section of the ball-and-socket hip joint. I measured the diameter of the femoral head. It was tiny, falling on the low end of the female range.

I studied the internal structure of the head, just below the articular surface. The spicules of bone showed the typical honeycombed pattern of an adult, with no thick line to indicate a recently fused growth cap. That was consistent with the completed molar roots I'd noticed earlier in the jaw. This victim was not a kid.

I looked at the outer edges of the cup that formed the hip socket, and at the lower border of the femoral head. On both the bone seemed to drip downward, like wax

56

overflowing a candle. Arthritis. The individual was not young.

I already suspected the victim was a woman. What remained of the long bones were small in diameter, with smooth-muscle attachments. I shifted my attention to the cranial fragments.

Small mastoids and brow ridges. Sharp orbital borders. The bone was smooth at the back of the skull and in all the places male bone would be rough and bumpy.

I examined the frontal bone. The upper ends of the two nasal bones were still in place. They met at a high angle along the midline, like a church steeple. I found two pieces of maxilla. The lower border of the nasal opening ended in a sharp ledge with a spike of bone projecting upward at its center. The nose had been narrow and prominent, the face straight when viewed from the side. I located a fragment of temporal bone and shone a flashlight into the ear opening. I could see a tiny round opening, the oval window to the inner ear. All good Caucasoid traits.

Female. White. Adult. Old.

I returned to the pelvis, hoping it would allow me to confirm the sex and be more precise about the age. I was particularly interested in the region where the two halves meet in front.

Gently, I teased away charred tissue, revealing the joint between the pubic bones, the pubic symphysis. The pubes themselves were wide, the angle below them broad. Each had a raised ridge angling across its corner. The lower branch of each pubic bone was gracile and gently recurved. Typical female features. I noted them on my case form and took more Polaroid close-ups.

The intense heat had shrunk the connective cartilage and pulled the pubic bones apart along the midline. I twisted and turned the charred mass, trying to peer into

57

the gap. It looked like the symphyseal surfaces were intact, but I couldn't make out any detail.

"Let's take the pubes out," I said to Lisa.

I smelled burned flesh as the saw buzzed through the wings connecting the pubic bone to the rest of the pelvis. It took just seconds.

The symphyseal joint was singed, but easily readable. There were no ridges or furrows on either surface. In fact, both faces were porous, their outer edges irregularly lipped. Erratic threads of bone projected from the front of each pubic element, ossifications into the surrounding soft tissue. The lady had lived a long time.

I turned the pubes over. A deep trench scarred the belly side of each. And she had given birth.

I reached again for the frontal bone. For a moment I stood there, the fluorescent light showing in harsh detail what I'd first suspected in the basement, and what the metallic scatter on the X-ray had confirmed.

I'd held my feelings at bay, but now I allowed myself to grieve for the ravaged human being on my table. And to puzzle over what had happened to her.

The woman had been at least seventy, undoubtedly a mother, probably a grandmother.

Why had someone shot her in the head and left her to burn in a house in the Laurentians?

5

By noon on Tuesday I was finishing my report. I'd worked past nine the night before, knowing Ryan would want answers. Surprisingly, I'd yet to see him.

I read what I'd written, checking for errors. Sometimes I think gender agreements and accent marks are Francophone curses specifically designed for my torment. I try my best, but I always blow a few.

In addition to a biological profile of the unknown, the report included an analysis of trauma. On dissection I found the radiopaque fragments in the femur were the result of postmortem impact. The small bits of metal were probably blasted into the bone by the explosion of a propane tank. Most of the other damage was also due to the fire.

Some was not. I read my summary.

Wound A is a circular defect, of which only the superior half is preserved. It is localized to the midfrontal region, lying approximately 2 centimeters above glabella and 1.2 centimeters to the left of mid-line. The defect measures 1.4 centimeters in diameter and presents characteristic beveling of the inner table. Charring is present along the margins of the defect. Wound A is consistent with a gunshot entrance wound.

Wound B is a circular defect with characteristic beveling of the outer table. It measures 1.6 centimeters in diameter endocranially, and 4.8 centimeters in diameter ectocranially. The defect is localized to the occipital bone, 2.6 centimeters superior to opisthion and 0.9 centimeters to the left of the midsagittal line. There is focal charring of the left, right, and inferior margins of the defect. Wound B is consistent with a gunshot exit wound.

While fire damage made a complete reconstruction impossible, I was able to piece together enough of the vault to interpret the fractures lacing between the exit and entrance holes.

The pattern was classic. The old woman had suffered a gunshot wound to the head. The bullet entered the middle of her forehead, traversed her brain, and exited at the back. It explained why the skull had not shattered in the flames. A vent for intracranial pressure had been created before heat became a problem.

I walked the report to the secretarial pool and returned to find Ryan sitting across from my desk, gazing out the window behind my chair. His legs stretched the length of my office.

"Nice view." He spoke in English.

Five floors down the Jacques Cartier Bridge arched across the St. Lawrence River. I could see minuscule cars crawling across its back. It *was* a nice view.

"It distracts me from thinking about how small this office is." I slipped past him, around the desk, and into my chair.

"A distracted mind can be dangerous."

"My bruised shins bring me back to reality." I swiveled sideways and propped my legs on the ledge below the window, ankles crossed. "It's an old woman, Ryan. Shot in the head."

60

"How old?"

"I'd say she was at least seventy. Maybe even seventy-five. Her pubic symphyses have a lot of miles on them, but folks are variable up in that range. She has advanced arthritis and she's osteoporotic."

He dipped his chin and raised his brows. "French or English, Brennan. Not doctor talk." His eyes were the shade of blue on the Windows 95 screen.

"Os-te-o-po-ro-sis." I spoke each syllable slowly. "I can tell from the X-rays that her cortical bone is thin. I can't see any fractures, but I only had parts of the long bones. The hip is a common site for breaks in older women because a lot of weight is transferred there. Hers were O.K."

"Caucasian?"

I nodded.

"Anything else."

"She probably had several kids." The laser blues were fixed on my face. "She has a trench the size of the Orinoco on the back of each pubic bone."

"Great."

"Another thing. I think she was already in the basement when the fire started."

"How's that?"

"There was absolutely no floor debris below the body. And I found a few tiny scraps of fabric embedded between her and the clay. She must have been lying directly on the floor."

He thought for a moment.

"So you're telling me someone shot Granny, dragged her down to the basement, and left her to fry."

"No. I'm saying Granny took a bullet in the head. I don't have a clue who fired it. Maybe she did. That's your job, Ryan."

"Did you find a gun near her?"

"No."

61

Just then Bertrand appeared in the doorway. While Ryan looked neat and pressed, his partner's creases were sharp enough to cut precious gems. He wore a mauve shirt keyed to the tones of his floral tie, a lavender and gray tweed jacket, and wool trousers a precise half note down from shade four in the tweed.

"What have you got?" Ryan asked his partner.

"Nothing we didn't already know. It's like these people were beamed down from space. No one really knows who the hell was living in there. We're still trying to track down the guy in Europe that owns the house. The neighbors across the road saw the old lady from time to time, but she never spoke to them. They say the couple with the kids had only been there a few months. They rarely saw them, never learned their names. A woman up the road thought they were part of some sort of fundamentalist group."

"Brennan says our Doe is a Jane. As in Baby Jane. A septuagenarian."

Bertrand looked at him.

"In her seventies."

"An old lady?"

"With a bullet in her brain."

"No shit?"

"No shit."

"Someone shot her and torched the place?"

"Or Granny pulled the trigger after having lit the barbecue. But, then, where's the weapon?"

When they'd gone I checked my consult requests. A jar of ashes had arrived in Quebec City, the cremains of an elderly man who died in Jamaica. The family was accusing the crematory of fraud, and had brought the ashes to the coroner's office. He wanted to know what I thought.

A skull was found in a ravine outside the Côte des Neiges Cemetery. It was dry and bleached, and had probably come from an old grave. The coroner needed confirmation.

Pelletiér wanted me to look at the baby for evidence of starvation. That would require microscopy. Thin sections of bone would have to be ground down, stained, and placed on slides so I could examine the cells under magnification. While high turnover of bone is typical of infants, I'd look for signs of unusual porosity and abnormal remodeling in the microanatomy.

Samples had been sent to the histology lab. I'd also study the X-rays and the skeleton, but that was still soaking to remove the putrefied flesh. A baby's bones are too fragile to risk boiling.

So. Nothing urgent. I could open Élisabeth Nicolet's coffin.

After a refrigerated sandwich and a yogurt in the cafeteria, I rode down to the morgue, asked to have the remains brought to room three, then went to change.

The coffin was smaller than I remembered, measuring less than three feet in length. The left side had rotted, allowing the top to collapse inward. I brushed off loose soil and took photos.

"Need a crowbar?" Lisa stood in the doorway.

Since this was not an LML case, I was to work alone, but I was getting a lot of offers. Apparently I was not the only one fascinated by Élisabeth.

"Please."

It took less than a minute to remove the cover. The wood was soft and crumbly, and the nails gave easily. I scooped dirt from the interior to reveal a lead liner containing another wood coffin.

"Why are they so little?" asked Lisa.

"This isn't the original casket. Élisabeth Nicolet was exhumed and reburied around the turn of the century, so they just needed enough space for her bones."

63

"Think it's her?"

I drilled a look at her.

"Let me know if you need anything."

I continued scooping dirt until I had cleared the lid of the inner casket. It bore no plaque, but was more ornate than the outer, with an elaborately carved border paralleling the hexagonal outside edge. Like the exterior coffin, the one inside had collapsed and filled with dirt.

Lisa returned in twenty minutes.

"I'm free for a while if you need X-rays."

"Can't do it because of the lead liner," I said. "But I'm ready to open the inner casket."

"No problem."

Again the wood was soft and the nails slipped right out.

More dirt. I'd removed only two handfuls when I spotted the skull. Yes! Someone was home!

Slowly, the skeleton emerged. The bones were not in anatomical order, but lay parallel to one another, as though tightly bound when placed into the coffin. The arrangement reminded me of archaeological sites I'd excavated early in my career. Before Columbus, some aboriginal groups exposed their dead on scaffolds until the bones were clean, then bundled them for burial. Élisabeth had been packed like this.

I'd loved archaeology. Still did. I regretted doing so little of it, but over the past decade my career had taken a different path. Teaching and forensic casework now occupied all my time. Élisabeth Nicolet was allowing me a brief return to my roots, and I was enjoying the hell out of it.

I removed and arranged the bones, just as I had the day before. They were dry and fragile, but this person was in much better shape than yesterday's lady from St-Jovite.

My skeletal inventory indicated that only a metatarsal

64

and six phalanges were missing. They did not show up when I screened the soil, but I did locate several incisors and a canine, and replaced them in their sockets.

I followed my regular procedure, filling out a form just as I would for a coroner case. I started with the pelvis. The bones were those of a female. No doubt there. Her pubic symphyses suggested an age of thirty-five to forty-five years. The good sisters would be happy.

In taking long-bone measurements I noted an unusual flattening on the front of the tibia, just below the knee. I checked the metatarsals. They showed arthritis where the toes join the feet. Yahoo! Repeated patterns of movement leave their marks on the skeleton. Élisabeth was supposed to have spent years in prayer on the stone floor of her convent cell. In kneeling, the combination of pressure on the knees and hyperflexion of the toes creates exactly the pattern I was seeing.

I remembered something I'd noticed as I removed a tooth from the screen, and picked up the jaw. Each of the lower central incisors had a small but noticeable groove on the biting edge. I found the uppers. Same grooves. When not praying or writing letters, Élisabeth sewed. Her embroidery still hung in the convent at Lac Memphrémagog. Her teeth were notched from years of pulling thread or holding a needle between them. I was loving this.

Then I turned the skull faceup and did a double take. I was standing there, staring at it, when LaManche entered the room.

"So, is this the saint?" he asked.

He came up beside me and looked at the skull.

"*Mon Dieu.*"

"Yes, the analysis is going well." I was in my office,

65

speaking with Father Ménard. The skull from Mem-phrémagog sat in a cork ring on my worktable. "The bones are remarkably well preserved."

"Will you be able to confirm that it's Élisabeth? Élisabeth Nicolet?"

"Father, I wanted to ask you a few more questions."

"Is there a problem?"

Yes. There may be.

"No, no. I'd just like a little more information."

"Yes?"

"Do you have any official document stating who Élisabeth's parents were?"

"Her father was Alain Nicolet, and her mother was Eugénie Bélanger, a well-known singer at that time. Her uncle, Louis-Philippe Bélanger, was a city councilman and a very distinguished physician."

"Yes. Is there a birth certificate?"

He was silent. Then,

"We have not been able to locate a birth certificate."

"Do you know where Élisabeth was born?"

"I think she was born in Montreal. Her family was here for generations. Élisabeth is a descendant of Michel Bélanger, who came to Canada in 1758, in the last days of New France. The Bélanger family was always prominent in city affairs."

"Yes. Is there a hospital record, or a baptismal certificate, or anything that officially records her birth?"

More silence.

"She was born more than a century and a half ago."

"Were records kept?"

"Yes. Sister Julienne has searched. But things can be lost over such a long time. Such a long time."

"Of course."

For a moment we were both silent. I was about to thank him when,

"Why are you asking these questions, Dr. Brennan?"

66

I hesitated. Not yet. I could be wrong. I could be right but it meant nothing.

"I just wanted a bit more background."

I'd hardly replaced the receiver when the phone rang.

"*Oui,* Dr. Brennan."

"Ryan." I could hear tension in his voice. "It was arson all right. And whoever planned it made sure the place went up. Simple but effective. They hooked a heat coil to a timer, same kind you use to turn on your lamps when you go off to the spa."

"I don't go to spas, Ryan."

"Do you want to hear this?"

I didn't answer.

"The timer turned on the hot plate. That set off a fire which ignited a propane tank. Most of the timers were destroyed, but we recovered a few. Looks like they were set to go off at intervals, but once the fire spread it was bombs away."

"How many tanks?"

"Fourteen. We found one undamaged timer out in the yard. Must have been a dud. It's the kind you can buy in any hardware store. We'll try for prints, but it's a long shot."

"The accelerant?"

"Gasoline, as I suspected."

"Why both?"

"Because someone friggin' wanted the place destroyed big time and didn't want a screw-up. Probably figured there wouldn't be a second chance."

"How do you know that?"

"LaManche was able to draw fluid samples from the bodies in the bedroom. Toxicology found celestial levels of Rohypnol."

"Rohypnol?"

"I'll let him tell you about it. It's called the date rape

drug or something because it's undetectable to the victim and knocks you flat on your ass for hours."

"I know what Rohypnol is, Ryan. I'm just surprised. It's not so easy to come by."

"Yeah. That could be a break. It's banned in the U.S. and Canada."

So is crack, I thought.

"Here's another weird thing. It wasn't Ward and June Cleaver up in that bedroom. LaManche says the guy was probably in his twenties, the woman closer to fifty."

I knew that. LaManche had asked my opinion during the autopsy.

"Now what?"

"We're heading back out there to take the other two buildings apart. We're still waiting for word from the owner. He's some kind of hermit buried in the Belgian boonies."

"Good luck."

Rohypnol. That kindled something way down in my memory cells, but when I tried to bring it up the spark went out.

I checked to see if the slides for Pelletiér's malnourished baby case were finished. The histology tech told me they'd be ready tomorrow.

I then spent an hour examining the cremains. They were in a jelly jar with a handwritten label stating the name of the decedent, the name of the crematorium, and the date of cremation. Not typical packaging for North America, but I knew nothing of practices in the Caribbean.

No particle was over a centimeter in size. Typical. Few bone fragments survive the pulverizers used by modern crematoriums. Using a dissecting scope, I was able to identify a few things, including a complete ear ossicle. I also located some small bits of twisted metal that I thought might be parts of a dental prosthesis. I saved them for the dentist.

Typically, an adult male will be reduced by firing and pulverization to about 3,500 cc's of ash. This jar contained about 360. I wrote a brief report stating that the cremains were those of an adult human, and that they were incomplete. Any hope at personal identification would lie with Bergeron.

At six-thirty I packed up and went home.

6

Élisabeth's skeleton troubled me. What I'd seen just couldn't be, but even LaManche had spotted it. I was anxious to resolve the question, but the next morning a set of tiny bones by the sink in the histo lab commanded my attention. The slides were also ready, so I spent several hours on Pelletiér's baby case.

Finding no other requisition on my desk, at ten-thirty I phoned Sister Julienne to find out as much as I could about Élisabeth Nicolet. I asked her the same questions I'd posed to Father Ménard, with similar results. Élisabeth was *"pure laine."* Pure-wool québécoise. But no papers directly establishing her birth or parentage.

"What about outside the convent, Sister? Have you checked other collections?"

"Ah, *oui*. I've researched all the archives in the archdiocese. We have libraries throughout the province, you know. I've gotten materials from many convents and monasteries."

I'd seen some of this material. Most was in the form of letters and personal journals containing references to the family. A few were attempts at historical narrative, but were not what my dean would call "peer reviewed."

70

Many were purely anecdotal accounts, made up of hearsay on top of hearsay.

I tried a different tack. "Until recently, the church was responsible for all birth certificates in Quebec, correct?" Father Ménard had explained that.

"Yes. Until just a few years ago."

"But none can be found for Élisabeth?"

"No." There was a pause. "We've had some tragic fires over the years. In 1880 the Sisters of Notre Dame built a beautiful motherhouse on the side of Mount Royal. Sadly, it burned to the ground thirteen years later. Our own motherhouse was destroyed in 1897. Hundreds of priceless documents were lost in those fires."

For a moment neither of us spoke.

"Sister, can you think of anywhere else I might find information on Élisabeth's birth? Or on her parents?"

"I . . . well, you could try the secular libraries, I suppose. Or the historical society. Or perhaps one of the universities. The Nicolet and Bélanger families have produced several important figures in French Canadian history. I'm certain they are discussed in historical accounts."

"Thank you, Sister. I'll do that."

"There's a professor at McGill who's done research in our archives. My niece knows her. She studies religious movements, but she's also interested in Quebec history. I can't remember if she's an anthropologist, or a historian, or what. She might be able to help." She hesitated. "Of course, her references would be different from ours."

I was certain of that, but said nothing.

"Do you remember her name?"

There was a long pause. I could hear others on the line, far away, like voices carrying across a lake. Someone laughed.

71

"It's been a long time. I'm sorry. I could ask my niece if you wish."

"Thank you, Sister. I'll follow up your lead."

"Dr. Brennan, when do you think you'll finish with the bones?"

"Soon. Unless something comes up, I should be able to complete my report on Friday. I'll write up my assessments of age, sex, and race, and any other observations I've made, and comment on how my findings compare to the facts known about Élisabeth. You can include whatever you feel is appropriate with your application to the Vatican."

"And you will call?"

"Of course. As soon as I'm done." Actually, I was done, and I had little doubt what my report would say. Why didn't I just tell them now?

We exchanged good-byes, then I disconnected, waited for the tone, and dialed again. A phone rang across town.

"Mitch Denton."

"Hi, Mitch. Tempe Brennan. Are you still head honcho at your place?"

Mitch was the anthropology chair who'd hired me to teach part-time when I first came to Montreal. We'd been friends ever since. His specialty was the French Paleolithic.

"Still stuck. Want to do a course for us this summer?"

"No, thanks. I've got a question for you."

"Shoot."

"Do you remember the historic case I told you about? The one I'm doing for the archdiocese?"

"The saint wanna-be?"

"Right."

"Sure. Beats the hell out of most of the stuff you work on. Did you find her?"

72

"Yes. But I've noticed something a bit odd, and I'd like to learn more about her."

"Odd?"

"Unexpected. Listen, one of the nuns told me someone at McGill does research involving religion and Quebec history. Does that ring a bell?"

"Dong! That would be our own Daisy Jean."

"Daisy Jean?"

"Dr. Jeannotte to you. Professor of Religious Studies and students' best friend."

"Back up, Mitch."

"Her name is Daisy Jeannotte. Officially she's on the Faculty of Religious Studies, but she also teaches some history courses. 'Religious Movements in Quebec.' 'Ancient and Modern Belief Systems.' That sort of thing."

"Daisy Jean?" I repeated the question.

"Just an in-house endearment. It's not for direct address."

"Why?"

"She can be a bit . . . odd, to use your expression."

"Odd?"

"Unexpected. She's from Dixie, you know."

I ignored that. Mitch was a transplanted Vermonter. He never let up on my Southern homeland.

"Why do you say she's the students' best friend?"

"Daisy spends all her free time with students. She takes them on outings, advises them, travels with them, has them to the house for dinner. There's a constant line of needy souls outside her door seeking solace and counseling."

"Sounds admirable."

He started to say something, caught himself. "I suppose."

"Would Dr. Jeannotte know anything about Élisabeth Nicolet or her family?"

"If anyone can help you it will be Daisy Jean."

He gave me her number and we promised to get together soon.

A secretary told me Dr. Jeannotte would be holding office hours between one and three, so I decided to drop in after lunch.

It takes analytical skills worthy of a degree in civil engineering to understand when and where one is allowed to leave a car in Montreal. McGill University lies in the heart of Centre-Ville, so even if one is able to comprehend where parking is permitted, it is almost impossible to find a space. I found a spot on Stanley that I interpreted to be legal from nine to five, between April 1 and December 31, except from 1 to 2 P.M. on Tuesdays and Thursdays. It did not require a neighborhood permit.

After five reversals of direction and much manipulation of the steering wheel, I managed to wedge the Mazda between a Toyota pickup and an Oldsmobile Cutlass. Not a bad job on a steep grade. When I got out I was sweating despite the cold. I checked the bumpers. I had at least twenty-four inches to spare. Total.

The weather was not as frigid as it had been, but the modest rise in temperature had come with an increased dampness. A cloud of cold, moist air pressed down on the city, and the sky was the color of old tin. A heavy, wet snow began to fall as I walked downhill to Sherbrooke and turned east. The first flakes melted when they touched the pavement, then others lingered and threatened to accumulate.

I trudged uphill on McTavish and entered McGill through the west gate. The campus lay above and below me, the gray stone buildings climbing the hill from Sherbrooke to Docteur-Penfield. People hurried about, shoulders rounded against the cold and damp, books and packages shielded from the snow. I passed the library and cut behind the Redpath Museum. Exiting the east gate, I turned left, and headed uphill on rue Universitie, my calves feeling as though I'd done three miles on a Nordic Track. Outside Birks Hall I nearly collided with a tall young man walking head down, his hair and glasses coated with snowflakes the size of luna moths.

Birks is from another time, with its Gothic exterior, carved oak walls and furniture, and enormous cathedral windows. It is a place that inspires whispering, not the chatting and swapping of notes that occurs in most university buildings. The first-floor lobby is cavernous, its walls hung with portraits of grave men looking down in scholarly self-importance.

I added my boots to the row of footwear trickling melted snow onto the marble floor, and stepped over for a closer look at the august artworks. *Thomas Cranmer, Archbishop of Canterbury*. Good job, Tom. *John Bunyan, Immortal Dreamer*. Times had changed. When I was a student abstract reverie in class, if detected, got you called on and humiliated for being inattentive.

I climbed a winding staircase, past two sets of wooden doors on the second floor, one to the chapel, the other to the library, and continued to the third. Here the elegance of the lobby gave way to signs of aging. Patches of paint peeled from walls and ceiling, and here and there a tile was missing.

At the top of the stairs I paused to get my bearings. It was strangely quiet and gloomy. On my left I could see an alcove with double doors opening on to the chapel balcony. Two corridors flanked the alcove, with wooden doors set at intervals along each hall. I passed the chapel and started up the far corridor.

The last office on the left was open but unoccupied.

75

A plaque above the door said "Jeannotte" in delicate script. Compared with my office, the room looked like St. Joseph's Oratory. It was long and narrow, with a bell-shaped window at the far end. Through the leaded glass I could see the administration building and the drive leading up to the Strathcona Medical-Dental Complex. The floor was oak, the planks buffed yellow by years of studious feet.

Shelves lined every wall, filled with books, journals, notebooks, videotapes, slide carousels, and stacks of papers and reprints. A wooden desk sat in front of the window, a computer workstation to its right.

I looked at my watch. Twelve forty-five. I was early. I moved back up the hall and began to examine the photos lining the corridor. School of Divinity, Graduating Class of 1937, and 1938, and 1939. Stiff poses. Somber faces.

I had worked my way to 1942 when a young woman appeared. She wore jeans, a turtleneck, and a wool plaid shirt that hung to her knees. Her blond hair was cut blunt at the jawline, and thick bangs covered her eyebrows. She wore no makeup.

"May I help you?" she asked in English. She tipped her head and the bangs fell sideways.

"Yes. I'm looking for Dr. Jeannotte."

"Dr. Jeannotte's not here yet, but I expect her any time. Can I do something for you? I'm her teaching assistant." With a quick gesture, she tucked hair behind her right ear.

"Thank you, I'd like to ask Dr. Jeannotte a few questions. I'll wait, if I may."

"Uh, oh, well. O.K. I guess that's O.K. She's just, I'm not sure. She doesn't allow anyone in her office." She looked at me, glanced through the open door, then back at me. "I was at the copy machine."

"That's fine. I'll wait out here."

76

"Well, no, she could be a while. She's often late. I . . ." She turned and scanned the corridor behind her.

"You could sit in her office." Again the hair gesture. "But I don't know if she'll like that."

She seemed unable to make a decision.

"I'm fine here. Really."

Her eyes moved past me, then back to my face. She bit her lip and did another hair tuck. She didn't seem old enough to be a college student. She looked about twelve.

"What did you say your name is?"

"Dr. Brennan. Tempe Brennan."

"Are you a professor?"

"Yes, but not here. I work at the Laboratoire de Médecine Légale."

"Is that the police?" A crease formed between her eyes.

"No. It's the medical examiner."

"Oh." She licked her lips, then checked her watch. It was the only jewelry she wore.

"Well, come in and sit down. I'm here, so I think it's O.K. I was just at the copy machine."

"I don't want to cause . . ."

"No. It's no problem." She gave a follow-me jerk of her head and entered the office. "Come in."

I entered and took a seat on the small sofa she indicated. She moved past me to the far end of the room and began reshelving journals.

I could hear the hum of an electric motor, but couldn't see the source. I looked around. I'd never seen books take up so much space in a room. I scanned the titles immediately across from me.

The Elements of Celtic Tradition. The Dead Sea Scrolls and the New Testament. The Mysteries of Freemasonry. Shamanism: Archaic Techniques of Ecstasy. The Kingship Rituals of Egypt. Peake's Commentary on the Bible.

77

Churches That Abuse. Thought Reform and the Psychology of Totalism. Armageddon in Waco. When Time Shall Be No More: Prophecy Belief in Modern America. An eclectic collection.

Minutes dragged by. The office was uncomfortably warm, and I felt a headache begin at the base of my skull. I removed my jacket.

Hmmmmmm.

I studied a print on the wall to my right. Naked children warmed themselves at a hearth, skin glowing in firelight. Below was written *After the Bath*, Robert Peel, 1892. The picture reminded me of one in my grandmother's music room.

I checked the time. One-ten.

"How long have you worked for Dr. Jeannotte?"

She was bending over the desk but straightened quickly at the sound of my voice.

"How long?" Bewildered.

"Are you one of her graduate students?"

"Undergraduate." She stood silhouetted by the light from the window. I couldn't see her features, but her body looked tense.

"I hear she is very involved with her students."

"Why are you asking me?"

Strange answer. "I was just curious. I never seem to have enough time to see my students outside the classroom. I admire her."

That seemed to satisfy her.

"Dr. Jeannotte is more than a teacher to many of us."

"How did you come to major in religious studies?"

For a while she didn't answer. When I thought she wasn't going to, she spoke slowly.

"I met Dr. Jeannotte when I signed up for her seminar. She . . ." Another long pause. It was hard to see her expression because of the backlighting. ". . . inspired me."

78

"How so?"

Another pause.

"She made me want to do things right. To learn how to do things right."

I didn't know what to say, but this time no prompt was necessary to keep her talking.

"She made me realize that a lot of the answers have already been written, we just have to learn to find them." She took a deep breath, let it out. "It's hard, it's really hard, but I've come to understand what a mess people have made of the world, and that only a few enlightened . . ."

She turned slightly, and I could see her face again. Her eyes had widened and her mouth was tense.

"Dr. Jeannotte. We were just talking."

A woman stood in the doorway. She was no more than five feet tall, with dark hair pulled tightly back from her forehead and knotted at the back of her head. Her skin was the same eggshell color as the wall behind her.

"I was at the copy machine before. I was only out of the office for a few seconds."

The woman remained absolutely still.

"She wasn't in here by herself. I wouldn't allow that." The student bit her lip and dropped her eyes.

Daisy Jeannotte never wavered.

"Dr. Jeannotte, she wants to ask you a few questions so I thought it would be O.K. if she came in to wait. She's a medical examiner." Her voice was almost trembling.

Jeannotte did not look in my direction. I had no idea what was going on.

"I . . . I'm shelving the journals. We were just making conversation." I could see drops of sweat on her upper lip.

For a moment Jeannotte continued her gaze, then, slowly, she turned in my direction.

"You have chosen a slightly inconvenient time, Miss . . .?" Soft. Tennessee, maybe Georgia.

"Dr. Brennan." I stood.

"Dr. Brennan."

"I apologize for coming unannounced. Your secretary told me that this is your time for office hours."

She took a long time to look me over. Her eyes were deep-set, the irises so pale they were almost without color. Jeannotte accentuated this by darkening her lashes and brows. Her hair, too, was an unnatural, dense black.

"Well," she said finally, "since you are here. What is it you are seeking?" She remained motionless in the doorway. Daisy Jeannotte was one of those people who possess an air of total calm.

I explained about Sister Julienne, and about my interest in Élisabeth Nicolet, without revealing the reasons for my interest.

Jeannotte thought a moment, then shifted her gaze to the teaching assistant. Without a word the young woman laid down the journals and hurried from the office.

"You'll have to excuse my assistant. She's very high-strung." She gave a soft laugh and shook her head. "But she is an excellent student."

Jeannotte moved to a chair opposite me. We both sat.

"This time of the afternoon I normally reserve for students, but today there seem to be none. Would you like some tea?" Her voice had a honeyed quality, like the country club ladies back home.

"No, thank you. I've just had lunch."

"You are a medical examiner?"

"Not exactly. I'm a forensic anthropologist, on the

80

faculty at the University of North Carolina at Charlotte. I consult to the coroner here."

"Charlotte is a lovely city. I've visited there often."

"Thank you. Our campus is quite different from McGill, very modern. I envy you this beautiful office."

"Yes. It is charming. Birks dates to 1931 and was originally called Divinity Hall. The building belonged to the Joint Theological Colleges until McGill acquired it in 1948. Did you know that the School of Divinity is one of the oldest faculties at McGill?"

"No, I didn't."

"Of course, today we call ourselves the Faculty of Religious Studies. So, you are interested in the Nicolet family." She crossed her ankles and settled back. I found the lack of color in her eyes unsettling.

"Yes. I'd particularly like to know where Élisabeth was born and what her parents were doing at the time. Sister Julienne has been unable to locate a birth certificate, but she's certain the birth was in Montreal. She felt you might be able to lead me to some references."

"Sister Julienne." She laughed again, a sound like water running over rocks. Then her face sobered. "There's been a great deal written about and by members of the Nicolet and Bélanger families. Our own library has a rich archive of historic documents. I'm sure you will find many things there. You could also try the Archives of the Province of Quebec, the Canadian Historical Society, and the Public Archives of Canada." The soft, Southern tones assumed an almost mechanical quality. I was a sophomore on a research project.

"You could check journals such as the *Report of the Canadian Historical Society*, the *Canadian Annual Review*, the *Canadian Archives Report*, the *Canadian Historical Review*, the *Transactions of the Quebec Literary and Historical Society*, the *Report of the Archives of the*

81

Province of Quebec, or the *Transactions of the Royal Society of Canada.*" She sounded like a tape. "And, of course, there are hundreds of books. I myself know very little about that period in history."

My face must have reflected my thoughts.

"Don't look so daunted. It just takes time."

I'd never find enough hours to wade through that volume of material. I decided to try another tack.

"Are you familiar with the circumstances surrounding Élisabeth's birth?"

"Not really. As I said, that's not a period for which I've done research. I do know who she is, of course, and of her work during the smallpox epidemic of 1885." She paused a moment, choosing her words carefully. "My work has focused on messianic movements and new belief systems, not on the traditional ecclesiastical religions."

"In Quebec?"

"Not exclusively." She circled back to the Nicolets. "The family was well known in its day, so you might find it more interesting to go through old newspaper stories. There were four English language dailies back then, the *Gazette, Star, Herald,* and *Witness.*"

"Those would be in the library?"

"Yes. And, of course, there was the French press, *La Minerve, Le Monde, La Patrie, L'Etendard,* and *La Presse.* The French papers were a bit less prosperous and somewhat thinner than the English, but I believe they all carried birth announcements."

I hadn't thought of press accounts. Somehow that seemed more manageable.

She explained where the newspapers were stored on microfilm, and promised to draw up a list of sources for me. For a while we spoke of other things. I sated her curiosity about my job. We compared experiences, two female professors in the male-dominated world of the university. Before long a student appeared in the doorway. Jeannotte tapped her watch and held up five fingers, and the young woman disappeared.

We both stood at the same time. I thanked her, slipped on my jacket, hat, and scarf. I was halfway through the door when she stopped me with a question.

"Do you have a religion, Dr. Brennan?"

"I was raised Roman Catholic, but currently I don't belong to a church."

The ghostly eyes looked into mine.

"Do you believe in God?"

"Dr. Jeannotte, there are some days I don't believe in tomorrow morning."

After I left, I swung by the library and spent an hour browsing the history books, skimming indexes for Nicolet or Bélanger. I found several in which one or the other name was listed, and checked them out, thankful I still had faculty privileges.

It was growing dark when I emerged. Snow was falling, forcing pedestrians to walk in the street or follow narrow trails on the sidewalks, carefully placing one foot in front of the other to keep out of the deeper snow. I trudged behind a couple, girl in front, boy behind, his hands resting on her shoulders. Ties on their knapsacks swung back and forth as hips swiveled to keep feet inside the snow-free passage. Now and then the girl stopped to catch a snowflake on her tongue.

The temperature had dropped as daylight had faded, and when I got to the car, the windshield was coated with ice. I dug out a scraper and chipped away, cursing my migratory instincts. Anyone with any sense would be at the beach.

During the short drive home I replayed the scene in Jeannotte's office, trying to figure out the curious behavior of the teaching assistant. Why had she been so

83

nervous? She seemed in awe of Jeannotte, beyond even the customary deference of an undergraduate. She mentioned her trip to the copy machine three times, yet when I'd met her in the hall she had nothing in her hands. I realized I'd never learned her name.

I thought about Jeannotte. She'd been so gracious, so totally composed, as if used to being in control of any audience. I pictured the penetrating eyes, such a contrast to the tiny body and soft, gentle drawl. She'd made me feel like an undergraduate. Why? Then I remembered. During our conversation Daisy Jean's gaze didn't leave my face. Never once did she break eye contact. That and the eerie irises made a disconcerting combination.

I arrived home to find two messages. The first made me mildly anxious. Harry had enrolled in her course and was becoming a guru of modern mental health.

The second sent a chill deep into my soul. I listened, watching snow pile up against my garden wall. The new flakes lay white atop the underlying gray, like newborn innocence on last year's sins.

"*Brennan, if you're there, pick up. This is important.*" Pause. "*There's been a development in the St-Jovite case.*" Ryan's voice was tinged with sadness. "*When we tossed the outbuildings we found four more bodies behind a stairway.*" I could hear him pull smoke deep into his lungs, release it slowly. "*Two adults and two babies. They're not burned, but it's grisly. I've never seen anything like it. I don't want to go into details, but we've got a whole new ball game, and it's a shitpot. See you tomorrow.*"

84

7

Ryan wasn't alone in his revulsion. I have seen abused and starved children. I have seen them after they were beaten, raped, smothered, shaken to death, but I had never seen anything like what had been done to the babies found in St-Jovite.

Others had received calls the night before. When I arrived at eight-fifteen several press vans had taken up stations outside the SQ building, windows fogged, exhaust billowing from tailpipes.

Although the workday normally begins at eight-thirty, activity already filled the large autopsy room. Bertrand was there, along with several other SQ detectives and a photographer from SIJ, La Section d'Identité Judiciaire. Ryan hadn't arrived.

The external exam was under way, and a series of Polaroids lay on the corner desk. The body had been taken to X-ray, and LaManche was scribbling notes when I entered. He stopped and looked up.

"Temperance, I am glad to see you. I may need help in establishing the age of the infants."

I nodded.

"And there may be an unusual" – he searched for a word, his long, basset face tense – ". . . tool involved."

85

I nodded and went to change into scrubs. Ryan smiled and gave a small salute as I passed him in the corridor. His eyes were teary, his nose and cheeks cherry red, as though he'd walked some distance in the cold.

In the locker room I steeled myself for what was to come. A pair of murdered babies was horror enough. What did LaManche mean by an unusual tool?

Cases involving children are always difficult for me. When my daughter was young, after each child murder I'd fight an urge to tether Katy to me to keep her in sight.

Katy is grown now, but I still dread images of dead children. Of all victims, they are the most vulnerable, the most trusting, and the most innocent. I ache each time one arrives in the morgue. The stark truth of fallen humanity stares at me. And pity provides small comfort.

I returned to the autopsy room, thinking I was prepared to proceed. Then I saw the small body lying on the stainless steel.

A doll. That was my first impression. A life-size latex baby that had grayed with age. I'd had one as a child, a newborn that was pink and smelled rubbery sweet. I fed her through a small, round hole between her lips, and changed her diaper when the water flowed through.

But this was no toy. The baby lay on its belly, arms at its sides, fingers curled into the tiny palms. The buttocks were flattened, and bands of white crisscrossed the purple livor of the back. A cap of fine red down covered the little head. The infant was naked save for a bracelet of miniature blocks circling the right wrist. I could see two wounds near the left shoulder blade.

A sleeper lay on the adjacent table, blue and red trucks smiling from the flannel. Spread next to it were a soiled diaper, a cotton undershirt with crotch snaps, a

86

long-sleeved sweater, and a pair of white socks. Every-thing was bloodstained.

LaManche spoke into a recorder.

"Bébé de race blanche, bien développé et bien nourri . . ."

Well developed and well nourished but dead, I thought, the outrage beginning to build.

"Le corps est bien préservé, avec une légère macération épidermique . . ."

I stared at the small cadaver. Yes, it was well preserved, with only slight skin slippage on the hands.

"Guess he won't have to check for defense wounds."

Bertrand had come up beside me. I didn't respond. I was not in the mood for morgue humor.

"There's another one in the cooler," he continued.

"That's what we'd been told," I said crisply.

"Yeah, but, Christ. They're babies."

I met his eyes and felt a stab of guilt. Bertrand was not trying to be funny. He looked as if his own child had died.

"Babies. Someone wasted them and stashed them in a basement. That's about as cold as a drive-by. Worse. The bastard probably knew these kids."

"Why do you say that?"

"Makes sense. Two kids, two adults who are prob-ably the parents. Someone wiped out the whole family."

"And burned the house as a cover?"

"Possible."

"Could be a stranger."

"Could be, but I doubt it. Wait. You'll see." He refocused on the autopsy proceeding, hands clutched tightly behind his back.

LaManche stopped dictating and spoke to the autopsy technician. Lisa took a tape from the counter and stretched it the length of the baby's body.

"Cinquante-huit centimètres." Fifty-eight centimeters.

Ryan observed from across the room, arms crossed,

right thumb grating the tweed on his left bicep. Now and then I saw his jaw tense and his Adam's apple rise and fall.

Lisa wrapped the tape around the baby's head, chest, and abdomen, calling out after each measurement. Then she lifted the body and laid it in a hanging scale. Normally the device is used to weigh individual organs. The basket swung slightly and she placed a hand to steady it. The image was heartrending. A lifeless child in a stainless steel cradle.

"Six kilos."

The baby had died weighing only six kilos. Thirteen pounds.

LaManche recorded the weight, and Lisa removed the tiny corpse and placed it on the autopsy table. When she stepped back my breath froze in my throat. I looked at Bertrand, but his eyes were now fixed on his shoes.

The body had been a little boy. He lay on his back, legs and feet splayed sharply at the joints. His eyes were wide and button round, the irises clouded to a smoky gray. His head had rolled to the side, and one fat cheek rested against his left collarbone.

Directly below the cheek I saw a hole in the chest approximately the size of my fist. The wound had jagged edges, and a deep purple collar circled its perimeter. A star burst of slits, each measuring one to two centimeters in length, surrounded the cavity. Some were deep, others superficial. In places one slit crossed another, forming L- or V-shaped patterns.

My hand flew to my own chest and I felt my stomach tighten. I turned to Bertrand, unable to form a question.

"Do you believe that?" he said dismally. "The bastard carved his heart out."

"It's gone?"

He nodded.

I swallowed. "The other child?"

He nodded again. "Just when you think you've seen it all, you learn that you haven't."

"Christ." I felt cold all over. I hoped fervently the children were unconscious when the mutilation took place.

I looked across at Ryan. He was studying the scene on the table, his face without expression.

"What about the adults?"

Bertrand shook his head. "Looks like they were stabbed repeatedly, throats slashed, but nobody harvested their organs."

LaManche's voice droned on, describing the external appearance of the wounds. I didn't have to listen. I knew what the presence of hematoma meant. Tissue will bruise only if blood is circulating. The baby had been alive when the cut was made. Babies.

I closed my eyes, fought the urge to run from the room. Get a grip, Brennan. Do your job.

I crossed to the middle table to examine the clothing. Everything was so tiny, so familiar. I looked at the sleeper with its attached footies and soft, fleecy collar and cuffs. Katy had worn a dozen of them. I remembered opening and closing the snaps to change her diaper, her fat little legs kicking like mad. What were these things called? They had a specific name. I tried to recall but my mind refused to focus. Perhaps it was protecting me, urging me to stop personalizing and get back to business before I began to weep or simply went numb.

Most of the bleeding had been while the baby lay on his left side. The right sleeve and shoulder of the sleeper were spattered, but blood had soaked the left side, darkening the flannel to shades of dull red and brown. The undershirt and sweater were similarly stained.

"Three layers," I said to no one in particular. "And socks."

Bertrand crossed to the table.

"Someone took care that the child would be warm."

"Yeah, I guess," Bertrand agreed.

Ryan joined us as we stared at the clothing. Each garment displayed a jagged hole surrounded by a star burst of small tears, replicating the injuries on the baby's chest. Ryan spoke first.

"The little guy was dressed."

"Yeah," said Bertrand. "Guess clothing didn't interfere with his vicious little ritual."

I said nothing.

"Temperance," said LaManche, "please get a magnifying glass and come here. I've found something."

We clustered around the pathologist, and he pointed to a small discoloration to the left and below the hole in the infant's chest. When I handed him a glass, he bent close, studied the bruise, then returned the lens to me.

When I took my turn I was stunned. The spot did not show the disorganized mottling characteristic of a normal bruise. Under magnification I could see a distinct pattern in the baby's flesh, a cruciate central feature with a loop at one end like an Egyptian ankh or Maltese cross. The figure was outlined by a crenulated rectangular border. I handed the glass to Ryan and looked a question at LaManche.

"Temperance, this is clearly a patterned injury of some kind. The tissue must be preserved. Dr. Bergeron is not here today, so I would appreciate your assistance."

Marc Bergeron, odontologist to the LML, had developed a technique for lifting and fixing injuries in soft tissue. Initially he'd devised it to remove bite marks from the bodies of victims of violent sexual assault. The method had also proved useful for excising and preserving tattoos and patterned injuries on skin. I'd seen Marc do it in hundreds of cases, had assisted him in several.

I got Bergeron's kit from a cabinet in the first autopsy room, returned to room two, and spread the equipment on a stainless steel cart. By the time I'd gloved, the photographer had finished and LaManche was ready. He nodded that I should go ahead. Ryan and Bertrand watched.

I measured five scoops of pink powder from a plastic bottle and placed it in a glass vial, then added 20 cc's of a clear liquid monomer. I stirred and, within a minute, the mixture thickened until it resembled pink modeling clay. I formed the dough into a ring, and placed it on the tiny chest, completely encircling the bruise. The acrylic felt hot as I patted it into place.

To accelerate the hardening process, I placed a wet cloth over the ring, then waited. In less than ten minutes the acrylic had cooled. I reached for a tube and began squeezing a clear liquid around the edges of the ring.

"What's that?" asked Ryan.

"Cyanoacrylate."

"Smells like Krazy Glue."

"It is."

When I thought the glue was dry, I tested by tugging gently on the ring. A few more dabs, more waiting, and the ring held fast. I marked it with the date, and case and morgue numbers, and indicated top, bottom, right, and left relative to the baby's chest.

"It's ready," I said, and stepped back.

LaManche used a scalpel to dissect free the skin outside the acrylic doughnut, cutting deep enough to include the underlying fatty tissue. When the ring finally came free, it held the bruised skin tightly in place, like a miniature painting stretched on a circular pink frame. LaManche slid the specimen into the jar of clear liquid that I held ready.

"What's that?" Ryan again.

"A solution of ten percent buffered formalin. In ten to twelve hours the tissue will be fixed. The ring will ensure that there's no distortion, so later, if we get a weapon, we'll be able to compare it to the wound to see if the patterns match. And, of course, we'll have the photos."

"Why not just use the photos?"

"With this we can do transillumination if we have to."

"Transillumination?"

I wasn't really in the mood for a science seminar, so I kept it simple. "You can shine a light up through the tissue and see what's going on under the skin. It often brings out details not visible on the surface."

"What do you think made it?" Bertrand.

"I don't know," I said, sealing the jar and handing it to Lisa.

As I was turning away I felt a tremendous sadness, and couldn't resist lifting the tiny hand. It felt soft and cold in my fingers. I rotated the blocks circling the wrist. M-A-T-H-I-A-S.

I'm so sorry, Mathias.

I looked up to see LaManche gazing at me. His eyes seemed to mirror the despair I was feeling. I stepped back, and he began the internal exam. He would excise and send upstairs the ends of all bones cut by the killer, but I wasn't optimistic. Though I'd never looked for tool marks on a victim this young, I suspected that an infant's ribs would be too tiny to retain much detail.

I stripped off my gloves and turned to Ryan as Lisa made a Y-shaped incision on the infant's chest.

"Are the scene photos here?"

"Just the backups."

92

He handed me a large brown envelope containing a set of Polaroids. I took them to the corner desk.

The first showed the largest of the outbuildings at the chalet in St-Jovite. The style was that of the main house: Alpine Tacky. The next photo was taken inside, shot from the top of a staircase looking downward. The passage was dark and narrow, with walls on both sides, wooden handrails on the walls, and junk heaped at both ends of each step.

There were several pictures of a basement taken from different angles. The room was dim, the only light coming from small rectangular windows close to the ceiling. Linoleum floor. Knotty pine walls. Washtubs. A hot water heater. More junk.

Several photos zoomed in on the water heater, then on the space between it and the wall. The niche was filled with what looked like old carpets and plastic bags. The next pictures showed these objects lined up on the linoleum, first unopened, then laid out to expose their contents.

The adults had been wrapped in large pieces of clear plastic, then rolled in rugs and stacked behind the water heater. Their bodies showed abdominal bloating and skin slippage, but were well preserved.

Ryan came and stood over me.

"The water heater must have been off," I said, handing him the picture. "If it was running the heat would have caused more decomposition."

"We don't think they were using that building."

"What was it?"

He shrugged.

I went back to the Polaroids.

The man and woman were both fully dressed, though barefoot. Their throats had been cut and blood saturated their clothing and stained the plastic shrouds. The man lay with one hand thrown back, and I could see

93

deep slashes across his palm. Defense wounds. He had tried to save himself. Or his family.

Oh, God. I closed my eyes for a moment.

With the infants the packaging had been simpler. They were bundled in plastic, placed in garbage bags, then stuffed in above the adults.

I looked at the little hands, the dimpled knuckles. Bertrand was right. There would be no defense wounds on the babies. Grief and anger merged in my mind.

"I want this son of a bitch." I looked up into Ryan's eyes.

"Yeah."

"I want you to get him, Ryan. I mean it. I want this one. Before we see another baby butchered. What good are we to anyone if we can't stop this?"

The electric blues stared straight back. "We'll get him, Brennan. No doubt about that."

I spent the rest of the day riding the elevator between my office and the autopsies. It would take at least two days to complete them since LaManche was doing all four victims. This is standard procedure in multiple homicides. Using one pathologist provides coherence in a case, and ensures consistency in testimony if it goes to trial.

When I looked in at one o'clock Mathias had been rolled back to the morgue cooler and the autopsy of the second infant was under way. The scene we'd played out in the morning was taking place again. Same actors. Same setting. Same victim. Except this one wore a bracelet that spelled out M-A-L-A-C-H-Y.

By four-thirty Malachy's belly had been closed, his tiny skullcap replaced, his face repositioned. Save for the Y-incisions and the mutilation to their chests, the babies were ready for burial. As yet we had no idea where that would be. Or by whom.

94

Ryan and Bertrand had also spent the day coming and going. Prints had been taken from both boys' feet, but the smudges on hospital birth records are notoriously unreadable, and Ryan was not optimistic about a match.

The bones in the hand and wrist represent over 25 percent of those in the skeleton. An adult has twenty-seven in each hand, an infant far fewer, depending on its age. I'd examined X-rays to see which bones were present and how well they were formed. According to my estimate, Mathias and Malachy were about four months old when they were killed.

This information was released to the media, but, aside from the usual loonies, there was little response. Our best hope lay with the adult bodies in the cooler. We were sure that when the identities of the adults were established, those of the children would follow. For the present the infants remained Baby Malachy and Baby Mathias.

8

On Friday I saw neither Ryan nor Bertrand. LaManche spent all day downstairs with the adult corpses from St-Jovite. I had the babies' ribs soaking in glass vials in the histology lab. Any grooves or striations that might be present would be so tiny I didn't want them damaged by boiling or scraping, and I couldn't risk introducing nicks with a scalpel or scissors, so all I could do at that point was periodically change the water and tease off flesh.

I was glad for the temporary lull in the level of activity, and was using the time to finalize my report on Élisabeth Nicolet, which I'd promised that day. Since I had to return to Charlotte on Monday, I planned to examine the ribs over the weekend. If nothing else came up, I thought I could get everything that was pressing done before Monday. I had not counted on the call I took at ten-thirty.

"I am very, very sorry to call you like this, Dr. Brennan." English, spoken slowly, each word chosen with care.

"Sister Julienne, it's nice to hear from you."

"Please. I apologize for the calls."

"The calls?" I riffled through the pink slips on my

96

desk. I knew she'd phoned back Wednesday, but thought it was a follow-up on our earlier conversation. There were two other slips with her name and number.

"I'm the one who should apologize. I was tied up all day yesterday, and didn't check my messages. I'm sorry."

There was no response.

"I'm writing the report now."

"No, no, it's not that. I mean, yes, of course, that is terribly important. And we are all anxious . . ."

She hesitated, and I could picture her dark brows deepening the perpetual frown she wore. Sister Julienne always looked worried.

"I feel very awkward, but I don't know where to turn. I've prayed, of course, and I know God is listening, but I feel *I* should be doing something. I devote myself to my work, to keeping God's archives, but, well, I have an earthly family too." She was forming her words precisely, shaping them like a baker molding dough.

There was another long pause. I waited her out.

"He does help those who help themselves."

"Yes."

"It's about my niece, Anna. Anna Goyette. She's the one I spoke of on Wednesday."

"Your niece?" I couldn't imagine where this was going.

"She's my sister's child."

"I see."

"She's . . . We're not sure where she is."

"Uh-huh."

"She's normally a very thoughtful child, very reliable, never stays out without calling."

"Uh-huh." I was beginning to get the drift.

Finally, she blurted it out. "Anna didn't come home last night and my sister is frantic. I've told her to pray, of course, but, well . . ." Her voice trailed off.

97

I wasn't sure what to say. This was not where I'd expected the conversation to go.

"Your niece is missing?"

"Yes."

"If you're worried, perhaps you should contact the police."

"My sister called twice. They told her that with someone Anna's age their policy is to wait forty-eight to seventy-two hours."

"How old is your niece?"

"Anna is nineteen."

"She's the one studying at McGill?"

"Yes." Her voice sounded tense enough to saw metal.

"Sister, there's really noth . . ."

I heard her choke back a sob. "I know, I know, and I apologize for bothering you, Dr. Brennan." Her words came out between sharply inhaled breaths, like hiccups. "I know you are busy, I know that, but my sister is hysterical and I just don't know what to tell her. She lost her husband two years ago and now she feels that Anna is all she has. Virginie is calling me every half-hour, insisting I help her find her daughter. I know this is not your job, and I would never call you unless I was desperate. I've prayed, but, oh . . ."

I was startled to hear her burst into tears. They engulfed her speech, obliterating her words. I waited, my mind in a muddle. What should I say?

Then the sobs receded and I heard the sound of tissues pulled from a box, then a nose being blown.

"I . . . I . . . Please forgive me." Her voice was trembling.

Counseling has never been my strong point. Even with those close to me, I feel awkward and inadequate in the face of emotion. I focus on the practical.

"Has Anna taken off before?" Solve the problem.

"I don't think so. But my sister and I don't always . . .

communicate well." She had calmed somewhat and was back to word sifting.

"Has she been having problems at school?"

"I don't think so."

"With friends? A boyfriend, perhaps?"

"I don't know."

"Have you noticed any changes in her behavior lately?"

"What do you mean?"

"Has she changed her eating habits? Is she sleeping more or less than usual? Has she become less communicative?"

"I . . . I'm sorry. Since she's been in university I haven't seen as much of Anna as I used to."

"Is she attending her classes?"

"I'm not sure." Her voice faded on the last word. She sounded completely drained.

"Does Anna get along with her mother?"

There was a very long pause.

"There is the usual tension, but I know Anna loves her mother."

Bingo.

"Sister, your niece might have needed some time to herself. I'm sure if you wait a day or two she'll either show up or call."

"Yes, I suppose you're right, but I feel so helpless for Virginie. She is totally distraught. I can't reason with her, and I thought if I could tell her the police were checking, she might be . . . reassured."

I heard another tissue pull and feared a second round of tears.

"Let me make a call. I'm not sure it will do any good, but I'll give it a try."

She thanked me and we hung up. For a moment I sat there, running through my options. I thought of Ryan, but McGill is located on the island of Montreal.

Communauté Urbaine de Montréal Police. CUM. I took a deep breath and dialed. When the receptionist answered, I made my request.

"Monsieur Charbonneau, *s'il vous plaît.*"

"*Un instant, s'il vous plaît.*"

She came back shortly and said Charbonneau was out for the afternoon.

"Do you want Monsieur Claudel?"

"Yes." Like I wanted anthrax. Damn.

"Claudel," said the next voice.

"Monsieur Claudel. It's Tempe Brennan."

As I listened to empty air, I pictured Claudel's beak nose and parrot face, usually set with disapproval of me. I enjoyed talking to this detective as much as I enjoyed boils. But since I didn't deal with juvenile runaways, I wasn't sure whom else to ask. Claudel and I had worked CUM cases before, and he had come to tolerate me, so I hoped he would at least tell me where to turn.

"*Oui?*"

"Monsieur Claudel, I have a rather odd request. I realize this isn't exactly you—"

"What is it, Dr. Brennan?" Abrupt. Claudel was one of the few who could make the French language sound cold. Just the facts, ma'am.

"I've just had a call from a woman who is concerned about her niece. The girl is a student at McGill and she didn't return home last night. I was wond—"

"They should fill out a missing person report."

"The mother was told that nothing could be done for forty-eight to seventy-two hours."

"Age?"

"Nineteen."

"Name."

"Anna Goyette."

"Does she live on campus?"

100

"I don't know. It didn't sound like it. I think she lives with the mother."

"Did she attend her classes yesterday?"

"I don't know."

"Where was she last seen?"

"I don't know."

Another pause. Then,

"There is a great deal you do not know, it appears. This may not be a CUM case, and, at this point, it is definitely not a homicide matter." I could picture him tapping something against something, his face pinched with impatience.

"Yes. I would simply like to know who I could contact," I spat. He was making me feel unprepared, which was making me irritable. And screwing up my grammar. As usual, Claudel did not bring out the best in me, particularly when his criticism of my methodology was in part legitimate.

"Try missing persons."

I listened to a dial tone.

I was still fuming when the phone rang again.

"Dr. Brennan," I barked.

"Is this a bad time?" The soft, Southern English was a sharp contrast to Claudel's clipped, nasal French.

"Dr. Jeannotte?"

"Yes. Please call me Daisy."

"Please excuse me, Daisy. I – it's been a rough couple of days. What can I do for you?"

"Well, I have found some interesting Nicolet materials for you. I hate to send them by courier, since some items are quite old and probably valuable. Would you like to drop by and pick them up?"

I looked at my watch. It was after eleven. Hell, why not. Maybe while on campus I might ask about Anna. At least I'd have something to tell Sister Julienne.

101

"I could come by about noon. Would that be convenient?"

"That would be just fine."

Again, I arrived early. Again, the door was open and the office empty except for a young woman shelving journals. I wondered if it was the same stack Jeannotte's assistant had been clearing on Wednesday.

"Hi. I'm looking for Dr. Jeannotte."

The woman turned and her large loop earrings swung and caught the light. She was tall, perhaps six feet, with dark hair shaved close to her head.

"She's gone downstairs for a minute. Do you have an appointment?"

"I'm a bit early. No problem."

The office was just as warm and just as cluttered as on my first visit. I took off my jacket and stuffed my mittens into the pocket. The woman indicated a wooden hall tree, and I hung the jacket there. She watched me wordlessly.

"She does have a lot of journals," I said, indicating the stack on the desk.

"I think I spend my life sorting these things." She reached up and slid a journal onto a shelf above her head.

"Helps to be tall, I guess."

"Helps with some things."

"I met Dr. Jeannotte's TA on Wednesday. She was reshelving, too."

"Um-hum." The young woman picked up another journal and examined its spine.

"I'm Dr. Brennan," I offered.

She slipped the journal into a row at eye level.

"And you are . . .?" I coaxed.

"Sandy O'Reilly," she said without turning. I wondered if my height remark had offended her.

102

"Nice to meet you, Sandy. After I left on Wednesday I realized I'd never asked the other assistant her name."

She shrugged. "I'm sure Anna didn't care."

The name hit me like a spitball. I couldn't be that lucky.

"Anna?" I asked. "Anna Goyette?"

"Yeah." Finally she turned to face me. "Know her?"

"No, not really. A student by that name is related to an acquaintance of mine, and I wondered if it might be the same person. Is she here today?"

"No. I think she's sick. That's why I'm working. I'm not scheduled on Fridays, but Anna couldn't, so Dr. Jeannotte asked me to fill in today."

"She's sick?"

"Yeah, I guess. Actually, I don't know. All I know is she's out again. It's O.K. I can use the money."

"Again?"

"Well, yeah. She misses quite a bit. I usually fill in. The extra money's nice, but it isn't helping my thesis get written." She gave a short laugh, but I could detect annoyance in her voice.

"Does Anna have health problems?"

Sandy tilted her head and looked at me. "Why are you so interested in Anna?"

"I'm not really. I'm here to pick up some research that Dr. Jeannotte has for me. But I am a friend of Anna's aunt, and I know that her family is worried because they haven't seen her since yesterday morning."

She shook her head and reached for another journal. "They ought to worry about Anna. She is one weird cookie."

"Weird?"

She shelved the journal then turned to face me. Her eyes rested on mine for a long time, assessing.

"You're a friend of the family?"

103

"Yes." Sort of.

"You're not an investigator or reporter or something?"

"I'm an anthropologist." True, though not fully accurate. But an image of Margaret Mead or Jane Goodall might be more reassuring. "I'm only asking because Anna's aunt called me this morning. Then when it developed that we were talking about the same person . . ."

Sandy crossed the office and checked the corridor, then leaned against the wall just inside the door. It was obvious that her height did not embarrass her. She held her head high and moved with long, languid strides.

"I don't want to say anything that will cost Anna her job. Or me mine. Please don't tell anyone where this came from, particularly Dr. Jeannotte. She would not like me talking about one of her students."

"You have my word."

She took a deep breath. "I think Anna's really messed up and needs help. And it's not just because I have to cover for her. Anna and I were friends, or at least we hung out a lot last year. Then she changed. Zoned out. I've been thinking of calling her mother for a while now. Someone should know."

She swallowed and shifted weight.

"Anna spends half her time over at the counseling center because she's so unhappy. She goes missing for days on end, and when she is around she doesn't seem to have any life, just hangs here all the time. And she always looks edgy, like she's ready to jump off a bridge."

She stopped, her eyes riveted on mine, deciding. Then,

"A friend told me Anna is involved in something."

"Yes?"

"I have absolutely no idea if this is true, or if I should even say it. It's not my style to pass on gossip, but if

104

Anna is in trouble, I'd never forgive myself for keeping quiet."

I waited.

"And if it is true she could be at risk."

"What is it you think Anna is involved in?"

"This sounds so bizarre." She shook her head and the earrings tapped her jaw. "I mean, you hear about these things, but it's never someone you know."

She swallowed again and glanced over her shoulder out the door.

"My friend told me that Anna joined a cult. A group of Satan worshipers. I don't know if . . ."

On hearing the creak of floorboards, Sandy crossed to the far end of the office and picked up several journals. She was busy shelving when Daisy Jeannotte appeared in the doorway.

9

"I am so sorry," Daisy said, smiling warmly. "I seem to always be keeping you waiting. Have you and Sandy introduced yourselves?" Her hair was in the same impeccable bun.

"Yes, we have. We've been talking about the joys of shelving."

"I do ask them to do a lot of that. Copying and shelving. Very tedious, I know. But a great deal of real research is just plain tedious. My students and helpers are very patient with me."

She turned her smile on Sandy, who gave her own brief version and returned to the journals. I was struck by how differently Jeannotte interacted with this student compared with what I'd seen with Anna.

"Now, then, let me show you what I've found. I think you'll like it." She gestured toward the sofa.

When we'd settled she lifted a stack of materials from a small brass table to her right, and looked down at a two-page printout. Her part was a stark white line bisecting the crown of her head.

"These are titles of books about Quebec during the nineteenth century. I'm sure you'll find mention of the Nicolet family in many of them."

She gave it to me and I glanced down the list, but my mind was not on Élisabeth Nicolet.

"And this book is about the smallpox epidemic of 1885. It may contain some mention of Élisabeth or her work. If nothing else, it will give you a sense of the times and the enormity of suffering in Montreal in those days."

The volume was new and in perfect condition, as though no one had ever read it. I flipped a few pages, seeing nothing. What had Sandy been about to say?

"But I think you're especially going to like these." She handed me what looked like three old ledgers, then leaned back, the smile still on her lips, but watching me intently.

The covers were gray, with deep burgundy binding and trim. Gingerly, I opened the top one and turned several pages. It smelled musty, like something kept for years in a basement or attic. It was not a ledger, but a diary, handwritten in a bold, clear script. I glanced at the first entry: January 1, 1844. I flipped to the last: December 23, 1846.

"They are written by Louis-Philippe Bélanger, Élisabeth's uncle. It is known that he was a prodigious journal keeper, so, on a hunch, I checked with our rare documents section. Sure enough, McGill owns part of the collection. I don't know where the rest of the journals are, or if they've even survived, but I could try to find out. I had to pledge my soul to get these." She laughed. "I borrowed the ones that date to the period of Élisabeth's birth and early infancy."

"This is too good to be true," I said, momentarily forgetting Anna Goyette. "I don't know what to say."

"Say you will take exceedingly good care of them."

"May I actually take them with me?"

"Yes. I trust you. I'm sure you appreciate their value and will treat them accordingly."

"Daisy, I'm overwhelmed. This is more than I'd hoped for."

She raised a hand in a gesture of dismissal, then refolded it quietly in her lap. For a moment neither of us spoke. I couldn't wait to get out of there and into the journals. Then I remembered Sister Julienne's niece. And Sandy's words.

"Daisy, I wonder if I could ask you something about Anna Goyette."

"Yes." She was still smiling, but her eyes grew wary.

"As you know I've been working with Sister Julienne, who is Anna's aunt."

"I didn't know they were kin."

"Yes. Sister Julienne called to tell me that Anna hasn't been home since yesterday morning, and her mother is very worried."

Throughout our conversation I'd been aware of Sandy's movements as she sorted journals and placed them on shelves. The far end of the office now grew very still. Jeannotte noticed, too.

"Sandy, you must be quite tired. You go on now and take a little break."

"I'm fi—"

"Now, please."

Sandy's eyes met mine as she slipped past us and out the office door. Her expression was unreadable.

"Anna is a very bright young woman," Jeannotte continued. "A bit skittish, but a good intellect. I'm sure she's fine." Very firm.

"Her aunt says it isn't typical for Anna to take off like this."

"Anna probably needed some time to reflect. I know she's had some disagreements with her mama. She's probably gone off for a few days."

Sandy had hinted that Jeannotte was protective of her

students. Was that what I was seeing? Did the professor know something she wasn't telling?

"I suppose I'm more of an alarmist than most. In my work I see so many young women who *aren't* just fine."

Jeannotte looked down at her hands. For a moment she was absolutely still. Then, with the same smile, "Anna Goyette is trying to extract herself from the influence of an impossible home situation. That's all I can say, but I assure you she is well and happy."

Why so certain? Should I? What the hell. I threw it out to see her reaction.

"Daisy, I know this sounds bizarre, but I've heard that Anna is involved in some kind of satanic cult."

The smile disappeared. "I won't even ask where you picked up that information. It doesn't surprise me." She shook her head. "Child molesters. Psychopathic murderers. Depraved messiahs. Doomsday prophets. Satanists. The sinister neighbor who feeds arsenic to trick-or-treaters."

"But those threats do exist." I raised my eyebrows in question.

"Do they? Or are they just urban legends? Memorates for modern times?"

"Memorates?" I wondered how this concerned Anna.

"A term folklorists use to describe how people integrate their fears with popular legends. It's a way to explain bewildering experiences."

My face told her I was still confused.

"Every culture has stories, folk legends that express commonly held anxieties. The fear of bogeymen, outsiders, aliens. The loss of children. When something happens we can't understand, we update old tales. The witch got Hansel and Gretel. The man in the mall got the child who wandered off. It's a way to make confusing experiences seem credible. So people tell stories of abductions by UFO's, Elvis sightings, Halloween poisonings. It always happened to a friend of a friend, a cousin, the boss's son."

"Aren't the Halloween candy poisonings real?"

"A sociologist reviewed newspaper accounts from the 1970s and 1980s and found that during that time only two deaths could be shown to have occurred due to candy tampering, both by family members. Very few other incidents could be documented. But the legend grew because it expresses deep-seated fears: loss of children, fear of the night, fear of strangers."

I let her go on, waiting for the link to Anna.

"You've heard of subversion myths? Anthropologists love to discuss these."

I dug back to a grad school seminar on mythology. "Blame giving. Stories that find scapegoats for complicated problems."

"Exactly. Usually the scapegoats are outsiders – racial, ethnic, or religious groups that make others uneasy. Romans accused early Christians of incest and child sacrifice. Later Christian sects accused one another, then Christians pointed the same finger at Jews. Thousands died because of such beliefs. Think of the witch trials. Or the Holocaust. And it's not just old news. After the student uprising in France in the late sixties, Jewish shopkeepers were accused of kidnapping teenage girls from boutique dressing rooms."

I vaguely remembered that.

"And most recently it's been Turkish and North African immigrants. Several years ago hundreds of French parents claimed children were being abducted, killed, and eviscerated by them, even though virtually no children had been reported missing in France.

"And that myth continues, even here in Montreal, only now there's a new bogeyman practicing ritual child

110

killing." She leaned forward, widening her eyes, and almost hissing the last word. "Satanists."

It was the most animated I'd seen her. Her words caused an image to take shape in my mind. Malachy lying on stainless steel.

"Not surprising, really," she continued. "Preoccupation with demonology always intensifies during periods of social change. And toward the end of millennia. But now the threat is from Satan."

"Hasn't Hollywood created a lot of that?"

"Not intentionally, of course, but it has certainly contributed. Hollywood just wants to make commercially successful films. But that's an age-old question: Does art shape the times or merely reflect them? *Rosemary's Baby, The Omen, The Exorcist.* What do these movies do? They explain social anxieties through the use of demonic imagery. And the public watches and listens."

"But isn't that just part of the increasing interest in mysticism in American culture over the past three decades?"

"Of course. And what's the other trend that has taken place during the last generation?"

I felt as if I was being quizzed. What did all this have to do with Anna? I shook my head.

"The rise in popularity of fundamentalist Christianity. The economy had a lot to do with it, of course. Layoffs. Plant closings. Downsizing. Poverty and economic insecurity are very stressful. But that isn't the only source of worry. People at every economic level are feeling anxiety due to shifting social norms. Relations have changed between men and women, within families, between generations."

She ticked the points off on her fingers.

"The old explanations are breaking down and new ones haven't been established yet. The fundamentalist

111

churches provide solace by presenting simple answers to complex questions."

"Satan."

"Satan. All the world's evil is due to Satan. Teen-agers are being recruited to devil worship. Children are being abducted and killed in demonic rituals. Satanic livestock killing is spreading across the country. The Proctor and Gamble logo contains a secret satanic symbol. Grass roots frustration locks on to these rumors and feeds them so they grow."

"So, are you suggesting that satanic cults don't exist?"

"I'm not saying that. There are a few, what shall we say, high-profile, organized Satanist groups, like that of Anton LaVey."

"The Church of Satan, out in San Francisco."

"Yes. But they're a small, small group. Most 'Sata-nists'" – she hooked both index fingers in the air, placing the term in quotation marks – "are probably just white, middle-class kids playing at devil worship. Occa-sionally these kids get out of line, of course, vandalize churches or cemeteries, or torture animals, but mostly they perform a lot of rituals, and go off on legend trips."

"Legend trips?"

"I believe that term came from the sociologists. Visits to spooky sites, like cemeteries or haunted houses. They light bonfires, tell ghost stories, cast spells, maybe do some vandalism. That's about it. Later, when police find graffiti, an overturned gravestone, a campfire site, maybe a dead cat, they assume the local youth are all in a satanic cult. The press picks it up, the preachers sound the alarm, and another legend takes flight."

She was, as usual, totally composed, but her nostrils dilated and contracted as she spoke, betraying a tension I hadn't seen before. I said nothing.

"I am suggesting that the threat of Satanism is vastly

112

overblown. Another subversion myth, as your colleagues would say."

Without warning her voice rose and sharpened, causing me to jump.

"David! Is that you?"

I hadn't heard a sound.

"Yes, ma'am." Muffled.

A tall figure appeared in the doorway, his face concealed by the hood of his parka and an enormous muffler wrapped around his neck. The hunched form looked vaguely familiar.

"Excuse me a moment."

Jeannotte rose and disappeared through the doorway. I caught little of their conversation, but the man sounded agitated, his voice rising and falling like a whining child's. Jeannotte interrupted him frequently. She spoke in short bursts, her tone as steady as his was volatile. I could make out only one word. "No." She repeated it several times.

Then there was silence. In a moment, Jeannotte returned, but did not sit.

"Students," she said, laughing and shaking her head.

"Let me guess. He needs more time to finish his paper."

"Nothing ever changes." She looked at her watch. "So, Tempe, I hope your visit has been helpful. You will take care of the diaries? They are very dear." I was being dismissed.

"Of course. I'll return them by Monday at the latest." I rose, slid Jeannotte's materials into my briefcase, and collected my jacket and purse.

She smiled me out of the room.

In winter, the Montreal sky displays mainly gray tones, shifting from dove, to iron, to lead, to zinc. When I

113

stepped out of Birks Hall moist clouds had turned the day a dull pewter.

I slung my purse and briefcase over my shoulder, stuffed my fists into my pockets, and turned downhill into a raw, damp wind. Before I'd taken twenty steps tears filled my eyes, making it hard to see. As I walked, an image of Fripp Island flashed across my mind. Palmetto palms. Sea oats. Sunlight glinting on the marsh.

Knock it off, Brennan. March is windy and cold in many parts of the planet. Stop using the Carolinas as a baseline against which to measure the weather of the world. It could be worse. It could be snowing. With that, the first fat flake struck my cheek.

As I opened the car door, I looked up to see a tall young man staring at me from the far side of the street. I recognized the parka and muffler. The hunched form was that of David, Jeannotte's unhappy visitor.

Our gazes locked for a moment, and the raw anger in his eyes startled me. Then, without a word, the student turned and hurried off down the block. Unnerved, I climbed into the car and locked the doors, thankful he was Jeannotte's problem and not mine.

On the drive back to the lab my mind went through its usual paces, rehashing the immediate, and worrying about things undone. Where was Anna? Should Sandy's concerns about a cult be seriously considered? Was Jeannotte right? Were satanic cults little more than youth clubs? Why had I not asked Jeannotte to elaborate on her remark that Anna was safe? Our conversation had gotten so fascinating I'd been side-tracked from asking further about Anna. Was that deliberate? Was Jeannotte purposefully concealing something? If so, what and why? Was the professor merely shielding her student from outsiders prying into a personal matter? What was Anna's "impossible home situation"? Why did David's behavior seem so sinister?

How would I ever get through the ledgers by Monday? My flight was at 5 P.M. Could I finish the Nicolet report today, do those for the babies tomorrow, and work through the ledgers on Sunday? No wonder I had no social life.

By the time I got to rue Parthenais, steadily falling snow was sticking to the street. I found a parking spot just outside the door, and said a prayer that the car wouldn't be plowed in when I came back.

The air in the lobby felt steamy and smelled of wet wool. I stomped my boots, contributing to the slick, shallow pool of melted snow spreading across the floor, and punched for an elevator. On the ride up I tried to clean streaked mascara from my lower lids.

There were two pink message slips on my desk. Sister Julienne had called. No doubt she wanted reports on Anna and Élisabeth. I wasn't ready on either. Next. Ryan.

I dialed and he answered.

"Long lunch."

I checked my watch. One forty-five.

"I'm paid by the hour. What's up?"

"We've finally tracked down the owner of the house in St-Jovite. Guy's name is Jacques Guillion. He's from Quebec City, but moved to Belgium years ago. His whereabouts remain unknown, but a Belgian neighbor says Guillion has been renting the St-Jovite place to an old lady named Patrice Simonnet. She thinks the tenant is Belgian, but isn't sure. She says Guillion also provides the tenant with cars. We're running a check."

"Pretty well-informed neighbor."

"Apparently they were close."

"The burned body from the basement could be Simonnet."

"Could be."

"We got good dental X-rays during the post. Bergeron has them."

"We've given the name to the RCMP. They're working with Interpol. If she's Belgian, they'll track her."

"What about the other two bodies in the main house and the two adults with the babies?"

"We're working on it."

We both thought for a moment.

"Pretty big place for one old lady."

"Looks like she wasn't all that alone."

I spent the next two hours in the histology lab teasing the last of the tissue from the babies' ribs and examining them under the microscope. As I'd feared, there were no unique nicks or patterns in the bone. There was nothing I could say except that the killer had used a very sharp knife with a blade which was not serrated. Bad for the investigation. Good for me. The report would be brief.

I'd just returned to my office when Ryan called back.

"How about a beer?" he asked.

"I don't keep beer in my office, Ryan. If I did, I'd drink it."

"You don't drink."

"Then why are you asking me for beer?"

"I'm asking if you'd like one. Could be green."

"What?"

"Aren't you Irish, Brennan?"

I glanced at my wall calendar. March 17. The anniversary of some of my best performances. I didn't want to remember.

"Can't do it anymore, Ryan."

"It's a generic way of saying 'Let's take a break.'"

"Are you asking me for a date?"

"Yes."

"With you?"

"No, with my parish priest."

"Wow. Does he cheat on his vows?"

"Brennan, do you want to meet me for a beverage this evening? Alcohol-free?"

"Ryan, I—"

"It's St. Paddy's Day. It's Friday night and snowing like a sonofabitch. Got a better offer?"

I didn't. In fact, I had no other offers. But Ryan and I often investigated the same cases, and I'd always had a policy of keeping work and home separate.

Always. Right. I'd been separated and living on my own less than two years of my adult life. And they hadn't been banner ones for male companionship.

"I don't think it's a good idea."

There was a pause. Then,

"We got a break on Simonnet. She popped right up on the Interpol search. Born in Brussels, lived there until two years ago. Still pays taxes on a piece of property in the countryside. Loyal old gal, went to the same dentist her whole life. The guy's been in practice since the Stone Age, keeps everything. They're faxing the records. If it looks like a match, we'll get the originals."

"When was she born?"

I heard a paper flip.

"Nineteen-eighteen."

"That fits. Family?"

"We're checking."

"Why did she leave Belgium?"

"Maybe she needed a change of scenery. Look, champ, if you decide *you* do, I'll be at Hurley's after nine. If there's a line, use my name."

I sat awhile, thinking about why I'd said no. Pete and I had reached an accord. We still loved each other, but

117

couldn't live together. Separated, we were once again able to be friends. Our relationship hadn't been as good in years. Pete was dating, I was free to do the same. Oh, God. Dating. The word raised images of acne and braces.

To be honest, I found Andrew Ryan extremely attractive. No zits or orthodontics. A definite plus. And technically we didn't work together. But I also found him extremely annoying. And unpredictable. No. Ryan is trouble.

I was finishing my report on Malachy and Mathias when the phone rang again. I smiled. O.K., Ryan. You win.

The voice of a security guard told me I had a visitor in the downstairs lobby. I looked at my watch. Four-twenty. Who would be coming this late? I didn't remember making any appointments.

I asked for the name. When he told me, my heart sank.

"Oh no." I couldn't help myself.

"*Est-ce qu'il y a un problème?*"

"*Non. Pas de problème.*" I told him I'd be right down.

No problem? Who was I kidding?

I said it again in the elevator.

Oh no.

10

"What are you doing here?"

"Well, you could look glad to see me, big sister."

"I—of course I'm glad to see you, Harry. I'm just surprised." I couldn't have been more astounded if the guard had announced Teddy Roosevelt.

She snorted. "That's about as heartfelt as grits."

My sister sat in the lobby of the SQ building surrounded by shopping bags from Nieman Marcus and canvas packs of varying shapes and sizes. She wore red cowboy boots engraved with black and white loops and swirls and a matching leather jacket with fringe. When she stood I could see jeans tight enough to cut off blood flow. We all could.

Harry hugged me, fully aware of but completely unself-conscious about her effect on others. Especially the others with Y chromosomes.

"Whew, it is bad-ass cold out there! I'm iced enough to freeze tequila." She hunched her shoulders and wrapped her arms around her rib cage.

"Yes." I didn't get the analogy.

"My flight was supposed to touch down at noon, but the pissant snow held us up. Oh well, here I am, big sister."

She dropped her shoulders and held out her arms, causing the jacket fringe to shimmy. Harry looked so out of place it was surreal. Amarillo comes to the tundra.

"O.K. Great. What a surprise. Well. I—What brings you to Montreal?"

"I'll tell you all about it. It's awesome. When I heard about it I just couldn't believe my ears. I mean, right here in Montreal and all."

"What is 'it', Harry?"

"The seminar I'd done. I told you about it, Tempe, when I called last weekend. I did it. I signed up for that training course in Houston and now I'm mainlinin' this stuff. I have never been so pumped. I cruised the first level. I mean cruised it. Some people take years to realize their own reality and I just whupped that puppy in a few weeks. I mean I am learning some powerful therapeutic strategies, and I am taking hold of my life. So when they invited me to this level-two workshop, and right here where my big sister lives, well, I packed my bags and pointed my nose north."

Harry beamed at me with clear, blue eyes surrounded by gobs of mascara.

"You're here for a workshop?"

"Exactamundo. All expenses paid. Well, almost all."

"I want to hear all about it," I said, hoping the course was short. I was unsure if Quebec Province and Harry could survive each other.

"This shit is awesome," she said, rephrasing her initial assessment, but adding little additional information.

"Let's go upstairs and I'll wrap up. Or would you rather wait here?"

"Hell, no. I want to see where the great cadaver doctor works. Lead on."

120

"You'll have to submit a photo ID to get a visitor's pass," I said, indicating the guard at the security desk.

He was observing the scene, a half smile on his face, and spoke before either of us could make a move.

"*Vôtre sœur?*" he bellowed across the lobby, exchanging looks with the other guards.

I nodded. Obviously everyone now knew that Harry was my sister, and found it terribly amusing.

The guard gave a sweeping gesture toward the elevators.

"*Merci,*" I mumbled, and shot him a withering glance.

"Mercy," Harry drawled, giving each guard a radiant smile.

We gathered her bundles and rode to the fifth floor, where I stacked everything in the hall outside my office. No way to fit it inside. The quantity of her gear raised apprehension as to the likely length of her stay.

"Hell, this office looks like a twister just traveled through here." Though she was only five feet nine and thin as a fashion model, Harry seemed to fill the small space.

"It's a little messy right now. Let me shut down the computer and collect a few things. Then we'll head out."

"Take your time, I'm in no hurry. I'll just chat with your friends." She was looking up at a row of skulls, her head tipped back so that the ends of her hair brushed the bottom fringe on her jacket. It looked blonder than I remembered it.

"Howdy," she said to the first, "decided to quit while you're a head, did you?"

I couldn't help but smile. Her cranial friend did not. While Harry worked her way along the shelf, I logged off and gathered the ledgers and books from Daisy

121

Jeannotte. I planned to be back first thing in the morning, so I didn't pack my unfinished reports.

"So, what's new with you?" Harry spoke to the fourth skull. "Not talking? Oh, you're so sexy when you're moody."

"She's always moody." Andrew Ryan stood in the doorway.

Harry turned and looked the detective up and down. Slowly. Then blue eyes met blue eyes.

"What the hey?"

My sister's smile for the security guards was nothing compared with the one she now beamed at Ryan. In that moment I knew calamity was predestined.

"We were just leaving," I said, zipping my computer case.

"Well?"

"Well what, Ryan?"

"Out-of-town company?"

"A good detective always notices the obvious."

"Harriet Lamour," said my sister, sticking out her hand. "I'm Tempe's younger sister." As usual, she emphasized the birth order.

"Reckon you're not from around these parts," Ryan drawled. The fringe went to town as they shook hands.

"Lamour?" I asked, incredulous.

"Houston. That's in Texas. Ever been there?"

"Lamour?" I repeated. "What happened to Crone?"

"Once or twice. Mighty pretty country." Ryan was still doing Brett Maverick.

"Or Dawood?"

That got her attention.

"Now why would I ever go back to using that retard's name? Do you *remember* Esteban? The only human being ever fired for being too dumb to stock the 7-Eleven?"

122

Esteban Dawood had been her third husband. I couldn't summon an image of his face.

"Are you and Striker divorced already?"

"No. But I have dumped his ass and scrapped that ridiculous name. Crone? What was I thinking? Who'd ever choose a handle like Crone? What kinda name is that for your descendants? Missus Crone? Cousin Crone? Great-granddaddy Crone?"

Ryan joined in. "Not bad if you're a lone Crone."

Harry giggled. "Yeah, but I don't ever want to be an old Crone."

"That's it. We're outta here." I reached for my jacket.

"Bergeron says we've got a positive," said Ryan.

I stopped and looked at him. His face had gone serious.

"Simonnet?"

He nodded.

"Anything on the bodies from upstairs?"

"Bergeron thinks they're probably European, too. Or at least they got drilled and filled over there. Something about their dental work. We had Interpol run a search in Belgium, because of the Simonnet link, but they came up empty. The old lady had no family, so that's a dead end. The RCMP got no hits in Canada. Same for NCIC. No matches in the States."

"Rohypnol's pretty hard to get here, and those two were loaded. A European connection might explain that."

"Might."

"LaManche says the bodies in the outbuilding were negative for drugs and alcohol. Simonnet was too badly burned to test."

Ryan knew this. I was thinking aloud.

"Jesus, Ryan, it's been a week and we still have no idea who these people are."

123

"Yip." He smiled at Harry, who was listening closely. Their flirting was starting to annoy me.

"You haven't found any leads in the house?"

"You may have heard about a little altercation on the West Island Tuesday? The Rock Machine blew the lights out on two Hell's Angels. The Angels returned fire and left one of the Machine dead and three others bleeding bad. So I've been otherwise engaged."

"Patrice Simonnet took a bullet in the head."

"The biker boys also took out a twelve-year-old kid who happened to be on his way to hockey practice."

"Oh, God. Look, I'm not suggesting you're dragging your feet, but surely someone must miss these people. We're talking about a whole damn family. Plus two others. There must be *something* in that house that provides a clue."

"Recovery took forty-seven cartons of crap out of there. We're sifting through it, but so far zippo. No letters. No checks. No photos. No shopping lists. No address books. The utility and phone bills are paid by Simonnet. Heating oil is delivered once a year, she pays in advance. We can't find anyone who's been into the place since Simonnet's been renting."

"What about property taxes?"

"Guillion. Pays by an official check drawn on Citicorp in New York."

"Were any weapons recovered?" I asked.

"Nope."

"Pretty much rules out suicide."

"Yeah. And it isn't likely Granny slashed the family."

"Did you run a history on the address?"

"It was negative. The police were never called there."

"Have you gotten the phone records?"

"They're coming."

"What about the cars? Weren't they registered?"

"Both to Guillion. At the St-Jovite address. He also pays the insurance by official check."

"Does Simonnet have a driver's license?"

"Yeah, Belgian. Clean record."

"Health insurance card?"

"No."

"Anything else?"

"Nothing comes up."

"Who serviced the cars?"

"Apparently Simonnet took them to a station in town. The description matches. She paid cash."

"And the house? A woman that age couldn't do her own repairs."

"Obviously there were other people living there. The neighbors say the couple with the babies had been around for several months. They'd seen other cars pull in, sometimes in large numbers."

"Maybe she took in boarders?"

We both turned to Harry.

"You know. Maybe she rented out rooms."

Ryan and I let her go on.

"You could check the newspapers for ads. Or church bulletins."

"She doesn't seem to have been a churchgoer."

"Maybe she ran a drug ring. With this dude Guillion. That's why she got killed. That's why there are no records or anything." Her eyes were round with excitement. She was getting into it. "Maybe she was hiding out there."

"Who is this Guillion?" I asked.

"He's got no police record here or there. The Belgian cops are checking him out. The guy kept to himself, so nobody knows much about him."

"Like the old lady."

Ryan and I stared at her. Good point, Harry.

A phone shrilled, indicating the lines had been

switched to the night service. Ryan glanced at his watch.

"Well, I hope I'll see y'all this evening." Maverick was back.

"Probably not. I've got to get through this Nicolet report."

Harry opened her mouth, but seeing my look, closed it.

"Thanks anyway, Ryan."

"*Enchanté*," he said to Harry, then turned and headed up the hall.

"That's one good-looking cowboy."

"Don't train your scope on him, Harry. His little black book has more entries than the Omaha white pages."

"Just lookin', darlin'. That's still free."

Though it was only five, we walked out into deep dusk. Headlights and streetlamps shone through falling snow. I unlocked and started the car, then spent several minutes cleaning the windows and windshield while Harry scanned the radio choices. When I got in, my usual Vermont Public Radio had been replaced by a local rock station.

"That is so cool." Harry voiced her approval of Mitsou.

"She's a québécoise," I said, shifting between drive and reverse to rock the Mazda out of the snow rut. "Been big here for years."

"I mean, rock and roll in French. That is too cool."

"Yeah." The front wheels caught pavement, and I joined the flow of traffic.

Harry listened to the lyrics as we wound our way west toward Centre-Ville.

"Is she singing about a cowboy? *Mon* cowboy?"

"Yes," I said, turning onto Viger. "I think she likes the guy."

We lost Mitsou when we entered the Ville-Marie Tunnel.

Ten minutes later I unlocked the door to my condo. I showed Harry the extra bedroom and went to the kitchen to check my food stock. Since I'd planned to hit the Atwater Market over the weekend, there wasn't much. When Harry joined me I was rummaging in the tiny closet I call a pantry.

"I'm taking you out to dinner, Tempe."

"You are?"

"Actually, Inner Life Empowerment is taking you to dinner. I told you. They're paying all my expenses. Well, at least up to twenty dollars for dinner tonight. Howie's Diners Club card will pick up the rest."

Howie was her second husband, and probably the source of whatever had been in the Nieman Marcus bags.

"Why is Inner Life whatever paying for this trip?"

"Because I did so well. Actually, it's a special deal." She gave an exaggerated wink, opening her mouth and scrunching the right side of her face. "They don't usually do that, but they really want me to go on with this."

"Well, if you're sure. What do you feel like?"

"Action!"

"I meant food."

"Anything but barbecue."

I thought a minute. "Indian?"

"Shawnee or Paiute?"

Harry hooted. She always loved her own jokes.

"The Etoile des Indes is just a few blocks from here. They make a great khorma."

"Yippee. I don't think I've ever eaten an Indian. And

127

I know I've never eaten a French Indian. Anyway, I don't think you can eat karma."

I could only shake my head.

"I look like forty miles of bad road," said Harry, singling out several long strands for inspection. "I'm going to do a few repairs."

I went to my bedroom, changed into jeans, then got pen and paper and propped myself against the pillows on my bed. I opened the first ledger and noted the date of the earliest entry: January 1, 1844. Selecting one of the library books, I flipped to the section on Elisabeth Nicolet and checked the day of her birth. January 18, 1846. Her uncle had begun this volume two years before she was born.

Though Louis-Philippe Bélanger wrote with a strong hand, time had faded his entries. The ink was a dull brown, and at places the words were too blurry to read. In addition, the French was antiquated and replete with unfamiliar terms. After thirty minutes my head was pounding and I'd taken few notes.

I lay back and closed my eyes. I could still hear water running in the bathroom. I was tired and discouraged and pessimistic. I'd never get through this in two days. I'd do better to spend a few hours at the copy machine, then work through the ledgers at my leisure. Jeannotte hadn't said anything about *not* copying the material. And it was probably safer for the originals, I reasoned.

And I didn't have to find the answer right away. After all, my report didn't require an explanation. I saw what I saw in the bones. I would report my findings, and let the good sisters come to me with theorizations. Or questions.

Perhaps they wouldn't understand. Perhaps they wouldn't believe me. They probably wouldn't welcome the news. Or would they? Would it affect their application to the Vatican? I couldn't help that. I was certain I

128

was right about Élisabeth. I just couldn't imagine what
it meant.

11

Two hours later Harry shook me awake. She had finished bathing, blow drying, and whatever else the repair process required. We bundled up and headed out, winding our way to rue Ste-Catherine. The snow had stopped, but a layer blanketed everything, slightly muffling the city clamor. Signs, trees, mailboxes, and parked cars wore fluffy caps of white.

The restaurant was not crowded and we were seated immediately. When we'd ordered, I asked about her workshop.

"It's awesome. I've learned whole new ways of thinking and being. I don't mean some kinda Eastern mysticism cow flop. And I'm not talking about potions or crystals or that astral projection shit. I mean I am learning how to take control of my life."

"How?"

"How?"

"How."

"I'm learning self-identity, I'm undergoing empowerment through spiritual awakening. I'm gaining internal peace through holistic health and healing."

"Spiritual awakening?"

"Now don't get me wrong, Tempe. This isn't some

130

rebirthing thing like the damn evangelists preach down home. There's none of that repenting, and making a joyful noise unto the Lord, and the righteous walking through flames and all."

"How is it different?"

"That all has to do with damnation, and guilt, and accepting your lot as a sinner, and turning yourself over to the Lord so He'll take care of you. I didn't buy that agenda from the nuns, and thirty-eight years of living haven't changed my mind."

Harry and I had spent our early days in Catholic schools.

"This has to do with me taking care of myself." She stabbed a manicured finger at her chest.

"How?"

"Tempe, are you trying to ridicule me?"

"No. I'd like to know how one does this."

"It's a matter of interpreting your own mind and body, then purifying yourself."

"Harry, you're just giving me jargon. How do you do this?"

"Well, you eat right and you breathe right and – did you notice that I passed up the beer? That's part of purifying."

"Did you pay a lot of money for this seminar?"

"I told you. They waived my fees and they flat out gave me the plane ticket."

"What about in Houston?"

"Well, yeah, of course I paid some fees. They have to charge something. These are very prominent people."

Just then our food arrived. I'd ordered lamb khorma. Harry had vegetable curry and rice.

"See?" She pointed to her dish. "No more dead carcasses for me. I am getting clear."

"Where did you find this course?"

"At the North Harris County Community College."

131

That sounded legit.

"When do you start here?"

"Tomorrow. The seminar goes for five days. I'll tell you all about it, really I will. I'll come home every night and fill you in on exactly what we did. It's O.K. if I stay with you, isn't it?"

"Of course. I truly am glad to see you, Harry. And I'm very curious about what you're doing. But I'm leaving for Charlotte on Monday." I rummaged in the back pocket of my purse for the emergency keys I keep there, and handed them to her. "You're more than welcome to stay as long as you need the place."

"No wild parties," she said, leaning forward and pointing a stern finger at me. "I have a lady watching the house."

"Yes, Mom," I answered. The fictitious house watcher was perhaps our oldest family joke.

She gave me a brilliant Harry smile and slid the keys into her jeans pocket.

"Thanks. Now, enough about me, let me tell you what Kit's up to."

For the next half-hour we talked about my nephew's latest scheme. Christopher "Kit" Howard had resulted from her second marriage. He'd just turned eighteen, and come into a sizable sum of money from his father. Kit had bought, and was renovating, a forty-eight-foot sailboat. Harry was unsure as to why.

"Tell me again how Howie got his name?" I knew the story, but loved to hear her tell it.

"Howie's mama took off right after he was born, and his daddy had left well before then. She left Howie on the steps of an orphanage in Basic, Texas, with a note pinned to his blanket. It said she'd be back, and that the baby's name was Howard. The folks at the orphanage weren't sure if Mama meant his first name or his family name, so they took no chances. They baptized him Howard Howard."

132

"What's Howie doing now?"

"Still bringing in gushers and chasing every skirt in West Texas. But he's generous to me and Kit."

When we'd finished, the waiter cleared the dishes and I ordered coffee. Harry passed, because stimulants interfered with her purification process.

We sat in silence awhile, then,

"So where's this cowboy want you to meet him?"

I stopped stirring, and my mind scanned for a connection. Cowboy?

"The cop with the great ass."

"Ryan. He's going to a place called Hurley's. Today is St. Pat—"

"Hell, yes." Her face went serious. "I feel we owe it to our heritage to join in the recognition of a truly great patron saint, in whatever small way we can."

"Harry, I've had a long—"

"Tempe, but for St. Pat snakes would have eaten our ancestors and we would never have been."

"I'm not suggesting—"

"And right now, at a time when the Irish people are in such turmoil—"

"That's not the point and you know it."

"How far is Hurley's from here?"

"A few blocks."

"No-brainer." She spread her hands, palms up. "We go over, we listen to a few songs, we leave. We're not committing to a night at the opera."

"I've heard that before."

"No. I promise. As soon as you're ready, we're outta there. Hey, I've got an early morning, too."

That argument did not impress me. Harry is one of those people who can go days with no sleep.

"Tempe. You've got to make some effort at a social life."

That argument did.

133

"All right. But—"

"Hee. Haw. May the saints preserve ye, ye rascal."

As she waved for the check, I was already feeling the knot below my sternum. There was a time I loved Irish pubs. Pubs of any kind. I didn't want to open that scrapbook, and had no intention of making new entries.

Lighten up, Brennan. What are you afraid of? You've been to Hurley's and you didn't drown yourself in beer. True. So why the trepidation?

Harry chatted amiably as we walked back up Ste-Catherine to Crescent. At nine-thirty the sidewalk crowd was already thick, the couples and cruisers mingling with the last of the shoppers and sightseers. Everyone wore heavy coats with hats and mufflers. People looked thick and bulky, like shrubbery wrapped and tied for winter.

The portion of Crescent above Ste-Catherine is the Anglo "Street of Dreams," lined on both sides with singles bars and trendy restaurants. The Hard Rock Café. Thursdays. Sir Winston Churchill's. In summer, the balconies are filled with spectators sipping drinks and watching the dance of romance below. In winter, the action moves inside.

Few but the Hurley's regulars frequent Crescent below Ste-Catherine. Except on St. Patrick's Day. When we arrived, the line from the entrance stretched up the steps and halfway to the corner.

"Oh hell, Harry. I don't want to stand out here freezing my butt." I didn't want to mention Ryan's offer.

"Don't you know anyone who works here?"

"I'm not a regular."

We joined the queue and stood in silence, shifting our feet to keep warm. The movement reminded me of the nuns at Lac Memphrémagog, which made me think of

134

the unfinished Nicolet report. And the ledgers on my bedside table. And the report on the dead babies. And the classes I had to teach in Charlotte next week. And a paper I planned to present at the Physical Anthropology meeting. I felt my face grow numb from the cold. How did I let Harry talk me into these things?

There is little patron exodus from pubs at 10 P.M. After fifteen minutes we'd advanced about two feet.

"I feel like one of those flash-frozen deserts," said Harry. "Are you sure you don't know someone inside?"

"Ryan did say I could use his name if there was a wait." My egalitarian principles were being sorely tested by encroaching hypothermia.

"Big sister, what are you thinking?" Harry had no qualms about exploiting any available advantage.

She shot up the sidewalk and disappeared into the head of the line. Moments later I saw her at a side door, flanked by a particularly large representative of the Irish National Football Club. They were both gesturing to me. Avoiding eye contact with those remaining in line, I scurried down the steps and slipped inside.

I followed Harry and her guardian through the labyrinth of rooms that make up Hurley's Irish Pub. Every chair, ledge, table, bar stool, and square inch of floor was filled with green-clad patrons. Signs and mirrors advertised Bass, Guinness, and Kilkenny Cream Ale. The place smelled of beer, and the smoke was thick enough to rest your elbows on.

We wormed our way along stone walls, between tables, leather armchairs, and kegs, and eventually around an oak and brass bar. The sound level exceeded that permitted on airport runways.

As we rounded the main bar I could see Ryan seated on a tall wooden stool outside a back room. He had his back to a brick wall, one heel hooked on the stool's bottom rung. The other leg stretched across the seats of two empty stools to his right. His head was framed by a square opening in the brick bordered with carved green wood.

Through the opening I could see a trio playing fiddle, flute, and mandolin. Tables ringed the room's perimeter, and five dancers cavorted in an impossibly small space in the middle. Three women did passable jigs, but the young men just hopped from foot to foot, sloshing beer on anything within a five-foot radius. No one seemed to care.

Harry hugged the footballer, and he melted back into the crowd. I wondered how Ryan had managed to keep two stools free. And why. I couldn't decide whether his confidence annoyed or pleased me.

"Well, bless my heart," said Ryan when he spotted us. "Glad you could make it, podnas. Sit down and rest a spell." He had to yell to be heard.

Ryan hooked his free foot around one of the empty stools, pulled it out, and patted the cushion. Without hesitation Harry slipped off her jacket, draped it across the seat, and settled herself.

"On one condition," I yelled back.

He raised his eyebrows and focused the blues on me.

"Lose the wrangler routine."

"That's about as kind as gravel in peanut butter." Ryan spoke so loud the veins stood out in his neck.

"I mean it, Ryan." I'd never be able to keep up this volume.

"O.K. O.K. Sit down."

I moved toward the end stool.

"And I'll buy you a soda pop, ma'am."

Harry hooted.

I felt my mouth open, then Ryan was up and unzipping my jacket. He laid it on the stool and I sat.

Ryan flagged a waitress, ordered Guinness for himself

136

and a Diet Coke for me. Again, I felt pique. Was I *that* predictable?

He looked at Harry.

"I'll have the same."

"Diet Coke?"

"No. The other."

The waitress disappeared.

"What about the purification?" I bellowed in Harry's ear.

"What?"

"The purification?"

"One beer won't poison me, Tempe. I'm not a zealot."

Since conversation required screaming, I focused on the band. I grew up with Irish music, and the old songs always summon childhood memories. My grandmother's house. Old ladies, brogue, canasta. The roll-away bed. Danny Kaye on the black-and-white TV. Falling asleep to John Gary L.P.s. I suspected these musicians were a bit loud for Gran's taste. Too much amplification.

The lead singer began a ballad about a wild rover. I knew the song and braced myself. At the chorus hands slammed in a five-strike staccato. Bam! Bam! Bam! Bam! Bam! The waitress arrived at the last pounding.

Harry and Ryan chatted, their words lost to the din. I sipped my drink and looked around. High on the wall I could see a row of carved wooden shields, totems of the old-line families. Or were they clans? I looked for one named Brennan, but it was too dark and smoky to read most of them. Crone? No.

The group began a tune Gran would have liked. It was about a young woman who wore her hair tied up with a black velvet band.

I studied a series of photographs in oblong oval frames, close-up portraits of men and women in their

137

Sunday best. When had they been taken – 1890? 1910? These faces looked as grim as those in Birks Hall. Maybe the high collars were uncomfortable.

Two schoolhouse clocks gave the time in Dublin and Montreal. Ten-thirty. I checked my watch. Yip.

Several songs later Harry got my attention by waving both arms. She looked like a referee signaling an incomplete pass. Ryan was holding up his empty mug.

I shook my head. He spoke to Harry, then raised two fingers above his head.

Here we go, I thought.

As the band began a reel, I noticed Ryan pointing in the direction from which we'd entered. Harry slid off her stool and disappeared into the mass of bodies. The price of tight jeans. I didn't want to think about how long her wait would be. Just another gender inequality.

Ryan lifted Harry's jacket, slid onto her stool, and placed the jacket where he'd been sitting. He leaned close and shouted in my ear.

"Are you sure you two have the same mother?"

"And father." Ryan smelled of something like rum and talcum powder.

"How long has she lived in Texas?"

"Since Moses led the Exodus."

"Moses Malone?"

"Nineteen years." I swirled and stared at the ice in my Coke. Ryan had every right to talk to Harry. Conversation was impossible anyway, so why was I pissed off?

"Who is this Anna Goyette?"

"What?"

"Who is Anna Goyette?"

The band stopped in midsentence, and the name boomed out in the relative quiet.

"Jesus, Ryan, why don't you take out an ad?"

"We're a little jumpy tonight. Too much caffeine?" He grinned.

I glared at him.

"It's not good at your age."

"It's not good at any age. How do you know about Anna Goyette?"

The waitress brought the drinks and showed Ryan as many teeth as my sister at her friendliest. He paid and winked at her. Spare me.

"You're not exactly poetry to be with," he said after placing one of the beers on the ledge above Harry's jacket.

"I'll work on it. How do you know about Anna Goyette?"

"I ran into Claudel on this biker thing, and we talked about it."

"Why in the world would you do that?"

"He asked me."

I could never figure out Claudel. He blows me off, then discusses my phone call with Ryan.

"So who is she?"

"Anna is a McGill student. Her aunt asked me to locate her. It's not the Hoffa case."

"Claudel says she's a very interesting young lady."

"What the hell does that mean?"

Harry chose that moment to rejoin us.

"Whoa, little buckaroos. If you have to pee you'd better plan ahead."

She took in the altered seating arrangement and slid onto the stool to Ryan's left. As if on cue the band began singing about whiskey in a jug. Harry swayed and clapped along until a geezer in a checkered cap and green suspenders jigged over and took her by the hand. She jumped up and followed him to the back room, where two young men were once again doing egret

139

imitations. Harry's partner had a substantial belly and a soft, round face. I hoped she wouldn't kill the guy.

I looked at my watch. Eleven-forty. My eyes burned from smoke and my throat was scratchy from shouting.

And I was enjoying myself.

And I wanted a drink.

Seriously.

"Look, I've got a headache. As soon as Ginger Rogers gets off the dance floor I'm going to cut out."

"Suit yourself, bucko. You've done very well for your first session."

"Jesus, Ryan. I've been here before."

"For the storyteller?"

"No!" I had thought about that. I love Irish folklore.

I watched Harry hop and twist, her long blond hair flying. Everyone watched her. After a while I shouted in Ryan's ear.

"Does Claudel know where Anna is?"

He shook his head.

I gave up. The potential for conversation was zero.

Harry and the geezer danced on. His face was red and covered with sweat, and his clip-on tie hung at an odd angle. When Harry's jig brought her round to face me I pantomimed a finger across the throat. Cut. Wrap.

She waved gaily.

I jabbed my thumb toward the exit, but she'd already rotated out of eye contact.

Oh, God.

Ryan watched me, an amused smile on his face.

I gave him a look that could freeze El Niño, and he slouched back and held both hands in a palms-out gesture.

The next time Harry circled toward me I gestured again, but she was staring at something over my shoulder, an odd look on her face.

At twelve-fifteen my prayers were answered as the

band took a break. Harry returned, flushed but beaming. Her partner looked like he needed a resuscitator.

"Whew! I feel rode hard and put away wet."

She ran a finger around her collar, hopped onto her stool, and chugged the beer Ryan had ordered. When the geezer made a move to settle next to her, she patted him on his cap.

"Thanks, big guy. I'll see y'all later."

He tipped his head and gave her a puppy look.

"Bye-bye."

Harry wriggled her fingers, and the geezer shrugged and blended back into the crowd.

Harry leaned across Ryan. "Tempe, who's that over there?" She tipped her head toward the bar behind us.

I started to turn.

"Don't look now!"

"What?"

"The tall skinny dude with the glasses."

I rolled my eyes, which didn't help my headache. Harry would use this routine in junior high when I wanted to leave and she wanted to stay.

"I know. He's cute and he's really interested in me. Only he's shy. Been there, done that, Harry."

The band started another reel. I stood and put on my jacket.

"Bedtime."

"No. Really. This guy was scoping you the whole time I was dancing. I could see him through the window."

I looked in the direction she'd indicated. No one fit her description.

"Where?"

She scanned the faces around the bar, then looked over her shoulder in the other direction.

"Really, Tempe." She shrugged. "I can't spot him now."

141

"He's probably one of my students. They're always amazed to see me out without a walker."

"Yeah, I guess. The guy looked pretty young for you."

"Thanks."

Ryan watched like Gramps observing the young 'uns.

"Are you ready?" I buttoned my jacket and pulled on my mittens.

Harry looked at her Rolex, then said exactly what I expected.

"It's just past midnight. Couldn't we—"

"I'm heading out, Harry. The condo's only four blocks from here and you've got a key. You can stay if you want."

For a moment she looked undecided, then she turned to Ryan.

"Are you going to be here awhile?"

"No problema, kiddo."

She gave me the same puppy look the geezer had used.

"You're sure you don't mind?"

"Of course not." Like hell.

I explained the keys and she gave me a hug.

"Let me walk you back," said Ryan, reaching for his jacket. My protector.

"No, thanks. I'm a big girl."

"Then let me call a taxi for you."

"Ryan, I am allowed to travel unaccompanied."

"Suit yourself." He settled back, shaking his head.

The cold air felt good after the heat and smoke of the pub. For about a millisecond. The temperature had dropped and the wind had picked up, plunging the chill factor to a billion degrees below zero.

Within steps my eyes were tearing and I could feel ice forming around the edges of my nostrils. I drew my muffler across my mouth and nose, and tied it in a big knot at the back of my head. I looked like a geek, but at least my orifices wouldn't freeze over.

I stuffed my hands deep into my pockets, lowered my head, and trudged on. Warmer, but barely able to see, I angled across Crescent and up to Ste-Catherine. There wasn't a soul in sight.

I'd just crossed MacKay when I felt my scarf tighten, and my feet go out from under me. At first I thought I'd slipped on ice but then I realized I was being pulled backward. I had passed the old York Theater and I was being dragged toward the side of the building. Hands spun me and shoved me face first against the wall. My own were still trapped in my pockets. As my face struck the brick I slid downward. When my knees hit the ground, I was shoved face-down into the snow. A heavy blow struck my back, as though a large person had dropped knees first onto my thoracic spine. Pain shot down my back and my breath exploded outward through my muffler. I was pinned to the ground in a prone position. I couldn't see, I couldn't move, and I couldn't breathe! I felt panic and air hunger. Blood pounded in my ears.

I closed my eyes and concentrated on turning my mouth to the side. I pulled a shallow breath. Then another. And another. The burning subsided and I began to exchange air.

I felt pain in my jaw and face. My head was locked at an awkward angle, my right eye pressed against the frozen snow. I felt a bulkiness below me and knew it was my purse. It had helped knock the wind out of me.

Give him the purse!

I wriggled to free myself, but my jacket and scarf still bound me like a straitjacket. I felt his body move. He seemed to stretch out on top of me. Then his breathing in my ear. Though muffled by the scarf, it sounded heavy and rapid, desperate, animal-like in its intensity.

Don't lose consciousness. Unconscious means dead in this weather. Move! Do something!

Under my heavy clothing I was covered in sweat. I inched my hand around inside my pocket, searching. My fingers felt slick inside the wool mitten.

There!

I gripped my keys. The instant he let up I'd be ready. Helpless, I waited for an opening.

"Leave it alone," a voice hissed in my ear.

He'd spotted the movement!

I froze.

"You don't know what you're doing. Back off!"

Back off what? Who did he think I was?

"Leave it alone," he repeated, his voice trembling with emotion.

I couldn't speak, and he didn't seem to expect an answer. Was it a madman and not a mugger?

We lay there for what seemed eternity. Cars whooshed past. I'd lost all feeling in my face, and my neck vertebrae felt as if they would crack. I breathed with my mouth open, saliva freezing on my muffler.

Stay calm. Think!

My mind raced through possibilities. Was he drunk? Stoned? Undecided? Was he savoring some sick fantasy that would trigger him to action? My heart pounded so loud I feared it would be the catalyst.

Then I heard footsteps. He must have heard them, too, for he tightened his grip on my scarf and placed a gloved hand over my face.

Scream! Do something!

I couldn't see him and it made me crazy.

"Get off me you goddamn dirtbag!" I yelled through my muffler.

144

But my voice came from a million miles away, smothered by the thick layer of wool.

I held the keys in a death grip, my hand slippery inside the mitten and tensed to drive them into his eye if I got an opening. Suddenly, I felt the scarf tighten and his body shift. He rose to his knees again, concentrating all of his weight in the center of my back. His weight and my purse compressed my lungs, making me gasp for air.

Using the scarf he lifted my head, then drove it down with his hand. My ear slammed into ice and gravel, and a cloud of sparks burst behind my eyes. He lifted and slammed down again and the sparks began to coalesce. I could feel blood on my face and taste it in my mouth. I thought I felt something snap in my neck. My heart thundered inside my rib cage.

Get off me you demented piece of shit!

I felt light-headed. My tortured brain foresaw the autopsy report. *My* autopsy. *Nothing under her nails. No defense wounds.*

Don't pass out!

I squirmed and tried to scream, but again my voice was barely audible.

Suddenly, the pounding stopped and my attacker leaned close again. He spoke, but I caught only garbled sounds through the ringing in my ears.

Then I felt his hands press against my back and his weight lifted. Boots crunched on gravel, and he was gone.

Dazed, I pulled my hands free, pushed myself to all fours, and rolled to a seated position. A wave of dizziness washed over me, and I raised my knees and lowered my head between them. My nose was running and either blood or saliva was oozing from my mouth. My hands trembled as I wiped my face with the end of my muffler, and I knew I was a hair away from tears.

Wind rattled the broken windows in the abandoned theater. What was the name? Yale? York? It seemed terribly important. I knew it before, so why couldn't I remember it now? I felt disoriented, and began shivering uncontrollably, from cold, from fear, and perhaps from relief.

When the dizziness passed I rose, inched my way along the building, and peeked around the corner. There was no one in sight.

I stumbled home on rubbery legs, looking over my shoulder every other step. The few pedestrians I passed looked away and gave me a wide berth. Just another drunk.

Ten minutes later I sat on the edge of my bed, checking myself for injuries. My pupils were even and coordinated. No numbness. No nausea.

The scarf had been a mixed blessing. While it provided my attacker a convenient handle, it had also cushioned the blows. I had a few cuts and abrasions on the right side of my head, but I believed I had not sustained a concussion.

Not bad for a mugging survivor, I thought as I slipped between the sheets. But had it been a mugging? The guy hadn't stolen anything. Why did he run? Did he panic and give up? Was he just a drunk? Did he figure out I wasn't who he thought I was? Subzero cold rarely inspires sexual assaults. What was his motive?

I tried to sleep but my mind was still on an adrenaline high. Or was it post-traumatic stress syndrome? My hands still shook and I jumped at every sound.

Should I call the cops? What for? I wasn't hurt much and nothing was stolen. And I never got a look at the guy. Should I tell Ryan? Not a chance in hell after my cocky departure. Harry? No way.

Oh, God. What if Harry walks home alone? Could he still be out there?

I rolled over and looked at the clock. Two thirty-seven. Where the hell was Harry?

I touched my broken lip. Would she notice? Probably. Harry had instincts like a wildcat. She missed nothing. I thought of cover stories. Doors are always good, or face-first falls on the ice while your hands are deep in your pockets.

My eyes drifted shut, then flew open as I felt the knee on my back and heard the rasping breath.

I checked the clock again. Three-fifteen. Did Hurley's stay open this late? Had Harry gone home with Ryan?

"Where are you, Harry?" I said to the glowing green digits.

I lay there, wishing she'd come home, not wanting to be alone.

147

12

I woke to bright sunlight and total silence, having slept fitfully. My brain cells had called an all-night meeting to organize input from the past few days. Missing students. Muggers. Saints. Murdered babies and grandmas. Harry. Ryan. Harry and Ryan. They broke around dawn, having accomplished little.

I rolled over on my back and a burst of pain in my neck reminded me of last night's adventure. I flexed and extended my neck and each arm and leg. Pretty good. In the morning light the attack seemed illogical and imaginary. But the memory of fear was very real.

I lay still for a while, exploring for damage to my face and listening for signs of my sister. Tender areas on the face. No noise from the sister.

At seven-forty I hauled myself out of bed and grabbed my ratty old robe and slippers. The guest room door was open, the bed made. Had Harry been home last night?

I found a Post-it on the refrigerator explaining the absence of two cartons of yogurt and saying she'd be back after seven. O.K. She'd come in, but had she slept here?

"Who cares," I said, reaching for the coffee beans.

148

Just then the phone rang.

I slammed down the canister and padded to the living room phone.

"Yeah."

"Hey, Mom. Rough night?"

"Sorry, honey. What's up?"

"Are you going to be in Charlotte the week after next?"

"I get in Monday and I'll be there until early April, when I go to the Physical Anthropology meetings in Oakland. Why?"

"Well, I thought I'd come home for a few days. This beach trip isn't working out."

"Great. I mean, great that we can spend some time together. Sorry your trip went bust." I didn't ask why. "Will you be staying with me or with Dad?"

"Yes."

"O.K. O.K. Classes going all right?"

"Yeah. I'm really enjoying the abnormal psych. The prof is so cool. And criminology's pretty good, too. We never have to turn anything in on time."

"Hm. How's Aubrey?"

"Who?"

"Guess that answers my question. How's the zit?"

"Gone."

"Why are you up so early on a Saturday?"

"I've got to write a paper for my crim class. I'm going to do something on profiling, maybe bring in stuff from abnormal psych."

"I thought you never had to hand anything in on time."

"It was due two weeks ago."

"Oh."

"Can you help me think of a project for my anthro class?"

"Sure."

149

"Nothing too elaborate. It's supposed to be something I can do in one day."

I heard a beep.

"I've got another call, Katy. I'll think about the project. Let me know when you're arriving in Charlotte."

"Will do."

I clicked over and was amazed to hear Claudel's voice.

"Claudel *ici*."

As usual there was no greeting, and he did not apologize for phoning me on Saturday morning. He dove straight to the point.

"Has Anna Goyette returned home?"

My chest went hollow. Claudel had never called me at home. Anna must be dead.

I swallowed and answered. "I don't think so."

"She is nineteen."

"Yes."

I saw Sister Julienne's face. I couldn't bear to think of telling her.

". . . *caractéristiques physiques*?"

"I'm sorry. What was that?"

Claudel repeated the question. I had no idea if Anna had any unusual physical features.

"I don't know. I'd have to ask the family."

"When was she last seen?"

"Thursday. Monsieur Claudel, why are you asking me these questions?"

I waited out a Claudel pause. I could hear commotion in the background and guessed he was calling from the homicide squad room.

"A white female was found early this morning, naked, with no identification."

"Where?" The hollow feeling pushed against my sternum.

150

"Île des Sœurs. At the back of the island there is a wooded area and a pond. The body was found" – he hesitated – "on the water's edge."

"Found how?" He was holding back.

Claudel considered my question for a moment. I could picture his beak nose, his close-set eyes narrowed in thought.

"The victim was murdered. The circumstances are . . ." Again the hesitation. ". . . unusual."

"Tell me." I shifted the phone to my other hand and wiped my palm on my robe.

"The body was found in an old steamer trunk. There were multiple injuries. LaManche is doing the autopsy today."

"What kinds of injuries?" I stared at a pattern of spots on my robe.

He took a deep breath. "There are multiple stab wounds and ligature marks around the wrists. LaManche suspects there has also been an animal attack."

I found Claudel's habit of depersonalizing annoying. A white female. The victim. The body. The wrists. Not even a personal pronoun.

"And the victim may have been burned," he continued.

"Burned?"

"LaManche will know more later. He is going to do the post today."

"Jesus." Though one pathologist from the lab is on call at all times, rarely is an autopsy carried out on a weekend. I knew the murder had to be extraordinary. "How long has she been dead?"

"The body wasn't fully frozen, so it was probably outside less than twelve hours. LaManche will try to narrow the time of death."

I didn't want to ask the next question.

151

"Why do you think it could be Anna Goyette?"

"The age and description fit."

I felt a little weak.

"What physical characteristic were you referring to?"

"The victim has no lower molars."

"Were they extracted?" I felt stupid as soon as the question was out.

"Dr. Brennan, I am not a dentist. There is also a small tattoo on the right hip. Two figures holding a heart between them."

"I'll call Anna's aunt and get back to you."

"I can—"

"No. I'll do it. I have something else to discuss with her."

He gave me his beeper number and hung up.

My hand trembled as I punched the digits for the convent. I saw frightened eyes gazing from below blonde bangs.

Before I could think of how to frame my questions, Sister Julienne was on the line. I spent several minutes thanking her for sending me to Daisy Jeannotte, and telling her about the journals. I was evading what I had to do, and she saw right through me.

"I know something bad has happened." Her voice was soft, but I could hear tension just below the surface.

I asked if Anna had turned up. She had not.

"Sister, a young woman has been found—"

I heard the swish of fabric and knew she was crossing herself.

"I need to ask a few personal questions about your niece."

"Yes." Barely audible.

I asked about the molars and tattoo.

The line was quiet only a second, then I was surprised to hear her laugh.

"Oh my, no, no, that isn't Anna. Oh heavens, no,

152

she'd never allow herself to be tattooed. And I'm certain Anna has all of her teeth. In fact she often mentions her teeth. That's how I know. She has a lot of trouble with them, complains about pain when she eats something cold. Or hot."

The words flew in such a torrent I could almost feel her relief rush across the line.

"But, Sister, it's possible—"

"No. I know my niece. She has all of her teeth. She isn't happy with them, but she has them." Again the nervous laugh. "And no tattoos, thank the Lord."

"I'm glad to hear that. This young woman is probably not Anna, but perhaps it would be best to have your niece's dental records sent over, just to be sure."

"I am sure."

"Yes. Well, perhaps to assure Detective Claudel. It can't hurt."

"I suppose. And I will pray for that poor girl's family."

She gave me the name of Anna's dentist and I called Claudel back.

"She's sure Anna didn't have a tattoo."

"Hi, Auntie nun! Guess what? I had my ass tattooed last week!"

"I agree. Not likely."

He snorted.

"But she's absolutely certain Anna has all of her teeth. She remembers her niece complaining about toothaches."

"Who has extractions?"

My thought precisely.

"It's usually not people with happy teeth."

"Yes."

"And this aunt also believes Anna never went off without telling her mother, right?"

"That's what she said."

"Anna Goyette has a better act than David Copperfield. She disappeared seven times in the last eighteen months. At least that's how many reports the mother filed."

"Oh." The hollowness spread from my breastbone to the pit of my stomach.

I asked Claudel to keep me informed, and hung up. I doubted he would.

I was showered, dressed, and in my office by nine-thirty. I finished my report on Élisabeth Nicolet, describing and explaining my observations, just as I would with any forensic case. I wished I could have included information from the Bélanger journals, but there just hadn't been time to go through them.

After printing the report, I spent three hours photographing. I was tense and clumsy, and had trouble positioning the bones. At two I grabbed a sandwich from the cafeteria, and ate it as I proofed my findings on Mathias and Malachy. But my mind was focused on the phone and wouldn't concentrate on the work at hand.

I was at the copy machine with the Bélanger journals when I looked up to see Claudel.

"It is not your young lady."

I stared into his eyes. "Really?"

He nodded.

"Who is she?" I asked.

"Her name was Carole Comptois. When the dentals excluded Goyette we ran the prints and got a hit. There were a couple of arrests for soliciting."

"Age?"

"Eighteen."

"How did she die?"

"LaManche is finishing the post now."

"Any suspects?"

"Many." He stared at my face a moment, said nothing, and left.

I continued photocopying, a robot with emotions swirling inside. The relief I'd felt at learning it wasn't Anna had immediately turned to guilt. There was still a girl on a table downstairs. A family to be told.

Lift the cover. Turn the page. Lower the cover. Push the button.

Eighteen.

I had no desire to see the autopsy.

At four-thirty I finished with the journals and returned to my office. I dropped the babies' reports in the secretarial office then left a note on LaManche's desk explaining about the photocopies. When I reentered the corridor LaManche and Bergeron stood talking outside the dentist's office. Both men looked tired and grim. As I approached they took in my face, but didn't inquire.

"Bad one?" I asked.

LaManche nodded.

"What happened to her?"

"What didn't," said Bergeron.

I shifted my gaze from one to the other. Even stooped the dentist was over six feet tall, and I had to look up to meet his eyes. His white frizz was backlit by a fluorescent ceiling light. I remembered Claudel's comment about an animal attack and suspected why Bergeron's Saturday had also been spoiled.

"It looks like she was hung by her wrists and beaten, then attacked by dogs," said LaManche. "Marc thinks there were at least two."

Bergeron nodded. "One of the larger breeds. Maybe shepherds or Dobermans. There are over sixty bite wounds."

"Jesus."

"A boiling liquid, probably water, was poured on her

155

while she was naked. Her skin is badly scalded, but I couldn't find traces of anything identifiable," LaManche continued.

"She was still alive?" My gut recoiled at the thought of her pain.

"Yes. She finally died as a result of multiple stab wounds to the chest and abdomen. Do you want to see the Polaroids?"

I shook my head.

"Were there defense wounds?" I recalled my own ordeal with the mugger.

"No."

"When did she die?"

"Probably late yesterday."

I didn't want to know the details.

"One other thing." LaManche's eyes were full of sadness. "She was four months pregnant."

I moved past them quickly and slipped into my office. I don't know how long I sat there, my eyes moving over the familiar objects of my trade, not seeing them. Though I had some emotional immunity, inoculated by years of exposure to cruelty and violence, some deaths still broke through. The recent onslaught of horrors seemed uglier than most I could remember. Or were my circuits simply overloaded to the point that I could not absorb more heinousness?

Carole Comptois was not my case, and I'd never laid eyes on her, but I couldn't control the visions surfacing from the darkest depths of my mind. I saw her in her last moments, her face contorted in pain and terror. Did she beg for her life? For her unborn baby? What kind of monsters were afoot in the world?

"Damn it to hell!" I said to the empty office.

I shoved my papers into my briefcase, grabbed my gear, and slammed the door behind me. Bergeron said something as I passed his office, but I didn't stop.

156

The six o'clock news began as I drove under the Jacques Cartier Bridge, the Comptois murder the lead story. I jammed the button, repeating my last thought.

"Damn it to hell!"

By the time I got home my anger had cooled. Some emotions are too intense to persist without ebbing. I phoned Sister Julienne and assured her about Anna. Claudel had already called, but I wanted to make personal contact. She will turn up, I said. Yes, she agreed. Neither of us fully believed it anymore.

I told her Élisabeth's skeleton was packed and ready, and that the report was being typed. She said the bones would be picked up first thing Monday morning.

"Thank you so much, Dr. Brennan. We await your report with great anticipation."

I did not avail myself of the opening. I had no idea how they'd react to what I'd written.

I changed to jeans, then prepared dinner, refusing to allow myself to think about what had been done to Carole Comptois. Harry arrived at half past seven and we ate, commenting on little but the pasta and zucchini. She seemed tired and distracted, and willing to accept my explanation of having fallen face forward on the ice. I was completely drained by the day's events. I didn't ask about the night before, or about the seminar, and she didn't offer. I think we both were glad to neither listen nor respond.

After dinner Harry read her workshop material and I started with the diaries again. My report to the sisters was complete, but I wanted to know more. The photocopying had not improved the technical quality, and I found it just as discouraging as I had on Friday. Besides, Louis-Philippe was not the most exciting chronicler. A young medical doctor, he wrote long accounts of his days at the Hôtel Dieu Hospital. In forty

157

pages I came across only a few references to his sister. It seemed he was concerned about Eugénie continuing to sing in public after her marriage to Alain Nicolet. He also disliked her hairdresser. Louis-Philippe sounded like a real prig.

Sunday Harry was gone again before I got up. I did laundry, worked out at the gym, and updated a lecture I planned to give in my human evolution class on Tuesday. By late afternoon I felt reasonably caught up. I lit a fire, made myself a cup of Earl Grey, and curled up on the couch with my books and papers.

I started where I'd left off in the Bélanger diary, but after about twenty pages I shifted to the smallpox book. It was as fascinating as Louis-Philippe was dull.

I read about the streets I walk every day. Montreal and its surrounding villages had over two hundred thousand inhabitants in the eighteen-eighties. The city stretched from Sherbrooke Street on the north to the port along the river on the south. To the east it was bounded by the industrial town of Hochelaga, and to the west by the working-class villages of Ste-Cunégonde and St-Henri, which lay just above the Lachine Canal. Last summer I'd pedaled the length of the canal bike path.

Then, as now, there was tension. Though most of Montreal west of rue St-Laurent was English-speaking, by the eighteen-eighties the French had become a clear majority in the city as a whole. They dominated municipal politics, but the English ruled in commerce and in the press.

The French and Irish were Catholic, the English, Protestant. The groups remained largely separate, both in life and in death. Each had its own cemetery high on the mountain.

I closed my eyes and thought about that. Even today language and religion determined so much in Montreal.

The Catholic schools. The Protestant schools. The Nationalists. The Federalists. I wondered where Élisabeth Nicolet's loyalties would lie.

The room dimmed and the lamps clicked to life. I read on.

In the late nineteenth century Montreal was a major commercial hub, boasting a magnificent harbor, huge stone warehouses, tanneries, soapworks, factories. McGill was already a leading university. But, like other Victorian cities, it was a place of contrasts, with the huge mansions of the merchant princes overshadowing the hovels of the working poor. Just off the wide, paved avenues, beyond Sherbrooke and Dorchester, lay hundreds of dirt lanes and unpaved alleys.

The city then was poorly drained, with garbage and animal carcasses rotting in vacant lots, and excrement everywhere. The river was used as an open sewer. Though frozen in winter, the offal and refuse rotted and reeked in the warmer months. Everyone complained of the foul odors.

My tea had grown cold so I uncurled, stretched, and made a fresh cup. When I reopened the book, I skipped ahead to a section on sanitation. It had been one of Louis-Philippe's recurring gripes about the Hôtel Dieu Hospital. Sure enough, there was a reference to the old boy. He'd gone on to become a member of the Health Committee of the City Council.

I read an engrossing account of the council discussing human waste. Disposal was chaotic at the time. Some Montrealers flushed excrement into city sewers that led into the river. Some used earth closets, sprinkling dirt over their deposits then putting them out for garbage collectors. Others defecated into outdoor privy pits.

The city's medical officer reported that inhabitants produced approximately 170 tons of excrement each day, or over 215,000 tons per year. He warned that the

159

10,000 privy pits and cesspools in the city were the primary source of zymotic diseases, including typhoid, scarlet fever, and diphtheria. The council decided in favor of a system of collection and incineration. Louis-Philippe voted yea. It was January 28, 1885.

The day after the vote, Grand Trunk Railway's western train pulled into Bonaventure Station. A conductor was ill and the railroad's doctor was called. The man was examined and diagnosed as having smallpox. Being Protestant, he was taken to the Montreal General Hospital, but was refused admission. The patient was allowed to wait in an isolated room in the contagious diseases wing. Finally, at the railroad doctor's pleading, he was grudgingly admitted to the Catholic Hôtel Dieu Hospital.

I got up to stoke the fire. As I rearranged the logs I pictured the rambling, gray-stone building that stood at avenue des Pins and rue St-Urbain. The Hôtel Dieu was still a functioning hospital. I'd driven past it many times.

I went back to the book. My stomach was growling, but I wanted to read until Harry arrived.

The doctors at the Montreal General thought those at the Hôtel Dieu had reported the smallpox to public health authorities. Those at the Hôtel Dieu thought the converse. No one told the authorities, and no one told the medical staff at either hospital. By the time the epidemic ended, over three thousand people were dead, most of them children.

I closed the book. My eyes were burning and my temples throbbed. The clock said seven-fifteen. Where was Harry?

I went to the kitchen, took out and rinsed the salmon steaks. As I mixed dill sauce I tried to picture my neighborhood a century earlier. How did one face smallpox in those days? To what home remedies did

160

one turn? Over two thirds of the dead were children. What was it like to see your neighbors' children die? How did one deal with the helplessness of caring for a doomed child?

I scrubbed two potatoes and put them in the toaster oven, then washed lettuce, tomatoes, and cucumbers. Still no Harry.

Though the reading had taken my mind off Mathias and Malachy and Carole Comptois, I was still tense and my head hurt. I ran a hot bath and added aromatherapy ocean mineral salts. Then I put on a Leonard Cohen CD and slipped in for a long soak.

I used Élisabeth to keep my mind off my recent homicide cases. The trip through history had been fascinating, but I hadn't learned what I needed to know. I was already familiar with Élisabeth's work during the epidemic through the volumes of information Sister Julienne had sent before the exhumation.

Élisabeth had been a recluse for years, but when the epidemic raged out of control she became an advocate for medical modernization. She wrote letters to the Provincial Board of Health, to the Health Committee of the City Council, and to Honoré Beaugrand, mayor of Montreal, begging for improved sanitation. She bombarded the French- and English-language papers, demanding the reopening of the city smallpox hospital and arguing for public vaccination.

She wrote to her bishop, pointing out that the fever was spread in places where crowds gathered, and begging him to temporarily close the churches. Bishop Fabre refused, stating that to close the churches would be to laugh at God. The bishop urged his flock to church, telling them that united prayer was more powerful than prayer in isolation.

Good thinking, Bishop. That's why French Catholics

161

were dying and English Protestants were not. The heathens got inoculated and stayed home.

I added hot water, imagining Élisabeth's frustration and how much tact I would have used.

O.K. I knew about her work, and I knew about her death. The nuns had gone to town on that. I'd read reams on her final illness and the public funeral that followed.

But I needed to know about her birth.

I took the soap and worked up a lather.

There was no avoiding the journals.

I ran the bar over my shoulders.

But I had the photocopies, so that could wait until I got to Charlotte.

I washed my feet.

Newspapers. That had been Jeannotte's suggestion. Yes. I'd use the time I had on Monday to view old newspapers. I had to go to McGill anyway to return the diaries.

I slid back into the hot water and thought about my sister. Poor Harry. I'd pretty much ignored her yesterday. I'd been tired, but was that it? Or was it Ryan? She had every right to sleep with him if she wanted. So why had I been so cold? I resolved to be more friendly tonight.

I was toweling off when I heard the beep of the security alarm. I dug out a flannel Disney nightshirt Harry had given me one Christmas, and pulled it over my head.

I found her standing in the living room, still wearing her jacket, gloves, and hat, her eyes fixed on something a million miles away.

"Long day, I'd say."

"Yeah." She refocused on the present, and gave me a half smile.

"Hungry?"

162

"I guess. Just let me have a few minutes." She threw her pack onto the couch and flopped down beside it.

"Sure. Take your coat off and stay awhile."

"Right. Damn, it gets cold here. I feel like a Popsicle just walking from the metro."

A few minutes later I heard her in the guest room, then she joined me in the kitchen. I grilled the salmon and tossed the salad while she set the table.

When we sat down to eat I asked about her day.

"It was fine." She cut her potato, squeezed it, and added sour cream.

"Fine?" I encouraged.

"Yeah. We covered a lot."

"You look like you covered forty miles of bad road."

"Yeah. I'm pretty beat." She didn't smile at my use of her expression.

"So what did you do?"

"Lots of lectures, exercises." She spooned sauce onto her fish. "What are these little green threads?"

"Dill. What kinds of exercises?"

"Meditation. Games."

"Games?"

"Storytelling. Calisthenics. Whatever they tell us to do."

"You just do whatever they say?"

"I do it because I choose to do it," she snapped.

I was taken aback. Harry rarely barked at me like that.

"Sorry. I'm just tired."

For a while we ate in silence. I didn't really want to hear about her touchy-feely therapy, but after a few minutes I tried again.

"How many people are there?"

"Quite a few."

"Are they interesting?"

"I'm not doing this to make new friends, Tempe. I'm

163

learning to be accountable. To be responsible. My life sucks, and I'm trying to figure out how to make it work."

She stabbed at her salad. I couldn't remember when I'd seen her so down.

"And these exercises help?"

"Tempe, you just have to try it for yourself. I can't tell you exactly what we do or how it works."

She scraped off the dill sauce and picked at her salmon.

I said nothing.

"I don't think you'd get it anyway. You're too frozen."

She picked up her plate and carried it to the kitchen. So much for my resolve to be interested.

I joined her at the sink.

"I think I'm just going to turn in," she said, laying a hand on my shoulder. "I'll talk to you tomorrow."

"I'm leaving in the afternoon."

"Oh. I'll call you."

In bed, I replayed the conversation. I'd never seen Harry so listless, or so snappish when approached. She must have been exhausted. Or maybe it was the thing with Ryan. Or her breakup with Striker.

Later, I'd wonder why I hadn't seen the signs. It might have changed so much.

13

On monday I got up at dawn, planning to make breakfast for Harry and myself. She declined, saying it was a fast day. She left before seven, wearing sweats and no makeup, a sight I had never expected to experience.

There are records identifying the coldest spot on earth, the driest, the lowest. The gloomiest is without doubt the serials and microform department of McGill's McLennan Library. It is a long narrow room on the second floor done in poured cement and fluorescent lighting, set off smartly by a bloodred floor.

Following the librarian's instructions, I worked my way past the stacks of serials and newspapers to rows of metal shelves holding tiny cardboard boxes and round metal tins. I found the ones I wanted and took them to the reading room. Deciding to start with the English press, I withdrew a roll of microfilm and wound it onto the reading machine.

In 1846 the *Montreal Gazette* was published triweekly, with a format like today's *New York Times*. Narrow columns, few pictures, numerous ads. My viewer was bad and so was the film. It was like trying to read under water. The print kept moving in and out of focus, and hairs and particles of debris migrated across the screen.

Ads extolled fur caps, British stationery, untanned sheepskins. Dr. Taylor wanted you to buy his balsam liverwort, Dr. Berlin, his antibilious pills. John Bower Lewis promoted himself as a worthy barrister and attorney-at-law. Pierre Grégoire would be pleased to do your hair. I read the ad:

Gentleman can accommodate respectable male and female clients. Will render hair soft and glossy, however harsh. Will use admirable preparations to produce beautiful curls and do excellent restoration. Reasonable prices. Select clients only.

And now for the news.

Antoine Lindsay died when his neighbor hit him in the head with a piece of wood. Coroner's finding: Willful Murder.

A young English girl, Maria Nash, lately landed in Montreal, was victim of an abduction and betrayal. She died in a state of madness at the Emigrant Hospital.

When Bridget Clocone gave birth to a male child at the Women's Lying-In Hospital, doctors found that the forty-year-old widow had recently delivered another child. Police searched her employer's home and found the body of a second male infant hidden under clothes in a box. The baby showed ". . . marks of violence as though occasioned by the strong pressure of fingers on the neck." Coroner's finding: Willful Murder.

Jesus. Does anything ever change?

I shifted gears and scanned a list of ships that had cleared the port, and a list of ocean passengers leaving Montreal for Liverpool. Pretty dry stuff.

Fares for the steamboat. Stagecoach service to Ontario. Notices of removal. Not many folks moving that week.

Finally I found it. Births, Marriages, Deaths. In this

city on the seventeenth, Mrs. David Mackay, a son. Mrs. Marie-Claire Bisset, a daughter. No mention of Eugénie Nicolet and her baby.

I noted the position of the birth notices within each paper, and fast-forwarded through the next several weeks, going right to that section. Nothing. I checked every paper on the reel. Through the end of 1846 there was no notice of Élisabeth's birth.

I tried the other English papers. Same story. No mention of Eugénie Nicolet. No birth of Élisabeth. I shifted to the French press. Still nothing.

By ten o'clock my eyes were throbbing and pain had spread throughout my back and shoulders. I leaned back, stretched, and rubbed my temples. Now what?

Across the room someone at another machine hit the rewind knob. Good idea. Good as anything. I'll go backward. Élisabeth was born in January. Let's check the period when the little sperm and egg were introducing themselves to each other.

I got the boxes and wound a film through the spools. April 1845. Same ads. Same notices of removal. Same passenger lists. English press. French press.

By the time I got to *La Presse* my eyes would hardly focus. I looked at my watch. Eleven-thirty. Twenty minutes more.

I rested my chin on my fist and hit rewind. When the film stopped I was in March. I was advancing manually, stopping here and there to scan down the middle of the screen, when I spotted the Bélanger name.

I sat up and brought the article into focus. It was brief. Eugénie Bélanger was off to Paris. The noted singer and wife of Alain Nicolet would be traveling with a company of twelve and would return after the season. Except for some verbiage saying how much she'd be missed, that was it.

So Eugénie had left town. When had she returned?

167

Where was she in April? Did Alain go with her? Did he join her there? I looked at my watch. Shit.

I checked my wallet, dug into the bottom of my purse, then printed as many pages as my coins would allow. I rewound and returned the films and hurried across campus to Birks Hall.

Jeannotte's door was closed and locked, so I found the department office. The secretary dragged her eyes from her computer screen long enough to assure me that the journals would be delivered safely. I attached a note of thanks and left.

Walking back to the condo, my mind was still on history. I imagined the grand old homes I was passing as they'd been a century ago. What had the occupants seen when they looked out across Sherbrooke? Not the Musée des Beaux-Arts or the Ritz-Carlton. Not the latest offerings of Ralph Lauren, Giorgio Armani, and the atelier of Versace.

I wondered if they would have liked such trendy neighbors. Surely the boutiques were more uplifting than the smallpox hospital that had reopened not far from their backyards.

At home I checked the answering machine, afraid that I'd missed Harry's call. Nothing. I quickly made a sandwich, then drove to the lab to sign reports. When I left I placed a note on LaManche's desk reminding him of my date of return. As a rule I spend most of April in Charlotte, with the understanding that I'd return to Montreal immediately for court appearances or urgent matters. Come May and the end of spring semester, I'm back for the summer.

Home again, I spent an hour packing and organizing work materials. While I am not exactly a light traveler, clothes are not the problem. After years of commuting between countries, I've found it's easier to keep two sets of everything. I have the world's largest suitcase on

168

wheels, and I load it with books, files, journals, manuscripts, lecture notes, and anything else on which I'm working. This trip it held several pounds of Xerox copies.

At three-thirty I took a taxi to the airport. Harry had not called.

I live in perhaps the most unique apartment in Charlotte. Mine is the smallest unit in a complex known as Sharon Hall, a two-and-a-half-acre property situated in Myers Park. Deeds don't record the original function of the little structure, and today, for lack of a better label, the residents call it the Coach House Annex, or just the Annex.

The main house at Sharon Hall was built in 1913 as home for a local timber magnate. On the death of his wife in 1954, the 7,500-square-foot Georgian was donated to Queens College. The buildings housed the college's music department until the mid-eighties, when the property was sold and the mansion and coach house were converted to condos. At that time wings and annexes with an additional ten town houses were added, all conforming to the style of the original home. Old brick from a courtyard wall was incorporated into the new buildings, and windows, moldings, and hardwood floors were made as similar to the 1913 style as possible.

In the early sixties a gazebo was built next to the Annex, and the tiny building served as a sort of summer kitchen. It eventually fell into disuse, then served as a storage shed for the next two decades. In 1993 a NationsBank executive bought the Annex and converted it into the world's smallest town house, incorporating the gazebo as part of the main living area. He was transferred just as my deteriorating marital situation

169

sent me into the market for alternative living arrangements. I have a little over eight hundred square feet on two floors and, though cramped, I love it.

The only sound in the town house was the slow, steady ticking of my schoolhouse clock. Pete had been there. How like him to wind it for me. I called Birdie's name, but he didn't appear. I hung my jacket in the hall closet and muscled the suitcase up the narrow staircase to my bedroom.

"Bird?"

No answering meow and no furry white face appearing around a corner.

Downstairs, I found a note on the kitchen table. Pete still had Birdie, but he was going to Denver on Wednesday for a day or two, and wanted the cat picked up no later than tomorrow. The answering machine was blinking like a hazard light, and appropriately so, I thought.

I looked at my watch. Ten-thirty. I really didn't want to go back out.

I dialed Pete's number. My number for so many years. I could picture the phone on the kitchen wall, the V-shaped nick in the right-side casing. We'd had good times in that house, especially in that kitchen, with its walk-in fireplace and huge old pine table. Guests always drifted to that room, no matter where I tried to steer them.

The machine came on and Pete's voice asked for a short message. I left one. I tried Harry. Same routine, my voice.

I played my own messages. Pete. My department chair. Two students. A friend inviting me to a party the previous Tuesday. My mother-in-law. Two hang-ups. My best friend, Ann. No land mines. Always a relief when the series of monologues runs its course without describing catastrophes concluded or in the making.

I'd zapped and eaten a frozen pizza, and was almost finished unpacking when the phone rang.

"Good trip?"

"Not bad. Same old."

"Bird says he's bringing suit."

"For?"

"Abandonment."

"He may have a case. Will you represent him?"

"If he can come up with the retainer."

"What's in Denver?"

"A deposition. Same old."

"Could I get Birdie tomorrow? I've been up since six and I'm really exhausted."

"I understand Harry paid you a visit."

"That's not it," I snapped. My sister had always been a source of friction with Pete.

"Hey, hey. Ease down. How is she?"

"She's terrific."

"Tomorrow is fine. What time?"

"It's my first day back, so I know I won't get away until late. Probably six or seven."

"No problem. Come after seven and I'll feed you."

"I—"

"For Birdie. He needs to see that we're still friends. I think he feels it's all his fault."

"Right."

"You don't want him in veterinary therapy."

I smiled. Pete.

"O.K. But I'll bring something."

"Fine with me."

The next day was even more hectic than I'd anticipated. I was up by six, on campus by seven-thirty. By nine I'd checked my e-mail, sorted my snail mail, and reviewed my lecture notes.

I handed back exams in both my classes, so I had to

171

extend office hours well beyond the normal time. Some students wanted to discuss their grades, others needed clemency for missing the test. Relatives always die during exams, and all manner of personal crises incapacitate the test takers. This midterm had been no exception.

At four I attended a College Course and Curriculum Committee meeting where we spent ninety minutes discussing whether the philosophy department could change the name of an upper-level course on Thomas Aquinas. I returned to my office to find my phone light blinking. Two messages.

Another student with a dead aunt. A taped message from campus security warning of break-ins in the Physical Sciences Building.

Next I turned to collecting diagrams, calipers, casts, and a list of materials I planned to have my assistant lay out for a lab exercise the next day. Then I spent an hour in the lab assuring that the specimens I'd chosen were appropriate.

At six I locked all the cabinets and the outer lab door. The corridors of the Colvard Building were deserted and quiet, but when I turned the corner toward my office I was surprised to see a young woman leaning against my doorway.

"Can I help you?"

She jumped at the sound of my voice.

"I—No. Sorry. I knocked." She spoke without turning, making it hard to see her face. "I have the wrong office." With that she bolted around the corner beyond my office and disappeared.

I suddenly recalled the message about break-ins.

Chill, Brennan. She was probably just listening to see if someone was inside.

I turned the handle and the door opened. Damn. I was sure I'd locked it. Or had I? My arms were so full I

172

had pulled the door closed with my foot. Maybe the latch hadn't caught.

I did a quick inventory of the room. Nothing looked disturbed. I pulled my purse from the bottom file drawer and checked. Money. Keys. Passport. Credit cards. Everything worth taking was there.

Maybe she *had* been at the wrong place. Maybe she'd looked in, realized her mistake, and was leaving. I hadn't actually seen her open the door.

Whatever.

I packed my briefcase, turned the key and tested the lock, then headed for the parking deck.

Charlotte is as different from Montreal as Boston is from Bombay. A city suffering from multiple personality disorder, it is at once the graceful Old South and also the country's second-largest financial center. It is home to the Charlotte Motor Speedway and to Nations-Bank and First Union, to Opera Carolina and Coyote Joe's. It is churches on every corner, with a few titty bars around the corner. Country clubs and barbecue joints, crowded expressways and quiet cul-de-sacs. Billy Graham grew up on a dairy farm where a shopping center now stands, and Jim Bakker had his start in a local church and his finish in a federal courthouse. Charlotte is the place where mandatory busing to achieve racial balance in public schools began, and the home of numerous private academies, some with a religious orientation, others entirely secular.

Charlotte was a segregated city going into the 1960s, but then an extraordinary group of black and white leaders began to work to integrate restaurants, public lodging, recreation, and transportation. When Judge James B. McMillan handed down the mandatory busing order in 1969, there were no riots. The judge

173

took a lot of personal heat, but his order stood, and the city complied.

I have always lived in the southeast part of town. Dillworth. Myers Park. Eastover. Foxcroft. Though a long way from the university, these neighborhoods are the oldest and prettiest, labyrinths of winding streets lined with stately homes and large lawns canopied by huge elms and willow oaks older than the pyramids. Most of Charlotte's streets, like most of Charlotte's people, are pleasant and graceful.

I cracked the car window and breathed in the late March evening. It had been one of those transitional days, not quite spring but no longer winter, when you slip your jacket on and off at least a dozen times. Already the crocuses were pushing through the earth, and soon the air would be lush with the smell of dogwoods, redbuds, and azaleas. Forget Paris. In spring, Charlotte is the most beautiful city on the planet.

I have several choices of routes going home from campus. Tonight I decided to take the highway, so I used the back exit to Harris Boulevard. Highways I-85 and I-77 were moving well, so in fifteen minutes I had cut through uptown and was heading southeast on Providence Road. I stopped at the Pasta and Provisions Company for spaghetti, Caesar salad, and garlic bread, and shortly after seven I was ringing Pete's doorbell.

He answered wearing faded jeans and a yellow and blue rugby shirt, open at the neck. His hair stuck up as though he'd just combed it with his fingers. He looked good. Pete always looks good.

"Why didn't you use your key?"

Why didn't I?

"And find a blonde in spandex in the den?"

"Is she here now?" he said, whipping around as if seriously searching.

174

"You wish. Here, boil water." I held out the pasta.

As Pete took the bag, Birdie made his appearance, stretching first one hind leg, then the other, then sitting with all four feet in a neat square. His eyes locked onto my face, but he did not approach.

"Hey, Bird. Did you miss me?"

The cat didn't move.

"You're right. He's pissed," I said.

I threw my purse onto the couch and followed Pete to the kitchen. The chairs on each end of the table were filled with stacks of mail, most unopened. The same was true of the buggy seat beneath the window and the wooden shelf below the phone. I said nothing. It was no longer my problem.

We passed a pleasant hour eating spaghetti and discussing Katy and other family. I told him his mother had called complaining of neglect. He said he'd represent her and Birdie in a package deal. I told him to call her. He said he would.

At eight-thirty I carried Birdie to the car, Pete following with the paraphernalia. My cat travels with more baggage than I do.

As I opened the door Pete placed his hand over mine.

"You're sure you don't want to stay?"

He tightened his fingers and, with the other hand, gently stroked my hair.

Did I? His touch felt so good, and dinner had seemed so normal so comfortable. I felt something inside me start to melt.

Think, Brennan. You're tired. You're horny. Get your ass home.

"What about Judy?"

"A temporary disturbance in the cosmic order."

"I don't think so, Pete. We've been over this. I enjoyed the dinner."

He shrugged and dropped his hands.

175

"You know where I live," he said, and walked back to the house.

I've read that there are ten trillion cells in the human brain. All of mine were awake that night, engaged in frenzied communication on one topic: Pete.

Why *hadn't* I used my key?

Boundaries, the cells agreed. Not the old "here's a line in the dirt, don't cross it" challenge, but the establishing of new territorial limits, both real and symbolic.

Why the breakup at all? There was a time I wanted nothing more than to marry Pete and live with him the rest of my life. What had changed between the me then and the me now? I was very young when I married, but was the me in the making so very different from the me today? Or had the two Petes diverged course? Had the Pete I married been so irresponsible? So unreliable? Had I once thought that was part of his charm?

You are starting to sound like a Sammy Cahn song, the cells piped up.

What along the way had led to our present separateness? What choices had we made? Would we make those choices now? Was it me? Pete? Fate? What had gone wrong? Or had it gone right? Was I now on a new but correct path, the road of my marriage having led as far as it was going to take me?

Tough ones, the brain cells said.

Did I still want to sleep with Pete?

A unanimous yes from the cells.

But it's been a lean year for sex, I argued.

Interesting choice of words, the id guys pointed out. Lean. No meat. Implies hunger.

There was that lawyer in Montreal, I protested.

That's not it, the higher centers said. That guy hardly

176

jiggled the needle. The voltage is in the red zone with this one.

There's no arguing with the brain when it's in that mood.

14

Wednesday morning I had just arrived at the university when my office phone rang. Ryan's voice took me by surprise.

"I don't want a weather report," he said by way of greeting.

"Low sixties and I'm wearing sunblock."

"You really do have a vicious streak, Brennan."

I said nothing.

"Let's talk about St-Jovite."

"Go ahead." I picked up a pen and began drawing triangles.

"We've got names on the four in back."

I waited.

"It was a family. Mother, father, and twin baby boys."

"Hadn't we already figured that out?"

I heard the rustle of paper.

"Brian Gilbert, age twenty-three, Heidi Schneider, age twenty, Malachy and Mathias Gilbert, age four months."

I connected my base series to a set of secondary triangles.

178

"Most women would be impressed with my detecting."

"I'm not most women."

"Are you pissed off at me?"

"Should I be?"

I unclenched my molars and filled my lungs with air. For a long time he didn't reply.

"Bell Canada was unhurried as usual, but the phone records finally came on Monday. The only nonlocal number called during the past year was to an eight-four-three area code."

I stopped in mid-triangle.

"Seems you're not the only one whose heart's in Dixie."

"Cute."

"Old times there are not forgotten."

"Where?"

"Beaufort, South Carolina."

"Are you on the level?"

"The old lady was a great dialer, then the calls stopped last winter."

"Where was she calling?"

"It's probably a residence. The local sheriff's going to check it out today."

"That's where this young family lived?"

"Not exactly. The Beaufort link started me thinking. The calls were pretty regular, then they stopped on December twelfth. Why? That's about three months before the fire. Something kept bugging me about that. The three-month part. Then I remembered. That's how long the neighbors said the couple and the babies had been at St-Jovite. You had said the babies were four months old, so I figured maybe those kids were born in Beaufort, and the calls stopped when they arrived in St-Jovite."

179

I let him go on.

"I called Beaufort Memorial, but there'd been no twin boys delivered there in the past year. Next I tried the clinics and hit pay dirt. They remembered the mother at . . ." More paper rustling. ". . . Beaufort-Jasper Comprehensive Health Clinic out on Saint Helena. That's an island."

"I know that, Ryan."

"It's a rural health clinic, mostly black doctors, mostly black patients. I spoke to one of the OB-GYNS, and, after the usual patient privacy bullshit, she admitted she treated a prenatal that fit my description. The woman had come in four months pregnant, carrying twins. Her due date was late November. Heidi Schneider. The doctor said she remembered Heidi because she was white, and because of the twins."

"So she delivered there?"

"No. The other reason the doctor remembered her was because she'd disappeared. The woman kept her appointments through her sixth month, then never went back."

"That's it?"

"That's all she'd give up until I faxed her the autopsy photo. I suspect she'll be seeing that in her sleep for a while. When she phoned back she was more cooperative. Not that the chart info was all that helpful. Heidi wasn't exactly forthcoming when she filled out the forms. She listed the father as Brian Gilbert, gave a home address in Sugar Land, Texas, and left the boxes for local address and phone number blank."

"What's in Texas?"

"We're checkin', ma'am."

"Don't start, Ryan."

"How schooled are the Beaufort boys in blue?"

"I don't really know them. Anyway, they wouldn't

180

have jurisdiction out on Saint Helena. It's unincorporated, so it's the sheriff's turf."

"Well, we're going to meet him."

"We?"

"I'm flying in on Sunday and I could use a local guide. You know, someone who speaks the language, knows local protocol. I have no idea how you eat grits."

"Can't do it. Katy's coming home next week. Besides, Beaufort is perhaps my favorite spot on the planet. If I ever do give you a tour, which I probably won't, it will not be while you're taking care of business."

"Or why."

"Why what?"

"Why anyone would eat grits."

"Ask Martha Stewart."

"Think about it."

No need. I had as much intention of meeting Ryan in Beaufort as I did of registering myself as an available single person in the People Meeting People section of my local paper.

"What about the two charred bodies upstairs?" Back to St-Jovite.

"We're still working on it."

"Has Anna Goyette turned up?"

"No idea."

"Any developments on Claudel's homicide?"

"Which one?"

"The scalded pregnant girl."

"Not that I'm aware of."

"You've been a fountain of information. Let me know what you find in Texas."

I hung up and got myself a Diet Coke. I didn't know at that point, but it was going to be a phone-intensive day.

All afternoon I worked on a paper I planned to

181

present at the American Association of Physical Anthropology meetings in early April. I felt the usual stress from having left too much until the last minute.

At three-thirty, as I was sorting photos of CAT scans, the phone rang again.

"You ought to get out more."

"Some of us work, Ryan."

"The address in Texas is the Schneider home. According to the parents, who, by the way, aren't ever going to win Final Jeopardy, Heidi and Brian showed up sometime in August and stayed until the babies were born. Heidi refused prenatal care and delivered at home with a midwife. Easy birth. No problems. Happy grandparents. Then a man visited the couple in early December, and a week later an old lady drove up in a van and they split."

"Where did they go?"

"The parents have no idea. There was no contact after that."

"Who was the man?"

"No clue, but they say this guy scared the crap out of Heidi and Brian. After he left they hid the babies and refused to go out of the house until the old lady got there. Papa Schneider didn't like him much either."

"Why?"

"Didn't like his looks. Said he brought to mind a . . . Let me get this exactly." I could picture Ryan flipping pages in his notebook. ". . . 'goddam skunk.' Kinda poetic, don't you think?"

"Dad's a regular Yeats. Anything else?"

"Talking to these folks is like talking to my parakeet, but there was one other thing."

"You have a bird?"

"Mama said Heidi and Brian had been members of some sort of group. That they'd all been living together. Ready for this?"

"I just swallowed four Valium. Hit me."

"In Beaufort, South Carolina."

"That fits."

"Like O.J.'s Bruno Maglis."

"What else did they say?"

"Nothing useful."

"What about Brian Gilbert?"

"He and Heidi met at college two years ago, both dropped out shortly after that. Mama Schneider thought he came from Ohio. She said he talked funny. We're checking it out."

"Did you tell them?"

"Yes."

For a moment neither of us spoke. Breaking the news of a murder is the worst part of a detective's job, the one they all dread the most.

"I still could use you in Beaufort."

"I still am not coming. This is detective work, not forensics."

"Knowing the hood speeds the process."

"I'm not sure Beaufort has hoods."

Ten minutes later the phone rang again.

"*Bonjour*, Temperance. *Comment ça va?*"

LaManche. Ryan had wasted no time, and had argued his case well. Could I possibly help Detective Lieutenant Ryan on the matter in Beaufort? This was a particularly sensitive investigation, and the media were becoming restive. I could bill my time and my expenses would be covered.

The message light came on as we were speaking, indicating I'd missed a call. I promised LaManche I'd see what I could work out, and hung up.

The message was from Katy. Her plans for next week had recrystallized. She'd still come home for the weekend, but then wanted to join friends on Hilton Head Island.

183

As I sat back to organize, my eyes drifted to the computer screen with its unfinished paper. Katy and I *could* go to Beaufort for the weekend, and I *could* work on it there. Then she'd move onto Hilton Head and I'd stay to help Ryan. LaManche would be happy. Ryan would be happy. And God knew I could use the extra income.

I also had reasons for not going.

Since Ryan's call an image of Malachy had been floating through my mind. I saw his half-open eyes and mangled chest, his tiny fingers curled in death. I thought of his dead sibling and his dead parents and his grieving grandparents. Thinking about that case plunged me into melancholy, and I wanted to get away from it for a while.

I checked my course syllabi for the next week. I had a film scheduled for Thursday in the human evolution course. I could switch that. Don Johanson would be just as enlightening on Tuesday.

A bone quiz in the osteology course, then open lab. I made a quick call. No problem. Alex would proctor if I organized everything for her.

I checked my agenda book. No more committee meetings this month. After tomorrow, no student appointments until late the following week. How could there be? I was sure I'd seen every student in the university yesterday.

It could work.

And the real truth was I had a duty to help if I could. No matter how small the contribution. I couldn't bring color back to Malachy's cheeks, or close the terrible wound in his chest. And I couldn't erase the older Schneiders' pain, or give them back their child and grandchildren. But I just might be able to help rein in the psychopathic mutant who had killed them. And maybe save a future Malachy.

If you're going to do this kind of work, Brennan, just do it.

I phoned Ryan and told him he could have me Monday and Tuesday. I'd let him know where I would stay.

I had another idea, so I made a second call, then dialed Katy. I explained my plan, and she was all for it. She'd meet me at home on Friday and we'd go down in my car.

"Go to the health clinic right now and get a TB test," I told her. "Subdermal, not just the scratch thing. Then have it read on Friday before you leave."

"Why?"

"Because I have a great idea for your project and that's a prerequisite. And while you're at the clinic get a photocopy of your immunization record."

"My what?"

"A record of all your shots. You had to put it on file to register at the university. And bring everything the professor handed out for the field project assignment."

"Why?"

"You'll see."

15

Thursday passed in a blur of teaching and student advising. After dinner I called to ask Pete to check on Birdie over the weekend. Harry phoned around ten to say that the seminar had ended. She'd been singled out to meet the professor, and would be dining at his home on Friday. She wanted to use the condo through the weekend.

I told her to stay as long as she wanted. I didn't ask where she'd been all week, or why she hadn't phoned. I'd called several times and never gotten an answer, including twice after midnight. I didn't point that out, either.

"You're meeting Ryan in the Land of Cotton next week?" she asked.

"It looks that way." I felt my molars reach for each other. How did she know that?

"Should be fun."

"It's strictly work, Harry."

"Right. He's still cute as a bean bug."

"His ancestors were bred to root truffles."

"What?"

"Never mind."

Friday morning I selected bone fragments, wrote out

186

questions, and set the assemblage up on trays. Alex, my teaching assistant, would arrange the cards and specimens in numerical order, and time the students as they moved from station to station. The ever-popular bone quiz.

Katy showed up right on time, and by noon we were cruising south. The temperature was in the high sixties, the sky the color portrayed in Grand Strand promotional posters. We put on our shades and rolled the windows down to let our hair blow. I drove and Katy chose the rock and roll.

We took I-77 south through Columbia, cut southeast on I-26, and south again on I-95. At Yemassee we left the interstate and flew along narrow low-country roads. We talked and laughed and stopped when we wanted. Barbecue at Maurice's Piggy Park. A snapshot at the Old Sheldon-Prince Williams Church ruins, burned by Sherman after his march to the sea. It felt wonderful to be schedule-free, and with my daughter, and heading for the place I love most on earth.

Katy told me about her classes, and about the men she was dating. In her words, no keepers. She shared the story of the rift, now patched, that had threatened her plans for spring break. She described the girls with whom she'd be sharing the Hilton Head condo, and I laughed until I hurt. Yes, this was my daughter, with a humor dark enough to house vampires. I'd never felt closer to her, and for a while I was young and free, and forgot about murdered babies.

In Beaufort we passed the marine air station, made a quick stop at the Bi-Lo, then wound our way through town and over the Woods Memorial Bridge to Lady's Island. At the top I turned and looked back at the Beaufort waterfront, a sight that always lifts my spirits.

I spent my childhood summers near Beaufort, and most of those as an adult, the chain being broken only recently, when I began my work in Montreal. I witnessed the mushrooming of fast-food strips and the construction of the county government center, dubbed the "Taj Mahal" by the locals. The roads have been widened, the traffic is heavier. The islands are now home to golf resorts and condos. But Bay Street remains unchanged. The mansions still stand in antebellum grandeur, shaded by water oaks draped in Spanish moss. So little in life is constant; I find reassurance in the languid pace of life in Beaufort. The tide of time itself ebbs tardily to the eternal sea.

As we descended the far side of the bridge, ahead and to the left I could see a colony of boats docked on Factory Creek, a small loop of water off the Beaufort River. The late-afternoon sun glinted off their windows and glowed white on masts and decks. I drove another half mile on Highway 21, then turned into the parking area at Ollie's Seafood restaurant. Winding my way through live oaks, I headed to the back of the lot and pulled in at the water's edge.

Katy and I gathered our groceries and duffel bags and crossed a walkway from Ollie's to the Lady's Island Marina. To either side lay mudflats, the new spring shoots green among last year's dark stubble. Marsh wrens rasped complaints at our passing, and darted in and out among the cordgrass and cattails. I breathed the gentle blend of brackish water, chlorophyll, and decaying vegetation, and felt glad to be back in the low country.

The walkway from the shore led like a tunnel through the marina headquarters, a square white building with a narrow third story running the length of its roof, and an open passage on the first floor. On our right, doors opened to washrooms and a laundry. The offices of Apex Realty, a sail maker, and the harbormaster occupied the space to our left.

We passed through the tunnel, descended a floating gangplank with horizontal wooden risers, and crossed to the farthest of the docks. As we walked its length, Katy scanned each of the boats we passed. The *Ecstasy*, a forty-foot Morgan out of Norfolk, Virginia. The *Blew Palm*, a custom-built fifty-three-footer with a steel hull and enough sail to go round the world. The *Hillbilly Heaven*, a classic nineteen-thirties power yacht, once elegant, now weathered and no longer seaworthy. The *Melanie Tess* was the last boat on the right. Katy eyed the forty-two-foot Chris Craft, but said nothing.

"Hold here a second," I said, dropping my bundles onto the dock.

I stepped onto the stern, climbed to the bridge, and worked the combination on a toolbox to the right of the captain's chair. Then I dug out a key, unlocked and opened the aft entrance, slid back the hatch, and lowered myself the three steps to the main cabin. Inside, the air was cool and smelled of wood and mildew and pine disinfectant. I unlocked the port-side entrance and Katy handed me our food and duffels, then came aboard.

Without a word my daughter and I left everything in the main salon, then darted around the boat, snooping out the decor. It was a habit we'd started when she was very young, and no matter how old I live to be, it will remain my favorite part of stays in unknown places. The *Melanie Tess* wasn't exactly unknown, but I hadn't been on her in five years, and was curious to see the changes Sam had described.

Our survey revealed a galley one step down and forward from the main salon. It had a two-burner stove, a sink, and a wooden refrigerator with an old-style icebox handle. The floor was parquet, the walls, as everywhere, teak. On the starboard side was a dining nook, its cushions covered in bold pinks and greens.

Forward of the galley were a pantry, a head, and a V-berth large enough to sleep two.

Aft lay the master stateroom with its king-size bed and mirrored closets. As in the main salon and dining nook, it was done in teak and bright cotton foliage. Katy looked relieved to see a shower in the master head.

"This is so cool," said Katy. "Can I have the V-berth?"

"Are you sure?" I asked.

"Totally. It looks so snug I'm going to make a little nest up there, put all my *stuff* along those shelves." She mimed lining up and straightening small objects.

I laughed. George Carlin's "stuff" routine was one of our favorite comedy bits.

"Besides, I'm only going to be here two nights, you take the large bed."

"O.K."

"Look, a communiqué with your name on it." She took an envelope from the table and handed it to me.

I tore the flap and shook out a note.

> *The water and electricity are hooked up so you should be set. Give me a call when you're settled. I want to take you out to feed. Enjoy.*
>
> *Sam*

We stowed the groceries, then Katy went to arrange her stuff while I dialed Sam.

"Hey, hey, darlin', you're all tucked in?"

"We've been here about twenty minutes. She looks beautiful, Sam. I can't believe it's the same boat."

"Nothing a little money and muscle can't accomplish."

"It shows. Do you ever stay on board?"

"Oh, yeah. That's why the phone and answering machine are there. It's a bit over the top for a boat, but I

190

can't afford to miss messages. You feel free to use that number."

"Thanks, Sam. I really appreciate this."

"Hell, I don't use her enough. Someone ought to."

"Well, thanks again."

"How about dinner?"

"I really don't want to impose on—"

"Hell, I need to eat, too. I'll tell you what. I'm going out to the Gay Seafood Market to buy grouper for some damn thing Melanie's cooking up tomorrow. How 'bout I meet you at Factory Creek Landing. It'll be on the right, just after Ollie's and just before the bridge. It isn't fancy, but they make some mean shrimp."

"What time?"

"It's six-forty now, so how 'bout seven-thirty. I want to go by the shop and pick up the Harley."

"On one condition. I'm buying."

"You're a tough woman, Tempe."

"Don't mess with me."

"Are we still on for tomorrow?"

"If it's O.K. with you. I don't want t—"

"Yeah. Yeah. Have you told her?"

"Not yet. But she'll figure it out once you meet. See you in an hour."

I tossed my bag onto my bed, then went up to the bridge. The sun was dropping, its last rays tinting the world a warm crimson. It flamed the marsh to my right and tinted a white ibis standing in the grass. The bridge to Beaufort stood out black against the pink, like the backbone of some ancient monster arching across the sky. The boats in the city marina winked across the river at our little pier.

Though the day had cooled, the air still felt like satin. A breeze lifted a strand of hair and wrapped it softly across my face.

"What's the agenda?"

191

Katy had joined me. I checked my watch.

"We're meeting Sam Rayburn for dinner in half an hour."

"*The* Sam Rayburn? I thought he was dead."

"He is. This one is the mayor of Beaufort and an old friend."

"How old?"

"Older than I am. But he's still ambulatory. You'll like him."

"Wait a minute." She pointed a finger at me, and I could see thought working in her eyes. Then a synapse. "Is this the monkey guy?"

I smiled and tipped my head.

"Is that where we're going tomorrow? No, don't answer. Of course it is. That's why I had to get the shots."

"You had it checked, didn't you?"

"Cancel the bed at the sanitarium," she said, holding out her arm. "I'm certified tuberculosis-free."

When we arrived at the restaurant Sam's motorcycle was parked in the lot. Last summer it had joined the Lotus, the sailboat, and the ultralight as the newest addition to a long list of playthings. I am never sure if these toys are Sam's way of fending off middle age, or his attempts at integration into the activities of people after years of focusing on the activities of primates.

Though he is a decade older, Sam and I have been friends for more than twenty years. When we met I was a college sophomore, Sam a second-year graduate student. We were drawn to each other, I suspect, because our lives to that point had been so different.

Sam is a Texan, the only child of Jewish boarding-house owners. At fifteen his father was killed defending a cash box that held twelve dollars. Following her husband's death, Mrs. Rayburn sank into a depression

192

from which she never emerged. Sam shouldered the burden of running the business while finishing high school and caring for his mother. Upon her death seven years later, he sold the boardinghouse and joined the marines. He was restless, angry, and interested in nothing.

Life in the military only fed Sam's cynicism. In boot camp he found the antics of his fellow recruits profoundly annoying, and drew deeper and deeper into himself. During his tour in Vietnam he spent hours watching birds and animals, using them as an escape from the horror around him. He was appalled by the carnage of war, and felt tremendous guilt about his role in it. The animals seemed innocent by contrast, not motivated by elaborate schemes designed to kill others of their own kind. He was especially drawn to the monkeys, to the orderliness of their society and the way they resolved disputes with minimal physical injury. For the first time Sam found himself truly fascinated.

Sam returned to the States and enrolled at the University of Illinois at Champaign-Urbana. He finished a bachelor's degree in three years, and when I met him was the teaching assistant for the section of introductory zoology to which I was assigned. He had a reputation among undergraduates for a quick temper, a harsh tongue, and being easily annoyed. Particularly by the slow-witted and the ill-prepared. He was meticulous and demanding, but scrupulously fair in his evaluation of student work.

As I got to know Sam I found that he liked few people, but was tenaciously loyal to those he admitted into his small circle. He once told me that, having spent so many years among primates, he felt he no longer fit in human society. The monkey perspective, as he called it, had shown him the ridiculousness of human behavior.

Sam eventually switched to physical anthropology, did field-work in Africa, and completed his doctorate. After stints at several universities, he ended up in Beaufort in the early 1970s as scientist in charge of the primate facility.

Though age has mellowed Sam, I doubt that it will ever change his discomfiture at social interaction. It isn't that he doesn't want to participate. He does. His seeking the office of mayor proves that. Life just doesn't operate for Sam the way it does for others. So he buys bikes and wings for flying. They provide stimulation and excitement, but remain predictable and manageable. Sam Rayburn is one of the most complex and most intelligent people I have ever met.

His mayoral honor was at the bar, watching a basketball game and drinking draft beer.

I made the introductions and, as usual, Sam took charge, ordering a refill for himself, Diet Coke for me and Katy, then herding us to a booth at the back of the restaurant.

My daughter wasted no time in confirming her suspicions regarding tomorrow's plans, then pummeled Sam with questions.

"How long have you directed this primate center?"

"Longer than I care to think about. I worked for someone else until about ten years ago, then bought the damn company for myself. Just about went to the poorhouse, but I'm glad I did it. Nothing beats being your own boss."

"How many monkeys live on the island?"

"Right now about forty-five hundred."

"Who owns them?"

"The FDA. My company owns the island and manages the animals."

"Where do they come from?"

"They were brought to Murtry Island from a research

194

colony in Puerto Rico. Your mom and I both did work there, somewhere back in the early Bronze Age. But they're originally from India. They're rhesus."

"*Macaca mulatta.*" Katy pronounced the genus and species in a lilting, singsong voice.

"Very good. Where did you learn primate taxonomy?"

"I'm a psych major. A lot of research is done using rhesus. You know, like Harry Harlow and his progeny?"

Sam was about to comment when the waitress arrived with plates of fried clams and oysters, boiled shrimp, hush puppies, and slaw. We all concentrated on spooning sauces onto our plates, squeezing lemons, and peeling a starter batch of shrimp.

"What are the monkeys used for?"

"The Murtry population is a breeding colony. Some yearlings are removed and sent to the Food and Drug Administration, but if an animal isn't trapped by the time it reaches a certain body weight, it's there for life. Monkey heaven."

"What else is out there?" My daughter had no reservations about chewing and talking at the same time.

"Not much. The monkeys are free-ranging so they go where they want. They set up their own social groups and have their own rules. There are feeder stations, and corrals for trapping, but outside camp the island is really theirs."

"What's camp?"

"That's what we call the area right at the dock. There's a field station, a small veterinary clinic, mostly for emergencies, some storage sheds for monkey chow, and a trailer where students and researchers can stay."

He dipped an oyster in cocktail sauce, tipped back his head, and dropped it in his mouth.

"There was a plantation on the island back in the

nineteenth century." Small drops of red clung to his beard. "Belonged to the Murtry family. That's where the island gets its name."

"Who's allowed out there?" She peeled another shrimp.

"Absolutely no one. These monkeys are virus-free and worth mucho dinero. Anyone, and I mean anyone, who sets foot on the island is cleared through me, and has to have a shitload of immunizations, including a negative TB test within the last six months."

Sam looked a question at me, and I nodded.

"I didn't think anyone caught TB anymore."

"The test isn't for your protection, young lady. The monks are very susceptible to TB. An outbreak can destroy a colony quicker than you can say jackshit."

Katy turned to me. "Your students had to do the shot bit?"

"Every time."

Early in my career, before I was lured into forensics, my research involved the use of monkeys to study the aging process in the skeleton. I'd taught all the primatology courses at UNCC, including a field school on Murtry Island. I'd brought students out for fourteen years.

"Hm," said Katy, popping a clam into her mouth. "This is going to be O.K."

At seven-thirty the next morning we stood on a dock at the northern tip of Lady's Island, eager to go to Murtry. The drive had been like traveling through a terrarium. A heavy mist covered everything, blurring edges and throwing the world slightly out of focus. Though Murtry was less than a mile out, I looked across the water into nothingness. Closer in, an ibis startled and lifted off, its long, slender legs trailing behind.

The staff had arrived and were loading the facility's

two open boats. They finished shortly and took off. Katy and I sipped coffee, waiting for Sam's signal. At last he whistled and gave a come-on gesture. We crumpled our Styrofoam cups, threw them into an oil drum turned trash barrel, and hurried down to the lower dock.

Sam helped each of us board, then untied the line and jumped in. He nodded to the man at the wheel, and we putted out into the inlet.

"How long is the ride?" Katy asked Sam.

"The tide's up, so we'll take Parrot Creek, then the back creek and cut through the marsh. Shouldn't be more than forty minutes."

Katy sat cross-legged on the bottom of the boat.

"You'd do better to stand and lean against the side," Sam suggested. "When Joey throttles down, this thing jumps. The vibration's enough to rattle your vertebrae."

Katy got up and he handed her a rope.

"Hang on to this. Do you want a life vest?"

Katy shook her head. Sam looked at me.

"She's a strong swimmer," I assured him.

Just then Joey opened the engine and the boat surged to life. We raced across open water, the wind snapping hair and clothes and ripping the words from our lips. At one point Katy tapped Sam's shoulder and pointed to a buoy.

"Crab pot," yelled Sam.

Farther on, he showed her an osprey nest atop a channel marker. Katy nodded vigorously.

Before long we left open water and entered the marsh. Joey stood with feet spread, eyes fixed straight ahead as he twisted and turned the wheel, piloting the boat through narrow ribbons of water. There couldn't have been more than ten feet of clearance in any of the alleys. We leaned hard left, then hard right, twisting

197

through the cut, our spray showering the grass to either side.

Katy and I clung to the boat and to each other, our bodies pitching with the centrifugal force of hard turns, laughing and enjoying the thrill of speed and the beauty of the day. Much as I love Murtry Island, I think I have always loved the crossing more.

By the time we reached Murtry the mist had burned away. Sunlight warmed the dock and dappled the sign at the entrance to the island. A breeze teased the foliage overhead, sending splotches of shadow and light dancing and changing shape across the words: GOVERNMENT PROPERTY. KEEP OUT. ABSOLUTELY NO ADMITTANCE.

When the boats were unloaded and everyone was inside the field station, Sam introduced Katy to the staff. I knew most of them, though there were a few new faces. Joey had been hired two summers earlier. Fred and Hank were still in training. As he made introductions, Sam gave a quick rundown of the operation.

Joey, Larry, Tommy, and Fred were technicians, their primary duties being day-to-day maintenance of the facility and transport of supplies. They did painting and repair, cleaned the corrals and feeder stations, and kept the animals supplied with water and chow.

Jane, Chris, and Hank were more directly involved with the monkeys, monitoring the groups for various types of data.

"Like what?" Katy asked.

"Pregnancies, births, deaths, veterinary problems. We keep close tabs on the population. And there are research projects. Jane's involved in a serotonin study. She goes out each day to record certain types of behavior, to see which monkeys are more aggressive, more impulsive. Then we run that data against their serotonin levels. We're also looking at their rank. Her

198

monkeys wear telemetric collars that send out a signal so she can find them. You'll probably spot one."

"Serotonin is a chemical in the brain," I offered.

"Yes," said Katy. "A neurotransmitter thought to be correlated with aggression."

Sam and I exchanged smiles. Atta girl!

"How do you gauge whether a monkey is impulsive?" Katy asked.

"He takes more risks. Makes longer leaps, for example, high up in the trees. Leaves home at an earlier age."

"He?"

"This is a pilot study. No girls."

"You may see one of my boys in camp," said Jane, strapping a box with a long antenna to her waist. "J-7. He's in O group. They hang around here a lot."

"He's the klepto?" Hank asked.

"Yeah. He'll snatch anything that isn't nailed down. He got another pen last week. And Larry's watch. I thought Larry'd have a stroke chasing him."

When everyone had stowed his or her gear, checked assignments, and gone out, Sam took Katy on a tour of the island. I tagged along, watching my daughter become a monkey spotter. As we meandered along the trails, Sam pointed out the feeder stations, and described the groups that frequented each. He talked about territory, and dominance hierarchies, and maternal lines while Katy held binoculars to her face and scanned the trees.

At feeder station E Sam threw dried corn kernels against the corrugated metal roof.

"Hold still and watch," he said.

Soon we heard the swish of foliage and saw a group move in. Within minutes monkeys surrounded us, some remaining in the trees, others dropping to the ground and darting forward to pick up corn.

199

Katy was enthralled.

"That's F group," said Sam. "It's small, but it's run by one of the highest-ranking females on the island. She's a ball buster."

By the time we got back to camp Sam had helped Katy design a simple project. She organized her notes while he got a bag of corn for her, then she headed back out. I watched her disappear into a tunnel of oak trees, the binoculars banging against her hip.

Sam and I sat on the screened porch and talked for a while, then he went to work and I got out the CAT scan draft. Though I tried, I found it hard to focus. Sinus patterns held little appeal when I could look up and see sunshine on a tidal estuary and smell air laced with salt and pine.

The staff came in at noon, Katy among them. After sandwiches and Fritos, Sam went back to his data, and Katy returned to the woods.

I resettled with my paper, but it was still no go. I drifted off after page three.

I woke to a familiar sound.

Thunk! Rat a tat a tat a tat a tat. Thunk! Rat a tat a tat tat tat.

Two monkeys had dropped from the trees and were running across the porch roof. Being as inconspicuous as possible, I opened the screen door and eased myself out and onto the steps. O group had entered camp and was resting in the branches above the field station. The pair that had wakened me now leaped from the field station to the trailer and settled on opposite ends of the roof.

"That's him." I hadn't heard Sam come up behind me. "Look." He handed me the binoculars.

"I can make out the tattoos," I said, reading the chest of each monkey. "J-7 and GN-9. J-7 has a collar."

I passed back the glasses and Sam took another look.

200

"What the hell's he got? You don't suppose the little shit's still toting Larry's watch?"

Another handoff.

"It's shiny. Looks like gold when the sun hits it."

Just then GN-9 lunged and gave a full, openmouthed threat. J-7 screeched and flew off the roof, launching himself from branch to branch until he was out of sight behind the trailer. His treasure slid down the roof and into the gutter.

"Let's find out."

Sam dragged a ladder from under the field house and propped it against the trailer. He brushed away spiderwebs, tested his weight on the first rung, then climbed up.

"What the hell?"

"What?"

"Sonofabitch."

"What is it?"

He rotated something in his hand.

"I'll be goddamned."

"What is it?" I tried to see what the monkey had dropped, but Sam's body obscured my view.

Sam stood motionless at the top of the ladder, his head bent.

"Sam, what is it?"

Without a word he climbed down and held the object out for my inspection. I knew instantly what it was and what it meant, and felt the sunshine go out of the day.

I met Sam's eyes and we stared at each other in silence.

16

I stood with the thing in my hand, unwilling to believe
what my eyes were telling me.

Sam spoke first.

"That's a human jaw."

"Yes." I watched lacy shadows slide across his face.

"Probably an old Indian burial."

"Not with this dental work." I rotated the mandible
and sunlight glinted off gold.

"That's what got J-7's attention," he said, staring at
the crowns.

"And this is flesh," I added, pointing to a brown glob
clinging to the joint.

"What does that mean?"

I raised the jaw and sniffed. It had the dank, cloying
odor of death.

"In this climate, depending on whether the body was
buried or left on the surface, I'd say this person has
been dead less than a year."

"How the fuck can that be?" A vein throbbed in his
forehead.

"Don't yell at me. Apparently everyone who comes to
this island does not clear through you!"

I glanced away from him.

"Where the hell did he get it?"

"He's your monkey, Sam. You figure it out."

"You damn well better believe I will."

He strode toward the field station, took the stairs two at a time, and disappeared inside. Through the open windows I heard him call to Jane.

For a moment I stood there, hearing the click of palmetto fronds and feeling surreal. Had death actually penetrated my island of tranquillity?

"No!" cried a voice in my head. "Not here!"

I heard the whirp of the spring as the screen door flew open. Sam emerged with Jane and called to me.

"Come on, Quincy. Let's round up the usual suspects. Jane knows where O group goes when it's not in camp, so we should be able to pick up J-7's collar. Maybe the little bugger will give something up."

I didn't move.

"Son of a buck, I'm sorry. I just don't like body parts showing up on my island. You know my temper."

I did. But it wasn't Sam's outburst that held me back. I smelled the pine and felt the warm breeze on my cheek. I knew what was out there and didn't want to find it.

"C'mon."

I took a deep breath, as enthused as a woman on her way to a meeting requested by an oncologist.

"Wait."

I went into the field station and rooted in the kitchen until I found a plastic tub. I sealed the jaw inside, hid the container in a cabinet in the back room, then left a note for Katy.

We took a trail behind the field station and followed Jane toward the center of the island. She led us to an area where the trees were the size of offshore rigs, the foliage a solid canopy overhead. The ground was a plush of humus and pine needles, the air heavy with the scent of decaying vegetation and animal matter. A swish in the branches told me monkeys were present.

"Someone's here," said Jane, turning on her receiver.

Sam searched the trees with his binoculars, trying to make out tattoo codes.

"It's A group," he said.

"Hunh!"

A juvenile crouched on a branch above me, shoulders down, tail in the air, eyes fixed on my face. The sharp, throaty bark was his way of saying "back off!"

When I met his gaze the monkey sat back, ducked his head, then raised it diagonally across his body. He repeated the bob several times, then spun and did a cannonball into the next tree.

Jane adjusted dials then closed her eyes to listen, face tense with concentration. After a while she shook her head and continued up the path.

Sam scanned the treetops as Jane stopped again and rotated clockwise, totally focused on the sounds in her headset. Finally,

"I've got a very faint signal."

She veered in the direction in which the cannonballer had disappeared, paused, pivoted again.

"I think he's over near Alcatraz." She pointed toward ten o'clock.

While most of the trapping pens on the island are designated by letter, a few of the older ones have names like O.K. Corral or Alcatraz.

We moved toward Alcatraz, but just south of the corral Jane left the path and cut into the woods. The vegetation was thicker here, the ground spongy underfoot. Sam turned to me.

"Watch yourself near the pond. Alice had a mess of babies last season, and I suspect she's not feeling sociable."

Alice is a fourteen-foot alligator who has lived on

Murtry for as long as anyone can remember. No one recalls who named her. The staff respects her right to be there and leaves her to her pond.

I gave Sam a thumbs-up sign. While they do not frighten me, gators have never been creatures whose company I sought.

We weren't twenty feet off the trail when I noticed it, faint at first, just a variation on the dark, organic forest smell. Initially I wasn't sure, but as we picked our way closer the odor grew stronger, and a cold band tightened on my chest.

Jane cut north, away from the pond, and Sam followed, binoculars trained on the overhead branches. I held back. The smell was coming from straight ahead.

I circled a fallen sweet gum and stopped. I could see a belt of brush and scrub palm bordering the pond. The forest grew silent as Jane and Sam pulled away, the rustling of their feet fading with each step.

The odor of decaying flesh is like no other. I'd smelled it on the jaw, and now the sweet, fetid scent tainted the afternoon air, telling me my quarry was near. Barely breathing, I pivoted as Jane had done, eyes closed, every fiber fixed on sensory input. Same motion, different focus. While Jane was tracking with her ears, I hunted with my nose.

The smell was coming from the direction of the pond. I moved toward it, my nose following the odor and my eyes on reptile alert. Overhead a monkey barked, then a stream of urine trickled to the ground. Branches stirred and leaves fluttered earthward. The stench grew stronger with each step.

I drew within ten feet, stopped, and trained my binoculars on the thicket of scrub palm and yaupon holly that separated me from the pond. An iridescent cloud formed and re-formed just outside its border.

I crept forward, carefully testing with each footfall. At

205

the edge of the bushes the smell of putrefaction was overpowering. I listened. Silence. I scanned the underbrush. Nothing. My heart raced and sweat poured down my face.

Move your ass, Brennan. It's too far from the pond for alligators.

I pulled a bandanna from my pocket, covered my mouth and nose, and squatted to see what the flies found so attractive.

They rose as one, whining and darting around me. I waved them away, but they returned immediately. Sweeping back flies with one hand, I wrapped the bandanna around the other and lifted the yaupon branches. Insects bounced off my face and arms, buzzing and swarming in agitation.

The flies had been drawn to a shallow grave, hidden from view by the thick leaves. Staring from it was a human face, the features shifting and changing in the shadowy light. I leaned close, then drew back in horror.

What I saw was no longer a face, but a skull stripped bare by scavengers. What appeared as eyes and nose and lips were, in fact, mounds of tiny crabs, parts of a seething mass that covered the skull and fed on its flesh.

As I looked around I realized there had been other opportunists. A mangled segment of rib cage lay to my right. Arm bones, still connected by tendrils of dried ligament, peeked from the undergrowth five feet away.

I released the bush and sat back on my heels, immobilized by a cold, sick feeling. On the edge of my vision I saw Sam approaching. He was speaking, but his words didn't penetrate. Somewhere, a million miles away, a motor grew louder then stopped.

I wanted to be somewhere else. To be some*one* else. Someone who had not spent years smelling death and seeing its final degradation. Someone who did not work day after day reassembling the human carnage left by macho pimps, enraged partners, wired cokeheads, and psychopaths. I had come to the island to escape the brutality of my life's work. But even here, death had found me. I felt overwhelmed. Another day. Another death. Death du jour. My God, how many such days would there be?

I felt Sam's hand on my shoulder and looked up. His other hand was cupped across his nose and mouth.

"What is it?"

I inclined my head toward the bush and Sam bent it backward with his boot.

"Holy shit."

I agreed.

"How long has it been here?"

I shrugged.

"Days? Weeks? Years?"

"The burial has been a bonanza for your island fauna, but most of the body looks undisturbed. I can't tell what condition it's in."

"Monkeys didn't dig this up. They won't have anything to do with meat. Must be the damn buzzards."

"Buzzards?"

"Turkey vultures. They love to chow down on monkey carcasses."

"I'd also question the raccoons."

"Yeah? Coons love the yaupon, but I didn't think they'd eat carrion."

I looked again at the grave.

"The body is on its side, with the right shoulder just below the surface. No doubt the smell attracted scavengers. The vultures and raccoons probably dug and ate, then pulled out the arm and the jaw when decomposition weakened the joints." I indicated the ribs. "They chewed off a section of the thorax and dragged that out, too. The rest of the body was

207

probably too deep, or just too hard to get at, so they left it."

Using a stick, I dragged the arm closer. Though the elbow was still connected, the ends of the long bones were missing, their spongy interiors exposed along rough, gnarled edges.

"See how the ends are chewed off? That's animals. And this?" I indicated a small round hole. "That's a tooth puncture. Something small, probably a raccoon."

"Son of a buck."

"And of course the crabs and bugs did their share."

He rose, did a half turn, and kicked the dirt with the heel of his boot.

"Jesus H. Christ. Now what?"

"Now you call your local coroner, and he, or she, calls his, or her, local anthropologist." I rose and brushed dirt from my jeans. "And everybody talks to the sheriff."

"This is a goddam nightmare. I can't have people crawling all over this island."

"They don't have to crawl all over the island, Sam. They just have to come out, recover the body, maybe run a cadaver dog around to see if anyone else is buried here."

"How the—? Shit. This is impossible." A bead of sweat trickled down his temple. His jaw muscles bunched and unbunched.

For a moment neither of us spoke. The flies whined and circled.

Sam finally broke the silence. "You've got to do it."

"Do what?"

"Whatever has to be done. Dig this stuff up." He swept an arm in the direction of the grave.

"No way. Not my jurisdiction."

"I don't give a flying rat's ass whose jurisdiction it is. I'm not going to have a bunch of yo-yos running around out here, sabotaging my island, fucking up my work schedule, and very possibly infecting my monkeys. It's out of the question. It's not going to happen. I'm the bloody mayor, and this is my island. I'll sit on the goddam dock with a goddam shotgun before I let that happen."

The vein was back in his forehead, and the tendons in his neck stood out like guy wires. His finger jabbed the air to emphasize each point.

"That was an Academy Award performance, Sam, but I'm still not doing it. Dan Jaffer is at USC in Columbia. He does the anthropology cases in South Carolina, so that's probably who your coroner will call. Dan is board-certified and he's very good."

"Dan fucking Jaffer could have fucking TB!"

There seemed no point, so I didn't answer.

"You do this all the time! You could dig the guy out and turn everything over to this Jaffer character."

Still no point.

"Why the hell not, Tempe?" He glared at me.

"You know I'm in Beaufort on another case. I've promised these guys I'll work with them, and I have to be back in Charlotte on Wednesday."

I didn't give him the real answer, which was that I wanted nothing to do with this. I wasn't mentally ready to equate my island sanctuary with ugly death. Since first seeing the jaw, broken images had been floating through my brain, shards of cases past. Strangled women, butchered babies, young men with slashed throats and dull, unseeing eyes. If slaughter had come to the island, I wanted no part of it.

"We'll talk about this at camp," said Sam. "Don't mention bodies to anyone."

Ignoring his dictatorial manner, I tied my bandanna to the holly bush, and we headed back.

When we drew close to the trail I could see a battered

pickup near the point at which we'd cut into the woods. The truck was loaded with bags of monkey chow and had a three-hundred-gallon water tank chained to the rear. Joey was inspecting the tank.

Sam called to him.

"Hold up a minute."

Joey wiped the back of his hand across his mouth and folded his arms. He wore jeans and a sweatshirt with the sleeves and neck cut out. His greasy blond hair hung like linguini around his face.

Joey watched us approach, his eyes hidden by sunglasses, his mouth a tight line across his face. His body looked taut and tense.

"I don't want anyone going near the pond," Sam said to Joey.

"Alice get another monkey?"

"No." Sam didn't elaborate. "Where's that chow going?"

"Feeder seven."

"Leave it and come right back."

"What about water?"

"Fill the tanks and get back to camp. If you see Jane, send her in."

Joey's shades moved to my face and rested there for what seemed a long time. Then he got into the pickup and pulled away, the tank clanking behind.

Sam and I walked in silence. I dreaded the scene about to take place, and resolved not to let him bully me. I recalled his words, saw his face as he uncovered the grave. Then something else. Just before Sam joined me, I thought I'd heard a motor. Had it been the pickup? I wondered how long Joey had been parked on the trail. And why right there?

"When did Joey start working for you?" I asked.

"Joey?" He thought a moment. "Almost two years ago."

210

"He's reliable?"

"Let's just say Joey's compassion exceeds his common sense. He's one of these bleeding-heart types, always talking about animal rights and worrying about disturbing the monkeys. He doesn't know jackshit about animals, but he's a good worker."

When we got to camp I found a note from Katy. She'd finished her observation and gone to the dock to read. While Sam got out the phone, I walked down to the water. My daughter sat in one of the boats, shoes off, legs stretched in front of her, her sleeves and pants legs rolled as high as they would go. I waved and she returned the gesture, then pointed at the boat. I wagged my head and held up both hands, indicating it wasn't time to leave. She smiled and resumed reading.

When I entered the field station Sam was at the kitchen table, talking on a cell phone. I slid onto the bench opposite him.

"When will he be back?" he asked into the mouthpiece. He looked more agitated than I'd ever seen him.

Pause. He tapped a pencil against the table, reversing from tip, to end, to tip as he slid it lengthwise through his fingers.

"Ivy Lee, I need to talk to him now. Can't you raise him somehow?"

Pause. Tap. Tap. Tap.

"No, a deputy will not do. I need Sheriff Baker."

Long pause. Tap. Ta—The lead snapped and Sam threw the pencil into a trash basket on the far side of the kitchen.

"I don't care what he said, keep trying. Have him call me here at the island. I'll wait."

He slammed down the receiver.

"How can both the sheriff and the coroner be out of contact?" He ran two hands through his hair.

I turned sideways on the bench, brought my feet up,

and leaned against the wall. Through the years I'd learned that the best way to deal with Sam's temper was to ignore it. It came and went like a flash fire.

He got up and paced the kitchen, punching one hand into the palm of the other. "Where the hell is Harley?"

He looked at his watch.

"Four-ten. Terrific. In twenty minutes everyone will be here, wanting to get back to town. Hell, they're not even supposed to be here on Saturday. This is a make-up day for bad weather."

He kicked a piece of chalk across the room.

"I can't make them stay here. Or maybe I should? Maybe I should tell them about the body, say 'nobody leaves the island,' then take each suspect into the back room and grill him, like Hercule fucking Poirot!"

More pacing. Watch checking. Pacing. Finally he dropped onto the opposite bench and rested his forehead on his fists.

"Are you finished with your tantrum?"

No response.

"May I make a suggestion?"

He didn't look up.

"Here it is anyway. The body is on the island because someone doesn't want it found. Obviously they didn't count on J-7."

I spoke to the top of his head.

"I see several possibilities. One. It was brought here by one of your employees. Two. An outsider dropped in by boat, possibly a local who knows your routine. The island is unguarded after the crews leave, right?"

He nodded without raising his head.

"Three. It could be one of the drug traffickers who cruise around these waters."

No response.

"Aren't you a deputy wildlife officer?"

He looked up. His forehead glistened with sweat.

212

"Yes."

"If you can't raise the coroner or Sheriff Baker, and you won't trust a deputy, call your wildlife buddies. They have jurisdiction offshore, right? Calling them won't arouse suspicion and they can get someone out here to seal off the site until you talk to the sheriff."

He slapped the tabletop. "Kim."

"Whoever. Just ask them to keep it cool until you've talked with Baker. I've already told you what he's going to do."

"Kim Waggoner works for the South Carolina Department of Natural Resources. She's helped me out in the past when I've had law enforcement problems out here. I can trust Kim."

"Will she stay all night?" While I've never been a timid woman, holding murderers or drug dealers at bay was not a job I would want.

"No problem." He was already dialing. "Kim is an ex-marine."

"She can handle intruders?"

"She eats nails for breakfast."

Someone answered and he asked for Officer Waggoner.

"Wait till you see her," he said, covering the mouthpiece with his hand.

By the time the staff reconvened everything had been arranged. The crew took Katy in their boat, while Sam and I stayed behind. Kim arrived shortly after five and was everything Sam had promised. She wore jungle fatigues, combat boots, and an Australian bush hat, and packed enough munitions to hunt rhino. The island would be safe.

On the drive back to the marina, Sam again asked me to do the recovery. I repeated what I'd told him earlier. Sheriff. Coroner. Jaffer.

"I'll talk to you tomorrow," I said as he pulled up to the walkway. "Thanks for taking us out today. I know Katy loved it."

"No problemo."

We watched a pelican glide over the water, then fold its wings and dive headlong into a trough. It reappeared with a fish, the afternoon light metallic on its wet scales. Then the pelican tacked and the fish dropped, a silvery missile plummeting to the sea.

"Jesus Christ. Why did they have to pick my island?" Sam sounded tired and discouraged.

I opened the car door. "Let me know what Sheriff Baker says."

"I will."

"You do understand why I can't do the scene, don't you?"

"Scene. Christ."

When I slammed the door and leaned in the open window he started with a new argument.

"Tempe, think about it. Monkey island. Buried corpse. The local mayor. If there's a leak the press will go crazy with this, and you know how sensitive the animal rights issue is. I don't need the media discovering Murtry."

"That could happen no matter who works the case."

"I know. It's—"

"Let it go, Sam."

As I watched him drive off, the pelican circled back and swooped low above the boat. A new fish glistened in its beak.

Sam had that same tenacity. I doubted he would let it go, and I was right.

214

17

After dinner at Steamers Oyster Bar, Katy and I visited a gallery on Saint Helena. We meandered the rooms of the creaky old inn, inspecting the work of local Gullah artists, appreciating another perspective on a place we thought we knew. But as I critiqued collages, paintings, and photos, I remembered bones and crabs and dancing flies.

Katy bought a miniature heron carved from bark and painted periwinkle blue. On the way home we stopped for coffee ice cream, then ate it on the bow of the *Melanie Tess*, talking and listening to the lines and halyards of the surrounding sailboats clicking in the breeze. The moon spread a shimmering triangle outward from the marsh. As we chatted I watched the pale yellow light ripple on the undulating blackness.

My daughter confided her ambition to be a criminal profiler, and shared her misgivings about attaining that goal. She marveled at the beauty of Murtry and described the antics of the monkeys she'd observed. At one point I considered telling her of the day's discovery, but held back. I didn't want to sully the memory of her visit to the island.

I went to bed at eleven and lay for a long time

listening to the creak of mooring lines and willing myself to sleep. Eventually I drifted off, taking the day with me and weaving it into the fabric of the last few weeks. I rode in a boat with Mathias and Malachy, desperately trying to keep them on board. I brushed crabs from a corpse, watched the seething mass re-form as fast as I scattered it. The corpse's skull morphed into Ryan's face, then into the charred features of Patrice Simonnet. Sam and Harry shouted at me, their words incomprehensible, their faces hard and angry.

When the phone woke me I felt disoriented, unsure where I was or why. I stumbled to the galley.

"Good morning." It was Sam, his voice sounding strained and edgy.

"What time is it?"

"Almost seven."

"Where are you?"

"At the sheriff's office. Your plan isn't going to work."

"Plan?" My brain fought to patch into the conversation.

"Your guy is in Bosnia."

I peeked through the blinds. At the inner dock, a grizzled old man sat on the deck of his sailboat. As I released the slats he tipped back his head and drained a can of Old Milwaukee.

"Bosnia?"

"Jaffer. The anthropologist at USC. He's gone to Bosnia to excavate mass graves for the UN. No one is sure when he'll be back."

"Who's covering his casework?"

"It doesn't matter. Baxter wants you to do the recovery."

"Who's Baxter?"

"Baxter Colker is the Beaufort County coroner. He wants you to do it."

216

"Why?"

"Because I want you to do it."

That was straightforward enough.

"When?"

"As soon as possible. Harley's got a detective and a deputy lined up. Baxter is meeting us here at nine. He has a transport team on call. When we're ready to leave Murtry, he'll phone over and they'll meet us at the Lady's Island dock to take the body to Beaufort Memorial. But he wants you to do the digging. Just tell us what equipment you need and we'll get it."

"Is Colker a forensic pathologist?"

"Baxter's an elected official and has no medical training. He runs a funeral home. But he's conscientious as hell and wants this thing done right."

I thought for a minute.

"Does Sheriff Baker have any idea who might be buried out there?"

"There's a lot of drug shit that goes on down here. He's going to talk to the folks over at U.S. Customs and the local DEA people. Also the wildlife agents. Harley tells me they were staking out the marshes in the Coosaw River last month. He thinks one of the drug brethren is our best bet, and I agree. These guys value life about as much as a used Q-Tip. You will help us, won't you?"

Reluctantly, I agreed. I told him what equipment to gather and he said he'd get right on it. I was to be ready at ten.

For several minutes I stood there, unsure what to do about Katy. I could explain the situation and leave it up to her. After all, there was no reason she couldn't go with us to the island. Or, I could simply tell her that something had come up and Sam had asked me for help. Katy could spend the day here, or leave for Hilton

217

Head earlier than planned. I knew the second was a better idea, but decided to tell her anyway.

I ate a bowl of Raisin Bran and washed the dish and spoon. Unable to sit still, I threw on shorts and a T-shirt, and went outside to check the lines and water tank. While there I realigned the chairs on the bridge. Inside again, I made my bed and straightened the towels in the head. I rearranged the pillows on the salon sofa and picked fluff from the carpet. I wound the clock and checked the time. Only seven-fifteen. Katy wouldn't be up for hours. Putting on running shoes, I quietly let myself out.

I drove down Route 21 east across Saint Helena to Harbor Island, then Hunting Island, and turned in at the state park. The narrow blacktop wound through a slough still and dark as an underground lake. Palmetto palms and live oaks rose from the murky bottom. Here and there a shaft of sunlight sliced through the canopy, turning the water a honey gold.

I parked near the lighthouse and crossed a boardwalk to the beach. The tide was out and the wet sand glistened like a mirror. I watched a sandpiper skitter between tidal pools, its long filament legs disappearing into an inverted image of itself. The morning was cool, and goose bumps formed on my arms and legs as I went through my warm-up.

I ran east beside the Atlantic Ocean, my feet sinking only slightly into the packed sand. The air was absolutely calm. I passed a formation of pelicans bobbing on the gently rolling water. The broom sedge and sea oats stood motionless on the dunes.

As I jogged I studied the ocean's offerings. Drift-wood, rippled and smoothed and covered in barnacles. Tangled seaweed. The shiny brown shell of a horseshoe crab. A mullet, its eyes and innards gnawed clean by crabs and gulls.

218

I ran until my lungs burned. Then I ran some more. When I got back to the boardwalk, my trembling legs could barely carry me up the stairs. But mentally I felt rejuvenated. Maybe it was the dead fish, or even the horseshoe crab. Maybe I'd simply raised my endorphin level. But I no longer dreaded the day ahead. Death occurred every minute of every day in every place on the globe. It was part of the cycle of life, and that included Murtry Island. I would unearth this corpse and deliver it to those in charge. That was my job.

When I slipped back onto the boat Katy was still asleep. I made coffee, then went to shower, hoping the sound of the pump wouldn't disturb her. When I'd dressed, I toasted two English muffins, spread them with butter and blackberry jam, and took them to the salon. Friends tell me that physical exertion is an appetite depressant. Not for me. Exercise makes me want to devour my body weight in food.

I clicked on the TV, surfed the channels, and chose one of the half dozen evangelists offering Sunday morning advice. I was listening to the Reverend Eugene Highwater describe the "endless bounty provided to the righteous" when Katy stumbled in and threw herself onto the couch. Her face was creased and puffy from sleep, and her hair looked like one of the seaweed tumbles I'd passed on the beach. She wore a Hornets T-shirt that hung to her knees.

"Good morning. You're lovely today."

No response from my daughter.

"Coffee?"

She nodded, eyes still shut.

I went to the kitchen, filled a mug, and brought it to her. Katy rolled to a semi-upright position, tentatively raised her lids, and reached for the coffee.

"I stayed up till two reading."

She took a sip, then held the mug out as she stood

219

and folded her feet under her, Indian style. Her newly opened eyes fell on the Reverend Highwater.

"Why are you listening to that twit?"

"I'm trying to find out how you get this endless bounty stuff."

"Write him a check and he'll send you a four-pack."

Charity was not on the list of my daughter's early morning virtues.

"Who was the moron that called at dawn?"

Nor was delicacy.

"Sam."

"Oh. What did he want?"

"Katy, something happened yesterday that I didn't tell you about."

Her eyes went to full attention and fixed on mine.

I hesitated, then launched into an account of the previous day's discovery. Avoiding details, I described the body, and how J-7 had led us to it, then told her of my phone conversation with Sam.

"So you're going back out there today?" She raised her mug to drink.

"Yes. With the coroner and a team from the sheriff's office. Sam is picking me up at ten. I'm sorry about our day. You're welcome to come along, of course, but I understand if you'd rather not."

For a long time she said nothing. The reverend blustered on about Jeee-sus.

"Do they have any idea who it is?"

"The sheriff is thinking drugs. Traffickers use the rivers and inlets around here to bring stuff in. He suspects a deal went bad and someone ended up with a body to off-load."

"What will you do out there?"

"We'll remove the body, collect samples, and take a lot of pictures."

220

"No, no. I mean, tell me exactly what you'll do. I might be able to use it for a paper or something."

"Step by step?"

She nodded and settled back into the cushions.

"It looks pretty routine. We'll clear the vegetation, then set up a grid with a reference point for drawings and measurements." The St-Jovite basement flashed through my mind. "When we're done with surface collection I'll open the grave. Some recovery teams excavate in levels, looking for layering and whatnot. I don't really think that's necessary in these situations. When someone digs a hole, drops in a body, and covers it up, there isn't going to be any stratigraphy. But I'll keep one side of the trench clean so I'll have a profile as I go down into the grave. That way I can see if there are tool marks in the soil."

"Tool marks?"

"A shovel, or maybe a spade or a pick that's left an imprint in the dirt. I've never seen one, but some of my colleagues swear they have. They claim you can take impressions then make molds and match them to suspect tools. What I *have* seen are footwear impressions in the bottom of graves, especially if there's a lot of clay and silt. I'll definitely check for those."

"From the guy that dug it?"

"Yeah. When the hole reaches a certain depth the digger may jump in and work from there. If so, he can leave shoe prints. I'll also take soil samples. Sometimes soil from a grave can be matched to dirt found on a suspect."

"Or on his closet floor."

"Exactly. And I'll collect bugs."

"Bugs?"

"This burial is going to be lousy with bugs. It's shallow to begin with, and the turkey vultures and raccoons have partially exposed the body. The flies are having a jamboree out there. They'll be useful for determining PMI."

"PMI?"

"Postmortem interval. How long the person's been dead."

"How?"

"Entomologists have studied carrion-eating insects, mostly flies and beetles. They've found that different species arrive at a body in regular sequence, then each goes through its life cycle just as predictably. Some fly species arrive within minutes. Others show up later. The adults lay their eggs, and the eggs hatch into larvae. That's what maggots are, fly larvae."

Katy gave a grimace.

"After a certain period the larvae abandon the body and encase themselves in a hard outer shell called a pupa. Eventually they hatch as adults and fly off to start the whole thing over again."

"Why don't all the bugs arrive at the same time?"

"Different species have different game plans. Some come to munch on the corpse. Others prefer to dine on the eggs and larvae of their predecessors."

"Gross."

"There's a niche for everyone."

"What will you do with the bugs?"

"I'll collect samples of larvae and pupal casings, and try to net some adult insects. Depending on the state of preservation, I may also use a probe to take thermal readings from the body. When maggot masses form they can raise the internal temperature of a corpse appreciably. That's also useful for PMI estimation."

"Then what?"

"I'll preserve all the adults and half the larvae in an alcohol solution. The other larvae I'll place in containers with liver and vermiculite. The entomologist will raise them to hatching and identify what they are."

I wondered where Sam would come up with nets, ice cream containers, vermiculite, and a thermal probe on a Sunday morning. Not to mention the screens, trowels, and other excavating equipment I'd requested. That was his problem.

"What about the body?"

"That will depend on its condition. If it's fairly intact I'll simply lift it out and zip it in a body bag. A skeleton will take longer since I'll have to do a bone inventory to be sure I have everything."

She thought about this.

"What's the best-case scenario?"

"All day."

"What's the worst-case scenario?"

"Longer."

Frowning, she ran her fingers through her hair, then tied it into a loose knot on her neck.

"You keep your appointment on Murtry. I think I'll hang here then catch a ride to Hilton Head."

"Your friends won't mind picking you up early?"

"Nah. It's on the way."

"Good choice." I meant it.

It went as I'd described to Katy, but for one major variation. There was stratigraphy. Below the body with the crab face I was shocked to find a second decomposing corpse. It lay on the bottom of the four-foot pit, facedown, arms tucked below its belly, at a twenty-degree angle to the body above.

Depth has its benefits. Though the upper remains had been reduced to bone and connective tissue, those below retained a large amount of flesh and soupy innards. I worked until dark, meticulously screening every particle of dirt, taking soil, flora, and insect samples, and transferring the corpses to body bags. The sheriff's detective took videos and stills.

Sam, Baxter Colker, and Harley Baker watched from a distance, occasionally commenting or stepping forward for a better look. The deputy searched the surrounding woods with a Sheriff's Department dog specially trained to alert to the smell of decomposition. Kim looked for physical evidence.

All to no avail. Except for the two bodies, nothing turned up. The victims had been stripped naked and dumped, robbed of everything that linked them to their lives. And as hard as I studied the details, neither the body positions nor anything I observed in the grave contour or fill revealed if the victims had been buried simultaneously, or if the upper corpse had followed at a later date.

It was almost eight when we watched Baxter Colker slam the door of the transport van and lock the handle in place. The coroner, Sam, and I were gathered beside the blacktop, above the dock where we'd moored the boats.

Colker looked like a stick figure in his bow tie and neatly pressed suit, his trousers belted high above the waist. While Sam had warned me of the Beaufort County coroner's fastidiousness, I'd been unprepared for business attire at an exhumation. I wondered what the man wore to dinner parties.

"Well, that does her," he said, wiping his hands on a linen handkerchief. Hundreds of tiny veins had burst and coalesced in his cheeks, giving his face a bluish cast. He turned to me.

"I guess I'll see you at the hospital tomorrow." It was more a statement than a question.

"Whoa. Hold on. I thought these cases were going to the forensic pathologist in Charleston."

"Well, now, I can send these cases up to the medical college, ma'am, but I know what that gentleman is

224

going to tell me." Colker had been "ma'aming" me all day.

"That's Axel Hardaway?"

"Yes, ma'am. And Dr. Hardaway is going to tell me that I need an anthropologist because he doesn't know beans about bones. That's what he's going to tell me. And I understand Dr. Jaffer, the regular anthropologist, isn't available. Now, where does that leave these poor folks?" He waved a bony hand at the van.

"No matter who does the skeletal analysis, you're still going to want a full autopsy on the second body."

Something startled in the river, breaking the moonlight into a thousand little pieces. A breeze had picked up and I could smell rain in the air.

Colker knocked on the side of the van and an arm appeared in the window, waved, and the van pulled away. Colker watched it for a moment.

"Those two souls are going to overnight at Beaufort Memorial, today being Sunday. In the meantime I'll get hold of Dr. Hardaway and see what his preference is. May I ask where you're staying, ma'am?"

As I was telling him, the sheriff joined us.

"I want to thank you again, Dr. Brennan. You did a fine job out there."

Baker stood a foot taller than the coroner, and Sam and Colker together did not equal his body mass. Under his uniform shirt the sheriff's chest and arms looked as if they'd been forged from iron. His face was angular, his skin the color of strong coffee. Harley Baker looked like a heavyweight contender and spoke like a Harvard grad.

"Thank you, Sheriff. Your detective and deputy were very helpful."

When we shook hands mine looked pale and slender inside his. I suspected his grip could crush granite.

225

"Thank you again. I'll see you tomorrow with Detective Ryan. And I'll take good care of your bugs."

Baker and I had already discussed the insects, and I'd given him the name of an entomologist. I'd explained how to ship them and how to store the soil and plant samples. Everything was now on its way to the county government center in the care of the Sheriff's Department detective.

Baker shook hands with Colker and gave Sam a friendly punch on the shoulder.

"I know I'll see your sorry face," he said to Sam as he strode away. A minute later his cruiser passed us on its way to Beaufort.

Sam and I drove back to the *Melanie Tess*, stopping for carryout on the way. We spoke little. I could smell death on my clothes and hair, and I wanted to shower, eat, and fall into an eight-hour coma. Sam probably wanted me out of his car.

By nine forty-five my hair was wrapped in a towel and I smelled of White Diamonds moisturizing mist. I was raising the cover of my carryout box when Ryan called.

"Where are you?" I asked, squeezing ketchup onto my fries.

"An enchanting little place called the Lord Carteret."

"What's wrong with it?"

"There's no golf course."

"We're to meet with the sheriff at nine tomorrow." I inhaled the fry.

"Zero nine hundred hours, Dr. Brennan. What are you eating?"

"A salami sub."

"At ten P.M.?"

"It was a long day."

"My day wasn't exactly a walk in the park." I heard a match, then a long exhalation of breath. "Three flights, then the drive from Savannah out here to Tara, and

226

then I couldn't even raise this yokel of a sheriff. He was out on some damn thing all day, and no one would say where he was or what he was doing. Very hush-hush. He and Aunt Bee probably work deep cover for the CIA."

"Sheriff Baker is solid." I slurped a spoonful of slaw.

"You know him?"

"I spent the day with him."

Hush puppy.

"That chewing sounds different."

"Hush puppy."

"What's a hush puppy?"

"If you chip in I'll get you one tomorrow."

"Yahoo. What is it?"

"Deep-fried cornmeal."

"What were you and Baker doing all day?"

I gave him a brief account of the body recovery.

"And Baker suspects the hookah boys?"

"Yes. But I don't think so."

"Why not?"

"Ryan, I'm exhausted, and Baker's expecting us early. I'll tell you tomorrow. Can you find the Lady's Island Marina?"

"My first guess would be Lady's Island."

I gave him directions and we hung up. Then I finished my dinner and fell into bed, not bothering with pajamas. I slept naked and like a rock, dreaming nothing that I could recall for a solid eight hours.

227

18

At eight o'clock on Monday morning traffic was heavy on the Woods Memorial Bridge. The sky was overcast, the river choppy and slate green. The news on the car radio predicted light rain and a high of seventy-two for the day. Ryan looked out of place in his wool trousers and tweed jacket, like an arctic creature blown to the tropics. He was already perspiring.

As we crossed into Beaufort, I explained jurisdiction in the county. I told Ryan that the Beaufort Police Department functions strictly within the city limits, and described the other three municipalities, Port Royal, Bluffton, and Hilton Head, each with its own force.

"The rest of Beaufort County is unincorporated, so it's Sheriff Baker's bailiwick," I summed up. "His department also provides services to Hilton Head Island. Detectives, for example."

"Sounds like Quebec," said Ryan.

"It is. You just have to know whose turf you're on."

"Simonnet phoned her calls to Saint Helena. So that's Baker."

"Yes."

"You say he's solid."

"I'll let you form your own opinion."

"Tell me about the bodies you dug up."

I did.

"Jesus, Brennan, how do you get yourself into these things?"

"It is my job, Ryan." The question irked me. Everything about Ryan irked me lately.

"But you were on holiday."

Yes. On Murtry. With my daughter.

"It must be my rich fantasy life," I snapped. "I dream up corpses, then poof, there they are. It's what I live for."

I clamped my teeth and watched tiny drops gather on the windshield. If Ryan needed conversation he could talk to himself.

"I may need a little guidance here," he said as we passed the campus of USC-Beaufort.

"Carteret will take a hard left and turn into Boundary. Go with it."

We curved west past the condominiums at Pigeon Point, and eventually drove between the redbrick walls that enclose the National Cemetery on both sides of the road. At Ribaut I indicated a left turn.

Ryan signaled, then headed south. On our left we passed a Maryland Fried Chicken, the fire station, and the Second Pilgrim Baptist Church. On our right sprawled the county government center. The vanilla stucco buildings house the county administrative offices, the courthouse, the solicitors' offices, various law enforcement agencies, and the jail. The faux columns and archways were intended to create a low-country flavor, but instead the complex looks like an enormous Art Deco medical mall.

At Ribaut and Duke I pointed to a sand lot shaded by live oaks and Spanish moss. Ryan pulled in and parked between a Beaufort City Police cruiser and the county Haz Mat trailer. Sheriff Baker had just arrived and was

229

reaching for something in the back of his cruiser. Recognizing me, he waved, slammed the trunk, and waited for us to join him.

I made introductions and the men shook hands. The rain had dwindled to a fine mist. "Sorry to have to put one through your basket," said Ryan. "I'm sure you're busy enough without foreigners dropping in."

"No problem at all," Baker replied. "I hope we can do something for you."

"Nice digs," said Ryan, nodding toward the building housing the Sheriff's Department.

As we crossed Duke, the sheriff gave a brief explanation of the complex.

"In the early nineties the county decided it wanted all its agencies under one roof, so it built this place at a cost of about thirty million dollars. We've got our own space, so does the city of Beaufort, but we share services such as communications, dispatch, records."

A pair of deputies passed us on their way to the lot. They waved and Baker nodded in return, then he opened the glass door and held it for us.

The offices of the Beaufort County Sheriff's Department lay to the right, past a glass case filled with uniforms and plaques. The city police were to the left, through a door marked AUTHORIZED PERSONNEL ONLY. Next to that door another case displayed pictures of the FBI's ten most wanted, photos of local missing persons, and a poster from the Center for Missing and Exploited Children. Straight ahead a hallway led past an elevator to the building's interior.

We entered the sheriff's corridor to see a woman hanging an umbrella on a hall tree. Though well past fifty, she looked like an escapee from a Madonna video. Her hair was long and jet-black, and she wore a lace slip over a peacock mini-dress with a violet bolero jacket

230

over that. Platform clogs added three inches to her height. She spoke to the sheriff.

"Mr. Colker just phoned. And some detective called 'bout half a dozen times yesterday with his balls on fire 'bout something. It's on your desk."

"Thank you, Ivy Lee. This is Detective Ryan." Baker indicated the two of us. "And Dr. Brennan. The department will be assisting them in a matter."

Ivy Lee looked us over.

"You want coffee, sir?"

"Yes. Thank you."

"Three, then?"

"Yes."

"Cream?"

Ryan and I nodded.

We entered the sheriff's office and everyone sat. Baker tossed his hat onto a bank of file cabinets behind his desk.

"Ivy Lee can be colorful," he said, smiling. "She did twenty with the Marines, then came home and joined us." He thought a moment. "That's about nineteen years now. The lady runs this place with the efficiency of a hydrogen fuel cell. Right now she's doing some . . ." He searched for a phrase. ". . . fashion experimentation."

Baker leaned back and laced his fingers behind his head. His leather chair wheezed like a bagpipe.

"So, Mr. Ryan, tell me what you need."

Ryan described the deaths in St-Jovite, and explained the calls to Saint Helena. He had just outlined his conversations with the Beaufort-Jasper Clinic obstetrician and with Heidi Schneider's parents when Ivy Lee knocked. She placed a mug in front of Baker, set two others on a table between Ryan and me, and left without a word.

I took a sip. Then another.

231

"Does she make this?" I asked. If not the best coffee I'd ever tasted, it was right near the top of the list.

Baker nodded.

I drank again and tried to identify the flavors. I heard a phone in the outer office, then Ivy Lee's voice.

"What's in it?"

"It's a 'don't ask don't tell' policy with regard to Ivy Lee's coffee. I give her an allowance each month, and she buys the ingredients. She claims no one knows the recipe but her sisters and her mama."

"Can they be bribed?"

Laughing, Baker lay his forearms on the desk and leaned his weight on them. His shoulders were wider than a cement truck.

"I wouldn't want to offend Ivy Lee," he said. "And definitely not her mama."

"Good policy," agreed Ryan. "Don't offend the mamas." He flipped the elastic from a corrugated brown folder, searched the contents, and withdrew a paper.

"The number phoned from St-Jovite traces to four-three-five Adler Lyons Road."

"You're right about that being Saint Helena," said Baker.

He swiveled to the metal cabinets, slid open a drawer, and pulled a file. Laying the folder on his desk, he perused its one document.

"We ran the address, and there's no police history. Not a single call in the past five years."

"Is it a private home?" asked Ryan.

"Probably. That part of the island is pretty much trailers and small homes. I've been living here off and on all of my life and I had to use a map to find Adler Lyons. Some of the dirt roads out on the islands are little more than driveways. I might know them to see

232

them, but I don't always know their names. Or if they even have names."

"Who owns the property?"

"I don't have that, but we'll check it out later. In the meantime, why don't we just drop in for a friendly visit."

"Suits me," said Ryan, replacing his paper and snapping the elastic into place.

"And we can swing by the clinic if you think that would be useful."

"I don't want to jam you up with this. I know you're busy." Ryan rose. "If you prefer to point us in the right direction, I'm sure we'll be fine."

"No, no. I owe Dr. Brennan for yesterday. And I'm sure Baxter Colker isn't through with her yet. In fact, would you mind waiting while I check something?"

He disappeared into an adjacent office, returned immediately with a message slip.

"As I suspected, Colker called again. He's sent the bodies up to Charleston, but he wants to talk to Dr. Brennan." He smiled at me. His cheekbones and brow ridges were so prominent, his skin so shiny black, his face looked ceramic in the fluorescent light.

I looked at Ryan. He shrugged and sat back down. Baker dialed a number, asked for Colker, then handed me the phone. I had a bad feeling.

Colker said exactly what I anticipated. Axel Hardaway would perform the autopsies on the Murtry bodies, but refused to do any skeletal analysis. Dan Jaffer couldn't be reached. Hardaway would process the remains at the med school facility following any protocol I specified, then Colker would transport the bones to my lab in Charlotte if I would do the examinations.

Reluctantly, I agreed, and promised to speak directly with Hardaway. Colker gave me the number and we hung up.

"*Allons-y*," I said to the others.

"*Allons-y*," echoed the sheriff, reaching for his hat and placing it on his head.

We took Highway 21 out of Beaufort to Lady's Island, crossed Cowan's Creek to Saint Helena, and continued for several miles. At Eddings Point Road we turned left, and drove past miles of weather-beaten frame houses and trailers set on pilings. Plastic stretched across windows and porches sagged under the weight of moth-eaten easy chairs and old appliances. In the yards I could see junked auto frames and parts, makeshift sheds, and rusted septic tanks. Here and there a hand-lettered sign offered collards, butter beans, or goats.

Before long the blacktop made a hard left and sandy roads took off ahead and to the right. Baker turned and we entered a long, shady tunnel. Live oaks lined the road, their bark mossy, their branches arching overhead like the dome on a green cathedral. To either side ran narrow moats of algae-coated water.

Our tires scrunched softly as we passed more mobile homes and run-down houses, some with plastic or wooden whirligigs, others with chickens scratching in the yards. Save for the model years of the beat-up cars and pickups, the area looked much as it must have in the nineteen-thirties. And forties. And fifties.

Within a quarter mile Adler Lyons joined us from the left. Baker turned and drove almost to the end and stopped. Across the way I could see mossy gravestones shaded by live oaks and magnolias. Here and there a wooden cross gleamed white in the murky shadows.

To our right stood a pair of buildings, the larger a two-story farmhouse with dark green siding, the smaller a bungalow, once white, its paint now gray and peeling. Behind the houses I observed trailers and a swing set.

A low wall separated the compound from the road. It

234

was built of cinder blocks laid sideways and stacked, so the centers formed rows and layers of small tunnels. Each hollow was packed with vines and creepers, and purple wisteria meandered the length of the wall. At the driveway entrance a rusted metal sign said PRIVATE PROPERTY in bright orange letters.

The road continued less than a hundred feet past the wall, then ended in a stand of marsh grass. Beyond the weeds lay water the color of dull pewter.

"That should be four-three-five," said Sheriff Baker, shifting into park and indicating the larger home. "This was a fishing camp years ago." He tipped his head toward the water. "That's Eddings Point Creek out there. It empties into the sound not too far up. I'd forgotten about this property. It was abandoned for years."

The place had definitely seen better times. The siding on the farmhouse was patched and covered with mildew. The trim, once white, was now blistered and flaking to reveal a pale blue underlayer. A screened porch ran the width of the first floor, and dormer windows projected from the third, their upper borders mimicking in miniature the angle of the roof.

We got out, rounded the wall, and headed up the drive. Mist hung in the air like smoke. I could smell mud and decomposing leaves, and from far off, the hint of a bonfire.

The sheriff stepped onto the stoop while Ryan and I waited on the grass. The inner door stood open, but it was too dark to see past the screen. Baker moved to the side and knocked, rattling the door in its frame. Overhead, birdsong mingled with the click of palmetto fronds. From inside, I thought I heard a baby cry.

Baker knocked again.

In a moment we heard footsteps, then a young man appeared at the door. He had freckles and curly red hair, and wore denim overalls with a plaid shirt. I had a feeling we were about to interview Howdy Doody.

"Yeah?" He spoke through the screen, his eyes moving among the three of us.

"How are you doing?" asked Baker, greeting him with the Southern substitute for "hello."

"Fine."

"Good. I'm Harley Baker." His uniform made clear this was not a social call. "May we come in?"

"Why?"

"We'd just like to ask you a few questions."

"Questions?"

"Do you live here?"

Howdy nodded.

"May we come in?" Baker repeated.

"Shouldn't you have a warrant or something?"

"No."

I heard a voice, and Howdy turned and spoke over his shoulder. In a moment he was joined by a middle-aged woman with a broad face and perm-frizzed hair. She held an infant to one shoulder, and alternately patted and rubbed its back. The flesh on her upper arm jiggled with each movement.

"It's a cop," he said to her, stepping back from the screen.

"Yes?"

While Ryan and I listened, Baker and the woman exchanged the same B-movie dialogue we'd just heard. Then,

"There's no one here right now. You come back some other time."

"You're here, ma'am," replied Baker.

"We're busy with the babies."

"We're not going away, ma'am," said the Beaufort County sheriff.

The woman made a face, shifted the baby higher on

her shoulder, and pushed open the screen door. Her flip-flops made soft popping sounds as we followed her across the porch and into a small foyer.

The house was dim and smelled slightly sour, like milk left overnight in a glass. Straight ahead, a staircase rose to the second floor, to the right and left archways opened on to large rooms filled with sofas and chairs.

The woman led us to the room on the left and indicated a grouping of rattan couches. As we sat she whispered something to Howdy, and he disappeared up the stairs. Then she joined us.

"Yes?" she asked quietly, looking from Baker to Ryan.

"My name is Harley Baker." He set his hat on the coffee table and leaned toward her, hands on his thighs, arms bent outward. "And you are?"

She placed an arm across the baby's back, cradled its head, and raised the other, palm toward him. "I don't mean to be unpolite, Sheriff, but I got to know what you want."

"Do you live here, ma'am?"

She hesitated, then nodded. A curtain rippled in a window behind me and I felt a damp breeze on my neck.

"We're curious about some calls made to this house," Baker went on.

"Phone calls?"

"Yes, ma'am. Last fall. Would you have been here at that time?"

"There's no phone here."

"No phone?"

"Well, just an office phone. Not for personal use."

"I see." He waited.

"We don't get phone calls."

"We?"

"There are nine of us in this house, four next door.

And of course the trailers. But we don't talk on no phones. It's not allowed."

Upstairs, another baby started to cry.

"Not allowed?"

"We're a community. We live clean and don't cause no trouble. No drugs, none of that. We keep to ourselves and follow our beliefs. There's no law against that, is there?"

"No, ma'am, there isn't. How large is your group?"

She thought a minute. "We're twenty-six here."

"Where are the others?"

"Some's gone off to jobs. Those that integrate. The rest are at morning meeting next door. Jerry and I are watching the babies."

"Are you a religious group?" Ryan asked.

She looked at him, back to Baker.

"Who are they?" She raised her chin toward Ryan and me.

"They're homicide detectives." The sheriff stared at her, his face hard and unsmiling. "What is your group, ma'am?"

She fingered the baby's blanket. Somewhere in the distance I heard a dog bark.

"We want no problems with the law," she said. "You can take my word on that."

"Are you expecting trouble?" Ryan.

She gave him an odd look, then glanced at her watch. "We are people wanting peace and health. We can't take no more of the drugs and crime, so we live out here by ourselves. We don't hurt no one. I don't have no more to say. You talk to Dom. He'll be here soon."

"Dom?"

"He'll know what to tell you."

"That would be good." Baker's dark eyes impaled her again. "I wouldn't want everyone to have to make that long trip into town."

238

Just then I heard voices and watched her gaze slide off Baker's face and out the window. We all turned to look.

Through the screen I saw activity at the house next door. Five women stood on the porch, two holding toddlers, a third bending to set a child onto the ground. The tot took off on wobbly legs, and the woman followed across the yard. One by one a dozen adults emerged and disappeared behind the house. Seconds later a man came out and headed in our direction.

Our hostess excused herself and went to the foyer. Before long we heard the screen door, then muted voices.

I saw the woman climb the stairs, then the man from next door appeared in the archway. I guessed he was in his mid-forties. His blond hair was going gray, his face and arms deeply tanned. He wore khakis, a pale yellow golf shirt, and Topsiders without socks. He looked like an aging Kappa Sigma.

"I'm so sorry," he said. "I didn't realize we had visitors."

Ryan and Baker started to rise.

"Please, please. Don't get up." He crossed to us and held out a hand. "I'm Dom."

We all shook, and Dom joined us on one of the sofas.

"Would you like some juice or lemonade?"

We all declined.

"So, you've been talking to Helen. She says you have some questions about our group?"

Baker nodded once.

"I suppose we're what you'd call a commune." He laughed. "But not what the term usually conjures up. We're a far cry from the counterculture hippies of the sixties. We are opposed to drugs and polluting chemicals, and committed to purity, creativity, and self-awareness. We live and work together in harmony. For

239

instance, we've just finished our morning meeting. That's where we discuss each day's agenda and collectively decide what has to be done and who will do it. Food preparation, cleaning chores, housekeeping mostly." He smiled. "Mondays can be long since that's the day we air grievances." Again the smile. "Although we rarely have grievances."

The man leaned back and folded his hands in his lap. "Helen tells me you're interested in phone calls."

The sheriff introduced himself. "And you are Dom . . .?"

"Just Dom. We don't use surnames."

"We do," said Baker, his voice devoid of humor.

There was a long pause. Then,

"Owens. But he's long dead. I haven't been Dominick Owens in years."

"Thank you, Mr. Owens." Baker made a note in a tiny spiral notebook. "Detective Ryan is investigating a homicide in Quebec and has reason to believe the victim knew someone at this address."

"Quebec?" Dom's eyes widened, revealing tiny white creases in his tan skin. "Canada?"

"Calls were made to this number from a home in St-Jovite," said Ryan. "That's a village in the Laurentian Mountains north of Montreal."

Dom listened, a puzzled look on his face.

"Does the name Patrice Simonnet mean anything to you?"

He shook his head.

"Heidi Schneider?"

More head shaking. "I'm sorry." Dom smiled and gave a light shrug. "I told you. We don't use last names. And members often change their given names. In the group one is free to choose whatever name one likes."

"What is the name of your group?"

"Names. Labels. Titles. *The* Church of Christ. *The*

240

People's Temple. *The* Righteous Path. Such egomania. We choose not to use one."

"How long has your group lived here, Mr. Owens?" Ryan.

"Please call me Dom."

Ryan waited.

"Almost eight years."

"Were you here last summer and fall?"

"On and off. I was traveling quite a bit."

Ryan took a snapshot from his pocket and placed it on the table.

"We're trying to track the whereabouts of this young woman."

Dom leaned forward and examined the photo, his fingers smoothing the edges. They were long and slender, with tufts of golden hair between the knuckles.

"Is she the one that was killed?"

"Yes."

"Who's the boy?"

"Brian Gilbert."

Dom studied the faces a long time. When he looked up his eyes had an expression I couldn't read.

"I wish I could help you. Really, I do. Perhaps I could ask at this evening's experiential session. That's when we encourage self-exploration and movement toward inner awareness. It would be an appropriate setting."

Ryan's face was rigid as his eyes held Dom's.

"I'm not in a ministerial mood, Mr. Owens, and I'm not particularly concerned with what you consider appropriate times. Here's chapter and verse. I know calls were made to this number from the house where Heidi Schneider was murdered. I know the victim was in Beaufort last summer. I'm going to find the connection."

"Yes, of course. How terrible. It is this kind of violence that causes us to live as we do."

He closed his eyes, as though seeking holy guidance, then opened them and gazed intently at each of us.

"Let me explain. We grow our own vegetables, raise chickens for eggs, we fish, and gather mollusks. Some members work in town and contribute wages. We have a set of beliefs that forces us to reject society, but we wish no harm to others. We live simply and quietly."

He took a long breath.

"While we have a core of longtime members, there are many that come and go. Our lifestyle is not for everyone. It's possible your young woman visited with us, perhaps during one of my absences. You have my word. I will speak to the others," said Dom.

"Yes," said Ryan. "So will I."

"Of course. And please let me know if there is anything else that I can do."

At that moment a young woman burst through the screen door, a toddler on her hip. She was laughing and tickling the child. He giggled and batted at her with pudgy fingers.

Malachy's pale little hands skittered across my mind.

When she saw us, the woman hunched and gave a grimace.

"Oops. Sorry." She laughed. "I didn't know anyone was here." The toddler thumped her head, and she scratched a finger on his stomach. He squealed and kicked his legs.

"Come in, Kathryn," said Dom. "I think we're finished here."

He looked a question at Baker and Ryan. The sheriff retrieved his hat and we all rose.

The child turned toward Dom's voice, spotted him, and began to wriggle. When Kathryn set him down, he teetered forward with outstretched arms, and Dom bent to scoop him up. His arms looked milky white around Dom's sun-darkened neck.

Kathryn joined us.

"How old is your baby?" I asked.

"Fourteen months. Aren't you, Carlie?" She extended a finger and Carlie grabbed for it, then held his arms out toward her. Dom returned the baby to its mother.

"Excuse us," Kathryn said. "He needs a nappy change."

"Before you go, may I ask you one question?" Ryan produced the photo. "Do you know either of these people?"

Kathryn studied the snapshot, holding it beyond Carlie's reach. I watched Dom's face. His expression never changed.

Kathryn shook her head, then handed back the photo. "No. Sorry." She fanned the air and wrinkled her nose. "Gotta go."

"The woman was pregnant," Ryan offered.

"Sorry," said Kathryn.

"He's a beautiful baby," I said.

"Thank you." She smiled and disappeared into the back of the house.

Dom looked at his watch.

"We'll be in touch," said Baker.

"Yes. Good. And good luck."

Back in the car, we sat and studied the property. I'd cracked the passenger-side window, and mist blew in and settled on my face. The flash of Malachy had depressed me, and the damp, gray weather mirrored my mood perfectly.

I scanned the road in both directions, then looked again at the houses. I could see people working in a garden behind the bungalow. Seed packets stuck on sticks identified the contents of each patch. Otherwise, there were no signs of life.

"What do you think?" I asked no one in particular.

"If they've been here eight years they've kept a very low profile," said Baker. "I haven't heard a thing about them."

We watched Helen leave the green house and walk to one of the trailers.

"But they're about to be discovered," he added, reaching for the ignition.

For several miles, no one spoke. We were crossing the bridge into Beaufort when Ryan broke the silence.

"There's got to be a link. It can't be coincidence."

"Coincidences do happen," said Baker.

"Yes."

"One thing bothers me," I said.

"What's that?"

"Heidi quit going to the clinic here in her sixth month. Her parents said she showed up in Texas in late August. Right?"

"Right."

"But the phone calls continued to the number here until December."

"Yes," said Ryan. "That's a problem."

19

The mist changed to rain as we drove to the Beaufort-Jasper Comprehensive Health Clinic. It turned the tree trunks dark and shiny and painted a sheen on the blacktop. When I cracked the window I could smell wet grass and earth.

We located the doctor with whom Ryan had spoken, and he showed her the photo. She thought she recognized Heidi as the patient she'd treated the previous summer, but couldn't be sure. The pregnancy was normal. She'd written the standard prenatal prescriptions. Beyond that, she could tell us nothing. She had no recollection of Brian.

At noon Sheriff Baker left us to handle a domestic situation on Lady's Island. We agreed to meet at his office at six, by which time he hoped to have information on the Adler Lyons property.

Ryan and I stopped for barbecue at Sgt. White's Diner, then spent the afternoon showing Heidi's snapshot around town, and asking about the commune on Adler Lyons Road.

By four o'clock we knew two things: No one had heard of Dom Owens or his followers. No one remembered Heidi Schneider or Brian Gilbert.

We sat in Ryan's rental car and stared up Bay Street. On my right customers entered and left the Palmetto Federal Banking Center. I looked across to the stores we'd just canvassed. The Cat's Meow. Stones and Bones. In High Cotton. Yes. Beaufort had embraced the world of tourism.

The rain had stopped but the sky was still dark and heavy. I felt tired and discouraged, and no longer sure about the Beaufort-St-Jovite connection.

Outside Lipsitz Department Store a man with greased hair and a face like bread dough waved a Bible and screamed about Jesus. March was the off season for sidewalk salvation, so he had the stage to himself.

Sam had told me about his war with the street preachers. For twenty years they'd been coming to Beaufort, descending on the city like pilgrims on hajj. In 1993 His Honor had the Reverend Isaac Abernathy arrested for harassing women in shorts, calling them whores and bellowing about eternal damnation. Suits were filed against the mayor and the city, and the ACLU jumped to the defense of the evangelists, the issue being one of First Amendment rights. The case was pending review by the Fourth Circuit Court of Appeals in Richmond, and the preachers still came.

I listened to the man rant about Satan and heathens and Jews, and felt tiny hairs rise on the back of my neck. I resent those who see themselves as God's spokesmen and next of kin, and am disturbed by people interpreting the Gospel to push a political agenda.

"What do you think of Southern civilization?" I asked Ryan, my eyes never leaving the preacher.

"Sounds like a good idea."

"Well, well. Stealing material from Gandhi," I said, turning to him in surprise. It was one of my favorite Gandhi quotes.

246

"Some homicide detectives *can* read." There was an edge to his voice.

Guilty, Brennan. Apparently the reverend isn't the only one harboring cultural stereotypes.

I watched an old woman circle wide to avoid the preacher, and wondered what sort of salvation Dom Owens promised his followers. I checked my watch.

"We're moving toward the dinner hour," I said.

"Could be a good time to catch folks mixing up tofu burgers."

"We can't meet Baker for another ninety minutes."

"You up for a surprise visit, skipper?"

"Beats sitting here."

Ryan was reaching for the ignition when his hand stopped. I followed his gaze and saw Kathryn coming up the sidewalk, Carlie on her back. An older woman with long, dark braids walked beside her. The damp breeze blew their skirts backward, molding fabric to hips and legs. They paused and Kathryn's companion spoke to the preacher, then the pair continued in our direction.

Ryan and I exchanged glances, then got out and crossed to the women. They stopped speaking when we approached, and Kathryn smiled at me.

"How's it going?" she asked, brushing back a tangle of curls.

"Not so good," I said.

"No luck finding your missing girl?"

"No one remembers her. I find that odd, since she spent at least three months here."

I watched for a reaction, but her expression didn't change.

"Where did you ask?" Carlie stirred and Kathryn reached over her shoulder to adjust his carrier.

"Shops, food stores, pharmacies, gas stations, restaurants, the library. We even tried Boombears."

247

"Yeah. That's a cool idea. If she was expecting she might have gone to a toy store."

The baby whimpered, then raised his arms and arched backward, pressing his feet against his mother's back.

"Guess who's up?" said Kathryn, reaching back to calm her son. "And no one knew her from that picture?"

"No one."

Carlie's whimpers grew more strident, and the older woman moved behind Kathryn and slid the baby from the carrier.

"Oh, sorry. This is El." Kathryn indicated her companion.

Ryan and I introduced ourselves. El nodded, but said nothing as she tried to calm Carlie.

"Could we buy you ladies a Coke or a cup of coffee?" Ryan asked.

"Nah. That stuff will mess up your genetic potential." Kathryn crinkled her nose, then broke into a smile. "But I could go for juice. So could Carlie." She rolled her eyes and reached for her baby's hand. "He can be a handful when he's not happy. Dom's not picking us up for another forty minutes, right, El?"

"We should wait for Dom." The woman spoke so softly I could hardly make out her words.

"Oh, El, you know he'll be late. Let's get some juice and sit outside. I don't want to ride back with Carlie fussing all the way."

El opened her mouth, but before she could speak Carlie twisted and let out a wail.

"Juice," said Kathryn, taking the baby and bouncing him on her hip. "Blackstone's has lots of choices. I've seen their menu in the window."

We entered the deli and I ordered a Diet Coke. The others asked for juice, then we took our drinks to an outside bench. Kathryn pulled a small blanket from her shoulder bag, spread it at her feet, and set Carlie on it. Then she dug out bottled water and a small yellow mug. The cup had a round bottom and a removable cover with a drinking spout. She filled it halfway with her Very Berry, added water, and handed it to Carlie. He made a two-handed grab and started sucking on the spout. I watched, remembering, and the sensation I'd had on the island washed over me again.

I felt out of sync with the world. The bodies on Murtry. Thoughts of infant Katy. Ryan in Beaufort, with his gun and badge and Nova Scotia speech. The world seemed strange around me, the space in which I moved transported from another place or time, yet somehow present and jarringly real.

"Tell me about your group," I said, forcing my thoughts back to the moment.

El looked at me but didn't speak.

"What do you want to know?" Kathryn asked.

"What is it you believe in?"

"Knowing our own minds and bodies. Keeping our cosmic and molecular energy clear."

"What is it you do?"

"Do?" The question seemed to puzzle her. "We grow our own food, and we don't eat anything polluting." She gave a slight shrug of the shoulders. As I listened to her, I thought of Harry. Purification through diet. ". . . we study. We work. We sing and play games. Sometimes we have lectures. Dom is incredibly smart. He's completely clear—"

El tapped her on the arm and pointed to Carlie's cup. Kathryn retrieved it, wiped the spout on her skirt, and held it out to her son. The baby grabbed the mug and pounded it on his mother's foot.

"How long have you lived with the group?"

"Nine years."

"How old are you?" I couldn't keep the amazement out of my voice.

"Seventeen. My parents joined when I was eight."

"And before that?"

She bent and redirected the cup to Carlie's mouth. "I remember I cried a lot. I was alone a lot. I was always sick. My parents fought all the time."

"And?"

"When they joined the group we underwent a transformation. Through purification."

"Are you happy?"

"The point of life is not happiness." El spoke for the first time. Her voice was deep and whispery, with just the trace of an accent I couldn't place.

"What is?"

"Peace and health and harmony."

"Can't that be attained without withdrawing from society?"

"We think not." Her face was bronzed and deeply lined, her eyes the color of mahogany. "In society, too many things divert us. Drugs. Television. Possessions. Interpersonal greed. Our own beliefs stand in the way."

"El says things a lot better than I do," said Kathryn.

"But why the commune?" asked Ryan. "Why not blow it all off and join an order?"

Kathryn gave El a "take it away" gesture.

"The universe is one organic whole composed of many interdependent elements. Every part is insepara-ble from and interacts with every other part. While we live apart, our group is a microcosm of that reality."

"Would you care to explain that?" Ryan.

"By living apart from the world we reject the slaughterhouses and chemical plants and oil refineries, the beer cans, and the tire heaps, and the raw sewage. By living together as a group we support each other, we feed each other both spiritually and physically."

250

"All for one."

El gave him a brief smile. "All the old myths have to be eliminated before true consciousness is possible."

"All of them?"

"Yes."

"Even his?" Ryan tipped his head in the direction of the preacher.

"All of them."

I circled the conversation back.

"Kathryn, if you wanted information on someone, where would you ask?"

"Look," she said, smiling, "you're not going to find her." She retrieved Carlie's cup again. "She's probably on the Riviera right now, smearing sunblock on her babies."

I looked at her a long time. She didn't know. Dom hadn't told her. She'd missed the introductions and had no idea why we were asking about Heidi and Brian. I took a deep breath.

"Heidi Schneider is dead, Kathryn. So is Brian Gilbert."

She looked at me as if I were crazy.

"Dead? She can't be dead."

"Kathryn!" El's voice was sharp.

Kathryn ignored her.

"I mean, she's so young. And she's pregnant. Or was." Her voice was plaintive, like a child's.

"They were murdered less than three weeks ago."

"You're not here to take her home?" Her eyes shifted from Ryan to me. I could see tiny yellow flecks in the green irises. "You're not her parents?"

"No."

"They're dead?"

"Yes."

"Her babies?"

I nodded.

251

Her hand went to her mouth, then fluttered to her lap, like a butterfly unsure where to light. Carlie tugged her skirt, and the hand dropped to stroke his head.

"How could someone do something like that? I mean, I didn't know them, but, how could someone kill a whole family? Kill babies?"

"We all pass through," said El, placing an arm around the girl's shoulders. "Death is merely a transition in the process of growth."

"A transition to what?" asked Ryan.

There was no answer. At that moment a white van pulled to the curb in front of the People's Bank on the far side of Bay Street. El squeezed Kathryn's shoulders and nodded toward it. Then she gathered Carlie, rose, and extended her hand. Kathryn took it and got to her feet.

"I wish you the best of luck," said El, and the two women set off toward the van.

I watched them a moment, then downed the last of my Coke. As I looked for a trash can something under the bench caught my eye. The cover to Carlie's cup.

I dug a card from my purse, scribbled a number, and snatched up the lid. Ryan looked amused as I bolted from the bench.

She was just climbing into the van.

"Kathryn," I called from the middle of the street.

She looked up, and I waved the cover in the air. Behind her the clock on the bank said five-fifteen.

She spoke into the van then walked toward me. When she reached out I gave her the lid with my card tucked inside.

Her eyes met mine.

"Call me if you'd like to talk."

She turned without a word, walked back to the van, and got in. I could see Dom's blonde head silhouetted behind the wheel as they disappeared up Bay Street.

*   *   *

Ryan and I showed the snapshot at another pharmacy and several fast-food restaurants, then drove to Sheriff Baker's office. Ivy Lee told us his domestic situation had turned into a standoff. An unemployed sanitation worker was barricaded in his house with his wife and three-year-old daughter, threatening to shoot everyone. Baker would not be joining us that evening.

"Now what?" I asked Ryan. We were standing in the Duke Street parking lot.

"I don't think Heidi was making the night scene, so we're not going to accomplish anything running around to bars and clubs."

"No."

"Let's call it a day. I'll drive you back to the Love Boat."

"It's the *Melanie Tess*."

"Tess. Is that something you eat with corn bread and greens?"

"Ham hocks and yams."

"Do you want the ride?"

"Sure."

We rode in silence most of the way. I'd found Ryan annoying all day and couldn't wait to be free of him. We were on the bridge when he broke the silence.

"I doubt she'd go to beauty parlors or tanning salons."

"That's amazing. I can see why you made detective."

"Maybe we should focus on Brian. Maybe he worked for a time."

"You've already run him. There's no tax record, right?"

"Nothing."

"He could have been paid in cash."

"That narrows the possibilities."

We turned in at Ollie's.

"So where do we go from here?" I asked.

253

"I never got that hush puppy."

"I meant the investigation. You're on your own for dinner. I'm going to go home, take a shower, and make myself a scrumptious plate of instant macaroni. In that order."

"Jesus, Brennan, that stuff has more preservatives than Lenin's cadaver."

"I've read the label."

"You might as well swallow industrial waste. You'll mess up your" – he mimicked Kathryn – "genetic potential."

Some half-forgotten thought started to seep into my mind, formless, like the morning's mist. I tried to reel it in, but the harder I concentrated the faster it dissolved.

"– Owens better keep his skivvies up. I'm going to be on his ass like flies on a Tootsie Roll."

"What sort of gospel do you suppose he preaches?"

"Sounds like some combination of ecological Armageddon and self-improvement through Wheaties."

When he pulled up at the pier the sky was beginning to clear over the marsh. Streaks of yellow lit the horizon.

"Kathryn knows something," I said.

"Don't we all."

"You can be a real pain in the ass, Ryan."

"Thank you for noticing. What makes you think she's holding out?"

"She said babies."

"So?"

"Babies."

I saw thought working in his eyes. Then,

"Son of a bitch."

"We never told her Heidi was carrying twins."

Forty minutes later I heard a knock at the port-side entrance. I was wearing the Hornets T-shirt Katy had

254

left, no panties, and a towel fashioned into a pretty slick turban. I peered through the blinds.

Ryan stood on the dock holding two six-packs and a pizza the size of a manhole cover. He'd abandoned his jacket and tie, and rolled his shirtsleeves to just below the elbows.

Shit.

I released the slats and pulled back. I could turn off the light and refuse to answer. I could ignore him. I could tell him to go away.

I peeked out again and found myself looking directly into Ryan's eyes.

"I know you're in there, Brennan. I'm a detective, remember?"

He dangled a six-pack in front of me. "Diet Coke."

Damn.

I didn't dislike Ryan. In fact, I enjoyed his company more than that of most people. More than I cared to admit. I liked his commitment to what he did, and the compassion he showed to victims and their families. I liked his intelligence and wit. And I liked the story of Ryan, the college kid gone wild, beaten up by a biker cokehead, then converted to the other side. Tough kid turned tough cop. It had a kind of poetic symmetry.

And I definitely liked the way he looked, but my better judgment told me not to get involved.

Oh hell. It beat noodles and synthetic cheese.

I dropped to my stateroom, grabbed a pair of cutoffs, and ran a brush through my hair.

I raised the blinds and slid back the screen to allow him in. He handed down the drinks and pizza, then turned and climbed aboard backward.

"I have my own Coke," I said, closing the screen.

"One can never have too much Coke."

I pointed to the galley and he set the pizza on the table, detached a beer for himself and a Diet Coke for

255

me, then placed the other cans in the refrigerator. I got out plates, napkins, and a large knife while he opened the pizza box.

"You think that's more nourishing than pasta?"

"It's a veggie supreme."

"What's that?" I pointed to a brown chunk.

"Side order of bacon. I wanted all the food groups."

"Let's take it into the salon," I suggested.

We spread the food on the coffee table and settled on the couch. The smell of marsh and wet wood floated in and mingled with the aroma of tomato sauce and basil. We ate and talked about the murders, and weighed the likelihood that the victims in St-Jovite had a connection to Dom Owens.

Eventually, we drifted to more personal topics. I described the Beaufort of my childhood, and shared memories of my summers at the beach. I talked about Katy, and about my estrangement from Pete. Ryan told stories of his early years in Nova Scotia, and disclosed his feelings about a recent breakup.

The conversation was easy and natural, and I revealed more about myself than I would ever have imagined. In the silences we listened to the water and the rustling of the spartina grass in the marsh. I forgot about violence and death and did something I hadn't done in a very long time. I relaxed.

"I can't believe I'm talking so much," I said, as I began to gather plates and napkins.

Ryan reached for the empty cans. "Let me help."

Our arms brushed and I felt heat race across my skin. Wordlessly, we gathered the dinner mess and brought it to the kitchen.

When we returned to the couch Ryan stood over me a moment, then sat close, placed both hands on my shoulders, and turned my body away from him. As I was about to object he began massaging the muscles at

256

the base of my neck, across my shoulders, and down my arms to just above the elbows. His hands slid down my back, then worked their way upward, each thumb moving in small circles along the edge of a shoulder blade. When he reached my hairline his fingers made the same rotating motions in the hollows below my skull.

My eyes closed.

"Mmmmm."

"You're very tense."

This was too good to ruin with talk.

Ryan's hands dropped to the small of my back, and his thumbs kneaded the muscles paralleling my spine, pressing higher inch by inch. My breathing slowed and I felt myself melt.

Then I remembered Harry. And my lack of underwear.

I turned to face him, to pull the plug, and our eyes met. Ryan hesitated a moment, then cupped my face in both his hands, and pressed his lips to mine. He ran his fingers along my jawline and backward through my hair, then his arms circled my shoulders and he pulled me close. I started to push away, then stopped, my hands flat on his chest. He felt lean and taut, his muscles molded to his bones.

I felt the heat of his body and smelled his skin, and my nipples hardened under my thin cotton shirt. Collapsing against his chest, I closed my eyes and kissed back.

He held me hard against him and we kissed a long time. When my arms went around his neck he slid his hand under my shirt and danced his fingers across my skin. His stroke felt cobweb light, and shivers raced up my back and across the top of my skull. I arched against his chest and kissed him harder, opening and closing my mouth to the rhythm of his breathing.

257

He dropped his hand and ran his fingers around my waist and up my stomach, circling my breasts with the same feathery touch. My nipples throbbed and fire surged through my body. He thrust his tongue into my mouth and my lips closed around it. His hand cupped my left breast, then gently bounced it up and down. Then he squeezed the nipple between his thumb and finger, compressing and releasing in time to the sucking of our mouths.

I ran my fingers along his spine and his hand traveled downward to the curve of my waist. He caressed my belly, circled my navel, then hooked his fingers inside the waistband of my shorts. Current shot through my lower torso.

Eventually, our lips separated and Ryan kissed my face and ran his tongue inside my ear. Then he eased me back against the cushions, and lay beside me, the off-the-chart blue eyes boring into mine. Shifting onto his side, he took me by the hips, and pulled me to him. I could feel his hardness, and we kissed again.

After a while he disengaged, crooked his knee, and pressed his thigh between my legs. I felt an explosion in my loins and found it hard to breathe. Again Ryan put one hand below the T-shirt and slid it upward to my breast. He made circular movements with his palm, then ran his thumb across my nipple. I arched my back and moaned as the sensation obliterated the world around me. I lost all sense of time.

Moments or hours later his hand dropped, and I felt a tugging on my zipper. I buried my nose in his neck and knew one thing with certainty. Regardless of Harry, I wouldn't say no.

Then the phone shrilled.

Ryan's hands went to my ears and he kissed me hard on the mouth. I responded, clutching the hair at the

258

back of his head, cursing Southern Bell. We ignored it through four rings.

When the answering machine clicked on the voice was soft and hard to hear, as though its owner were speaking from the end of a long tunnel. We both lunged, but it was too late.

Kathryn had hung up.

20

There was no salvaging the situation after Kathryn's call. While Ryan was up for giving it a go, rational thought had returned and I was not in a good mood. Not only had I missed the opportunity to talk with Kathryn but I knew I'd have to live with Detective Dick's new sense of sexual prowess. While the orgasm was overdue and would certainly have been welcome, I suspected the cost was already too high.

I hustled Ryan out and fell into bed, ignoring teeth and my nightly routine. My last image before drifting off came to me from the seventh grade: Sister Luke lecturing on the wages of sin. I supposed my romp with Ryan would goose these wages well above minimum.

I woke to sunshine and the cry of gulls, and an immediate flash-back to my roll on the couch. I cringed and covered my face with both hands, feeling like a teen who'd given it up in a Pontiac.

Brennan, what were you thinking?

That was not the issue. The problem lay in what I'd been thinking *with*. Edna St. Vincent Millay had written a poem about that. What was it called? "I Being Born a Woman and Distressed."

Sam called at eight to say the Murtry case was going

nowhere. No one had seen anything unusual. No strange boats had been spotted approaching or leaving the island in the past few weeks. He wanted to know if I'd heard from Hardaway.

I told him I hadn't. He said he was going to Raleigh for a few days and wanted to be sure I was taken care of.

Oh, yeah.

He explained how to close up the boat and where to leave the key, and we said good-bye.

I was scraping pizza into the garbage when I heard a knock at the port entrance. I had a feeling who was there and ignored it. The banging continued, relentless as a National Public Radio fund drive, and after a while I couldn't take it. I raised the blinds to see Ryan standing exactly where he'd been the night before.

"Good morning." He held out a bag of doughnuts.

"Expanding into food delivery?" I lowered the screen. One innuendo and I knew I'd rip his throat out.

He climbed in, grinned, and offered high-calorie, low-food-value treats. "They go well with coffee."

I went to the galley, poured two cups, and added milk to mine.

"It's a beautiful day out there." He reached for the milk carton.

"Mm."

I helped myself to a chocolate-glazed and leaned against the sink. I had no intention of resettling on the couch.

"I've already spoken to Baker," said Ryan.

I waited.

"He'll meet with us at three."

"I'll be on the road at three." I reached for another doughnut.

"I think we should make another social call," said Ryan.

"Yes."

"Maybe we can get Kathryn alone."

"That seems to be your specialty."

"Are you going to keep this up all day?"

"I'll probably sing when I'm on the road."

"I didn't come out here intending to seduce you."

That piqued me even more.

"You mean I'm not in my sister's league?"

"What?"

We drank in silence, then I refilled my mug and pointedly replaced the pot. Ryan watched, then crossed to Mr. Coffee and poured himself a second cup.

"Do you think Kathryn actually has something to tell us?" he asked.

"She probably phoned to invite me for tuna casserole."

"Now who's being a pain in the ass?"

"Thanks for noticing." I rinsed my mug and placed it upside down on the counter.

"Look, if you're embarrassed about last night . . ."

"Should I be?"

"Of course not."

"What a relief."

"Brennan, I'm not going to go berserk in the autopsy room or grope you on a stakeout. Our personal relationship will in no way affect our professional behavior."

"Small chance. Today I'm wearing underwear."

"See." He grinned.

I went aft to gather my things.

Half an hour later we were parked in front of the farmhouse. Dom Owens sat on the porch talking with a group of people. Through the screen it was impossible to tell anything about the others but gender. All four were male.

A crew was at work in the garden behind the white

bungalow, and two women pushed children on the swings by the trailers while several others hung laundry. A blue van was parked in the driveway, but I saw no sign of the white one.

I scanned the figures at the swing set. I didn't see Kathryn, though I thought one of the infants looked like Carlie. I watched a woman in a floral skirt push the baby back and forth in smooth metronomic arcs.

Ryan and I walked to the door and I knocked. The men stopped talking and turned in our direction.

"May I help you?" said a high-pitched voice.

Owens held up a hand. "It's fine, Jason."

He rose, crossed the porch, and pushed open the screen door.

"I'm sorry, but I don't think I ever got your names."

"I'm Detective Ryan. This is Dr. Brennan."

Owens smiled and stepped out onto the stoop. I nodded and took my turn at shaking hands. The men on the porch grew very still.

"What can I do for you today?"

"We're still trying to determine where Heidi Schneider and Brian Gilbert spent last summer. You were going to raise the question during family hour?" Ryan's voice held no warmth.

Owens smiled again. "Experiential session. Yes, we did discuss it. Unfortunately, no one knew anything about either of them. I'm so sorry. I had hoped we could be of help."

"We'd like to speak to your people, if we may."

"I'm sorry, but I can't encourage that."

"And why is that?"

"Our members live here because they seek peace and refuge. Many want nothing to do with the filth and violence of modern society. You, Detective Ryan, represent the world they have rejected. I cannot violate their sanctuary by asking them to speak to you."

"Some of your members work in town."

Owens tipped his head and looked to heaven for patience. Then he gave Ryan another smile.

"One of the skills we nurture is encapsulation. Not everyone is equally gifted, but some of our members learn to function in the secular yet remain sealed off, untouched by the moral and physical pollution." Again the patient smile. "While we reject the profanity of our culture, Mr. Ryan, we are not fools. We know that man does not live by spirit alone. We also need bread."

While Owens talked I checked the gardeners. No Kathryn.

"Is everyone here free to come and go?" I asked, turning back to Owens.

"Of course." He laughed. "How could I stop them?"

"What happens if someone wants to leave for good?"

"They go." He shrugged and spread his hands.

For a moment no one spoke. The creak of the swings carried across the yard.

"I thought your young couple might have stayed with us briefly, perhaps during one of my absences," Owens offered. "Though not common, that has happened. But I'm afraid that is not the case. No one here has any recollection of either of them."

Just then Howdy Doody appeared from behind the neighboring house. When he spotted us he hesitated, then turned and hurried back in the direction from which he'd come.

"I'd still like to speak to a few folks," said Ryan. "There could be something someone knows that they just don't think is important. That happens all the time."

"Mr. Ryan, I will not have my people harassed. I asked about your young couple and no one knew them. What more is there to say? I'm afraid I really can't have you disturbing our routine."

Ryan cocked his head and made a clucking sound. "I'm afraid you're going to have to, Dom."

"And why is that?"

"Because I'm not going to go away. I have a friend named Baker. You do remember him? And he has friends who give him things called warrants."

Owens and Ryan locked eyes, and for a moment no one spoke. I heard the men on the porch rise, and in the distance a dog barked. Then Owens smiled and cleared his throat.

"Jason, please ask everyone to come to the parlors." His voice was low and even.

Owens stood back and a tall man in a red warm-up suit slipped past him and angled toward the neighboring property. He was soft and overweight, and looked a little like Julia Child. I watched him stop to stroke a cat, then continue toward the garden.

"Please come in," said Owens, opening the screen. We followed him to the same room we'd occupied the day before and sat on the same rattan couch. The house was very quiet.

"If you'll excuse me, I'll be right back. Would you care for anything?"

We told him no, and he left the room. Overhead, a fan hummed softly.

Soon I heard voices and laughter, then the creak of the screen door. As Owens' flock filtered in I studied them one by one. I sensed Ryan doing the same.

Within minutes the room was full, and I could conclude only one thing. The assembly looked totally unremarkable. They might have been a Baptist study group on its annual summer picnic. They joked and laughed and looked anything but oppressed.

There were babies, adults, and at least one septuagenarian, but no adolescents or children. I did a quick count: seven men, thirteen women, three kids. Helen had said there were twenty-six living at the commune.

I recognized Howdy and Helen. Jason leaned against a wall. El stood near the archway, Carlie on her hip. She stared at me intently. I smiled, remembering our meeting in Beaufort the previous afternoon. Her expression didn't change.

I scanned the other faces. Kathryn was not present.

Owens returned and the room fell silent. He made introductions, then explained why we were there. The adults listened attentively, then turned to us. Ryan handed the photo of Brian and Heidi to a middle-aged man on his left, then outlined the case, avoiding unnecessary detail. The man looked at the picture and passed it on. As the snapshot circulated I studied each face, watching for subtle changes of expression that might indicate recognition. I saw only puzzlement and empathy.

When Ryan finished, Owens again addressed his followers, soliciting input on the couple or the phone calls. No one spoke.

"Mr. Ryan and Dr. Brennan have requested permission to interview you individually." Owens looked from face to face. "Please feel free to talk to them. If there is a thought you harbor, please share it with honesty and compassion. We did not cause this tragedy, but we are part of the cosmic whole and should do what is in our power to set this dislocation in order. Do it in the name of harmony."

Every eye was on him, and I felt a strange intensity in the room.

"Those of you who cannot speak should feel no guilt or shame." He clapped his hands. "Now. Work and be well! Holistic affirmation through collective responsibility!"

Spare me, I thought.

When they'd gone Ryan thanked him.

"This is not Waco, Mr. Ryan. We have nothing to hide."

"We were hoping to speak with the young woman we met yesterday," I said.

He looked at me a moment then said, "Young woman?"

"Yes. She came in with a child. Carlie, I believe?"

He looked at me so long I thought perhaps he didn't remember. Then the Owens smile.

"That would be Kathryn. She had an appointment today."

"An appointment?"

"Why are you concerned with Kathryn?"

"She seems close to Heidi's age. I thought they might have known each other." Something told me not to discuss our juice party in Beaufort.

"Kathryn wasn't here last summer. She'd gone to visit with her parents."

"I see. When will she be back?"

"I'm not certain."

The screen door opened and a tall man appeared in the hallway. He was scarecrow thin, and had a white streak across his right eyebrow and lashes, giving him an oddly lopsided look. I remembered him. During the assembly he'd stood near the hall, playing with one of the toddlers.

Owens held up one finger, and scarecrow nodded and pointed to the back of the house. He wore a bulky ring that looked out of place on his long, bony finger.

"I'm sorry, but there are things I must do," said Owens. "Talk with whomever you like, but please, respect our desire for harmony."

He ushered us to the door and extended a hand. If nothing else, Dom was a great shaker. He said he was glad we had stopped by and wished us luck. Then he was gone.

Ryan and I spent the rest of the morning talking to the faithful. They were pleasant, and cooperative, and totally harmonious. And they knew zilch. Not even the whereabouts of Kathryn's appointment.

By eleven-thirty we knew nothing more than when we'd arrived.

"Let's go thank the reverend," said Ryan, taking a set of keys from his pocket. They hung from a large plastic disk, and were not the ones for the rental car.

"What the hell for?" I asked. I was hungry and hot and ready to move on.

"It's good manners."

I rolled my eyes, but Ryan was already halfway across the yard. I watched him knock on the screen door, then speak to the man with the pale eyebrow. In a moment Owens appeared. Ryan said something and extended his hand and, like marionettes, the three men squatted then rose quickly. Ryan spoke again, turned, and walked toward the car.

After lunch we tried a few more pharmacies, then drove back to the government center. I showed Ryan the records offices, then we crossed the grounds to the law enforcement building. A black man in a tank top and fedora was crisscrossing the lawn on a small tractor, his bony knees projecting like legs on a grasshopper.

"How y'all doin'?" he said, putting one finger to his brim.

"Good." I breathed in the smell of fresh-cut grass and wished it were true.

Baker was on the phone when we entered his office. He gestured us to chairs, spoke a few more words, and hung up.

"So, how's it going?" he asked.

268

"It isn't," said Ryan. "Nobody knows squat."

"How can we help?"

Ryan lifted his jacket, pulled a Ziploc bag from the pocket, and laid it on Baker's desk. Inside was the red plastic disk.

"You can run this for prints."

Baker looked at him.

"I accidentally dropped it. Owens was kind enough to pick it up for me."

Baker hesitated a moment, then smiled and shook his head. "You know it may not be usable."

"I know. But it may tell us who this puke is."

Baker laid the bag aside. "What else?"

"How about a wiretap?"

"No way. You haven't got enough."

"Search warrant?"

"What's your probable cause?"

"Phone calls?"

"Not enough."

"Didn't think so."

Ryan let out a breath and stretched his legs.

"Then I'll do it the hard way. I'll start with deeds and tax records, see who owns the country club on Adler Lyons. I'll check the utilities, find out who pays the bills. I'll talk to the postal boys, see if anyone gets *Hustler* or orders from J. Crew. I'll run Owens for a Social Security number, former wife, that sort of thing. I assume he has a driver's license, so that should take me somewhere. If the reverend's ever taken an illegal piss, I'll nail him. Maybe I'll do a little surveillance, see what cars go in and out of the compound, run the tags. Hope you don't mind my hanging around for a while."

"You are welcome in Beaufort for as long as it takes, Mr. Ryan. I'll assign a detective to help you. And, Dr. Brennan, what are your plans?"

269

"I'm heading out shortly. I have classes to prepare for and Mr. Colker's cases from Murtry to look at."

"Baxter will be glad to hear that. He called to say that Dr. Hardaway would like to speak with you as soon as possible. In fact, he's rung us three times today. Would you like to use my phone to call up there?"

No one can say I can't take a hint.

"Please."

Baker asked Ivy Lee to get Hardaway on the line. In a moment the phone rang and I picked it up.

The pathologist had finished with what he felt he could do. He was able to determine the gender of the corpse in the bottom of the grave, and that the race was probably white. The victim had died of what he thought were incised injuries, but the body was too badly decomposed to determine their exact nature.

The burial had been shallow enough that insects had gained access, probably using the body above as a conduit. The open wounds had also encouraged colonization. The skull and chest contained the largest maggot masses he'd ever seen. The face was not recognizable and he was unable to estimate an age. He thought he might have some usable prints.

In the background Ryan and Baker discussed Dom Owens.

Hardaway went on. The upper body was largely skeletonized, though some connective tissue remained. He could do little with it, and asked me to do a full analysis.

I told him to send me the skull, the hip blades, the clavicles, and the chest ends of the third through fifth ribs from the bottom body. I would need the entire skeleton from the upper burial. I also asked for a series of X-rays on each victim, a copy of his report, and a full set of autopsy photos.

Last, I explained how I preferred to have the bones

270

processed. Hardaway was familiar with the routine and said both sets of remains and all documents would arrive in my lab in Charlotte on Friday.

I hung up and looked at my watch. If I had any hope of getting everything done before my conference trip to Oakland, I had to get moving.

Ryan and I crossed to the lot, where I had left my car that morning. The sun was hot and the shade felt good. I opened the door and leaned my arm on the upper edge.

"Let's have dinner," said Ryan.

"Sure. Then I'll put on pasties and we'll take pics for the *New York Times*."

"Brennan, for two days now you've been treating me like I'm gum on the sidewalk. Actually, now that I think about it, you've had some kind of burr up your ass for a couple of weeks. Fine. I can live with that."

He took my chin in his hands and looked straight into my eyes.

"But I want you to know one thing. That was not just a chemical event last night. I care about you and I was enjoying the hell out of being close. I'm not sorry it happened. And I can't say I won't try again. Remember, I might be the wind, but you control the kite. Drive safely."

With that he released my chin and walked to his car. Unlocking the door, he threw his jacket on the passenger seat and turned back to me.

"By the way, you never told me why you doubt the Murtry victims are dealers."

For a moment I could only stare. I wanted to stay, but I also wanted to be continents away from him. Then my mind snapped back.

"What?"

271

"The bodies from the island. Why do you question the drug burn theory?"

"Because they're both girls."

21

During the drive I played some tapes, but the news from Lake Wobegon didn't hold my attention. I had a million questions and very few answers. Had Anna Goyette returned home? Who were the women buried on Murtry Island? What would their bones tell me? Who killed Heidi and her babies? Was there a connection between St-Jovite and the commune on Saint Helena? Who was Dom Owens? Where had Kathryn gone? Where the hell had Harry gone?

My mind spun off thoughts of all I had to do. And wanted to do. I hadn't read a word about Élisabeth Nicolet since leaving Montreal.

By eight-thirty I was back in Charlotte. In my absence the grounds at Sharon Hall had put on their finest springtime attire. Azaleas and dogwoods were in full bloom, and a few Bradford pears and flowering crabapples still retained blossoms. The air smelled of pine needles and bark chips. Inside, my arrival at the Annex was a replay of the week before. The clock was ticking. The message light was flashing. The refrigerator was empty.

Birdie's bowls were in their usual place under the bay

window. Odd that Pete hadn't emptied them. Disorderly with everything else, my estranged husband was fastidious about foodstuffs. I did a quick patrol to see if the cat was skulking under a chair or in a closet. No Bird.

I called Pete, but, as before, he wasn't in. Neither was Harry at the condo in Montreal. Thinking perhaps she'd gone home, I tried her number in Texas. No answer.

After unpacking, I fixed a tuna sandwich and ate it with dill pickles and chips while I watched the end of a Hornets' game. At ten I turned off the TV and tried Pete again. Still no answer. I considered driving over to collect Birdie, but decided to let it go until morning.

I showered, then propped myself in bed with the Bélanger photocopies and escaped into the world of nineteenth-century Montreal. The hiatus had not improved Louis-Philippe, and within an hour my lids were drooping. I turned off the light and curled into a tuck position, hoping a good long rest would bring order to my mind.

Two hours later I was sitting bolt upright, my heart hammering, my brain struggling to know why. I clutched the blanket to my chest, barely breathing, straining to identify the threat that had sent me into full alert.

Silence. The only light in the room came from my bedside clock.

Then the sound of shattering glass sent the hairs straight up on my arms and neck. My adrenals went to high tide. I had a flashback to another break-in, reptilian eyes, a knife flashing in moonlight. A single thought crackled in my brain.

Not again!
Crash! Thud!

Yes, again!

The noise wasn't outside! It was downstairs! It was in my house! My mind sprinted through options. Lock the bedroom. Check it out. Call the police.

Then I smelled smoke.

Shit!

I threw back the covers and fumbled across the room, digging below the terror for elements of rational thought. A weapon. I needed a weapon. What? What could I use? Why did I refuse to keep a gun?

I stumbled to the dresser and felt for a large conch I'd collected on the Outer Banks. It wouldn't kill, but the point would penetrate flesh and do damage. Turning the sharp end forward, I wrapped my fingers inside and braced my thumb against the outer surface.

Hardly breathing, I crept toward the door, my free hand sliding over familiar surfaces as if seeking guidance in Braille. Dresser. Doorjamb. Hallway.

At the top of the stairs I froze and peered downward into the blackness. Blood pounded in my ears as I clutched the shell and listened. Not a sound from below. If there was someone there I should stay upstairs. Phone. If there was fire downstairs, I needed to get out.

I took a breath and placed one foot on the top stair, waited. Then the second. Third. Knees bent, shell raised to shoulder level, I crept toward the first floor. The acrid smell grew stronger. Smoke. Gasoline. And something else. Something familiar.

At the bottom I stopped, my mind playing back a scene from Montreal less than a year ago. That time he'd been inside, a killer, waiting to attack.

That isn't going to happen again! Call 911! Get out!

I rounded the banister and looked into the dining room. Blackness. I doubled back toward the parlor. Darkness, but strangely altered.

275

The far end of the room looked bronzed in the surrounding gloom. The fireplace, the Queen Anne chairs, all the furnishings and pictures glimmered gently, like objects in a mirage. Through the kitchen door I could see orange light dancing on the front of the refrigerator.

Eeeeeeeeeeeeeeeeeeeeeeeeeeeeeeeeeeee!

My chest constricted as the silence was split by a high-pitched wail. I jerked and the shell struck plaster. Trembling, I pressed backward against the wall.

The sound was from the smoke detector!

I watched for signs of movement. Nothing but darkness and the eerie flickering.

The house is on fire. Move!

My heart drumming, my breath coming in short gasps, I lunged toward the kitchen. A fire crackled in the center of the room, filling the air with smoke and reflecting off every shiny surface.

My shaking hand found the switch and I threw on the light. My eyes darted left and right. The burning bundle lay in the middle of the floor. The flames hadn't spread.

I put down the shell and, holding the hem of my nightie across my mouth and nose, I bent low and circled to the pantry. I pulled the small extinguisher from the top shelf. My lungs drew in smoke and tears blurred my vision, but I managed to squeeze the handle. The extinguisher only hissed.

Damn!

Coughing and gagging, I squeezed again. Another hiss, then a stream of carbon dioxide and white powder burst from the spout.

Yes!

I aimed the nozzle at the flames and in less than a minute the fire was out. The alarm still screamed, the sound like shards of metal piercing my ears and dragging across my brain.

I opened the back door and the window above the sink, then crossed to the table. No need to open that one. The panes were shattered, and glass and splintered wood covered the sill and floor. Tiny gusts of wind played with the curtains, tugging them in and out of the jagged opening.

Circling the thing on the floor, I turned on the ceiling fan, grabbed a towel, and fanned smoke from the room. Slowly, the air began to clear.

I wiped my eyes and made an effort to control my breathing.

Keep fanning!

The alarm shrieked on.

I stopped waving the towel and looked around the room. A cinder block lay beneath the table, another rested against the cabinet below the sink. Between them were the charred remains of the bundle that had been burning. The room reeked of smoke and gasoline. And another odor I knew.

With shaky legs, I crossed to the smoldering heap. I was staring, not comprehending, when the alarm stopped. The silence seemed unnatural.

Dial 911.

It wasn't necessary. As I reached for the phone I heard a distant siren. It grew louder, very loud, then stopped. In a moment a fireman appeared at my back door.

"You O.K., ma'am?"

I nodded and folded my arms across my chest, self-conscious about my state of undress.

"Your neighbor called." His chin strap dangled.

"Oh." I forgot my nightie. I was back in St-Jovite.

"Everything under control?"

Another nod. St-Jovite. Almost a synapse.

"Mind if I make sure?"

I stepped back.

He sized it up in one look.

"Pretty mean prank. Know who might have heaved this through your window?"

I shook my head.

"Looks like they broke the glass with the cinder blocks, then chucked that thing in." He walked over to the smoldering mound. "They must've soaked it in gasoline, lit it, and pitched it."

I heard his words but couldn't speak. My body had locked up as my mind tried to rouse some shapeless notion sleeping in the core of my brain.

The firefighter slipped a shovel from his belt, snapped open the blade, and poked at the heap on my kitchen floor. Black flecks shot upward, then rejoined the rubble below. He slid the blade below the object, flipped it over, and leaned in.

"Looks like a burlap sack. Maybe a seed bag. Damned if I can tell what's inside."

He scraped the object with the tip of the shovel and more charred particles spiraled up. He prodded harder, rolling the thing from side to side.

The smell grew stronger. St-Jovite. Autopsy room three. Memory broke through and I went cold all over.

With trembling hands I opened a drawer and withdrew a pair of kitchen scissors. No longer concerned about my nightie, I squatted and cut the burlap.

The corpse was small, its back arched, its legs contracted by the heat of the flames. I saw a shriveled eye, a tiny jaw with blackened teeth. Anticipation of the horror that the sack held made me begin to feel faint.

No! Please no!

I leaned in, my mind recoiling from the smell of burned flesh and hair. Between the hind legs I saw a curled and blackened tail, its vertebrae protruding like thorns on a stem.

278

Tears slid down my cheeks as I cut further. Near the knot I saw hairs, scorched now, but white in spots.

The half-full bowls.

"Noooooooooooooooooo!"

I heard the voice, but did not connect it to myself.

"No! No! No! Birdie. Please God, no!"

I felt hands on my shoulders, then on my hands, taking the scissors, gently pulling me to my feet. Voices.

Then I was in the parlor, a quilt around me. I was crying, shaking, my body in pain.

I don't know how long I'd been sobbing when I looked up to see my neighbor. She pointed at a cup of tea.

"What is it?" My chest heaved in and out.

"Peppermint."

"Thanks." I drank the tepid liquid. "What time is it?"

"A little past two." She wore slippers and a trench coat that didn't cover her flannel gown. Though we'd waved to each other across the lawn, or exchanged hellos on the walk, I hardly knew her.

"I'm so sorry you had to get up in the middle of the nigh—"

"Please, Dr. Brennan. We're neighbors. I know you'd do the same for me."

I took another sip. My hands were icy, but trembled less.

"Are the firemen still here?"

"They left. They said you can fill out a report when you feel better."

"Did they take—" My voice broke and I felt tears behind my eyes.

"Yes. Can I get you anything else?"

"No, thank you. I'll be fine. You've been very kind."

"I'm sorry about your damage. We put a board across the window. It's not elegant, but it will keep the wind out."

"Thank you so much. I—"

"Please. Just get some sleep. Perhaps this won't seem so bad in the morning."

I thought of Birdie and dreaded the morning. In desperate hope I picked up the phone and dialed Pete's number. No answer.

"You will be O.K.? Shall I help you upstairs?"

"No. Thank you. I'll manage."

When she'd gone I crawled into bed and cried myself to sleep with great, heaving sobs.

I awoke with the feeling that something was wrong. Changed. Lost. Then full consciousness, and with it, memory.

It was a warm spring morning. Through the window I could see blue sky and sunlight and smell the perfume of flowers. But the beauty of the day could not lift my depression.

When I called the fire department I was told the physical evidence had been sent to the crime lab. Feeling leaden, I went through the morning motions. I dressed, applied makeup, brushed my hair, and headed downtown.

The sack contained nothing but the cat. No collar. No tags. A hand-lettered note was found inside one of the cinder blocks. I read it through the plastic evidence bag.

Next time it won't be a cat.

"Now what?" I asked Ron Gillman, director of the crime lab. He was a tall, good-looking man with silver-gray hair and an unfortunate gap between his front teeth.

"We've already checked for prints. Zippo on the note and blocks. Recovery will be out to your place, but you

280

know as well as I do they won't find much. Your kitchen window is so close to the street the perps probably pulled up, lit the bag, then threw everything in from the sidewalk. We'll look for footprints, and we'll ask around, of course, but at one-thirty in the morning it's not too likely anyone was awake in that neighborhood."

"Sorry I don't live on Wilkinson Boulevard."

"You get into enough trouble wherever you are."

Ron and I had worked together for years. He knew about the serial murderer who had broken into my Montreal condo.

"I'll have recovery go over your kitchen, but since these guys never went inside, there won't be any trace. You didn't touch anything, I assume."

"No." I hadn't gone near the kitchen since the night before. I couldn't bear the sight of Birdie's dishes.

"Are you working on anything that could piss folks off?"

I told him about the murders in Quebec and about the bodies from Murtry Island.

"How do you think they got your cat?"

"He may have run out when Pete went in to feed him. He does that." A stab of pain. "Did that."

Don't cry. Don't you dare cry.

"Or . . ."

"Yes?"

"Well, I'm not sure. Last week I thought someone might have broken into my office at school. Well, not exactly broken in. I may have left the door unlocked."

"A student?"

"I don't know."

I described the incident.

"My house keys were still in my purse, but I suppose she could have made an impression."

"You look a little shaken up."

281

"A little. I'm fine."

For a moment he said nothing. Then,

"Tempe, when I heard about this I assumed it was a disgruntled student." He scratched the side of his nose. "But this could be more than a prank. Watch yourself. Maybe tell Pete."

"I don't want to do that. He'd feel obligated to baby-sit me, and he doesn't have time for that. He never did."

When we'd finished talking, I gave Ron a key to the Annex, signed the incident report, and left.

Though traffic was light, the drive to UNCC seemed longer than usual. An icy fist had hold of my innards and refused to let go.

All day the feeling was there. Through task after task I was interrupted by images of my murdered cat. Kitten Birdie sitting upright, forepaws flapping like a baby sparrow's. Birdie, flat on his back beneath the sofa. Rubbing figure eights around my ankles. Staring me down for cereal leavings. The sadness that had plagued me in recent weeks was deepening into unshakable melancholy.

After office hours I crossed campus to the athletic complex and changed into running gear. I pushed myself as hard as I could, hoping physical exertion would relieve the ache in my heart and the tension in my body.

As I pounded around the track my mind shifted gears. Ron Gillman's words replaced the images of my dead pet. Butchering an animal is cruel but it's amateur. Was it merely an unhappy student? Or could Birdie's death be a real threat? From whom? Was there a link to the mugging in Montreal? To the Murtry investigation? Had I been drawn into something far bigger than I knew?

I kicked it hard and with each lap the tightness drained from my body. After four miles I collapsed on the grass. Breath rasping, I watched a miniature rainbow shimmer in the spray of a lawn sprinkler. Success. My mind was blank.

When my pulse and breathing had slowed, I returned to the locker room, showered, and dressed in fresh clothes. Feeling better, I climbed the hill to the Colvard Building.

The sensation was short-lived.

My phone was flashing. I punched in the code and waited.

Damn!

I'd missed Kathryn again. As before, she'd left no information, only a statement that she'd called. I rewound the message and listened a second time. She sounded breathless, her words tense and clipped.

I played the message again and again, but could make nothing of the background noise. Kathryn's voice was muffled, as though she were speaking from inside a small space. I imagined her cupping the receiver, whispering, furtively checking her surroundings.

Was I being paranoid? Had last night's incident sent my imagination into overdrive? Or was Kathryn in real danger?

The sun through the venetian blinds threw bright stripes across my desk. Down the hall, a door slammed. Slowly, an idea took shape.

I reached for the phone.

22

"Thanks for making time for me this late in the day. I'm surprised you're still on campus."

"Are you implying that anthropologists work harder than sociologists?"

"Never," I laughed, settling into the black plastic chair he indicated. "Red, I'd like to pick your brain. What can you tell me about local cults?"

"What do you mean by cult?"

Red Skyler slouched sideways behind his desk. Though his hair had gone gray, the russet beard explained the origin of the nickname. He squinted at me through steel-rimmed glasses.

"Fringe groups. Doomsday sects. Satanic circles."

He smiled and gave me a "carry on" gesture.

"The Manson Family. Hare Krishna. MOVE. The People's Temple. Synanon. You know. Cults."

"You're using a very loaded term. What you call a cult someone else may see as a religion. Or family. Or political party."

I had a flashback to Daisy Jeannotte. She, too, had objected to the word, but there the similarity ended. In that interview I sat across from a tiny woman in a huge office. Now I faced a large man in a space so small and crowded I felt claustrophobic.

"All right. What's a cult?"

"Cults are not just groups of crazies who follow weird leaders. At least the way I use the term, they are organizations with a set of common features."

"Yes." I leaned back in my chair.

"A cult forms around a charismatic individual who promises something. This individual professes some special knowledge. Sometimes the claim is access to ancient secrets, sometimes it's an entirely new discovery to which he or she alone is privy. Sometimes it's a combination of both. The leader offers to share the information with those who follow. Some leaders offer utopia. Or a way out. Just come along, follow me. I'll make the decisions. All will be fine."

"How does that differ from a priest or rabbi?"

"In a cult it's this charismatic leader who eventually becomes the object of devotion; in some cases he's actually deified. And as that happens, the leader comes to hold extraordinary control over the lives of his followers."

He removed his glasses and rubbed each lens with a square of green material he took from his pocket. Then he replaced them, wrapping each bow behind an ear.

"Cults are totalistic, authoritarian. The leader is supreme and delegates power to very few. The leader's morality becomes the only acceptable theology. The only acceptable behavior. And, as I said, veneration is eventually centered on him, not on supreme beings or on abstract principles."

I waited.

"And often there is a double set of ethics. Members are urged to be honest and loving to each other but to deceive and shun outsiders. Established religions tend to follow one set of rules for everybody."

"How does a leader gain such control?"

"That's another important element. Thought reform. Cult leaders use a variety of psychological processes to manipulate their members. Some leaders are fairly benign, but others are not and really exploit the idealism of their followers."

Again I waited for him to go on.

"The way I see it, there are two broad types of cults, both of which use thought reform. The commercially packaged 'awareness programs'" – he gestured quotation marks – "use very intense persuasion techniques. These groups keep members by getting them to buy more and more courses.

"Then there are the cults that recruit followers for life. These groups use organized psychological and social persuasion to produce extreme attitudinal changes. As a result they come to exert enormous control over the lives of their members. They are manipulative, deceptive, and highly exploitative."

I digested that.

"How does thought reform work?"

"You begin by destabilizing a person's sense of self. I'm sure you discuss this in your anthropology classes. Separate. Deconstruct. Reconstruct."

"I'm a physical anthropologist."

"Right. Cults cut newcomers off from all other influences, then get them to question everything they believe in. Persuade them to reinterpret the world and their own life history. They create a whole new reality for the person, and in so doing they create a dependence on the organization and its ideology."

I thought back to the cultural anthropology courses I'd taken in graduate school.

"But you're not talking about rites of passage. I know in some cultures kids are isolated for a period in their lives and subjected to training, but the process is meant

286

to reinforce ideas the child has grown up with. You're talking about getting people to reject the values of their upbringing, to toss out everything they believe in. How is that done?"

"The cult controls the recruit's time and environment. Diet. Sleep. Work. Recreation. Money. Everything. It creates a sense of dependency, of powerlessness apart from the group. As it does that it instills the new morality, the system of logic to which the group adheres. The world according to the leader. And it is definitely a closed system. No feedback allowed. No criticism. No complaints. The group suppresses old behaviors and attitudes and, bit by bit, replaces them with its own behaviors and attitudes."

"Why does anyone go along with that?"

"The process is so gradual the person isn't aware of what's happening. You're taken through a series of tiny steps, each one seemingly unimportant. Other members grow their hair. You grow your hair. Others speak softly, so you lower your voice. Everyone listens docilely to the leader, asking no questions, so you do the same. There is a sense of approval by the group and of acceptance into it. The new recruit is totally unaware of the double agenda that's operating."

"Don't they eventually see what's happening?"

"Usually new members are encouraged to break all contact with friends and family, to cut themselves off from their former networks. Sometimes they're taken to isolated places. Farms. Communes. Chalets.

"This isolation, both physical and social, strips them of their normal support systems and increases their sense of personal powerlessness and need for group acceptance. It also eliminates the normal sounding boards we all use for evaluating what we're being told. The person's confidence in his or her own judgment

287

and perception deteriorates. Independent action becomes impossible."

I thought of Dom and his group on Saint Helena.

"I can see how a cult has control if you live under its roof twenty-four hours a day, but what if members work outside the headquarters?"

"Easy. Members are given instructions to do chants or meditation whenever they're not working. Lunch hour. Coffee break. The mind is occupied by cult-directed behaviors. And outside the job all their time is devoted to the organization."

"But what is the appeal? What drives someone to reject his past and turn himself over to a sect?"

I couldn't wrap my mind around this. Were Kathryn and the others automatons, controlled in their every move?

"There is a system of rewards and punishments. If the member behaves, talks, and thinks appropriately he or she is loved by the leader and by the peer group. And, of course, he or she will be saved. Enlightened. Taken to another world. Whatever the ideology promises."

"What *do* they promise?"

"You name it. Not all cults are religious. The public has that idea because back in the sixties and seventies a lot of groups registered as churches for the tax break. Cults come in all shapes and sizes and promise all kinds of benefits. Health. Overthrow of the government. A trip to outer space. Immortality."

"I still don't see why anyone but a nutcase would fall for such crap."

"Not at all." He shook his head. "It's not just marginal people who get sucked in. In some studies approximately two thirds of the respondents came from normal families and were demonstrating age-appropriate behavior when they entered a cult."

I looked at the tiny Navajo rug beneath my feet. The mental itch was back. What was it? Why couldn't I bring it to the surface?

"Has your research shed light on why people seek out these movements?"

"Often they don't. These groups seek you. And as I've said, these leaders can be incredibly charming and persuasive."

Dom Owens fit that description. Who was he? An ideologue forcing his whims on malleable followers? Or just a health-fad prophet trying to grow organic butter beans?

Again I thought of Daisy Jeannotte. Was she right? Had the public become overly fearful of Satan worshipers and doomsday prophets?

"How many cults exist in the U.S.?" I asked.

"Depending on your definition" – he gave a wry smile and spread his hands – "anywhere from three to five thousand."

"You're kidding."

"One of my colleagues estimates that over the past two decades as many as twenty million people have had some involvement with a cult. She believes that at any given time the number is two to five million people."

"Do you agree?" I was astounded.

"It's awfully hard to know. Some groups inflate their numbers by counting as a member anyone who ever attended a meeting or requested information. Others are very secretive, and keep as low a profile as possible. The police discover some groups only indirectly, if there's a problem, or if a member leaves and files a complaint. The small ones are particularly hard to track."

"Ever hear of Dom Owens?"

He shook his head. "What's the name of his group?"

"They don't use one."

Down the hall a printer whirred to life.

"Are there any organizations in the Carolinas that the police are monitoring?"

"Not my area, Tempe. I'm a sociologist. I can tell you how these groups work, but not necessarily who's at the plate at any given time. I can try to find out if it's important."

"I just don't get it, Red. How can people be so gullible?"

"It's seductive to think that you're elite. Chosen. Most cults teach their members that only they are enlightened and everyone else in the world is left out. Lesser in some way. It's powerful stuff."

"Red, are these groups violent?"

"Most aren't, but there are the exceptions. There was Jonestown, Waco, Heaven's Gate, and the Solar Temple. Obviously their members didn't fare too well. Remember the Rajneesh cult? They attempted to poison the water supply in some town in Oregon, and made threatening moves toward the county officials. And Synanon? Those fine citizens placed a diamond-back in the mailbox of a lawyer who brought suit against them. The guy barely survived."

I vaguely recalled the incident.

"What about small groups, the ones with less profile?"

"Most are harmless, but some are sophisticated and potentially dangerous. I can think of only a few that have crossed the line in recent years. Does this have to do with a case?"

"Yeah. No. I'm not sure." I picked at a hangnail on my thumb.

He hesitated. "Is it Katy?"

"What?"

"Is Katy involved with . . ."

"Oh no, nothing like that. Really. It's related to a

case. I came across this commune in Beaufort and they got me thinking."

The border of my nail began to bleed.

"Dom Owens."

I nodded.

"Things aren't always what they seem."

"No."

"I can make a few calls if you'd like."

"I'd appreciate that."

"Do you want a Band-Aid?"

I dropped my hands and stood.

"No, thanks. I really won't keep you any longer. You've been very helpful."

"Any more questions, you know where I am."

Back in my office, I sat and watched shadows lengthen across the room, the feeling of an unformed thought still teasing my mind. The building was heavy with after-hours quiet.

Was it Daisy Jeannotte? I'd forgotten to ask Red if he knew her. Was that it?

No.

What was it that kept calling from the labyrinth of my neural wiring? Why couldn't I drag it into consciousness? What link did my id see that I did not?

My eyes fell on the small collection of mystery writers I keep on campus for exchange with colleagues. What did these authors call it? The "Had-I-But-Known" technique. Was that it? Was tragedy approaching because of a subconscious message I couldn't manage to retrieve?

What tragedy? Another death in Quebec? More killings in Beaufort? Harm to Kathryn? Another attack on me, with more serious consequences?

Somewhere a phone rang and rang, then stopped abruptly as the messaging service cut in. Silence.

291

I tried Pete's number again. No answer. He was probably off on another deposition trip. It didn't matter. I knew Birdie wasn't there.

I got up and started filing papers, sorted through a stack of reprints, then switched to shelving books. I knew it was avoidance, but couldn't help myself. The thought of going home was unbearable.

Ten minutes of restless activity. Don't think. Then, "Oh hell, Birdie!"

I slammed a copy of *Baboon Ecology* onto the desk and slumped into my chair.

"Why did you have to be there? I'm so sorry. I'm so very, very sorry, Bird."

I lay my head on the blotter and sobbed.

23

Thursday was deceptively pleasant.

In the morning I had two small surprises. The call to my insurance carrier went well. Both repairmen I phoned were available and would start work immediately.

During the day I taught my classes and revised the CAT scan paper for the physical anthropology conference. Late in the afternoon Ron Gillman reported that the Crime Scene Recovery unit had found nothing useful in the debris from my kitchen. No surprise there. He'd asked patrol to keep an eye on my place.

I also heard from Sam. He had no news, but was becoming increasingly convinced the bodies had been dropped on his island by dope dealers. He was taking it as a personal challenge and had dug out an old twelve gauge and stashed it under a bunk in the field station.

On the way home from the university I stopped at the Harris Teeter superstore across from the Southpark Shopping Center and bought all of my favorite foods. I worked out at the Harris YMCA and arrived at the Annex around six-thirty. The window had been fixed and a workman was just finishing sanding the floor.

Every surface in the kitchen was coated in fine white dust.

I cleaned the stove and counters, then fixed crab cakes and a goat cheese salad and ate them while watching a rerun of "Murphy Brown." The Murph was tough. I resolved to be more like her.

During the evening I revised the CAT scan paper again, watched a Hornets' game, and thought about my taxes. I resolved to do that, too. But not this week. At eleven I fell asleep with the copies of Louis-Philippe's journal spread across the bed.

Friday was scripted by Satan. It was then I got my first inkling of the horror about to unfold.

The Murtry victims arrived from Charleston early in the morning. By nine-thirty I was gloved and goggled and had the cases spread out in my lab. One table held the skull and bone samples Hardaway had removed during his autopsy of the lower corpse. The other held a full skeleton. The technicians at the medical university had done an excellent job. All the bones looked clean and undamaged.

I started with the body from the bottom of the pit. Though putrefied, it had retained enough soft tissue to allow a full autopsy. Sex and race were evident, so Hardaway wanted my help only in assessing age. I left the pathologist's report and photos until later since I didn't want to bias my conclusions by knowing his.

I popped the X-rays onto the light box. Nothing unusual. In the cranial views I could see that all thirty-two teeth were erupted, their roots fully formed. There were no restorations or missing teeth. I noted this on a case form.

I walked to the first table and looked at the skull. The gap at the cranial base was fused. This was not an adolescent.

294

I studied the rib ends and the surfaces where the halves of the pelvis join in front, the pubic symphyses. The ribs had moderately deep indentations where cartilage had connected them to the breastbone. Wavy ridges ran across the pubic symphyseal faces, and I could see tiny nodules of bone along the outer border of each.

The throat end of each collarbone was fused. The upper edge of each hip blade retained a thin line of separation.

I checked my models and histograms, and wrote down my estimate. The woman was twenty to twenty-eight years of age when she died.

Hardaway wanted a full analysis on the subsurface burial. Again I started with the X-rays. Again they were unremarkable, except for the perfect dentition.

I already suspected this victim was also female, as I'd told Ryan. As I'd laid out the bones, I'd noted the smooth skull and delicate facial architecture. The broad, short pelvis with its distinctly feminine pubic area confirmed my initial impression.

This woman's age indicators were similar to those of the first victim, though her pubic symphyses showed deep ridges across their entire surfaces and lacked the little nodes.

I estimated this victim had died slightly younger, probably in her late teens or early twenties.

For the question of ancestry, I returned to the cranium. The mid-face region was classic, especially the nasal features: high bridge between the eyes, narrow opening, prominent lower border and spine.

I took measurements that I would analyze statistically, but I knew the woman was white.

I measured the long bones, fed the data into the computer, and ran the regression equations. I was entering a height estimate into the case form when the phone rang.

"If I stay here one more day I'm going to need complete linguistic retraining," Ryan said, then added, "y'all."

"Catch a bus north."

"I thought it was just you, but now I see it's not your fault."

"It's hard to overcome one's roots."

"Yo."

"Have you learned anything new?"

"I saw a great bumper sticker this morning."

I waited.

"Jesus loves you. Everyone else thinks you're an asshole."

"Is that what you called to tell me?"

"That was the bumper sticker."

"We are a religious people."

I looked at the clock. Two-fifteen. I realized I was famished and reached for the banana and Moon Pie I'd brought from home.

"I've spent some time observing Dom's little ashram. Not very useful. Thursday morning three of the faithful piled into a van and drove off. Other than that I saw no traffic in or out."

"Kathryn?"

"Didn't see her."

"Did you run the plates?"

"Yes, ma'am. Both vans are registered to Dom Owens at the Adler Lyons address."

"Does he have a driver's license?"

"Issued by the great Palmetto State in 1988. No record of a previous license. Apparently the reverend just walked in and took the exam. He pays his insurance right on time. In cash. No record of claims. No record of traffic arrests or citations."

"Utilities?" I tried not to crinkle the cellophane.

"Phone, electric, and water. Owens pays cash."

"Does he have a Social Security number?"

"Issued in 1987. But there's no record of any activity. Never paid in, never requested benefits of any kind."

"Eighty-seven? Where was he before that?"

"An insightful question, Dr. Brennan."

"Mail?"

"These folks are not great correspondents. They get the usual personal greetings addressed to 'Occupant,' and the utility bills, of course, but that's it. Owens has no box, but there could be a drop under another name. I staked the post office briefly, but didn't recognize any of the flock."

A student appeared in the doorway and I shook my head.

"Were there prints on your key chain?"

"Three beauties, but no hits. Apparently Dom Owens is a choir-boy."

Silence stretched between us.

"There are kids living at that place. What about Social Services?"

"You're not half bad, Brennan."

"I watch a lot of television."

"I checked with Social Services. A neighbor called about a year and a half ago, worried about the kids. Mrs. Joseph Espinoza. So they sent a caseworker out to investigate. I read the report. She found a clean home with smiling, well-nourished young'uns, none of which was of school age. She saw no cause for action, but recommended a follow-up visit in six months. That was not done."

"Did you talk to the neighbor?"

"Deceased."

"How about the property?"

"Well, there is one thing."

297

Several seconds passed.

"Yes?"

"I spent Wednesday afternoon going through property deeds and tax records."

He went quiet again.

"Are you trying to annoy me?" I prompted.

"That piece of land has a colorful history. Did you know there was a school out there from the early 1860s until the turn of the century? One of the first public schools in North America established exclusively for black students."

"I didn't know that." I opened a Diet Coke.

"And Baker was right. The property was used as a fishing camp from the thirties until the mid-seventies. When the owner died it passed to her relatives in Georgia. I guess they weren't big on seafood. Or maybe they got fed up with the property taxes. Anyway, they sold the place in 1988."

This time I waited him out.

"The purchaser was one J. R. Guillion."

It took a nanosecond for the name to register.

"Jacques Guillion?"

"*Oui, madame.*"

"The same Jacques Guillion?" I said it so loudly a student turned in the corridor to peer in at me.

"Presumably. The taxes are paid . . ."

"With an official check from Citicorp in New York."

"You got it."

"Holy shit."

"Well put."

I was unnerved by the information. The owner of the Adler Lyons property also held title to the burned-out house in St-Jovite.

"Have you talked to Guillion?"

"Monsieur Guillion is still in seclusion."

"What?"

298

"He hasn't been located."

"I'll be damned. There really is a link."

"Looks that way."

A bell rang.

"One other thing."

The hall filled with the commotion of students passing between classes.

"Just to be perverse I sent the names out to Texas. Came up empty on the Right Reverend Owens, but guess who's a rancher?"

"No!"

"Monsieur J. R. Guillion. Two acres in Fort Bend County. Pays his taxes . . ."

"With official bank checks!"

"Eventually I'll head out that way, but for now I'm letting the local sheriff snoop around. And the gendarmerie can flush Guillion. I'm going to hang here a few more days and turn the heat up on Owens."

"Locate Kathryn. She called here, but I missed her again. I'm sure she knows something."

"If she's here, I'll find her."

"She could be in danger."

"What makes you say that?"

I thought of describing my recent conversation about cults, but since I'd only been fishing I wasn't sure if I'd learned anything relevant. Even if Dom Owens was leading some type of cult, he was not Jim Jones or David Koresh, of that I was certain.

"I don't know. Just a feeling. She sounded so edgy when she called."

"My impression of Miss Kathryn is that all her lobes may not be firing."

"She is different."

"And her friend El doesn't look like a candidate for Mensa. Are you keeping busy?"

I hesitated, then told him about my own attack.

"Sonofabitch. I'm sorry, Brennan. I liked that cat. Any idea who did it?"

"No."

"Have they put a unit on your place?"

"They're doing drive-bys. I'm fine."

"Stay out of dark alleys."

"The cases from Murtry arrived this morning. I'm pretty tied up in the lab."

"If those deaths are drug-related, you could be pissing off some heavy characters."

"That's breaking news, Ryan." I tossed the banana peel and Moon Pie wrapper into the trash. "The victims are both young, white, and female, just as I thought."

"Not your typical trafficker profile."

"No."

"Doesn't rule it out. Some of these guys use women like condoms. The ladies might have been at the wrong place at the wrong time."

"Yes."

"Cause of death?"

"I haven't finished yet."

"Go get 'em, tiger. But remember, we're going to need you on the St-Jovite cases when I nail these bastards."

"What bastards?"

"Don't know yet, but I will."

When we disconnected I stared at my report. Then I got up and paced the lab. Then I sat. Then I paced some more.

My mind kept throwing up images from St-Jovite. Doughy white babies, eyelids and fingernails a delicate blue. A bullet-pierced skull. Slashed throats, hands scored with defense wounds. Scorched bodies, their limbs twisted and contorted.

What linked the Quebec deaths to the point of land on Saint Helena Island? Why babies and fragile old

300

women? Who was Guillion? What was in Texas? Into what form of malignancy had Heidi and her family stumbled?

Concentrate, Brennan. The young women in this lab are just as dead. Leave the Quebec murders to Ryan and finish these cases. They deserve your attention. Find out when they died. And how.

I pulled on another pair of gloves and examined every bone of the second victim's skeleton under magnification. I found nothing to tell me what caused her death. No blunt instrument trauma. No gunshot entry or exit. No stab wound. No hyoid fracture to indicate strangulation.

The only damage I observed was caused by animals scavenging on her corpse.

As I replaced the last foot bone, a tiny black beetle crawled from under a vertebra. I stared at it, remembering an afternoon when Birdie had tracked a June bug in my kitchen in Montreal. He'd played with the creature for hours before finally losing interest.

Tears burned my eyelids, but I refused to give in.

I collected the beetle and put it in a plastic container. No more death. I would release the bug when I left the building.

O.K., beetle. How long have these ladies been dead? We'll work on that.

I looked at the clock. Four-thirty. Late enough. I flipped through my Rolodex, found a number, and dialed.

Five time zones away a phone was answered.

"Dr. West."

"Dr. Lou West?"

"Yes."

"A.k.a. Kaptain Kam?"

Silence.

"Of Spam fame?"

301

"It's tuna fish. Is that you, Tempe?"

In my mind's eye I saw him, thick silver hair and beard framing a face permanently tanned by the Hawaiian sun. Years before I'd met him, a Japanese ad agency spotted Lou and cast him as spokesman for a brand of canned tuna. His earring and ponytail were perfectly suited to the sea captain image they wanted. The Japanese loved Kaptain Kam. Though we teased him unmercifully, no one I knew had ever seen the ads.

"Ready to give up bugs and hawk tuna full time?"

Lou holds a doctorate in biology and teaches at the University of Hawaii. In my opinion he is the best forensic entomologist in the country.

"Not quite." He laughed. "The suit itches."

"Do it in the buff."

"I don't think the Japanese are ready for that."

"When has that ever stopped you?"

Lou and I, and a handful of other forensic specialists, teach a course on body recovery at the FBI Academy in Quantico, Virginia. It's an irreverent group, composed of pathologists, entomologists, anthropologists, botanists, and soil experts, most with academic backgrounds. One year a zealously conservative agent suggested to the entomologist that his earring was inappropriate. Lou listened solemnly, and the next day the small gold loop was replaced by an eight-inch Cherokee feather with beads, fringe, and a small silver bell.

"I've got your bugs."

"They came through intact?"

"Unscathed. And you did a great job collecting. In the Carolinas the insect assemblage associated with decomposition includes over five hundred and twenty species. I think you sent me most of them."

"So what can you tell me?"

"You want the whole rundown?"

"Sure."

"First of all, I think your vics were killed during the day. Or at least the bodies were exposed during daylight hours for a while before burial. I found larviposition by *Sarcophaga bullata*."

"Give that to me in English."

"It's a species of flesh fly. You collected empty *Sarcophaga bullata* puparial cases and intact puparia from both bodies."

"And?"

"The *Sarcophagidae* aren't too spunky after sundown. If you drop a body right next to them they might larviposit, but they're not very active at night."

"Larviposit?"

"Insects use larviposition or oviposition. Some lay eggs, some lay larvae."

"Insects lay larvae?"

"First instar larvae. That's the very first larval stage. The *Sarcophagidae* as a group larviposit. It's a strategy that gives them a head start on the rest of the maggots, and also provides some protection against predators that feed on eggs."

"Then why don't all these insects larviposit?"

"There's a downside. The females can't produce nearly as many larvae as they can eggs. It's a trade-off."

"Life is compromise."

"Indeed. I also suspect the bodies were exposed outside, at least for a short period. The *Sarcophagidae* aren't quite as willing to enter buildings as some other groups. The *Calliphoridae*, for example."

"That makes sense. They were either killed on the island or the bodies were transported there by boat."

"In any event, I'd guess they were killed during the day, then spent some time outside and aboveground before being buried."

"What about the other species?"

"You want the whole party?"

"Definitely."

"For both corpses burial would have delayed the normal insect invasion. Once the top body was exposed by the scavengers, however, the *Calliphoridae* would have found it irresistible for egg laying."

"*Calliphoridae?*"

"Blowflies. They usually arrive within minutes of death, along with their friends the flesh flies. They're both strong fliers."

"Bully."

"You collected at least two species of blowflies, *Cochliomyia* . . ."

"Maybe we should stick to common names."

"O.K. You collected first, second, and third instar larvae and intact and empty puparial cases for at least two species of blowflies."

"Which means what?"

"O.K., class. Let's review the life cycle of the fly. Like us, adult flies are concerned with finding suitable places to rear their young. A dead body is perfect. Protected environment. Lots to eat. The perfect neighborhood to raise the kids. Corpses are so attractive, blowflies and flesh flies may arrive within minutes after death. The female will either oviposit immediately, or feed for a while on the fluids seeping from the remains, and then lay her eggs."

"Nice."

"Hey, the stuff is very rich in protein. If there's trauma to the corpse, they'll go for that, if not they'll settle for orifices – eyes, nose, mouth, anus . . ."

"I get the picture."

"Blowflies lay huge clusters of eggs that can completely fill natural body openings and wound sites. You say it's been cool there, so there may not have been quite as many in your grave."

304

"When the eggs hatch, the maggots take center stage."

"Exactly. Act two. Maggots are really pretty cool. On the front end they have a pair of mouth hooks that they use for feeding and locomotion. They breathe through little flat structures on the back end."

"They breathe through their asses."

"In a sense. Anyway, eggs laid at the same time hatch at the same time and the maggots mature together. They also feed together, so you can get these enormous maggot masses moving around the body. The group feeding behavior results in the dissemination of bacteria and the production of digestive enzymes which permit maggots to consume most of the soft tissues of a corpse. It's all highly efficient.

"Maggots mature rapidly, and when they reach maximum size they undergo a dramatic change in behavior. They stop feeding and look for drier digs, usually away from the body."

"Act three."

"Yep. The larvae burrow in and their outer skins harden and form protective encasements called puparia. They look like tiny footballs. The maggots stay inside the pupal casings until their cells have reorganized, then emerge as adult flies."

"That's why the empty puparial cases are significant?"

"Yes. Remember the flesh flies?"

"The *Sarcophagidae*. The larvipositers."

"Very good. They're usually the first to emerge as adults. It takes them anywhere from sixteen to twenty-four days to mature, given temperatures around eighty degrees Fahrenheit. They'd be slowed under the conditions you describe."

"Yes. It wasn't that warm."

"But the empty puparial casings mean some of the flesh flies had finished their development."

"Flown the pupae, as it were."

"It takes the blowfly about fourteen to twenty-five days to mature, probably longer in the wet environment on your island."

"Those estimates tally."

"You also collected what I'm pretty sure are *Muscidae* larvae, maggots of the housefly and its relatives. Typically these species don't show up for five to seven days after death. They prefer to wait for what we call the late fresh or early bloat stages. Oh, and there were cheese skippers."

Cheese skippers are maggots that jump. Though not always easy, I've learned to ignore them while working on putrefied bodies.

"My personal favorites."

"Everybody's got to make a living, Dr. Brennan."

"I suppose one has to admire an organism that can jump ninety times its body length."

"Have you measured?"

"It's an estimate."

"A particularly useful critter for estimating PMI is the black soldier fly. They don't usually show up until twenty days after death, and they're fairly consistent, even with buried remains."

"They were present?"

"Yes."

"What else?"

"The beetle assemblage was more limited, probably due to the wet habitat. But the typical predator forms were there, no doubt munching happily on the maggots and soft-bodied forms."

"So what's your estimate?"

"I'd say we're talking about three to four weeks."

"Both bodies?"

"You measured four feet to the bottom of the pit, three feet to the top of the lower body. We've already discussed the preburial larviposition by the flesh flies, so that explains the puparial cases you found on and above the deeper body. Some held adults, half in and half out. They must have been trapped by the soil while trying to exit. The *Piophilidae* were there, also."

"Lou?"

"Cheese skippers. I also found some coffin flies in the soil sample you took from above the lower body, and some larvae on the body itself. These species are known to burrow down to corpses to deposit their eggs. The soil disturbance in the grave and the presence of the upper body would have facilitated their access. I forgot to mention I found coffin flies on the upper body."

"Were the soil samples useful?"

"Very. You don't want to hear about all the critters that chow down on maggots and decompositional materials, but I found one form that's helpful with PMI. When I processed the soil I collected a number of mites which support a minimum time since death of three weeks."

"So you're saying three to four weeks for both bodies."

"That's my preliminary estimate."

"This is very helpful, Lou. You guys amaze me."

"Does all this square with the condition of the remains?"

"Perfectly."

"There's one other thing I want to mention."

What he told me next sent an icy wind rocketing through my soul.

24

"I'm sorry, Lou. Go over that again."

"It's not new. The increase in drug-related deaths in recent years has prompted research into testing for pharmaceuticals in carrion-feeding insects. I don't have to tell you that bodies aren't always found right away, so investigators may not have the specimens they need for tox analysis. You know, blood, urine, or organ tissues."

"So you test for drugs in maggots?"

"You can, but we've had better luck with the puparial casings. Probably because of the longer feeding time compared to the larvae. We've also played with beetle exuviae and frass . . ."

"Which is?"

"Cast-off beetle skins and fecal matter. We're finding the highest drug levels in the fly puparia, though. That probably reflects feeding preference. While beetles prefer dried integument, flies go for soft tissues. That's where drug concentrations are likely to be greatest."

"What's been found?"

"The list is pretty long. Cocaine, heroin, methamphetamine, amitriptyline, nortriptyline. Most recently we've been working with 3,4-methylenedioxymethamphetamine."

308

"Street name?"

"Ecstasy is the most common one."

"And you're finding these substances in puparial casings?"

"We've isolated both the parent drugs and their metabolites."

"How?"

"The extraction method is similar to that used on regular pathology samples, except that you have to break down the tough chitin/protein matrix in the insect puparia and exuviae so the toxins can be released. You do that by crushing the casings, then using either a strong acid or base treatment. After that, and a pH adjustment, you just use routine drug-screening techniques. We do a base extraction followed by liquid chromatography and mass spectrometry. The ion breakdown indicates what's in your sample and how much."

I swallowed.

"And you're telling me you found flunitrazepam in the puparial casings I sent?"

"The ones associated with the upper body contained flunitrazepam and two of its metabolites, desmethylflunitrazepam and 7-aminoflunitrazepam. The concentration of the parent drug was much greater than the metabolites."

"Which is consistent with acute rather than chronic exposure."

"Exactamundo."

I thanked Lou and hung up.

For a moment I just sat there. The shock of discovery had curdled my stomach and I felt I might throw up. Or maybe it was the Moon Pie.

Flunitrazepam.

The word had finally roused the stored memory.

Flunitrazepam.

Rohypnol.

That was the wake-up call my brain had been sounding.

With trembling hands I dialed the Lord Cartaret Motel. No answer. I redialed and left my number on Ryan's pager.

Then I waited, my sympathetic nervous system broadcasting a low-level alert, telling me to fear. Fear what?

Rohypnol.

When the phone rang I lunged for it.

A student.

I cleared the line and waited some more, feeling a dark, cold dread.

Rohypnol. The date rape drug.

Glaciers formed. Ocean levels rose and fell. Somewhere a star spun planets from dust.

Eleven minutes later Ryan called.

"I think I've found another link."

"What?"

Slow down. Don't let the shock interfere with your thinking.

"The Murtry Island and St-Jovite murders."

I told him about my conversation with Lou West.

"One of the women on Murtry had massive amounts of Rohypnol in her tissue."

"So did the bodies in the upstairs bedroom at St-Jovite."

"Yes."

Another memory had slammed to the surface when Lou spoke the name of the drug.

Boreal forest. Aerial views of a smoldering chalet. A meadow, shrouded bodies arranged in a circle. Uniformed personnel. Stretchers. Ambulances.

"Do you remember the Order of the Solar Temple?"

310

"The wing nut worshipers that offed themselves en masse?"

"Yes. Sixty-four people died in Europe. Ten in Quebec."

I fought to steady my voice.

"Some of those chalets were wired to explode and burn."

"Yeah. I've thought of that."

"Rohypnol was found in both locations. Many of the victims had ingested the drug shortly before they died."

Pause.

"You think Owens is rezoning for the Temple?"

"I don't know."

"Think they're dealing?"

Dealing what? Human lives?

"I suppose it's a possibility."

For several moments neither of us spoke.

"I'll run this past the guys who worked Morin Heights. Meantime, I'm going to shove a deadbolt up Dom Owens' ass."

"There's more."

The line hummed softly.

"Are you listening?"

"Yes."

"West estimates the women died three to four weeks ago."

My breath sounded loud in the receiver.

"The fire in St-Jovite was on March tenth. Tomorrow's the first."

I listened to the hum as Ryan did the math.

"Holy Christ. Three weeks ago."

"I have a feeling something terrible is going to happen, Ryan."

"Roger that."

Dial tone.

★ ★ ★

In looking back I always have the sense events accelerated after that conversation, gathered speed and grew more frantic, eventually forming a vortex that sucked everything into itself. Including me.

That evening I worked late. So did Hardaway. He called as I was pulling his autopsy report from the envelope.

I gave him the profile for the subsurface body, and my age estimate for the deeper one.

"That squares," he said. "She was twenty-five."

"You've got an ID?"

"We were able to lift one readable print. Got nothing from the local or state files, so they sent it up to the FBI. Nothing in their AFIS.

"Screwiest thing, though. Don't know what made me do it, probably 'cause I know you work up there. When the guy at the bureau suggested we try the RCMP I said, what the hell, fire it through. Damned if she doesn't pop up Canadian."

"What else did you find out about her?"

"Hang on."

I heard the creak of springs, then the rustle of paper.

"The sheet came through late today. Name's Jennifer Cannon. White race. Height five foot five, weight one hundred thirty pounds. Hair brown. Eyes green. Single. Last seen alive . . ." There was a pause while he calculated. ". . . two years, three months ago."

"Where's she from?"

"Let's see." Pause. "Calgary. Where's that?"

"Out west. Who reported her missing?"

"Sylvia Cannon. It's a Calgary address, so it must be the mother."

I gave Hardaway the pager number and asked him to phone Ryan.

"When you speak to him, please have him call me. If I'm not here I'll be at home."

312

I boxed and locked up the Murtry bones. Then I stuffed my diskette and case forms, Hardaway's autopsy report and photos, and the CAT scan paper into my briefcase, secured the lab, and left.

The campus was deserted, the night still and moist. Unseasonably warm, the broadcasters would call it. The air was heavy with the smell of grass just cut and rain about to fall. I heard the faint rumble of distant thunder, and pictured the storm rolling down from the Smokies and across the Piedmont.

On the way home I stopped for take-out at the Selwyn Pub. The after-work crowd was dispersing, and the younger set from Queens College had not yet arrived to take over the premises for the evening. Sarge, the rascally Irish co-owner, sat on his usual corner stool dispensing opinions on sports and politics, while Neal the bartender dispensed any one of a dozen draft beers. Sarge wanted to discuss the death penalty, or rather have his say about the death penalty, but I was not in the mood for banter. I took my cheeseburger and left quickly.

The first drops were patting the magnolias as I slipped my key into the Annex lock. Nothing greeted me but a soft, steady ticking.

It was almost ten when I heard from Ryan.

Sylvia Cannon had not lived at the address provided in the missing person report for over two years. Nor was she residing at the one given the post office for forwarding.

Neighbors at the earlier address remembered no husband and only one daughter. They described Sylvia as quiet and reclusive. A loner. No one knew where she had worked, or where she had gone. One woman thought there was a brother in the area. The Calgary PD were trying to locate her.

313

Later in bed, up under the eaves, I listened to rain tick on the roof and leaves. Thunder rumbled and lightning popped, now and then backlighting the silhouette of Sharon Hall. The ceiling fan brought in a cool mist, and with it the smell of petunias and wet window screen.

I adore storms. I love the raw power of the spectacle: Hydraulics! Voltage! Percussion! Mother Nature has dominion and everyone awaits her whim.

I enjoyed the show as long as I could, then got up and crossed to the dormer. The curtain felt damp and water was already pooling on the sill. I closed and latched the left window, took hold of the right, and breathed deeply. The thundershower cocktail triggered a flood of childhood recollections. Summer nights. Lightning bugs. Sleeping with Harry on Gran's porch.

Think about that, I told myself. Listen to those memories, not the voices of the dead clamoring in your brain.

Lightning flashed and my breath froze in my throat. Was something moving under the hedge?

Another flicker.

I stared, but the shrubs looked still and empty.

Could I have imagined it?

My eyes searched the dimness. Green lawn and hedges. Colorless walks. Pale petunias against the darkness of pine chips and ivy.

Nothing moved.

Again the world lit up and a loud crack split the night.

A white form burst from the bushes and tore across the lawn. I strained to see, but the image was gone before my eyes could focus.

My heart beat so frantically I could feel it in my skull. I threw back the window and leaned into the screen, searching the darkness where the thing had disappeared. Water soaked my nightgown and goose bumps spread across my body.

I scanned the yard, trembling.

Stillness.

Forgetting the window, I turned and raced down the stairs. I was about to throw open the back door when the phone shrilled, sending my heart pounding into my throat.

Oh, God. What now?

I grabbed the receiver.

"Tempe, I'm sorry."

I looked at the clock.

One-forty.

Why was my neighbor calling?

". . . he must have gotten in there on Wednesday when I showed the place. It's empty, you know. I went over just now to check on things, with the storm and all, and he came tearing out. I called, but he just took off. I thought you'd want to know . . ."

I dropped the receiver, threw open the kitchen door, and rushed outside.

"Here, Bird," I called. "Come on, boy."

I stepped off the patio. In seconds my hair was drenched and my nightie clung like wet Kleenex.

"Birdie! Are you there?"

Lightning flared, illuminating walkways, bushes, gardens, and buildings.

"Birdie!" I screamed. "Bird!"

Raindrops pounded brick and slapped at leaves above my head.

I shouted again.

No response.

Over and over I called his name, a madwoman, prowling the grounds of Sharon Hall. Before long I was shaking uncontrollably.

315

Then I saw him.

He was huddled under a bush, head down, ears forward at an odd angle. His fur was wet and clumped, revealing ribbons of pale skin, like cracks on an old painting.

I walked over to him and squatted. He looked like he'd been dipped then rolled. Pine needles, bark chips, and minced vegetation clung to his head and back.

"Bird?" I said in a soft voice, holding out my arms.

He raised his head and searched my face with round yellow eyes. Lightning flicked. Birdie rose, arched his back, and said, "Mrrrrp."

I turned my palms up. "Come on, Bird," I whispered.

He hesitated, then crossed to me, pressed his body sideways against my thigh, and repeated himself. "Mrrrrrp."

I scooped my cat up, hugged him close, and ran for the kitchen. Birdie draped his front paws over my shoulder and pressed himself to me, like a baby monkey clinging to its mother. I felt his claws through my rain-soaked gown.

Ten minutes later I'd finished rubbing him down. White fur coated several towels and drifted in the air. For once there'd been no protest.

Birdie wolfed down a bowl of Science Diet and a saucer of vanilla ice cream. Then I carried him up to bed. He crawled under the covers and stretched full length against my leg. I felt his body tense then relax as he extended his paws, then settled into the mattress. His fur was still damp but I didn't care. I had my cat back.

"I love you, Bird," I said to the night.

I fell asleep to a duet of muffled purring and pelting rain.

25

The next day was Saturday so I didn't go to the university. I planned to read Hardaway's findings, then write my reports on the Murtry victims. After that I would purchase flowers at the garden center and transplant them to the large pots I keep on my patio. Instant gardening, one of my many talents. Then a long talk with Katy, quality time with my cat, the CAT scan paper, and an evening with Élisabeth Nicolet.

That's not how it turned out.

When I woke Birdie was already gone. I called but got no response, so I threw on shorts and a T-shirt and went downstairs to find him. The trail was easy. He'd emptied his dish and fallen asleep in a patch of sunlight on the couch in the living room.

The cat lay on his back, hind legs splayed, front paws dangling over his chest. I watched him a moment, smiling like a kid on Christmas morning. Then I went to the kitchen, made coffee and a bagel, collected the *Observer*, and settled at the kitchen table.

A doctor's wife was found stabbed to death in Myers Park. A child had been attacked by a pit bull. The parents were demanding the animal be destroyed, and

317

the owner was indignant. The Hornets beat Golden State 101 to 87.

I checked the weather. Sunshine and a high of seventy-four predicted for Charlotte. I scanned world temperatures. On Friday the mercury had climbed to forty-eight degrees in Montreal. There is a reason for Southern smugness.

I read the entire paper. Editorials. Want ads. Pharmacy-flyers. It's a weekend ritual I enjoy, but one I'd had to forgo in the past few weeks. Like a junkie on a binge I absorbed every printed word.

When I'd finished I cleared the table and went to my briefcase. I stacked the autopsy photos to my left and lay Hardaway's report in front of me. My pen gave out with the first notation. I rose and went to the living room to find another.

When I saw the figure on the front stoop my heart slipped in an extra beat. I had no idea who it was or how long it had been there.

The figure turned, stepped up against the outer wall, and leaned into the window. Our eyes met and I stared in disbelief.

Immediately, I crossed and opened the door.

She stood with hips thrust forward, hands clutching the straps of a backpack. The hem of her skirt billowed around her hiking boots. The morning sun caught her hair, outlining her head in a copper glow.

Sweet Jesus, I thought. Now what?

Kathryn spoke first.

"I need to talk. I—"

"Yes, of course. Please, come in." I stood back and held out a hand. "Let me take your pack."

She stepped inside, slipped off the backpack, and dropped it to the floor, her eyes never leaving my face.

"I know this is a terrible imposition, and I—"

"Kathryn, don't be silly. I'm glad to see you. I was just so surprised my brain locked up for a second."

Her lips parted but no words came out.

"Would you like something to eat?"

The answer was in her face.

I put my arm around her and took her to the kitchen table. She complied meekly. I stacked the photos and report to the side and sat her down.

As I toasted a bagel, spread it with cream cheese, and poured orange juice, I stole glances at my visitor. Kathryn stared at the tabletop, her hands smoothing nonexistent wrinkles from the mat I'd placed in front of her. Her fingers arranged and rearranged the fringe, straightening each clump and laying it parallel to the next.

My stomach was tied in a granny knot. How had she gotten here? Had she run away? Where was Carlie? I held my questions while she ate.

When Kathryn had finished and declined seconds, I cleared the dishes and rejoined her at the table.

"So. How did you find me?" I patted her hand and smiled encouragingly.

"You gave me your card." She dug it from her pocket and laid it on the table. Then her fingers went back to the place mat. "I called the number in Beaufort a couple of times, but you were never there. Finally some guy answered and said you'd gone back to Charlotte."

"That was Sam Rayburn. I was staying on his boat."

"Anyway, I decided to leave Beaufort." She raised her eyes to mine, then quickly dropped them. "I hitched up here and went to the university, but it took longer than I'd figured. When I got to campus you were gone. I crashed with someone, then this morning she dropped me here on her way to work."

"How did you know where I live?"

"She looked you up in some kind of book."

"I see." I was sure my home address was not listed in the faculty directory. "Well, I'm glad you're here."

Kathryn nodded. She looked exhausted. Her eyes were red and a dark crescent underscored each lower lid.

"I would have returned your calls but you left no number. When Detective Ryan and I visited the compound on Tuesday we didn't see you."

"I was there, but . . ." Her voice faded out.

I waited.

Birdie appeared in the doorway then withdrew, deflected by the tension. The clock chimed the half-hour. Kathryn's fingers worked the fringe.

Finally, I could take it no longer.

"Kathryn, where's Carlie?" I placed my hand on hers.

She raised her eyes to mine. They looked flat and empty.

"They're taking care of him." Her voice was small, like a child answering an accusation.

"Who is?"

She pulled her hand free, rested her elbows on the table, and rubbed small circles on each of her temples. Her eyes were back on the place mat.

"Is Carlie on Saint Helena?"

Another nod.

"Did you want to leave him there?"

She shook her head and her hands slid upward so the palms pressed against her temples.

"Is the baby all right?"

"He's my baby! Mine!"

The vehemence took me by surprise.

"I can take care of him." When she raised her head a tear glistened on each cheek. Her eyes bored into mine.

"Who says you can't?"

"I'm his mother." Her voice trembled. With what? Exhaustion? Fear? Resentment?

320

"Who is taking care of Carlie?"

"But what if I'm wrong? What if it's all true?" Her gaze went back to the tabletop.

"What if *what* is true?"

"I love my baby. I want the best for him."

Kathryn's answers were unrelated to my questions. She was probing her own dark places, reworking a familiar discourse with herself. Only this time it was in my kitchen.

"Of course you do."

"I don't want my baby to die." Her fingers trembled as they caressed the tassels on the mat. It was the same movement I'd seen her use to stroke Carlie's head.

"Is Carlie sick?" I asked, alarmed.

"No. He's perfect." The words were almost inaudible. A tear dropped to the mat.

I looked at the small, dark spot, feeling completely inept.

"Kathryn, I don't know how to help you. You have to tell me what's going on."

The phone rang, but I ignored it. From the other room I heard a click, my message, then a beep followed by a tinny voice. More clicks, then silence.

Kathryn didn't move. She seemed paralyzed by the thoughts that tortured her. Across the silence I felt her pain, and waited.

Seven spots darkened the blue linen. Ten. Thirteen.

After what seemed an eternity Kathryn raised her head. She wiped each cheek and brushed back her hair, then intertwined her fingers and placed her hands carefully in the center of the mat. She cleared her throat twice.

"I don't know what it's like to live a normal life." She gave a self-deprecating smile. "Until this year I didn't know that I wasn't."

She dropped her eyes.

321

"I guess it had to do with having Carlie. I never doubted anything before he was born. It never occurred to me to ask questions. I was home-schooled so what I knew—" Again the smile. "What I know of the world is limited." She thought for a moment. "What I know of the world is what they want me to know."

"They?"

She clutched her hands so tightly the knuckles grew white.

"We're never supposed to talk about group matters." She swallowed. "They're my family. They've been my world since I was eight years old. He's been my father and counselor and teacher and—"

"Dom Owens?"

Her eyes flew to mine. "He's a brilliant man. He knows all about health and reproduction and evolution and pollution and how to keep the spiritual and biological and cosmic forces in balance. He sees and understands things the rest of us don't have a clue about. It's not Dom. I trust Dom. He would never hurt Carlie. He does what he does to protect us. He's watching out for us. I'm just not sure—"

She closed her eyes and tipped her face upward. A small vessel throbbed in the side of her neck. Her larynx rose and fell, then she took a deep breath, lowered her chin, and looked directly into my eyes.

"That girl. The one you were looking for. She was there."

I had to strain to hear her.

"Heidi Schneider?"

"I never knew her last name."

"Tell me what you remember about her."

"Heidi joined somewhere else. Texas, I think. She lived on Saint Helena for about two years. She was older than me, but I liked her. She was always willing to talk or to help me out. She was funny." She paused. "Heidi was supposed to procreate with Jason—"

"What?" I thought I'd heard incorrectly.

"Her procreation partner was Jason. But she was in love with Brian, the guy she was with when she joined. He's the one in your snapshot."

"Brian Gilbert." My mouth felt dry.

"Anyway, she and Brian used to sneak off to be together." Her eyes went to a point somewhere in the distance. "When Heidi got pregnant she was terrified because the baby wouldn't be sanctified. She tried to hide it, but eventually they found out."

"Owens?"

Her eyes refocused on mine and I could see real fear.

"It doesn't matter. It affects everyone."

"What does?"

"The order." She rubbed her palms on the mat then reclasped her hands. "Some things I can't talk about. Do you want to hear this?" She looked at me and I could see that her eyes were starting to water again.

"Go on."

"One day Heidi and Brian didn't show up for morning meeting. They were gone."

"Where?"

"I don't know."

"Do you think Owens sent someone to find them?"

Her eyes slid to the window, and she bit down on her lower lip.

"There's more. One night last fall Carlie woke up fussy, so I went downstairs to get him milk. I heard movement in the office, then a woman speaking, real quiet like she didn't want anyone to hear. She must have been on the phone."

"Did you recognize her voice?"

"Yes. It was one of the women who worked in the office."

323

"What did she say?"

"She was telling someone that someone else was O.K. I didn't hang around to hear more."

"Go on."

"About three weeks ago the same thing happened, only this time I overheard people arguing. They were really angry, but the door was closed, so I couldn't make out their words. It was Dom and this same woman."

She wiped a tear from her cheek with the back of her hand. She still did not look at me.

"The next day she was gone and I never saw her again. She and another woman. They just disappeared."

"Don't people come and go from the group?"

Her eyes locked on to mine.

"She worked in the office. I think she was the one taking the calls you were asking about." I could see her chest rise and fall as she fought back the tears. "She was Heidi's best friend."

I felt the knot tighten in my stomach. "Was her name Jennifer?"

Kathryn nodded.

I took a deep breath. Stay calm for Kathryn's sake. "Who was the other woman?"

"I'm not sure. She hadn't been there long. Wait. Maybe her name was Alice. Or Anne."

My heart changed speed. Oh, God. No.

"Do you know where she came from?"

"Somewhere up North. No, maybe it was Europe. Sometimes she and Jennifer spoke a different language."

"Do you think Dom Owens had Heidi and her babies killed? Is that why you're afraid for Carlie?"

"You don't understand. It isn't Dom. He's just trying to protect us and get us across." She gazed at me

324

intently, as though trying to reach inside my head. "Dom doesn't believe in Antichrists. He just wants to transport us out of the destruction."

Her voice had grown tremulous and short gasps punctuated the spaces between her words. She rose and crossed to the window.

"It's the others. It's her. Dom wants us all to live forever."

"Who?"

Kathryn paced the kitchen like a caged animal, her fingers twisting the front of her cotton blouse. Tears slid down her face.

"But not now. It's too soon. It can't be now." Pleading.

"What's too soon?"

"What if they're wrong? What if there isn't enough cosmic energy? What if there's nothing out there? What if Carlie just dies? What if my baby dies?"

Fatigue. Anxiety. Guilt. The mix won over and Kathryn began to weep uncontrollably. She was growing incoherent and I knew I would learn nothing further.

I went to her and hugged her with both arms. "Kathryn, you need rest. Please, come and lie down for a while. We'll talk later."

She made a sound I couldn't interpret, and allowed herself to be led upstairs to the guest room. I got towels and went down to the parlor for her pack. When I returned, she lay on the bed, one arm thrown across her forehead, eyes shut, tears sliding into the hair at her temples.

I left the pack on the dresser and pulled the window shades. As I was closing the door she spoke softly, eyes still closed, lips barely moving.

Her words frightened me more than anything I had heard in a long time.

26

"'Eternal life'? Those were her exact words?"

"Yes." I clutched the phone so tightly the tendons in my wrist ached.

"Give it to me again."

"'What if they go and we're left behind?' 'What if I deny Carlie eternal life?'"

I waited while Red considered Kathryn's words. When I switched hands I could see a print where my palm had sweated onto the plastic.

"I don't know, Tempe. It's a tough call. How can we ever know when a group will turn violent? Some of these marginal religious movements are extremely volatile. Others are harmless."

"Are there no predictors?"

What if my baby dies?

"There are a number of factors that feed back on each other. First there's the sect itself, its beliefs and rituals, its organization and, of course, its leader. Then there are the outside forces. How much hostility is directed toward the members? How stigmatized are they by society? And the mistreatment doesn't have to be real. Even perceived persecution can cause an organization to become violent."

He just wants to transport us out of the destruction.

"What types of beliefs push these groups over the line?"

"That's what concerns me about your young lady. Sounds like she's talking about a voyage. About going somewhere for eternal life. That sounds apocalyptic."

He's just trying to protect us and get us across.

"The end of the world."

"Exactly. The last days. Armageddon."

"That's not new. Why does an apocalyptic worldview encourage violence? Why not just hunker in and wait?"

"Don't get me wrong. It doesn't always. But these groups believe the last days are imminent, and they see themselves as having a key role in the events that are about to unfold. They're the chosen ones who will give birth to the new order."

She was terrified because the baby wouldn't be sanctified.

"So what develops is a kind of dualism in their thinking. They are good, and all others are hopelessly corrupt, totally lacking in moral virtue. Outsiders come to be demonized."

"You're with me or you're against me."

"Exactly. According to these visions the last days are going to be characterized by violence. Some groups go into a sort of survivalist mode, stockpiling weapons and setting up elaborate surveillance systems against the evil social order that's out to get them. Or the Antichrist, or Satan, or whatever they see as the perceived threat."

Dom doesn't believe in Antichrists.

"Apocalyptic beliefs can be especially volatile when embodied in a charismatic leader. Koresh saw himself as the Lord's appointed."

"Go on."

"You see, one of the problems for a self-appointed prophet is that he has to constantly reinvent himself. There's no institutional support for his long-term

327

authority. There are also no institutional restraints on his behavior. The leader runs the show, but only as long as his disciples follow. So these guys can be very volatile. And they can do whatever they choose within their sphere of power.

"Some of the more paranoid respond to perceived threats to their authority by becoming oppressively dictatorial. They make increasingly bizarre demands, insisting their followers comply in order to show loyalty."

"Such as?"

"Jim Jones had tests of faith, as he called them. Members of the People's Temple would be forced to sign confessions or suffer public humiliations to prove their devotion. One little ritual required the participant to drink unidentified liquids. When told it was poison, the testee wasn't supposed to show fear."

"Charming."

"Vasectomy is another favorite. It's said that the leadership of Synanon required some of the male members to go under the knife."

Her procreation partner was Jason.

"What about arranging marriages?"

"Jouret and DiMambro, Jim Jones, David Koresh, Charles Manson. They all used controlled coupling. Diet, sex, abortion, dress, sleep. It really doesn't matter what the idiosyncrasy is. As a leader conditions his followers to abide by his rules he breaks down their inhibitions. Eventually this unquestioning acceptance of bizarre behaviors may habituate them to the idea of violence. At first it's small acts of devotion, seemingly harmless requirements like hairstyles or meditation at midnight, or sex with the messiah. Later his demands may become more lethal."

"Sounds like the deification of insanity."

"Well put. The process has another advantage for the

328

leader. It weeds out the less committed, since they get fed up and leave."

"O.K., fine. You have these fringe groups living a life orchestrated by some nutcase. What makes them turn violent at any given time? Why today and not next month?"

It's too soon. It can't be now.

"Most outbreaks of violence involve what sociologists refer to as 'escalating boundary tensions.'"

"Don't feed me jargon, Red."

"O.K. These fringe groups usually are concerned with two things, getting members and keeping members. But if a leader feels threatened the emphasis often shifts. Sometimes recruitment stops and existing members are monitored more closely. The demand for commitment to eccentric rules may intensify. The theme of doom may become more pronounced. The group can grow increasingly isolated and increasingly paranoid. Tensions with the surrounding community, or with the government, or law enforcement may escalate."

"What could possibly threaten these megalomaniacs?"

"A member who leaves could be seen as a defector."

We woke up and Heidi and Brian were gone.

"The leader might feel he's losing control. Or if the cult exists in more than one place, and he can't always be there, he might feel his authority is slipping during his absences. More anxiety. More isolation. More tyranny. It's a paranoid spiral. Then all it takes is some external factor to pull the pin."

"How disruptive would the outside event have to be?"

"It varies. At Jonestown it took only the visit by a congressman and his press entourage, and their attempt to return to the U.S. with a handful of defectors. At

329

Waco it took a military-style raid by the Bureau of
Alcohol, Tobacco, and Firearms, and the eventual
insertion of CS gas and the breaching of the compound
walls by armored vehicles."

"Why the difference?"

"That has to do with ideology and leadership. The
settlement at Jonestown was more internally volatile
than the community at Waco."

My fingers felt cold on the handset.

"Do you think Owens has a violent agenda?"

"He definitely bears watching. If he's holding your
friend's baby against her will that should get you a
warrant."

"It's unclear whether she agreed to leave him there.
She's very reluctant to talk about the cult. She's been
raised by these people since she was eight years old. I've
never seen anyone so torn. But the fact that Jennifer
Cannon was living at the Owens compound when she
was killed should do it."

For a while neither of us spoke.

"Could Heidi and Brian have sent Owens over the
edge?" I asked. "Could he have ordered someone to kill
them and their babies?"

"Could be. And don't forget, he's had some other
blows. Sounds like Jennifer Cannon may have concealed those phone calls from Canada, then refused to
go along with something Owens wanted when he found
out. And of course there's you."

"Me?"

"Brian gets Heidi pregnant against cult orders. Then
the couple splits. Then the thing with Jennifer. Then
you and Ryan show up. Odd coincidence in names, by
the way."

"What?"

"The congressman who showed up in Guyana. His
name was Ryan."

330

"Give me a prediction, Red. Based on what I've told you, what do you see in your crystal ball?"

There was a long pause.

"From what you've told me Owens may fit the profile of a charismatic leader with a messianic self-image. And it sounds like his followers have accepted that vision. Owens may feel he's losing control over his members. He may see your investigation as an additional threat to his authority."

Another pause.

"And this Kathryn is talking about crossing over to eternal life."

I heard him take a deep breath.

"Given all of that, I'd say there is a high potential for violence."

I disconnected and dialed Ryan's pager. While I waited for him to phone back I returned to the Hardaway report. I'd just pulled it from the envelope when the phone rang. Had I not been so agitated it might have been amusing. I seemed destined never to read that document.

"You must have hit the floor running this morning." Ryan's voice sounded tired.

"I'm always up early. I have a visitor."

"Let me guess. Gregory Peck."

"Kathryn showed up this morning. She says she spent the night at UNCC and found me through the faculty directory."

"Not smart to list your home address."

"I don't. Jennifer Cannon lived at the Saint Helena compound."

"Damn."

"Kathryn overheard an argument between Jennifer and Owens. The next day Jennifer was gone."

"Good stuff, Brennan."

"It gets better."

I told him about Jennifer's access to the phone and her friendship with Heidi. He came back with his own shocker.

"When you talked to Hardaway you asked when Jennifer Cannon was last seen alive. What you didn't ask was where. It wasn't Calgary. Jennifer hadn't lived there since she went off to school. According to the mother they kept in close contact until shortly before she disappeared. Then her daughter's calls became less frequent, and when they spoke Jennifer seemed evasive.

"Jennifer called home at Thanksgiving two years ago, then nothing. The mother phoned the school, contacted her daughter's friends, even visited the campus, but she never discovered where Jennifer had gone. That's when she filed the missing person report."

"And?"

I heard him draw a deep breath.

"Jennifer Cannon was last seen leaving the McGill University campus."

"No."

"Yes. She didn't take her finals or withdraw from her classes. She just packed up and left."

"Packed up?"

"Yeah. That's why the police didn't pursue the case too vigorously. She packed her belongings, closed her bank account, left a note for her landlord, and vanished. It didn't look like an abduction."

My mind threw up an image, then resisted bringing it into focus. A face with bangs. A nervous gesture. I forced my lips to form the words.

"Another young woman disappeared from the compound at the same time Jennifer Cannon did. Kathryn didn't know her since she was a newcomer." I swallowed. "Kathryn thought the girl's name might have been Anne."

"I don't follow."

332

"Anna Goyette was" – I corrected myself – "is a McGill student."

"Anna is a common name."

"Kathryn heard Jennifer and this girl speak a foreign language."

"French?"

"I'm not sure Kathryn would know French if she heard it."

"You think the second Murtry victim could be Anna Goyette?"

I didn't answer.

"Brennan, just because some girl showed up on Saint Helena who may have been called Anna doesn't mean it was a McGill class reunion. Cannon left the university over two years ago. Goyette is nineteen. She wasn't there yet."

"True. But everything else fits."

"I don't know. And even if Jennifer Cannon lived with Owens it doesn't mean he killed her."

"They fight. She disappears. Her body turns up in a shallow grave."

"Maybe she was into dope. Or her friend Anne was. Maybe Owens found out and threw them out. They've got nowhere to go so they squeeze their business associates. Or they take off with a bag of the merchandise."

"Is that what you think happened?"

"Look, all we know for sure is that Jennifer Cannon left Montreal a couple of years ago and her body turned up on Murtry Island. She may have spent time with the community on Saint Helena. She may have argued with Owens. If so, those facts may or may not be relevant to her death."

"They're sure as hell germane to the question of her whereabouts for the past several years."

"Yes."

333

"What are you going to do?"

"First I'm going to visit Sheriff Baker to see if this gets us a warrant. Then I'm going to light a fire under the boys in Texas. I want to know about every cell this Owens has ever shed. Then it's back out to Happy Acres for some high-visibility surveillance. I want to see what color the guru sweats, and I don't have much time. They want me in Montreal on Monday."

"I think he's dangerous, Ryan."

He listened without interrupting as I outlined my conversation with Red Skyler. When I'd finished there was a long silence as Ryan integrated the sociologist's words with what we'd just discussed.

"I'll call Claudel and get a status on Anna Goyette."

"Thanks, Ryan."

"Keep an eye on Kathryn," he said solemnly.

"I will."

I didn't get that opportunity. When I went upstairs, Kathryn was gone.

27

"Damn!" I said to the empty air.

Birdie had followed me up the stairs. He froze at my outburst, lowered his head, and regarded me with a steady gaze.

"Damn!"

No one answered.

Ryan was right. Kathryn was not stable. I knew I couldn't assure her safety, or that of her baby, so why did I feel responsible?

"She split, Bird. What can you do?"

The cat had no suggestions, so I followed my usual pattern. When anxious, I work.

I returned to the kitchen. The door was ajar and wind had scattered the autopsy photos.

Or had it? Hardaway's report lay exactly as I'd left it.

Had Kathryn viewed the pictures? Had the grisly tableau sent her fleeing in panic?

Feeling another surge of guilt, I sat down and sorted through the stack.

Cleaned of its shroud of maggots and sediment, Jennifer Cannon's body was better preserved than I'd expected. Though decomposition had ravaged her face and viscera, wounds were clearly evident in the bloated and discolored flesh.

Cuts. Hundreds of them. Some circular, others linear, measuring one to several centimeters. They clustered near her throat, in her thorax, and ran the length of her arms and legs. All over her body I could see what looked like superficial scratches, but skin slippage made these lesions difficult to observe. The mottling of hematoma was everywhere.

I examined several close-ups. While the chest wounds had smooth, clean edges, the other cuts looked jagged and uneven. A deep gash circled her upper right arm, exposing torn flesh and splintered bone.

I moved to the cranial photos. Though sloughing had begun, most of the hair was still in place. Oddly, the posterior views showed bone gleaming through the tangled mat, as though a section of scalp were missing.

I'd seen that pattern before. Where?

I finished with the photos and opened Hardaway's report.

Twenty minutes later I leaned back and closed my eyes.

Probable cause of death: exsanguination due to stabbing. The smooth-bordered chest wounds were made by a blade that had severed critical vessels. Due to decomposition, the pathologist was uncertain as to the cause of the other lacerations.

I passed the rest of the day in a state of agitation. I wrote my reports on Jennifer Cannon and the other Murtry victim, then turned to the CAT scan data, stopping frequently to listen for Kathryn.

Ryan phoned at two to say that the Jennifer Cannon link had convinced a judge, and a search warrant was being issued for the Saint Helena compound. He and Baker were heading out as soon as they had the paper.

I told him about Kathryn's disappearance, and

listened to his assurances that I was not to blame. I also told him about Birdie.

"At least there's some good news."

"Yeah. Any word on Anna Goyette?"

"No."

"Texas?"

"Still waiting. I'll let you know what goes down here."

As I hung up, I felt fur brush my ankle, and looked down to see Birdie worming figure eights between my feet.

"Come on, Bird. How 'bout a treat?"

My cat is inordinately fond of canine chew toys. I've explained that these products are for dogs, but he will not be dissuaded.

I dug a small rawhide bone from a kitchen drawer and sailed it into the living room.

Birdie raced across the room, pounced, then rolled onto his prey. He righted himself, positioned the object between his front paws, and began gnawing on his kill.

I watched, wondering about the appeal of slimy hide.

The cat chewed a corner, then turned the toy and dragged his teeth the length of one edge. The object fell sideways and Bird nudged it back and sank a canine into the leather.

I watched, transfixed.

Was that it?

I went to Birdie, squatted, and pried his quarry from him. The cat placed his front paws on my knee, stood on hind legs, and tried to retrieve his prize.

My pulse quickened as I stared at the mangled leather.

Sweet Jesus.

I thought of the puzzling wounds in Jennifer Cannon's flesh. Superficial scratches. Jagged tears.

I ran to the living room for my lens, then raced to the

337

kitchen and rifled through Hardaway's photos. I selected the head views and studied each under magnification.

The balding was not due to decomposition. The strands that remained were firmly rooted. The detached segment of skin and hair was neatly rectangular, its edges torn and ragged.

Jennifer Cannon's scalp had been ripped from her skull.

I thought of what that meant.

And I thought of something else.

Could I have been so thick? Could a preconceived mind-set have blinded me to the obvious?

I grabbed my keys and purse and flew out the door.

Forty minutes later I was at the university. The bones of the unidentified Murtry victim stared accusingly from my lab table.

How could I have been so careless?

"Never assume a single source of trauma." My mentor's words floated back across the decades.

I'd fallen into the trap. When I saw the destruction on the bones I'd thought raccoons and vultures. I hadn't looked closely. I hadn't measured.

Now I had.

While there was extensive damage on the skeleton due to post-mortem scavenging, other injury had gone before.

The two holes in the occipital bone were the most telling. They measured five millimeters each, with a distance between them of thirty-five. These punctures were not made by a turkey vulture, and the pattern was too large for a raccoon.

The dimensions suggested a large dog. So did parallel scratches on the cranial bones, and similar perforations in the clavicle and sternum.

Jennifer Cannon and her companion had been attacked by animals, probably large dogs. Teeth had torn their flesh and scored their bones. Some bites had been powerful enough to pierce the thickness at the back of the skull.

My mind made a leap.

Carole Comptois, the Montreal victim who had been hung by her wrists and tortured, had also been mauled.

That's reaching, Brennan.

Yes.

It's ridiculous.

No, I told myself. It's not.

Up to now my skepticism had done nothing for these victims. I'd been slack about the animal damage. I'd doubted the link between Heidi Schneider and Dom Owens, and I'd failed to see his connection to Jennifer Cannon. I hadn't helped Kathryn or Carlie, and I'd done nothing to locate Anna Goyette.

From now on, if necessary, I *would* reach. If there was a remote possibility that Carole Comptois and the women on Murtry Island were linked, I would consider it.

I phoned Hardaway, not expecting him to be working late on Saturday. He wasn't. Neither was LaManche, the pathologist who had done the Comptois autopsy. I left messages for both.

Frustrated, I took out a tablet and began to list what I knew.

Jennifer Cannon and Carole Comptois were both from Montreal. Each died following an animal attack.

The skeleton buried with Jennifer Cannon also bore the marks of animal teeth. The victim died with levels of Rohypnol indicative of acute intoxication.

Rohypnol was isolated in two of the victims found with Heidi Schneider and her family in St-Jovite.

339

Rohypnol was found in bodies at the murder/suicide sites of the Order of the Solar Temple.

The Solar Temple operated in Quebec and Europe.

Phone calls were made from the house in St-Jovite to Dom Owens' commune on Saint Helena. Both properties were owned by Jacques Guillion, who also owned property in Texas.

Jacques Guillion is Belgian.

One of the St-Jovite victims, Patrice Simonnet, was Belgian.

Heidi Schneider and Brian Gilbert joined Dom Owens' group in Texas and returned there for the birth of their babies. They left Texas and were murdered. In St-Jovite.

The St-Jovite victims died approximately three weeks ago.

Jennifer Cannon and the unidentified victim on Murtry died three to four weeks ago.

Carole Comptois died a little less than three weeks ago.

I stared at the page. Ten. Ten people dead. Again the odd phrase ricocheted through my brain. Death du jour. Death of the day. We'd found them day by day, but they'd all died around the same time. Who would be next? Into what circle of hell had we stumbled?

When I got home I went directly to the computer to revise my report on the Murtry skeleton to include injury due to animal attack. Then I printed and read what I'd written.

As I finished, the clock chimed the full Westminster refrain, then gave six low bongs. My stomach growled a reminder that I'd eaten nothing since the bagel and coffee.

I went to the patio and snipped basil and chives. Then I cut chunks of cheese, took two eggs from the fridge, and scrambled everything together. I toasted another bagel, poured a Diet Coke, and returned to the desk in the living room.

When I reviewed the list I'd made at the university, an unsettling thought popped into my mind.

Anna Goyette had also disappeared a little less than three weeks ago.

My appetite vanished. I left the desk and crossed to the couch. I lay down and allowed my mind to drift, willing associations to rise to the surface.

I went through names. Schneider. Gilbert. Comptois. Simonnet. Owens. Cannon. Goyette.

Nothing.

Ages. Four months. Eighteen. Twenty-five. Four score.

No pattern.

Places. St-Jovite. Saint Helena.

A connection?

Saints. Could that be a link? I made a note. Ask Ryan where the Guillion property is located in Texas.

I chewed my thumbnail. What was taking Ryan so long?

My eyes drifted over the shelves that line six of the eight sunroom walls. Floor-to-ceiling books. It's the one thing I can never bring myself to discard. I really needed to sort and eliminate. I had dozens of texts I'd never open again, some dating to my undergraduate days.

University.

Jennifer Cannon. Anna Goyette. Both were students at McGill.

I thought of Daisy Jeannotte, and the odd words she'd spoken about her teaching assistant.

My eyes wandered to the computer. My screen saver sent vertebrae in a sinuous snake dance around the monitor. Long bones replaced the spinal column, then

341

ribs, a pelvis, and the screen went black. The performance began anew with a slowly rotating skull.

E-mail. When Jeannotte and I had exchanged
addresses I'd asked her to contact me if Anna returned.
I hadn't checked my messages in days.

I logged on, downloaded my mail, and skimmed the
names of the senders. There was nothing from Jeannotte. My nephew, Kit, had sent three messages. Two
last week, one this morning.

Kit never sent me e-mail.

I opened the most recent communication.

From: khoward
To: tbrennan
Subject: Harry

Aunt Tempe:
I called but you must not be there. I am ferociously
worried about Harry.
Please call.

                                                    Kit

From age two Kit had called his mother by name.
Though his parents disapproved, the boy refused to
change. Harry simply sounded better to his ear.

As I worked my way backward through my nephew's
messages, I experienced a mix of emotions. Fear for
Harry's safety. Annoyance at her cavalier attitude.
Compassion for Kit. Guilt at my own inconsideration.
His must have been the call I ignored while talking with
Kathryn.

I went to the hall and hit the button.

Hi, Aunt Tempe. It's Kit. I'm calling about Harry.
When I call your condo in Montreal she doesn't answer, and
I have no idea where she's gone. I know she was there until a
few days ago. Pause. *Last time we talked she sounded*

342

strange, even for Harry. Nervous laugh. *Is she still in Quebec? If not, do you know where she is? I'm worried. I've never heard her sound like this before. Please give me a call. Bye.*

I pictured my nephew, with his green eyes and sandy hair. It was hard to believe Howard Howard had made any genetic contribution to Harry's son. Six foot two and thin as a ladder, Kit was an exact replica of my father.

I replayed the message and considered whether something was amiss.

No, Brennan.

But why was Kit so concerned?

Call him. She's fine.

I hit the speed dial button. No answer.

I tried my number in Montreal. Ditto. I left a message.

Pete. He hadn't heard from Harry.

Of course not. He was as fond of my sister as he was of nail fungus. She knew that.

Enough, Brennan. Back to the victims. They need you.

I turned my thoughts from my sister. Harry had gone off before. I had to assume she was all right.

I went back to the sofa and lay down. When I woke I was in my clothes, the portable phone ringing on my chest.

"Thanks for calling, Aunt Tempe. I—Maybe I'm jumping the gun, but my mother sounded very depressed the last time I talked to her. And now she's disappeared. It's not like Harry. To sound so down, I mean."

"Kit, I'm sure she's fine."

"You're probably right, but, well, we'd made these plans. She's always complaining that we never spend

343

time together anymore, so I promised to take her out on the boat next week. I've pretty much finished the renovations, so Harry and I were going to sail around the Gulf for a few days. If she's changed her mind, she could at least call."

I experienced the usual anger at my sister's thoughtlessness.

"She'll get in touch, Kit. When I left she was pretty caught up in her workshop. You know how your mother is."

"Yeah." He paused. "But that's just it. She sounded so . . ." He searched for a word. "Flat. Not like Harry."

I remembered my last evening with Harry.

"Maybe it's part of the new persona. A lovely, exterior calm." My words even sounded false to me.

"Yeah. I guess. Did she mention she was going someplace else?"

"No. Why?"

"Something she said made me think she might have a trip planned. But, like, it wasn't her idea, or she didn't want to? Oh hell, I don't know."

He let out a sigh. In my mind's eye I saw my nephew run a hand backward through his hair, then rub the top of his head. Kit frustration.

"What did she say?" Despite my resolve, I felt the beginnings of anxiety.

"I don't remember exactly, but get this. It wouldn't matter what she wore or how she looked. Does that sound like my mother?"

No. It didn't.

"Aunt Tempe, do you know anything about this outfit she's hooked up with?"

"Just the name. Inner Life Empowerment, I think. Would you feel better if I made some inquiries?"

"Yeah."

"And I'll call my neighbors in Montreal and see if they've seen her. O.K.?"

"Yeah."

"Kit. Remember when she met Striker?"

There was a pause.

"Yeah."

"What happened?"

"She set off for a balloon rally, went missing for three days, then turned up married."

"Remember how freaked you were?"

"Yeah. But she didn't give up her curling iron. Just have her call me. I've left messages on the machine up there but, hell, maybe she's pissed off about something. Who knows?"

I clicked off and looked at the clock. Twelve-fifteen. I tried Montreal. Harry didn't answer, so I left another message. As I lay in the dark my mind positioned itself for cross-examination.

Why *hadn't* I checked out ILE?

Because there was no reason to do so. She took the course through a legitimate institution, and there was no cause for alarm. Besides, to research each of Harry's schemes would take a full-time investigator.

Tomorrow. I'll make some calls tomorrow. Not tonight. I shut down the inquisition.

I mounted the stairs, stripped, and slid under the covers. I needed sleep. I needed a respite from the turmoil that dominated my conscious thought.

Overhead, the ceiling fan hummed softly. I thought of Dom Owens' parlor, and, though I fought them, the names drifted back.

Brian. Heidi. Brian and Heidi were students.

Jennifer Cannon was a student.

Anna Goyette.

My stomach turned over.

Harry.

345

Harry had registered for her first seminar at the North Harris County Community College. Harry was a student.

The others had been killed or had disappeared while in Quebec.

My sister was in Quebec.

Or was she?

Where the hell was Ryan?

When he finally called my trepidation escalated to real fear.

28

"Gone? what do you mean, gone?"

I'd slept fitfully, and when Ryan woke me at dawn, I felt headachy and out of sorts.

"When we arrived with the warrant the place was deserted."

"Twenty-six people just vanished?"

"Owens and a female companion gassed up the vans around seven yesterday morning. The attendant remembered because it wasn't their normal routine. Baker and I got to the commune around five P.M. Sometime in between the padre and his disciples took the big powder."

"They just drove off?"

"Baker's put out an APB, but so far the vans haven't been spotted."

"For God's sake." I wasn't believing this.

"Actually, it's worse."

I waited.

"Another eighteen people have vanished in Texas."

I felt myself go cold.

"Turns out there was another little band on the Guillion property out there. The Fort Bend County Sheriff's Department has been monitoring them for

347

several years and weren't all that adverse to taking a closer look. Unfortunately, when the team showed up, the brethren had split. They bagged one old man and a cocker spaniel hiding under the porch."

"What's his story?"

"The guy's in custody, but he's either senile or feebleminded and hasn't given much up."

"Or cagey as hell."

I watched the gray outside my window lighten.

"Now what?"

"Now we toss the Saint Helena compound and hope the state boys can discover where Owens has led the faithful."

I glanced at the clock. Seven-ten and already I was at the thumb-nail.

"How's your end?"

I told Ryan about the tooth marks on the bones, and about my suspicions concerning Carole Comptois.

"Not the right MO."

"What MO? Simonnet was shot, Heidi and her family were slashed and stabbed, and we don't know how the two in the upstairs bedroom died. Cannon and Comptois were both attacked by animals and knives. That's not a common occurrence."

"Comptois was killed in Montreal. Cannon and friend were found twelve hundred miles south of there. Did this dog catch a shuttle?"

"I'm not saying it's the same dog. Just the same pattern."

"Why?"

I'd been asking myself that question all night. And who?

"Jennifer Cannon was a McGill student. So is Anna Goyette. Heidi and Brian were also in school when they joined Owens' group. Can you find out if Carole

348

Comptois had any university ties? Took a course or worked at a college?"

"She was a hooker."

"Maybe she won a scholarship," I snapped. His negative attitude was irritating me.

"O.K., O.K. Don't get your bra in a twist."

"Ryan . . ." I hesitated, not wanting to give reality to my fear by shaping it into words.

He waited.

"My sister registered for her seminar at a community college in Texas."

The line was quiet.

"Her son called me yesterday because he can't contact her. Neither can I."

"She may be hunkered in as part of the training. You know, like a retreat. Maybe she's laid a grid map over her soul and she's combing it inch by inch. But if you're really worried, call the college."

"Yeah."

"Just because she enrolled in the Lone Star State doesn't m—"

"I realize I'm being absurd, but Kathryn's words frightened me, and now Dom Owens is out there planning God knows what."

"We'll nail his ass."

"I know."

"Brennan, how do I say this?" He drew a long breath, let it out. "Your sister is going through a transition, and right now she's open to new relationships. She may have met someone and gone off for a few days."

Without her curling iron? Anxiety lodged like a cold, dense mass inside my chest.

When we disconnected I tried Harry again. In my mind's eye I saw the phone ringing in my empty condo. Where could she be at seven on a Sunday morning?

349

Sunday. Damn! I couldn't call the college until tomorrow.

I made coffee then rang Kit, even though it was an hour earlier in Texas.

He was polite but groggy, and didn't follow my line of questioning. When he finally began to comprehend, he was unsure if his mother's course had been a regular college offering. He thought he remembered literature, and promised to drop by her house to check.

I couldn't sit still. I opened the *Observer*, then the Bélanger journals. I even tried the Sunday morning evangelists. Neither crime nor Louis-Philippe nor Jeeee-zus could hold my attention. I was a mental cul-de-sac with no outlet.

Not really in the mood, I threw on running gear and headed out. The sky was clear, the air soft and balmy as I followed Queens Road West, then cut over on Princeton to Freedom Park. Sweat droplets changed to rivulets as my Nikes pounded past the lagoon. Little ducks glided single file behind their mother, their quacks drifting on the Sunday morning air.

My thoughts remained jumbled and useless, the players and events of the past weeks running in circles around my brain. I tried to focus on the steady beat of my sneakers, the rhythm of my breath, but I kept hearing Ryan's phrase. New relationships. Is that what he and Harry had called their Hurley's night? Is that what I'd danced into with my adventure with Ryan on the *Melanie Tess*?

I traversed the park, ran north past the medical clinic, then snaked my way through the narrow streets of Myers Park. I passed flawless gardens and parklike lawns, here and there tended by an equally impeccable homeowner.

I'd just crossed Providence Road when I nearly collided with a man in tan slacks, a pink shirt, and a rumpled seersucker sports jacket that looked like a Sears original. He carried a battered briefcase and a canvas bag bulging with slide carousels. It was Red Skyler.

"Slumming in southeast?" I asked, trying to catch my breath. Red lived on the opposite side of Charlotte, near the university.

"My lecture at Myers Park Methodist is today." He gestured at the gray stone complex across the street. "I've come early to set my slides."

"Right." I was slick with sweat, and my hair hung in stringy, wet clumps. I pinched my T-shirt and flapped it away from my skin.

"How is your case progressing?"

"Not well. Owens and his followers have gone to ground."

"They're in hiding?"

"Apparently. Red, can I follow up on something you said?"

"Of course."

"When we discussed cults, you mentioned two broad types. We talked so much about one I forgot to ask about the other."

A man passed with a black Standard poodle. Both needed a trim.

"You said you would include some of the commercially packaged awareness programs in your definition."

"Yes. If they rely on thought reform to get and keep members." He set the bag on the sidewalk and scratched the side of his nose.

"I think you said these groups fill their ranks by persuading participants to buy more and more courses?"

"Yes. Unlike the cults we discussed, these programs don't intend to keep people forever. They exploit participants as long as they're willing to buy more courses. And bring in others."

"So why do you consider them cults?"

"The coercive influence that these so-called self-improvement programs exert is amazing. It's the same old thing, behavioral control through thought reform."

"What goes on in these awareness training programs?"

Red glanced at his watch.

"I finish at ten forty-five. Let's meet for breakfast and I'll share what I know."

"It's known as large group awareness training."

As he spoke Red spread red-eye gravy over his grits. We were at Anderson's, and through the window I could see the hedges and brick of Presbyterian Hospital.

"They're packaged to sound like seminars, or college courses, but the sessions are scripted to get participants emotionally and psychologically aroused. That part isn't mentioned in the brochure. Neither is the fact that attendees will be brainwashed into accepting an entirely new worldview." He forked a piece of country ham.

"How do they work?"

"Most programs last four or five days. The first day is devoted to establishing the leader's authority. Lots of humiliation and verbal abuse. The next day pounds in the new philosophy. The trainer convinces participants their lives are crap and that the only way out is to accept the new way of thinking."

Grits.

"Day three is typically filled with exercises. Trance inducement. Memory regression. Guided imagery. The trainer gets everyone to dredge up disappointments, rejections, bad memories. It really lays people out emotionally. Then the following day there's a lot of warm fuzzy group sharing, and the leader morphs from

352

the hard taskmaster to the loving mommy or daddy. It's the beginning of the pitch for the next series of courses. The last day is fun and happy, with lots of hugs and dancing and music and games. And the hard sell."

A couple in khakis and identical golf shirts slid into the booth to our right. He was seashell, she was foam green.

"The damaging thing is that these courses can be incredibly stressful, both physically and psychologically. Most people have no idea how intense it's going to be. If they did, they wouldn't sign up."

"Don't participants talk about the program afterward?"

"They're told to be vague, that to discuss the experience would spoil it for others. They're instructed to rave about how their lives have changed, but to conceal how confrontational and unnerving the process was."

"Where do these groups recruit?" I feared I already knew the answer.

"Everywhere. On the street. Door to door. At schools, businesses, health clinics. They advertise in alternative newspapers, New Age magazines—"

"What about colleges and universities?"

"Very fertile ground. On bulletin boards, in dorms and eating halls, at student activity sign-up days. Some cults assign members to hang around campus counseling centers looking for students who come in alone. The schools don't condone or encourage these outfits, but there's little they can do. The administrations have the flyers removed from bulletin boards, but the ads go right back up."

"But this is a separate animal, right? These awareness seminars are unrelated to the type of cults we discussed before?"

"Not necessarily. Some programs are used to recruit

members to background organizations. You take the course, then you're told that you've performed so well you've been singled out to go to a higher level, or meet the guru, or whatever."

The words hit me like a blow to the chest. Harry's dinner at the leader's house.

"Red, what sort of people fall for these things?" I hoped my voice sounded calmer than I felt.

"My research shows that there are two important factors." He ticked them off on greasy fingers. "Depression and broken affiliations."

"What do you mean?"

"Someone who is in transition is often lonely and confused, and therefore vulnerable."

"In transition?"

"Between high school and college, college and a job. Recently separated. Recently fired."

Red's words blurred into the breakfast clatter. I had to talk to Kit.

When I refocused Red was eyeing me strangely. I knew I had to say something.

"I think my sister may have signed on to one of these group training courses. Inner Life Empowerment."

He shrugged. "There are so many. It's not one that I know."

"Now she's gone incommunicado. No one can raise her."

"Tempe, most of these programs are fairly benign. But you should talk to her. The effects can be very damaging for certain individuals."

Like Harry.

The usual mix of fear and aggravation seethed inside me.

I thanked Red and paid the bill. On the sidewalk I remembered another question.

354

"Have you ever heard of a sociologist named Jean-notte? She studies religious movements."

"Daisy Jeannotte?" One eyebrow rose, sending lop-sided furrows across his forehead.

"I met her at McGill several weeks ago and I'm curious about how she's viewed by her colleagues."

He hesitated. "Yes. I'd heard she was in Canada."

"Do you know her?"

"I knew her years ago." His voice had gone flat. "Jeannotte is not considered mainstream."

"Oh?" I searched his face but it was blank.

"Thank you for the ham and grits, Tempe. I hope you got your money's worth." His grin looked strained.

I touched his arm. "What aren't you telling me, Red?"

The grin faded. "Is your sister a pupil of Daisy Jeannotte?"

"No. Why?"

"Jeannotte was at the center of a controversy some years back. I don't know the real story, and I don't want to spread gossip. Just be cautious."

I wanted to ask more, but with that he nodded and set off toward his car.

I stood in the sunshine with my mouth open. What the hell did that mean?

When I got home Kit had left a message. He'd located a course catalog, but there was nothing that sounded like Harry's workshop in the North Harris County Community College listings. He had found an Inner Life Empowerment flyer on his mother's desk, however. The paper had a thumbtack hole, and he suspected it had come from a bulletin board. He'd called the number. It was no longer in service.

Harry's course had nothing to do with the college!

Red's words intertwined with Ryan's, heightening my

355

feeling of dread. New relationships. In transition. Unaffiliated. Vulnerable.

For the rest of the day I skittered from task to task, my concentration destroyed by worry and indecision. Then, as shadows lengthened across my patio, I took a call that jarred me into more organized thinking. I listened in shock as the story unfolded, then I made a decision.

I dialed my department head to tell him that I would be leaving earlier than planned. Since I'd scheduled an absence for the physical anthropology conference my students would miss only one additional class period. I was sorry, but I had to go.

When we disconnected I went upstairs to pack. Not for Oakland, but for Montreal.

I had to find my sister.

I had to stop the madness that was rolling in like Piedmont thunder.

29

As the plane took off I closed my eyes and leaned into the seat, too exhausted from another restless night to notice my surroundings. Normally I enjoy feeling the acceleration as I rise and watch the world grow small, but not at that moment. The words of a frightened old man rebounded through my brain.

I stretched, and my foot tapped the package I'd placed beneath the seat. Hand-carried. Always in view. Chain of custody could be important.

Beside me, Ryan flipped through the USAirways magazine. Unable to get a flight from Savannah, he'd driven to Charlotte for the six thirty-five. At the airport he'd elaborated on the statement taken in Texas.

The old man had fled to protect his dog.

Like Kathryn, I thought, afraid for her baby.

"Did he say exactly what they intend to do?" I asked Ryan in a low whisper. The attendant demonstrated seat belts and oxygen.

Ryan shook his head. "The guy's a zomboid. He was at the ranch because they gave him a place to stay and let him keep his dog. He wasn't really tuned in to the credo, but he picked up enough." The magazine dropped to his lap.

357

"He's rambling on about cosmic energy and guardian angels and fiery inhalation."

"Annihilation?"

Ryan shrugged. "He says the people he lives with don't belong to this world. Seems they've been battling the forces of evil and now it's time to go. Only he couldn't bring Fido."

"So he hid under the porch."

Ryan nodded.

"Who are these forces of evil?"

"He's not sure."

"And he can't say where the righteous are going?"

"North. Remember, Gramps is not at the top of the bell curve."

"He's never heard of Dom Owens?"

"No. His troop leader was someone named Toby."

"No last name."

"Last names are of this world. But that's not who frightens him. Apparently Toby and the cocker got along. It's some woman that scares the shit out of him."

What had Kathryn said? "It's not Dom. It's her." A face flashed in front of me.

"Who is she?"

"He doesn't have a name, but he says this chick told Toby that the Antichrist had been destroyed and doomsday was at hand. That's when the wagon train rolled."

"And?" I felt numb.

"The dog wasn't invited."

"Nothing else?"

"He says the lady is definitely mother superior."

"Kathryn also spoke of a woman."

"Name?"

"I didn't ask. It just didn't sink in at the time."

"What else did she say?"

I repeated what I could remember.

358

Ryan placed a hand on mine.

"Tempe, we really don't know anything about this Kathryn except that she's spent her life with the encounter culture. She shows up at your place claiming she found you through the university. You say your address isn't listed. That same day forty-three of her closest friends take a hike in two states and the lady does her own vanishing act."

True. Ryan had voiced misgivings about Kathryn earlier.

"You never found out who pulled the cat trick?"

"No." I withdrew my hand and went to work on the thumbnail.

For a while neither of us spoke. Then I remembered something else.

"Kathryn also made reference to an Antichrist."

"How?"

"She said Dom didn't believe in Antichrists."

Ryan was quiet a long time. Then,

"I talked to the guys who worked the Solar Temple deaths in Canada. Do you know what went down in Morin Heights?"

"Just that five people died. I was in Charlotte, and the American media focused mostly on Switzerland. The Canadian end got very little press."

"I'll tell you what happened. Joseph DiMambro sent a team of assassins to kill a baby." He paused to let that sink in. "Morin Heights was the kickoff for the fireworks overseas. Seems this kid's birth hadn't been approved by Big Daddy, so he viewed him as the Antichrist. Once the tyke was dead the faithful were free to make the crossing."

"Jesus Christ. Do you think Owens really is one of these Solar Temple fanatics?"

Ryan shrugged again. "Or it could be some sort of

359

copycat shuck. It's hard to know what the Adler Lyons babble means until the psychologists work it out."

A treatise had been found at the compound on Saint Helena. And a map of Quebec Province.

"But I don't give a hog's tit which looney is in the lead if innocent people are trailing along to their deaths. I'm going to catch this bastard and gut him and fry him up myself."

His jaw muscles bunched as he picked up the magazine.

I closed my eyes and tried to rest, but the images wouldn't settle.

Harry, buoyant and full of life. Harry in sweats and no makeup.

Sam, unnerved by the invasion of his island.

Malachy. Mathias. Jennifer Cannon. Carole Comptois. A charred cat. The contents of the package at my feet.

Kathryn, eyes pleading. As if I could help her. As if I could take her life and somehow make it better.

Or was Ryan right? Had I been set up? Was Kathryn sent for some sinister purpose of which I was unaware? Was Owens responsible for the slaughtered cat?

Harry had spoken of order. Her life sucked and the order was going to pull her clear. So had Kathryn. She said the order affects everyone. Brian and Heidi had broken it. What order? Cosmic order? An order from on high? The Order of the Solar Temple?

I felt like a moth in a jar, batting against the glass with random thought after random thought, but unable to escape the cognitive restraints of my own jumbled thinking.

Brennan, you're making yourself crazy! There's nothing you can do at thirty-seven thousand feet.

I decided to break free by dropping back a hundred years.

I opened my briefcase, pulled out a Bélanger diary, and skipped to December of 1844, hoping the holidays had put Louis-Philippe in a better mood.

The good doctor enjoyed Christmas dinner at the Nicolet house, liked his new pipe, but did not approve of his sister's plan for a return to the stage. Eugénie had been invited to sing in Europe.

What he lacked in humor, Louis-Philippe made up for in tenacity. His sister's name was written often in the early months of 1845. He apparently expressed his views frequently. But, much to the doctor's annoyance, Eugénie would not be dissuaded. She was leaving in April, would do concerts in Paris and Brussels, then spend the summer in France, returning to Montreal at the end of July.

A voice ordered trays and chair backs into full upright and locked position for landing in Pittsburgh.

An hour later, again airborne, I skimmed through the spring of 1845. Louis-Philippe was busy with hospital and city affairs, but made weekly visits to his brother-in-law. Alain Nicolet, it appears, did not travel to Europe with his wife.

I wondered how Eugénie's tour had gone. Apparently Uncle Louis-Philippe had not, since she was mentioned little during those months. Then an entry caught my eye.

July 17, 1845. Due to irregular circumstances, Eugénie's stay in France would be prolonged. Arrangements had been made, but Louis-Philippe was vague as to their nature.

I stared at the whiteness outside my window. What "irregular circumstances" had kept Eugénie in France? I calculated. Élisabeth was born in January. Oh, boy.

Throughout the summer and fall Louis-Philippe made only brief reference to his sister. Letter from Eugénie. Doing well.

As our wheels touched pavement at Dorval Airport, Eugénie reappeared. She, too, had returned to Montreal. April 16, 1846. Her baby was three months old.

There it was.

Élisabeth Nicolet was born in France. Alain could not be her father. But who was?

Ryan and I deplaned in silence. He checked his messages while I waited for the baggage. When he returned his face told me the news was not good.

"They found the vans near Charleston."

"Empty."

He nodded.

Eugénie and her baby faded into another century.

The sky was nickel and a light rain blew across the headlights as Ryan and I drove east along Highway 20. According to the pilot, Montreal was a balmy thirty-eight degrees Fahrenheit.

We rode in silence having already agreed on our courses of action. I wanted to rush home, to find my sister and relieve myself of a building sense of foreboding. Instead, I would do as Ryan asked. Then I would pursue a plan of my own.

We parked in the lot at Parthenais and Ryan and I picked our way toward the building. The air smelled of malt from the Molson brewery. Oil filmed the pools of rainwater collecting on the uneven pavement.

Ryan got off on the first floor and I continued to my office on the fifth. After removing my coat, I dialed an inside extension. They'd gotten my message and we could begin as soon as I was ready. I went at once to the lab.

I gathered scalpel, ruler, glue, and a two-foot length of rubber eraser material and set them on my worktable. Then I opened my carry-on package, unwrapped and inspected the contents.

The skull and mandible of the unknown Murtry victim had made the trip undamaged. I often wonder what the airport scanner operators think when my skeletal parts go through. I placed the skull on a cork ring in the middle of the table. Then I squeezed glue into the temporomandibular joint and fixed the jaw in place.

While the Elmer's dried, I found a chart of facial tissue thicknesses for white American females. When the jaw felt firm I slid the skull onto a holder, adjusted the height, and secured it with clamps. The empty orbits stared directly into my eyes as I measured and cut seventeen tiny rubber cylinders and glued them onto the facial bones.

Twenty minutes later I took the skull to a small room down the corridor. A plaque identified the section as Section d'Imagerie. A technician greeted me and indicated that the system was up and running.

Wasting no time, I placed the skull on a copy stand, captured images of it with a video camera, and sent them to the PC. I evaluated the digitized views on the monitor and chose a frontal orientation. Then, using a stylus and drawing tablet attached to the computer, I connected the rubber markers projecting from the skull. As I directed the crosshairs around the screen a macabre silhouette began to emerge.

When satisfied with the facial contour, I moved on. Using the bony architecture as a guide I sampled eyes, ears, noses, and lips from the program's database, and fitted predrawn features onto the skull.

Next I tested hair, and added what I thought would be the least distracting style. Knowing nothing of the victim, I decided it was better to be vague than wrong. When I was happy with the components I'd added to the captured cranial image, I used the stylus to blend and shadow to make the reconstruction as lifelike as possible. The whole process took less than two hours.

I leaned back and looked at my work.

A face gazed from the monitor. It had drooping eyes, a delicate nose, and broad, high cheekbones. It was pretty in a robotic, expressionless way. And somehow familiar. I swallowed. Then with a touch of the stylus I modified the hair. Blunt cut. Bangs.

I drew in a breath. Did my reconstruction resemble Anna Goyette? Or had I simply created a generic young female and given the hair a familiar cut?

I returned the hair to the original style and evaluated the likeness. Yes? No? I had no idea.

Finally, I touched a command on the drop-down menu, and four frames appeared on the screen. I compared the series, looking for hints of inconsistency between my merged image and the skull. First, the unaltered cranium and jaw. Next, a peel image, with bare bone on the skull's left, fleshed features on the right. Third, the face I'd created superimposed in ghostly translucence over bone and tissue markers. Last, the finished facial approximation. I clicked the final image to full screen and stared at it a long time. I still wasn't sure.

I printed, then stored the image, and hurried to my office. As I left the building I dropped copies of the sketch on Ryan's desk. The attached note consisted of two words: Murtry, *Inconnue*. Unknown. I had other things on my mind.

When I climbed out of the taxi the rain had eased, but the temperature had plummeted. Thin membranes were forming on puddles and crystallizing on wires and branches.

The apartment was as dim and still as a crypt. Dropping my coat and bags in the hall, I went directly to the guest room. Harry's makeup lay scattered across the dresser. Had she used it this morning or last week? Clothes. Boots. Hair dryer. Magazines. My search turned up nothing to indicate where Harry had gone or when she had left.

I'd expected that. What I'd not expected was the alarm that gripped me as I rummaged from room to room.

I checked the machine. No messages.

Calm down. Maybe she phoned Kit.

Negative.

Charlotte?

No word from Harry, but Red Skyler had called there to say he'd contacted the Cult Awareness Network. They had nothing on Dom Owens, but there was a file on Inner Life Empowerment. According to CAN, the outfit was legit. ILE operated in several states, offering insight seminars that were useless but nontoxic. Confront the intimate you and the intimate other. Crap, but probably harmless and I shouldn't be too concerned. If I wanted more information I could call him or CAN. He left both numbers.

I hardly listened to the other voices. Sam, wanting news. Katy reporting her return to Charlottesville.

So ILE was not dangerous and Ryan was probably right. Harry had gone off again. Anger made my cheeks feel warm.

Like a robot I hung my coat and rolled my suitcase to the bedroom. Then I sat on the edge of the bed, kneaded my temples, and let my thoughts roll. The digits on my clock slowly marked the minutes.

These last few weeks had been some of the most difficult of my career. The torture and mutilation these victims had endured far surpassed what I normally saw. And I couldn't remember when I'd worked so many deaths in so short a period of time. How were the

365

murders on Murtry linked to those in St-Jovite? Was Carole Comptois killed by the same monstrous hand? Had the slaughter in St-Jovite been merely the beginning? At this moment was some maniac scripting a bloodbath too terrible to contemplate?

Harry would have to deal with Harry.

I knew what I was going to do. At least I knew where I would start.

It was raining again and the McGill campus was covered with a thin, frozen crust. The buildings stood out as black silhouettes, their windows the only light in the dreary, wet dusk. Here and there a figure moved in an illuminated square, a tiny puppet in a shadow-box theater.

A porous ice shell crumbled to the steps as I gripped the handle to Birks Hall. The building was empty, abandoned by occupants fearing the storm. No raincoats on hooks, no boots melting along walls. The printers and copy machines were still, the only sound the tick of raindrops high above on leaded glass.

My steps echoed hollowly as I climbed to the third floor. From the main corridor I could see that Jeannotte's door was closed. I didn't really think she'd be here, but had decided it was worth a try. She didn't expect me, and people say odd things when caught outside their normal routines.

When I turned the corner I saw yellow light spilling from below the door. I knocked, unsure what to expect.

When the door opened my jaw dropped in amazement.

30

Her eyes were red along the rims, her skin pale and drawn. She tensed when she recognized me, but said nothing.

"How are you, Anna?"

"O.K." She blinked and her lids made the bangs hop.

"I'm Dr. Brennan. We met several weeks ago."

"I know."

"When I returned they told me you were ill."

"I'm fine. I was gone for a while."

I wanted to ask her where she'd been, but held back. "Is Dr. Jeannotte here?"

Anna shook her head. She did a slow-motion hair tuck, absently circling her ear.

"Your mother was worried about you."

She shrugged, the movement sluggish and barely noticeable. She didn't question my knowledge of her home life.

"I've been working on a project with your aunt. She was also concerned."

"Oh." She looked down so I couldn't see her face. Hit her with it.

"Your friend said you might be involved with something that's upsetting you."

Her eyes came back to mine. "I have no friends. Who are you talking about?" Her voice was small and flat.

"Sandy O'Reilly. She was replacing you that day."

"Sandy wants my hours. Why are you here?"

Good question.

"I wanted to talk to you and to Dr. Jeannotte."

"She's not in."

"Could you and I talk?"

"There's nothing you can do for me. My life is my own business." The listlessness chilled me.

"I appreciate that. But, actually, I thought you might be able to help me."

Her glance slid down the corridor then back to me.

"Help you how?"

"Would you like some coffee?"

"No."

"Could we go somewhere else?"

She looked at me a long time, her eyes flat and empty. Then she nodded, took a parka from the hall tree, and guided me down the stairs and out a back door. Bending into the frigid rain we trudged uphill to the center of campus, and circled to the back of the Redpath Museum. Anna took a key from her pocket, opened a door, and led me into a dim corridor. The air smelled faintly of mildew and decay.

We climbed to the second floor and sat on a long wooden bench, surrounded by the bones of creatures long dead. Above us hung a beluga whale, casualty of some Pleistocene misfortune. Dust motes drifted in the fluorescent light.

"I don't work in the museum anymore, but I still come here to think." She gazed at the Irish elk. "These creatures lived millions of years and thousands of miles apart and now they're fixed at this one point in the universe, forever motionless in time and place. I like that."

"Yes." That was one way to view extinction. "Stability is a rare thing in today's world."

She gave me an odd look, then turned back to the skeletons. I watched her profile as she studied the collection.

"Sandy talked about you, but I didn't really listen." She spoke without turning to face me. "I'm not sure who you are or what you want."

"I'm a friend of your aunt."

"My aunt is a nice person."

"Yes. Your mother thought you might be in trouble."

She gave a wry smile. Obviously this was not a happy subject for her.

"Why do you care what my mother thinks?"

"I care that Sister Julienne was distressed by your disappearance. Your aunt is not aware that you've taken off before."

Her eyes left the vertebrates and swung to me. "What else do you know about me?" She flicked her hair. Perhaps the cold had revived her. Perhaps escape from her mentor's presence. She seemed slightly more animated than she'd been in Birks.

"Anna, your aunt begged me to find you. She didn't want to pry, she simply wanted to reassure your mother."

She looked uncertain. "Since you seem to have made me your pet project, you must also know that my mother is crazy. If I'm ten minutes late she calls the cops."

"According to the police your absences lasted a bit longer than ten minutes."

Her eyes narrowed slightly.

Good, Brennan. Put her on the defensive.

"Look, Anna, I don't want to meddle. But if there's anything I can do to help you, I'm more than willing to try."

369

I waited but she said nothing.

Turn it around. Maybe she'll open up.

"Perhaps you can help me. As you know I work with the coroner, and some recent cases really have us baffled. A young woman named Jennifer Cannon vanished from Montreal several years ago. Her body was found last week in South Carolina. She was a McGill student."

Anna's expression did not change.

"Did you know her?"

She was as silent as the bones around us.

"On March seventeenth a woman named Carole Comptois was murdered and dumped on Île des Sœurs. She was eighteen."

A hand slid to her hair.

"Jennifer Cannon wasn't alone." The hand dropped to her lap, floated back to her ear. "We haven't identified the person buried with her."

I withdrew the composite sketch and held it out. She took it, her eyes avoiding mine.

The paper trembled slightly as she stared at the face I'd created.

"Is this for real?"

"Facial approximation is an art, not a science. One can never be certain about the accuracy."

"You did this from a skull?" There was a tremor in her voice.

"Yes."

"The hair is wrong." Barely audible.

"You recognize the face?"

"Amalie Provencher."

"Do you know her?"

"She works in the counseling center." She kept her eyes averted.

"When did you last see her?"

370

"It's been a couple of weeks. Maybe longer, I'm not sure. I was gone."

"Is she a student?"

"What did they do to her?"

I hesitated, uncertain how much to reveal. Anna's mood swings made me suspect she was either unstable or taking drugs. She didn't wait for my answer.

"Did they murder her?"

"Who, Anna? Who are 'they'?"

Finally, she looked at me. Her pupils glistened in the artificial light.

"Sandy told me about your conversation. She was right, and she was wrong. There is a group here on campus, but they have nothing to do with Satan. And I have nothing to do with them. Amalie did. She got the job in the counseling center because they told her to."

"Is that where you met?"

She nodded, ran a knuckle under each eye, and wiped them on her pants.

"When?"

"I don't know. Awhile back. I was pretty bummed, so I thought I'd try counseling. When I went to the center Amalie always made a point of chatting with me, acting really concerned. She'd never talk about herself or her problems. She really listened to what I had to say. We had a lot in common, so we became friends."

I remembered Red's words. Recruiters are instructed to learn about potential members, to convince them of their common ground and earn their trust.

"She'd talk about this group she belonged to, said it turned her life around. I finally went to one of the meetings. It was O.K." She shrugged. "Someone spoke and we ate and did breathing exercises and stuff. It didn't really grab me, but I went back a couple of times because everyone acted as if they really liked me."

Love bombing.

"Then they invited me to the country. That sounded cool, so I went. We played games and listened to lectures and chanted and did exercises. Amalie loved it, but it wasn't for me. I thought it was a lot of gobbledygook, but you couldn't disagree. Plus they never left me alone. I wasn't allowed a minute to myself.

"They wanted me to stay for a longer workshop, and when I said no, they got kind of huffy. I had to get pretty bitchy to get a ride back to town. I avoid Amalie now, but I see her from time to time."

"What's this group called?"

"I'm not sure."

"Do you think they killed Amalie?"

She wiped her palms on the sides of her thighs.

"There was a guy I met out there. He signed up through a course someplace else. Anyway, after I left he stayed, so I didn't see him for a long time. Maybe a year. Then I ran into him at a concert on Île Notre Dame. We saw each other for a while, but that didn't work out." Another shrug. "By then he'd left the group, but he had some spooky stories about what went on. Mostly, he wouldn't talk about it, though. He was pretty freaked."

"What was his name?"

"John something."

"Where is he now?"

"I don't know. I think he moved away." She wiped tears from her lower lashes.

"Anna, is Dr. Jeannotte connected with this group?"

"Why do you ask that?" Her voice broke on the last word. I could see a small blue vein pulsing in her neck.

"When I first met you, in her office, you seemed very nervous around Dr. Jeannotte."

"She's been wonderful to me. She's a lot better for my head than meditation and heavy breathing." She

372

snorted. "But she's also demanding, and I worry all the time that I'll mess up."

"I understand you spend a lot of time with her."

Her eyes went back to the skeletons. "I thought you were concerned about Amalie and these dead people."

"Anna, would you be willing to talk to someone else? What you've told me is important, and the police will definitely want to follow up on it. A detective named Andrew Ryan is investigating these homicides. He's a very kind man, and I think you'll like him."

She gave me a confused look and whipped hair behind both ears.

"There's nothing I can tell you. John could, but I really don't know where he's gone."

"Do you remember where this seminar took place?"

"Some kind of farm. I rode in a van and didn't pay much attention because they had us playing games. Coming back, I just slept. They kept us up a lot and I was exhausted. Except for John and Amalie, I never saw any of them again. And now you say she's—"

Downstairs a door opened, then a voice rolled up the stairs.

"Who's there?"

"Great. Now I'll lose the key," Anna whispered.

"Are we not supposed to be here?"

"Not exactly. When I stopped working in the museum I just sort of kept the key."

Terrific.

"Go along with me," I said, rising from the bench.

"Is someone there?" I called out. "We're here."

Footfalls on the stairs, then a security guard appeared in the doorway. His knitted cap stopped just above his eyes, and a water-soaked parka barely covered his paunch. He was breathing hard, and his teeth looked yellow in the violet light.

"Oh, God, are we glad to see you." I overacted. "We

373

were sketching *Odocoileus virginianus* and lost track of time. Everyone left early because of the ice, and I guess they forgot about us. We got locked in." I gave a silly-me smile. "I was about to call security."

"You can't be in here now. The museum's closed," he rasped.

Obviously my performance had been wasted.

"Of course. We really need to be on our way. Her husband will be crazy wondering where she is." I gestured at Anna, who was nodding like a box turtle.

The guard shifted watery eyes from Anna to me, then tipped his head toward the stairs.

"Let's go, then."

We wasted no time.

Outside, rain was still falling. The drops were thicker now, like the Slushes my sister and I had bought from summer vendors. Her face rose from a niche in my mind. Where are you, Harry?

At Birks Hall Anna gave me a funny look.

"*Odocoileus virginianus?*"

"It popped into my head."

"There is no white-tailed deer in the museum."

Did the corners of her mouth pucker, or was it merely the cold? I shrugged.

Reluctantly, Anna gave me her home number and address. We parted, and I assured her that Ryan would call soon. As I hurried down University something made me turn back. Anna stood in the archway of the Gothic old building, motionless, like her Cenozoic comrades.

When I got home I dialed Ryan's pager. Minutes later the phone rang. I told him that Anna had surfaced and outlined our conversation. He promised to inform the coroner so a search could begin for Amalie Provencher's medical and dental records. He rang off quickly,

374

intending to contact Anna before she left Jeannotte's office. He would phone later to fill me in on what he'd learned during the day.

I ate a supper of salad niçoise and croissants, took a long bath, and slipped into an old sweat suit. I still felt chilled, and decided to light a fire. I'd used the last of my starter logs so I wadded newspaper into balls and overlaid them with kindling. Ice was ticking against the windows as I lit the pile and watched it catch.

Eight-forty. I got the Bélanger journals and turned on "Seinfeld," hoping the rhythm of the dialogue and laughter would have a soothing effect. Left on their own I knew my thoughts would run like cats in the night, rooting and snarling, and raising my anxiety to a level where sleep would be impossible.

No go. Jerry and Kramer did their best, but I couldn't concentrate.

My eyes drifted to the fire. The flames had dwindled to a few sparse tongues curving around the bottom log. I went to the hearth, separated a section of paper, tore and balled up several pages, and stuffed them into the embers.

I was poking the logs when recall kicked in.

Newspapers!

I'd forgotten about the microfilm!

I went to the bedroom, pulled out the pages I'd copied at McGill, and took them back to the sofa. It took only a moment to locate the article in *La Presse*.

The story was as brief as I remembered it. April 20, 1845. Eugénie Nicolet was sailing for France. She would sing in Paris and Brussels, summer in the south of France, and return to Montreal in July. The members of her entourage were listed, as were her upcoming concert dates. There was also a brief summary of her career, and comments as to how she would be missed.

My coins had taken me through April 26. I skimmed everything I'd printed, but Eugénie's name did not reappear. Then I went back through, strip-searching every story and announcement.

The article appeared on April 22.

Someone else would appear in Paris. This gentleman's talent lay not in music, but in oratory. He was on a speaking tour, denouncing the selling of human beings and encouraging commerce with West Africa. Born in the Gold Coast, he'd been educated in Germany and held a professorship in philosophy at the University of Halle. He'd just completed a series of lectures at the McGill School of Divinity.

I backpedaled through history. Eighteen forty-five. Slavery was in full swing in the United States, but had been banned in France and England. Canada was still a British colony. Church and missionary groups were begging Africans to stop exporting their brothers and sisters, and encouraging Europeans to engage in legal commerce with West Africa as an alternative. What did they call it? The "legitimate trade."

I read the passenger's name with growing excitement.

And the name of the vessel.

Eugénie Nicolet and Abo Gabassa had made the crossing on the same ship.

I got up to poke the fire.

Was that it? Had I stumbled on the secret hidden for a century and a half? Eugénie Nicolet and Abo Gabassa? An affair?

I slipped on shoes, went to the French doors, flipped the handle, and pushed. The door was frozen shut. I leaned hard with my hip and the seal cracked.

My woodpile was frozen, and it took me some time to hack a log free with a garden trowel. When I finally got back inside I was shivering and covered with tiny pellets. A sound stopped me dead as I crossed to the hearth.

My doorbell doesn't ring, it twitters. It did so now, then stopped abruptly, as if someone had given up.

I dropped the log, raced to the security box, and hit the video button. On the screen I saw a familiar figure disappearing through the front door.

I grabbed my keys, ran to the lobby, and opened the door to the vestibule. The outer door was settling into place. I depressed the tongue and pulled it wide.

Daisy Jeannotte lay sprawled across my steps.

31

Before I could reach her, she moved. Slowly, she drew in her hands, rolled, and pushed to a sitting position, her back to me.

"Are you hurt?" My throat was so dry my words came out high and stretched.

She flinched at the sound of my voice, then turned.

"The ice is treacherous. I slipped, but I'm quite fine."

I reached out and she allowed me to help her up. She was trembling, and didn't look fine at all.

"Please, come inside and I'll make some tea."

"No. I can't stay. There's someone waiting for me. I shouldn't be out on such a dreadful night but I had to speak to you."

"Please come in where it's warmer."

"No. Thank you." Her tone was as cold as the air.

She retied her scarf, then looked directly into my eyes. Behind her, bullets of ice sliced through a cone of streetlight. The tree limbs looked shiny black through the sodium vapor.

"Dr. Brennan, you must leave my students alone. I've tried to be helpful to you, but I do believe you are abusing my kindness. You cannot pursue these young people in this manner. And to give my number to the police for the purpose of harassing my assistant is simply unthinkable."

A gloved hand wiped her eye, leaving a dark smear trailing across her cheek.

Anger flared like a kitchen match. My arms were wrapped around my midriff, and through the flannel I felt my nails dig into my flesh.

"What the hell are you talking about? I'm not *pursuing* Anna." I spat the word back at her. "This isn't some goddam research project! People are dead! Ten for certain, God knows how many others."

Pellets bounced off my forehead and arms. I didn't feel them. Her words enraged me, and I vented all the anguish and frustration that had built in me over the past few weeks.

"Jennifer Cannon and Amalie Provencher were McGill students. They were murdered, Dr. Jeannotte. But not just murdered. No. That wasn't enough for these people. These maniacs threw them to animals, then watched their flesh torn and their skulls pierced right into their brains."

I ranted on, no longer in control of my voice. I noticed a passing couple quicken their pace, despite the glassy sidewalk.

"A family was slashed and mutilated and an old woman shot in the head not two hundred kilometers from here. Babies! They slaughtered two little babies! An eighteen-year-old girl was torn apart, stuffed in a trunk, and dumped right in this city. They're dead, Dr. Jeannotte, murdered by a group of loonies who think they're the posse for all morality."

I felt flushed, despite the freezing cold.

"Well, let me tell you something." I jabbed a trembling finger. "I'm going to find these self-righteous, malevolent bastards and put them out of business, no matter how many altar boys, or guidance counselors, or

379

Bible-toting swamis I have to harass! And that includes your students! And that may include you!"

Jeannotte's face looked ghostly in the darkness, the smeared mascara transforming it into a macabre mask. A lump had formed above her left eye, throwing it into shadow and causing the right to look strangely light.

I dropped my finger and rewrapped the arm around my body. I had said too much. My outburst spent, the cold was causing me to shiver.

The street was deserted and utterly silent. I could hear the rasping of my breath.

I don't know what I expected to hear, but it was not the question that came from her lips. "Why do you use such imagery?"

"*What?*" Was she questioning my prose?

"Bibles and swamis and altar boys. Why do you make these references?"

"Because I believe these murders were committed by religious fanatics."

Jeannotte held herself completely still. When she spoke her voice was icier than the night, and her words chilled me more than the weather.

"You are out of your depth, Dr. Brennan. I'm warning you to leave this alone." The colorless eyes bore into mine. "If you persist, I will be forced to take action."

A car crept down the alley opposite my building and stopped. As it turned onto the street, the headlights made a wide arc, sweeping the block and momentarily illuminating Jeannotte's face.

I tensed, and my nails dug deeper into my sides.

Oh, God.

It was not an illusion created by shadow. Jeannotte's right eye was eerily pale. Stripped of makeup, the brow and lashes flared white in the passing beams.

She may have seen something in my face, for she

380

pulled her scarf forward, turned, and picked her way down the steps. She did not look back.

When I got inside, the message light was flashing. Ryan. I phoned him back with shaky hands.

"Jeannotte's involved," I said, wasting no time. "She was just here telling me to back off. Seems your call to Anna really irked her. Listen, when we went back to Saint Helena, do you remember the man with the white streak?"

"Yeah. Skinny guy, scarecrow-thin, tall. He came in to talk to Owens." Ryan sounded exhausted.

"Jeannotte has the same pattern of depigmentation, same eye. It's not obvious because she hides it with makeup."

"Same hair streak?"

"I couldn't tell, but she probably uses dye. Look, these two must be related. The trait's just too unusual to be a coincidence."

"Siblings?"

"I didn't pay much attention at the time, but I think the guy on Saint Helena was too young to be her father and too old to be her son."

"If she's from the Tennessee mountains there are limited genetic possibilities."

"Funny." I was not in the mood for redneck jokes.

"Could be whole clans that share the gene."

"This is serious, Ryan."

"You know, different stripes in different hollers." He imitated Jeff Foxworthy. "If your stripe is the same as your sister's, then you may be—"

Stripes. Something about stripes pulled at me.

"What did you say?"

"Hollers, it's what you folk—"

"Will you stop it! I just thought of something else. Do

381

you remember what Heidi Schneider's father said about their visitor?"

The line was quiet.

"He said the guy looked like a skunk. A goddam skunk."

"Shit. So maybe Daddy wasn't being poetic."

In the background a phone rang and rang. No one answered it.

"You think Owens sent Streak to Texas?" Ryan asked.

"No, not Owens. Kathryn and the old man both talked about a woman. I think it's Jeannotte. She probably directs the show from here and has lieutenants at her other camps. I also think she recruits on campus through some sort of seminar network."

"What else can you tell me about Jeannotte?"

I related everything I knew, including her behavior toward her assistant, and asked what he'd learned in his conversation with Anna.

"Not much. I think there's a shitload she's keeping bottled up. This kid makes Zelda look stable."

"She could be on drugs."

The ringing started up again.

"Are you alone there?" Save for the phones, the squad room sounded unnaturally quiet.

"Everyone's been pulled out for this friggin' storm. Are you having problems?"

"Like what?"

"Don't you listen to the news? The ice is really screwing things up. They've closed the airport, and a lot of the minor roads are impassable. Power lines are cracking like dry spaghetti, and stretches of the south shore are cold and dark. The city fathers are starting to worry about old folks. And looters."

"I'm fine so far. Did Baker's men find anything to tie Saint Helena to the group in Texas?"

382

"Not really. The old guy with the dog talked a lot about meeting his guardian angel. Seems Owens and his disciples had the same idea. It's all through their journals."

"Journals?"

"Yeah. Apparently some of the faithful had the creative urge."

"And?"

I heard him inhale, then exhale slowly.

"Tell me, goddamit!"

"According to some expert down there, it's definitely apocalyptic and it's now. They're heading for the big one. Sheriff Baker's taking no chances. He's called in the feds."

"And they found no clue as to destination? The earthly destination, I mean."

"To meet their guardian angel and make the crossing to a better place. That's the kind of crap we're dealing with. But they're well organized. Apparently the trip has been planned for a long time."

"Jeannotte! You've got to find Jeannotte! It's her! She's the guardian angel!"

I knew I sounded frantic, but I couldn't help myself.

"O.K. I agree. It's time to drive Miss Daisy hard. When did she leave your place?"

"Fifteen minutes ago."

"Where was she going?"

"I don't know. She said she was meeting someone."

"O.K., I'll find her. Brennan, if you're right about this, the little professor is a very dangerous woman. Do *not*, I repeat, do not do anything on your own. I know you're worried about Harry, but if she's been sucked into this thing it may take professionals to get her out. Do you understand?"

"May I brush my teeth? Or is that considered risky?"

I snapped. His paternalism did not bring out the best in me.

"You know what I mean. Find yourself some candles. I'll get back to you as soon as I learn anything."

I hung up and walked to the French doors. I wanted more space around me and slid the curtain aside. The courtyard looked like a mythological garden, the trees and shrubs fashioned of spun glass. Filmy nets covered the upstairs balconies and clung to the brick chimneys and walls.

I located candles, matches, and a flashlight, then dug my radio and headphones from my gym bag and placed everything on the kitchen counter. Back in the living room, I settled on the couch and clicked to the CTV news.

Ryan was right. The storm was big news. Lines were down throughout the province and Hydro-Québec could not say when power would be restored. Temperatures were dropping and more precipitation was on the way.

I threw on a jacket and made three trips for logs. If the electricity failed, I would have heat. Next, I got extra blankets and placed them on the bed. When I returned to the living room a grim-looking newscaster was listing events that would not take place.

It was a familiar ritual, and oddly comforting. When snow threatens in the South, schools close, public activities cease, and frenzied homeowners strip store shelves. Usually the blizzards never come, or if snow falls, it disappears the following day. In Montreal storm preparations are methodical, not frantic, dominated by an air of "we will cope."

My preparations occupied me for fifteen minutes. The TV held my attention for another ten. A brief respite. When I clicked off, my agitation returned full force. I felt stuck, a bug on a pin. Ryan was right. There was nothing I could do, and my powerlessness made me all the more restless.

I went through my nighttime routine, hoping to keep bad thoughts at bay a little longer. No go. When I crawled into bed, the neural floodgates overflowed.

Harry. Why hadn't I listened to her? How could I have been so self-absorbed? Where had she gone? Why hadn't she called her son? Why hadn't she called me?

Daisy Jeannotte. Who had she been going to meet? What crazed course was she mapping? How many innocent souls did she intend to take with her?

Heidi Schneider. Who had felt so threatened by Heidi's babies as to resort to brutal infanticide? Were these deaths the herald of more bloodshed?

Jennifer Cannon. Amalie Provencher. Carole Comptois. Were their murders part of the madness? What demonic mores had they violated? Had their deaths been the choreography of some hellish ritual? Had my sister suffered the same fate?

When the phone rang I jumped and knocked the flashlight to the floor.

Ryan, I prayed. It's Ryan and he's got Jeannotte.

My nephew's voice came across the line.

"Oh hell, Aunt Tempe. I think I've really screwed up. She called. I found it on the other cassette."

"What other cassette."

"I've got one of these old answering machines with the tiny tapes. The one I had wasn't rewinding right so I put in a new one. I didn't think about it until a friend came by just now. I was pretty hacked off at her because we were supposed to go out last week, but when I went to get her she wasn't home. When she dropped by tonight I told her to kiss off, and she insisted she'd left a message. We got into a hassle so I got out the old tape and played it. She was on there, all right, but so was Harry. Right at the end."

385

"What did your mother say?"

"She sounded pissed off. You know how Harry is. But she sounded scared at the same time. She was at some farm or something and wanted to split but no one would drive her back to Montreal. So I guess she's still in Canada."

"What else did she say?" My heart was pounding so hard I thought my nephew would hear it.

"She said things were getting creepy and she wanted out. Then the tape quit or she was cut off or something. I'm not sure. The message just ended."

"When did she call?"

"Pam phoned Monday. Harry's message was after that."

"There's no date indicator?"

"This thing was made during the Truman years."

"When did you change the tape?"

"I think maybe Wednesday or Thursday. I'm not sure. But before the weekend, I know that."

"Think, Kit!"

The line buzzed.

"Thursday. When I got home from the boat I was tired and the tape wouldn't rewind, so I popped the cassette and pitched it. That's when I put in the new one. Shit, that means she phoned at least four days ago, maybe even six. God, I hope she's all right. She sounded pretty panicky, even for Harry."

"I think I know who she's with. She'll be fine." I didn't believe my own words.

"Let me know as soon as you talk to her. Tell her I feel bad about this. I just didn't think."

I went to the window and pressed my face to the glass. The coating of ice turned the streetlights into tiny suns, and my neighbors' windows into glimmering rectangles. Tears ran down my cheeks as I thought of my sister, somewhere in that storm.

386

I dragged myself back to bed, turned on the lamp, and settled in to await Ryan's call.

Now and then the lights dimmed, flickered, then returned to normal. A millennium passed. The phone sat mute.

I drifted off.

It was the dream that provided the final epiphany.

32

I stand gazing at the old church. It is winter and the trees are bare. Though the sky is leaden, the branches send spider-webs of shadow crawling across the weathered gray stone. The air smells of snow, and the prestorm silence is thick around me. In the distance I see a frozen lake.

A door opens and a figure is silhouetted against the soft yellow of lamplight. It hesitates, then walks in my direction, head lowered against the wind. The figure draws near, and I see she is female. Her head is veiled and she wears a long black gown.

As the woman comes closer the first powdery flakes appear. She carries a candle, and I realize her crouching is to protect the flame. I wonder how it survives.

The woman stops and beckons with her head. Already the veil is flecked with snow. I strain to recognize her face, but it moves in and out of focus, like pebbles at the bottom of a deep pool.

She turns and I follow.

The woman pulls farther and farther ahead. I feel alarm and try to catch up, but my body does not respond. My legs are weighted and I cannot hurry. I see

388

her disappear through the door. I call out, but there is no sound.

Then I am inside the church and everything is dim. The walls are stone, the floor dirt. Huge carved windows disappear into darkness overhead. Through them I see tiny flakes wafting like smoke.

I can't remember why I've come to the church. I feel guilty, because I know it is important. Someone has sent me, but I can't recall who.

As I walk through the dusklike gloom I look down and see that my feet are bare. I am ashamed because I don't know where I've left my shoes. I want to leave, but don't know the way. I feel if I abandon my task I won't be able to leave.

I hear muffled voices and turn in that direction. There is something on the ground but it is obscure, a mirage I can't identify. I move toward it and the shadows congeal into separate objects.

A circle of wrapped cocoons. I stare down at them. They are too small to be bodies, but are shaped like bodies.

I go to one and loosen a corner. There is a muffled buzzing. I pull back the cloth and flies billow out and float to the window. The glass is frosted with vapor and I watch the insects swarm across it, knowing they are wrong in the cold.

My eyes drop back to the bundle. I don't hurry because I know it isn't a corpse. The dead are not packaged and arrayed in this manner.

Only it is. And I recognize the face. Amalie Provencher stares at me, her features a cartoon portrait in shades of gray.

Still, I cannot hurry. I move from bundle to bundle, unbinding fabric and sending flies rising into the shadows. The faces are white, the eyes fixed, but I do not recognize them. Except for one.

389

The size tells me before I open the shroud. It is so much smaller than the others. I don't want to see, but it is impossible to stop.

No! I try denial, but it doesn't work.

Carlie lies on his stomach, hands curled into upturned fists.

Then I see two others, tiny, side by side in the circle.

I cry out, but again there is no sound.

A hand closes around my arm. I look up and see my guide. She is changed, or just more clearly visible.

It is a nun, her habit frayed and covered with mold. When she moves I hear the click of beads and smell wet earth and decay.

I rise and see cocoa skin covered with oozing, red sores. I know it is Élisabeth Nicolet.

"Who are you?" I think the question, but she answers.

"All in robe of darkest grain."

I don't understand.

"Why are you here?"

"I come a reluctant bride of Christ."

Then I see another figure. She stands in a recess, the dim snowfall light obscuring her features and turning her hair a lackluster gray. Her eyes meet mine and she speaks, but the words are lost.

"Harry!" I scream, but my voice is thin and weak.

Harry doesn't hear. She extends both arms and her mouth moves, a black oval in the specter that is her face.

Again I shout, but no sound emerges.

She speaks again and I hear her, though her words are distant, like voices drifting across water.

"Help me. I am dying."

"No!" I try to run, but my legs won't move.

Harry enters a passageway I haven't noticed. Above it

I see an inscription. GUARDIAN ANGEL. She becomes shadow, merges with the darkness.

I call but she won't look back. I try to go to her, but my body is frozen, nothing moves but the tears down my cheeks.

My companion transforms. Dark feathered wings sprout from her back, and her face grows pale and deeply creviced. Her eyes congeal into chunks of stone. As I stare into them the irises go clear and color drains from the brows and lashes. A white streak appears in her hair and races backward, separating a flap of scalp and throwing it high into the air. The tissue flutters to the floor and flies swarm from the window and settle on it.

"The order must not be ignored." The voice comes from everywhere and nowhere.

The dreamscape shifts to the low country. Long rays of sun slant through Spanish moss, and giant shadows dance between the trees. It is hot and I am digging. I sweat as I scoop mud the color of dried blood and fling it to a mound behind me.

The blade hits something and I scrape the edges, carefully revealing the form. White fur clotted with brick-red clay. I follow the arch of the back. A hand with long, red nails. I work my way up the arm. Cowboy fringe. Everything shimmers in the intense heat.

I see Harry's face and scream.

Heart pounding and bathed in sweat, I sat upright. It took me a moment to reconnect.

Montreal. Bedroom. Ice storm.

The light still burned and the room was quiet. I checked the clock. Three forty-two.

Calm down. A dream is just a dream. It reflects fears and anxieties, not reality.

Then another thought. Ryan's call. Had I slept through it?

I threw back the quilt and moved to the living room. The answering machine was dark.

Back in the bedroom, I took off my damp clothes. As I dropped the sweatpants to the floor I could see fingernail-shaped moons in the flesh of my palms. I dressed in jeans and a heavy sweater.

More sleep did not seem likely, so I went to the kitchen and set water to boil. I felt queasy from the dream. I didn't want to bring it back, but the vision had knocked something loose in my mind, and I needed to make sense of it. I took my tea to the sofa.

My dreams as a rule are not particularly wondrous nor frightening or grotesque. They are of two types.

Most commonly, I cannot dial the phone, see the road, catch the plane. I must take an exam but have never attended the class. Piece of cake: anxiety.

Less frequently the message is more baffling. My subconscious sifts material that my conscious mind has amassed, and weaves it into surreal tableaux. I am left to interpret what my psyche is saying.

Tonight's nightmare was clearly of the cryptic type. I closed my eyes to see what I could decode. Images flashed, like glimpses through a picket fence.

Amalie Provencher's computer face.

The dead babies.

A winged Daisy Jeannotte. I remembered my words to Ryan. Was she truly an angel of death?

The church. It resembled the convent at Lac Memphrémagog. Why was my brain beaming that to me?

Élisabeth Nicolet.

Harry, beckoning for help, then disappearing into a dark tunnel. Harry, dead with Birdie. Was Harry at serious risk?

A reluctant bride. What the hell did that mean? Was

392

Élisabeth held against her will? Was that part of her saintly truth?

I had no time to sort it further, for just then the doorbell sounded. Friend or foe, I wondered as I stumbled to the security panel and picked up the handset.

Ryan's tall, lanky frame filled the screen. I buzzed him in and watched through the peephole as he trudged up the corridor. He looked like a survivor of the Trail of Tears.

"You look exhausted."

"It's been a long one and we're still in overtime. I'm on my own, thanks to the storm."

Ryan wiped his boots and unzipped his parka. Ice cascaded to the floor when he pulled off his tuque. He didn't question why I was dressed at four o'clock in the morning, and I didn't ask why he was dropping in at that hour.

"Baker's found Kathryn. She had a last-minute change of mind and bailed on Owens."

"The baby?" My heart raced.

"He's there too."

"Where?"

"Got coffee?"

"Yeah, sure."

Ryan threw his hat on the hall table and followed me to the kitchen. He talked as I ground beans and measured water.

"She's been in hiding with some guy named Espinoza. Remember the neighbor who called Social Services about Owens?"

"I thought the neighbor was dead."

"She is. This is her son. He's one of the faithful, but he holds a day job and lives down the road in Mama's house."

"How did Kathryn get Carlie?"

"He was already there. Ready for this? Someone drove the vans to Charleston while the group went to ground in the Espinoza house. They were all on the island the whole time. Then, when the heat cooled they left."

"How?"

"They split up and everybody boogied to a different tune. Some were picked up by boat, others were smuggled in pickups and car trunks. Seems Owens has quite an underground. And like schmucks, we just focused on the vans."

I handed him a steaming mug.

"Kathryn was supposed to go with Espinoza and some other guy, but she talked him into staying put."

"Where's the other guy?"

"Espinoza turns into igneous rock on that topic."

"Where did everyone go?" My throat felt tight. I already knew the answer.

"I think they're here."

I said nothing.

"Kathryn isn't sure where they were heading, but she knows it involved a border crossing. They're traveling in twos and threes and they've got directions for roads that aren't patrolled."

"Where?"

"She thinks she heard talk of Vermont. The highway patrol and INS have been alerted, but it's probably too late. They've had almost three days and Canada isn't exactly Libya when it comes to border security."

Ryan sipped his coffee.

"Kathryn claims she didn't pay much attention because she never thought they'd really go. But she is clear on one thing. When they find this guardian angel, everyone will die."

I began wiping the counter, though it was already clean.

For a long time neither of us spoke. Then,

"Any word from your sister?"

My stomach constricted anew. "No."

When he spoke again his voice had softened.

"Baker's boys found something in the Saint Helena compound."

"What?" Fear shot through me.

"A letter to Owens. In it someone named Daniel is discussing Inner Life Empowerment." I felt a hand on my shoulder. "It looks like the organization was a front, or else Owens' followers infiltrated the courses. That part's not clear, but what is clear is that they used ILE to recruit."

"Oh, my God."

"The letter's dated about two months ago, but there's nothing to indicate where it came from. The wording's vague, but it sounds like there was some sort of quota to be met, and this Daniel is promising he'll deliver."

"How?" I could hardly speak.

"He doesn't say. There's nothing else that makes reference to ILE. Just that one letter."

The dream slammed back in vivid detail and I felt ice slide through my veins.

"They've got Harry!" I said with trembling lips. "I have to find her!"

"We will."

I told him about Kit's call.

"Shit."

"How can these people remain invisible for years, then we turn over their rock and they slither away and vanish?" My voice was quavery.

Ryan set down his mug and turned me around with both hands. I was squeezing the sponge so hard it made small hissing sounds.

"There's no trail because these people have a tremendous source of clandestine income. They deal exclusively in cash but don't seem to be involved in anything illegal."

"Except murder!" I wanted to pace but Ryan held me firmly.

"What I'm saying is these assholes can't be tied to drugs or theft or credit card scams. There's no money trail and no evidence of crime, and that's usually where the break comes." His eyes were hard. "But they've fucked up badly by coming into my backyard and I'm going to nail the rabid little pricks."

I ripped free of his grasp and threw the sponge across the kitchen.

"What did Jeannotte say?"

"I tried her office, then staked her pad. No-show at either place. Don't forget I'm working this alone, Brennan. This storm has shut down the province."

"What did you find out about Jennifer Cannon and Amalie Provencher?"

"The university is pulling the usual student-privacy crap. They won't release a thing without a court order."

That did it. I pushed past him and went to the bedroom. I was pulling on wool socks when he appeared in the doorway.

"What do you think you're doing?"

"I'm going to get some answers from Anna Goyette, then I'm going to find my sister."

"Whoa, scout. There's a blanket of polar ice out there."

"I'll manage."

"In a five-year-old Mazda?"

I was shaking so badly I couldn't lace my boots. I stopped, untangled the knot, and crisscrossed the cord carefully through the prongs. Then I did the other foot, stood, and turned to Ryan.

"I am not going to sit here and allow these fanatics to murder my sister. They may be consumed with suicidal obsession, but they are not taking Harry with them. With or without you I'm going to find her, Ryan. And I'm going to do it *now!*"

For a full minute he simply stared. Then he breathed deeply, exhaled through his nose, and opened his mouth to speak.

It was then the lights flared, dimmed, and died.

33

The floor of Ryan's Jeep was wet with melted slush. The wipers slapped back and forth, now and then skipping on a patch of ice. In the fans of cleared windshield I could see millions of silvery slivers slicing through the beams from our headlights.

Centre-Ville was dark and deserted. No street or building lights, no neon signs, no traffic signals. The only cars I saw were police cruisers. Yellow tape cordoned off sidewalks adjacent to high-rises to prevent injuries from falling ice. I wondered how many people would really try to go to work today. Now and then I heard a crack, then a frozen sheet exploded on the pavement. The landscape brought to mind news clips of Sarajevo, and I pictured my neighbors hunkered in cold, dark rooms.

Ryan was blizzard driving, shoulders tense, fingers tightly clutching the wheel. He kept the speed low and even, accelerating gradually and easing off the gas well in advance of intersections. Even so we fishtailed often. Ryan was right to drive his Jeep. The cruisers we saw were sliding more than rolling.

We crawled up rue Guy and turned east onto Docteur-Penfield. Above us I could see Montréal

General glowing under the power of its own generator. My fingers strangled the armrest on the right, and my left hand was in a fist.

"It's colder than crap. Why isn't this snow?" I snapped. Tension and fear were showing.

Ryan's eyes never left the road.

"According to the radio there's some sort of inversion working, so it's warmer in the clouds than on the ground. The stuff is forming as rain, but freezing when it gets down here. The weight of the ice is taking out whole power stations."

"When is it going to let up?"

"The weather guy says the system is stuck and going nowhere."

I closed my eyes and focused on sound. Defroster. Wipers. Whistling wind. My pounding heart.

The car swerved and my lids flew open. I unclenched a hand and punched the radio.

The voice was solemn but reassuring. Much of the province was without electricity, and Hydro-Québec had three thousand employees on the job. Crews would work around the clock, but no one could say when the lines would be repaired.

The transformer serving Centre-Ville had blown because of overload, but was being given top priority. The filtration plant was down and residents were advised to boil their water.

Tough without power, I thought.

Shelters had been set up, and police would start going door to door at dawn to locate stranded seniors. Many roads were closed and motorists were advised to stay home.

I clicked the radio off, desperately wishing I were at home. With my sister. The thought of Harry set something pounding behind my left eye.

Ignore the headache and think, Brennan. You'll be of no use if you become distracted.

The Goyettes lived in an area known as the Plateau, so we cut north, then east on avenue des Pins. Uphill, I could see lights at Royal Victoria Hospital. Below us McGill was a black swatch, beyond that the city and waterfront, where the only thing visible was Place Ville-Marie.

Ryan turned north on St-Denis. Normally teaming with shoppers and tourists, the street was abandoned to the ice and wind. A translucence blanketed everything, obliterating the names of boutiques and bistros.

At Mont-Royal we headed east again, turned south on Christophe Colomb, and a decade later pulled up at the address Anna had given me. The building was a typical Montreal three-flat, bayed in front, with narrow metal stairs sweeping to the second floor. Ryan nosed the Jeep toward the curb and left it in the street.

When we got out the ice stung my cheeks like tiny cinders and brought tears to my eyes. Head down, we climbed to the Goyette flat, slipping and sliding on the frozen steps. The bell was encased in solid gray, so I pounded on the door. In a moment the curtain moved and Anna's face appeared. Through the frosted pane I could see her head wag from side to side.

"Open the door, Anna!" I shouted.

The head shaking intensified, but I was not in a mood to negotiate.

"*Open the goddam door!*"

She went still, and a hand flew to her ear. She stepped back and I expected her to disappear. Instead, I heard the sound of a key, then the door opened a crack.

I didn't wait. I pushed hard and Ryan and I were inside before she could react.

Anna backed away and stood with arms crossed, hands clutching the sleeves of her jacket. An oil lamp

400

sputtered on a small wooden table, sending shadows twitching high up the walls of the narrow hallway.

"Why can't you all just leave me alone?" Her eyes looked huge in the flickering light.

"I need your help, Anna."

"I can't do it."

"Yes, you can."

"I told her the same thing. I can't do it. They'll find me." Her voice trembled and I saw real fear on her face. The look sent a shaft straight to my heart. I'd seen it before. A friend, terrified by a stalker. I'd convinced her the danger wasn't real and she died because of it.

"Told who?" I wondered where her mother was.

"Dr. Jeannotte."

"She was here?"

A nod.

"When?"

"Several hours ago. I was sleeping."

"What did she want?"

Her eyes flicked to Ryan, then dropped to the floor.

"She asked odd questions. She wanted to know if I'd been seeing anyone from Amalie's group. I think she was going to the country, to the place I did the workshop. I – she hit me. I never had someone hit me like that. She was like a crazy person. I'd never seen her that way."

I heard anguish and shame in her voice, as if the attack were somehow her fault. She looked so small standing in the dark that I went to her and wrapped my arms around her.

"Don't blame yourself, Anna."

Her shoulders began to heave and I stroked her hair. It shimmered in the flickering lamplight.

"I would have helped her, but I honestly don't remember. I – it was one of my bad times."

"I know, but I want you to go back to that time and

401

think hard. Think of everything you remember about where you were."

"I've tried. It just isn't there."

I wanted to shake her, to jar loose the information that would save my sister. I remembered a course in child psychology. No abstracts, ask specific questions. Gently, I pushed her to arm's length and raised her chin with my hand.

"When you went to the workshop did you leave from school?"

"No. They picked me up here."

"Which way did you turn off from your street?"

"I don't know."

"Do you remember how you left town?"

"No."

Abstract, Brennan.

"Did you cross a bridge?"

Her eyes narrowed, then she nodded.

"Which one?"

"I don't know. Wait, I remember an island with lots of tall buildings."

"Île des Sœurs," said Ryan.

"Yes." Her eyes opened wide. "Someone made a joke about nuns living in the condos. You know, *sœurs*. Sisters."

"The Champlain Bridge," said Ryan.

"How far was the farm?"

"I—"

"How long were you in the van?"

"About forty-five minutes. Yeah. When we got there the driver bragged that he'd made it in less then an hour."

"What did you see when you got out of the van?"

Again I saw doubt in her eyes. Then, slowly, as if she were describing a Rorschach spatter,

"Right before we got there I remember a big tower

with lots of wires and antennae and disks. And then a tiny little house. Someone probably built it for their kids to wait for the school bus. I remember thinking it was made of gingerbread and decorated with frosting."

At that moment a face materialized behind Anna. It wore no makeup and looked shiny and pale in the flickering light.

"Who are you? Why do you come in the middle of the night?" The English was heavily accented.

Without waiting for an answer the woman grabbed Anna's wrist and pulled the girl behind her.

"You leave my daughter alone."

"Mrs. Goyette, I believe people are going to die. Anna may be able to help save them."

"She is not well. Now go." She pointed at the door. "I order you or I will call the police."

The ghostly face. The dim light. The tunnel-like hall. I was back in the dream, and suddenly I remembered. I knew, and I had to get there!

Ryan started to speak but I cut him off.

"Thank you. Your daughter has been very helpful," I managed.

Ryan glared as I pushed past him and out the door. I nearly fell in my plunge down the stairs. I no longer felt the cold as I stood at the Jeep, impatient for Ryan to speak to Mrs. Goyette, snug his tuque, then pick his way to ground level.

"What the hell—"

"Get me a map, Ryan."

"That little loony may be—"

"Do you have a goddam map of this province?" I hissed.

Without a word Ryan circled the Jeep and we both got in. He took a map from a holder on the driver's-side door, and I dug a flashlight from my pack. As I

403

unfolded the province he started the engine, then got out to scrape the windshield.

I located Montreal, then followed the Champlain Bridge across the St. Lawrence and on to 10 East. With a numb finger I traced the route I had taken to Lac Memphrémagog. In my mind's eye I saw the old church. I saw the grave. I saw the signpost, half covered in snow.

I moved my finger along the highway, estimating driving time. The names wavered in the flashlight beam.

Marieville. St-Grégoire. Ste-Angèle-de-Monnoir.

My heart stopped when I saw it.

Please, God, let us be in time.

I lowered the window and screamed into the wind.

The grating stopped and the door opened. Ryan threw the scraper into the back and slid behind the wheel. He pulled off his gloves and I handed him the map and flashlight. Wordlessly, I pointed to a small dot on the square I'd folded upward. He studied it, his breath like fog in the yellow beam.

"Holy shit." An ice crystal melted and ran from his lash. He swiped at the eye.

"It makes sense. Ange Gardien. It's not a person, it's a place. They're going to meet *at* Ange Gardien. It should be about forty-five minutes from here."

"How did you think of it?" he asked.

I didn't want to go into the dream. "I remembered the sign from my drive to Lac Memphrémagog. Let's go."

"Brennan—"

"Ryan, I'll say this one more time. I am going to get my sister." I fought to keep my voice steady. "I am going with or without you. You can take me home or you can take me to Ange Gardien."

He hesitated, then,

"Fuck!" He got out, flipped his seat forward, and dug around in back. As he slammed the door I saw him drop something into his pocket and yank the zipper. Then he resumed scraping.

In a minute he was back. Without a word he clicked his seat belt, put the Jeep in gear, and accelerated. The wheels spun but we went nowhere. He changed to reverse, then quickly back to first. The car rocked as Ryan shifted from first gear to reverse and back again. The Jeep broke free and we moved slowly up the block.

I said nothing as we crept south on Christophe Colomb, then west on Rachel. At St-Denis Ryan turned south, reversing the route we'd just driven.

Damn! He was taking me home. My blood went cold as I thought of the drive to Ange Gardien.

I closed my eyes and leaned back to prepare myself. You have chains, Brennan. You will put them on and drive as Ryan is doing. Dickhead Ryan.

Silence intruded on my lecture. I opened my eyes to pitch-black. Ice no longer pelted the windshield.

"Where are we?"

"Ville-Marie Tunnel."

I said nothing. Ryan raced through the tunnel like a starship threading a wormhole in space. When he took the exit for the Champlain Bridge I felt both relief and apprehension.

Yes! Ange Gardien.

Ten light-years later we were crossing the St. Law-rence. The river looked unnaturally dense, the buildings of Île des Sœurs black against the predawn sky. Though their scoreboards were out I knew the players. Nortel. Kodak. Honeywell. So normal. So familiar in my world at the end of the second millennium. I wished I were approaching their well-ordered offices instead of the madness that lay ahead.

The atmosphere in the Jeep was tense. Ryan focused

405

on the road and I worked the thumbnail. I stared out the window, avoiding thoughts of what might await us.

We crawled through a cold and forbidding landscape, a vista beamed from a frozen planet. As we moved east the ice increased visibly, robbing the world of texture and hue. Edges were blurred and objects seemed to blend together like parts of a giant plaster sculpture.

Guideposts, signs, and billboards were obliterated, erasing messages and boundaries. Here and there through the darkness wisps of smoke could be seen curling from chimneys, otherwise everything seemed frozen in place. Just over the Richelieu River the road curved, and I saw a beached car, belly-up like a loggerhead turtle. Stalactites hung from the bumpers and tires.

We'd been driving almost two hours when I spotted the sign. It was dawn, and the sky was changing from black to murky gray. Through the ice I could see an arrow and the letters *nge Gardi*.

"There."

Ryan released the gas and eased onto the exit. When it ended at a T-intersection he pumped the brake and the Jeep crunched to a stop.

"Which way?"

I grabbed the scraper, got out, and struggled to the sign, slipping once and cracking my knee. As I hacked away, the wind stood my hair on end and drove icy granules into my eyes. Overhead it hissed through branches and rattled power lines with an odd clacking sound.

I chopped at the ice as though demented. Eventually the blade snapped, but I jabbed on until the plastic was completely shattered. Using the wooden handle I scraped and clawed until finally, I could see letters and an arrow.

As I scrambled back to the Jeep something in my left knee felt terribly wrong.

"That way." I pointed. I didn't apologize for the scraper.

When Ryan turned, the rear spun out and we swerved wildly. My feet flew forward and I grabbed the armrests.

Ryan regained control and my teeth unclenched.

"There's no brake on your side."

"Thanks."

"This is the Rouville district. There's an SQ post not far from here. We'll go there first."

Though I begrudged the lost time, I didn't argue. If we walked into a hornet's nest I knew we might need backup. And, while Ryan's Jeep was good on ice, it had no radio.

Five minutes later I saw the tower. Or what was left of it. The metal had cracked under the weight of the ice, and beams and girders lay twisted and scattered like parts of a giant Erector set.

Just beyond the collapsed tower, a road took off to the left. Ten yards down I could see Anna's gingerbread hut.

"It's here, Ryan! Turn here!"

"We're doing this my way or not at all." He continued without slowing.

I was frantic. Any argument.

"It's getting light. What if they've decided to act at dawn?" I thought of Harry, drugged and helpless while zealots lit fires and prayed to their god. Or loosed wild dogs onto sacrificial lambs.

"We're going to check in first."

"We could be too late!" My hands trembled. I couldn't bear it. My sister could be ten yards away. I felt my chest begin to heave and turned my back to him.

A tree decided it.

We hadn't gone a quarter mile when an enormous pine blocked our way. It had fallen, bringing up a twelve-foot root wad and dragging power lines across the road. We would not be continuing in that direction.

Ryan struck the wheel with the heel of his hand.

"Jesus Christ in a peach tree!"

"It's pine." My heart hammered.

He stared at me, unamused. Outside, the wind moaned and threw ice against the windows. I saw Ryan's jaw muscles bunch, relax, bunch again. Then,

"We do this my way, Brennan. If I say wait in the Jeep, that's where your ass will be. Is that clear?"

I nodded. I would have agreed to anything.

We did an about-face and hung a right at the toppled tower. The road was narrow and littered with trees, some uprooted, others snapped where their trunks had failed. Ryan wove in and out among them. To either side poplars, ashes, and birches formed inverted U's, their crowns bent toward earth by the burden of ice.

A split-log fence began just beyond the gingerbread shelter. Ryan slowed and crept along it. At several places toppled trees had crushed the rails. Then I spotted the first living thing since Montreal.

The car was nose-down in a gully, wheels spinning, enveloped in a cloud of exhaust. The driver's door was open and I could see one booted leg planted on the ground.

Ryan braked and shifted to park.

"Stay here."

I started to object, thought better of it.

He got out and walked to the car. From where I sat the occupant could have been male or female. As Ryan and the driver exchanged words I lowered the window, but I couldn't make out what was said. Ryan's breath spurted like jets of mist. In less than a minute he was back in the Jeep.

"Not the most helpful character."

"What did he say?"

"*Oui* and *non*. He lives just up the road, but the cretin wouldn't notice if Genghis Khan moved in next door."

We moved on to where the fence ended at a gravel drive. Ryan pulled in and switched off the engine.

Two vans and a half dozen cars were scattered in front of a ramshackle lodge. They looked like rounded humps, frozen hippos in a river of gray. Ice dripped from the eaves and sills of the building and turned the windows milky, eliminating any view of the inside.

Ryan turned to me.

"Now listen. If this is the right place we're going to be about as welcome as a cottonmouth." He touched my cheek. "Promise me you'll stay here."

"I—"

His fingers slid to my lips.

"Stay here." His eyes were blindingly blue in the dreary dawn light.

"This is bullshit," I said into his fingertips.

He withdrew the hand and pointed at me.

"Wait in the car."

He pulled on gloves and stepped into the storm. When he slammed the door I reached for my mittens. I would wait two minutes.

What happened next comes back as disjointed images, shards of memory fragmented in time. I saw, but my mind did not accept the whole. It collected the memory and stored it away as separate frames.

Ryan had taken a half dozen steps when I heard a pop and his body jerked. His hands flew up and he started to turn. Another pop and another spasm, then he dropped to the ground and lay still.

"Ryan!" I yelled as I threw open the door. When I jumped out pain shot up my leg and my knee buckled. "Andy!" I screamed at his inert form.

Then lightning burst inside my skull and I was engulfed in darkness thicker than the ice.

34

My next conscious sensation was also of blackness. Blackness and pain. I sat up slowly, unable to see any form to the darkness. Fierce pain shot into my head and I thought I would vomit. More pain as I raised my knees and hung my head between them.

In a moment the queasiness passed. I listened. Nothing but the pounding of my own heart. I looked at my hands but they were lost to the darkness. I inhaled. Rotten wood and damp earth. Gingerly, I reached out.

I was sitting on a dirt floor. Behind me and to both sides I could feel a wall of rough, round stones. Six inches above my head my hand met wood.

My breath came in short, rapid gasps as I fought panic.

I was trapped! I had to get out!

Noooooooo!

The scream was in my mind. I hadn't entirely lost my self-control.

I closed my eyes and tried to control the hyperventilation. Clasping my hands, I tried to concentrate on one thing at a time.

Breathe in. Breathe out. In. Out.

Slowly the panic receded. I got to my knees and

stretched a hand straight out in front of me. Nothing. The pain in my left knee brought me to tears, but I crawled forward into the inky void. Two feet. Six. Ten.

As I moved unobstructed my terror receded. A tunnel was better than a stone cage.

I sat back and tried to connect with a functioning portion of my brain. I had no idea where I was, how long I'd been there, or how I'd arrived.

I began to reconstruct.

Harry. The lodge. The car.

Ryan! God, my God, oh, God!

Please, no! Please, please, not Ryan.

My stomach roiled again and a bitter taste rose to my mouth. I swallowed.

Who shot Ryan? Who brought me in here? Where was Harry?

My head pounded and I was becoming stiff with cold. This was no good. I had to do something. I took a deep breath and rolled back to my knees.

Step by throbbing step I crept along the tunnel. I'd lost my gloves, and the frigid clay numbed my hands and jarred my injured patella. The pain kept me focused until I touched the foot.

As I recoiled my head cracked wood and the start of a scream froze in my throat.

Goddam it, Brennan, get ahold of yourself. You are a crime scene professional, not a hysterical onlooker.

I crouched, still paralyzed with dread. Not of the tomblike space, but of the thing with which I shared it. Generations were born and died as I waited for a sign of life. Nothing spoke, nothing moved. I breathed deeply, then inched forward and touched the foot again.

It wore a leather boot, small, with laces like mine. I found its partner and followed the legs upward. The body was lying on its side. Cautiously, I rolled it over and continued my exploration. Hem. Buttons. Scarf.

412

My throat constricted as my fingertips recognized the clothing. Before I touched the face I knew.

But it couldn't be! It didn't make sense.

I pulled off the scarf and felt the hair. Yes. Daisy Jeannotte.

Jesus, God! What was going on?

Keep moving! a portion of my brain commanded.

I dragged myself forward on one knee and one hand, bracing a palm against the wall. My fingers touched cobwebs and things I didn't want to consider. Debris crumbled and trickled to earth as I moved slowly along the tunnel.

After several more feet the gloom lightened almost imperceptibly. My hand struck something and I followed it. Wooden rails. Trestles. When I looked up I could see a faint rectangle of amber light. Steps leading up.

I eased up the stairs, testing for sound at each riser. Three steps brought me to the ceiling. My hands identified the borders of a cover, but when I pushed it didn't budge.

I pressed my ear to the wood and the barking of dogs sent adrenaline to every part of my being. The sound seemed far off and muffled, but I could tell the animals were excited. A human voice yelled some command, then silence, then the yapping started again.

Directly overhead, no sounds of movement, no voices.

I pressed with my shoulder and the panel shifted slightly, but didn't give. When I examined the strips of light I could see a shadow at the midpoint of the right side. I tried poking it with my fingertips, but the gap was too narrow. Frustrated, I inserted my fingers farther up and slid them along the crack. Splinters pierced my flesh and tore at my nails, but I could not reach the retaining point. The opening around the edges wasn't wide enough.

Damn!

I thought of my sister and dogs and Jennifer Cannon. I thought of me and dogs and Jennifer Cannon. My fingers were so cold I could no longer feel them, and I slid them into my pockets. My right knuckle struck something hard and flat. Puzzled, I withdrew the object and held it up to the crack.

The broken scraper blade!

Please!

With a silent prayer, I inserted an edge. The blade fit! Trembling, I wiggled it toward the retaining point. The scraping seemed loud enough to be heard for miles.

I froze and listened. No movement overhead. Barely breathing, I nudged the shard farther. Inches short of what I hoped was a latch it snagged, popped from my hand, and fell into darkness.

Damn! Damn! Sonofabitch!

I bumped down the stairs on my hands and bum, and seated myself on the ground. Cursing my clumsiness, I began a miniature grid search across the dank clay. Within moments my fingers came down on the broken scraper.

Back up the stairs. By now movement sent searing pain firing up and down my leg. Using both hands I reinserted the blade and pushed up on the latch. No go. I withdrew and repositioned the shard, then swiped it sideways along the crack.

Something clicked. I listened. Silence. I pushed with my shoulder and the trapdoor lifted. Grabbing the panel along its edges, I eased it up, then lowered it quietly to the floor above. Heart racing, I raised my head and peeked around.

The room was lit by a single oil lamp. I could tell it was a pantry of some sort. Shelves lined three walls, some of which held boxes and cans. Stacks of cartons filled the corners ahead and to my left and right. When I looked to my rear a chill far greater than any caused by the weather overcame me.

Dozens of propane tanks lined the wall, their enamel luminous in the soft light. An image flitted through my mind, a wartime propaganda photo of armaments stockpiled in orderly rows. With shaking hands I eased myself down, and perched on the top step.

What could I do to stop them?

I glanced down the steps. A square of yellowish light fell across the cellar floor, just reaching Daisy Jeannotte's face. I looked at the cold, still features.

"Who are you?" I muttered. "I thought this was your show."

Total stillness.

I drew a few steadying breaths, then ascended into the pantry. Relief at escaping the tunnel alternated with fear of what I would encounter next.

The pantry opened onto a cavernous kitchen. I hobbled to a door on the far side, pressed my back against the wall, and sifted sounds. The creak of wood. The hiss of wind and ice. The click of frozen branches.

Barely breathing, I eased around the doorjamb and entered a long, dark hall.

The storm sounds faded. I could smell dust and wood smoke and old carpet. I limped forward, supporting myself against the wall. Not a sliver of light penetrated to this part of the house.

Where are you, Harry?

I came to a door and leaned close. Nothing. My knee trembled and I wondered how much farther I could go. Then I heard muffled voices.

Hide! the brain cells screamed.

The knob turned and I slipped into blackness.

415

The room smelled dank and sweet, like flowers left to die in a vase. Suddenly, the hair on my arms and neck stood straight. Was that movement? Again, I held my breath and sorted sounds.

Something was breathing!

Mouth dry, I swallowed and strained for the tiniest motion. Save for the steady rhythm of inhaling and exhaling, the room was devoid of sound. Slowly, I crept forward until objects emerged from the darkness. A bed. A human form. A nightstand with water glass and adjacent a vial of pills.

Two more steps and I could see long blond hair on a patchwork quilt.

Could it be? Could my prayers possibly be answered this quickly?

I stumbled forward and turned the head to expose the face.

"Harry!" God, yes. It was Harry.

Her head rolled and she gave a low moan.

I was reaching for the vial of pills when an arm caught me from behind. It wrapped around my throat, crushing my windpipe and cutting off my air. A hand clamped across my mouth.

My legs thrashed and I clawed to break free. Somehow I got hold of the wrist and twisted the hand off my face. Before it arched back I saw the ring. A black rectangle with a carved ankh and crenulated border. As I thrashed and clawed I remembered a bruise in soft, white flesh. I knew I was in hands that would not hesitate to end my life.

I tried to scream but Malachy's killer had me in a grip that compressed my throat and muffled my mouth. Then my head was yanked sideways and pressed against a bony scarecrow chest. In the murky gloom I saw one pale eye, a white hair streak. Light-years passed as I

416

struggled for air. My lungs burned, my pulse pounded, and I slipped in and out of consciousness.

I heard voices, but the world was receding. The pain in my knee faded as a numbness overtook my mind. I felt myself being being dragged. My shoulder struck something. Softness underfoot. Hard again. We banged through another doorway, the arm a vise on my trachea.

Hands grabbed me and something rough slid over my wrists. My arms shot up, but the pressure on my head and throat was released and I could breathe! I heard a moan from my own throat as my lungs gulped precious air.

As I reestablished contact with my body, the pain returned.

My throat ached and my breath was labored. My shoulders and elbows were stretched from the traction, and my hands felt cold and numb above my head.

Forget your body. Use your brain.

The room was large, the kind you see in inns and lodges. It had a wide plank floor and heavy log walls, and was lit only by candle-light. I was roped to an overhead beam, my shadow a Giacometti figure with arms held high.

I turned my head and the ovoid shadow skull elongated in the flickering light. Double doorway straight ahead. Stone fireplace to my left. Picture window to my right. I stored the blueprint.

Hearing voices behind me, I threw one shoulder forward, retracted the other, and pushed with my toes. My body twisted, and for a split second I saw them before the ropes spun me back. I recognized the streaked hair and eye of the man. But who was the other?

The voices paused, then continued in hushed tones. I heard footsteps, followed by quiet. I knew I wasn't alone. I held my breath and waited for them.

417

When she stepped in front of me I was startled but not shocked. Today the braids were coiled on her head, not hanging down as they had been when she had walked the streets of Beaufort with Kathryn and Carlie.

She reached out and wiped a tear from my cheek.

"Are you frightened?" Her eyes looked cold and hard.

Fear will rouse her like a junkyard dog!

"No, Ellie. Not of you or your band of zealots." The pain in my throat made it hard to talk.

She ran the finger down my nose and across my lips. It felt rough against my skin. "Not Ellie. *Je suis Elle*. I am She. The female force."

I recognized the deep, breathy voice.

"The high priestess of death!" I spat.

"You should have left us alone."

"You should have left my sister alone."

"We need her."

"Didn't you have enough others? Or does each kill excite you so much?"

Keep her talking. Buy time.

"We punish the intractable."

"Is that why you killed Daisy Jeannotte?"

"Jeannotte." Her voice grew harsh with contempt. "That vicious, meddling old fool. Finally, she'll let him be."

What's the right thing to say to keep the conversation going?

"She didn't want her brother to die."

"Daniel will live forever."

"Like Jennifer and Amalie?"

"Their weakness was going to hold us back."

"So you take the weak and watch them torn to bits?"

Her eyes narrowed into something I couldn't interpret. Bitterness? Regret? Anticipation?

"I brought them out of the famine and showed them how to survive. They chose cataclysm."

418

"What was Heidi Schneider's sin? Loving her husband and babies?"

The eyes hardened.

"I revealed the way and she brought poison into the world! Evil in duplicate!"

"The Antichrist."

"Yes!" she hissed.

Think! What were her words in Beaufort?

"You say death is a transition in the growth process. Do you nurture by slaughtering babies and old women?"

"The corrupt cannot be permitted to pollute the new order."

"Heidi's babies were four months old!" Fear and anger made my voice crack.

"They were perversion!"

"They were babies!" I struggled and tried to lunge at her, but the ropes held firm.

Beyond the doorway I could hear the sound of others moving around. I thought of the children at the Saint Helena compound, and felt my chest heave.

Where was Daniel Jeannotte?

"How many children will you and your henchman kill?"

The corners of her eyes pinched almost imperceptibly.

Keep her talking.

"Are you going to ask all your followers to die?"

Still she said nothing.

"Why do you need my sister? Have you lost your ability to motivate followers?" My voice sounded tremulous and two octaves too high.

"She will take the place of another."

"She doesn't believe in your Armageddon."

"Your world is ending."

"The last I looked it was doing fine."

419

"You kill redwoods to make toilet paper and pour poisons into the rivers and oceans. Is that doing fine?" She thrust her face so close to mine I could see vessels throbbing at her temples.

"Kill yourself if you must, but let the others make their own choices."

"There must be perfect balance. The number has been revealed."

"Really? And is everyone else here?"

She drew back her head but didn't speak. I saw something spark in her eye, like light skipping off broken glass.

"They're not all coming, Elle."

The eyes never faltered.

"Kathryn's not going to die for you. She's miles from here, safe with her baby."

"You lie!"

"You're not going to hit your cosmic quota."

"The signs have been sent. The apocalypse is now and we will rise from the ashes!"

Her eyes were black holes in the flickering light. I recognized the look for what it was. Madness.

I was about to respond when I heard the snarling and yapping of dogs. The sound was coming from deep inside the lodge.

I yanked desperately, but the ropes only tightened. My breathing turned to frenzied gasping. It was reflex, unthinking struggle.

I couldn't do it! I couldn't get free! And what if I did? I was there among them.

"Please," I begged.

Elle stared, her eyes unfeeling.

A sob escaped me as the barking grew louder. I continued to thrash. I would not submit passively, however hopeless my resistance.

What had the others done? I saw the torn flesh and

punctured skulls. The barking turned to growls. The dogs were very near. Fear beyond control overcame me.

I twisted to see and my eyes swept across the bay window. My heart froze. Had I seen figures moving outside?

Don't draw attention to the window!

I dropped my gaze and rotated back to Elle, still straining, but my thoughts now on the outside. Was there still hope of rescue?

Elle watched me wordlessly. One second passed. Two. Five. I spun myself to the right and stole another peek.

Through the ice and condensation I saw a shadow slide from left to right.

Distract her!

I pivoted back and fixed my eyes on Elle. The window was to her left.

The barking grew louder. Closer.

Say anything!

"Harry doesn't believe in—"

The door burst inward, then I heard deep voices. "Police!"

Boots chocked on hardwood.

"Haut les mains!" Hands up!

Snarling and yelping. Shouts. A scream.

Elle's mouth turned to an oval, then to a thin, dark line. She drew a gun from the folds of her dress and aimed it at something behind me.

The instant her eyes left me I wrapped my fingers around the ropes, threw my hips forward, kicked out with my feet, and arched toward her. Pain screamed through my shoulders and wrists as my body swung out, my arms in full extension. I flexed my hips and brought my boots up, hitting her arm with the full force of my weight. The gun flew across the room and out of my field of vision.

My feet slammed to the floor and I scrabbled backward to relieve the pressure on my upper limbs. When I looked up, Elle stood frozen, an SQ muzzle trained on her chest. One dark braid had fallen and looped her forehead like a brocade sash.

I felt hands on my back and heard voices speak to me. Then I was free and strong arms half dragged, half carried me to a couch. I smelled wintry air and wet wool. English Leather.

"*Calmez-vous, madame. Tout va bien.*"

My arms were lead, my knees were jelly. I wanted to sink back and sleep forever but I struggled to stand.

"*Ma soeur*! I have to find my sister!"

"*Tout va bien, madame.*" Hands pressed me back into the cushions.

More boots. Doors. Shouted commands. I saw Elle and Daniel Jeannotte handcuffed and led away.

"Where's Ryan? Do you know Andrew Ryan?"

"Take it easy, you're going to be fine." English.

I tried to pry myself loose.

"Is Ryan all right?"

"Relax."

Then Harry was beside me, eyes enormous in the dreamlike gloom.

"I'm scared," she murmured in a thick, slurry voice.

"It's O.K." I wrapped my deadened arms around her. "I'm taking you home."

Her head dropped onto my shoulder, and I rested mine against it. I held her a moment, then released her. Summoning up memories of religious education from my childhood, I closed my eyes, clasped my hands in front of my chest, and wept quietly as I prayed to God for the life of Andrew Ryan.

35

One week later I was sitting on my patio in Charlotte, thirty-six exam booklets stacked to my right, the thirty-seventh on a lap table in front of me. The sky was Carolina blue, the yard a deep, rich green. In the adjacent magnolia, a mockingbird strove for a personal best.

"Brilliantly average job," I said, marking a C+ on the blue cover and circling it several times. Birdie looked up, stretched, and slithered from the chaise.

My knee was healing well. The small hairline fracture in my left patella had been nothing compared with the injuries to my psyche. After the terror in Ange Gardien I'd spent two days in Quebec, recoiling at every sound and every shadow, barking dogs in particular. Then I returned to Charlotte to hobble through the remainder of the semester. I filled the days with relentless activity, but the nights were difficult. In the dark my mind loosened, releasing visions the daytime had locked away. Some nights I slept with the lamp on.

The phone rang and I reached for the handset. It was the call I'd been expecting.

"*Bonjour*, Dr. Brennan. *Comment ça va?*"

"*Ça va bien*, Sister Julienne. More important, how is Anna?"

"I think the medication is helping." Her voice went low. "I don't know anything about bipolar disorder, but the doctor gave me a great deal of material and I am learning. I had never understood her depression. I thought Anna was moody because that's what her mother said. Sometimes she'd be down, then suddenly she'd be full of energy and feeling good about herself. I didn't know that was, what is it called . . .?"

"A manic phase?"

"*C'est ça*. She seemed to go up and down so quickly."

"I'm so glad she's better."

"Yes, God be praised. Professor Jeannotte's death hit her hard. Please, Dr. Brennan, for Anna's sake, I must know what went on with that woman."

I took a deep breath. What to say?

"Professor Jeannotte's troubles stemmed from her love for her brother. Daniel Jeannotte spent his life organizing one cult group after another. Daisy believed he was well intentioned and wrongly scorned by mainstream society. Her career in American academia was compromised following complaints to her university by parents of students she had steered to Daniel's conferences and workshops. She took a leave from teaching to do research and write, and resurfaced in Canada. For years she continued to be supportive of her brother.

"When Daniel hooked up with Elle, Daisy began to lose confidence. She thought Elle was a psychopath, and a struggle developed between the two women for Daniel's allegiance. Daisy wanted to protect her brother, but was afraid of something catastrophic.

"Jeannotte knew that Daniel and Elle's group was active on campus, though the university had tried to

424

drive them off. So when Anna had her encounter with them, Daisy wanted to monitor them through Anna.

"Daisy was never a recruiter for the group. She learned that cult members had infiltrated the counseling center, looking for students to befriend. My sister was recruited that way at a community college in Texas. This agitated Daisy all the more because she feared being blamed because of the episode in her past."

"Who is this Elle?"

"Her real name is Sylvie Boudrais. What we know is patchy. She's forty-four, born in Baie Comeau of an Inuit mother and québécois father. Her mother died when she was fourteen, her father was an alcoholic. The old man beat her regularly and forced her into prostitution when she was fourteen. Sylvie never finished high school, but she tests in the stratosphere for IQ.

"Boudrais disappeared after dropping out of school, then showed up in Quebec City sometime in the mid-seventies offering psychic healing for a moderate fee. She acquired a small following, and eventually became the leader of a group that took up residence in a hunting lodge near Ste-Anne-de-Beaupré. There was constant money pressure, and problems developed because of underaged members. A fourteen-year-old turned up pregnant, and the parents went to the authorities.

"The group disbanded and Boudrais moved on. She did a brief stint with a sect called the Celestial Pathway in Montreal, but left. Like Daniel Jeannotte, she wandered from group to group, turning up in Belgium around 1980, where she preached a combination of shamanism and New Age spiritualism. She established a band of followers, including a very wealthy man named Jacques Guillion.

"Boudrais had met Guillion early through the Celestial Pathway, and saw him as the answer to a group's

425

cash flow problems. Guillion fell under her spell, and was eventually persuaded to sell his properties and turn over his assets."

"No one objected?"

"The taxes were paid and Guillion had no family, so no questions arose."

"*Mon Dieu.*"

"In the mid-eighties the group left Belgium for the U.S. They established a commune in Fort Bend County, Texas, and Guillion shuttled back and forth to Europe for several years, probably transferring money. He last entered the U.S. two years ago."

"What happened to him?" Her voice was small and tremulous.

"The police think he's buried somewhere on the ranch."

I heard the swish of fabric.

"Jeannotte's brother met Boudrais in Texas and was captivated. By then she was calling herself Elle. That's also where Dom Owens came into the picture."

"He is the man from South Carolina?"

"Yes. Owens was a small-time dabbler in mysticism and organic healing. He visited the Fort Bend ranch and was infatuated with Elle. He invited her to the South Carolina compound on Saint Helena, and she seized control of his group."

"But it all sounds so harmless. Herbs and spells and holistic medicine. How did it come to violence and death?"

How does one explain madness? I didn't want to discuss the psychiatric evaluation lying on my desk, or the rambling suicide notes found at Ange Gardien.

"Boudrais read extensively, especially philosophy and ecology. She was convinced the earth would be destroyed, and before that happened she would take her followers away. She believed herself to be the guardian angel of those devoted to her, and the lodge at Ange Gardien was the jumping-off point."

There was a long pause. Then,

"Did they really believe it?"

"I don't know. I don't think Elle was willing to trust entirely to the power of her oratory. She relied in part on drugs."

Another pause.

"Do you think they believed enough to be willing to die?"

I thought of Kathryn. And Harry.

"Not all of them."

"It is mortal sin to orchestrate the loss of life, or even to hold another living soul as a captive."

A perfect bridge.

"Sister, did you read the information I sent regarding Élisabeth Nicolet?"

The pause at her end was longer. It ended with a deep sigh.

"Yes."

"I've done a lot of research on Abo Gabassa. He was a well-respected philosopher and public speaker, known all over Europe, Africa, and North America for his efforts to end the slave trade."

"I understand that."

"He and Eugénie Nicolet sailed for France on the same ship. Eugénie returned to Canada with an infant daughter." I took a breath. "The bones don't lie, Sister Julienne. And they are not judgmental. From the moment I looked at Élisabeth's skull, I knew she was a person of mixed race."

"That doesn't mean she was a prisoner."

"No, it does not."

Another pause. Then she spoke slowly.

"I agree that an illegitimate child would not have been well received in the Nicolet circle. And in those days a mixed-race black baby might have been impossible. Perhaps Eugénie viewed the convent as the most humane solution."

"Perhaps. Élisabeth may not have chosen her own fate, but that doesn't diminish her contribution. According to all accounts, her work during the smallpox epidemic was heroic. Thousands may have been spared by her efforts.

"Sister, are there any saints from North America whose bloodlines included Native American, African, or Asian ancestry?"

"Why, I'm not sure." I heard something new in her voice.

"What an extraordinary role model Élisabeth could be to people of faith who suffer prejudices because they were not born Caucasian."

"Yes. Yes, I must speak to Father Ménard."

"May I ask you a question, Sister?"

"*Bien sûr.*"

"Élisabeth appeared to me in a dream and spoke a line I cannot place. When I asked who she was she said, 'All in robe of darkest grain.'"

"Come pensive nun devout and pure; Sober steadfast and demure; All in robe of darkest grain; Flowing with majestic train.' John Milton's *Il Penseroso*."

"The brain is an amazing archive," I said, laughing. "It's been years since I read that."

"Would you like to hear my favorite?"

"Of course."

It was a lovely thought.

When we hung up I looked at my watch. Time to go.

During the drive I turned the radio on and off, tried

428

to identify a rattle in the dashboard, and just drummed my fingers.

The traffic signal at Woodlawn and the Billy Graham Parkway took a lifetime.

This was your idea, Brennan.

Right. But does that make it a good one?

I arrived at the airport and went directly to baggage claim.

Ryan was draping a garment bag over his left shoulder. His right arm was in a sling and he moved with an uncharacteristic stiffness. But he looked good. Very good.

He's here to recover. That's all.

I waved and called to him. He smiled and pointed to an athletic bag circling toward him on the carousel.

I nodded and began sorting my keys, deciding which should go to another chain.

"*Bonjour*, y'all."

I gave him a minimal-contact hug, the kind people use when picking up in-laws. He stepped back, and the too-damn-blue eyes looked me up and down.

"Nice outfit."

I was wearing jeans and a shirt that didn't bunch too high with the crutches.

"How was your trip?"

"The flight attendant took pity and moved me up front."

I'll bet she did.

On the ride home I asked about the state of his injuries.

"Three fractured ribs and one perforated a lung. The other bullet preferred muscle. It was no big deal, except for some blood loss."

The no big deal had taken four hours of surgery.

"Are you in pain?"

"Only when I breathe."

429

When we got to the Annex, I showed Ryan the guest room and went to the kitchen to pour iced tea.

Minutes later he joined me on the patio. Sunlight was slanting through the magnolia, and a troupe of song sparrows had replaced the mockingbird.

"Nice outfit," I said, handing him a glass.

Ryan had changed to shorts and a T-shirt. His legs were the color of uncooked cod, and athletic socks bagged around his ankles.

"Been wintering in Newfoundland?"

"Tanning causes melanoma."

"I'll need shades for the glare."

Ryan and I had already reviewed the events in Ange Gardien. We'd discussed it at the hospital, then later by phone as more information came to light.

Ryan had used his cell phone to call the Rouville district SQ post while I was outside scraping the road sign. When we didn't appear – there the dispatcher sent a truck to clear the road so a unit could investigate. The officers found Ryan unconscious and called in backup and ambulances.

"So your sister is through with cosmic healing?"

"Yeah." I smiled and shook my head. "She came down here for a few days, then headed back to Texas. It won't be long before she becomes enthused by some other alternative agenda."

We sipped our tea.

"Have you read the psychiatric stuff?"

"Delusional misidentification with significant components of grandiosity and paranoia. What the frig does that mean?"

That same question had already sent me to the psychiatric literature.

"The Antichrist delusion. People see themselves or others as demonic. In Elle's case, she projected the delusion onto Heidi's babies. She'd read about matter

430

and antimatter, and believed everything has to be in balance. She said one of the babies was the Antichrist, the other some type of cosmic backup. Is she still talking?"

"Like a DJ on uppers. She admits to sending the hit team to St-Jovite to kill the kids. Simonnet tried to intervene, so they shot her. Then the killers downed the drugs and started the fire."

I thought of the old lady whose bones I'd examined.

"Simonnet must have tried to protect Heidi and Brian. All those calls to Saint Helena, then the rescue mission to Texas after Daniel Jeannotte showed up at the Schneider home." My fingers made oval prints in the condensation on my tea glass. "Why do you suppose Simonnet kept phoning after Heidi and Brian left Saint Helena?"

"Heidi kept in contact with Jennifer Cannon, and Simonnet phoned for reports. When Elle found out, she had Cannon killed."

"The same exorcism by dogs, knives, and scalding liquid she'd ordered when Carole Comptois got pregnant."

The image still made me shudder.

"Was Comptois still working as a hooker?"

"She'd given it up. Ironically, she was introduced to Elle by a former customer. Though Comptois lived with the group off and on, apparently she maintained outside interests, since her baby's father was not a member and therefore not an approved sperm donor. That's why Elle ordered the exorcism."

"Why Amalie Provencher?"

"That's unclear. Amalie may have gotten in the way of the elimination of Jennifer."

"Elle believed she needed the psychic strength of fifty-six souls to muster the energy for the final crossing.

431

She hadn't counted on losing Comptois. That's why she needed Harry."

"Why fifty-six?"

"It has something to do with the fifty-six Aubrey holes at Stonehenge."

"What are Aubrey holes?"

"Small pits that were dug and filled in immediately. They were probably used to predict lunar eclipses. Elle has woven all kinds of esoterica into her delusions."

I took a sip of tea.

"She was obsessed with the idea of balance. Matter and antimatter. Controlled coupling. Exactly fifty-six people. She chose Ange Gardien not just because of the name, but because it's equidistant from there to the communes in Texas and South Carolina. It's an amazing coincidence, isn't it?"

"What's that?"

"My sister lives in Texas. I work in Quebec, and have lifelong ties to the Carolinas. Everywhere I turned, Elle's influence was there. Her reach was awesome. How many lives do you suppose these cults affect?"

"There's no telling."

The sound of Vivaldi drifted from my neighbor's patio.

"How did your friend Sam take the news that one of his employees brought bodies to Murtry?"

"He wasn't thrilled." I remembered Joey's nervousness by the water truck when we emerged from the burial location. "Joey Espinoza had been working for Sam for almost two years."

"Right. He was an Owens follower, but lived in his mother's house. She's the one who phoned Social Services. Well, it turns out he's also Carlie's father. That's why Kathryn fled to him when things got ugly. It seems she didn't know anything about the murders."

"Where are they now?"

432

"She and the baby are with some cousin of hers. Joey is discussing the recent past with Sheriff Baker."

"Has anyone been charged?"

"Elle and Daniel have each been charged with three counts of first-degree murder for the deaths of Jennifer Cannon, Amalie Provencher, and Carole Comptois."

Ryan picked up a magnolia leaf and trailed it across his thigh.

"What else was in the evaluation?"

"According to the court-appointed shrink Elle suffers from an elaborate multidelusional psychosis. She's convinced that the apocalypse will occur soon in the form of a giant environmental disaster, and that she's destined to preserve humanity by transporting followers away from the apocalypse."

"Where were they going?"

"She's not saying. But you aren't on her manifest."

"How do people buy into such crap?" Ryan echoed my question to Red Skyler.

"The group recruited people who were disillusioned with their lot and attracted by group acceptance, being accorded a sense of worth and importance, and being given simple answers to all questions, with a little drug therapy thrown in."

A breeze lifted the branches of the magnolia, bringing with it the smell of wet grass. Ryan said nothing.

"Elle may be crazy, but she's smart and extraordinarily persuasive. Even now her followers are loyal. While she's pontificating, they're not saying a word."

"Yeah." He stretched, raised his bandaged arm, and repositioned it on his chest. "She's cunning, all right. She was never after a huge following. She wanted a small but loyal band. That and Guillion's money let her keep a low profile. Until it began to unravel, she made very few mistakes."

"What about the cat? That was brutal but stupid."

433

"That was Dom Owens. Elle ordered him to stop your meddling. He claims he was not into physically harming people, so he directed some student followers in Charlotte to do something to frighten you off. They devised the cat trick. Got the poor thing from the animal shelter."

"How did they find me?"

"One of them took a bill or something from your office. It had your home address."

Ryan sipped his tea.

"By the way, your St. Paddy's Day adventure in Montreal was also student-inspired."

"How did you know about that?"

He smiled and waggled the teacup. "It seems the protective attitude went both ways between Jeannotte and her students. One of them saw that she was upset, and concluded your visits were the cause. He decided to freelance and deliver a personal message."

I changed the subject. "Do you believe Owens was involved in killing Jennifer and Amalie?"

"He denies it. Claims that after he confronted Jennifer about the phone calls he reported to Elle. Says Elle told him she and Daniel were taking Jennifer and Amalie back to Canada."

"Why was Owens not at Ange Gardien?"

"Owens had decided to bail. He either became afraid over what Elle might do because he had lost track of Joey, Kathryn, and Carlie, or he didn't have confidence in the cosmic crossover. Either way, he had over two hundred thousand dollars of Guillion's money left, so he gathered it up and went west as everyone else headed north. The American feds caught up with him at a naturalist commune in Arizona. Elle would not have had her fifty-six souls even with Harry."

"Hungry?"

"Let's eat."

We made salad, then skewered chicken and vegetables for shish kebabs. Outside the sun had dropped below the horizon, and the deepening dusk filled the trees and grounds with dark shadows. We ate on the patio, talking and watching night settle in. Inevitably, the conversation drifted back to Elle and the murders.

"I guess Daisy Jeannotte felt she could confront her brother and force him to stop the madness."

"Yeah, but Elle spotted Daisy first and had Daniel eliminate her and throw her into the crawl space where they later stashed you. You had been perceived as a lesser threat and had simply been rapped over the head and stuck in the hole. When you responded by getting free and causing more trouble, Elle was outraged and committed you to the same murder-exorcism that she had lavished on Jennifer and Amalie."

"Daniel helped Elle kill Jennifer and Amalie, and he's the main suspect in the Carole Comptois murder. Who were the assassins in St-Jovite?"

"We may never know. No one has told that story yet."

Ryan finished his tea and leaned back. Crickets had taken over for birds. Far off a siren moaned in the night. For a long time we didn't speak.

"Do you remember the exhumation I did in Lac Memphrémagog?"

"The saint."

"One of the nuns in that order is Anna Goyette's aunt."

"Thanks to nuns I still have limited use of my knuckles."

I smiled. Another gender inequality.

I told him about Élisabeth Nicolet.

"They were all captives in one way or another. Harry. Kathryn. Élisabeth."

"Elle. Anna. Prisons take many forms."

"Sister Julienne shared a quote with me. In *Les Misérables* Victor Hugo refers to the convent as an optical device whereby man gains a glimpse of infinity."

The crickets chirped.

"It's not infinity, Ryan, but we're barreling toward the end of a millennium. Do you suppose there are others out there preaching Armageddon and orchestrating rituals of group death?"

For a moment he didn't answer. The magnolia rustled overhead.

"There will always be mystic hustlers who will play upon disillusionment, despair, low self-esteem, or fear to promote their own agendas. But if any of these psycho charlatans get off the bus in my town the reckoning will be swift and certain. Revelation according to Ryan."

I watched a leaf tumble across the brick.

"What about you, Brennan? Will you be there to help me?"

Ryan's form was black against the night sky. I couldn't see his eyes, but I knew they were looking straight toward mine.

I reached over and took his hand.

436